"If I don't relieve and pity thee," said the miller, "may Heaven, which
Pities all, forget me!"

PHŒBE;

OR,

THE MILLER'S MAID.

A ROMANCE OF DEEP INTEREST.

BY THE AUTHOR OF "ADELINE," ETC.

"And mingling with the storm, confused and wild,'
They heard, or thought they heard, a screaming child."

BLOOMFIELD.

LONDON:

PUBLISHED BY E. LLOYD, AT THE OFFICE OF "THE PENNY SUNDAY TIMES," 231, SHOREDITCH,

1842.

PHŒBE;

OR,

THE MILLER'S MAID.

A ROMANCE OF DEEP INTEREST.

CHAPTER I.

"It is a fearsome night, dame, and the old mill shakes at every gust. Pray Heaven it stands the storm. The mill is an old friend, dame. My father, and his father afore him, owned the old mill; but it be like us, dame, getting past work. Ah! well, well, I should grieve to see it stopped. We have had our troubles, dame; but the mill—the dear old mill—it's an old friend, and I tell 'e, I would not see it down for—no, not for—a—a—"

"Now, don't 'e take on about the old mill, Gilbert. Thee'll find it, man, in the morning just all right, like——. Dost thou not hear that, Gilbert?"

A clap of thunder, so loud, long, and terrible, now shook the Heavens, that the miller and his wife, who were sitting by the cheerful blaze of a wood fire, in their little cottage, which joined the mill, looked at each other in fear and consternation, and were too much alarmed, for some minutes, to speak.

"Was ever the like,"—exclaimed the miller's homely, but good-hearted helpmate—"was ever the like o' that, Gilbert?"

"Why, dame, dame, what 'e frightened at? Thee's heard thunder afore belike, and now thee tremblest like—a—a—"

No. 1

"Thee tremblest, too, Gilbert—thee dost, and thee can hardly speak. Oh! Gilbert, Gilbert! there may be some poor souls without a home, a morsel of bread, or a roof to shelter them in such a storm as this."

"Thee says true, dame; thee says true; there may, indeed. God help them."

"As He has helped us," replied the dame with a tear glistening in her eye; "thee hast worked hard, Gilbert, early and late, for me and mine, and the poor never pass empty handed by the door. Thee hast been a good husband, Gilbert, to me."

"Well, well, don't 'e take on so. I—I—I declare thee, foolish old dame—thee—thee be'st a going to cry now—don't 'e; now, don't 'e."

"Ah, Gilbert, I see the tear is in thy own eye. Take thy pipe, and make thyself happy."

"Don't be faint-hearted, dame.; the storm will blow over; can't 'e behave thyself like a man?"

"What! hast lost thy wits, Gilbert, that 'e tells me to behave myself like a man?"

"Nay, dame, I want 'e not to be afeard like—Goodness gracious."

A flash of lightning at this moment, so vivid and intense, that it for an instant lit up the little cottage with an awful light, in spite of the fire and the candle which burnt upon the table, caused the honest miller and his wife to shake with apprehension.

They looked at each other without speaking, and the old dame made a trembling effort to reach the old family Bible which stood on a shelf hard by.

Before they had time to recover from their fear, a clap of thunder seemed to shake the very earth on which the cottage and the mill stood, and then died away in the distance in endless reverberations.

The mill of the worthy couple, whom we have introduced to the reader, was situated on a little eminence, adjoining a lovely valley in one of the richest corn counties of England.

The mill had descended from generation to generation. It had been for many years in the possession of Gilbert, the present miller, and he and his good dame were as respected as they were well known, for many a mile round their happy, though humble, home.

The day had been cloudy and unusually close for the season of the year, for the winter was rapidly approaching; but towards evening a cold wind had set in, which was quickly followed by the storm, which now howled and roared round the old mill,

When the thunder for a moment died away, the wind might be heard sweeping along in violent gusts, which threatened destruction to everything that opposed its furious progress. For a moment there would be a lull in the tempest, and the silence of the elements permitted Gilbert and his alarmed dame to exchange a few cheering words; but then again, with a low moaning noise, as coming afar off, the wind would make known its approach, and in a few moments the gale would sweep, howling and tearing round the mill and the cottage, like some wild animal seeking for prey.

The mill creaked and shook at every gust, and the terrified and afflicted Gilbert expected nothing less than that his old friend, which had supported so many happy and contented families so long, must yield to the fury of the storm, and be swept from the little knoll on which it stood.

"Dame, dame," he cried, "thee art the same to me; but thee art not young; and in all thee life did thee ever hear a storm like this? The poor old mill;—it must go at last. Father would have broke his heart had he lived to see an end to the old mill."

"Dost thee not remember a storm, Gilbert, thirty-eight years ago, when we were courting, Gilbert? Oh, good man, you were a comely youth, though I say it, and faith you're not the worst of the gust now, for when you stand upright, Gilbert, and call 'Giles, Giles, put a hand to the hopper,' I just think you young again, not that you are old, though, now."

Gilbert smiled and shook his head, but the smile was one of pleasure, and the shake of the head only implied a modest doubt on the subject of his age.

"Aye, aye, dame," he said, "thee would flatter your old man. Heaven bless you, dame; you—you are the same merry, light-hearted, fair-haired Mary, that I lent my jacket to in the storm you speak of. I remember it well. Ah, yes,—well, well. And you crept under a hedge.—Oh! yes,— it seems but yesterday. Don't 'e fear, my pretty Mary, the storm were at the worst that ever blew o' the earth, could not have the heart to injure you."

"Ah, Gilbert! Gilbert! those were, indeed, the very words you said. Bless you, Gilbert!—bless you!"

The good dame was quite overcome by her recollection of former years, and she bent her head upon her husband's shoulder, and sobbed loudly.

"Well,—well, dame," said the happy, good man; "you are—no—you— I declare, your tears have just wetted my face—you—you see."

"Ah, Gilbert, bless you! they are your own tears. You have a good heart. And have we not much to thank Providence for, Gilbert?"

"Much, much, indeed, dame! But, hark 'e; the storm seems to get worse, and I hear the hail pattering like stones upon the window."

"It can't last long," replied the dame; "but there's no telling, everything is altered; and storms are not like they were in our young days."

"Oh, wife! wife! that's your outcry. The corn is not so full, and the winters get colder, somehow, I think; but storms are much alike, and yet this be no more like the storm we were in so long ago, than—than—a—a—"

"Ha! Gilbert, man, you are always just comparing things to something, and 'a forgets what it is."

"Well,—well, dame, I'll just put my head out at the door, and take a look at the old mill. It stood the wind as bravely as an oak tree. There never was such a mill, dame, and I very much doubt if there ever will be such another."

The miller walked to the door of his cottage, and carefully opened it to a small extent; but, the moment that he did so, he encountered such a volley of hail, rain, and sleet, which was driven in upon him by the wind which still raged around his dwelling, that after one slight glance up at the mill, which satisfied him that it still stood, he was fain to use all his strength against the wind to shut again his cottage-door, and he returned to his fire-side, half-blinded and dripping from the storm.

"God help whoever is out to-night!" cried Gilbert, as he threw another log on the fire; "the old mill stands, dame; but, 'tis an awful night surely."

"It be, Gilbert; it be, indeed. Here's some hail stones that have bounced in to the very hearth."

"Aye, dame, I see; we'll just bar the door and go to rest; and somehow, dame, I don't know how it is, but I feel as if I had something to do, and ought to keep up."

"What dost mean, Gilbert? Thou hast nothing to do, man."

"Not that I know of, dame; but I feel a sort uneasy like; and I'll just sit a little longer."

The miller, as he spoke, stirred the fire, and a warm, dancing flame lit up the snug little cottage, and was reflected brightly from the highly-polished pots and pans which the dame prided herself upon arranging, in spotless order, on the shelves of the humble dwelling.

The lightning and thunder had now considerably abated, and it was only occasionally that a brilliant flash for a moment shot across the latticed window of the cottage, and was succeeded at a longer interval, by the solemn boom of the thunder in the distance. The storm of wind and hail, and the noise was so great sometimes, that the honest miller and his dame could hardly hear each other speak.

The miller sat down by the fire-side, and listened for some time in silence to the storm, while his wife pursued her knitting opposite to him ; and, between them, on the hearth, sat a large black cat, which kept up a gentle purring, and continually winked at the fire, as if very sleepy, but determined not to give way to it till its master and mistress retired to rest.

Stretched partly under the old-fashioned arm-chair, on which Gilbert sat, and partly on the hearth, was a large handsome dog ; but he was fast asleep, and the cat now and then seemed to peer at him out of her half-closed eyes, and with a drowsy shake of the head, reprove him for his laziness. Occasionally, she would bob her head forwards quite overcome by her disposition to sleep, and bring her nose in close contact to one of the hot logs—then a sneeze would ensue, and a violent rubbing on the injured nose with one of her fore paws ; and the dog would open his eyes for a moment and look at her, as much as to say,—"there, now ; don't you see you can't keep up. You'd better be down at once."

" I'm thinking, Gilbert," said the dame ; " upon who'll have the old mill when we are gone."

" But we are not going, dame ; and such another storm as this, and we may last out the old mill after all. Dost hear ?—the wind is worse and worse, dame, only more steady like."

Suddenly, as if both were actuated by one impulse, the dame dropped her knitting, and Gilbert started up from his arm-chair, and stood erect on his feet.

They neither of them spoke for several moments, and the miller held up his finger as if enjoining silence.

" Listen, dame," he cried ; " didst hear nothing?"

" Oh, Gilbert ! I thought I heard a cry, but it might be the wind. It do cry and howl for all the world like a Christian."

" No, dame ; I tell 'e no ;—it be not the wind. Look—look at Andy ; he knows it be not the wind. See dame."

" Andy," for so the large dog was named, had risen to his feet, and walked to the door of the cottage, where he stood and appeared to listen attentively.

" Hark !—there, again, dame," cried the miller in a loud voice ; " I tell 'e it be not the wind. There be some poor soul calling for help in the storm."

The dog now commenced a low whining sound, and scratched with his foot at the door.

" Oh ! Gilbert, I heard it then," said the dame ; " it seemed like a child crying."

" My staff, dame—quick !— there be some one in trouble. Dost hear ? There again. Quiet, Andy—quiet ; thou see'st I be coming."

A low plaintive wailing cry now might be distinctly heard accompanying the wind, as it howled and moaned round the cottage.

It was a cry of deep distress. It was not a shout for help, but it sounded like a cry wrung from a despairing heart, amid the terrors of the fearful storm.

The dame handed her husband his hat, and after much tugging and struggling, he was equipped in a large coat, and grasping his staff firmly in his hand, he was ready to brave the fury of the tempest, at the call of humanity.

Again and again they heard the cry, and each time it sounded nearer and nearer, as if the person who was in distress was rapidly approaching the cottage.

The dog barked loudly, and the miller in a moment opened the door of his dwelling. He was almost staggered by the torrent of hail, rain, and sleet, which he encountered; but he stepped forward, accompanied by Andy, who, with a loud bark, bounded through the open door.

"Dame!—dame!" cried the miller from the outside of the door; "dame, I say, will 'e come hither?—Don't 'e cry, poor thing! don't 'e cry.—I will carry thee in."

The dame, as she was hurrying to the door, heard a low, but extremely sweet and plaintive voice, say, "Oh! good sir, have pity on a poor orphan.—I have no home, and am cold and weary.—Good sir, have pity on a poor orphan."

"If I don't relieve and pity thee," said the miller, in accents of emotion, "may Heaven, which pities all, forget me!"

In a moment he met the dame at the door of the cottage, and in his arms he carefully and tenderly carried a little girl, who had fainted on his breast.

The miller carried his insensible burthen direct to the fire side, and placed the immoveable child in his own great chair.

"Alack! alack! poor child," cried the dame. "To be out such a night as this!—bless her heart, poor thing!—how she must have suffered!"

"Don't 'e say another word," cried the miller. "Get thee some cordial, dame. The poor dear thing has fainted.—How pale and ill she do look to be sure;—and as cold as an icicle. Dame! dame! it was the Almighty that kept me from going to bed, that I might be a help to this poor unfortunate child."

"It was, indeed, you may depend, Gilbert," replied the dame. "Poor dear thing! how fair and beautiful she be, to be sure."

And, in truth, she was a fair and beautiful child.—Her features were thin and pale, but there was a world of sweetness and beauty in her innocent face—her long flaxen hair hung in luxuriance, although it was soaked by the sleet and rain, upon her neck and shoulders—her eyes were closed, but her long silken lashes hung upon her cheeks, which was as white as marble.

There was an expression upon the delicate and beautiful face of the child of suffering and privation, which was heart-rending to behold; and the good dame's tears dropped upon the little suffer's pallid cheek, as she hung over her endeavouring to administer to her a few drops of reviving cordial, which was the manufacture of her own hands.

The little stranger seemed to be about eleven or twelve years old, and her dress was tattered and torn in many places. It would seem as if harshness, misery, and absolute want, had long been familiar to that fair and gentle-looking child,

"Poor thing! poor thing!" cried the miller, "my heart do bleed for thee. If thee art as good as thee art fair, thee shall be as a treasure to us, bestowed by the hand of Heaven."

"Who," said the good dame—"oh! who, Gilbert, could be other than kind to his sweet little creature? Bless her heart, poor thing!"

"She said she was an orphan, dame.   It seems to me as if the Almighty had sent her to us.   And—and, dame, I feel happy as I look at her."

The miller stooped as he spoke, and kissed the pale cheek of the little sufferer, while a tear gathered in his eye.

"To think, Gilbert, that this delicate little creature should have been in such a storm!   But see, bless her, she opens her dear eyes—see, Gilbert, see!"

"She does! she does!" cried the miller, joyfully.   "My poor thing, look up; you are with friends.   How dost thee, my dear?"

"Oh! what sweet eyes," cried the dame.   "Did you ever, Gilbert, see such?"

"Never mind the eyes, dame.   It be the pure heart that shines through them, that be truly beautiful!"

The child moaned as she opened her sweet blue eyes, and said, in heart-rending accents,—

"Oh! mercy—mercy.   Do not beat me any more."

"Beat thee!" cried the miller; "who could—who would beat thee?   I could as soon beat a little gentle lamb that scarcely knew its mother, as thee.   No, no—no one shall beat thee while the old mill goes round in a merry gale."

"Oh! sir, I am a poor orphan—I am, indeed.   You—you will not turn me out?"

"Turn thee out!—no.   Thee shalt stay here and be happy.   Thee art not an orphan, for thee hast a Father above who has sent thee here.   Bless thee sweet pretty face!"

The dame was most assiduous in her kind attentions, and after swallowing a small drop of the cordial, the child seemed much revived.

The warmth and comfort of the fire had soon a beneficial effect upon the child; and a slight tinge of colour returned to her pale cheeks.   She was about to speak again, but the good dame imposed immediate silence.

"Thee be'st tired and hungry, little one, I tell 'e, and thee must eat and sleep before thee tell us thee story."

"Aye, aye, that be the best," said the miller.   "Thee must get strong and hearty.   My heart seems to worm to thee; and—and if thee stay with us, I think thee will be the darling of Gilbert, the old miller; I am sure thee will."

The child smiled as she looked up in the honest miller's good-humoured and kind face, beaming as it was with benevolence and good-feeling.   It was a smile; it fleeted across the fair child's face like a gleam of bright sunshine upon a wintry heath.   In a moment it was gone, and the features of the gentle girl resumed their pale melancholy expression.   It would seem that such smiles were unfrequent guests; but the words of the miller had broken through the gloom of the young thing's heart, and that one sweet smile was the harbinger of future hapiness—the beginning of a new existence to the child.

Slowly she closed her eyes and sinking far down into the miller's armchair, she dropt into a quiet slumber, and happy visions of joy and hope seemed to visit her repose, for the smile of dawning happiness again and again played upon her lips, and the good dame took down her bible, and thanked God that had brought the little stranger to their door.

The miller drew a chair opposite to his usual seat, on which reposed the child, and there he sat and watched her as she slept, and wondered much as he gazed upon her slender, delicate form, and pale, though beautiful, features, what train of circumstances could have heaped misfortune and destitution upon so young a head, and who could have had the heart to expose her to all the horrors of homeless want.

"Poor thing! poor thing!" he said, in a low tone. "Thee art an orphan, thee says. Well, well, 'tis better that thee should suffer from the want of a father and mother, than that they had been unkind to thee. I have found thee, poor young thing; I have taken thee from the storm. Thee art the gift of Heaven, and I will make much of thee; thee shall not want; and I hope to see thee smile the whole day long. Thee art an orphan, and thee art friendless, or thee would not have been out in the storm. Dame, dame, we will be the father and mother to this poor child, and no one can take her from us."

"We will, Gilbert; we will," replied the dame. "And see, even Andy has taken to the sweet young thing."

The little white hand of the child hung over one of the arms of the chair, and the large faithful dog, Andy, had sat by the side of the miller, watching with the greatest attention, the slumbering girl, and he now, with a low whine of affection, rose and licked the little hand which might have belonged to a child of half her age, it was so small and fair.

With the action the child awoke, and for a moment she looked alarmed, for she forgot her situation; but when she saw the honest miller seated opposite to her, and watching her, with anxious kindness depicted in his face, she remembered all that had occurred, and clasping together her little hands, she cried, while the tears covered each other down her cheeks.

"Oh, sir, and you, madam, do not send me away; let me work for you, I can work; indeed I can, the whole day long—I shall never complain—I am an orphan—do not, oh! do not turn me away."

"Thee hast neither father nor mother?"

"Oh, no," answered the child, "They are both gone—gone."

"Nor friends who love thee?"

"Love me! Oh, no—no one ever loved me but my poor mother, and—and she is dead!"

"Then," cried the miller, joyfully, "thee art mine—thee shalt be my child, my own, my darling child. God bless thee, and as I hope for peace, I will never desert thee."

As he spoke, he upset the seat on which he had sat, and catching the orphan child in his arms, he kissed her tenderly.

"Here, dame, here, dame," he continued, "she is ours—our own. Take her good wife, and as we do by her, may Heaven do by us. Ha! ha! ha! I could laugh, dame, with joy. Let's see thee smile again, little one. What's 'e name?"

"Phœbe," answered the child, and she smiled amid her tears.

"Then thee shalt be called Phœbe Marks, for my name be Gilbert Marks and thee shalt be named after us:—but thee hast another name?"

"Phœbe Grainger," said the child.

The good dame had taken the young thing on her knee, and was parting from her fair forehead the luxuriant and beautiful flaxen hair.

"Ha!" she cried, "my dear child, thee wilt turn all the young men's heads in the village, if thee grow up half so beautiful as thee art now. Bless thee! Wilt thou be my dear child?"

"Oh, yes, yes, I will, indeed I will—I will be good always. I can work—I can—you—you make me think of—of——"

The child burst into tears, and hid her cherub face upon the good dame's bosom.

"Of who, my dear?—of who?" said the dame, tenderly.

"Of—of my poor mother; for she used to speak to me, and look as you do now."

"And hast thee had no one to be ever kind to thee but thy poor mother, my darling Phœbe?" said the miller, much affected.

"Oh! oh, no," replied the girl, with a shudder. "I—I could not do work enough, and they beat me."

She covered her face with her hand, as if to shut out some dreadful recollections, and trembled as she spoke.

"Beat thee!" cried the miller.

"Oh, yes—yes—often," sobbed the child;—but—but—you will not let them now? I will stay with you."

The indignant miller opened his mouth several times, but as he could not think of anything sufficiently strong and powerful in his stock of language to express his feelings, he said nothing; but catching up the poker as the first implement of defence that caught his eye, he flourished it round his head to the surprise and consternation of the good dame,

The moment the dog Andy saw the belligerent action of his master, he set up a loud barking of defiance, apparently in the full supposition that his master was about to engage in single combat with somebody, and he was determined to be in the fray.

"Why, Gilbert! Gilbert!" cried the dame; "what dost e' mean? Thee act beside thyself."

"Never mind," said the miller, laying down the poker; "beat thee, did they?—never mind. Andy, dost see that be thy young mistress."

Andy shook his tail, and whining, he crept to the side of the dame, and laid his head on Phœbe's knees.

"We will all love thee, Phœbe," continued the miller, "and no one shall lay a finger on thee, but in kindness while I live."

The child looked from one to the other, with a face beaming with happiness, and said, in her soft silvery voice :—

"I love you—all of you; I do love you; you will never beat me, and I will do anything; indeed I will; you look so kind. Since mother died, nobody looked kind at poor Phœbe."

The old-fashioned clock which had ticked for many years in one corner of the cottage, now struck twelve.

"Why, dame," cried Gilbert; "it be twelve o'clock; thee shall make a warm bed for Phœbe, and Andy will take care of her."

"The storm be gone quite away," said the dame.

"Indeed it be passed," replied the miller.

He opened the door of the cottage and looked out as he spoke. The sky was clear and serene, and spangled with stars. Not a breath of wind was stirring, and nature seemed to be resting after the war with the elements.

The dame placed an ample, though homely repast before the little stranger, who partook of it cheerfully. Her two hours of happiness beneath that humble roof, seemed already to have imparted a lustre to her eyes, and a bloom to her cheeks. She appeared, however, to be very weary, and the dame having made her arrangements for the night, the good miller rose to retire to his bed, to enjoy that sweet and calm repose which ever waits upon the pure-minded and the good.

"Good night to thee, my Phœbe,—God bless thee;" said the miller.

The little thing turned her sweet face to him, and stretched out her arms. He came to her, and she twined them round his neck, and kissed him, and he felt a tear wet his cheek. He could not speak, but he pressed her to his heart, and then hurried from the room.

The affectionate and thankful child then embraced the dame tenderly, and kissed her aged cheeks.

"My mother," she said, "used to tell me there were good people in the world, who would love me and be kind to me."

Mr. Bung stating the case of the "wicious orphans" to the parochial authorities.

"Sleep, my darling, you are tired, I know," said the dame, "and Andy will take care of you."

"Andy!" cried the child, and she laughed joyously, and threw her arms round the dog's neck. "I love him, too. Andy—Andy!"

The dog in an instant was up, and had commenced a furious licking of Phœbe's face, that she was fain to fly to the dame for refuge.

"And there's Bardons, too," said the dame. "That's the cat's name. Gilbert calls her Bardons."

"Oh, Bardons!" laughed the child; "I will love you, too, Bardons."

But Bardons only winked more than ever, and sneezed out loudly twice, which was quite as great a demonstration as was to be expected from so grave a personage.

"And now good night, my dear, and God bless you!" said the dame, kissing her, and wrapping her carefully in the little bed she had prepared for her.

The dame turned to the door, but the child called her back once more, and twining her little arms round her, she said—

"And I shall never leave you? Never?"

"Never, my dear, while Heaven will permit us to keep you with us."

The child smiled, and kissed her; then, still holding her, dropped into a happy sleep.

After a time, the good wife quietly disengaged the little thing's arms, and kissing her as she slept, retired to her own apartment, murmuring a blessing upon the innocent orphan whom God had committed to her care.

Deep repose—the repose of innocence and virtue, closed their eyelids, and peace and joy, unbroken by a sigh, were beneath the humble roof of Gilbert, the miller.

No. 2

CHAPTER II.

THREE years before the eventful evening of the storm when the benighted orphan sought and obtained shelter and sympathy at the cottage of Gilbert, the miller, sounds of woe might have been heard coming from a poor hovel in a little village on the coast of Kent.

There was the feeble voice of some one weakened by illness and pain, and the sobbing of young children in that poor dwelling.

The room from whence the sounds of lamentation proceeded was scantily furnished, although the cottage had, at one time, been the pride of the village, from its neatness and beauty.

It had been for some years inhabited by an industrious woman, who was the wife of a soldier, who was reported to have died in India. He had left with his disconsolate widow two young children, a girl and a boy for whom she alone lived, and strove to quench her tears.

By her own industry the widow Grainger had for some time supported her helpless children, and the little cottage in which they dwelt was the abode of peace and love. When the widow thought of the fate of him to whom she had given her young affections, she checked the rising tear by pressing her darlings to her heart, and in their smiles and dear caresses she would strive to forget her grief, and thank Heaven for the blessings she enjoyed.

The boy George was ten years of age, and the little garden in the front of their cottage won many a glance of admiration from passers-by, in consequence of his careful tending.

Phœbe, the girl, was a fair and delicate child, two years younger than her more robust brother, and she would sit with her mother in the summer's evenings at the opened casement, surrounded by flowers, and listen to the songs of the birds as they chirruped among the trees, and dashed in and out the sweet flowers which adorned the garden.

Often would the fond mother check a rising sigh as she thought how friendless and hopeless would be her darling children if she were called away by the stern mandate of death, and she prayed to Heaven for life, that she might see them pass the years of helpless infancy.

But who shall question the decrees of Heaven? The widow's health gradually sunk—the colour left her cheek—her strength declined, and want and misery usurped the places of contentment and peace in her humble dwelling. She felt her end approaching, and she was no longer able to do the scanty work which she could obtain, and which she had hitherto toiled at early and late for her young treasures.

The villagers were kind, but they were poor; and one by one the treasured relics of former happy days were parted with to support existence.

The widow's malady advanced with rapid strides—consumption was performing his fell work, and the delusion of hope was past. She felt that she was no longer for this world; and one calm autumn evening, just as the glorious sun was sinking to its rest, the dying mother called her children to her side with feeble voice, to listen to her last injunctions.

The weeping children hung over the humble couch in heartfelt grief. Their mother was all to them in the wide world; they had felt want and misfortune, but she had ever cheered them with her sweet smile, and now, with bursts of grief, they gazed upon her strangely altered form and bloodless lips, as she called them faintly to her side.

She drew them gently to her, and kissed them both; but Phœbe she held in her arms, and seemed loath to part from her. She kissed her frequently, and clung to her with frantic eagerness.

"Listen, George," she said; "and—and Phœbe—my Phœbe—listen. You will soon be alone—alone in the world."

"Oh, no—oh, no, mother," sobbed the children; "stay with us—stay, dear mother, stay."

"It is God's will, my babes, that I should go. But He will protect and raise up friends for the orphans. His will be done!"

She sunk exhausted upon the bed, and the children sobbed loudly, and called her to speak to them once more.

Their cries reached the ears of a compassionate neighbour or two, who entered the house of mourning, and soon saw that the children would shortly be without a mother.

They compassionately strove to remove them from the scene of death, but the dying mother spoke again, although feebly.

"Let them remain—oh, let them stay!" she cried. Phœbe — my Phœbe!"

The child threw herself into her mother's arms, and sobbed upon her breast as if her little heart would break.

"Stay, mother, stay!" she cried—"oh, stay, stay!"

"Hush, my child, hush," replied the mother, feebly. "Perhaps I may still be permitted to watch over thee, my darling, and shield thee from harm. God bless you, my child, bless you!"

"Can we do anything for thee, Dame Grainger?" said one of the neighbours, kindly.

"Not for me—no, not for me, but for these—these little ones. Oh, help them, and Heaven will reward you."

As she spoke, and before any one could reply, a loud knocking sounded at the little door of the cottage.

The dying woman looked up alarmed, and, fixing her eyes on the door of the room, she clasped the weeping Phœbe closer to her breast.

"What's that?" she cried, "who knocks? Not yet—I—I—oh, no—not yet! My children—my dear children!"

One of the neighbours had opened the door, and an altercation was evidently taking place between her and some men, whose harsh tones sounded through the nearly empty dwelling.

The voice of the neighbour was heard to say something, but in too low a tone to be distinctly heard by the widow and her children, and the man's voice replied loudly and harshly—

"Dying!—dying be bothered! What do people mean by dying till they have paid their rent and taxes, I should like to know?"

Again a neighbour was heard in a tone of expostulation.

"Oh, don't tell me," cried the man. "It is all very fine for people to owe three quarters, and then set about dying. I can't be put off in that way, you know. This comes of letting widows into houses; they are always dying, or some botheration or another."

"Wait till to-morrow, then," said the neighbour—"only to-morrow." Then something was added in a low tone, as before; but the widow caught the word "dead," and she said—

"Yes—yes, my children, dead—dead to-morrow! and you will be left to the mercy of such as he! Oh, Heaven! can this be possible? Protect and save my children!"

"Oh, to-morrow, indeed," cried the man; "that won't do for me. Why, I should be three-and-sixpence clean out of pocket! What do you think of that, eh?"

The kind neighbour found that remonstrance was useless, and she returned into the room to break the matter gently to the widow. She was followed by the man, who walked into the room with a noisy air of consequence.

"Get out! get out!" cried George, placing himself before the intruder.

"Get out, indeed! Oh, that's all very fine, my little chap. Now, now, don't lay hold of my waistcoat: I call you to witness, Mrs. Grainger, and you, Mrs. Thingamy What's-your-name, that I am assaulted."

"Cruel man," said the widow, feebly, "I shall witness against thee elsewhere shortly. Leave me to die in peace."

"Witness against me, well! Oh, no, not at all— it's all right—quite a legal distress. You young villain, don't you see you've torn two buttons off my waistcoat?"

"Go away, then," cried the boy, "and don't disturb my mother."

"Disturb your mother! Well, that's good. I believe I stand here representative of the Lord Chancellor, his gracious Majesty, and the church-wardens. What do you think of that, eh?"

"Listen to me, my darlings, said the widow to the children. "This hour is my last. Be good to each other in after life, and——"

"Three quarters church-rate," interposed the man, consulting his book, and speaking with a pen in his mouth.

"And Heaven will send you friends—dear friends, who will love——"

"Three quarters assessed taxes. Two quarters paving and lighting——"

"Who will love you and cherish you. Do not cry for me, but pray to the just God for aid and support. Fear nothing but——"

"Three quarters poor-rates—registration, one shilling."

"Yes, dear mother, yes," cried the children. "But you will stay with us yet?"

"Fear nothing but wickedness, my dear children. Be good and virtuous, and you will be happy."

"And always pay your rates and taxes down on the nail," said the man, "whatever you do."

"God bless you, my children, into His hands I commit you."

"Two quarters rate for repairing high-ways, bye-ways, public-ways, and private-ways, in and about the parish of Bungleum, and for beautifying the church thereof."

"You—you will be kind to them when—when I am gone," said the dying mother to the poor woman who had in vain tried to interrupt the district tax-collector, broker, and parish clerk—for those offices were all combined by the important personage who had so rudely intruded into the chamber of death.

"I will—indeed I will, Mrs. Grainger," said the compassionate neighbour.

"Ha! Mrs. Thingamy, mind what you say," cried the man; "your last quarter's rate ain't paid yet."

"George," said the widow, speaking so faintly and feebly, that her voice could scarcely be heard, "you will always love Phœbe?"

"I will, dear mother, I will."

"You will protect her through—life—and—and be good to her—for my sake."

"Dear Phœbe," said George, "I will always love you; and when I am a man nobody shall harm you."

"Bless you both," sobbed the widow. "One thing more I—would say.——I—I—"

"Nine and four's thirteen," said the broker, "and seven is twenty; and six—and six is twenty-six and six—and three is twenty-nine and six—levy ten and six, forty—valuation five, forty-five."

"Peace," said the widow, sitting up in her bed. "Peace, man; the shadow of God is in this house now. His—His hand is upon my heart. Phœbe—George—Phœbe—*when I am gone do not separate the children ; they are not both mine—but——*"

She sunk slowly backwards—then tried hard to articulate something, and all was still. The widow was dead.

With a burst of grief, George and Phœbe threw themselves upon the body of their dear mother, and called to her to speak to them once more by every tender epithet of loving childhood ; but that dear voice to them was for ever mute, and they were alone in the world!

"What can be done?" cried the compassionate neighbour. "These poor children are left destitute."

"Making a total of two pound five shillings—not reckoning the man in possession," said the broker, closing his book. "Now, Mrs. Grainger, have you got the money, or must I call in my man, eh ?—what do you think of that ?"

"Unfeeling man," cried the woman who was present. "Do you not see what has happened ?"

"Eh—what ?—bless me she is really dead, is she ? Well, I declare ! How obstinate some people are. She said she would die and so she has."

"Come with me, my dears," said the neighbour to Phœbe and George. "You shall stay with me to-day, but Heaven knows what will become of you, for I cannot keep you."

"Here, Muggins! Muggins !" cried the broker, opening the window, "come up here. You must take possession. What was that you said, Missus, about keeping the young uns, eh ?"

"I said I could not keep them. I wish I could."

"Woman, woman, ain't there the parish—the glorious parish ? Send them to the workus."

"Not yet! not yet!" replied the woman. "Come, George, come my dear Phœbe—this is no place for you. Come away."

"One flock bed—one ditto mattrass—one ditto pillow,—one——"

The broker was proceeding with his inventory as George and Phœbe, each holding a hand of the kind-hearted but poor neighbour, and sobbing bitterly, left the house.

That night the weeping children lay in the cottage of the poor woman, and the next morning with her they visited the humble home, where lay in the calm sleep of death, all that was dear to them.

Thus day after day wore on in tears and lamentations, on the part of the orphan children, until the succeeding Sunday arrived, on which their poor mother was to be consigned by the parish authorities to her last home.

The poor woman who had so kindly extended her hospitality to the friendless children, tied upon each of their arms a piece of crape, and with this simple insignia of mourning, and tears of sympathy in her own eyes, she took a hand of each, and followed the mournful cavalcade to the parish church-yard. There, amid moss-covered graves, in the little grave-yard of the picturesque village church, was the grave dug of the widow.

There were few to mourn over her hasty interment. The children knelt by the grave side as the clergyman read the service of the dead, and when he had finished, and had handed his surplice to the clerk in waiting, he asked who the children were, and being told they were the children—the orphan children of her who had just been consigned to the silent tomb, he looked at them with an eye of pity—he was a poor curate, and could only pity. He fumbled in several pockets, and at last found half-a-crown, which he handed to George.

"God help the poor things," he said, "for I cannot."

"There's the parish, sir—the parish," said the clerk. "Dear me, paupers are well off."

The clergyman made no reply, but walked slowly away.

"And what do you mean to do with the young 'uns, eh, Mrs. Thingamy?" asked the official, who in the course of his duty, had come to say "Amen" at the grave of the woman upon whose dying moments he had so grossly intruded.

"Alas! poor things, I cannot help them. I must take them to the parish. I have no resource. Poor things, poor things. I would cheerfully keep them if I could."

The children were weeping bitterly and standing by the little wicket gate which led into the humble church-yard where slept their mother.

"Come, George, come," said the little Phœbe, and led by her he walked back to the grave, which was now filled up and deserted.

They threw themselves upon the green turf, and called wildly upon their mother.

"Oh, mother, mother," cried Phœbe, "come to us again. Come to us again."

"I'll tell you what it is," said the broker, tax-collector, and clerk. "Them there children will be a precious plague to this here parish. I never knowed no good come o' feelings in my life. Ah, Mr. Bung, how do?—how do? You are looking charmingly."

This salutation was addressed to the no less important a functionary than the parish beadle, who at that moment issued from the church-porch, in all the dignity of cocked hat and laced coat.

"Ah, Mr. Seely," said the beadle, who luxuriated in the name of Bung. "How do? how do?"

"Why, pretty well, thank you," replied Mr. Seely. "Do you see them there young 'uns?"

"I does, I does," said Bung.

"Them is orphans," continued Seely; "and they'll be up afore the blessed board, afore another blessed day is passed over our blessed heads— blow me if they won't."

"You don't say so?" cried the beadle.

"Don't I?" replied Mr. Seely; "you'll see. They're a evincing their feelings a bit just now."

"Ah, orphans is a sad plague to the parish. They're always a complaining, and when they're brought afore the board, all they says—'Oh, we're orphans,' and then they excites sympathy, and people says—'Oh! orphans, is they?—give 'em a extra ounce o' gruel a week.'"

"Ah, that's the way, Bung—that's the way. Sympathy's horrid. I never has no sympathy."

"Oh, I knows orphans well. I'd know a orphan a mile off, I would," continued Mr. Bung, warming himself into a fury of indignation. "We're orphans, they always says—and I say, what right have they to be orphans —or, if so be they can't help it, through the obstinacy and wickedness of parents, why don't they conceal it?—that's what I should like to know— why don't they conceal it?"

"It's a indelicate thing o' them to be always a mentioning it," cried Mr. Seely. "A most indelicate thing indeed—werry."

"Uncommon—werry. But it's their malice—their parochial malice, Mr. Seely. I know 'em, don't I—that's all."

"And what's to be done with the poor dear children?" asked the compassionate neighbour, humbly appealing to the important Mr. Bung.

"Done," cried Bung; "why that boy 'll be bound a apprentice to some most respectable man as sits on a wisp o' straw, and breaks big stones into little 'uns."

"Apprentice to stone-breaking?" cried the woman, in great surprise.

"Yes, ma'am, apprentice. And the parish may give with that ere widow's orphan a matter of—let me see. What had the last orphan? him as sweeps the blessed chimbleys, and was killed in a hot flue—oh, a matter of thirty shillings down plump."

"Alas! poor boy—poor George," said the woman. "So well brought up, too, as he has been."

"Eh? What do you say? Poor boy! Well, I never. Did you ever, Mr. Seely?"

"Never, Mr. Bung, never—in all my life, never."

"And the girl—the little girl, Mr. Bung? What will be done with her, sir?"

"Why, she'll be sent out as a maid of all work, in some highly respectable family. That's what she will."

"What little Phœbe? Poor delicate little Phœbe? She is only eight years old, Mr. Bung, I assure you."

"Paupers is deceiving," said Mr. Bung, "particular orphans. Mr. Seely, look at her—look at her, Mr. Seely, what do you think, sir? I say that's a particular strong young female orphan pauper, Mr. Seely. I shouldn't wonder if she pretended she was weak and delicate."

"She might, Mr. Bung," replied Mr. Seely; "and I dare say she'll live in idleness and luxury in the blessed workus."

"Yes," said the beadle, "and with nothing in the world to do for B. B. W. L. but to pick some oakum for eleven hours a day."

"Pray, Mr. B. what's B. B. W. L.?" asked the astonished woman, who was much afflicted at the probable fate of the children.

"It's bed, board, washing, and lodging, ma'am," said Mr. Seely, "what the paupers gets for nothing at all by no means."

"And yet they never is satisfied," said Mr. Bung. "Never, not at all. A old woman the werry other day as ever was, wanted a allowance of quarter of a ounce of snuff every week."

"And did she have it, Mr. Bung?"

"No, ma'am. The werry board got up with indignation, ma'am—and, and—sat down again."

"Dear, dear," said the woman. "Well, sir, I must bring the children to-morrow before the board, and I hope they will be well and kindly done by. I am sorry for the poor things. Come Phœbe,—come George."

"Hilloa!" cried Mr. Bung, as the children passed him. "Hilloa—oa—oa. Do you know who I am?"

"Yes," said George, looking stedfastly at him.

"Well!" cried Mr. Bung. "Well!"

"You are the beadle," said George, "but I don't like you. Come along, Phœbe, dear. Come along."

"There's wice!" cried Mr. Bung, when he had recovered from his utter astonishment. "There's wice!—Did you ever, Mr. Seely, I say? Did you ever?"

"No, I never," cried Mr. Mr. Seely, "never."

"Didn't I tell you, orphans were the very deuce? That comes of being orphans. There's wice in them 'ere paupers!"

Mr. Bung, with this conclusion, knocked his cocked hat more firmly on his head, and walked into the church, and Mr. Seely departed home—wards.

The next day, when George and Phœbe thought once more to have visited the cottage in which they had passed so many happy days, they were rudely repulsed from the door, and they saw that the pretty little garden had been trampled under foot.

With heavy hearts they once more visited their poor mother's grave, and mingled their tears upon the spot which contained the mortal remains of the only being upon earth to whom they had been accustomed to look up for protection and kindness.

"Phœbe," said George, "my dear Phœbe, they say we are to go to the workhouse."

"What is that, dear George? I don't mind, dear, if you go too. Shall we see poor dear mamma ever again, George?"

"Never, Phœbe. You are too young to understand; but she is gone to Heaven, dear."

"Oh, George, why don't we go too?"

"She used to tell me, dear, that she would meet us there some day; but I will always love you, dear, and take care of you till we meet mamma again."

"And shall I always be with you, George?"

"Always, dear, Didn't mamma tell us to stay by one another, and love one another, dear?"

"Oh, yes, she did, George—and we will, won't we?"

"For ever, Phœbe; but we must come home now, for we are to go to the workhouse this morning, dear. They are sure to be kind to you, Phœbe, and if they want any work done, I will do mine and your's too, you know."

The children walked homewards, or at least to what had been their home for a week, trying to cheer each other by their innocent prattle and conjectures of the future. Alas! how little did they know the stormy sea into which they were embarking. Many and many a painful lesson of life had those young things to learn.

Had the hand of kindness and sympathy been now held out to them, time would have obliterated the keenness of their grief for their poor mother's death, and their thoughts of her would have been calm and rational. They would have thought of her as a dear mother who had been called from them in the due course of earthly things to taste of that everlasting joy in a life to come, which is the blest heritage of the virtuous. But from that day on which they walked hand in hand from that dear parent's grave, they for a long time met with no sympathizing tear—no smile of love; and they hugged to their young hearts the memory of their kind and good mother with more pertinacity, and regretted her loss more bitterly at each harsh word or action they were forced to endure.

Before mid-day they were brought before the parochial board of the parish of Bungleum, and then and there duly questioned and examined touching their condition.

Mr. Bung acted on these occasions as master of the ceremonies, and he did not forget the little incident of the day before, when George actually braved him by expressing a sentiment very distinct from that degree of admiration and veneration which he, as a beadle, thought he undoubtedly ought to inspire.

When George and Phœbe were called before the awful parochial board, Mr. Bung seized George by the ear, and so conducted him into the presence, followed by the weeping Phœbe.

"No crying here!" said a gentleman with a very purple face, and a gold guard-chain tied round his waistcoat in so many folds and convolutions that it might be supposed he was held together solely by its agency.

"Do—you—hear?" said Mr. Bung, looking awfully grand at Phœbe:
"the sentiment of the board is, no crying here."

Phœbe dried her tears as quickly as she could, for Mr. Bung had inspired
her with great terror.

"Well, George Grainger," said one of the board, reading from a paper
where's your father, eh?"

"Dead, sir," replied George.

"Fled?" said an old gentleman, with an ear-trumpet; "a pretty fellow!
—and left his brats chargeable to the parish, eh? What's your name—Joe
Manger?"

"No, George Grainger," cried George; "and father's not fled—he's dead
—long, long ago."

"If you please, your washup," said Mr. Bung, "the willin is dead."

"Oh, dead!—very well. Who said he wasn't, eh? Perhaps you think
I'm deaf, eh?"

"Please you, gentlemen," said Mr. Bung, "these here is wicious orphans. You'd hardly believe it, your washups, but the mother on 'em died
to-day was a week."

"Eh, what?" said the deaf gentleman; "their mother was weak, eh?
Don't think I can't hear."

"They belong to this parish, do they, Bung?" said the gentleman with
the purple face.

"They has that 'ere honour, an' it please your washup, but they're uncommon wicious. This here boy orphan, he says, says he, 'I don't like
nobody,' says he; oh, he's a wicious one. And this here gal, she aids and
assistises this here boy, by female orphan arts, your washups."

"Take them into the house," growled another of the board.

"There," cried Mr. Bung, "do you hear that, you wictims of liberality?
No. 3

You are to be tooked into the house. Yes, your washup." And grasping George's ear again, Mr. Bung conveyed him out of the awful presence of the authorities.

The children were soon conveyed with heavy hearts to the workhouse; and there the hardest trial of all, since their mother's death, awaited them. A trial which, in their innocent contemplation, they had never thought possible—they were to be separated.

In vain did Phœbe cling, screaming, to George, and in vain did George hold Phœbe in his arms—they were torn asunder with violence.

"Here's wiciousness," cried Mr. Bung. "Look at my nose!—look at my nose, that's all!"

Mr. Bung had, indeed, received in the struggle, a scratch of alarming length on his nose; and, as he could not exactly say from which of the extremely wicious orphans he had received it, he privately resolved to take every opportunity of revenging himself upon both.

The terrified and sobbing Phœbe was conducted to a spacious hall, where were assembled a large collection of unfortunates, who regarded the newcomer with vacant stares of enquiry.

She was handed over to the tender mercies of a coarse herculean woman, who had the superintendence of several kinds of work; and the child in vain looked round for one kind or friendly-looking face. It was in vain—all was cold, chilling despair; and being neglected for a moment, she crept into a corner, and sobbed bitterly, and called in a low voice upon her dear mother, to come and take her away.

George was conducted to a place similar in appearance, and immediately set to work in tearing wool. His heart was swelling in his bosom, and ready to burst, but he would not cry. Nature, however, at length overcame his boyish, but brave spirit, and he dropped his head upon his knees, and wept.

"Phœbe! Phœbe!" he cried, "where have they taken you, dear?"

A blow with a cane, across his shoulders, brought him in an instant to his feet, and he saw standing before him a stout, rough-looking man, who said—

"Just let me catch you at that snivelling again, my youngster, that's all."

This was George's first real lesson in life. For the first time he had received a blow, and felt that he must submit. His young heart was hardened in a moment, and it was many years before George Grainger shed another tear.

Several weeks passed thus to George and Phœbe in their painful prison-house, and, save at a distance, they had never seen each other.

It was soon seen that Phœbe could not possibly perform hard work, and she was chiefly employed in errands from one part of the building to another.

It happened that once she was sent on an errand to the room of the master, and in passing through the large building, she passed the door of a room in which the boys worked. It was standing partially open, and George—yes, it was dear George—was near it.

She paused, and with a fluttering heart advanced close to the door, but so as not to be seen by those within, for she knew that severe punishment would follow any infraction of the rules of the place, and she gently called "George! George!—Dear George!"

He heard the well-known voice, and watching his opportunity, when the eyes of his task-master were off him, he slipped, unobserved, out at the door.

"Hush! dear Phœbe—hush!" he said, and taking her by the hand, he led her quietly and as gently as feet could fall, to a distance from the door. Then clasping her in his arms, he kissed her a hundred times.

"Dear Phœbe," he said, "how have you have been, dear? They will not let me see you."

"Oh, George!" cried Phœbe, "I am so sorry I called you out, for they will beat you, dear George."

"Never mind, Phœbe; they might do what they liked with me if they let me see you, dear. Oh, Phœbe, I wanted to see you to tell you something."

"What is it, George? Is it about your poor dear mamma, and when we shall see her again?—Oh, tell me, dear—tell me."

"No, Phœbe; but I can't tell you now, for I must go back; but I have a book, dear, and it's about that."

"What book, George? Ah, our dear mamma used to read to us often —very often. Do you often think of poor mamma, George? Oh, when shall we see her again?"

"Often, dear!—often!—I can't sleep for thinking of her. But when I'm a man, Phœbe, dear, you sha'n't stay here—oh no—I've read the book."

"What book is it, George? Mamma, you know, dear, taught me to read a little."

"I have hidden it, Phœbe," said George. "It's about a brave sailor that goes in a ship. And, oh! he sees such things, and he comes home and makes everybody so happy."

"I've seen a ship often," said Phœbe; "a ship is very pretty."

"Oh, yes, Phœbe, and brave. But I must go back now, dear. They'll wonder where I've gone, dear."

"Oh, George, stay, stay—don't go away any more."

Phœbe sobbed upon his breast, and clasped her little arms around him.

"I must, dear—I must. Come again to-morrow. and I'll bring the book. "Oh, it's fine! I mean to go myself, Phœbe, I must run away from here. A boy, that I see in the church, told me how to run away."

"The church, George? Is not poor mamma there? I think she sometimes seems to speak along with the organ, dear George."

"She is close to the church, Phœbe. But to-morrow, dear, come again, —Oh, do come, Phœbe."

"Yes, yes; but I want to go with you in the fine ship."

"It's only boys, Phœbe, that can go," said George, mournfully.

"Is it not? Oh, George, I wish I was a boy to go with you. We could talk about dear mamma all day long."

"But I will come back, you know, dear."

"Soon, soon, George. Oh, stay with dear Phœbe, stay, stay."

George kissed her again and again, and saying, "Remember to-morrow, dear," he crept softly back, and Phœbe, with a lightened heart, performed her errand.

The children of the rich and happy may long remain children in idea and action, but how soon does poverty wage a war with the innocence and simplicity of childhood. In the few weeks that George Grainger had been an inhabitant of the workhouse, he had learnt more of the world and the world's ways than he would have learnt in the humble and virtuous abode of his mother in so many years.

Dissimulation and deceit became necessary to the poor and dependant in self defence. It is sad that it is so, but it is, nevertheless, a truth, although a melancholy one. Those upon whom the poor and needy are dependant, are never satisfied with their simple due of gratitude or service. They must have something over and above an account of their preference, and that something is generally from the impossibility of giving anything else—cringing servility, falsehood, and deceit ; and then, the rich, having themselves, by their insatiable vanity, enacted this evil, turn round and say, " What cringing sycophants the poor are !"

George and Phœbe never had had, nor dreamt of having a secret from their mother, or of covering any action whatever, with the cloak of falsehood, but now they lived in an atmosphere of dissimulation—a place in which everything was artificial from the morning's bow to the master, to the loud monotonous response to the church-prayers on a Sunday from " the poor gallery."

The next day how anxiously did the little Phœbe wait to be sent with some message which might enable her to pass the door of the room where George worked.   But alas ! for a long time no opportunity presented itself, and the little girl performed the various tasks which were assigned to her, with tears starting from her eye.

It was towards evening that Phœbe, despairing of being enabled to meet George by stealth, determined to risk the serious displeasure of the woman who superintended, by asking leave to see her brother for a few moments only.

She, accordingly, approached to where, in solemn state and magnificence, sat this awful dignitary.   As has been said, she was a large, coarse woman, and her appearance was not improved by a very high colour, which, however, was not exactly one which might be compared to the rose, for a strange thought always struck every one that saw it, that it had somewhat the appearance of being produced by a long indulgence in potations somewhat stronger than pure water.

In fact, this lady, at sundry periods of the day, was in the habit of looking out at the window for a moment or two, and then drawing in her head again, with a face redder than usual, and something in her hand which bore a marked resemblance to that most unfashionable article—a black bottle, while, at the same time, a bland odour of gin would pervade the apartment.   The Cardigan was, however, always with great expedition deposited in an enormous pocket, which the distinguished female wore for the purpose of holding waifs and strays in the shape of marbles—now and then an apple, and perchance a halfpenny which the paupers in their love of wealth and thirst for this world's wholly enjoyments, might have possessed themselves of.

It was unfortunate for Phœbe that it was upon one of the interesting occasions alluded to, when the lady's head was out of the window, that she approached to tender her modest request to be permitted to see George.

It is true it was out of the power of the lady to grant so much, had she been inclined, for the master himself, and under him, Mr. Bung were the only persons cloathed with such awful and onerous authority.   But they were all powerful tyrants alike to poor Phœbe, and she had no idea of their difference of rank.

" Please, ma'am," said Phœbe, in her mild soft voice.

She was unheeded ; for if the truth must be told, the neck of the black bottle was deep in the lady's mouth, and a soft stream of the cordial balm of Juniper was passing down her throat, and lulling her senses into sweet oblivion of everything else.

" Please ma'am," said Phœbe, again, " may I——"

The child saw she was unattended to, and she gently plucked the illustrious female by the gown.   Now the lady had not the remotest idea that any pauper would have done so much as to dream of the possibility of plucking her gown ; and as she afterwards declared, she thought it must be a " wisiting justice " at least.   And so, indeed, it seemed a visitation of justice; for the lady at once, in her extreme terror and fright at being, as she conceived, fully caught in the illegal act of drinking gin, when it was quite notorious that her private apartment was adorned with no less than five temperance medals, as well as a framed and glazed solemn oath upon the subject, dropped the black bottle into the paved yard, where it fell with an awful crash.

"Please, ma'am, may I go and see George, again?" said Phœbe, in an imploring tone.

"What!" demanded the insulting female; "and was it you—you—you; dear me, was it you as pulled my gownd?"

"Yes, please, ma'am," said Phœbe.

The lady looked round at the assembled pauper children with an air as much as to say, "Are you not, all of you, old and young, at once struck dumb, and deprived of your senses at this awful effrontery?"

"You little wretch!" screamed the lady, when she had fully remarked the horror depicted on each countenance; "you vile little monster! I'm Macadamized—I am—I'm Macadamized at your presumption."

"I—I only wanted to see brother George," said the terrified child.

"If a hangel had comed out of Heaven and a told me a pauper—and a orphan pauper too—would a catched hold of my gownd, I'd a said, 'Ho! thank you. I doesn't believe it not at all.'"

The children looked at each other in consternation, and thought how thoroughly taken aback and dumb-founded the angel would have been.

"As for you, you little villain, I'll—I'll—I don't know what I won't do yet. I'll——"

"Ah, ah! Mrs. Fungus, what's the matter?—what's the matter?" said Mr. Bung, as he appeared at the door of the room.

"Oh, Mr. Bung, sich a occurrence? You can't think, Mr. Bung!—you can't, indeed."

"Eh? What? Anything wrong, Mrs. Fungus? Paupers is paupers."

"You won't believe it, Mr. Bung—you won't. This here orphan pauper has been a pulling and a hauling at my gownd."

"What!—a assault? Was there ever? This comes of encouraging people to see orphans. Oh, Mrs. Fungus—Mrs. Fungus, that's a wicious piece of goods, that ere female orphan."

"And what do you think she wants? The impertinence! I'm astound-ified."

"What is it, Mrs. Fungus—what is it?" cried Mr. Bung, casting a withering look at the trembling and alarmed Phœbe, who stood transfixed and wondering what she had done to produce such an ebullition of rage and indignation.

"She wants, Mr. Bung, to hold an assassination with the other wicious orphan."

"What! Mrs. Fungus? A assignation you mean."

"Well, perhaps it's both, Mr. Bung. Oh, the hardened hussey! I declare I hav'n't no sort of patience whatsomdever—not at all."

"I only want," said Phœbe, "to see George. He is my brother. Oh, sir, let me see him! Do, sir,—do—just for a little while, sir. I won't stay long—indeed I won't."

"Paupers is horrid plagues," cried Mr. Bung. "What can you want to see your brother for?"

"Mother told us to love each other, sir, and I love George."

"What! do I live to hear it? Love among paupers! That all comes of letting paupers into the house. There ought to be a law—a wery strong law, Mrs. Fungus, for the abolition of orphans, and pertickler of these here, as we has in this here workus. There's nine orphans in this here house, and I wonders the blessed roof don't fall in pop upon 'em, they is such ungrateful wretches."

"Do you hear, you little object, what Mr. Bung says? Listen and improve yourself."

"That ere female orphan," continued Mr. Bung, "is always a bothering about her mother and her brother, as if it wasn't the law of the land that paupers shouldn't have no such things."

"Very true, Mr. Bung; you know what's what as well as most folks. I just dropt a vial of liquid in the yard, and while you are here——"

"Don't think of it, Mrs. Fungus. I heard it—I heard it, and (in a low tone) I chucked the pieces away, and nobody knows nothing."

"Dear Mr. Bung, it was all a owing to that 'ere wicious little brat."

"It were—it were, I know. But she is going to service soon. The board have set upon her, Mrs. Fungus."

"Have they, indeed, Mr. Bung? There, you wretch, do you hear? The board has been a setting on you, and maybe they'll set on you again."

"She is to be brought afore their washups this day week," continued Mr. Bung, "and she'll be sent to service, Mrs. Fungus."

"And wery proper, too. A little idle wretch. I'm always a whopping of her, but nothing 'll do—she's wicious—she's wicious."

"Very well, we'll see, that's all. She'll be sent to a place, ma'am, where she'll be learnt her business, ma'am, and if she don't learn it quick she'll be made."

"Ah, Mr. Bung, the board, I suppose, will wash their hands in her when they've once done for her?"

"Their washups will, Mrs. Fungus, wash their blessed hands of her."

"But will they—oh, will they let me see George? They may kill me and let me go to mamma, if they let me see George."

Phœbe clasped her little hands together, and dropped on her knees before the potentates, Mr. Bung and Mrs. Fungus, and sobbed forth her humble petition to see her dear brother.

"There's artfulness," said Mr. Bung. "Mrs. Fungus, I haven't no doubt but she's a inwoking curses on us at this wery moment."

"No doubt—no doubt. Oh, you wicked hussey! You little hardened wretch! Where do you expect to go to—eh?"

"To see George," sobbed the child. "Oh, do let me go."

"And to talk of the blessed board a imbruing of their blessed hands in her gore!" said Mr. Bung. "It's horrid—dreadful! You sanguinary little brute!"

"Oh, mother, mother!" sobbed the child, convulsively, "where are you? George—George!"

"Take that, will you?" said Mrs. Fungus, bestowing a hearty cuff upon the weeping child.

"It sarves her right—wery," cried Mr. Bung. "Paupers is paupers."

The lady who superintended the children and the black bottle, would have followed up her brutal attack upon the little Phœbe, but the door burst open, and George, rushing in, caught her in his arms.

CHAPTER IV.

"Phœbe—Phœbe!" he cried, "what's the matter, dear? What is it? Oh, you cruel woman, how I hate you! You wicked woman! Never mind her, dear."

Mrs. Fungus was thunder-stricken, and Mr. Bung actually dropped his cocked hat upon the floor.

Phœbe wept in her brother's arms convulsively, and clung to him for protection.

"George—dear George," she cried, "they beat me. Stay with me, George. Don't go away—oh, don't."

"Is the precious world turned topsy-turvy?" asked Mrs. Fungus.

"It is—it is," cried Mr. Bung; "and paupers is beadles and beadles is paupers."

"We're all on our blessed heads," screamed Mrs. Fungus, "and our heelseses is a kicking."

"Paupers sits on boards," continued Mr. Bung, "and orphans is washups."

"Help! help! Murder!" cried Mrs. Fungus rushing to the door.

In an instant divers parochial authorities, of an under grade, rushed into the room.

"Seize them ere able-bodied paupers," cried she. "Oh, the wicious willains! I'm Macadamized again—I am, indeed."

George was immediately laid hold of.

It appeared that, hearing Phœbe's cry, he had, in defiance of everybody, left his work, and guided by the sound of her sobs, reached the room, where he found her on her knees before the incensed Mrs. Fungus.

Before, however, they could tear him from Phœbe, he had whispered in her ear,—

"Phœbe, dear, hide in the church on Sunday."

"Drag him away," cried Mr. Bung; "he has the wery malice of—of—of a steam-engine."

"I'll have 'em both afore the board, I will," shrieked Mrs. Fungus. "Oh, Mr. Bung, you can't think how I'm flurried—you can't, Bung—you can't indeed!"

"My dear Mrs. Fungus, you ought really to take a—a drop of—a—hem!"

"Oh, no, Mr. Bung! not for worlds; not for lots of bright spears and planets. What does the dear medal say?—'Don't drink nothing, and repent always.' That's my motto, Mr. Bung."

"Ah, Mrs. Fungus, you are too strict; you are, indeed. Now, just a small drop of—of—"

"Medicine, Bung—medicine I do'sn't object, perticker if it's—"

"Rather strong," interrupted the beadle. "You are a woman of a thousand—you are, indeed."

"I rather thinks I is, Mr. Bung, but I ain't proud."

"No, no—not at all. Well, good by, good by, ma'am. You have many trials, you have."

"I has—I has. But yer know, Mr. Bung, that——"

"Paupers is paupers, Mrs. Fungus, and partikler orphans is orphans."

So saying, Mr. Bung walked slowly, and in a highly dignified manner, after George, who was conducted forthwith to the black-hole, as a warning to all paupers who dared to possess them ere wery troublesome things—feelings.

Phœbe was sent to work, with a promise of some unheard-of punishment being in store for her.

"Hide in the church," she kept repeating to herself. "Hide in the church. What could George mean?" Phœbe liked the church; she loved to listen to the solemn swelling of the organ, and she knew, likewise, that her dear mother lay close at hand; and she could think of her during the service without being chidden or struck. In the low tones of the swelling music she could fancy she heard her mother's sweet low voice breathing comfort to her dear children, and the little Phœbe would sit listening to the harmonious sounds, while the tears bedewed her cheeks—but they were tears of pleasure: and the Sunday to the little orphan child was truly a day of hope, joy, and deep thankfulness.

The next day was Sunday, and the prisoner, George, was taken from the black-hole to be led to church, to hear the doctrines of love and mercy preached, and then, with threats and blows, to be again thrust into his dungeon—and for what?

Two-and-two the melancholy-looking children were marched into the gallery of the sacred edifice, which was appropriated to their use; and divers old ladies who had arrived early to pay off their weekly debt of religion, exclaimed, "What a pretty sight!"

The girls occupied one side of the gallery, and the boys the other; and many were the keen glances which George cast from where he stood, with the hope of catching, if but for a moment, the eye of Phœbe.

She, too, looked anxiously for him; and the usual smiling recognition between the children took place. They were both sad and unhappy, but they forgot it for a moment to smile at each other from their respective situations.

"Hide in the church," thought Phœbe. "Oh, how? How hide in the church?"

Again she looked at George. He was very pale; now the slight smile and flush of pleasure at the sight of her, had passed away, and he looked at her anxiously and imploringly.

The little Phœbe cast her eyes round what, in her simple estimation, was the immense building in which they were, and she repeated over and over to herself the question of "Where shall I hide?—Where shall I hide?"

She looked carefully around her, but no place of concealment could she see. Her eyes wandered to the roof—from the roof to the pulpit—then to the pews beneath her—to the little communion table—the humble aisle— all were familiar to her, for she had watched them many hours. But where to hide?—that was the question.

She could not think what to do. The organ began to play, but it seemed to her to say, "Hide in the church! Hide in the church." The oppressed child leant her head upon her lap, and wept bitterly but silently, for she knew not what to do.

The prayers were over; the service proceeded, and the clergyman ascended the pulpit, and commenced his sermon. He was the same who had read the solemn service for the dead over Phœbe's mother, and she never forgot him. He always seemed to her like some dear friend. She fancied as if he must have known her dear mother, and the words of hope which he had spoken by her grave-side, had made a deep and lasting impression upon the child's young and susceptible heart.

The discourse of the preacher was mild, earnest, and serious. He was a man who had himself known trouble and the real sickness of the heart, and he spoke calmly and sadly of vice and its consequences—but eloquently and warmly of the dear hopes of the good and the virtuous in the world which was to come. Then his pale face brightened, and his eye dilated, and the poor scholar and divine forgot a world of care and trouble in the fervour of his invocation to his hearers, to repent and "do unto others as they would that others should do unto them."

Mr. Bung meanwhile walked about the aisle, and in, and about, and round the free seats, and blew his nose very often with a bright yellow silk handkerchief, with white spots, which he flourished about as if it had been some flaming banner of grace; and he looked awful and big at little children who had the hardihood to bring an apple or some nuts to church, and

took partial opportunities of eating the same when his awful back was turned. When all the congregation coughed, according to custom, at the end of the prayers, Mr. Bung coughed louder than anybody, and held the yellow handkerchief by an extreme corner, and flashed it in the eyes of all beholders, and he punched the heads and ribs of the aforesaid little boys with the knob at the top of his cane, as a gentle admonishment to keep quiet and acknowledge their unworthiness.

In fact, the clergyman was nothing at all to the beadle—a mere cypher. Mr. Bung was not only much more imposing in his personal appearance, but at the same time much more terrible in his denunciations ; for whereas the clergyman only mildly, and in Christian charity urged his hearers to do right, Mr. Bung proved that in this world there is a retributive justice, which invariably visits apple-munchers, and crackers of nuts, in what he called "a place of washup."

The sermon was over—the blessing was given, and the organ burst forth into a swelling voluntary.

Slowly the people rose, and thronged the little door-way of the beautiful suburban church ; and Phœbe looked anxiously to the opposite gallery, to catch another glimpse of George. She saw him but for a moment—he looked flushed, and his eyes wandered over the sacred edifice. Then in an instant he was gone—she could not say where. Two-and-two the children were marshalled forth as they arrived at the doors of their respective galleries—and the boys going first, Phœbe had an opportunity of striving to catch another glimpse of her brother. But no—she could not see him. The last couple went on—or rather the last three or four boys left in a straggling manner, as was the usual custom—but he was not among them— he had not passed out. " Oh," thought Phœbe, " where can I hide ? Poor George has stayed behind."

No. 4

The bustle around her warned her to depart. She clasped her hands in grief, and wept bitterly.

The other girls passed her one by one, and some paid no attention at all to her, others looked at her for a moment with a curious gaze, and then passed on without even an inquiry as to the cause of her tears. Poor things ! they had all had feelings, but they had seen so many tears, and so much misery, that their hearts had become hardened.

The weeping Phœbe lingered till the last two or three were leaving the gallery,—she felt that she must go too.

" Hide in the church" seemed to ring in her ears, and she cast many a wistful glance towards the boys' gallery, where she felt sure was dear George.

Slowly she reached the door of the gallery. It was small, and opened inwards. A thought struck her in a moment, and her little heart fluttered with anxiety. She was the last, and instead of going out, she shrunk behind the little door. It opened into a little corner, and Phœbe jammed herself up behind it quite close. She feared even to breathe, and trembled in every limb.

The door shut—she heard it locked, but she could not move. She might be alone in that solemn building. How still and calm it looked.

The frightened child sunk upon her knees in the corner where she stood —she burst into tears. She had hidden in the church, and where was George ?

" Phœbe—dear Phœbe," cried a voice.—It was George's. She sprang to her feet.

" George—George,—oh, come to me—come to me, dear George."

She saw him in the other gallery. They were divided by the organ-loft ; but he climbed in a moment round the narrow rail, and clasped in the next instant the smiling Phœbe in his arms.

" Phœbe—dear Phœbe," he cried, " how frightened I was that you would not know where to hide, dear."

" George, I did not know. But I don't know dear, how I came to go behind the door ; indeed I don't. But they will come and find us, George."

" Phœbe, dear, they can't have the heart to beat you, and—and they won't find me long."

" Oh, George ! what do you mean ?"

" I'm going to be a man, dear, and a sailor, and to bring you home lots of guineas and a fine ship, all to yourself."

" Oh, George, dear, are you, indeed ? Let me go too."

" I can't Phœbe—they won't have you. I wanted to tell you, Phœbe—I mean to run away to-night or to-morrow night, and then when I come home with a ship, I'll run here for you, dear."

" How long will it be, George ?"

" Not long Phœbe. I've read all about it. Oh, they are fine brave fellows ! I'll be a sailor. Father was a soldier, but he never came home to poor mother, but I'll be a sailor."

" What shall I do, George, when your are gone ? Oh, what shall I do ?" cried Phœbe, throwing herself into his arms, and clasping him round the neck.

" I—I must not cry any more, dear, so—so don't, dear, make me."

" But you will take me, George ?—Yes, you will. They'll beat me worse when you are gone."

" Tell them, Phœbe, that if they dare to touch you, I'll come and fight them all."

" To-night, George ? Did you mean to go to-night ? Oh, how I shall cry."

"To-night or to-morrow night, Phœbe, I shall slip out when they're all in bed, 'and I know a way how to get out by the back garden."

"We sleep near there, George, dear—all the girls do."

"Then, perhaps, I can come and bid you good-bye, dear. I'll try, at all risk. They sha'n't catch me though."

"Oh, do try—do try, George. I won't go to sleep all night, nor take off my things. I sleep near the door, dear. If you say Phœbe, ever so softly, I shall hear you."

"I will, Phœbe, I will; and when I come back, we shall be so happy, and I'll build you a nice little cottage."

"And we'll have a little garden, George, and flowers."

"Yes, dear Phœbe, and a grotto."

"And dear chickens, George, and a pussy. Oh, dear, oh, dear, we shall be so happy."

"We shall, Phœbe; and it shall be near poor mamma's grave, and we'll sit there, and talk about her all day."

"Yes, George, oh, yes. Poor mamma! When shall we see her again? Oh, dear George, if we could have her in the cottage, she would never cry then."

"Hush, Phœbe!—hush!—Stoop down, dear. What noise was that?"

The children both hid trembling under the seats of the gallery, and they heard some one slowly unlocking the church door.

They peered cautiously from their place of concealment, and saw no less a personage than Mr. Bung himself enter the church.

He took the key from the lock, and slammed the door, arousing many an echo in the old building. He then blew his nose, with a loud trumpet-like sound, and walked slowly up the aisle towards the pulpit.

The children dared not move, or hardly breathe, and they watched his movements in silent and trembling dread of what might be his errand in the church.

"It's very odd, very," remarked Mr. Bung, "that I have been a coming into this ere church for a matter of fifteen years or more atween the services to dust the pulpit cushions, and put things a little tidy, and I always feels a little uncomfortable when I comes. This is a great mercy, though." As Mr. Bung spoke, he took a small bottle from his pocket, and indulged in a deep draught, after which he smacked his lips with a sound equal to the smack of a cart-whip. "It's a wery lonely place is a church, wery; and ever since old Mumbles, the sexton, said he thought he heard, he saw, something speak in the church, ——Eh; Oh Lord! what's that? eh—dear me—ha!—I'm all over of a muck inspiration."

Mr. Bung trembled excessively, and looked cautiously around him for several minutes.

The fact was, that a slight movement of George's had produced a sound in the gallery, which, in the dead stillness of the building, had reached Mr. Bung's ears.

"Well, I declare," he said, "I thought I heard something; it must have been the ratseses and the miceses. Well, it's a wery agreeable thing to have rats and mice; for if one hears an odd noise, it's a great comfort to think it may be only them ere warment."

With this bit of practical philosophy, Mr. Bung proceeded to the communion table, and begun dusting away with great assiduity.

"What it were as old Mumbles seed, or thought he heard he seed, I doesn't know, but it must have been something uncommon horrid, for old Mumbles never could tell exactly what it were."

Mr. Bung having finished the communion table, walked through the little rails, and shutting the little gilt gate, he prepared to ascend to the pulpit.

The children meanwhile watched, with the greatest anxiety, all these movements of Mr. Bung's, and felt considerably relieved upon finding that their first fear, namely, that he had come to search [for them, was groundless.

"George," said Phœbe, in a whisper close to his ear, while she held tightly by his arm, "what shall we do? How shall we go away, dear?"

"Hush Phœbe, hush," said George; "Don't speak. He'll go away soon, dear, and then we'll see. Oh! I wish I was a man."

"And if you had your ship here, George," sighed Phœbe.

"Some of these ere days the old pulpit will come down," said Mr. Bung, standing on the stairs which led up to it. "It will come down with a blessed whop uncommonly slap on Mrs. Birdwinkle's old head, for her pew is just under it, and it's very old and crazy. I never walks near it, never—it creaks uncommon—and I seed it wibrate on'y this very morning."

Mr. Bung now ascended the pulpit, and leaning his elbows upon the cushion, he looked over right into Mrs. Birdwinkle's pew, and seemed for a time lost in the consideration of the vanity of all worldly tidings.

The old pulpit seemed, indeed, frail and weak, for it creaked and groaned under Mr. Bung's weight. He sighed, "afore I was beadle, I seed this ere pulpit a swagging about when old Reverend Josiah Perkinwobble used to preach in it. Mrs. Birdwinkle, she only gave a sixpence last boxing-day, and I sha'n't say nothing more about the pulpit to nobody whatsomever. Some people isn't no loss to society even if pulpits does fall on 'em with a blessed crunch."

Having uttered this discursive and humane sentiment, Mr. Bung sighed deeply, and proceeded to thump the cushions and turn them over, and make other tidy preparations for the afternoon service.

CHAPTER V.

"Phœbe! Phœbe," said George, in a whisper; "perhaps Mr. Bung would let us out, and not say anything."

"Oh, no, no," said Phœbe; "he is a cruel man—he would not, George, dear—I think he would not—don't ask him, dear."

"But, Phœbe, you know it isn't right to speak as he does in the church and to drink, too. We would tell of him if he was to beat us."

"After all," suddenly said Mr. Bung, as if he had come to the conclusion of an intricate train of thought; "after all, what is parsons? Ain't they old pumps? They is, they is; and they know it. It's beadles as keeps parochial affairs a-going, not parsons. They is pumps, they is pumps." Mr. Bung clenched his argument with a thump upon the pulpit cushion, as much as to say, dispute who can.

"There, Phœbe," whispered George; "do you hear that? He would not like us to tell that he got into the pulpit, and called the good minister who said such kind things to God about mother such a name. Oh! I hate him."

"The short and the long, and the wery middle on it is," said Mr. Bung, warming with his subject, "beadles is neglected and not fattened as they ought to be."

"I'll speak to him, Phœbe, dear," said George; "he'll be afraid not to let us go."

"Parishes is stark staring mad," continued Bung from the pulpit; "they look on beables as mere individuals, they does. Now, who am I? What am I? Who—am—I? Why, in course, I answers——"

"Mr. Bung," cried George, from the gallery,

Mr. Bung had just made a thump at the cushion as the voice reached his ears, and his hair bristled upon his head with fright.

"Ha!—oh!—O Lord—O Lord—oh—oh—oh—oh!" he cried, beginning very high, and diminishing to a low tone. "Who—who—who are you?—I—I—oh, dear; oh, dear. I'm a sinner, a great sinner."

Mr. Bung dropped down to the very bottom of the pulpit, from whence only could be heard a low, murmuring sound, and from the vibration of the old pulpit, it might be conjectured that Mr. Bung trembled excessively therein.

"Mr. Bung!" again called George, as loud as he could.

"Oh, dear, dear!" cried the beadle; "there again. Oh! oh! oh! it must be old Mumbles. Oh, Lord! oh, Lord! I—I did steal the wine; I—I did take the coals from the blessed westry fire. Oh, dear! oh, dear! I once sold a dead pauper—oh, Lord! oh, dear!"

George and Phœbe now both stood up perfectly amazed at Mr. Bung's ejaculations and spontaneous confessions, and looked anxiously about for that gentleman for some moments in vain. At length a few groans attracted their notice to the pulpit in which the beadle was ensconced.

"He's in the pulpit, George," said Phœbe; "is he trying to frighten us, dear? Oh, let us go."

"No, Phœbe; the door is locked, and he has got the key. Perhaps he's ill."

"What shall we do, George? He won't speak to us. Suppose we run away now, dear?"

"No, Phœbe, we can't. I must go when it's all dark."

"What does he say, George? He is speaking something. Listen dear."

Mr. Bung's voice was tremulous and solemn, as he spoke from the very bottom of the pulpit.

"Parsons," he said, "is—is—not p—pu—pumps; b—b—beadles is pumps; they is, they is. I—I—I am wery sorry. Oh, dear; oh, dear."

"He says he is very sorry, George. What does he mean, dear? Will he let us go?"

"Beadles," continued Mr. Bung; "is—is human beans, and mere mortals. They imposes on—on paupers—they does. Parsons is wery—wery great guns, and beadles is—is dirt. Oh, wery—wery——I'm a sinner, I'm a sinner."

Mr. Bung here groaned about sixteen tolerably long groans, with the hope of at once producing an extraordinary and merciful feeling in the whole supernatural world, with the members of which he supposed himself now to be conversing.

"Oh, hide, George, hide," cried Phœbe; "there's somebody else opening the church-door."

The children again shrunk down beneath the seats as they heard the rattle of a key in the lock of the door.

In a moment it opened, and Mr. Seely, attired in his Sunday's suit of solemn clerk-like black, entered the church, and closed the door behind him.

"Where can Bung be?" he said, as he stood in the aisle, and looked round the church.

The beadle heard the enquiry, but he was too terrified to recognise the voice of his friend, the clerk, broker, and tax collector, and he burst into another volley of groans.

Mr. Seely's nerves were tolerably well strung, but he started a step or two back at this sudden volley of woe and grief, and turned rather pale.

"Why, w—w—what's that?" he said.—"Eh!—Dear me, what's that?"

Again Bung groaned, and Mr. Seely heard that the sound came from the pulpit, and he thought that surely some cow must have got in. He, however, thought it prudent to retire and summon assistance, so he carefully backed to the church-door.

Mr. Seely's steps, however, were aroused by the voice of Bung.

"I've boned things from the paupers—I'm a rum 'un and a sinner. I pisoned the public mind agin Simmons when I was made the beadle instead of him, oh! wery much—I gets something on the coffins, I does. Oh, dear, oh, dear—I'm a sinner beadle."

"Why, that's surely Bung's voice," said Mr. Seely. "Bung! Bung!"

"Oh, yes! oh, yes! I hears," roared Bung. "Would you like to know about Mrs. Fungus?—She's a sinner, too. Oh, dear, oh, dear."

"Bung! I say, Bung!"—again cried Mr. Seely, advancing, "why, what the devil————"

The pulpit shook more violently than ever as Mr. Seely spoke, and Bung out with such a volley of groans, that Mr. Seely stood aghast for a moment.

"He's ill, he must be unkimmon ill," cried the clerk; "and he'll shake down the very pulpit. Bung, Bung! come down. What's the matter?"

Mr. Seely aproached the pulpit as he spoke, and to the horror of the alarmed beadle, began to ascend the stairs.

"Oh, dear, oh, dear," cried Bung; "it's of no use of denying it; I've sold a precious lot of paupers, but they all went low—very low. Oh, lauk, oh, dear."

"He must be mad," thought the clerk, as he tugged and tugged in vain at the pulpit door.

"What shall we do, dear George?" said Phœbe. "What do they mean, dear?"

"I don't know," replied George. "Mr. Bung is in the pulpit, and won't come out, and Mr. Seely's trying to open the door."

"Shall we creep down stairs, George, and try to get away?"

"We can't dear Phœbe; we can't; they would see us; let us wait a little, dear."

Mr. Seely tugged at the pulpit door, and called loudly to Bung, who groaned as loudly within, and held it close, with his hands upon the lock, with all the energy of despair, for he expected neither more nor less than that the devil himself was on the outside. The clerk, however, proved the stronger, and at last, with a vigorous effort, he pulled the door open, leaving the handle in the inside in Mr. Bung's hands.

The beadle immediately rolled out head foremost, and coming against the feet of Mr. Seely, that humane individual lost his footing, and they both rolled, swearing and groaning, and shouting down the steps, and on to the pavement of the church.

Mr. Bung now fought with great desperation, and in vain Mr. Seely shouted————

"Bung! Bung! are you mad?—Don't you know me?—What are you at?—Here's a go. Bung's in high astericks."

From sheer exhaustion the beadle paused, and staring at the clerk, recognised him.

"What!" he cried, "you, Seely!—Was there ever?—Here's a world."

"Why, what the deuce do you mean? You have nearly broke my back upon the stairs, and then you pummels me down here, and tells me here's a world."

" Did you call ' Bung !' from the gallery ?"

" No, I didn't. What do you mean ?—I've only just come, and then you begins all this here knocking and wallopping."

" Then it were a ghostesses arter all," cried the beadle, making a rush to the door.

" What were a ghostesses ?" cried the clerk, somewhat alarmed.

" That ere woice—that ere woice," cried Bung, " what called to me in an uncommon and wery solemn manner, saying——"

" Mr. Bung !" cried George from the gallery.

" Oh, lauks ! oh, lauks ; there it is again. Don't stop me—let me go— let me go."

" Why," said Mr. Seely, looking up, " that ere is one o' them ere or-phans."

" What !" cried Bung.

" Them ere wicious orphans that as been afore the board and com-plained."

" What !" again cried Mr. Bung, looking positively purple with indig-nation ; " where is we ? Is this me ?—is this you ? Them ere orphans up there ? It's impossible—it's dreadful ; it's—it's—it's everything in the world."

" Mr. Bung," said George, " we want to go back, we won't tell anything you've said—we won't, indeed, if you will let us go."

" Come down, warmints, come down," cried the beadle. " Oh, dear, oh, dear. That I should have been frightened out of my seven senses by paupers. Paupers is paupers after all. Come down, will you ? Come down."

" We won't tell, sir, indeed we won't," cried Phœbe. " I came, sir, to see George, and we staid to see each other, sir. Oh, do not beat George, sir."

" Oh, you—you wagabones : I don't know what you shall be done to. You shall be—let me see—you shall be——"

" Punished, if necessary, but not otherwise ; and pardoned, if possible," said a mild voice, close to Mr. Bung.

The beadle turned, and saw the clergyman standing at his side.

" What is all this about ?" he asked, taking Phœbe gently by the hand ; " what have these poor children done ? Nothing, I dare say, that we may not easily and pleasantly forgive."

Mr. Bung was forced to bottle up his wrath ; and he said, in soft, insi-nuating accents,—

" Oh, Lor ! sir ; please, sir, they have been and hid their wery selves in the blessed church."

" Why did you hide yourselves in the church ?" said the clergyman, mildly, to the children.

Phœbe looked in his mild, benevolent face for a moment, and then burst into tears.

" Do not be frightened, my dear," said the minister ; " no one will harm you. Speak the truth, and it will be hard, indeed, if we cannot forgive young things, such as you."

" Sir," said George, " I persuaded dear Phœbe to hide in the church, to meet me."

" You are brother and sister ?" asked the clergyman.

" We are, sir," replied George ; " and our dear mother told us to love each other always, and speak the truth."

" Your mother told you what was right. Do not do this again, and I will see that you see each other sometimes. God bless you, poor children, you are forgiven. Take them to the house, Mr. Bung, with my compliments, and I request they may be forgiven for this fault, which more concerns me than any one else."

"Oh, dear, yes, sir," replied Bung. "Orphans, come. You sha'n't be whopp'd—oh, no, not at all. You are so very good, sir, everybody says, as you are——"

"Well,—enough, enough. Take the children back."

As he spoke, the bell tolled for afternoon service; and with a beaming smile to the poor children, the clergyman walked slowly into the vestry.

"Did you ever?" said the beadle to the astonished clerk.

"Never," cried Mr. Seely. "He's always a interesting himself about paupers, he is. Ha! he won't get on, not he."

"Yes, it's all very fine, but paupers is paupers. Beadles is rum ones, and knows a thing or two; but parsons is—hem! Come along you brats."

The beadle seized the children each by an arm, and dragged them back to the workhouse, where he was compelled to deliver the clergyman's message, but he added a rider of his own, to the effect that the whipping might only be deferred until some more favourable opportunity.

CHAPTER VI.

PHŒBE lay awake for many hours that night, in the expectation that George might have an opportunity of putting his project of escape into execution, and find some means of seeing her before he went. She wept incessantly; for young as she was, she keenly felt the misery of being parted from her brother, who was now the only being in the world from whom she could claim a kindred or sympathy. She might be days and weeks in that dismal house of wretchedness and woe, without exchanging a word with him, but still she knew dear George was there, and that the same roof covered them both. The sound of her voice could reach him, and she was comparatively happy; but now he was going—going far away, and the sensitive child sobbed in the anguish of her heart, and called upon him by name to stay with his dear Phœbe.

It was near the dawning of morning before Phœbe dropped into a peaceful slumber, exhausted and weary from her night's watching and weeping.

The sun rose bright and clear, and George had not visited her according to promise. Oh, how anxiously she wished to ask some one if he was still there. The bustle of the day began—the harsh voice of Mrs. Fungus summoned the girls to work, and she reluctantly commenced her daily duties.

She thought that, if George had, indeed, left the place, she should hear of it in some way or another; for even during her brief sojourn in that last place of refuge for misery before the grave, one boy had escaped, and a hue and cry had been raised about him, for he was supposed to have gone, filled with complaints, to make dire charges against the parish.

The morning, however, wore on, and Phœbe heard no alarm of any kind, and about mid-day Mrs. Fungus, after bestowing upon Phœbe's head a great number of raps with a brass thimble—a species of quiet punishment to which that lady was much attached, to awaken thoroughly her attention —told her to go immediately, and run all the way, and ask the porter if Mr. Bung was in the house.

"And do you hear, you warmint? If I finds you loitering and stravaging on the road, I'll do for you, you abominable little wretch; I'll teach you to get clergymen to send messages here, you ungrateful horrid hussey. Oh, you artful designing minx—I hate you, I do. Go along now, and be

back in no time at all. It flutters my wery nerves to speak to you, it does, indeed—it's a aggrawation."

Phœbe departed on her errand, with a fluttering hope at her heart that she might see George, if even it was but for a moment, as she passed, which she must necessarily do, the door of the room in which he worked. She forgot the pain of the knocks with the thimble of Mrs. Fungus, and with trembling eagerness walked along the various passages, till she came near the place where all her hopes were concentrated. There she paused. The door, however, was closed, but she could hear the low hum of the boys within. They dared not talk, but there were enough of them always to disturb the silence by clandestine whispers.

Phœbe waited for five or ten minutes in anxious expectation that the door would open. She felt conscious that by so doing she was rendering herself peculiarly obnoxious to Mrs. Fungus, and that she should most probably suffer for her delay; but then the dear hope of seeing George rose superior to all other considerations, and Mrs. Fungus and her awful powers of punishment were all forgotten. The door did at lentgth open, and a tall, raw-boned boy came out. He had not observed Phœbe. He made a low and reverential bow as he stood in the door, before Phœbe could get a glimpse into the room.

The child was about to attract his attention by an enquiry for George, but she shrunk back in amazement, and thought he must be deranged, by the singular proceedings which he immediately commenced indulging in.

No sooner had he fairly closed the door, than the boy threw himself into a striking attitude, and placing his thumb upon the extreme tip of his nose, he achieved that expressive gesture which is denominated ' taking a sight.' Then kicking his legs up as high as his head, and alighting again in another attitude upon the ground, he repeated the operation, only both

No. 5

hands being this time employed, a 'double sight' was the result. This he continued for some moments, accompanying it by a playful waggle of the outstretched finger and a gentle shake of the head, all of which seemed to imply great contempt and everlasting defiance to somebody within the room.

He then stooped down, and in a singular manner grasping his ancles, he looked clean through his legs, and advanced to the door, and retreated several times till his face got very red, and he rose and nodded at the door, and rapped his elbow with his open hand a great many times. All these feats being accomplished, to the surprise and consternation of Phœbe, he opened his mouth, as if he were going to deafen every one by the loudness of his voice, and set his arms a-kimbo; but he closed his mouth again, and merely said in a whisper,—

"What do you think o' that, old stick in the mud?"

With another flourish of his long thin legs, which hardly seemed to belong to him, he was about to depart, having evidently greatly eased his mind, and poured an unheard-of quantity of balm into his wounded spirit by the gymnastic and singular exercise he had indulged in, when his eye suddenly rested upon the alarmed Phœbe.

"Ellow, young 'un," he said, "what's the ticket?—Vot does you bring it in?—Vilful murder?"

"I—I want to know," said Phœbe—"I want to know, please, if George is there. Oh, tell me, is he?"

"Hurrah, my flunkey," cried the boy, "how's your mother?"

"She's dead!" sobbed Phœbe.

"Oh, is she? Wery good. Flare away, then."

"It's George I want to know about," again said Phœbe. "Is he in there? Do tell me?"

"George who? my volloping kid. There a many Georges, my vonder o' the vurld. How can I tell vich is yourn, my pennywinkle?"

"George Grainger," said Phœbe; "that's his name; I'm his sister Phœbe, I am."

"Oh, you are, are you? Yes, he's there; but he's a precious sap, he is; he ain't up to nothing, no how."

"Oh, thank you, thank you," cried Phœbe. "Will you tell him I'm here?"

"Vy, I doesn't mind, if you'll vait till I comes back. I've been sent in a whacking hurry to see vot's a clock, I has."

With that the boy, legs and all, skipped, rolled, and jerked himself out of sight of Phœbe on his errand.

In a few moments he returned, and addressing Phœbe, said,—

"It's wery near half arter twelve, it is. Jist you vait a bit. That ere George is wery near the prisoner's door. P'r'aps he'll saw his timber, and come out."

The boy then retreated a good distance from the door, and folding his arms upon his breast, he walked up to it with a stately air, and a dense frown of defiance upon his brow, and Phœbe thought that without more ado he would kick it open and bounce in, to the consternation and astonishment of the constituted authorities, and she was somewhat surprised when, upon getting quite close she saw the frown vanish, and he opened the door very gently, made a low bow in the entrance, and glided in with an appearance of great humility and respect.

In a few moments, to Phœbe's great joy, the door slightly opened, and George appeared.

"Hilloa!" cried a voice within, "where are you going?"—

For one moment George clasped the little girl in his arms, and kissed her tenderly.

"To-night, Phœbe, dear, to-night," he said, hurriedly; "I'll go to-night, dear, but I will come to you first."

"Dear George, I wish ——"

"What do you mean, you young rarcal?" said a man, rushing suddenly out, and seizing upon George violently; "I'll teach you to slink out when you please. Come along, here's pretty doings, indeed; I say, Scroggs, you run and tell Mrs. Fungus here's one of her young 'uns a coming here and getting out the boys. A precious little warmint you are, to be sure."

Scroggs, who was no other than the boy who had told George that Phœbe was outside the room, now immediately appeared.

"Here, you Scroggs, be off directly and fetch Mrs. Fungus. Here's goings on."

Scroggs, with great humility, storked off, but he whispered to Phœbe as he passed her:—

"Won't you catch it neither."

Mrs. Fungus soon arrived at the scene of action, and darting a lightning glance at Phœbe, she said, in a voice something between a bawl and a scream:—

"Oh, you—you—baggage. You oudacious, unkimmon little beast. How dare you? I declare I am quite putrified,—send for Mr. Bung directly, she shall go up to the board this precious minute, they'll sit upon her I knows. This come of brats having brothers and mothers, and them ere things. You horrid, atrocious little wretch, you'll come to a end, you will, I knows it."

"I asked her to come," said George. "You may beat me for it, it is not her fault; I persuaded her to come. Let her off, and beat me. Dear Phœbe, don't cry."

"Do you hear the warmint?" continued Mrs. Fungus. "He wishes as how she would harden her heart worser nor it is. Oh, you'll come to a end, too, you will, you miss; you will."

"Well, Mrs. Fungus," said the man, who had hold of George, "I've nothing to do with her; you had better take her back; I'll cure you, my lad, of trolling out without leave. Come along."

"Oh, George, George, dear George," cried Phœbe, rushing forward, and throwing herself into his arms, "it was my fault—it was—it was. I asked George to come out."

"Oh, you're a unkimmon nice pair both ov you," screamed Mrs. Fungus. "A precious job we has had. Come along, you little warmint. You haven't got no person to speak for you now."

"Good-by, Phœbe, dear," said George. "Don't cry—never cry, dear—good-by."

"Good-by, George," sobbed Phœbe; "I can't help crying, dear, indeed I can't; good-bye."

George was dragged into the room, and so suddenly, too, by the man who had the charge of the boys, that he nearly caught the whole room at once in the flagrant act of making sights at him through the half-closed door, headed by the incorrigible Scroggs, who was actually looking through his legs, and hopping about in imitation of an enormous crab.

The highly incensed Mrs. Fungus lost no time in summoning to her aid Mr. Bung, and with that gentleman she remained in consultation what should be done with the contumacious and incorrigible Phœbe.

The beadle, upon a careful consideration of the occurrences in the church, had reluctantly come to the conclusion that it would be not at all desirable that the 'wicious orphans' should be goaded to relate what they had heard.

So he strove to calm the wrath of Mrs, Fungus, and to advise pacific measures.

"You see, my dear Mrs. Fungus," he said, "these here orphans have been taken notice of by the wery Reverend Mr. Hamilton, and he's a wery unkimmon persewering indiwidual he is."

"But what's to be done with the little wretch?" cried Mrs. Fungus; "oughtn't she to be flead alive? What a example she do set, to be sure, to the orphans in this here blessed house wot have been wolloped into wirtue, Mr. Bung."

"It's wery bad, indeed, Mrs. Fungus—wery bad; but we must look to ourselves, mum; and that ere wery reverend parson said as how he'd come and see arter those ere orphans, mum, and he says to me, says he, 'Bung,' that is the morning when I went to him, he says, 'Bung,' says he, 'how is them ere orphans?'"

"Oh, it's enough to produce a conflagration," cried Mrs. Fungus.

"Wery, mum, wery; a great confirmation, indeed. It ought to make all parishes tremble."

"It ought, Mr. Bung; it ought. Them ere orphans is radicals, Mr. Bung, I feels them is."

"No doubt, no doubt; but I'll tell you, mum, what I'll do; I am to see the board on Wednesday, and make a wery strong report, mum."

"Dear me, Mr. Bung, are you indeed?"

"Well, mum, the report is to be as to how many able-bodied young paupers there is as is fit to go to service, mum."

"Yes, Mr. Bung—ha! I begin to see. You'll just pop down this wicious young orphan's name. It's a uncommon good idea."

"I will, Mrs. Fungus, I will; and the board, mum, will give a matter of five-and-thirty shillings with her, mum, to teach her some honest trade, or to be a precious out and out servant, Mrs. Fungus, and you'll be rid of her for ever and ever—Amen—Mrs. Fungus."

"That'll do, Mr. Bung. On Wednesday, you say. I'll have her ready, in case the board wants to see her. They may, you know."

"Yes, mum, they may; and as for the boy orphan as owned a dislike to me—me, the very beadle of Bungleum,—I'll have bound a apprentice to—to—to something unkimmon ugly, mum—I will, indeed—something unkimmon ugly."

"It's wery right of you, Mr. Bung. Oh, he's a villain, that boy. Such wice, such wice."

"Well, consider that as settled, mum, then," continued the beadle. "They'll both be gone this day week, Mrs. Fungus, and our blessed minds will be easy."

"What a manager you is, Mr. Bung. Hem!—Would you like a small—hem!—drop of something—some—some medicine, Mr. Bung, if you please, just to calm your spirits? I'm quite flurried myself."

"Oh, dear, Mrs. Fungus, now you mention it, I declare—I——"

"Well, Mr. Bung, just step into my room."

"With the wery extremity of pleasure, mum. I'm a slave—a slave, Mrs. Fungus, to—to—to the parish, mum—and to you, mum—to your blessed charms, mum."

"Oh, what a man you are. Lor!"

"I'm a beadle, mum—a authority, Mrs. Fungus—and a faithful, attached beau, mum."

The beadle and Mrs. Fungus retired into the private apartment of the lady, and a strong smell of medicine, which some low people would have mistaken for gin, pervaded the place.

CHAPTER VII.

THE day wore on in anxious expectation on the parts of both the orphan children. Phœbe was the saddest, for she looked forward with dread to a separation from her dear George, and she watched with fearful anxiety the approach of evening.

George had but one drawback to his elated hopes, and that was the absolute necessity which, boy as he was, he fully saw there was of leaving the little Phœbe behind him, exposed to all the miseries of a workhouse. His own fate, in the fervour of his imagination, seemed painted in radiant colours in the coming future. A sea-port town was not four miles from the house, and he felt convinced, that could he once reach there, he should be able to gain some gallant ship, and realize in his own person all the wonders and pleasures of a sailor's life, as he had read depicted in books, which presented but the sunny side of existence to the readers. He was a bold and daring lad, and dangers he despised; the dear reward of enterprize and bravery he coveted; and oh, how his heart thrilled with pleasure as he thought of the day upon which he might return and rescue his dear sister from the gloomy abode in which, alas! she was compelled to waste what ought to have been some of the purest, happiest, and sunniest hours of her time. How he would clasp her to his heart, and kiss away her tears; and then, bearing her to his gallant ship, up anchor, and away to happy lands, where pearls floated in the clear streams, and tempting fruit and flowers were free to every hand to pluck,—where there were no work-houses—no beadles—nothing but joy, music, laughter, and delight, the whole day long.

These were the sunny dreams which had long haunted the fancy of the romantic boy. He lived in a world of dear imaginings; he had read of such things, and his mind became tinged with the bright hue of romance, which never, even when the stern realities of existence in after years, had scattered his air-built castles to the wind, wholly left it.

These thoughts supported him under punishment, harshness, and a thousand miseries. His couch at night was converted into a resting-place of joy, for his sleep was visited by bright phantoms. The teeming thoughts of the day were presented in all the vivid colouring of reality to the romantic boy in the still hours of the night, and he rose each morning with a flushed cheek and sparkling eye, for his visions had been those of hope and joy. The evening deepened into night, and the children were conducted to their dormitory.

Phœbe slept with a companion near the door of the long room, in which, nightly, there reposed fifty unfortunate little beings, who had all been, like herself, thrown on the parish for support. The room opened upon a long passage, at the end of which was a staircase, which led at once to the basement story and back of the house. There was a garden at the back, in which were grown vegetables for the master's table, and beyond that a paddock, which was used for all sorts of purposes.

The garden opened into the paddock by a little gate, and the paddock was only divided from the open country by a thick-set hedge.

George's principal difficulty in escaping from the house, would be to get at all into the garden. After that, if unpursued, all was easy.

At the bottom of the staircase was a stone-paved room, which led into the garden, but the door of it was usually at night securely fastened, and if he could not pass that, all his hopes of escaping by means of the garden were at an end. There was but one chance, the door was always locked, but the key was frequently left in the inside, and, in addition, a heavy bar was commonly put up at night.

Phœbe was in great anxiety as the order for bed was given, and she marched along, with her poor companions, to the long room, in which they all slept, and adjoining which was a small apartment, which was the chamber of Mrs. Fungus.

She sat down on her little bed, and trembled excessively, while the usual prayers were being read; and oh, how fervently did she beseech Heaven to prosper her George, and give him success in his scheme.

Poor Phœbe had been quite converted by her brother to the opinion that the best thing he could possibly do for them both was to go to sea; and the poor child had so indefinite an idea of time, that she would not have been surprised to have seen him return in a few weeks with everything that his fervid imagination had painted to her fully accomplished, and that then they could immediately live together in the state of pure enjoyment they had together so fondly pictured to themselves, when they conversed in the church.

Phœbe's bed-fellow undressed and retired to rest, but still Phœbe sat absorbed in thought, and apparently unconscious that she was the only one in the room who was not in bed.

She was, however, quickly roused by sundry thumps from Mrs. Fungus, and proceeded hastily to prepare for bed.

"You little, lazy, idle wagabond," screamed the incensed lady; "as I live, here you is, and not a blessed rag off yet. What do you mean by flying in my face in this here manner? It's really past nothing I never heard on."

"I'm going to bed, please ma'am," said Phœbe, beseechingly, and taking off her things as fast as her trembling hands would let her.

"It's wery well for you that I've the temper of a blessed angel, else I really doesn't know what I wouldn't do. Oh, you odious little troublesome thing."

Phœbe crept trembling to bed, and covering her face with the scanty clothing, laid quietly until Mrs. Fungus had exhausted her stock of invectives, and retired.

That lady paused at the threshold of her own chamber, and, in a loud voice, said,—

"Now just listen to me;—if I hears so much as a blessed mouse stir all this here night, I'll be among you, and you'll wish as you was skeletons rather than what you is."

With this admonitory threat she retired, and shut the door behind with a bang which startled every one, and awoke fear and dread in their breasts.

Phœbe suppressed her sobs, and listened attentively for the least sound. She heard the low breathing of the children, as they subsided one by one into sleep; and her eyes becoming accustomed to the darkness of the room, she could see the dim outline of each of the little beds, where slept the young things who were commencing life under such wretched auspices. The nights were moonlight, but the cheering luminary had not yet risen from below the horizon, and the place was dark and dismal.

A long time, Phœbe thought, must have passed, and still George comes not. She sat up in her bed, and strained her ears to catch the least sound. No one stirred; all was calm and still.

She was sufficiently near the door to see it tolerably well, and she fixed her eyes upon it for a long time, with the hope of seeing it open, and George appear.

Sleep nearly overcame the poor child once or twice during her melancholy watch, but she roused herself, and shook off the insidious infection.

Hour after hour thus passed, and Phœbe heard, amid the stillness of the night, the clock of the church strike twelve clearly and distinctly, but still he came not.

"Come, George; oh, come, come," she murmured, gently.

The silver light of the moon now came stealing into the room, and fell upon the sleepers.

The apartment was as light as day, and Phœbe could note the position of each particular child, as it rested on its humble couch in blessed tranquil sleeep.

How many might be dreaming of home, once happy home, and smiling faces of dear friends and kindred now in the silent tomb.

Phœbe started—some one spoke—it was a young child in her slumbers.

"Mother! mother!" it cried; "dear mother!" and the little voice died away in indistinct mutterings and tearful sighs.

Alas! poor Phœbe! What a sound was that of 'Mother!' for awakening echoes in her own young heart. She burst into tears, and repeated the words,—

"Mother! mother! dear mother!"

And now the solemn sound of the church clock again broke the stillness of the night, and one struck. The sound died away apparently in the far distance, and Phœbe started, and again fixed her gaze upon the door.

"Dear George," she thought, "cannot come. He said to-night, but they won't let him. No, no, he cannot come."

The exhausted girl dropped upon her humble pillow, and after a few ineffectual efforts to keep her eyes fixed upon the door, and murmuring exclamations of her brother's name, she dropt into a restless slumber, with the radiant moon-beams resting on her gentle and beautiful face, making her look like some fair and exquisite marble statue, which in some moment of inspiration had been wrought to 'enrich the world with loveliness.'

Phœbe could not tell how long she had slept, but she was suddenly awoke by some one laying a hand lightly upon her face, and the voice of George said, in a whisper in her ear,—

"Phœbe—Phœbe dear—awake, dear Phœbe—I am here—hush! hush!"

She opened her eyes, and saw George bending over her. He was very pale, and the moonbeams fell upon his face, and gave it a spectral appearance.

Phœbe sprung up in the bed, and threw her arms round his neck.

"Hush, hush," said George; "speak low, Phœbe, dear. I—I—am going—I will come back for you—God bless you, dear Phœbe—bless you, love."

"Oh, George, dear, dear George, what shall I do when you are gone? What shall poor Phœbe do?"

"Hush, hush, dear, you will waken some one. I must go now, love Good-by, dear; good-by, dear, dear Phœbe."

"Oh a minute—a minute more, dear—stay a minute—come soon, George —oh, come back soon, dear—can't I go, too, George?—Oh, let me come— I will come now, dear."

"No, Phœbe, no; it can't be; they won't have little girls, dear; they can't fight, you know, and be brave."

"Oh, but I will fight, dear, and be brave. Oh, take me, take me."

Phœbe got out of bed, and hung round the distressed George.

"Phœbe, dear Phœbe," he cried; "you will spoil it all. Let me go, dear, and I will come back again so soon—I will, indeed, dear. Good-by, good-by."

Phœbe's sudden moving from the bed awakened the girl who slept with her, who, opening her eyes slowly, was for a moment perfectly bewildered to see Phœbe kneeling in the moonlight at the foot of George, whom she at once magnified into a robber and a murderer, and everything else terrible, including a ghost.

"Oh, dear! oh, lauk!" she screamed.   "Murder! murder! murder!"

In an instant the whole room full were awake, and a yell and a scream arose sufficiently loud to arouse the whole village.

George kissed Phœbe fervently, and then freeing himself at once from her clinging grasp, he rushed out at the door.

"Murder! murder!" cried the fifty girls all at once, and in a few moments the door of Mrs. Fungus's chamber burst open, and out she rushed, screaming—

"Fire! fire!"

"A ghost! a ghost!" shouted Phœbe's bed-fellow; and the cry of a ghost! a ghost! rung through the room.

"A what?" cried Mrs. Fungus; "a ghostesses. Oh, lauks! oh, lauks!" Phœbe had sprung after George when when he left the room, and being missed by her bed-fellow, the latter immediately cried,—

"Oh, ma'am, oh, ma'am, the ghost has run away with Phœbe Grainger."

A crowd of persons now appeared at the door of the room, among whom was Mr. Bung, with his state coat hanging down in front of him, for he had thrust his arms in it as if it had been an immense laced pinbefore, and he made frantic exertions to button it, wondering where the buttons and button-holes could have possibly got to.

"W—w—what's the matter?" he cried; "is the blessed house a fire? Oh, dear, oh, dear."

"We're all a fire," screamed Mrs. Fungus, who was attired in a night-cap, kept fast upon her head by a black handkerchief, which passed under her chin, and a frilled jacket and short petticoat; "we are all a fire—we is, we is."

"I don't see it," said Mr. Bung, still vainly endeavouring to button his coat.

"It's a ghostesses as has comed and took Phœbe Grainger away," cried Phœbe's bed-fellow, pertinaciously.

"I smell a rat," cried Mr. Bung.

"Oh, Mr. Bung," cried Mrs. Fungus; "do you, indeed; the odious monster."

"Them ere orphans has been at it again, mum. I'll just step back, and slip on my—a—a—athingumys, mum, and be back directly."

"Why, really Mr. Bung, you don't mean to say you've comed here into this wery room without your—oh!—good gracious."

"I was in a hurry, mum, and forgot 'em," cried the beadle; "and all the blessed buttons, mum, has come off my coat, and the button-holes seems to have cut arter them ere."

"Why, Mr. Bung, Mr. Bung, you've got on that sweet coat the backer-dermost part afore," cried Mrs. Fungus, with a scream.

"Eh? what? Bless me, so I have;" cried the beadle, and he rushed out of the room.

He was hardly outside the room, when he raised a shout of exultation—

"Mrs. Fungus! Mrs. Fungus! Mum, mum, mum, didn't I say it was them ere wicious orphans? Here they is, a veeping on the blessed stairs, both on 'em. Now one on 'em has cut his stick; he's becomed a figurative; now the tother on 'em faints on the blessed stairs. Now the boy orphan cuts along like bricks, and undoes the yard-door. Oh, you willain, you willain, you would run away, would you. Catch him, catch him."

Mr. Bung made a rush to overtake George, who had staid but another moment to kiss the weeping Phœbe, but the coat was in his way, and down he rolled from the top to the bottom.

Mrs. Fungus thought it was more prudent to remain where she was, so after a little consideration, she fell into hysterics and screamed violently, in which exercise she was joined by all the girls in full chorus.

Mr. Bung's fall had precipitated several others, who had been aroused by the outcries in the girls' sleeping-room, down the stairs; and George, finding, fortunately, the key in the lock of the door, had barely time to turn it, and pull down the bar, when Mr. Bung, despite his bruises, made a rush towards him.

George, however, was far too nimble for the embarrassed beadle, and he slipped out at the door, and darted through the garden.

Mr. Bung now, in the ardour of the pursuit, threw down the coat, and appeared very lightly clad indeed.

George gained the little gate, and clambered over it in an instant into the paddock, still hotly followed by the beadle. They reached the hedge nearly together, and George, without hesitation, burst through it, and was off into the open fields.

Mr. Bung was not exactly in a fit state to burst through a prickly hedge, but he was at the top of his speed, and could only just check himself sufficiently to stick fast in the very middle of a blackberry bush.

"Oh! oh! oh!—the deuce—the deuce," shouted Mr. Bung, and with all the desperation of heart, from numberless pricks and scratches, he emerged, leaving his only garment behind him.

Back towards the house he bounded, and flew as never beadle bounded and flew before, and frantically rushing up the stairs, he sought his own room, amid a shout from many of the boys who had risen and witnessed his singular situation.

No. 6

Phœbe had been dragged back by the enraged Mrs. Fungus to the sleeping-room, and the whole house was in the greatest confusion and alarm.

George Grainger, however, was fairly off. Before half an hour he was several miles from the place, and twelve long years passed over his head before he again saw the workhouse of Bungleum.

CHAPTER VIII.

IT was a beautiful and serene night that George had accidentally chosen to execute his darling project of escape from the monotonous wretchedness and petty tyranny of the workhouse. The moon was high in the Heavens, and its beams fell upon the leaves of the trees and the waving grass, changing their bright green into a silvery hue. Not a cloud obscured the brilliant lustre of the scene; not a breath of wind stirred the leaves of the tenderest wild flower that slept in beauty by the hedge side.

So calm and serene a night had seldom come out of the Heavens; and it would seem as if the white light, which, like a sheet of pure molten silver, spread itself over all objects, had exercised a holy and calming influence upon the elements, and hushed them to repose.

George Grainger, when he felt himself free from the pursuit of the beadle, looked all about him, anxiously to obtain his true direction to the sea-port town, which he knew was within an easy distance of the spot where he stood, provided he took the right road towards it.

The various objects and buildings in the neighbourhood were familiar to his eye, and lit up, as they now were, he had no difficulty in ascertaining his true path.

Fearful, then, of further pursuit, he started off at a good speed, which he did not relax till he had accomplished more than two-thirds of his journey.

Exhausted then, both in body and in mind, he sat down on the roots of an aged oak-tree, which grew by the way-side, and his thoughts reverted painfully and bitterly to the situation of the poor and friendless Phœbe, whom he had left among persons so little calculated to sympathize with her griefs, or soothe her distresses. He had foresworn weeping, or his tears would now have flown at the situation of his gentle sister.

"The time will come, however," said he, "and it may come soon, when I can take care of poor Phœbe myself, and then she will be so happy that she will forget everything that has ever vexed her, and I think we will go and live somewhere else, where we shall never see that hateful workhouse again."

The morning was beginning gently to dawn as the wearied George Grainger rested himself upon the root of the aged tree. The moon-beams were growing paler and paler, and the stars were, one by one, gradually fading away and disappearing from the blue vault of Heaven.

The birds were beginning their morning's song, numberless insects began to buzz and flit about as the day approached, and a slight breeze began to blow from the sea, from which George was not now above a mile. George turned his face in the direction from which it blew, and he could taste in his mouth the saline flavour of the wind, which, probably, ere it reached him, had swept over the wide Atlantic Ocean.

George Grainger was without a cap, and the delightfully refreshing breeze waved and tossed about his clustering hair, and imparted to his frame a sensation of health, strength, and elasticity, which he had been a stranger to in the gloomy workhouse. His eyes sparkled with pleasure as he inhaled the pure air. "It comes," he cried, "from the sea, the beautiful sea, where I am to make a fortune for Phœbe. Dear Phœbe, oh, if you were but here this moment to feel this pleasant wind blowing upon your pale, pretty face—but it shall be soon, very soon—I'll come home a man and a sailor, and a lot of money, all for Phœbe."

"That's right, my man," cried a voice behind him; "that's a brave fellow; you'll get on in the world, though you have got all your troubles before you, and may get more kicks than coppers, like the galley monkey.'"

George Grainger turned abruptly round upon hearing this singular address behind him, and he saw a rough, weather-beaten, but withal, good-looking sailor standing close to him.

He was attired in a small blue jacket and trowsers, and on the front of his shirt, which was visible, was worked the word "Flame."

"Well, my hearty," he said, smiling at George's confusion, "you are a sweet lad enough, and you want a trip on the blue waters, do you?"

"I want to go to sea," replied George, "and be a brave sailor."

The tar took out his tobacco-box, and deliberately placing a fresh quid in his mouth, said:—

"Hark'ye, my lad. I'll tell you what our skipper once said about that very thing, and he was a devil of a fellow for an argeyment, he was. Bless you, he'd argey, and argey about anything, he would. It's not him as I sails under now, for he was paid off, and I've joined the marchant service. Well, I'll tell you how he argeyed once. We was sent along of a squadron to the Mediterranean, we was, and we expected a little fighting, you see, for the Turks was obstinate, and wouldn't ewacuate a fort, as we wanted 'em to ewacuate, you see. But, howsomdever, when we gets there, there was a summut they called a—let me see—a armistice, which meant no go. Now our captain he didn't at all like that ere, and he'd have all the officers up, and he'd say,—'I'll argey any on you, this here damned armistice won't last. And then they all grinned, and bowed, and said nothin', for they knew if they once began a argeying with the captain, it would last for ever, cos they all knew how he argeyed three different doctors out of the ship, and so he had. Well, this here was always his argeyment:—'I don't think the armistice will last.' One day, howsomever, the admiral of the station comes aboard, and he says, says he,—'Captain Newcombe, this here's wery dull work.' So our captain he looks round on the officers, and he says,—'Why,' says he, 'that ere admits of argeyment,' says he.—'Wery probable,' says the admiral, with a smile and a wery fine bow. But cos captain wasn't to be choused out of argeyment that way, so he says:—'I don't think that this ere armistice will last.'—'Nor I, either,' says the admiral, says he. But our captain wasn't a bit to be done out of his argeyment like that, so he says:—'But you know there's something to be said on both sides of that ere question,' says he.—'Very true,' says the admiral, says he, 'and at all events it will last another week.'—'No, excuse me,' says our captain, quite pleased at the argeyment, 'it won't; oh, no.'—'I thinks as it will,' says the admiral, says he.—'We'll argey that,' says our captain.—'No, no,' says the admiral; 'I haven't time,' says he; 'but you must get a cable's length or two further in shore, for you could not hit a man on the batteries from here.' Well, our captain was wery much pleased, for here was another argeyment. Nevertheless, it were uncommon true that we were far out, 'cause o' a shoal close in shore; but he had aboard a long forecastle gun, which turned on a swivel, and would carry ever so far, point blank. Our captain he takes the admiral to the gangway, and he says, says he, a pointing to the battery, and a winking at the the gunner. 'Don't you see,' just for the sake of argeyment, 'that fellow there smoking a pipe through that port hole?'—'Yes,' says the admiral, 'I do. It's a good range,' says he. Well, there was, sure enough, an old

Turk of a fellow, a winking and dozing away, and a smoking his long pipe out at a port-hole. Now the captain he keeps a leading the admiral to this forecastle gun, and all the while, a argeying away like mad. Then he winks again at the gunner, and he looks at the old fellow a smoking, and the gunner he pints the gun, and waits to see the end of the argeyment, and so did the old Turk. 'You maintain this here,' said our captain, almost skipping with pleasure. 'You say as the guns won't reach the batteries, and the armistice will last another week.'—'I do,' says the admiral; 'most certainly I do; that's my argeyment.'—'Hurra, then,' cried our captain. 'I'll have the best o' that ere argeyment any way.' With that, round he turns, and catches hold of a pipe from a man's mouth, and pops it to the gun. Bang it goes, and a round shot went whack into the port-hole of that ere battery, and took the Turk's head clean off. 'What do you think o' that for an argeyment?' cries our captain. 'There's an end of the argeyment and the armistice too.' Hurrah! hurrah!"

George listened, much astonished, to this story, and the seaman was not a little pleased at the interest his narrative had excited.

"I tell you what, my fine fellow," he cried, "I think I can get you a berth if so be as you likes to come along o' me."

"With pleasure," said George; "I wish, indeed, to go to sea, and to go soon, too."

"Keep in the mind, then," cried the sailor, "and I'll make a man of you. You're the right sort, you are. You'll live to be an admiral."

"I don't mind fighting," said George. "I want to be a brave sailor."

"And a brave sailor you must be, if so be you be one at all. Our captain he used to say, 'all men are sailors or swabs.' If so be they are sailors, they are out and outers; if so be they are swabs, then they are only fit to holy-stone hell, and feed the devil's jackdaws."

"If you will help me, sir," said George, "to go to sea, I will always be willing to do everything I can to please you, I'm sure."

"But what makes you so anxious to go to sea, my lad?"

"Oh, sir, I've—I've run away and——"

"Whew," whistled the sailor. "You've run away? and from where?"

"From the workhouse."

"The workhouse! the workhouse! Then if ever you run back again, you're not fit to fetch a swop to sick monkies. Why, who wouldn't run away from a workhouse? The worst ship that ever swam on the blue waters is better than all the workhouses and slow-going charities that ever sailed."

"Oh, yes, I know it; I'm sure of it," cried George.

"Why, if the ship's bad, and the captain's bad, and the grog's bad, and the beef and biscuit's walking about, there's the blue sky and the blue water; the bright and the free air; the merry laugh; the song and the yarn, and the kind messmate."

"There are, there are," cried George, his eyes sparkling with pleasure, "I've read of all that; I know it all well. Oh, it's delightful."

"Workhouse!" repeated the tar, with great indignation. "You've done right, indeed, to run away from a workhouse. Damn their workhouses. They put my old mother into a workhouse, because she wouldn't pay a matter of two pound a year rent for the little cottage, and I—I was far, far at sea. I made a calculation when I come home, and I found that when they put her in the workhouse I was off the Horn."

"Off the what?" said George, much interested.

"Cape Horn. We calls it the Horn. Well, when I comed home, I goes to the little cottage, and I knocks in the door, and says,—'How are you, mother?' But mother weren't there by no means, but there sat a fellow, a reading summut, and a turning up his eyes to the ceiling, and a saying—'The Lord forgive us.' Well, I says, 'Hilloa, old chap, where's my old mother as lived here?' So he says, a closing of his book, and giving his face a sort o' conwulsion, says:—'If so be you means the wicked woman who lived here, who would not be awakened to the new light, she's in the workhouse, a miserable sinner.' So I says to him:—'You be damned,' and I gives him a good 'un jist on his figure head, and away he goes into the corner. Then off I starts to the workhouse, and when I gets there, I says, 'Hilloa! hilloa! workhouse, ahoy!' Then a fellow opens a little port-hole, and pops his head out, which I claws hold on. So he hilloas and I says, in a mild and civil sort of way, 'Damn you all, you pirates, where's my mother?' So a chap says, says he, 'You can't have her, cos the board don't meet afore this day week, and they must make a order,' he says. So I knocks him down for being so wery unsatisfactory; and mother, she heard my voice, and comes running out, and a precious old female galley a giving chase. Well, I takes mother under my arm, and the old 'un as was a follering says, says she,—'She can't go; we can't permit it,' she says. So I says,—'Who the devil are you?' quite in a civil shore-going way, you see, and she says,—'I'm the matron.'—'Wery well,' says I. Then she says again,—'I'll alarm the ship—no, no, the house.'—'Will you?' says I; 'then I'll shew you how to do it, my old carittee war canoe.' With that I goes up to her, and holds her headway tight, and gives a kind o' hilloa in her ear, which was cut exactly in a whisper, and away she goes into what they calls high strokes. With that I knocks down another fellow at the door wot looked cross, and I walked off with mother. I'd got my pay in my pocket, and I took her a hundred miles round the coast, and settled her in a nice little crib, where she could sit at her own door and see the crafts come down the channel. I've been to see her now, I have."

"Oh," cried George, clasping his hands, "if I could but come back so, and take poor Phœbe away, how happy I should be."

"Who's Phœbe, my lad?" asked the sailor.

"My dear little sister," replied George, mournfully. "Mother's dead, and I want to go to sea, to get money for poor dear Phœbe."

"Bless your heart, youngster, you're the right sort," cried the warm-hearted tar, grasping the little hand of George; "I'll be your friend, my boy; I'll ship you with myself, if I can, and I don't doubt it, for our captain is as good a fellow as ever shipped between stem and starn."

"How can I thank you?" said George; "you are very kind. I should, indeed, like to go with you above all things."

"Come along, then, my boy; we won't lose no more time; we sail with the first wind."

The seaman took George's hand as he spoke, and they bent their course rapidly towards the town, which was not half an hour's walk from where they stood.

George felt the first sensations of sanguine hope full realized in this fortunate and unexpected encounter with the kind-hearted sailor. He fancied now he saw his way clearly before him, and his heart panted for the time when, like the brave man who held him by the hand, he could return to the workhouse, and snatch from its dreary walls, with pride and exultation, the being who was most dear to his heart in the whole world, the only one for whom he sighed, and for whom he would, fearlessly, meet any difficulties or dangers that might present themselves in the course of his career on the sea, to which he now looked forward with a heart elate with hope.

As they walked along he would look timidly, but trustingly, up to the weather-beaten face of the honest seaman, and he felt it was a face that he could love, for its expression was genuinely kind and good-humoured.

"See," said the tar, as they reached a little eminence which overlooked the town and harbour, "see, my boy, 'tis nearly light enough to see the 'Flame;' that's the name of my ship; that's her with the blue pennant."

George looked earnestly in the direction the sailor pointed out. A crowd of vessels, presenting to the eye a forest of masts, stood in the capacious harbour. He saw the blue flag gently fluttering in the morning air. A bright gleam of the mornnig sun now fell upon the sea, the shipping, and the picturesque town; it was the first beam from the orb of light as it rose from the bosom of the sea. That gleam of sunshine fell likewise upon the heart of George Grainger—his face flushed with joyous expectation—he stretched his arm towards the vessel, and for a moment he could not speak.

"For Phœbe, dear Phœbe," he cried, at length. "For her! for her!"

CHAPTER IX.

It was between five and six o'clock in the morning when George and his companion entered the town.

The morning was beautiful, and the sun was shining upon every object with a mild, yellow radiance, gilding into beauty the most worthless things and the meanest houses that it fell upon. The streets were beginning to be thronged with persons, and everything seemed bustle, activity, and cheerfulness. A fair wind for many outward-bound vessels was blowing, and the cheerful 'yieve ho' of the sailors, and the clicking of the capstans as the anchors were raised, came pleasantly to George's ears.

"We shall be off in half an hour," cried the sailor, as he hurried to the quay. "See that ship—that's the 'Angelica;' she's going to trade in the South Sea Islands."

George looked at the vessel indicated by his companion, with extreme interest and delight. Sheet after sheet of white canvass seemed to spread themselves like the wings of some large bird. The anchor was up, the pilot was on board, and for a few moments the greatest bustle seemed to prevail. Then a command was heard, and, with a fluttering noise, a broad sail was bent to the wind. It flapped for a moment against the cordage, and then, slowly curving seawards, it caught the breeze, and, amid a breathless silence on board the vessel, the stately fabric, to which was committed the lives and fortunes of so many human beings, slowly moved through the water.

A cheer burst from the crew as they felt she had her way, and a responsive cheer burst from those on shore.

The gallant ship was off. She cleared the harbour. The captain stood with his speaking-trumpet in his hand; he lifted his cap for a moment as the vessel left the harbour, and another cheer, both from the crew and the spectators on the shore, rent the air.

"Oh, was there ever music like that?" thought George.

"Shake a reef out there," shouted the captain.

"Keep her easy," cried the pilot; "the breeze freshens."

"Aye, aye, sir," cried the crew.

Onwards flew the gallant vessel.

"Oh!" cried George, clapping his hands in an extacy of enjoyment, "that is fine—beautiful. Shall we go like that?—shall we, indeed?"

"We shall, my boy," replied the sailor, "and quickly, too. We are going to Havannah. Come, quick—on board—on board!"

In a few moments George found himself on the well-kept deck of a stately vessel. The man whom George had so fortunately encountered was the mate of the 'Flame,' and he well knew he could take a youngster on board without much difficulty.

The captain stepped forward to look at George, after a few moments' conversation with the mate, and then nodded his head in acquiescence.

They were clearing out, and already had the immense fabric began to feel the influence of the outward breeze. She swung round only by her head ropes.

"Clear away!" was shouted; and in a few more moments the vessel had no connexion with the shore.

George stood, holding by a rope, looking upon the animated scene with a bewildered eye. The bustle to him was new and strange. The fluttering of the sails—the commands of the pilot and captain—the cheers of the men —all formed a scene of so much animation, that George, while he was delighted, yet, at the same time, felt himself utterly confounded.

There was one circumstance, however, which gave him great joy, namely, that all chance of capture from the parish authorities was at an end. They were free from the shore, and the distance every moment increasing.

The motion of the vessel was very gentle, and it appeared to George as if it was the people and the harbour and the town that were moving away, and not the ship.

The mate had left him on the spot where he stood, and had told him not to stir till he came to him, and George had only now and then observed his figure in different parts of the vessel, as he attended to his numerous duties.

As George was just flattering himself upon having thoroughly escaped the clutches of the parish of Bungleum, he happened to cast his eyes shoreward; and what was his dismay and surprise to see Mr. Bung, in full official costume, standing on the extreme edge of the quay, and shaking his staff of office at the retreating vessel, in which he had been informed by some idlers on the quay there was a boy, who had been taken on board by the mate, answering the description of George Grainger.

George started at this fearful apparition of parish authority, and, clasping his hands in despair, he gave himself up for lost.

"What's the matter, youngster?" said the mate, who at the moment was passing him.

"Look! look!" cried George. "See, there's the beadle—Mr. Bung. He's come for me."

"The what?" cried the mate, shading his eyes with his hand, and looking in the direction which George indicated.

"The beadle. See, he's been sent for me. They want to drag me back to the workhouse."

"Oh, that's the beadle, is it? I'm thinking he'll have a long arm to reach you here. Now, I'd a given a month's pay to have had him aboard. I never heard of a beadle aboard of a vessel in my life. What glorious fun it would have been, to be sure. A beadle! Oh, I've seed sich a thing afore to-day," continued the seaman, after taking another long look at Mr. Bung. "Why, he's going to hail us, I declare. Oh, it's glorious!—a beadle a hailing of the 'Flame!'—ha! ha! ha! It's—it's—ha! ha! ha! —like a elephant a reefing top-sails, it is. Oh, dear! oh, dear! We sees rum starts in this ere world; but if any one had told me a beadle would a hailed the 'Flame,' I'd a said it's a —— lie, I would."

George kept his eyes fixed intently upon Mr. Bung, who, after some conversation with a bystander, actually borrowed a speaking-trumpet, and, holding on to a capstan with one hand, and standing on his tip-toes, as if by that means his voice would certainly reach further, he placed the trumpet to his mouth.

"Mr. Flame," cried the beadle; "Mr. Flame! Stop! stop! sto—p!"

A shout of laughter sounded from the quay as Mr. Bung spoke, which was echoed by the crew, many of whom nearly fell into convulsions of mirth at the ship being called 'Mr. Flame.' The captain of the 'Flame' had gone below, but, hearing the laughter and confusion, he came on deck to enquire the cause, and stepping up to the mate, he said—

"What is this?—what's all this?"

"It's a beadle, sir," said the mate, smothering with difficulty his laughter; "it's a beadle, sir, as has come for the boy."

"Indeed," said the captain. "Bless me—a beadle?"

"Don't you see him? There he stands, sir, a hailing on us, a few pints east, sir, of the church steeple."

"Mr. Flame!" again shouted Mr. Bung, and again the people roared with laughter.

The captain smiled, and said—

"I don't know what authority he has, but I don't see him, really—you will recollect I couldn't see him—I don't see any beadle at all."

"Aye, aye, sir," said the mate, with a knowing wink.

The captain immediately descended again, with a broad grin upon his face, and the moment he disappeared, the crew burst into a roar of mirth.

The vessel was very slowly working out of the harbour, and the distance between Mr. Bung and George was momentarily increasing, to the great joy of the latter.

Mr. Bung, it appeared, had now prevailed upon some one to hail for him, and a voice reached the ship clearly and distinctly.

"Flame, ahoy!"

"Damn him!" cried the mate, "he has got one of the harbour-muggers to hail for him. Give me a trumpet—we must answer. Beadle, ahoy!" sung out the mate.

"Send the boy ashore," cried the voice.

"What workhouse?" shouted the mate; and another roar of laughter followed, both from ship and shore.

Mr. Bung might now be seen stamping with great indignation, and flourishing over his head his official staff, with the little gilt crown on the top of it.

A pause ensued, and it appeared as if the person who had hailed for Mr. Bung had thrown up his office, and that gentleman himself was utterly unable to make his voice reach so far. The mate now again placed the trumpet to his mouth, and, after asking of George the beadle's name, he shouted—

"Bung, ahoy!"

Mr. Bung upon this might be seen to flourish his staff more energetically than before.

"We're bound to Havannah," shouted the mate. "Hold on till we come back, and then you shall have him."

Another roar followed, and the discomfited beadle held out his staff like a gun towards the ship, in indication of future vengeance, while he stamped with great strength and energy upon the quay, to the immense amusement of the idlers there assembled.

The ship was out of the harbour, the breeze blew fresh and free, and the last George Grainger ever saw of Mr. Bung was a great bustle upon the quay, and an apparent fight between that functionary and some one.

The orphan boy still held by the rope, and gazed towards the land—that land which he could have freely left without a sigh of regret, had it not been for the friendless and unfortunate Phœbe. Of her he thought as the

gallant ship foamed through the dashing waters. Less and less distinct grew the town. The individuality of the people was lost, and they presented but one dark mass.

The sounds of life from the shore grew each moment more indistinct, and shortly entirely subsided. Lower and lower sunk the vessel on the sea, and George could soon see nothing of the land but a low black line on the horizon; then a choking sensation arose in his throat, and he stretched his hands towards the shore, which was now nearly merged in the swelling sea, and cried—

"Mother, mother!—Phœbe, dear Phœbe!"

The wind whistled through the cordage; the ship rode on her way triumphantly, and George Grainger lost sight of his native land for many a weary day.

CHAPTER X.

THERE was great confusion and consternation and vociferation, and all sorts of bustle, at the workhouse of Bungleum, on the morning after George's escape.

It was soon ascertained who was the culprit who had disturbed the serenity of the establishment on the previous night, and George Grainger was spoken of and anathematized as an extraordinary villanous production of nature, who, not content with running away from his B. B. W. L., had, no doubt, penetrated to the sleeping-room of the girls with all sorts of sinister objects; and a diligent search was made, and much anger and disappointment occasioned to Mr. Bung, by finding, as the result of it, that George had not robbed the house.

No. 7

"I'll tell you what it is," said Mr. Bung, at about four o'clock in the morning, to Mrs. Fungus, "that wretch of a boy orphan was on the wery eve, no doubt, of finding his way into your blessed room, mum, where you sleeps the blessed sleep of wirtue and wery incommon innocence, mum."

"Oh, goodness gracious me, Mr. Bung," cried Mrs. Fungus. "If the willain really had—oh, dear! oh, dear! The hardened monster. I dread to think, Mr. B., I does, I does."

"I'm determined, Mrs. Fungus, to make a wery horrid example o' that ere wicious boy orphan, mum," continued Mr. Bung, "and wot I wants is, to question the female orphan as to vere he has gone, and then won't I cotch him soon, mum, that's all?"

"Certainly, Mr. Bung. I'll fetch the little wretch here directly."

So saying, Mrs. Fungus departed, and presently appeared, dragging in the weeping Phœbe, who, still half clad, mourned George's departure.

"You abominable wixen," cried Mr. Bung, "what have you got to say for yourself? Don't you know you ought to be hung?"

"No sir," stammered Phœbe. "I—I am very sorry George is gone. What shall I do now?"

"Wice! wice! wice!" cried Mr. Bung.—"Wice you see, mum."

"Oh, yes, Mr. Bung. You little wretch, where's your brother gone? Tell instantly, or else you'll be flead alive, you will, you baggage."

"George has gone to sea," sobbed the child.

"To sea!" cried the beadle. "Wery well, wery good. Then, Mrs. Fungus, I'll soon have him back. I'll go to the town myself, armed with authority, mum, and drag him back by the hair of his wicious orphan head."

"Oh, dear, Mr. Bung," cried Mrs. Fungus, "don't go into any danger. Recollect how the hardened willain behaved last night."

"It's wery true, Mrs. Fungus. He, mum, and five strong men, assaulted me in the paddock, and stole my shirt, mum."

"Oh, dear, oh, dear; I know they did, the wretches. Oh, the murderers, I wish I had 'em here."

"I wish you had, mum—I wish you had. You'd soon let 'em know, mum, who they was. Good bye, Mrs. Fungus; good bye. I'll bring back the monster, mum."

So saying, the beadle departed on his errand in pursuit of George. Of his non success we are aware.

It was nearly mid-day when Mr. Bung arrived back to the workhouse; and as he entered the gate, it was noted that his official hat flapped down behind somewhat like a coalheaver's, and his highly-imposing laced coat was sadly begrimed with mud and dirt, and torn in many places, and he carried his staff of office in a smaller compass than when he started, for it was broken into three pieces, so that it became like a jointed flute, much more convenient to carry.

Mr. Bung's face, likewise, was expressive of much chagrin and bitter disappointment, and it had acquired a curious and knowing aspect, by being ornamented with a long scratch, which commenced exactly under one eye, and then took a slanting direction to the extreme tip of his official nose.

He walked solemnly across the yard, with the broken cocked hat flapping slowly against his back.

He walked directly to the room, in which were usually assembled some of the magnates of the parish, and there, sure enough, were Mr. Seely and one or two of 'the Board.'

Mr. Bung walked in to the surprise of every one, and, with a rueful countenance, he turned himself slowly round three times, like a joint of meat roasting.

"My eye," cried Mr. Seely, but the beadle did not notice this interruption, and slowly placing upon the table, side by side, the three pieces of the official wand which he had taken out with him in the morning in all the glory of paint and gilding, he solemnly looked into the faces of those present, and said—

"Is this the world, or isn't it? I asks no more. Is we here? or is we there?—Here yesterday, and gone to-day. Is parishes obliterated, and wice a ruling like mad? Is nothing everything to nobody? and is orphan paupers emperors and great commanders? Is ships and wessels wessels of wrath? Is beadles——"

"Why, Bung," interrupted the astonished Mr. Seely, "what's the meaning of all this here? Is you gone crazy? Wot do you mean?"

"Is this," continued Mr. Bung, with a disdainful sneer, "the times wot we lives in? Is there law, or isn't there law? Is there authorities of all kinds and sorts, from a lord chancellor up to a beadle? Where's Bungleum?—no where's. Where's me?—no where's. Where's paupers?—why, a riding on the backs of steeds, and a galloping over boards and workhouses, and kings and queens, and beadles and princesses, and all them ere."

Mr. Bung sunk upon a chair, and taking up the tail of his tattered coat, he wiped his eye, and thereon deposited a quantity of mud. He then passed the coat skirts generally round his face, and transferred to it various streaks of dirt from his garment.

"Where am I now?" he continued. "Look at me—I was Bung—I was beadle—whom is I now?—am I changed?"

"I'm blessed if you ain't," said Mr. Seely.

The two gentlemen belonging to the board had looked at Bung, and then at each other in horror, at the extremely revolutionary and singular doctrine which that gentleman gave utterance to in the despair of his heart, and they were so thunderstricken, for a few moments after the beadle had ceased his extraordinary and eloquent harangue, that they could not speak. At length one said—

"Mr. Bung, Mr. Bung, this is a—a—really—I—I—bless me."

"Precisely my opinion," said the other. "Precisely."

"Why, gentlemen," said Mr. Seely, "this ere's all along no doubt o' that ere orphan pauper as tried to fire the workhouse last night, murder Mrs. Fungus and Mr. Bung, and ruinate all the gals!"

"Ive been a—assaulted," said Bung; "assaulted in the exercise of parochial duties, I has, I has—by willains who laughed at the wery parish wot holds a blessed canopy of pertection over their ungrateful heads. They broke my wery stick—bonnetted me so wiolently that I couldn't see, and fity thousand of 'em, all at once, rolled me in the kennel."

"And did you catch the boy, Mr. Bung?" asked one of the board.

"No, I didn't," said Mr. Bung; "I was opposed by a wast population; I took 'em all into custody immediately, though."

"And where are they, Mr. Bung?"

"Why, sir, you'd hardly believe it, but not one on 'em would come, sir; and cos that ere boy orphan couldn't have Phœbe here whensoever he liked, they halloed to me through a speaking-trumpet that he was a going to have Ama."

"Well, summon a special meeting of the board," said the gentlemen, both together. "To morrow, Mr. Bung, you'll attend, and explain all this sadbusiness."

"I will, gentlemen," said Mr. Bung, "you may depend I will—it's wery afflicting—I don't want a commotion, or a revolution, or a war with France or America, on my account ; but I thinks as some bloodshed can't be wery well avoided, when beadles is bonnetted, and rolled uncommonly in dirty kennels."

The next day saw the board assembled specially to hear the report of Mr. Bung, of the circumstances attending the escape of a pauper, and the assault upon him, their officer, in the discharge of his duty in attempting to re-capture the same pauper.

There was the deaf gentleman looking highly intelligent, and alive to everything, which he did not hear, and there was the gentleman with the faint purple face, and the still deeper purple nose, and various other gentlemen, in all the beautiful variety of a parochial board.

Phœbe was dragged in the awful presence as being a culprit of no ordinary magnitude in the matter, since she was last seen with George upon the night when he had left the workhouse.

Mrs. Fungus, too, with some flaring new cap ribbons, was there, with a bottle of hartshorn in her hand, which, whenever her feelings nearly overcome her strength, she applied violently to her nose, and so recovered more fortitude.

Mr. Bung thought proper on this occasion to appear in the identical torn coat, and dilapidated hat which had suffered so much on the quay.

He had, moreover, been to the town and procured the attendance of the man who had hailed the ' Flame' for him, and the identical trumpet, with the assistance of which that feat was accomplished.

Mrs. Fungus was the first witness examined, and she deposed as follows :—

" Your wurships, there has been conflicting conflicts ever since these two orphan Graingers comed into the house.   My wery great affection for children is wery well known, and I showed that ere female orphan as was under my presiding care the wery extremityist of indulgences."

" Very good," cried one of the board.

" Wery good, sir," repeated Mrs. Fungus.   " I always allows the children to sit down when they don't want, and stand up when they are tired, I does ; and I never wollops 'em, oh, never, wery seldom, leastways."

" She's tender, yer woshups, wery tender," said Mr. Bung.

" What's that ?" cried the deaf gentleman ; " did he steal a fender ? eh ? eh ? oh!"

" Well, your wurships, I sees 'em all abed, and I says, ' if any on you is ill in the night, never mind disturbing me, but vake me up at once.' "

" It's quite affecting, it is," cried Mr. Bung, with a great flourish of the yellow handkerchief.

" Then, your worshops, I goes to bed myself, but I was soon awaked by a willain a grasping of my throat, and a woice said,—' You're a ornament to the parish, and I'll murder you all at once.' "   Mr. Bung groaned and blew his nose violently.   " Then I starts up, and I sees it was that ere orphan what's runned away, and I says to him, says I, ' Repent, and I'll forgive you,' which wur wery forgiving of me."

" Oh, wery, wery," said the beadle.

" Oh, so he went in a wherry, did he ?" cried the deaf gentleman.

" Well, then, his conscience was alarmed, and he rushes out and tries to cut everybody's throat as he meets, and this ere female orphan a encourages of him, and runs arter him down the stairs most undecent, oh, wery."

" Well," said the purple-nosed gentleman, " this is a serious affair. What have you got to say to this, eh ?" to Phœbe.

"Nothing, sir," said Phœbe, "but George just come inside the door to bid me good-by."

"He broke open the door and wanted to get by," said the deaf gentleman, recording a note of the evidence.

"Mr. Bung," said the purple-nosed man, "what have you got to say about the matter?"

"Yer wershups," said Mr. Bung, "jist look at me."

The board did so, and inclined their heads to signify that they saw him, and he then continued :—

"Do I, yer woshups, look like a parochial officer?—Do I look like a beadle?—no, I do not.—I'll tell yer woshups why. I was sleeping wery sound, and a dreaming o' the wast trouble the blessed board always had with wicious orphans, when I heard some one scream a scream, and call 'Fire and murder!' and as a parochial officer, I got up to see what the blessed skrimmage was about."

"At one o'clock in the morning," suggested Mrs. Fungus. "It was my woice he heard."

"Well, yer woshups, I rushed to my coat, and on I puts it, this here wery identical coat wot's now so anti-parochial, yer woshups, with mud and tears, and on I puts it."

"The hindermost part the forrerdest," said Mrs. Fungus.

"Wery true. Well, I runs to the screams, and I seed this here female pauper a wopping everybody, and the boy pauper flourishing three carving knives and forks, with bone handles."

"Ha!" sighed Mrs. Fungus, "I quite forgot the knives, but it's wery true, oh, wery. Then he rushes down stairs; all the young females was a laying about promicious, and the female orphan, with a wery short female shirt on, was a cutting arter him."

"The female orphan," said the deaf gentleman, making a note, "run after everybody, and cut their shirts? Dear me."

"Then, yer worshups, I cuts away arter them, and falls wop down the blessed stairs, along o' Mr. Seely."

"Wery true," cried Mrs. Fungus; "I seed it—I seed it."

"Having the interest of this here parish wery much at heart, I jumps up, and follers him hard. Then he undoes the door and bundles out, and I throws down this here coat and bundles arter him. Then he blows a immense whistle, and fifteen men jumps up, and tears my wery shirt off my back, and I comed back like a ordinary indiwidual, and no beadle at all, yer woshups."

"A daring outrage," cried the purple-faced gentleman.

"He got a great blow on his whistle, and comes back an ordinary man to wash up. Eh?" said the deaf gentleman, "a very singular occurrence, indeed. I hear you perfectly well, Mr. Bung. Go on, go on."

"Well, yer woshups, the female orphan confesses as he, the boy orphan, intends to go to sea, so Mrs. Fungus mildly wollops her, and I goes to the harbour to cotch the boy, and when I gets there, I sees him jist a going in a whacking ship, as they told me was the 'Fame.' So I hollers and holles, and they merely says—'Beadle a-hoy,' and sails away. Then a woman comes up, and she says ,says she, 'I knows that ere beadle; he belongs, he does, to Bungleum, where they killed my child, and—' a hem!"

"What else?" said the purple-faced gentleman; "eh?—speak out.—What did she say?"

"Smugged the body," groaned Mr. Bung, "as if—oh, lor! Well, yer woshups," continued Mr. Bung, "then they pitches into me, and the mob says, hurray, and they wollops me, and breaks this here staff into three

separate and indiwidual pieces, and bonnets me in a most absurd and horrible manner wery much, and rolled me in the kennel."

"A terrible outrage," cried the purple-faced member.

"Then, yer woshups, that wery woman she scratches my face in this ere
way as you sees, yer woshups, and makes me a object to behold."

Mr. Bung had finished his narration, and he wiped his face with the
yellow handkerchief, and flourished the same very much before the eyes of
the board.

"Are there any witnesses to all this?" said one of the board.

"There was a wet nurse at all this," wrote down the deaf gentleman very
carefully among his notes of the case.

"Yes, yer woshups," said Mr. Bung, with a tone of exultation, and he
immediately produced the speaking-trumpet.

"That ere, yer woshups, is the wery trumpet as the indiwidual hailed
that ere wessel with, as the boy wicious orphan went away on board on."

A great sensation was produced at the board by the production of this
remarkable piece of corroborative testimony, and it was handed from one
to the other, and examined with very great curiosity and attention.

"This is conclusive," said one of the board; "most conclusive."

"It's been once japanned," said another. "Most singular."

"The production of such things as these here," said another, "gives a
wery great finish to a case, indeed; oh, it looks so real."

All doubts seemed removed by the production of the trumpet but those
of one gentleman, who rose, and said:—

"Mr. Chairman and gentlemen, this board ought to decide upon the most
conclusive evidence possible. Now I am told that the man who blew
through this trumpet is actually here in this house, (hear, hear). If so, gentlemen of this highly honourable board, I suggest we ought, to remove all
doubt whatever, to hear him actually hilloa through it the wery words he
used to the ship; and if the carving knives and forks could be produced, it
would be better still."

Loud cries of "Hear, hear, hear," followed this speech, and the gentleman sat down, very hot, but with a nod of the head, which plainly indicated
that he thought he had made rather a hit than otherwise.

"Please yer woshups," said Mr. Bung, when the excitement caused by
the brilliant display which had just been made had partially subsided, "it's
thought as the uncommonly persewering and wicious boy pauper swallowed
them ere carving knives and forks, with the bone handles, and took 'em all
to sea with him."

"Ha!" cried Mrs. Fungus; "I seed him a trying them."

"But, yer woshups, here's the wery man as blew the wery trumpet."

The man was here introduced, and the purple gentleman said,—

"Who are you?"

"Vy," said the man, in a voice that made the board jump, "they calls
me 'Dick Martin.'"

"Dear me," said the board; "and what are you?"

"A gallows mugger."

"A what?—What's a—mugger?"

"A feller as warps out wessels from the harbour," replied the man.

"Is that a speaking-trumpet?"

The trumpet was handed to the witness.

"Why, yes to be sure. Every fool knows that, I should think."

"Are there any initials or other stamp on that trumpet?" asked one of
the board.

"No, there isn't," exclaimed its owner.

"I'm perfectly satisfied," said the questioner, making a note in a great hurry, and nodding his head a great number of times, to indicate how easy his mind now was upon that most important point of evidence.

"Will you now," said the purple-faced gentleman, "place yourself in the precise attitude that you were in when you hailed the ship, at the request of the beadle of this highly respectable and most populous parish?"

The man seized the trumpet, and putting it to his lips, he shouted, in a voice that made the house echo,—

"Flame ahoy."

"God bless us!" cried the board; "that'll do. That's conclusive evidence, indeed;" but the man was determined to give the whole of his evidence clearly, as he shouted again,—

"Send the boy ashore."

The board gave another jump, and placed its fingers in its ears.

"But they did not?—Oh, dear, dear George, they did not send you back?" cried Phœbe.

"No," cried the man, "they didn't; but they walloped the precious beadle."

Phœbe clasped her hands in thankfulness, and said, while tears of joy coursed each other down her cheeks,—

"Poor dear George, he's gone—he's gone. They did not catch him. He'll come back and take me away. Dear, dear George."

"Stop that riot," cried the purple-faced gentleman.

"You warmint," cried Mr. Bung, "don't you know as there's no feeling allowed here? Hold your noise, can't ye, ye reprobate?"

A little gentleman now rose, with a thin perked-up face, and a pair of spectacles, which he looked over, not through, and said,—

"Richard Martin, attend."

"Eh?" said the man, looking round him. "Do you mean me? Lor' I'm never spoked to in that ere way. Call me Dick."

"Did you," continued the little gentleman, counting off each word upon his fingers, and when he had got through both hands, beginning calmly over again. "Did you see, observe, notice, or otherwise become cognizant of an assault, battery, insolence, push, blow, thump, scratch, by person, or persons, men, women, or children,—upon or against the person of this parochial officer—or beadle? Eh?"

"Vot do you mean, spooney? I seed the beadle walloped."

"Were the party or parties who gave, or caused to be given, by deed, word, action, or otherwise, or in any way, or in no way whatever, and notwithstanding the beating, thumping, or walloping to the aforesaid beadle, or parish officer, residents or non-residents of—the town—manor—borough, or otherwise denominated place where the aforesaid assault, battery, or——"

"You be blowed," said Dick Martin, and catching up his speaking-trumpet, he very abruptly left the court.

The little man looked perfectly aghast at this contempt of court, and sat down, muttering unutterable things.

"Clear the room, clear the room," cried the purple-nosed gentleman. "We will consider and make known the result. Clear the room."

The room was cleared, and the board sat in profound deliberation till nearly dinner time.

CHAPTER XI.

THE honourable board having been further informed that Phœbe Grainger was an able-bodied and an uncommonly strong, as well as vicious pauper, by Mrs. Fungus, determined forthwith upon sending the delicate and fragile little girl to service.

With this intent Phœbe was duly ranked up with such of the inmates of the workhouse as were declared fit for service, and submitted to the inspection of divers females, who, to save proper wages and food for their domestics, usually selected them from the unfortunates at the parish poor-house.

These ladies who visited the workhouse, were commonly of middle age, with vinegar-looking visages, illustrious females, who prided themselves wonderfully upon their household attainments, which commonly resulted in the acquirement of the full art and mystery of living upon so slender a larder, and reducing the household economy to such a depth of meagreness, that their husbands have been eventually driven from home in dire despair, and flown, with reckless joviality, to cook-shops and public-houses.

It was about four or five days after the decision of the board with respect to the unfortunate little Phœbe, that she, with some others, was ranked up to be duly inspected by a " lady," to choose a slave from among its pallid and spirit-broken inmates.

Mr. Bung had been provided with a new coat and hat, and a new staff of office was in active preparation, so that that individual again appeared in very nearly his former splendour.

There was a look of fixed determination upon the brow of the beadle, as he walked with great majesty across the yard on that morning, and all sorts of kings and emperors might have seen and profited by his appearance.

He carried in his hand a paper, on which appeared some printing, and in his mouth he carried four red wafers, and in his official pocket was a wafer stamp, which belonged to the board.

Mr. Bung met several persons as he proceeded to the outer gate of the workhouse, but he spoke not, merely contenting himself with a nod and a smile, which plainly indicated to those who were used to Mr. Bung's symbolical language, that he rather thought he had settled some one's hash in a complete and satisfactory manner, and that the world might prepare to open its eyes, and express its admiration in any other manner it pleased, for he, Mr. Bung, was fraught with some important act, which would cause a cold shudder to run through society, and force it to have immediate recourse to a glass of something strong to recover itself, and cause its blood again to flow freely.

To the outer gate, then, Mr. Bung wended his way, and, without the least hesitation, clapped the same on the gate, at about the height of his own official nose, and completed the whole proceedings by four vigorous impressions of the wafer stamp, one upon each corner.

Mr. Bung then thrusting his hands under his coat tails, retired backwards to see the effect of the announcement he had just posted. He read it slowly, and with fearful distinctness.

" ABSCONDED.—Twenty shillings reward.—Whereas ! whereas ! an orphan of the name of George Grainger, after assaulting, in a ruffianly and disorderly manner, the parish officers, with four carving knives and forks, has absconded, with property belonging to the parish, consisting of one pair of shoes marked ' Bungleum.' Whoever will lodge the said George Grainger

in any of his Majesty's gaols, shall receive the above reward. He is an able-bodied pauper, and is expected to resist, as he has a gang of fifty ruffians with him, who were all apprehended by Mr. Bung, parish beadle, &c. &c. &c., but none of them would proceed in custody. One shilling each will be given for the apprehension of these men, who assaulted Bung, and tore one shirt, his lawful property.

        "By order of the Board,

                   "OLIANTHUS SNIFFLEUM, Clerk.

"Bungleum.   "JEREMIAH BUNG, Beadle."

"I rather think," cried Mr. Bung, "as that ere 'll be a warning to paupers, partickler orphan paupers, to take wery great care how they insults beadles in the wery pursuit of their wocation. It looks uncommon well. I got the printer to put them ere &c. &c's. arter my name, and he's done it amazing."

Mr. Bung then walked some distance down the wall of the workhouse, and then returning quick, in the manner of a chance passenger, in order to bring vividly before his mind the effect which the bill was likely to have upon persons passing, he affected to stop very abruptly, and read the placard.

"Wery good, wery good," he cried; "it'll do unkimmon well, and 'Jeremiah Bung, beadle,' looks wery imposing indeed. I rather think I has settled them ere orphans at last. The warmint of a boy orphan said as he didn't like me. He'll find as beadles isn't to be disliked with impunity."

Mr. Bung was not a selfish man in his gratifications, and he proceeded into the building, and brought out Mrs. Fungus, to observe the effect which the bill might have upon that lady's wounded feelings.

No. 8

"You and me, mum," said Mr. Bung, as they proceeded across the yard, "is wery peculiarly interested in this ere business. You were insulted, Mrs. Fungus, by your wirtuous chamber being made the resort, mum, of a male orphan, mum, and you was seen, Mrs. Fungus, in a nightcap, mum, and while the female paupers, mum, were observed by that horrible, wicious male orphan, mum, in their wery beds, mum."

"It's dreadful to think of, Mr. Bung," replied Mrs. Fungus; "it is, indeed. There wasn't a bit of starch in the borders of my cap; and to think that on that wery occasion I should be, as it were, dragged out clean from my bed, to be exposed to the wicious gaze of such a hindiwidual. It's been a sewere shock to me, it has."

"And no wonder, Mrs. Fungus. Orphans is always hardened characters, mum."

They had now arrived at the outer gate, and Mrs. Fungus read the bill with highly gratified feelings, and intimated to Mr. Bung, that she felt very much relieved in her mind now that there was a strong probability that George would be hung some day soon, or, if not hung, at least transported for the term of his natural life.

Just as Mr. Bung and Mrs. Fungus were retiring from the gate, a lady arrived at it, and darting a glance at the bill, then another at Mr. Bung, and a third at Mrs. Fungus, she inquired, in a voice which sounded not much unlike the notes produced by the sharpening of a saw, if the paupers could be seen.

"Why, yes, ma'am," replied Mrs. Fungus; "you comes, I 'spose, to choose a sarvent, ma'am?"

"Yes, I do," replied the lady. "I'm a housekeeper of this parish, and I'm sick of dirty idle sluts of servants. I've turned off twenty-six within four months, and I hear that you've got here strong girls, who—who don't eat much, and want to learn their business."

"They is instructed, ma'am," said Mrs. Fungus, "to controul their horrid appetites, and we has some as is much stronger than brewers' horses, ma'am."

"Well, I think such a one as that would do," replied the lady. "I'm not particular, but I expect them to be clean—tidy—good plain cook—smart—quick—understand getting up fine linen—boot and shoe cleaning—active—good at her needle—know how to clean plate—pickle onions, and make herself generally useful. I'll teach her anything else that I want her to do at her spare time myself; but servants are such an idle, dirty, filthy set of wretches. The more you do for them the more you may. I parted with my last because, forsooth, she could not bring her ladyship to sleep for a few weeks in a wooden chair in the kitchen, while I had a boarder staying with me."

"They is, indeed, wretches," replied Mrs. Fungus. "They is luxurious, oh, wery, wery."

"My husband is out all day," continued the lady, "and a servant has nothing in the world to do but attend upon me—the back parlour—the first floor—the two pair front—the two pair back, and the attics (they are mostly single men)—do the washing, ironing, and getting up—work at her needle, and keep the house clean."

"Ah, what a place, ma'am," cried Mrs. Fungus; "but sarvents, ma'am, never knows when they is well off; they lives in a agony for change."

"My name's Marrables," continued the lady. "I reside at No. 10, Pleasant-row."

"Mum," said Mr. Bung, with a flourish of his hand, "we has got in this ere workus a female orphan, mum, as 'll suit you, mum. She's little, mum, but she's wery strong. She conceals her real age, which is sixteen, and makes herself out much younger, to escape working, mum; but she'd wallop a horse-soldier, she would."

"Oh, that she would," interrupted Mrs. Fungus. "She wants a missus, mum, as would look sharp arter her."

The lady answered this indirect appeal to her sharpness by such a lightning glance, that Mr. Bung involuntarily retreated two or three steps.

"She belongs, mum," he said, "to a strong family. The mother died very hard; and her brother, mum, arter walloping loads of people, took a ship, and went to sea. That's him, mum, as this bill speaks on. I'll read it to you, mum, if your please, all but the last line, which speaks, mum, of a garment which I won't mention."

Mr. Bung read the bill, and then winked at Mrs. Fungus, as much as to say, we'll get rid o' that ere female orphan. But the lady was one of that class who in the world are demoninated clever managing women, which, generally, are most uncomfortable females as to temper and general characteristics, and she saw the wink in a moment.

"What are you winking at?" she said in a tone which made Mr. Bung jump.

"Eh? wink, mum; it's a affection of the eye, mum."

"Indeed it is, mum," said Mrs. Fungus. "He winks at the board even, and they knows it."

Mrs. Fungus might have added, that a great many things were winked at in the workhouse of Bungleum which would not bear a steady gaze.

"Well, can I see the girl?" asked Marrables.

"Yes, ma'am," answered Mrs. Fungus. "If so be, ma,am, you'll be as good as to follow along o' me, I'll shew her to you directly."

The lady inclined her head in token of gracious assent to this proposition, and she and Mrs. Fungus proceeded forthwith to the house.

Mrs. Fungus left her visitor in her own private room while she went to fetch poor Phœbe to be examined, and if approved, taken by Mrs. Marrables into service.

Phœbe Grainger, although a delicate child, and as fragile as could be, was yet tall of her age, and would, had she been in robust health, have been easily taken to have been several years older than she really was; but her slender form and pale face gave to the beholder anything but a notion of her hardihood and strength. Her mild blue eyes betokened softness and pure affection, and her voice was sweet and low. Had she now fallen into the hands of any one who would have shewn real kindness to the poor orphan, what a pure and tender heart they would have attached to them, and what a mine of affection and gratitude would they have sprung to repay them.

But it was not yet to be so. The time was to come when kind faces would beam affection upon her, when she would be greeted by smiles and tears of pure joy and love, but the dark cloud of her destiny still hovered over her, and the fair sun which was to gild her happy days had not yet shone through the thick mists of sorrow and adversity.

Poor Phœbe's was a hard fate. She had just felt sufficient of a mother's care and tenderness to awaken into life the sweet blossoms of affection, which would have matured into a lovely flower, when that dear parent was snatched from her by the ruthless hand of death, and the budding beauty and sweetness of the gentle girl's mind was blighted for a time.

The germ, however, of goodness and purity was not destroyed. It wanted but the general sunshine of the happy mind to make it again spring forth in luxuriant beauty. The affections and feelings, pure, high, and holy as they were, only slept in the breast of the beautiful orphan. They waited to be awakened by the smile of dear love and the gentle hand of affectionate sympathy.

Mrs. Fungus wished heartily to get rid of Phœbe Grainger, for there was something about the mild and uncomplaining countenance of the girl which always produced an uneasy sensation in that lady's breast. She would rather have been defied, for then she could have proceeded " *con amore,*" in all sorts of infliction, but the patient endurance of the mild and tender Phœbe was quite of an annoying character, and a course of action which Mrs. Fungus was not at all accustomed to ; and there was probably, no one wish of her heart which would have come more uppermost, had she been suddenly asked to name one, than the desire to get rid of Phœbe Grainger.

" How dare you look so pale and miserable, you odious little troublesome thing ?" cried Mrs. Fungus, as she clutched Phœbe by the arm to drag her to Mrs. Marrables.

" I cannot help it," sighed Phœbe.

" Ah, that's your constant outcry ; you can't help this, and you can't help t'other ; I'll help you to a little colour though, I'll be bound."

Mrs. Fungus then bestowed upon the poor child a slap upon each side of her face, which immediately reddened the delicate cheeks of Phœbe.

" Now, you little wretch, if you dare to cry, I'll—I don't know what I won't do to you."

" I don't cry now," said Phœbe, mournfully. " George, dear George, is gone, and—and I won't cry till he comes back again."

" Oh, you won't, won't you, you obstinate little mortal ? Now, I'll tell you what—if you dare to say that you can't do anything that the lady you're going to see asks you if you can do, I'll just be the death of you ;— now come along."

Mrs. Fungus soon dragged Phœbe to the presence of Mrs. Marrables ; and that lady darted a sharp and searching glance at Phœbe, which seemed to say—I shall see in a moment what you are, and all about you.

" She's small," said Mrs. Marrables ; but that lady did not speak in altogether in a disapproving tone, for she saw that, in the mild, humble little creature before her, she would most likely have an abject, submissive slave, whom she could command and browbeat at her sublime will and pleasure, without the least chance of resistance.

" Are you willing to work ?" said Mrs. Marrables, sharply, to Phœbe.

" Yes," she replied, " I am."

" Oh, well, we'll see. I'm afraid she's a great deal too good-looking to be a good servant."

" Do you hear ?" cried Mrs. Fungus ; " do you hear what the lady says, you little hypocrite ? How dare you have such a appearance, hussey, as interferes with your daily bread, you little abominable wretch ?"

Mrs. Marrables listened to this speech with a great deal of satisfaction, for it let her at once see that poor Phœbe might be grossly abused, and for nothing at all, with the greatest impunity, which was a very gratifying reflection to a lady of Mrs. Marrables' turn of mind.

" I don't mind," said that lady, " if I take her on trial for a month."

" Do you hear ?" cried Mrs. Fungus ; " the lady will give you a chance of making your fortin. You ought to go down on your blessed knees and pray."

Phœbe, however, did not at the moment perceive any urgent cause for thanksgiving, so she remained standing, and fixing her mild blue eyes upon her future mistress.

There was something in Mrs. Marrables' face peculiarly attractive. She was considered to be a handsome woman, and she, indeed, possessed that masculine form and features which passed among the ignorant and uncultivated for handsome, fine, &c.; for by some singular process of mind on the parts of many people, the more a woman differs from all those feminine and gentle characteristics of her sex, which constitute their great claim to the admiration and affectionate care of man, the more she is applauded and cried up as fair, handsome, slap-up, &c., making no mention whatever as to whether she be amiable and kind, or not. Nay, if in addition to being like a bold-faced man in petticoats, she has a temper as sharp as verjuice, and a manner as brisk and unpleasant as possible—bullies her husband, if she have one—beats the children—scolds the servants, and generally rides rough-shod over everybody, she is forthwith declared to be a marvellously "clever," as well as a "fine woman," and people wonder what poor Mr. such-an-one would do without his wife, who manages everything, herself included, so well.

The husbands of these kind of women generally resist at first, but who can stand out against public opinion?

"You can have her when you like, ma'am," said Mrs. Fungus to Mrs. Marrables. "She's ordered by the board to be put to place, and you can take her, ma'am, whenever you please."

"Then," said Mrs. Marrables, "I shall take her home with me. I—I suppose she's had her dinner?"

"Oh, yes, ma'am; leastways she doesn't require more, ma'am, to-day; she gormandized so yesterday."

"Oh, very well," said Mrs. Marrables. "She—looks—a little eater."

"A wery little eater, mum—a wery little eater," said the voice of Mr. Bung at the door. "Orphans, mum, principally lives on wice, mum; their wiciousness is to them equal to the whole world, mum. They always has feelings, as they calls 'em, which is nothing but wice, and they prefers them ere feelings to nothing, mum."

"Indeed," said Mrs. Marrables, looking sharply at Mr. Bung; "I don't like servants that have feelings; it interferes too much with their work."

"Wery much indeed, mum," continued Mr. Bung. "Feelings, mum, and wice, is all the same to some paupers, partiklar orphans, as soup and fish, joints, poultry, and pies and puddings; they lives upon 'em. Their feelings and wice, mum, is perpetual glasses of brandy and water to them."

"Dear me," replied Mrs. Marrables, "you don't say so! In imagination, you mean?"

"Yes, mum, in imagination; I speak parabolically, mum, which means warious figures of speech, and ideas, mum."

"Well, then, notwithstanding her bad propensities for feelings, I'll take her on trial. I like to do things off hand, and at once—it's my way; so if you will have the kindness to get her things together, I'll take her home with me now, and see what I can make of her."

"Yes, ma'am, directly," replied Mrs. Fungus.

Poor Phœbe's "things" consisted of what might very easily have been carried in an exceedingly small pocket handkerchief, and they, consequently, offered no great impediment to her instant departure with Mrs. Marrables.

The party, including Mr. Bung, as well as Mrs. Fungus, proceeded in a body to the outer gate, to see Phœbe fairly off the premises.

When there Mr. Bung paused, and casting first an eye at the bill, offering the stupendous reward for George, which stuck there, and then at Phœbe, and then at Mrs. Marrables, he said to the latter, with an insinuating smile and a flourish of his hand—

"Excuse me, mum. One word of adwice I wishes to give this ere orphan afore she goes from the blessed workus. You wicious female orphan, always in arter life——"

"Pho! pho!" cried Mrs. Marrables, darting a look at Mr. Bung, compounded of iron spikes and vinegar; "my time is valuable, if yours is not. Come along, girl."

With that Mrs. Marrables seized Phœbe by the shoulder, and dragged her through the gate, leaving Mr. Bung with his mouth wide open, and standing in an attitude of the greatest surprise and dismay, for he had meditated an astounding speech upon the departure of Phœbe, which should at once convince Mrs. Marrables that he was something far above common men, and, indeed, common beadles."

"That ere woman," he said, after a few ominous shakes of the head, "is a rum 'un, she is. She may be a very clever woman, and a very fine woman, but she ain't by no means genteel. She'd a heard something, Mrs. Fungus, to her adwantage, if she had but a staid."

"No doubt, Mr. Bung—no doubt. She's a wiolent woman, I could see that; and what a eye, Mr. Bung—what a eye!"

"You may say that, Mrs. Fungus; it's like a wery uncommon sharp gimblet."

"Well, well, that little brat, I hope, is off our hands at last, Mr. Bung. A precious deal of trouble we have had with her and her brother, to be sure."

"We has, we has, mum. Ain't you—fatigued, Mrs. Fungus, eh? Don't you really think, mum, you ought to take a little—eh?—hem."

"Composing medicine, I suppose you mean, Mr. Bung? Why, I think I requires it, and so do you; you look wery pale."

"Well, then, Mrs. Fungus, perhaps you've got a small quantity—eh?"

"I think I have. Medicine's a great relief, Mr. Bung."

"Partiklar, Mrs. Fungus, when it's rather strong, you know, mum. A wery great relief—wery."

Mrs. Fungus smiled a bland smile, and, with Mr. Bung, proceeded to the private room, from whence again issued the singular and unaccountable smell of gin, which occasionally saluted the noses of the longing paupers from Mrs. Fungus's sanctum.

CHAPTER XII.

PHŒBE followed Mrs. Marrables in silence, and with a heavy heart, towards No. 10, Pleasant Row, which was a flaming new brick-built row of houses, about half-way between the village and the town; indeed, it formed nearly the last street in the suburbs of the latter.

They soon arrived at their place of destination, and Mrs. Marrables knocked at the door in a manner which would at once have been the envy and admiration of any footman; but, then, Mrs. Marrables was a vastly clever woman, and knew how to do everything—but be amiable. The door was opened by Mr. Marrables in person, who was a tall, sickly-looking man, attired in rusty black clothes.

"Oh!" said Mr. Marrables, when he opened the door.

"Now, Marrables," said his lady, "it's high time you were gone; here every morning I have you loitering about the house when you ought to be off and about your business."

"But, my dear," humbly suggested Mr. Marrables, "you know you told me to wait till you come in, in case any of the lodgers rung."

"Now, do," cried Mrs. Marrables, in a high tone, "do stay and be aggravating; make me as wretched as possible, will you?"

"Well, well, my dear, I won't say any more," said the thoroughly subdued Mr. Marrables. "I'm going directly."

"I desire that you be home at one to a minute to dinner, Marrables," screamed his wife; "I'm not going to make myself a thorough slave to you, and then you won't come home. This house and you, together, will be the death of me, they will. I'm a slave to you, if ever there was one; late and early, it's all the same; nobody would credit the handful I've got. You'll see me in my grave some day, and then I wonder what will become of you. You'll find it out then, I'll be bound. Everybody knows how I work."

"Yes, yes, my dear," interposed Mr. Marrables, "you do, indeed; I'm quite aware of it; and this is the new girl is it?"

"And pray what's that to you, Mr. Marrables, whether this is a new girl or an old girl?" shrieked Mrs M. "Oh, you wretch; you must begin at your time of life to talk about girls, must you?"

"Why, my dear, I only asked the question; but it's no matter."

"Oh, yes, it is a matter, Mr. Marrables, a very great matter; I'll spare you the trouble of finding out. This is the new girl, Mr. Marrables."

Mrs. Marrables pronounced these last few words in so startling a tone, that Mr. Marrables gave a great jump, and very nearly fell down.

"What is there for dinner, my love?" Mr. Marrables ventured timidly to ask, with a propitiating smile upon his face.

"Breast of mutton," replied the lady; "and if you can't do anything better than laugh at my domestic arrangements, perhaps you'd like to see me in my grave?"

"Is—is—is it very fat?" enquired the poor man, with considerable hesitation.

"Now, really, oh, dear," cried Mrs. Marrables, "you'd like to see me in my coffin—that is what you want—I know it—I know it. I may work my fingers to the bones; but what do you care?—nothing. Oh—oh —oh!"

Mrs. Marrables here pressed her hand to her side, and sat down, shewing strong symptoms of going off immediately into hysterics, or some other dreadful state.

Mr. Marrables immediately looked very much alarmed, and turned round and round, looking for some restorative.

"My dear, my dear," he cried, "I'm very sorry—really I did not mean —dear me—dear me, this going off."

"When—I'm—in my—grave," sobbed Mrs. Marrables, "then he'll—know—his loss. Oh—oh—oh!"

"Here, little girl," cried Mr. Marrables to Phœbe, "here, take this tea-cup, and get half a quartern of the best brandy; do you hear? There's a public-house at the corner. Here's sixpence; make haste, make haste."

Mrs. Marrables got much worse as Phœbe started upon her errand, and betrayed great difficulty in breathing, and looked very wildly about her.

"Here, my dear—here, drink this," said Mr. Marrables, when Phœbe returned with the brandy; "it will do you good, my love; do now take it."

No—no—no—no," gasped the lady; "I cannot—no—no;" and she took the cup in her hand and tossed off the contents.

"Are you better, my dear?" asked the husband, bending over her.

After a few spasms, Mrs. Marrables spoke.

"Oh, Marrables! Marrables! you are killing me; you know you are; my constitution won't stand these attacks, you know it won't; but never mind—never mind."

"My dear," said Mr. Marrables," in a very contrite tone, "forgive me this once. I am really very sorry."

"Well, let it pass—it's over now—I only feel a little weak—don't mention it again."

"I won't indeed; I won't," replied Mr. Marrables, although he had not a very clear idea of what he had done or said, which was so highly reprehensible.

"You—you had sixpence, Marrables?" said the lady.

"Yes, my dear; didn't you know I had it, my love? Don't you recollect, my dear, last Friday you gave me a shilling to change for——"

"Never mind—never mind," cried the lady; "have you got any more money? Now speak the truth; I am still very weak."

"No my dear, not a penny; don't you know I gave you three-halfpence yesterday?"

"Very well," said Mrs. Marrables, plunging her hand into a large pocket, and making an awful rattling of keys, halfpence, a thimble, the key of a beer-tap, and sundry other articles. "Here's fourpence; you'd better dine out, Marrables."

"Very well, my dear," replied he; "I will, my love, I'll be back by seven, my dear."

"I sha'n't eat anything to-day," said Mrs. Marrables, faintly; "at least, not till you come home. I never eat when you are out—never."

"I know you don't, my dear," said Mr. Marrables; "but you really ought. Now do, dear, to-day."

"No, no; go and enjoy yourself. Don't be saving that fourpence, and then coming home at night and eating all before you."

"Oh, no, no," cried Mr. Marrables. And he departed with a floating, indistinct idea in his mind that he had not behaved quite well to Mrs. Marrables, who was a wonderful woman, and the best manager in the world, and, although a little hasty in temper, really a treasure.

The moment the door closed upon her husband, Mrs. Marrables wonderfully revived, and turning to poor Phœbe, who had witnessed the whole scene with the greatest surprise, she said, in a voice which might have well become a magistrate, when committing some hardened rogue and vagabond to the treadmill for three calendar months,—

"What's your name?—I forget it."

"Phœbe Grainger, ma'am," replied the trembling girl.

"Well, take this eighteen-pence, go to the public-house, and get me a bottle of their best stout; and there's a butcher's shop in the next street, bring me in three quarters of a pound of rump-steak; say it's for Mrs. Marrables, and they'll know how to cut it. Come, be quick—I declare I feel quite a sinking—I must have some lunch."

Phœbe entertained a wholesome dread of Mrs. Marrables after the scene which had been enacted between her and her husband, who, by some unaccountable means, thus truckled to a woman, his inferior in every respect, for Mr. Marrables was a man of ability and education, and she performed her errands so quickly, that Mrs. Marrables actually condescended to smile and nod at an old trunk which stood in one corner of the kitchen, which Phœbe understood as a gracious permission, to seat herself thereon, which she timidly did, wondering all the while in her own mind what Mrs. Marrables meant to do with the stout and the steak, as poor Phœbe implicitly believed the lady's assertion that she never ate in the absence of Mr. Marrables.

The clever woman—and fine woman—and managing woman, however, quickly set Phœbe's mind at rest upon the subject, for she cooked the steak, swallowed it down, together with a due assortment of pickles, bread, &c., and finally washed down the whole with the bottle of stout.

Phœbe looked perfectly amazed at this feat in the way of a lunch merely, and wondered very much what the delicate Mrs. Marrables would have for dinner.

Mr. Marrables had some employment out of doors which occupied him till seven o'clock in the evening usually, and he was accustomed to come home to dinner in the middle of the day, excepting upon those occasions when Mrs. Marrables pensioned him off for the day, which it will be remembered, she had done on the present occasion.

The house, No. 10, Pleasant-row, was a speculation altogether of Mrs. Marrables, who thought herself peculiarly qualified to let lodgings and "do for" young men.

The front parlour was reserved as a room in which people when they came to take lodgings, and so forth, were ushered, but Mrs. Marrables never permitted her husband to enter it, except on Sunday afternoon to tea, and then he saw as little of it, excepting the walls and the ceiling, as possible, for everything was covered up with the nicest art.

There was a drugget upon the carpet—the rug turned upside down—cheap chintz covers upon the chairs—gauze over the glass and pictures—a full suit of Holland upon the sofa, and something upon everything; in fact, the furniture appeared as well packed up, as if some long journey was immediately contemplated.

Mr. Marrables once turned up the corner of one of the chair covers, and saw that the seat was actually of a bright green, and he conjectured that the sofa might match them, but he never dared to hint at the possibility of taking off the suit of Holland from the latter; and upon the whole, he rather considered that the covering up of the parlour and its precious contents was a wonderful clever thing on the part of Mrs. Marrables, although he had no very distinct idea of when they were to be uncovered, or on what stupendous occasion their glories would be brought to light.

No. 9

There was throughout the house a shabby appearance, which arose from one peculiarity on the part of Mrs. Marrables, which, by the by, is not so uncommon a feeling as one would suppose.

Every article had been purchased, not for its beauty, its fineness, or ornamental appearance, but for its durability; that is to say, its durability of appearance, not structure.

Thus, Mrs. Marrables, being well aware that bright colours in process of time would fade and become dull colours, bethought herself of a scheme of preventing such a catastrophe, which was certainly efficacious, and that was to purchase dull and bad colours at first of carpets, &c., thus effectually giving the go-by to Time, and its destroying and blighting effects.

Mr. Marrables did, certainly, on one occasion, humbly suggest that things might as well be purchased handsome at first, for that until they did fade one had the enjoyment of their beauty, and that when that beauty was gone, they were then as good-looking as the dull, sombre things she was buying; and he further had the temerity to say, that one might as well punch out all one's teeth in early life, to prevent their gradual decay, and hinted at some pig which was killed to save its life; but Mrs. Marrables at once fell into a fit of strong hysterics, and the question was settled for ever. Mr. Marrables was shortly afterwards thoroughly conquered upon this point in the following manner:—

An ingenious hatter, knowing that there existed many persons of Mrs. Marrables' way of thinking, invented a hat, (which is exceedingly popular among noodles at the present day,) from off which the nap could never by any accident be rubbed, for the simple reason that it never had any on.

Mrs. Marrables knew well that in process of time the nap would come off Mr. Marrables' hats, and she forthwith insisted upon his possessing and wearing a napless hat, which, being from the first day as hideous and ugly as possible, could not by any means change for the worse. So Mr. Marrables, with many groans, became a walking illustration of the argument, that it's better to have things at first artfully constructed, in imitation of worn-out beauty and brightness, and then you will not be annoyed by a change in their appearance.

By the time Mrs. Marrables had finished her lunch a bell rung violently, and that lady, casting her eyes up to the kitchen ceiling, at once ascertained which one of the six, which were against the wall in a row, was agitated.

" It's the two pair front," she exclaimed; " run and see what Mr. Wattles wants. Be quick."

Phœbe started from the chest on which she was sitting, and proceeded to the two pair front. She knocked timidly at the door, and was answered by a loud " Come in!"

Phœbe opened the door, and advanced a few steps into the room.

A rather small young gentleman, of rather slender dimensions, was assiduously brushing his hair at the glass. He did not condescend to turn round, but, in an exceedingly affected voice, said:—

" Eh!—ha—a—a—my boots—e—ha."

" Yes, sir," said Phœbe, and was about to retire, but the sound of her sweet voice had taken Mr. Wattles quite by surprise, and he turned very abruptly, with the hair brush in one hand and the comb in the other:—

" Eh?—ha!—stop—eh?—are you ha—the—a—a—new slave?—eh?"

" Sir?" said Phœbe.

" Eh?—ha—the—the candidate for—ah—ah!—the honour of attending upon me."

" Mrs. Marrables told me to come and see what you wanted," replied Phœbe, with great simplicity of manner.

"Oh—oh—ah—green—green," said Mr. Wattles, "decidedly verdant. My boots—my boots."

Mr. Wattles was a young gentleman, who condescended to sit upon a stool in an attorney's office, in the town, upon the consideration of receiving weekly fifteen shillings; but he considered himself a very great man, notwithstanding, and absolutely killing in his personal appearance.

"Clean these immediately," said Mrs. Marrables, pointing to a pair of boots, when Phœbe returned to the kitchen. "When you've done them, take them up, then you can wash up these things—clean these knives and forks, mop up the area—do the door step—light the copper fire—black-lead the parlour stove, and make all tidy, and be sure you attend to the rings. Now look at these bells; that next the door is the first floor, and so on in regular order—second floor front—second floor back—back parlour—front attic—back attic."

"Yes, ma'am," said Phœbe, "I won't forget."

"The first floor," continued Mrs. Marrables, "is not up—the back is gone out—but I expect the back parlour to ring for his shoes. I'm going to dress. If you don't attend to everything, I'll pinch you black and blue, and wring your ears off."

Mrs. Marrables sailed out of the kitchen, and left Phœbe in undisturbed possession of the lower regions.

Phœbe had hardly cleaned one of Mr. Wattles' boots, when that gentleman's bell again rung violently; and Phœbe, very much alarmed at the consequences, rushed up stairs with the one; but she had hardly reached the first landing, when some other bell smote her ears. She, however, hurried onwards to Mr. Wattles, and knocked at his door.

"Come in! come in!" cried he.

Phœbe walked timidly in with the one boot, and said:—

"The other is coming, sir; I'll soon do it."

"The—ah—ah—eh!—the devil," cried Mr. Wattles. "I'm too late already."

Phœbe rushed down stairs again, and she heard two bells trying to out-ring each other, and keeping up a constant alarm.

As she passed the first floor, an old lady suddenly popped out her head adorned by an immense red turban, and a still redder face, and flourishing her arms wildly above her, she arrested the steps of the startled Phœbe.

"Am I to ring, ring, ring, ring," she cried, "for ever? I believe a drawing-room bell is a drawing-room bell, and requires answering afore a beggarly two pair front, or a attic!"

"Please ma'am," said Phœbe, mildly, "what do you want?"

"Want! what do I want! I want everything. Who are you? I shall give Mrs. Marrables warning. I want——"

Tingle, tingle, tingle, went some other bell, and Phœbe rushed a step or two down stairs.

"My boots!" screamed Mr. Wattles, from above, and throwing down the one that had been brought up, which narrowly missed hitting the "first floor" on the gigantic turban.

"Is this to be beared?" cried the old lady. "Am I to be insulted by a wretched lawyer's clerk, and boots shyed down on my head?"

"Damn it all," roared a voice from the parlour, "am I to have any breakfast, or not? Damn it all, am I to keep ringing here for a week? Damn it all, am I——"

"My boots!" roared Mr. Wattles.

"My breakfast!" shouted the back parlour.

"Hot water!" screamed the old lady.

Phœbe was bewildered. She sat down upon the stairs in despair, and burst into tears.

Mrs. Marrables had heard the commotion, but she was dressing, and could not very well make her appearance for some minutes; but when she did so, her face beat the old lady's face and turban combined, all to nothing.

She had been in the back-room second floor, and as she sailed out, she came full upon Mr. Wattles, who was leaning over the bannisters.

"Mr. Wattles!" she screamed in his ear, in such a voice that he very nearly overbalanced himself, and fell down stairs. He recovered himself, however, in a moment, and darting into his room, shut the door in an instant.

Mrs. Marrables having thus silenced one claimant, proceeded down stairs, and encountered the furious old lady.

Mrs. Marrables shook her head from side to side, and the old lady shook hers.

"What may you please to want, mem?" said Mrs. Marrables, in a voice perfectly tremulous with rage.

"Hot water, mem," said the old lady, with a vibration of the turban.

"Very well, mem," replied Mrs. Marrables; "anything else, mem?"

"No, mem," said the old lady, "but I shall leave these apartments, mem."

"You may, mem, when you've paid your rent, mem, and given a week's warning, you filthy old woman; I'm sick of you."

"You wretch! you drunken wretch!" cried the old lady, vibrating the turban fearfully, "you're intoxicated now, you know you are. I saw the girl bring in a bottle of stout, mem, and, previous, a half quartern of something, mem. Oh! you vile woman!"

"What!" screamed Mrs. Marrables, "me drunk—me drunk, you horrid, old, good-for-nothing cat—you frightful old hag!"

"Damn it all, my breakfast!" roared the back parlour.

"Where is that hussey?" cried Mrs. Marrables, looking round for Phœbe, and as she did so, the old lady, finding that she was no match for Mrs. Marrables, retired, turban and all, and shut her door with a bang.

"You little, ungrateful, idle, wretched slut," cried Mrs. Marrables, as she observed Phœbe, weeping and sitting upon the extreme corner of a stair. "You little filthy wretch; you abominable hussey."

Mrs. Marrables flew at Phœbe to execute summary justice upon her, but it happened that Mr. Wattles, in utter despair, had put on a pair of decayed pumps, and was rushing down stairs at the moment to depart to his office, and he came, opportunely for Phœbe, exactly between her and the enraged Mrs. Marrables, and that with such force, too, that the lady was compelled by the concussion to drop down very suddenly into a sitting position on the landing, which she did a very off-hand manner, and with a thump, which gave a shake to her whole system.

Mr. Wattles could not stop himself, for he was at full speed, and he made an attempt to jump over Mrs. Marrables as he would a post in the street. In this he was, however, signally defeated, for that lady caught him frantically, by one of his legs, and he fell, in a very complicated manner, right over Mrs. Marrables, who, on the occasion, did not betray the slightest weakness, but commenced such a furious attack upon the young gentleman, that he roared for mercy, and kicked and plunged in an agony.

"I'll teach you, you beggarly lawyer's fag, to come trundling down my stairs like a hoop," cried Mrs. Marrables, "you ignorant puppy! you half-starved bundle of wretchedness! you conceited, ill-looking baboon!"

"Murder! murder!" cried Mr. Wattles.

"Damn it all, my breakfast," roared the back parlour.

"I'll be down to you in a minute," cried Mrs. Marrables, still cuffing Mr. Wattles.

"The devil you will," said the back parlour, suddenly rushing into his room, and locking the door in the inside.

Mrs. Marrables now suddenly released Mr. Wattles, who forthwith rolled down stairs on to the mat, from whence he gathered himself quickly up, and made a grand rush from the house.

CHAPTER XIII.

MRS. MARRABLES now turned her attention to Phœbe, who was dreadfully alarmed, and bestowing upon her sundry boxes on the ears, and a fearful shake, she ordered her at once to the kitchen to take up the hot water to the first floor, while she, Mrs. Marrables, prepared the back parlour's breakfast.

Peace was shortly restored, and thus passed poor Phœbe Grainger's first introduction to service.

Bewildered—beaten—spiritless and wretched, the poor child, when Mrs. Marrables again left the kitchen, sat down on the chest, and wept and sobbed as if her heart would break.

The next few days presented but little variety to the poor orphan. She was miserably fed, and her place of nightly repose was upon the kitchen floor.

Mr. Marrables regularly departed each morning to his business, and Mrs. Marrables as regularly took her lunch.

When the gentleman came home to dinner, instead of solacing himself with the produce of his fourpence out of doors, Mrs. Marrables would invariably affect to be very much shocked at his gross and vulgar appetite.

Mrs. Marrables would sometimes comfort herself with a little ardent spirits along with the bottled stout, and on such occasions she would be unusually gracious to Phœbe, and relate to her divers of the villanies of former servants as so many rocks for her to shun.

The dinners, of which Mr. Marrables partook when he did come home, were by no means to be compared to the luncheons which the lady solaced herself with in his absence.

It was the custom of Mrs. Marrables to keep on the tap constantly a small cask of exceedingly small beer, the key to the tap of which she always kept in her capacious side pocket. This beer was especially intended for the use of Mr. Marrables; and, moreover, the prudent lady would condescend to retail the same to her lodgers, when, in an unusual fit of thirst, they hurriedly sent for some porter, at a fair public-house price.

Many were the wry faces which Mr. Wattles and the back parlour (the first floor drank strong liquors) used to make over their porter; but they, for a long time, were in ignorance of the fact that Mrs. Marrables enacted the publican, and took their money for strong beer, at the same time that she supplied them with very short measure from the cask of small, the current value of which was three halfpence per pot.

Mrs. Marrables was particularly partial to fat breasts of mutton for several reasons. She knew perfectly well that Mr. Marrables could by no means eat much of such joints, and they were always cheap. She would produce one cold at least four times, until at last Mr. Marrables, in the despair of his heart, would rush out of the house, dinnerless, and without even fourpence.

"My dear Mrs. Marrables," said he, one day, in a deprecating tone, "could you vary the dish a little, eh? and have, my love, some other joint?"

"There it is, Marrables—there it is," shrieked Mrs. M.; "let me have what I will, it's always, could you not let me have something else? I declare if I were to set you down before a roast goose, you would ask me why I could not have a pair of ducks instead."

"A roast goose!" cried Mr. Marrables, opening his eyes very wide; "oh, dear! oh dear!"

"What do you mean, Mr. Marrables, by speaking in that manner? Are all my exertions to make your home comfortable and keep a roof over your head to be met in this way? I declare I'm positively faint."

"Well, well, my dear, never mind," cried the alarmed husband; "I did not mean any reflection upon you, my dear; I was only thinking that—that we had not had a roast goose for a long time—I believe, I may say, for some years."

"And where do you suppose, Mr. Marrables, that roast goose money is to come from?"

"Why, my dear, you know you're saving money, and it's put in the bank in your name, my love, so I don't know how much there is exactly."

"Reproach me, do reproach me," cried Mrs. Marrables, "for providing for you against your old age; oh, yes, have roast geese, do. Perhaps, in addition, you would like to have the dish placed on the top of my coffin?"

"My dear," replied Mr. Marrables, taking up the knife to cut a small piece of brown from the roast breast of fat mutton, "I really——"

"You really shall not eat any more, Mr. Marrables," said the lady, suddenly whipping up the dish from the table; "do you want to die of apoplexy? I believe you would cheerfully die of apoplexy, Mr. Marrables, if by so doing you thought you would bring me to want and wretchedness."

Mrs. Marrables popped the joint into the safe, of which she kept the key, and the subdued man, with a sigh, gave up the bit of brown.

"I'll take a little more beer, my dear," said Mr. Marrables, peeping furtively into a little empty jug, which stood on the table.

"Indeed you'll do no such thing; I believe you've had a full half pint already."

"Oh, very well, my dear, very well; but you really have eaten nothing yourself, my love. I have not seen you touch the meat, my dear."

"When do you see me make a hog of myself, Mr. Marrables, as you do? You know how little I take; I slave for you all day long, but you never see me eating your substance."

It was strictly true that Mr. Marrables never saw his lady touch much at dinner, a fact which the lunches fully accounted for; and seeing that that very day Mrs. Marrables had indulged herself with two thick rashers of ham, four eggs, a bottle of stout, and half a quartern of the best gin, it was not surprising that the fat mutton should remain untasted.

Mr. Marrables bid Mrs. Marrables an affectionate adieu, and walked from the kitchen, and the lady, in a few minutes, heard the street-door close, as she thought, after him; but such was not the case, for Mr. Marrables had only opened it, and closed it again with a bang, to give the appearance of having gone out.

He then crept cautiously along the passage and up the staircase, as softly as possible, till he arrived at the door of Mr. Wattles' room, where that gentleman was, as it was his dinner hour, assiduously dining upon two-pennyworth of shrimps, some bread and butter, and half a pint of Mrs. Marrables' small beer, which he had obtained from that lady upon credit, as his exchequer was rather low, it being Saturday.

Now it generally happened that on Thursday Mr. Wattles had succeeded in exhausting his pecuniary resources, and was indebted to credit granted by Mrs. Marrables for the provender of the two remaining days, that is, until about seven or eight o'clock on Saturday evening, when Mr. Wattles received his fifteen shillings in one glorious lump. Thus it was that Mrs. Marrables always held Mr. Wattles in her clutches, and made a tolerable profit besides.

Mr. Lose, who occupied the back parlour, whose great principle of action was never to pay anybody at all, if possible, pretended to be an author, but he was, in reality, a trafficker in small literary wares, which were the produce of other men's brains. This gentleman Mrs. Marrables held likewise in the clutches of her gigantic power, for he owed three weeks' rent, rather than pay which, contrary to his genius in such matters, he would put up with anything whatever.

Mr. Marrables knocked gently at Mr. Wattles' door, and was requested to "bundle in," which he did forthwith.

"How are you, Wattles?" said Mr. Marrables; "how are you?"

"Tolerable," said Mr. Wattles; "how are you, old cock?"

"I say," continued Mr. Marrables, "I've got eighteen-pence, and I'm thinking of going to the play to-night; could not you go?"

"Why, yes, I could after seven," said Mr. Wattles, with a sigh; "but is the thingumy, you know—the conscience keeper—the female Marrables agreeable, eh?"

"Mrs. Marrables," said the poor man, "is an excellent woman; I often wonder what I should do without her; but, Wattles, you know, she is rather too hasty."

"I believe I do," replied Mr. Wattles; "but that's your look out, Marrables. If that splendid creature was Mrs. Wattles, which the fates forbid, I'd—but never mind—go on."

"Ah, poor thing, she has very bad health, and half starves herself. We all have our faults, Wattles, but you know she's a slave to the house."

"Oh, bother," cried Mr. Wattles, "drop her, drop her; about the play, now?"

"Why, you see, Wattles, if, just for the sake of peace, for Mrs. M. don't know I've got eighteen-pence, you'd say that you had an order, you know, to the play, and ask me to go with you, don't you see?"

"Oh, yes, the old joke; but, Marrables, what a precious ass you are, to be sure."

"Why?—How, Wattles?—What do you mean?"

"Why don't you keep your own money, man? Now I'll be bound you don't know what you're worth at this time?"

"No, Mrs. Marrables manages all that; she's a wonderful woman—a wonderful woman, Wattles; she always knows when I've got any money to receive. It was but t'other day I had five guineas to take, so I came home, and said to Mrs. M. 'Here's the five pounds,' thinking to keep the five shillings myself, you know, but she said, in a moment, 'It was guineas!—where's the shillings?'—so I had, you know, to give them to her."

"Excuse me, Marrables, but you're an ass, an emphatic ass, and Mrs. Marrables is ——"

"An admirable woman," cried Mr. Marrables; "and such a manager."

Mr. Wattles rose from his seat, and danced a *pas de zephyr* round the room, in intimation of his dissent from Mr. Marrables.

"Well," he said, "now that's settled, I'll speak about the play; leave me alone, I'll manage the old 'un, Marrables."

"Old 'un, Wattles; Mrs. Marrables is a fine woman, Wattles, a very fine woman; I really don't know what I should do without her. She often makes the same remark, and she's a woman of great understanding; but I must be off; she don't know I'm here; I thought it would look more natural of you to do it without my having seen you to-day."

"Very well," cried Mr. Wattles; "come home by seven, and we'll make a night of it."

Mr. Marrables nodded his head, and glided softly down the stairs again into the passage. He then slipped to the street door, opened it, and closing it as softly as he could, but not without some unavoidable noise, he took to his heels and ran as if he had just stolen something, and expected instant pursuit.

He stopped at the corner of a street to take breath.

"I don't think she could have seen me," he said. "Ah, Wattles may insinuate what he likes, but Mrs. Marrables is a fine woman, and a capital manager. Why, let me consider. I've had this coat a year and eleven months, and she says now it's to last me till Christmas. Oh, she's a treasure. I wonder what I should do without her?"

Seven o'clock arrived, and Mr. Marrables came home true to his engagement with Mr. Wattles, and that gentleman soon after arrived with his fifteen shillings, in current coin of the realm.

Mrs. Marrables was wont on these occasions to intercept Mr. Wattles on the stairs, and to thrust into his hand a dirty piece of paper, on which was written the two days' account, together with the sum of five shillings added to it for rent.

"Oh, oh—a—a—the pecuniary matter," said Mr. Wattles, who always wore a gay and fashionable manner when he had money in his pocket; "eight and four-pence halfpenny farthing. Hem! Beer, seven-pence; dear me, I didn't—ah—ah—think I'd imbibed so much a—a—ah."

Mrs. Marrables, upon finding her account thus remarked upon, looked clean over Mr. Wattles' head, and, as if addressing the mat, which was just behind him, said—

"Mr. Wattles, when I do you the favour to put my hand into my pocket for——"

"Oh, it's all right," interrupted Mr. Wattles, "I recollect, it's all right; here's the tin."

"I rather think, Mr. Wattles, it is all right. I'm a slave to my lodgers, and you know it. A farthing, Mr. Wattles, if you please."

"Why, really," said Mr. Wattles, "I haven't such a thing, but I'll owe you one, you know."

"I'll owe you one, if you please," said Mrs. Marrables, counting into his hand three-pence halfpenny out of nine shillings which he had given to her.

"An old wretch!" thought Mr. Wattles; "she'd hang a man for a farthing."

"Is Marrables at home?" asked Mr. Wattles.

"He is at home, sir, and he ain't going out. He has no money to waste in extravagance and beastly dissipation."

"Oh!" cried Mr. Wattles, in a loud voice, so that Mr. Marrables might hear him in the kitchen, "because I've got an order for the play, and I thought Marrables would like to go."

"Eh?" said Mr. Marrables, from the kitchen; "oh!—ah!—yes, yes—oh, yes—I should like very well, very well, indeed."

"No doubt you would," screamed his wife, "no doubt you would; and pray what sort of enjoyment am I to have while you are engaged in all sorts of extravagance and vice?"

"Why, really, my dear, I—I—you know it won't cost anything."

"No, and he won't be at home to supper," said Mr. Wattles; "it's an order, you know."

"Marrables!" cried his wife, "speak. Have you really any money?"

"No, my dear; oh, no—how should I, my love?—oh, dear, no."

"Then you may go; but don't be one minute after ten, not one moment. I can't sit up, you know, after ten—my constitution won't stand it."

"Half-past, my dear, say half-past," urged Mr. Marrables; "ten is very early."

"You don't come into this house to-night," said Mrs. Marrables, "either of you, if you are one minute after ten, you understand."

Mr. Marrables put on his hat, and slowly walked up the kitchen stairs, followed by Phœbe, while Mrs. Marrables descended them.

"My dear," said Mr. Marrables to Phœbe, "if we should be a little late, you'll let us in?"

"Yes, sir," replied Phœbe, "I will."

Mr. Marrables had always spoken and behaved kindly to her since she had been in the house, and the poor child felt a kind of attachment to him, and looked upon him as a kind of fellow sufferer with herself from Mrs. Marrables' tyranny.

In high glee Mr. Wattles and his companion started for the little theatre, which was in the town, and which was now open, although it boasted of but little support from the loungers of London, who made the town a

No. 10

fashionable resort in the summer season, for the sea-bathing, and the beauty of its situation, as well as its easy distance from London, from which it was but a day's journey.

CHAPTER XIV.

THE evening wore on, and Mrs. Marrables sat dozing and grumbling by the kitchen fire, and Phœbe, upon the chest, was striving to shake off the influence of the sleep which oppressed her.

Nine o'clock was told by the kitchen time-piece, and Mrs. Marrables started and sharply reproved Phœbe for not telling her that the clock was going to strike, for that sudden noises shattered her nerves.

"You may take your supper," said Mrs. Marrables, going to the everlastingly-locked safe, and taking therefrom a lump of dry bread, and a knuckle of ham, the former of which she handed to Phœbe, and the latter she placed before herself.

Phœbe drew for herself a little jug of water, and placing it along with the bread upon the top of the chest, the knelt before it, and partook of a humble repast.

Mrs. Marrables mixed for herself a tolerable stiff tumbler of brandy-and-water, and commenced picking the ham bone, and quaffing the steaming liquor with marks of the most lively satisfaction.

There is in time an end of all things, and by ten minutes to ten the ham was finished, the bone put carefully away in the safe to make pea-soup for Mr. Marrables, when next he adventured home to dinner, and the brandy-and-water was getting low in the tumbler.

Mrs. Marrables looked earnestly at the clock; minute after minute passed away, and, at length, ten struck.

The incensed lady at one gulp finished the brandy-and-water, and rose immediately. She approached Phœbe, and placing her clenched fist within a tenth of an inch of her nose, she said :—

"You little wretch! you know there's no key to the street-door, so I can't lock it, but I shall put up the chain and bolt it, and if you dare to presume to let in that wretch, Marrables, to-night, I'll be the death of you."

Phœbe answered not, and Mrs. Marrables proceeded to the fire, which she carefully poked out, and then ordered Phœbe, as was her nightly custom, to make her bed, and lie down at once, for she, Mrs. Marrables would never allow her a candle.

Phœbe dragged forth from a cupboard her humble bed, and spreading it upon the floor, undressed herself, and laid down. Then, and not till then, did Mrs. Marrables, with a withering look, leave the kitchen, and Phœbe heard her bolt the street-door and put up the chain, with a crash and a clatter, and then immediately ascend to her chamber. The little Phœbe rose then, and again put on her clothes, for she was mindful of her promise to poor Mr. Marrables to let him in, which she determined to do, at all hazards to herself from Mrs. Marrables' vengeance.

Mr. Marrables was for all the world like a great school-boy when he was from home, and upon any pleasure expedition, in defiance of Mrs. Marrables. He and Mr. Wattles, therefore, proceeded to the little theatre with great gaiety and light-heartedness.

Mr. Marrables was induced, by the earnest persuasion of Mr. Wattles, to imbibe something before they entered the place of entertainment. Accordingly, they sallied into a public-house, and Mr. Marrables, making a rattling in his pocket by means of the shilling and sixpence which he was possessed of, boldly ordered two glasses of rum and shrub, which he paid for, looking all the time very hard at Mr. Wattles, as much as to say, you see I am paying for this, but it's your turn next, you know.

The rum and shrub was disposed of; and Mr. Marrables, upon the strength of so unusual a potation, became exceedingly facetious, and actually winked three times consecutively at the bar-maid.

"Come on, old fellow," cried Mr. Wattles, "the play's began by this time; we're always late."

Thus urged, Mr. Marrables left off winking, and carefully pocketing his two-pence change out his sixpence, he left the public-house.

The theatre was very close at hand, and in a few minutes they were at the door, deeply immersed in reading the bill of the performances, which set forth, that on that evening, and during the week, was to be performed—"The Horrible Blood-stained Bandit; or, the Vengeance of the Spectre Monk of the Haunted Abbey." To be followed by a hornpipe in fetters, which was to be succeeded by a burletta, and then a comic song, which was to be followed by a melo-dramatic, wild extravaganza, pictorial, historical, hyperbolical, and diabolical, supported by the strength of the company. The whole to conclude with a display of fire-works.

"This is very promising," said Mr. Marrables; "I dare say we shall be very much amused, indeed; let's lose no time. You'd better take my shilling, you know, and that will save trouble."

"Exactly," said Mr. Wattles; "but I'll show you how to manage here. They don't do much business, and two shillings is an object, old file. Now, you see, a shilling a-piece is half price to the boxes. The play's began, so we'll offer them half price, and go to the boxes, instead of the pit; don't you see?"

"But will they really, Mr. Wattles? You know half price don't begin for two hours nearly."

"You'll see, won't they. Come along, old fellow; I'll manage it."

So saying, Mr. Wattles walked boldly up to the box entrance, and asked, in a tone of great authority, if half price had commenced.

"Half price!" repeated the money-taker, whose office was nearly a sine-cure; "half price, sir!—oh, dear, no—nine o'clock, sir. The doors haven't been open half an hour."

"Oh, very well," returned Mr. Wattles, "I didn't know. We won't give more than a shilling each, and, of course, we can't go anywhere but to the boxes—ah—a—ah—eh? We are out for a walk merely; we may come back again, or we may not—it's no matter. Come along, Marrables."

Now Mr. Wattles was right when he said two shillings were thought something of at a theatre; for when the money-taker saw that Mr. Wattles was fairly about to walk away, he winked at that gentleman, and said,—

"Well, well, come along—come along, go up;" and, taking the two shillings, he allowed them to pass to the boxes of the establishment.

"That's the way to do it," said Mr. Wattles, giving Mr. Marrables a peg in the ribs, which caused that gentleman to double himself up in a singular attitude.

"Oh! dear me!" cried Mr. Marrables, "don't do that again. I see, I see."

They seated themselves in the front row of the boxes, and Mr. Wattles dragged on a half-dirty pair of straw-coloured kid gloves, which he had carried in his pocket all the way, and which he informed Mr. Marrables, with a smile, and another threatened peg in the ribs, which made him give a great sympathetic start, he always kept for such occasions.

The play of the " Horrible Blood-stained Bandit," &c. &c. had begun ; and upon the entrance of Mr. Wattles and his companion, there were two murdered bodies lying upon the stage, and a terrific combat going on between a gentleman, with a child on his back, and three ruffians, with black hair and dirty faces.

The gentleman with the child was hard pressed, but he fought well, and kept saying such cutting and reproachful things to the three ruffians, that they were goaded to desperation, and became very furious, repeatedly requesting him to give up the brat to their sanguinary vengeance.

At last the gentleman was beaten on to one knee, but he fought on with great desperation, until his sword was beaten from his grasp, and at that moment an interesting young female rushed on to the stage, and snatching two horse pistols from one of the ruffian's belts, she gave one to the child, and with the other in her own hand, she stood upon one leg, and leaned over the gentleman, in a threatening manner, to the ruffians.

The ruffians were perfectly nonplussed at this sudden and unexpected appearance, and gave utterance to sundry expressions, signifying their fury and disappointment.

" Villains !" cried the gentleman, very much excited ; " poltroons and base cowards, how are you off for soap ?"

" Hurrah ! hurrah !" shouted five boys in the gallery.

The three ruffians were goaded to fury by this cruel taunt, and, stooping down, strove to injure the gentleman's legs, but the young lady and the child presented the pistols, and completely foiled the nefarious attempt.

The young lady, then, by a dexterous movement, took a dagger from the belt of one of the ruffians, and handed it to the gentleman ; then the little child dismounts, and the gentleman engaged in combat with the ruffians again, and he is just upon the point of being overpowered, when the child and the young lady both fire their pistols, and the gentleman exclaims,—

" Pepper for two."

" Hurrah ! hurrah !" again shouted the boys.

Two of the ruffians were by this means killed, and the third apparently dangerously wounded, for he staggered to the side, and remarked, that " like a wounded vulture he must seek his lair," and then at once absconded. The lady and gentleman and the little child then embraced each other to solemn music, and the act closed, leaving them in a bunch in each other's arms. Mr. Wattles had, during the progress of the scene, affected to be not in the least interested ; in fact, he had only glanced furtively at the stage, but had allowed his eyes to wander over the theatre with an air as much as to say my mind is thoroughly satiated with all kinds of gorgeous entertainments, and I merely came here to pass an hour, and am not so vulgar as to be at all interested with the play, a course of proceeding on the part of Mr. Wattles which induced several people to believe that he must be somebody uncommonly used to amusements and theatres, &c., for he evidently did not care at all about them.

" That was very good, Wattles, don't you think ?" said Mr. Marrables, when the act drop had descended.

" Eh—ah—ah—what, my dear fellow ?"

" Why, the play, to be sure !"

" Oh—ah—ah—eh ?—the play ?—Why—ah—ah—really I—I so seldom look at plays—ah.—I believe they are acting some play, eh ?—ah."

This speech of Mr. Wattles was heard by two young ladies, and a raw, overgrown youth who was with them, with undisguised admiration, and they looked at Mr. Wattles with profound respect, which was greatly increased when that gentleman pulled from his pocket a white handkerchief with a little border of lace, and holding it in his hand, gently tapped his, face therewith. The effect of the kid gloves and the handkerchief, and the edging together, was very great, and the young ladies nudged each other, and intimated their firm conviction that Mr. Wattles was somebody in disguise.

The overgrown, raw-looking young gentleman was very much annoyed at the proximity of so very superior a being as Mr. Wattles, and he affected to laugh in a very boisterous and manly manner, and then turned very red in the face at attracting so much attention. He was one of those youths who are so very common in London at the present time; a description of one describes the whole class. They are not tall, but lanky; their shoulders invariably curve outwards, and measure across about five inches; and their mothers and aunts, of whom they are especial darlings, always proclaim how exceedingly delicate they are, and yet what a spirit they possess. They have invariably grown far out of their trousers; and their jackets, by being suspended on their projecting blade-bones, stick out in a great flute at their waists. Moreover, they wear their shirt collars over their jackets, and no gloves. According to the taste of the present day, they are especial favourites with young ladies fresh from school, because they are lanky, slim, and pale, and consumptive-looking, which constitutes all the attributes of gentility. These youths are the pests of society; they are too lanky to be kept in the nursery, and washed and combed by the maids, and they are too childish and ridiculous to mix in society. In the few years that a man remains in this state of being, he generally does more little gaucheries and little stupidities, which give him future annoyance to think about, than in all his after life.

Mr. Felix Flurryman was one of those interesting long boys, and one of the young ladies was his sister, Miss Laura Flurryman, and the other was his sister's great friend and crony, Miss Theodosia Clements, for whom the gentle Felix entertained a great passion.

When Mr. Felix laughed, Mr. Wattles turned his face half round, and stared very hard at him, with a face of inconsiderable gravity, which was wormwood to Mr. Felix, who turned uncommonly red, and looked a little hysterical, and put himself into about twenty different positions in the course of three minutes, to prove how very much at his ease he was.

At this moment the curtain drew up to allow a young lady to perpetrate a dance between the acts, while the ruffians and the oppressed gentleman were regaling themselves with a pot of half-and-half in great amity and good fellowship.

In a moment on rushed the young lady, apparently with an intention of scrambling clean over foot lights and orchestra right into the pit, but she stopped short within an inch of the floats, and with a most insinuating smile, made a magnificent obeisance to the audience; then lifting up one leg, she spun round with the greatest dexterity upon the other toe.

"Fine gal," cried Mr. Wattles,—"ah! ah! belongs to the *corps de ballet* of the opera—ah! ah!"

The young lady was attired in the Highland costume, and was most liberal and gracious in the display of her legs, which, certainly, were not to be sneezed at, as Mr. Marrables remarked in a whisper.

"Ah! ah!—ah!—yes—yes," cried Mr. Wattles, loudly; "a fine girl; oh, very."

Now Mr. Felix Fluryman heard this, and was determined not to be outdone and completely ridden over by Mr. Wattles, particularly as he saw that Miss Theodosia Clements cast several approving glances towards that gentleman; so he exclaimed, in a nervous and agitated manner,—

"Ah! ah!—yes—a fine gal—a fine gal—eh! eh!—ha! ha!—I—I—'

Mr. Felix had frightened himself by his own boldness and stopped in the greatest alarm at the consequences of his temerity.

"Felix," cried his sister, "how can you admire that thing? I declare I'm surprised they allow anything so improper. She's a forward minx, don't you think, Dosia, dear?"

"Oh, yes," said Theodisa, who was very romantic, stealing a glance at Mr. Wattles; "and yet it reminds one very much of Sir Walter Scott, don't it you, dear?"

"Oh, oh! very good, 'pon my soul, eh! eh! eh!" cried Mr. Felix, coming out in great force, and actually clapping his hands close to Mr. Wattles' ear.

Mr. Wattles partially turned, and with a wave of the handkerchief and a glance right over Mr. Felix's shoulder at Miss Clements, said,—

"Ah, ah! my good lad—ah!—eh!—be quiet. There's something, Miss, classical and poetical about the refulgent grandeur of the sublimity of motion."

"Ye—ye—yes," replied Miss Theodosia, reddening; "yes sir, there is."

"The poetry of action, Miss, is singularly developed in the—ah!—ah!—female operatic specimen on the boards. The mind wavers on the wing of fancy, and the ærial fabric of the imagination is at once plunged into commiserian gloom in the bright abyss of the heart's high aspirations."

"Yes, yes, sir," replied Miss Clements, "very true, sir. Laura, dear (in a whisper), how uncommonly like poor dear Lord Byron. Did you ever! I could really scream."

And so it would appear by the appearance of Mr. Felix that he, too, could have screamed. He was so thunderstruck by the cool audacity of Mr. Wattles in calling him, him Mr. Felix, for whom a coat with skirts was actually ordered, and who, for all Mr. Wattles knew to the contrary, might be in the constant habit of wearing a hat like a man, a mere lad, and a good lad. It surpassed belief; and Mr. Felix laughed on in a kind of awful, hysterical manner, while Mr. Wattles was explaining to Miss Theodosia Clements the poetry of motion.

"The mind," continued Mr. Wattles, unheedful of many nudges from Mr. Marrables—" the mind is a tangled skein—a concatenation of brilliant images—a stone house of beauty—a mine of glorious gems, which shine with a lustre surpassing earth's richest treasures. The imagination—the bright sunshine of the soul casts its beams upon all things, and life becomes a gilded dream."

"Oh, dear! yes," said Miss Theodosia Clements, with a sympathetic sigh, and Mr. Wattles, to the horror of Mr. Felix, continued, for he had by heart plenty of similar rhapsodies.

"If there be light, dazzling light, to be found on the green earth to cheer the musing poet, and light up in his mind a flame of hope, 'tis, Miss, to be looked for in the eyes of beauty—the cheek of beauty—the—the beauty which now confounds my optics, and breathes soft incense to my enraptured mind."

The last of this speech was uttered in a low voice and with a tender accent, at the same time that Mr. Wattles flourished the bordered handkerchief in a highly amorous and exciting manner.

Mr. Felix heard the speech, and he saw the handkerchief floating about like the victorious banner of a bitter enemy. It was more than human nature could bear, or at least, lanky boys' nature, and, in a moment of fierce desperation, Mr. Felix made a snatch at the handkerchief, and with a very wild and insane look about the eyes, called out,—

"Never! never!"

Everybody looked aghast, and Mr. Felix flourished the handkerchief, and seemed not exactly to know what to do next, although he felt a disposition to cry rather than otherwise.

Miss Theodosia screamed, and looked tenderly at Mr. Wattles, and Miss Laura Flurryman screamed, and laid violent hands on Mr. Wattles in her terror.

Mr. Felix spoke.

"You—you—oh, dear! oh, dear! You may be Conrad, the Corsair, or the—the poet, Montgomery, or—or Lord Byron—but I hate you. I love—oh, dear—oh, dear."

Mr. Wattles stopped the current of his eloquence by taking the nose of Mr. Felix between his finger and thumb, and shaking his head violently thereby.

Mr. Felix was too much amazed for a moment to resist, and when he did do so, he unfortunately struck the first blow clean into the stomach of a middle-aged gentleman, who sat close at hand, and who had leaned forward to see the row.

"The devil!" cried the middle-aged gentleman.

"I'll fight—fight. I won't play any more—no, I mean—I—am a man," shrieked Mr. Felix. "I won't be flogged any more. I—I—oh, dear! oh, dear!"

Miss Theodisa screamed at intervals, and laid her hand tenderly upon Mr. Wattles' coat-sleeve, and Miss Laura Flurryman nearly embraced Mr. Marrables, who sat looking the picture of consternation and despair.

A roar of laughter followed the wild speech of Mr. Felix from the scanty audience, and the middle-aged gentleman clasped him tightly round the waist, and laughed so loudly in Mr. Felix's ear, that he was nearly deafened.

"What's the matter?" cried several voices. "What is it?—what is it?"

"Dosia, dear, I think I shall faint," cried Miss Laura. "Felix is such a fool and so indelicate."

"No, dear, don't; oh, don't faint," replied Theodosia. "Think of Medora, dear, and Gulmane, love."

"The boy took my handkerchief, ah! ah!" said Mr. Wattles; "and—ah, ah!—I chastised him—eh!—ah!"

"Let me go," cried Felix. "Fair play—no, no—I'll tell my mother."

Another roar of mirth followed Felix's expostulation, and Miss Theodosia Clements made a mental resolve to cast him from her for ever, and, if possible, in favour of the gifted individual who now pressed her hand in his.

"Felix, Felix," said his sister, "you're a fool. Go home, you great baby, and don't interfere with us. How dare you," said Miss Theodisia, "take the—the gentleman's handkerchief? Restore it, rash boy; you know not who you have insulted. Go home, child. This comes, sir (turning to Mr. Wattles), of bringing boys to public places, where they come in contact with men of distinguished genius and the nobility of the country in disguise."

"Ha!" cried Mr. Wattles, as if suddenly very much alarmed at the most distant supposition that he was a distinguished person in disguise. "I—I—excuse me, my name is—is Smith—yes, Smith."

Miss Theodosia Clements smiled, and shook her head.

"You do not know me?" asked Mr. Wattles, mysteriously.

"No," cried Miss Theodisa, tenderly. "My heart—that is—oh, no—not at all."

Mr. Felix said no more, but throwing down Mr. Wattles' handkerchief, he burst out of the box, muttering some dire threats in the name of his mother.

CHAPTER XV.

HARMONY was restored by the abrupt exit of Mr. Felix Flurryman; and the dance being ended, an animating conversation upon polite literature and the fine arts commenced between Mr. Wattles and Miss Theodosia Clements.

Mr. Marrables was quite astounded, and taken aback by the whole proceedings ; and when Miss Laura Flurryman said, in a low voice,—

"Theatrical entertainments are charming food for the mind," he actually groaned, and a cold perspiration came over him at the thought of what Mrs. Marrables would say, if some one, with malice aforethought, were to go and tell her that he, Mr. Marrables, actually made acquaintance with a young lady in the boxes of the theatre, and then and there conversed with her.

"Yes, Miss," he replied ; "very, oh, very ; I'm afraid I sha'n't be able to stay long."

Here he gave a nudge to Mr. Wattles, and winked at the box-door, to intimate the propriety of immediately retiring, but Mr. Wattles, not being oppressed with Mr. Marrables' fear, had no such intention, and only replied by a wink at Miss Laura Flurryman, which said, as plain as any wink could say,—

"Enjoy your luck, old Marrables, and leave me alone. This was farther accompanied by a peg in the ribs, which caused Mr. Marrables to cry, "Oh!" and double himself nearly right across Miss Laura.

Mr. Marrables was so confounded at this, that he at once burst into a wandering discourse upon all sorts of matters ; and Miss Flurryman (who was nine-and-twenty) thought him a very agreeable man, although he was on the wrong side of thirty.

Dreadful deeds were committed upon the stage—murders were perpetrated, pistols were fired, trap-doors opened and shut, and blue fire and green fire and red fire were all in their glory ; and Mr. Wattles talked poetry to Miss Theodosia at a great rate, while that young lady sighed responsively, and made up her own mind most decidedly that the individual who choose to call himself Smith was no more Smith than she was, but either Tom Moore, Lord Byron, or Robert Montgomery.

Mr. Marrables was a desperate man ; he knew it was past ten o'clock ; he felt all the dangers of his awful situation, but he was too far gone to retreat ; he felt himself, as Mr. Wattles would have said, emphatically, "in for it," and he dashed on. He was no longer the shy, retiring Mr. Marrables, but he rattled on surprisingly. Mr. Wattles was astonished, for Mr. Marrables went on at a great rate about music, novels, plays, dancing, flirting, and so on, with surprising facility. He pressed Miss Laura's hand in an insinuating and tender manner, and once or twice very nearly forgot the existence of such a person as Mrs. Marrables.

The play was over, the hornpipe in fetters was danced, Mr. Marrables applauded ; and, with a recklessness as to the flight of time, called, "encore !" The burletta began—Mr. Marrables laughed amazingly, and Miss Laura simpered behind her handkerchief.

The fair Theodosia and Mr. Wattles were on the best possible terms. The

gentleman had spent ninepence, sterling, for refreshments, which had been brought into the box, and he had generously handed some to Mr. Marrables, who had but twopence to bestow upon Miss Flurryman, which Mr. Marrables did with quite a gallant air.

The burletta was not of the most novel description. There was an old gentleman, who had a niece, who was, likewise, his ward ; and there was a young gentleman, who met the said niece at a ball, and fell desperately in love with her forthwith. Then there was another old gentleman, who has a son, and the first old gentleman argues with the second old gentleman that his son shall marry the niece ; and the lovers rave, and the old gentlemen storm and knock their sticks against the ground, and finally it turns out that the ball-room lover and the son of the second old gentleman are one and the same persons.

Mr. Marrables roared at the jokes in the burletta, and looked tender at Miss Laura Flurryman when the lovers were on the stage ; and Miss Laury Flurryman blushed a little, and coughed slightly, when the lover kissed the young lady ; and the first old gentleman, most opportunely rushing in, cried,—

"Hilloa ! hilloa !—poaching !"

"You write, of course ?" said Miss Theodesia to Mr. Wattles, with a languishing air.

"Shall I own," said Mr. Wattles, looking intently at a hole in the ceiling ;—"shall I own that I have, on Parnassian Mount, the fair-named muses wooed ?"

"Oh, yes ; delightful," cried Miss Clements ;—"do own it—do."

"I will. The mind, oppressed with teeming fancies, seizes madly upon the lyre, and bursts into extatic song."

"Dear me, Mr. Smith—hem !—you don't say so ? What song, sir ? I am so fond of songs."

No. 11

The comic song advertised in the bill was sung, and Mrs. Theodosia Clements and Miss Laura Flurryman both intimated their opinions that it was rather low; and so, indeed, it was to a certain degree, for its humour and comicality seemed altogether to depend upon the coincidence of a blow being given upon the great drum at the end of each verse, at the precise moment that the facetious singer dropped upon that part of his person, which Liston says is at the other end.

Certainly painful thoughts, like barbed sorrows, would occasionally fly across Mr. Marrables' brow as the time sped onwards, and he felt convinced that twelve o'clock must be fast approaching. He pictured Mrs. Marrables with a very red face, awaiting his return, and he groaned.

"Are you ill, sir?" asked Miss Theodosia. "Dear me, Mr. —— ah! ah!"

"Wilkins!" cried Mr. Wattles, who saw the hesitation for a name, "Mr. Peter Wilkins."

"No," said Mr. Marrables, "I am very well, thank you. I only—that is, I—nothing—oh!—nothing," and Mr. Marrables laughed and quoted poetry, and flirted with increased vigour.

The extravaganza followed and finished. The fireworks lived for a moment, ond then died away—the curtain dropped—the play was over, and a damp chilliness came over Mr. Marrables' heart as he thought of home and Mrs. Marrables.

"They rose and left the theatre, and Mr. Wattles offered his arm gallantly to Miss Clements, and Mr. Marrables could do no less to Miss Flurryman.

"Permit us the exquisite honour, ladies," said Mr. Wattles, "to escort so many charms to their home."

"Oh! dear me," said Miss Theodosia, "I really—Laura, dear—what do you say?"

"She says," replied Mr. Wattles for her, "that she can discriminate between mere forward gallantry and those whose hearts beat in unison with chivalric feelings."

This was quite irrisistible, and the two couples proceeded, arm in arm, down the thronged street in which the little theatre stood.

Mr. Wattles had just turned the corner with Miss Theodosia Clements, when some one stopped abruptly before them, trembling quite palpably.

Miss Theodosia screamed, "it's Felix!—it's Felix."

"Who?" cried Mr. Wattles, with a momentary fright that it might be the paternal Clements, if there were such a being; but his doubts were soon solved, for the mysterious being lifted up a hat, which, being a vast deal too large, came down to his chin, in the manner that an ancient warrior would have raised his viser, and cast a withering look at Mr. Wattles, who then saw that he was no other than the redoubtable young gentleman whose nose he had made free with in the theatre.

"Oh, dear! oh, dear!" cried Miss Theodosia. "Felix, how could you think of coming out in your pa's hat?"

"Sir," said Mr. Felix, clenching his teeth, and addressing Mr. Wattles; but upon his letting go the hat, it immediately descended, and Mr. Felix's face was hidden from mortal gaze, and only a muffled sound arose from the interior.

Miss Laura Flurryman now arrived at the spot; and when she saw her brother stamping and bawling about, apparently without a face at all, she screamed, and seized Mr. Marrables so tightly by the cravat, that he was very near strangulation, and in the agony of his feelings he crushed Miss Laura's bonnet wofully.

"Sir!" shrieked Mr. Felix, again succeeding in raising the extinguisher, "you're a perjured villain—a—a. You're a cheat, sir—a cheat—you'd swindle anybody, sir. Diamonds—marbles—gold—buttons—tops—hoops, or gingerbread—it would be all the same to you, sir; you'd cheat any boy; that is, any gentleman out of them, sir. There's my card, at least, it's father's card, but I'm named after him, sir, so it's all the same; I demand satisfaction, sir. Blood! blood! blood!"

"Eh!—ah!—ah! Poor lad!" replied Mr. Wattles. "Eh!—ah! Peter Wilkins, my good fellow, ah!—ah!—eh! Don't you think this poor boy's wits are—ah!—ah!—gone?"

"I'm ashamed of you, Felix!" cried his sister, in great wrath. "Go home—do."

"Your card, sir!—your card!" continued the young gentleman. "Blood, sir; blood. Perhaps you're an officer, sir, but I don't care; I'll fight you, sir, I will. Here's my card."

"Eh!—ah!" said Mr. Wattles. "When do you return—ah!—ah!—to the preparatory school, eh?"

"Fury and death!" cried Mr. Felix; "I wish I may be kept in for ever if I put up with this. I'd rather be sent to bed at six. Oh! the devil!—the devil!"

Mr. Wattles had allowed the card to fall upon the pavement, and he now affected to stoop, with great curiosity, to read it.

"Eh!—ah! 'F. Flurryman, grocer and family tea dealer.' Ah! ah!"

"Your card, sir!—where's your card?" shrieked Mr. Felix.

"'The best Mocha coffee ground upon the premises.'—Ah!—ah!"

"The devil!—oh! the devil!"

"'Mould and store candles'—eh! ah!—'mixed pickles—pepper.'—Ah!—ah!"

Mr. Felix could stand the thing no longer, and he threw himself upon Mr. Wattles with a shout, which might have been, in ancient times, the Flurryman warwhoop.

Miss Flurryman screamed—Miss Theodosia screamed, a crowd collected in a moment, and all was bustle and confusion.

Mr. Wattles did not expect the attack, and was rather taken by surprise than otherwise, and he very nearly fell upon his nose; but in an instant he recovered himself, and giving Master Felix a tremendous bonneter on the top of the large hat, the young gentleman was instantly lost, and fought and screamed, and cried, and kicked at everybody.

"Cut, Marrables, cut," whispered Mr. Wattles, and in a moment he cleared himself of the throng, followed by Mr. Marrables, and started off at full speed.

When they were three or four streets off, Mr. Wattles stopped, and setting down on a door step, he laughed outrageously.

"That's what I call a jolly spree, Marrables," he said.

"Oh, yes," replied Mr. Marrables, "an uncommon jolly spree; but have you any notion of what o'clock it is, eh, Wattles?"

"Not the least, old boy. This is life—life, old cut and come again."

"I'm afraid," said Mr. Marrables, "it's death to me; what will Mrs. Marrables say?"

"Hang what she says, Marrables. We're jolly dogs—lads of spirit—we've done it well."

"Oh! uncommonly well. But you know, Wattles, Mrs. Marrables is a woman who——"

"Don't mention her," shouted Mr. Wattles. "Come, old stew-pot, what'll you have to drink?"

"To drink, Mr. Wattles?—at this time of night, too? Why, there is not a public-house open in the whole town; besides, I really—you know

sixteen-pence out of eighteen-pence, leaves only two-pence; and Mrs.
Marrables——"

"Be damned!" cried Mr. Wattles. "I've got the tin—the circulating
medium. Come along; I know where to get a drop of brandy that's
never heard of at the Custom-house. Come on, old blacking brush; come
on."

"Why, really—" Mr. Marrables began; but his resistance was feeble,
and he suffered Mr. Wattles to lead him astray.

They arrived at the side door of a public-house, which was closed, but
at which Mr. Wattles knocked, and a voice from within asked—"Who's
there?"

"A trump!" cried Mr. Wattles, and the door was opened immediately.
"Two glasses of brandy and water, as hot as the devil, and as little water
as possible. Would you like a cigar, Marrables?"

"Dear me," replied Mr. Marrables, "I haven't smoked a cigar I don't
know how long; Mrs. Marrables, you see, Wattles, has an——"

"Oh! the devil take her," cried Wattles. "Two cigars. Here's the
brandy and water; drink Marrables. Here's better luck still, old time-
piece."

"Thank you," said Mr. Marrables, and he took a draught of the liquor,
which seemed to rush like liquid fire through his veins.

The brandy and water was drunk; and Mr. Marrables, who was utterly
unused to anything stronger than Mrs. Marrables' small beer, was nearly
drunk, too, and laughed and slapped Mr. Wattles on the back, and even
went so far as to say—

"Damn Mrs. Marrables, who—who—who—(hiccup)—who cares for
her?"

"Not you, my old tomahawk," replied Mr. Wattles; "keep it up, man.
'Luck in a bag, and shake it out as you want it.'"

"Ex—ex—ex—actly," said Mr. Marrables. "Hurrah! — hurrah! —
hurrah!"

"That's it, my old chronometer. Bravo! bravo!"

"I—I feel warm, Wattles—warm. My throat is—is ho—t."

"Have a pint of ale to cool it."

"But, Wattles, my dear fellow, w—will ale m—m—mix well with
brandy and water?"

"Oh, uncommonly. Didn't you know that, my ancient Greek?"

"Oh! yes; I—I—forgot—forgot. Give us a pint of ale, Hurrah!
hurrah!"

The pint of ale was brought, and that finished Mr. Marrables' business.
Like most sober men, when he did get drunk he was wild and desperate;
and when he and Mr. Wattles sallied forth from the public-house, each
with his cigar, Mr. Marrables danced several comic dances in the road, and
raised a lengthened yell, which might have been heard all over the town.
Mr. Wattles was rather gone than otherwise, and urged poor Marrables to
all sorts of extravagance and wild behaviour.

It was now about half-past two in the morning when they arrived at
Pleasant-row, and staggered up to No. 10.

Mr. Marrables was singing "All's well," and Mr. Wattles was helping
him out.

"I'll show you how to knock, Wattles," said Mr. Marrables. "Here
goes;" and he laid hold of the knocker, and executed such a peel, that Pleasant-row became in a moment unpleasant row, and various windows were
thrown up, and night-capped heads popped out, and an old lady who lived
at No. 8, sprung a watchman's rattle, and screamed.

Even Mr. Wattles was astonished, for Mr. Marrables never left off knocking for a moment, and seemed perfectly delighted with the noise, and shouted "Hurrah!" incessantly.

Poor Phœbe had waited long and anxiously for Mr. Marrables to come home; and at length, quite exhausted with watching, she had sank into a slumber about two o'clock—a slumber which she had held off as long as she could, for she thought that Mr. Marrables would adopt, as a matter of course, some very quiet and unobtrusive method of letting her know he was at the door; and when she was awakened suddenly by the awful knocking which at that still hour sounded terrifically loud, she was thoroughly bewildered, and rushed to the street-door in anticipation of some fearful calamity or fire at the very least. That it was Mr. Marrables she could not for a moment suppose.

Mrs. Marrables, who had fallen into a troubled sleep, and was dreaming of knocking Mr. Marrables' head against Mr. Wattles' head, and his against the kitchen table, was awakened in a great fright by the combination of noises. The old lady's rattle and screams—the laughter of Mr. Wattles— the perpetual knocking and shouts of triumph of Mr. Marrables—altogether made up a concert, which for a few moments deprived Mrs. Marrables of the power of thought or action. The lady's usual presence of mind, how- ever, soon returned, and she dashed to the window, and opening it, looked into the street, and there beheld Mr. Marrables, by the grey light of the morning, hanging on to the knocker, and knocking away, while Mr. Wat- tles sat on the step, roaring with laughter. For one moment a wild thought darted across Mrs. Marrables' brain of throwing herself clean out of the window, in the sanguine hope of accomplishing the destruction of both Mr. Marrables and Mr. Wattles, by falling upon them.

There was a pail, however, in the landing outside the bed-room; and in an incredible short space of time Mrs. Marrables filled it with water from the water-jug, and anywhere else, and flying to the window again, she precipitated the contents exactly on to the step of the door, and then threw down the pail with an awful force.

Phœbe had meanwhile opened the street-door, and Mr. Marrables had reeled into the passage, but Mr. Wattles was still on the step, and caught the whole of the shower bath from above, and would likewise have caught the pail, had he not sprung forward into the middle of the passage with a shout of surprise and indignation just before that missile fell on the step with an astounding crash.

"How are you?" said Mr. Marrables, nodding at Phœbe, and support- ing himself by placing his back against the wall; "how are—you, my— dear, eh? How's the old woman, Mrs. M—M—arrables, eh? Give us a kiss, my love. You—you're a damned fine girl, by Jove—hurrah! hurrah! hurrah!"

The shout of Mr. Marrables reached Mrs. Marrables' chamber; and, without waiting to dress herself, she seized a cloak belonging to Mr. Mar- rables, which fastened in front by a large brass claw and a chain, she im- mediately put it on, and rushed down stairs.

When Mrs. Marrables arrived in the passage, she seemed either to have lost the power of utterance, or to be totally unable to find words sufficiently strong to express her horror and indignation, for she stood arrayed in the cloak, and fencing with her arms like one possessed.

"Ha! old 'un!" cried Mr. Marrables, "how are you? You—you need not—have—got up, you know. This is—m—my house—hurrah!"

"How are you, old 'un?" echoed Mr. Wattles. "I say, the next time you throw a pail out at the window, just cry ' below there!' will you?"

"Wretches!—devils!" screamed Mrs. Marrables; "am I mad?—do I dream?"

"You be damned!" replied Mr. Marrables; "you—you're drunk—that's what you are. Woman, you're drunk—you—you—you're a beast!"

"An old beast!" suggested Mr. Wattles, shaking the water from his head.

"A damned old beast!" cried Mr. Marrables; "hurrah! Phœbe, you'll be a fine girl, you will, when the old 'un is—is under ground. I—I admire you. Let's have supper—hurrah! hurrah!—supper for ever. Mrs. Marrables go to bed, and—sleep off your in—intox—tox—toxication."

"Ah, do," said Mr. Wattles. "I suppose you mistook the window for the sink in the back kitchen. We've had a spree, Mrs. Marrables—a jolly spree. Marrables is a trump—a king of clubs, old lady—he's down as fifteen hammers, he is, my old vinegar cruet."

Poor Phœbe was not less astounded at this scene than was Mrs. Marrables. The poor child had accustomed herself to look upon her mistress as such an absolute monarch, that she heard Mr. Marrables' words of defiance with astonishment and horror.

Mrs. Marrables' rage quite overcame her reason, and, without another word, she flew at Mr. Marrables, and commenced an attack of the most alarming nature.

Mr. Wattles joined in the mill, and the combatants rolled about the passage. Mrs. Marrables got hold of Mr. Wattles by the hair, and dealt that facetious gentleman a blow on the nose, which drew first blood.

"Murder!" screamed Mr. Wattles—"murder! murder!"

"Hurrah! hurrah!" still shouted Mr. Marrables, who was reduced to a sitting posture.

"You wretches!" shrieked Mrs. Marrables, "I'll teach you to come home in this state; I'll let you know who's master here. Take that, and that. And you, you little shameless hussey," turning suddenly to Phœbe, and dealing her a random blow, "you little villain, you'll bring drunken wretches into the house, will you?"

"Hurrah!" said Mr. Marrables; "she—she's a trump, and—and uncommonly handsome."

"I'll handsome you, you little wretch. Troop!—troop! Get out this instant."

Poor Phœbe was terrified nearly to death at Mrs. Marrables' violence, and trembled from head to foot as she stood by the street door.

"Oh, ma'am," she said, "do not turn me out—oh! do not—what shall I do?"

Mrs. Marrables answered this appeal by a rush at Phœbe, who, in great fear, sprung out at the door, and into the street, followed by her mistress, who, not observing the pail which was lying on the step, fell over it, and rolled, enveloped in the cloak, into the road.

"Hurrah! hurrah!" shouted Mr. Marrables.

"Go it, old 'un," cried Mr. Wattles; "three to two on the pail."

Phœbe looked for a moment at the prostrate Mrs. Marrables; then clasping her hands, she cried—

"Heavens help me!" and fled from the place.

CHAPTER XVI.

THE morning was dawning as Phœbe, urged by fear, rushed from the house of the violent and capricious Mrs. Marrables. A cold grey light was upon everything; the streets were utterly deserted, and a solemn stillness reigned through the town.

Onwards, but not knowing whither, the alarmed girl rushed, until she had placed many streets between her and Pleasant-row. She then paused; and, tottering with fatigue and excitement of mind, she sunk upon a door step and wept bitterly.

Poor Phœbe Grainger was utterly destitute. She felt bitterly the misery of her situation. Return to Mrs. Marrables she could not, for what cruelties might she not dread from her vindictive spirit.

"No, no," cried Phœbe, "I will die here. Oh! George! George! where are you now?"

For an hour, or more, the unhappy Phœbe sat upon the step and wept; but as the day broke, and the sounds of life and bustle began slowly to arise from the houses, she became alarmed at the possibility of being claimed either by Mrs. Marrables, or some of the workhouse people, and she dried her eyes, and started from the step.

"Where—oh! where shall I go?" she cried, clasping her little hands in despair. "They will take me back to the cruel workhouse if I stay here, or to Mrs. Marrables; and—and I'd rather die, and go to poor dear mother."

"What are you crying at, eh?" said a rough man, as he passed her.

"Nothing—nothing," said Phœbe, and she hastened onwards.

She felt that she was in danger in the streets of momentarily meeting some one who might offer her interruption, and she walked rapidly, to get, if possible, into the open country.

She was dressed, but she had nothing on her head. The weather, however, was fine, and that might escape observation, or, at least, not expose her to suspicion.

Her fair hair hung in beautiful luxuriance about her neck and shoulders, and many a glance of curiosity and admiration was bestowed upon the houseless orphan as she walked through the suburbs of the town.

"I will go," she thought, "into the beautiful green fields, and where the yellow corn grows. There I can rest, and no one can see me. Perhaps I shall see some little cottage like—like poor dear mother's, and they who live in it may pity me."

She cleared the town, and the blithe song of the birds came sweetly to her ears. She was in the fields; fertile meadows and waving corn fields were all around her. The swallows shot across her path, almost touching her face with their wings, and the hedge-sparrow chirruped and whistled from every green shrub.

Phœbe crept under a stile, and entered a field of wheat. She plucked a few ears, and made a simple breakfast from the corn. She was weary and oppressed with sleep. She sat down by the hedge-side, and watched for a time the flight of the birds as they skimmed along the blue vault of Heaven. The rustling of the corn was a soothing, grateful sound to her ears; it was the only one, save the sweet notes of the feathered tribe, that disturbed the stillness of the scene.

A drowsy feeling came more and more over the gentle Phœbe. She leaned her head upon her hand, and muttered something about her dear mother and George—her eyes slowly closed—a smile played for a moment on her lips—and there, amid the luxuriance and beauty of nature, with the light sea breeze fanning her delicate cheek, the fair and gentle orphan, Phœbe Grainger, slept the sweet sleep of purity and innocence.

How many of the rich and powerful might have well envied the sweet untroubled sleep of that orphan child! Destitute of friends or a home, as she was, how much happier was she than many who were then surrounded with magnificence and luxury on their gilded couches, sighing for that sweet repose which visited so calmly the gentle girl, as she lay upon that verdant bank, with no canopy but that of Heaven above her head.

Many who have toiled through a long life of treachery, deceit, and ennui, to amass that wealth which they fondly thought would bring them happiness, would gladly give it all for the calm heart's guileless innocence with which they began existence. Many, oh, how many, would, with tears of joy and thanksgiving, gladly have exchanged inexhaustible treasures but to be as that fair young girl who slept so sweetly and so calmly on the breast of Nature. How they, who had grown weary of the world's pleasures and its vanities, would have laughed to scorn the destitution which they would have had to embrace by the exchange. The pure heart's joy would have been a kingdom—the freshness of the soul a glorious treasure.

The morning was advanced considerably when Phœbe awoke from her happy sleep. For an instant she looked alarmed, and started; but memory came to her aid, and she smiled, for there was no harsh mistress to quiet her with a word and a blow for sleeping too long.

The birds and the butterflies were flitting about, and they seemed to consider the fair child almost as one of themselves, for the sparrows moved not from her; and a goldfinch went through the whole of his sweet song on a bough not two feet from where she lay.

She rose much refreshed by her happy, quiet slumber, and walked along the hedge without a thought of the future. She plucked a few wild flowers, and twined them in her flowing hair, and then gathering some more ears of corn, she again made a frugal meal, with the addition of some water, which she lifted in the palm of her hand, from a little clear rivulet, which took its murmuring way on the other side of the verdant hedge.

Phœbe was now but in her ninth year, but she had latterly seen enough of the world to be well aware that she could not remain long without pursuing some particular course; and after a time, when the heat of the sun forced her to shelter herself beneath the shady boughs of a tree, and she sat down, the question again recurred to her of "What shall I do?"

Her knowledge of society and its resources was too slight for her to decide so intricate a question, but she resolved to walk onward through the fields until she came to some cottage, where, perhaps, she might be sufficiently encouraged by the kindness of the people to tell her tale, and crave counsel and assistance. She recollected poor wanderers coming occasionally to her mother's cottage, and being received with kindness and hospitality, and she thought that all who lived in pretty cottages and loved flowers, would be good and kind to her.

With this idea she rose, and taking the path by the side of the hedge on which she was sheltered from the sun, she walked forwards, not knowing where it might lead her to, nor caring, so it was away from Mrs. Marrables and the dreaded workhouse.

Phœbe had not proceeded very far before she saw a white-fronted cottage, from the chimney of which the smoke was ascending in the pure air. A neat garden appeared in front, in which were some bee-hives and roses, and honeysuckles decked the front of the pretty and picturesque dwelling.

"Here," thought Phœbe, "here I will ask for a drop of milk, and they may be good people, and ask me what I mean to do, and then I will tell them I am poor, and have no mother, and George is gone, and they will, perhaps, have pity on me."

She approached a little wicket gate, which opened into the garden, and, pushing it open, stood upon the neat gravelled walk.

A window suddenly opened, and a woman put her head out and surveyed the intruder.

"What do you want?" she cried.

"A draught of milk," said Phœbe, "or a bit of bread, if you please, ma'am, for I have no home."

"Oh! a beggar!" cried the woman. "Be off, will you, or else I'll make you; we don't encourage vagrants here; go to your parish, you little vagabond. I dare say you come to see what you can pick up. Be off!—be off!"

Poor Phœbe needed no urging to quit the inhospitable threshold. She passed the wicket again with a sigh, and wondered how people could like to be cruel and unfeeling, when it was so pleasant and delightful to be kind and good.

The poor orphan's faith in human nature had been considerably shaken by her residence at the workhouse, and by the outrageous bad temper of the frightful Mrs. Marrables, but she had still thought that in humble cottages, such as her mother's had been, she should find comfort and assistance, and she was particularly disappointed at this harsh result of her first application.

Slowly she took her way along a narrow pathway which presented itself; and although she saw several cottages in sight, yet she dreaded another repulse, and, with a shudder, she passed them by, and did not offer again to solicit the kind feelings of her fellow creatures.

For a long time she then wandered onwards without any settled purpose whatever. Her feet began to get tired, and she felt generally weary and weak. Again the thought occurred to her that it would be great happiness to lie down and fall asleep in the fields, and never awaken again.

The wild flowers had faded in her hair, and she let them fall out one by one without endeavouring to replace them. She had lost her spirits—there

No. 12

was no longer any hope to sustain her—her eyes filled with tears, and she was about to allow herself to sink to the ground in pure exhaustion and despair, when the low tinckling of some bells at a distance came faintly to her ears.

She listened attentively, and hope again renewed its blossoms in her heart. Nearer and nearer came the sound, and Phœbe hurried forwards in the direction from whence it seemed to proceed.

She found herself in a few moments close to the highway, and creeping through a hedge, she stood in the dusty country road.

The tinkle of the bells came clearly and sweetly to her ears, and shading her eyes with her hand, she looked down the road, and saw, at some distance off, a waggon and a train of horses slowly approaching. The bells were at the horses' heads; and as they slowly stepped along, in drowsy strength, the bells just sufficed to keep them sufficiently alert to their duty to prevent them from going off quite asleep, and dropping down upon the road.

Nearer and nearer they came, accompanied by a cloud of dust, and Phœbe could see that it was a large covered waggon, drawn by eight lazy fat horses. The waggoner was seated on one of them, half asleep, and nodding his head to the tread of the horses, who all seemed nearly asleep, too.

The foremost two horses, when they approached to where Phœbe stood, stopped short, and the two behind them took the hint, after running their heads against them, and stopped, too, and so on did the whole lot come to a stand still, and the waggon creaked a great deal, and then was perfectly quiet.

The waggoner suddenly opened his eyes, greatly astonished at the stillness, and immediately offered Phœbe a turnpike ticket, remarking, that he believed that cleared the gate.

Phœbe looked surprised, first at the ticket and then at the waggoner and the sleepy horses.

"I'm poor, sir," she said, "and have no mother."

"Eh!—ah!—what?—eh!" cried the man, rubbing his eyes; oh, dear! heart alive. I thought we'd a got to Clonney Gate, dang'd if I didn't. Woa! wa! wa! What dost want, wench?"

"I am poor, sir, and hungry, and have no home."

The waggoner whistled a long shrill whistle, and looked hard at Phœbe.

"And thee stopped all the horses, did thee? Dang'd if that ain't a good 'un. He! he! he!"

"No, sir, I did not stop them; they stopped themselves, sir, indeed they did."

"Well, doan't 'e mind. The more sensible they be's to stop o' themselves. Come, thee shall have summut for thy pretty face, thee shall. Heart alive, where did thee come from?"

"I've been in service; but they, she, I mean, was so cruel, and turned me away."

"She be domned!" said the waggoner, going to a little box attached to the side of the waggon, and taking therefrom some bacon, cheese, and bread—

"Come, my dear, eat thee breakfast, for thee lookest as thee had had none. Woa! woa!"

The compassionate waggoner then produced an immense clasp knife, and sitting down by the roadside, he invited Phœbe to sit by him, and partake of the repast.

Phœbe looked in the man's face for a moment, for children are great physiognomists, and then sat down.

The waggoner was a man of at least fifty years of age, but as hearty as possible. His broad good-humoured face was radiant with glee. No single line of care was on his brow, and he often broke out into an extemporaneous laugh at nothing at all, but in pure joyous light-heartedness.

He cut off about half a pound of bacon in one slice, and handed it to Phœbe, upon a large lump of bread, saying—

"Take that, my little lass— heart alive. It will do to begin with whiles I cut some more."

He then fumbled about a long time in various pockets till he produced a little knife, which he handed to Phœbe.

"Danged if I woren't a taking that knife to my grandson, but thou shall have it."

Phœbe eat some of the bread and bacon, and the waggoner finished the remainder.

"Where art thee going, heart alive?" cried he to Phœbe. "Thee don't mean, thee little thing, to tell me that thee has no hoame to go to!"

"It is true," said Phœbe with a sigh. "Mother died, and they took me to the workhouse."

"Poor thing! poor thing! Take some more bacon, will 'e?"

"Then I was sent to service, and my mistress beat me, and turned me out this morning, because I only—"

"Hold 'e tongue, will 'e? I doan't care what thee did. She who turned thee out of doors, my poor girl, had no heart at all, and I'm danged if she were a true woman. Poor thing, thee could do nothing to her half bad enough for that. Thee wert honest?"

"Oh! indeed, yes," cried Phœbe; "I would not tell a story for anything. Mother always told me to tell the truth."

"Then she was worth fifty of thy missus, my wench. Thee must not want. Did they use thee bad at the workhouse?"

"They did—they did," sobbed Phœbe. "Oh! do not tell me to go there again. I would rather die in the pretty fields among the dear birds, indeed I would."

"Then thee sha'n't go, that's settled. I don't know what to do with thee. My old woman would be good to thee, but she is a long way off—in London, heart alive; but I must do something for thee, my little wench."

As the waggoner spoke, a rattling, jerking noise came down the road, in the opposite direction to that which the waggon was travelling, and Phœbe started up, with an undefined sensation of danger, and looked down the road. The chaise cart, for such it was, that was approaching, was just in sight, and Phœbe's young eyes in an instant recognized it as a vehicle belonging to the parish of Bungleum, which was used for a variety of purposes, and in it was seated Mr. Bung, and Mrs. Marrables.

Poor Phœbe clasped her hands in despair.

"They are coming to take me—they are coming—oh! they will beat me so—oh! dear—oh, George!—mother! mother!"

"Who's coming?" cried the waggoner, jumping up, and seizing his whip; "who is it?"

"The beadle and my mistress who turned me out," cried Phœbe. "Oh don't let them take me. Protect me, sir—do, sir, do—I have no mother nor friends."

"Hold thee tongue, will 'e?" cried the waggoner, rushing to the back of the waggon, and thrusting aside several things which impeded the entrance.

"Come here, do—be quick, my wench—come here."

Phœbe was at his side in a moment. He took her in his arms, and immediately lifted her into the waggon, and she sank down among the straw.

"Bide there, my little wench; bide there—they sha'n't have 'e—doan't 'e speak—they sha'n't have 'e; noa, noa, I be danged if they shall. I do hate a beadle, surely."

It was, indeed, Mr. Bung and Mrs. Marrables who were in the parish cart; and Mr. Bung was in full costume, and driving in a very energetic manner.

Mrs. Marrables, upon cool reflection, very much regretted having turned away the submissive and gentle Phœbe, for she had never before had any one over whom she could so thoroughly tyrannize as the poor orphan child; who, with the consciousness that she was friendless, joined to her natural yielding and gentle disposition, put up quietly with Mrs. Marrables' blows and reproaches. She likewise felt some little alarm as to the extent of her responsibility in the matter of the friendless child; and, therefore, after terminating her conflict with Mr. Marrables and Mr. Wattles, which ended in the complete discomfiture of them both, and her signal triumph, she had at an early hour in the morning, walked down to Bungleum work-house, and informed Mr. Bung that Phœbe had eloped, and asked his advice what to do.

"What a horrid extremity of williany," said Mr. Bung, "them two orphans has gived way to. We never allows, mum, paupers to come into the house until we can't help it, mum; but we never allows them to come and go as they pleases, or to leave their blessed sitivations as we procure for 'em, and where they lives on the fat of the land, without no notice at all, it's a encouraging of wice, mum."

"I hasn't a doubt but that little odious Phœbe Grainger has formed some horrid connection," said Mrs. Fungus, who assisted at the council. "She's wice itself. I think I see her now, ma'am, nearly in a horrid state of nudity, ma'am, a running arter a he pauper, just because he was her brother, ma'am. Oh! she's very immoral; she's enough to conterminate a city, ma'am."

"Continate! Mrs. Fungus," said Mr. Bung, "you mean; she is, indeed; but I'll get out the chay, mum, and drive to the town, and I'll find her, you may depend."

"Unless," said Mrs. Fungus, "she's gone into keeping with some odious nobleman."

"She's a little wretch!" said Mrs. Marrables. "What do you think of my husband intimating his affections for the little slut, and speculating on my decease?"

"Horrid! horrid!" said Mrs. Fungus.

"It's the wery height of willany, mum," said Mr. Bung.

In a short time the chaise cart was at the door, and Mr. Bung gallantly helped in Mrs. Marrables, and then seizing the reins, off they set to the town, with a determination of capturing poor Phœbe, forthwith, and then it was they encountered the waggon, which was coming from the town on the London road, and in which Phœbe had so opportunely been hidden.

Mr. Bung drew in the reins as he approached near the waggoner, and assuming an air of great authority, he looked hard at him, and said:—

"My good fellow, have you seen a little girl, with long light hair on the road?"

"Wa—woa!" cried the waggoner, giving a smack to his whip, which so alarmed the chaise horse, that he immediately stood on his hind legs, to the great consternation of Mr. Bung and Mrs. Marrables.

"Wa—wa—wo—a," said Mr. Bung to the horse. "Poor fellow—poor fellow—wa—a—a—o."

"What did thee say?" enquired the waggoner.

"I asked, low man," replied Mr. Bung, "if you hadn't a happened to see a young girl on this here road? She's a escaped pauper, she is."

"Oh! be she?" replied the waggoner. "No, I ha'n't seen no pauper at all, not I. Gee—come up—come up."

The waggoner's horses acknowledged immediately the propriety of proceeding, and they shook their heads and wakened up, and the bells began to tinkle as they slowly walked along.

"Do you," said Mr. Bung, rising in a very frantic manner, "mean to jam the parish chay into smash?"

"There be room enough," replied the waggoner.

"But, individual, don't you see as my precious veel 'ill go into the ditch, and we shall be upset werry near?"

"Let 'e be upset, then," replied the waggoner, with another smack of the whip, which alarmed Mr. Bung so much, that he backed the chaise by a sudden tug at the reins right into a stagnant ditch by the road-side.

"Murder! murder!" cried Mrs. Marrables.

"Fire!" screamed Mr. Bung, scrambling out of the chaise, and alighting up to his knees in the ditch.

The waggoner paid not the least attention to the situation of the chaise cart, or its occupants, but, again speaking to his horses, he trudged along at their head, without once looking behind him, or taking further heed.

"You wretch!" screamed Mrs. Marrables, "I'll have you prosecuted. You shall be properly and quickly punished."

"You will, wagabond," said Mr. Bung. "I'll have you afore the blessed board, or else my name isn't Bung, by no means, and I'm a spurious beadle."

The waggoner smacked his whip, spoke to his horses, and paid no more attention to the vociferations of Mr. Bung and Mrs. Marrables than he would have done to two yelping curs who might have followed his waggon.

CHAPTER XVII.

PHŒBE had remained in the waggon in an agony of apprehension the whole of the time. Through a little creviee in the awning she had seen all that had occurred, and she trembled at the thought of how near she had been of falling into the power of Mr. Bung and the relentless Mrs. Marrables, from whom she knew she need expect no mercy.

With breathless attention she watched the whole scene, and when the waggon moved on, and she found herself really rescued from Mr. Bung and Mrs. Marrables, she sunk down amongst the straw; and when the waggoner, after a turn of the road, which brought them quite out of sight of the parish chaise, went to the back of the waggon, and removed the things he had placed to hide the interior, he found Phœbe weeping and sobbing violently.

"Why, my little wench," he cried, "don't cry. Heart alive, they shall not have thee. Thee heard them, my dear. Keep up thee heart; I've been thinking of thee."

"Oh! you have saved me from them," cried Phœbe. "They would have been so cruel. You have been very good to me, you have, indeed. I love you for it, and will always love you, indeed I will."

"Doan't say no more," cried the honest waggoner, with a tear ready to start from the corner of his eye. "I have done to thee as I would wish a poor little wench of my own done by. God bless thee, my pretty dear, thee shall not want a friend while I, Robert Greenfield, live."

"Thank you—thank you," cried Phœbe. "My poor mother said, if I told the truth, Heaven would make me friends, and so it has."

"Thee art a good girl, and I tell e' what, thee shalt go, if thee like, to London with me, and my wife, who be as good a woman as ever wore shoe leather, though I say it myself, will take care of thee, and put thee in some honest way. Heart alive, I would not have thee come to harm with thy pretty face, bless thee, for the best team of horses in the whole land; but trust theeself to me, my little wench."

"Yes," cried Phœbe, "I will—I will. You are good and kind, and I will go with you."

"It's a long way," said the waggoner; "it's to London."

"Mother's dead," said Phœbe, sorrowfully, "and dear George is gone."

"And you have no friends here, poor thing?"

"None! oh, none!" cried Phœbe, "except you. You are good to me."

"And, please Heaven, I will strive to be so still, my little wench. Keep up thy heart; thee shall not want one friend. Gee—come up—gee—gee—up—up."

The horses looked a little more brisk, and the waggon proceeded at the full rate of five miles an hour on the high road to London.

The day was hot, and the sun shone upon the road with unclouded splendour. The dust rose from every tread of the horses in clouds, and Phœbe sat at the back of the waggon admiring the country, rich in all kinds of vegetation, which, like a moving panorama, slowly shifted its aspect as the clumsy vehicle, in which she was seated, moved along the road; corn-fields, meadows, orchards, lakes, plantations, cottages, all seemed to move slowly past her, and fade away in the distance.

Travelling in any vehicle whatever was quite new to poor Phœbe, and she was wonderfully delighted at the succession of objects which met her eyes as she was borne along. The tinkling of the bells at the horses' heads kept up a pleasant rural sound; and when nothing more interesting presented itself to her eyes than, apparently, endless corn fields or large tracts of grass land, she would talk to the honest and kind-hearted waggoner, whose quaint and kindly remarks were quite as amusing to Phœbe, as were her artless answers and innocent questions to him.

Thus the time passed happily to both until the middle of the day, when they halted to refresh both themselves and the horses, which latter had performed for them a wonderful morning's work.

It was a mere village at which they stopped, and the waggoner assisting Phœbe to alight, took her into the little ale-house of the place, and calling to the landlady by name, he said:—

"Here Dame—Dame Wilks, will 'e just look a bit to my little wench here?"

The landlady looked astonished at Phœbe, and turned to the waggoner, with an enquiring gaze.

"She be," said the man, "a little wench that my wife be going to take care of, and I be taking her to town, you see. Heart alive, she be a rare good little wench, she be."

The landlady was kind and hospitable, and paid the kindest attention to Phœbe, whose young heart already began to expand with joy and thankfulness at finding herself so unexpectedly thrown among persons who spoke and acted so kindly to her.

For many a day she had heard nothing but taunts and the constant language of reproach and censure, and kindness and consideration now quite overcame her.

The waggoner took his humble dinner, and the landlady provided Phœbe a repast of a more delicate nature than bread and bacon, from her own larder, and then loading her with fruit from the garden, she assisted her into the waggon.

Phœbe, with childish thankfulness and affection, stretched out her arms and kissed while she embraced the buxom landlady, who, as she retired into the house, might have been observed with the corner of her apron very near her eye, into which something might have flown, for it looked red, and winked very much. Phœbe thought she had dropped a tear upon her cheek, and she called after her—

"Good-bye, ma'am—good-bye, ma'am. I'll come and see you again some day."

"God bless you, dear," cried the landlady; "good-bye."

The waggon was once more in motion, the horses had had rest and refreshment, and they went off at a very respectable walk, tinkling the bells in an exceedingly pleasant way, and kicking up the dust most beautifully.

The waggoner seated himself at the back of the waggon, and left the horses to keep on the right side of the road, which they knew as well as he, and he entered into conversation with Phœbe.

"My wench," he said, "my wife and myself we be poor people, but thee shall stay with us as long as thee please. We be old, too, and when we be gone, thee would have no friend, my wench, so I think we must try to put thee, heart alive, into some way of doing for theeself, my dear, as soon as we can."

"Oh, yes," cried Phœbe, "I could not think of staying always with you, although you are so kind to me—that is, unless you had work for me to do. I would go to place again with—with—anybody who was kind to me."

"And you sha'n't go to anybody that isn't, my little thing. You shall always have a home with us while we live and have got one. My old woman will find a good place, and if thee don't like it, thee shall come hoame again to us."

"Thank you, thank you," cried Phœbe, with fervent gratitude—" and—and sometimes you will let me come and see you?"

"Thee shall come when thee likes, my wench, and thee cannot come too often. The sight of thee sweet face has made me happy all day, bless thee."

The day wore on, and the waggoner intimated his intention of baiting for the night at a small town they were now approaching.

Again Phœbe met with a kind reception from the persons who kept the inn at which the waggon stopped, and that night she slept profoundly and happily.

In the morning she was awakened by the various noises proceeding from the inhabitants of the farm-yard, and she opened the little casement of her bed-room to look out upon the kitchen and flower garden, which was immediately outside of it.

Oh! how delightful was the pure morning air that visited her cheek. A sensation of joy and deep thankfulness came over the heart of the child, and she thought how happy her poor mother would be if from her long home she could see that her dear Phœbe was kindly treated. Of George, too, she thought and wondered now that she had left the workhouse, if she should ever see him again. She determined, when she was arrived in London, to request the good waggoner to adopt some means of ascertaining, if possible, when George arrived at the sea-port she was now leaving, for she never doubted his ultimate arrival and the realization of all their childish and bright anticipations of future happiness in a sweet cot, like their mother's had been.

The waggon was again brought from a shed, where it had been placed for the night. The horses were attached—breakfast was over—and Phœbe bade adieu to the inmates of the inn, and resumed her place in the comfortable interior of the humble vehicle.

"Did you ever hear of Canterbury?" said the waggoner. "We shall pass through it in about an hour, for we are not far off, now, and the team is fresh."

"Yes," said Phœbe; "I've heard my poor dear mother speak of Canterbury. There's a church."

"And a main fine one, too," said the waggoner; "it's what they call a cathedral, not a church, my wench; oh! it's uncommon grand, it is."

As the waggoner predicted, in the course of the next hour they arrived at Canterbury, and Phœbe gazed up at the sombre but beautiful and massive cathedral with admiration and awe. She had never seen a building at all approaching it in size and magnificence; and as the waggon rolled lazily past it and she felt its gigantic shadow upon her face, she could not believe it to be the work of human hands, as she had been told it was.

But little incident diversified the remainder of their journey. They passed through Feversham and Milton, Chatham and Gravesend, and finally, on the fifth morning of their journey, the dim smoke of London became visible in the horizon.

Vehicles of all kinds and descriptions now began to crowd the roads. An appearance of bustle and animation might be noticed in the people, and there was all that restless activity which denoted the proximity of an immense city, and the capital of a densely populated country.

Greenwich was passed. They toiled along the Old Kent Road, and arriving at London Bridge, Phœbe caught the first close view of the majestic Thames.

The tumult and bustle seemed to poor Phœbe prodigious, and she shrunk back in the waggon as it crossed the bridge in apprehension that some riot or disturbance was about to occur. The throngs of people passing in all directions, and with a speed totally unknown out of London, bewildered and astonished her. The multitude of vehicles rushing at terrific speed past the waggon, and almost grating its very wheels, alarmed her exceedingly, and she sat trembling in momentary expectation of some dreadful catastrophe.

The waggoner's whole care was now directed to his horses, and Phœbe was left to the solitude of her own reflections, and truly solitary she felt, more so than in the depth of the country, and in the green fields near her native village.

In London there was no sympathy, because she saw there was no observation. No man looked even at his neighbour. The great object of the pedestrians seemed to be to pass each other as quickly as possible. Each had some object in view, to which he alone looked, and everything on his road was merely an encumbrance in the way.

They proceeded onwards, through two or three streets, and then suddenly turned into one of those narrow thoroughfares in the city, which, as if by magic takes the passenger at once from the extreme noise and bustle to the greatest stillness, a stillness which, perhaps, is more marked and conspicuous, from the invasion of the distant turn of the riot and disorder in the main street.

The waggoner now guided his horses under an archway which led into an old inn-yard, which formed the terminus of his journey. He transacted some business in a dingy office with another gentleman with spectacles, and then, coming to the back of the waggon, he addressed Phœbe kindly.

"Come, my little wench, we are in London now. Doan't 'e be afeard, no one shall do thee a harm, heart alive. Come along; we will go home, my dear, and I'm sure my old dame will be main glad to see thee."

He had helped the trembling Phœbe from the waggon, and, with the child clinging to his arm, he left the inn yard.

"Doan't 'e be scared, my wench," he continued; "thee bee'st all of a tremble loike."

"There is such a crowd," replied Phœbe. "There's something the matter."

"No, there be nothing the matter. There be always a great row in London all the day."

"And where are they all going?" enquired Phœbe.

"My wench, a great many are going after no good, and a great many more are going to try to hinder them, any a very many, my wench, don't know where they are going. London be main full of wickedness, but still it be not all bad."

In a humble court, at the back of Finsbury-square, dwelt the honest waggoner and his wife. They had brought up a large family, and placed them out in the world as well as their humble means would permit, and the heart of the old man warmed to the young child, which Heaven seemed, in his declining years, to have thrown upon his protection and kindness.

Phœbe's heart beat with anxiety and expectation as the waggoner knocked at the door of his little dwelling. It was opened in a moment, and Phœbe saw him immediately clasped in the embraces of a homely, but kind-looking woman, who seemed but a few years younger than the honest man himself.

"Wife," cried the waggoner, "before thee says a word, I have got a word to say to thee. Look at this little one!"

The waggoner's wife turned her attention with surprise to Phœbe,

o. 13

who stood, silently gazing in her face, to read the nature of her welcome."

"Why, Robert, who is she?" asked the good woman, kindly.

"She be an orphan child, Nancy. She be without father, mother, or friends. She be destitute. Shall we turn her out, Nancy? Shall—shall we turn her out?"

"Robert!" said the waggoner's wife, in a tone of surprise, and she immediately took Phœbe upon her lap, and kissed her tenderly.

"What shall we do, wife, I ask thee?"

"We are poor, Robert, but a part of what we have shall this sweet child have, and—and if we have not enough, God will give us more, or a good heart to make a little do. Bless thee, my dear, how pretty you are, to be sure."

"Hurrah!—gee up—come up," shouted the waggoner. "Did I not tell thee my little wench, that the old woman would be main good to thee?"

Phœbe could not speak, for she was weeping upon the good woman's breast; but, amid her tears she looked round with a sweet smile at the waggoner, which spoke the gratitude of her young heart more eloquently than any words could have done.

The prospects and expectations of Phœbe were thus talked of by the honest couple at great length, and it was decided that she should remain with them until some unexceptionable place in some family, where she may be kindly treated, could be procured for her, and then she was to go to it with the full understanding that she was to consider the honest couple's home as her home, and a place of refuge from all disasters and misfortunes whatever.

Phœbe felt now very happy, and as day after day passed in the calm enjoyment of sweet peace of mind, she recovered, even though she was in smoky mirky London. The charming bloom of her complexion, and her beauty and sweet disposition, were the theme of the neighbourhood. The waggoner and his wife became more and more attached to her, and felt the greatest reluctance in allowing her to quit their roof; but they were not so selfish as to prefer their own temporary gratification to a consideration of Phœbe's ultimate welfare, and the good woman made every exertion to procure for Phœbe a suitable situation.

Many would have taken her, but the waggoner's wife was most particular with whom she trusted her pretty charge, and rejected, firmly, all offers which did not promise a comfortable home for the dear child, whom she now loved as tenderly and devotedly as if she had been one of her own children.

At length, however, the good dame thought she saw an opening for Phœbe in the family of a Mr. Spangle, who had retired from business. Mrs. Spangle, she knew to be a good-hearted, though a weak woman; but she was perfectly sure that even should the situation not be the most desirable for Phœbe, yet she would receive no sort of ill-usage from Mrs. Spangle, who was by far too indolent a person to ill-use anybody.

With many tears, it was accordingly settled that the waggoner's wife should introduce Phœbe to Mrs. Spangle; and should they be mutually pleased with each other, that the dear child should stay one week to see if she liked it. After which period she was to be at liberty either to stay, or return home, where she was, over and over again, by the good woman, with tears in her eyes, assured her of a warm and affectionate welcome.

Phœbe was pleased at this arrangement; for although young in years, she had a quick comprehension, and had seen enough of life to feel (although such a thing was never hinted at by the waggoner or his wife) that she was a burthen to the compassionate old couple.

The thought that she had a home to fly to in distress or misfortune, made her happy, and she earnestly entreated that no time might be lost in establshing her at Mr. Spangles, where she determined to stay even in the face of any trifling disagreeables, for she knew how much pleasure it would give her kind protectors to see her independent of their poor resources, and able to help herself.

CHAPTER XVIII.

MANY a time as Phœbe lay upon her little couch at the honest waggoner's did she think over the scenes of life which, young as she was, she had passed through.

In the dim distance of memory appeared the death-bed of her mother, and the heartless broker standing by and enumerating the schedule of his rates and taxes. Further back than that, as her memory travelled, and she recollected the happy cottage, in which reigned peace and plenty—the peace of innocence and guileless hearts—and the plenty of cheerful content. The little garden, with its roses and all its sweet smelling plants and fair flowers, came before her mind's eye; and George, who worked so gaily and so happily, while the face of her dear mother beamed with pleasure from the little casement of the cottage.

" Further—further back in the dim obscurity of early thought, she recollected being kissed fondly and strained to the breast of a man in gay and glittering attire, and she guessed that it must have been her father, who had thus taken the last kiss of his dear child; and he died, she thought. far off, and I never saw him again; and then the gloomy workhouse would rise up in her imagination, and the tyranny of Mrs. Fungus and Mr. Bung, and her subjection to Mrs. Marrables, and hence the picture, at which she shuddered, ended. She had slept so happily, and the birds had sung so sweetly in the corn field, and then she had met with her present protector, and peace and joy fell upon her heart.

Heartless prayers would then ascend to Heaven for a blessing upon them and theirs, who had been so kind and good to her, the poor, forsaken, destitute orphan; and surely, if prayers are wafted gently to the sublime throne of the Almighty, and there received with favour, they are such prayers as these that flow from the deep gratitude of a pure and gentle heart, untainted by one unholy wish.

The morning came when Phœbe was to accompany the waggoner's wife to meet Mrs. Spangles by appointment, and there and then settle the preliminaries of Phœbe's engagement.

The orphan child had now been some months, in fact, nearly a year at the waggoner's, and the good man himself had made many journeys to and from the place from whence he had brought Phœbe. He brought her, however, no intelligence of George, although he had done his best, with caution, to set enquiry on foot.

Phœbe had grown taller, and she looked healthy and reputatively handsome. Her clustering fair hair was now carefully tended, and she was neatly, though plainly dressed. In truth, at this period, she was a most lovely girl; and many were the high and wealthy who would stop her in the streets, when she was walking with the good dame, whom she now called by the endearing name of mother, to speak a word to the beautiful girl.

We must now, however, say a few words of the family into which for a year, Phœbe was to be domesticated—a year which did not pass altogether unhappily, but which was the forerunner of many months of bitter sorrow—— a sorrow, however, which a black cloud, which in the glorious summer will sometimes obscure the fair sun and casts a dismal shadow over the fair face of Nature, for a time, only serves when it is gone, to render the succeeding sunshine more beautiful and brilliant.

Thus dim eclipses in early life chasten the heart, and prepare it, with a tranquil and a holy spirit, to a more true enjoyment of any after happiness which may be in store. The pilgrim of life looks back upon the dreary wastes he has passed and the storms he has encountered before he at length reached the sweet haven of rest, with a similar look to that with which the weary traveller thinks upon the dangers and miseries of his journey when he is comfortably seated at the fireside of a happy home, and all his dangers are past, and seem but to enhance by their recollection the comparative happiness of the present moment.

At the period of our tale, and before the march of bricks and mortar had quite transformed the quiet suburban districts of London into clay-pits and brick-kilns, there dwelt in a small house situated in a new street, midway between Somers Town and Camden Town, Mr. and Mrs. Charles Spangle. The street, as we have remarked, was new, then, although it now no longer, by its neatness and trimness, puts, in the slightest degree, to the blush the surrounding locality. But few of the houses in the street were inhabited; in fact, few were sufficiently completed in their details to become human dwellings. Some rash speculator, afflicted with a mania for building, had erected the brickwork, or shells of the houses, and there paused, until, in the cycle of events, they became, duly and legally, the property of the ground landlord, for certain arrears of payment. An equally hardy adventurer had then essayed to make them tenantable.

The pools of stagnant water which had collected in the basement stories were, in some cases, partially dislodged by ingeniously-shaped shovels; and, in others, boarded over; doubtless from a conviction that too dry an atmosphere might not agree with the constitutions of some of the future inhabitants. The dilapidations occasioned by the sportive rambles of the juveniles of the neighbourhood, to whom the shells of houses had for some years afforded most seducing opportunities of dislocating and fracturing their limbs, were repaired, and placards shortly announced the " desirable premises to let," and two or three were absolutely let, in one of which resided Mr. Charles Spangle and his wife, together with two infantine Spangle, namely, Master Adolphus and Miss Caroline Spangle.

Mr. Charles Spangle was a mild, good-humoured-looking, thin, spare man, with a sparkling eye, and an eager, anxious expression of countenance; which latter peculiarity, probably, mainly arose from an intolerable deafness with which he was afflicted, and which induced him to seek for a person's meaning, more by the expression of the features than the tones of the voice. He walked with a brisk, quick step, and something of a spring in his gait, which assimilated very much with business, and business of importance too.

The prime of his existence has been passed in the drudgery of a counting-house attached to some public body; and the number of years during which he had faithfully performed his duty, together with the knowledge that his increasing infirmities unfitted him for further toil, had induced his (barely humane) employers to confer upon him a retiring stipend for the few years he might yet encumber the earth. He had married late in life; Master Adolphus Spangle and Miss Caroline Spangle being at the date of Phœbe Grainger's arrival in London, of the respective ages of twelve and ten.

Mrs. Spangle was an amiable, although unlearned, woman. She loved her children extravagantly ; she had sacrificed much for their welfare, and she did not scruple, upon a proper occasion, offering to state so much to all and every one within hearing. Her errors were all those of judgment ; and if she had one pride overbearing and triumphing over all others, it was the pride of managing her household affairs with exceeding skill, and that was a subject upon which she likewise loved to talk, which talking generally ended in the remark of how much better still would everything have been managed if Mr. Spangles had possessed any spirit, and had not been so entirely helpless and handless an individual as she, Mrs. Spangle, and every one else, well knew him to be ; to all of which she joined many expressions of wonder and intense curiosity to know what Mr. Spangle could possibly have done without her. In short, the good lady was quite willing to bear any burthen, always provided society at large were made accurately acquainted with its weight, and fully aware of the onerous situation in which it placed her.

From the back parlour to the front parlour was generally the extent of Mrs. Spangle's locomotive exertions, for rheumatism, acquired in consequence of a cold caught by rising in the night upon a false alarm of fire, and projecting Master Adolphus and Miss Caroline Spangle through an exceedingly small hole in the roof of the house, facetiously called a " fire-escape," had for some time deprived her of the due use of her limbs, therefore it was from an easy chair to the parlour that her mandates for the government of the household were issued.

Now Mr. Spangle had one peculiarity which vexed and annoyed Mrs. Spangle, and that was an earnest desire to repair to the City each morning in an omnibus, and after there remaining the usual hours of business, return by the same conveyance, as if a mighty day's work had been accomplished, when, in reality, he had done nothing but commune with the disturbed spirits of the Stock Exchange, ascertain the whole particulars of any newly-started commercial enterprise, and wander, with listless apathy, among the numberless small courts and alleys around the Bank, Royal Exchange, and Lombard-street. He, moreover, had a passion for collecting the prospectuses of public companies ; and while immersed in a contemplation of the numerous and tempting prospects of fortune held out by those flattering announcements, he became, in imagination, the actual possessor, for the time being, of boundless wealth, and revelled in the sunshine of prosperity.

The good waggoner's wife and Phœbe, after a long walk, arrived, at length, at the house of Mr. Spangle.

They knocked three several times before obtaining admission, and, at length, the door was opened by the lady of the house herself.

" Dear me," said she, " I thought you would never have been let in, Mrs. Greenfield. I couldn't get either of those tiresome children to open the door ; and I was so untidy myself, that not knowing who it was, I really couldn't come to the door till I'd just slipped on this dress."

As Mrs. Spangle spoke, she walked listlessly into the parlour, followed, respectfully, by the waggoner's wife and Phœbe.

Mrs. Spangle certainly had the dress she spoke of on her, but there was not the least attempt to fasten it ; in fact, it was a peculiarity of that lady never to fasten, tie, or hook-and-eye, or button or pin any of her cloths ; and when she rose from her chair, she usually, with great tact, acquired by long experience only, took so admirable a grasp of her cloths, that she kept them from falling clean off until she sat down again."

" This, ma'am, if you please," said Phœbe's dear friend, " is the little orphan girl you were so kind as to say you would take on trial. We know you will be kind to her ma'am."

"Oh! dear me, yes. I—I'm sure I'm kind to everything. Everybody does just what they like. I am sure I would not have the trouble of beating, or being—oh! dear me—unkind to anybody, no, not for the world."

"I am sure of it, ma'am," said Mrs. Greenfield; "and you'll find little Phœbe a dear, kind little creature. It nearly breaks our hearts to let her go, but we are getting old, and we know it's for her good, ma'am."

"Oh! dear me, yes, no doubt. Did you ever read 'The Exquisite Entanglement,' Mrs. Greenfield, in six volumes, octavo?"

"The what, ma'am?" cried the waggoner's wife.

"'The Exquisite Entanglement,'" repeated Mrs. Spangle. "I read a great deal—I've been crying now for a week—it's a most affecting work—I often forget that volume I'm in; but when I take it up, I know the place very well, for I always shed tears at page three hundred and forty-seven of of the third volume,"

"Surely, ma'am—indeed."

"Well, little girl, you can stay, you know. While the wind blows, then the mill goes. What can't be cured must be endured. Dear me, I'd shew you the kitchen myself, but I'm uncommonly tired, indeed I am. I so seldom open the door, but the children, you see, are so very—that is, oh! dear, they quite lead me a life——Adolphus! Adolphus! Adolphus!"

A child's voice answered from the back parlour.

"What is it?—oh! bother—what? what?"

"Just look, my dear, under the sofa, and see if there's a book there with greasy corners, that's a love, and bring it to me, my dear."

"I sha'n't," cried Master Adolphus.

"Oh! dear me," said his mother, "you wouldn't credit, Mrs. Greenfield, how Mr. Spangle spoils that boy. He'll do anything in the world for me, but Mr. Spangle spoils him. I think, my dear, you'd, perhaps, better just see for the book for me. What's your name, Phœbe? Oh! dear me, yes, I recollect, now, it is Phœbe. It's a greasy book, on a horse-hair sofa."

Phœbe went into the back parlour immediately; and, despite the resistance of Master Adolphus, she brought out the book, followed by that young gentleman, shrieking,—

"You sha'n't have it, you sha'n't," he cried. "No—no—no—you sha'n't."

"Dear me," cried Mrs. Spangle, "Phœbe—ah! that's your name—you'll have to go and put the book back again. Adolphus is a very good child; his father utterly spoils him, though. He'll do anything for me in the world."

Phœbe took the book back, and deposited it under the sofa, to the great triumph of Master Adolphus Spangle, who grumbled his satisfaction thereat.

"Perhaps," said Mrs. Spangle, "you'll have the kindness, Mrs. Greenfield, just to show the little girl the kitchen yourself. I declare I'm quite fatigued."

In accordance with this request, Mrs. Greenfield and Phœbe proceeded to the lower regions. Everything was in the greatest confusion. A gridiron stood on the table—a frying-pan on the dresser—a tea-kettle had overturned and put out the fire—a broken plate lay on the hearth, and everything betokened an ill-regulated household.

The waggoner's wife shook her head as she surveyed the kitchen, and said to Phœbe :—

"My dear, I don't think you can stay long here. Everything seems in confusion and disorder in this house, and I fear you will have too much to do to put all to rights."

" Never fear, dear mamma," said Phœbe, with a smile. " Mrs. Spangle is not cross, or cruel, and I don't mind anything else."

The willing child then set to work clearing the litter of the kitchen, and in a short time had produced something like order, and before Mrs. Greenfield departed, a great change was effected.

" I will see you to-morrow, dear," said the good woman, as she parted from Phœbe, and kissed her, and in a few moments more the orphan girl was alone in her new place.

The day gradually passed away, and Phœbe was happy, because she was light-hearted. It was half-past four o'clock in the afternoon; heavy rain had been descending for the last two hours, and the drops hung, bead-like, upon the window-frames. The gutter down the side of the house kept up a constant gurgling, melancholy sound, as the rain from the roof descended it, ere it burst out upon the pavement in a copious stream. The air within the house was damp, chilling, and comfortless, and nothing was heard without, but, occasionally, the solitary foot fall of some bedraggled passenger, and the monotonous pothering of the shower.

" Do stir the fire, Addy, my dear," said Mrs. Spangle to Master Adolphus.

" Don't bother," replied the young gentleman, who was jocularly and scientifically employed in rubbing the nose of a large cat with great energy against the wire of the cage of a canary bird, in order to induce a degree of amity and acquaintanceship between the two; but neither the cat nor the bird appeared to enter into Master Adolphus's views.

" Carry, my dear," said Mrs. Spangle, addressing her second born, " you stir it, there's a love."

" Lor, ma," said a little shrill voice from under the table, which proceeded from Miss Caroline Spangle, whose ingenuity was actively engaged in devising some new mode of torture for a kitten; " why can't Addy do it ?"

" Because Addy's a naughty boy, my love. I can't stir to-day, so you do it, and be mother's girl, and shut the door, my dear. I declare I never was in such a *draughty* house."

Mrs. Spangle was peculiarly happy at introducing new words into the English language.

" I sha'n't," replied Master Adolphus. " Call the new servant, ma."

" Well, was there ever such children ? Your father spoils you both. Call Betsey, and I insist upon you not tying the kitten's legs to its head in that way; its enough to *enstrangle* it. I wonder where your father is ?— that odious City."

As Mr. Spangle concluded, and the fire had been poked by Phœbe, who was shouted for by both children at once, a knock and a ring at the door now announced Mr. Spangle, who, in a few moments, entered the apartment, looking very shining from the rain, with a bundle of green cotton and sticks in his hand, which might once have been an umbrella.

" Ain't you very wet, my love ?" said Mrs. Spangle, elevating her voice to an extraordinary scream on account of Mr. Spangle's infirmity.

Mr. Spangle looked at his hat, passed his hand down his coat-sleeve, and said, " Likely."

" Did you come in the omnibus, my dear ?"

Mr. Spangle did not exactly hear the question, so he said—

" Very well."

" I suppose you want your dinner ?"

" True," said Mr. Spangle, wringing his pocket handkerchief, with which he had wiped his hat, in the coal-scuttle.

"Bless me, what's the matter with the umbrella?"

"Ah! a contingency—turned inside out at the corner of the street. There, Phœbe, take my coat, and—and spread my hat out to dry."

So saying, Mr. Spangle sat down to a chop and two potatoes, which having finished, he took from his pocket a variety of printed papers, and became immersed in their contents. Master Adolphus, meanwhile, was making a needle red-hot, for the purpose of running through the cat's nose, he having been informed by his mother that by so doing, the said cat's feelings towards the canary would be considerably appeased and ameliorated; and Miss Caroline Spangle, with that spirit for overcoming obstacles so peculiar to active intellects, had tied the kitten's legs to its head in defiance of its anatomical construction, and was dragging it across the wrong way of its fur.

"My love," said Mrs. Spangle, after a pause of some duration, "Adolphus is growing quite tall."

Mr. Spangle upon this only muttered something about "picking him up if he was going to fall;" for in addition to not thoroughly comprehending the question, he was intently reading the prospectus of 'The Royal Universal Patent Consolidated Magnetic Influence to and from the Margate Company,' which proposed fixing a large magnet at Margate, and letting off cast iron ships at London Bridge, the only difficulty being how to get them back again.

"And he's not a bad looking lad, either," continued Mrs. Spangle as if following out the train of some previous cogitations.

"Beautiful!" said Mr. Spangle—"superb."

"He is my son, Mr. S.; and, although I say it, he is, indeed——"

"A horse-shoe magnet."

"A what, my love?"

"Repulsion and attraction, my dear, you know."

"You are a fool, Mr. Spangle. Dear me!"

Mr. Spangle did not offer the least contradiction to this assertion, so Mrs. Spangle collapsed into silence, contenting herself by glancing at her liege lord with a peculiar expression, compounded of distilled vinegar and iron spikes, at the same time mentally contrasting his conduct with that of the Count Adolphe de Weremwiski, in the 'Exquisite Entanglement;' and Mr. Spangle, quite unknowing of the odious comparison, commenced reading the flaming prospectus of 'The Patent Imperial Domestic Telegraphic Communication, from all Parts of the House to the Kitchen, Association,' in great abstraction of mind.

CHAPTER XIX.

Poor Phœbe, although not altogether unhappy in the Spangles' family, was, nevertheless, much harassed both by the eternal fidgetty indolence of Mrs. Spangle and the self-willed obstinacy of the completely spoiled children.

A circumstance however occurred, which, for a time, absorbed every other feeling in the one painful one, that she was, probably, about to lose her best friend. Mr. Greenfield, the good waggoner's wife, became seriously ill, and sent for Phœbe to stay with her for a day or two, with the permission of Mrs. Spangle, and to receive, perhaps, her last kind wishes and advice.

With the tears coursing each other down her cheeks, Phœbe appeared at the abode of the benevolent, but poor couple, who had befriended her in the hour of her destitution.

Phœbe felt for the kind-hearted woman, who now lay on her death-bed, all the affection which a daughter could feel for a mother. There was no relation of Mrs. Greenfield's in London. Her illness had been sudden, and her own children were spread far and wide over the country. To the gentle and grateful Phœbe, alone, then devolved the task of soothing, with kind attention, the last moments of her dear friend.

For several nights did Phœbe sit by the expiring woman; and it was on the third evening of her arrival at the house that Mrs. Greenfield suddenly spoke to her, in a voice of great strength, and with a clearness of intonation, which astonished Phœbe.

"Phœbe," she said, "my dear child, you know my dear husband is far from us, and little thinks what is about to happen here. He is, I believe, at the place from where he brought you, my dear child, now nearly a whole year since."

"Oh! compose yourself, dear mamma, and lie down. He will be back, you know soon."

"No, Phœbe, no; he does not return for a month; and—and, my child, I wish you to be the first to see him when he does return, and comfort him, and tell him I died with you, my dear child, by my side, and happy."

Phœbe wept bitterly to hear her speak thus of death, and said,—

"Oh! no, no, no, mamma, you must not leave us."

"It is the will of Heaven, my dear child," said the woman, fervently, "and shall we murmur?"

"But you will get well; oh! yes, you will, indeed. What would poor

No. 14

Phœbe do if you were gone? Once before I lost a dear mother, and now that you have supplied her place, and I love you as I did her, how can I think of losing you, too?"

" We cannot, my child, struggle against the decrees of God. Go to the sideboard, dear, and give me the little box you see there. The key is on the shelf."

Phœbe brought the box, and the kind woman unlocked it, and took out fifteen pounds.

"Phœbe," she said, "this is mine, and I give it to you. Save it, love. Keep it till some sad and trying hour, when you want, bitterly, a friend."

Phœbe could not speak for weeping.

" What noise is that, child?" cried the dying woman.

"What?" said Phœbe. "I hear nothing."

"There, again—singing—he's singing. Hark! hark!"

Phœbe listened attentively, and heard nothing. A death-like stillness reigned in the chamber.

"Dear mamma," said Phœbe, " I hear nothing. Do you hear it now? What is it like?"

She looked in the face of her dear friend as she spoke—it was calm and still, and a faint smile seemed to linger on her lips. A horrid suspicion darted across Phœbe's mind.

"Mother! mother!" she cried. "Speak, oh! speak, one word—but one word."

The kind-hearted Mrs. Greenfield was dead.

With a loud scream Phœbe fell insensible across the bed.

The cry brought in the neighbours, and, in a few moments, the room was full of persons. They removed Phœbe to another apartment, and applied to every restorative they could think of, but it was long before she recovered consciousness, and then it was but to sob, as if her heart would break for the loss of the kindest and most disinterested friend that Heaven could ever bestow upon her.

The next day was one of great wretchedness to poor Phœbe. One of the neighbours had stayed with her since the death of Mrs. Greenfield, and had taken care of the money which Phœbe had left lying on the bed.

Phœbe, in answer to all her inquiries, could get no information of the address of the honest waggoner, and she was thus prevented from acquainting him with his melancholy bereavement, which she would fain have done, before the remains of her dear friend were consigned to the silent tomb.

Ten days elapsed in anxious expectation that he might return, but he came not; and, attended by the weeping Phœbe and a few kind neighbours, the mortal remains of Phœbe's second mother were placed in the churchyard of old Bishopsgate Church.

" Phœbe, after paying the expenses of the funeral, found she had still seven pounds left of the sum which Mrs. Greenfield had placed in her hands, and this she intended to hand to the good waggoner as soon as she could see him. To accomplish this object, there was no resource but to wait patiently until the expiration of the month, which period his deceased wife had fixed for his return.

Phœbe, with a heavy heart, returned to Mrs. Spangle, and strove, by an assidious attention to her duties, to banish from her mind the bitter sorrow and dejection which she felt for the loss of so dear a friend. The poor orphan felt as if she was once more alone in the world, and never had she felt such bitterness of woe since the death of her real mother.

Phœbe would weep bitterly as old, well-remembered words of kindness and sympathy from her who was now so cold and still, recurred to her memory, and her health suffered greatly from her mental disquietude.

Meantime things wore much the same aspect at the Spangles'. Mrs. Spangle, after a few dear me's and ejaculations of the sort, dismissed the subject of Mrs. Greenfield's death from her thoughts, and was as deeply immersed in her novels as ever. In point of fact, Mrs. Spangle had read novels and romances for so many years, and had witnessed in imagination so many horrors, murders, death beds, executions, and so on, that she had become quite steeled against any ordinary calamity, except when it touched herself or her children. The distress of mankind and their common-place misfortunes and deaths failed to have the least effect upon one whose mind was so crammed with the most exciting and alarming incidents which the fertile imaginations of romancists could devise.

Had Mrs. Greenfield jumped into the crater of Mount Vesuvius, or made any other equally extraordinary exit from this world, Mrs. Spangle might have been interested, but she had no patience with people who died quietly of some disorder, and she interrupted Phœbe in an account of the illness of her dear friend with a yawn and a request for her to go immediately to the nearest circulating library, and enquire for the first volume of " Slaughtered Innocence ; or, The Sanguinary Fisherman of the Blood Stained Bay."

Phœbe might have staid, however, a long time at the abode of the Spangles', but for an incident which occurred to change the current of her destiny, for the evils of the abode they were all rather of a negative character than positive and unbearable.

It would seem that upon the death of Mrs. Greenfield, as upon the death of her mother, a series of evils were to arise, and that poor Phœbe should be for a time persecuted by ill fortune.

Little did the kind old waggoner imagine that, during his month's absence from London, he should not only lose the dear companion of his life —she who had lightened every sorrow, and gilded every joy—but that the orphan child, whom he had rescued from poverty and want, and taught to bless him in her prayers to Heaven, should again be exposed to the same horrors, with the scantiest means of averting them ; but so it was. The hours were numbered that Phœbe Grainger was to reside with the Spangle family, and she lay down one night on her little bed with not the most wild and distant idea that it was for the last time in that house.

One morning it happened, about a week after Mrs. Greenfield's burial, that Mr. Spangle had departed as usual, in great haste, to the City, and Mrs. Spangle had duly seated herself, that lady most graciously intimated to Master Adolphus and Miss Caroline that they might take a walk in the neighbourhood, which permission being responded to by a declaration on the part of Master Adolphus that he intended to go before his mother spoke, the pair, in all brotherly and sisterly affection, the peculiar manifestations of which seemed to consist in sundry pinches, kicks, cuffs, and scratches, prepared to depart. Miss Caroline Spangle was the very personification of a nice little girl. Her fair hair hung in admired disorder upon her shoulders, and her rosy, healthful complexion more frequently gladdened the eye of the beholder, though under a thick coating of dirt, than any other medium, for Mrs. Spangle loved her children too fondly to vex them, as some unnatural mothers do, by continually washing their faces. She was, really, a graceful, animated, and intelligent child, with but few faults but those of home education to contend against.

Upon this occasion she was under the protection of a shawl of her mother's, which being entwined in many folds around her slender form, and firmly pinned in front to prevent the darling from catching cold, effectually precluded all observations upon the personal graces of the young lady, who, after a violent struggle for the use of her feet, even to a limited extent, walked forth, a corner of the shawl hanging gracefully to the pavement, and leaving on its dirty surface a trail, which might puzzle the beholders to account for.

And Master Adolphus was, truth to say, a fine, bold-looking lad, with a cheerful countenance and an open brow; but a close observer might easily detect in the ever-varying glances of his eyes, that irresolution of purpose which proved so long the bane of his future years.

Somers Town is a delightful locality for the lovers of both nature and art; for there nature talks with a loud voice, and art assists her wonderfully in a choice of terms. The feelings, habits, and modes of living of the population southward of the New Road, are as different from those of the population in the northern direction as any two very different things can well be.

The whole district of Somers Town may be divided into two distinct portions. There are the long, narrow, bustling streets, which are lines of shops, the principal peculiarities of which are, that in the first place they are almost entirely devoted to the sale of articles of diet; and in the second place, there exists an apparently earnest desire on the part of the shopkeepers that their wares should project as far as possible into the carriage-road; and when to this amiable peculiarity are added the hundreds of itinerant dealers occupying the centre of the road, it may be readily conceived that no ordinary patience and skill are required on the part of a pedestrian in threading his way through the intricate mazes of cabbage-stalls, potato dealers, ambulatory fishmongers, lucifer-match vendors, and dealers in every common and low-priced article of human, canine, and feline consumption that the most luxuriant imagination can suggest. Should a coach or other vehicle attempt a passage, the remarks made both on the part of the driver and the distrusted populace are exceedingly edifying to hear; and although not strictly grammatical, or couched in the most courtly language, are nevertheless very intelligible, and produce all the necessary effect.

Such streets are never clean and dry, for the constant washing of fish and other edibles, combined with the refuse of vegetable and animal matter in abundance, form an upper stratum in the road-way, which may be exceedingly delightful to philosophic pigs, who, believing that dirt and filth are merely acquired ideas, very properly disregard them; but upon a biped of tolerably acute perceptions, the effects are neither salutary nor agreeable. Passing from these crowded thoroughfares, there are many narrow, ill-paved streets, the houses in which are universally of a dirty and dingy aspect. The very bricks of which they are composed appear to be of a different colour to those of the rest of London. The lengthened traces of recent showers exhibit themselves in long dark streaks down the fronts of the houses; and the unclean windows and doorways present a most uninviting appearance. The greater number of persons occupying these tenements take them upon the speculation of letting them to young men as bed-rooms; and many a gay and bejewelled spark, who sports his person in the various promenades of the metropolis, at a late hour of the night, or early one of the morning, wends his solitary way towards Somers Town, to ensconce himself in some back attic of that delightful region, at an expense of perhaps three shillings, or four at the utmost, weekly. The abodes of such gentlemen are, even to their intimate acquaintance, like so many unfathomable mysteries; and then there is the luxury of a latch-key, with which all lodgers are provided, there being but little danger in leaving doors so unsecurely fastened, as there is no temptation to the robber. Law clerks have a peculiar adoration for Somers Town. It is cheap, and therefore suits their, in many cases, slender incomes. The free egress and in-

gress at all hours assimilates delightfully with their pursuits : moreover,
law clerks are great men in Somers Town ; they compose the well-dressed,
or rather the showily-dressed portion of the population. Now, a young
gentleman may, when walking down St. James's-street, look very like an
inhabitant of Somer's Town ; but the same young gentleman, owing to the
peculiarity of tolerably clean linen and a pair of white Berlin gloves, may,
in Somers Town, be supposed to appear very much like " the glass of
fashion," and venerated accordingly. How these legal offshoots contrive
to dress so much to the admiration of their dazzled beholders, must ever,
to a great extent, remain a mystery known only to their fraternity ; but the
changes of costume and *Brummagum* jewellery are to be accounted for by
the passion for bargain-making, roffling, and changing garments with each
other, which forms a feature in their character.

Somers Town is likewise intersected, like a little rabbit-warren, with
many small winding courts and alleys, which, apparently, lead to nowhere
but into each other, forming delightful retreats for many families who prefer retirement for more reasons than one ; and when upon any occasion of
unusual out-of-door interest, the population show their faces *en masse* from
their dark and wretched hiding-places, a casual spectator might well wonder from whence the squalid dirty tide of humanity had emerged. Then
might be seen the wretched mother with her palid, sickly infant at her
breast ; the lady who " sees company," aroused from her morning slumbers, partly attired in the tawdry finery of the preceding evening, with the
heavy eye and bloated cheek of intemperance and vice ; the shoeless and
half-clad children, with want and suffering stamped upon their young brows ;
and here and there a lad approaching to manhood, in that complicated
garb which bespeaks the wearer of no honest occupation, gazing with
sunken eyes and sullen contracted brows upon the sunlight, as if it was
painful even for an instant to crawl from his dark abode until day had departed, and all was as black as his own heart ; the tottering step, and
shrill accent of age might likewise be remarked among the throng, but,
alas ! " with nothing that should accompany old age." Those endearing
ties of kindred which bind families together in love and fellowship, are
nearly unknown. The haggard and intemperate mother nurses her infant
as if by mere animal instinct ; the association of the children is a scene of
strife and bitter contention ; and the father is but too often known only by
his family as a drunken brawler, whose hand is ready to strike his unof-
fending wife or helpless infants. Such are the lowest districts of Somers
Town ; and yet in that locality there are more religious meeting houses,
and more Scriptural fanaticism and cant, than in any other part of London, except Spitalfields.

It was Saturday morning when Miss Caroline and Master Adolphus
Spangle walked forth to enjoy their morning promenade. The young lady,
with the natural love of expenditure inherent in the female breast, and the
particular attachment to cherries in her own, took the first opportunity of
expending a small sum in the purchase of that fruit ; and with an ingenuity
far beyond her years, she placed two, the stalks of which were united
over each ear, thus forming a blooming pair of ear-rings, which bobbed
about in the most approved style of those semi-barbarous appendages, to
the intense admiration and envy of numerous small feminine pledges of
affection who crossed her path. The brother and sister ultimately arrived
at Skinner-street, which leads into the New Road. Now Master Adolphus had passed thus far in unwonted equanimity and peace with all mankind and boykind likewise, and had just paused for a moment to consider
of his route, when a butcher-boy in the luxuriance of a youthful imagination, conceived and executed the feat of bonneting Master Spangle, by

which ingenious and facetious process the rim of his hat was brought into sudden and severe proximity with his nose, and having passed that obstacle, finally enshrouded the whole of the countenance of our youthful hero, to the extravagant and uproarious delight of many young ladies and gentlemen who witnessed the humourous achievement.

Now Master Adolphus Spangle was a lad of both energy and courage, and when this interlude was performed, he struck out manfully, with clenched fists to the right and to the left, and straight before, and in fact all ways, with astonishing quickness : but his opponent had carried his drollery elsewhere, and Adolphus accomplished no other result than that of knocking in a most unchivalric manner, the cherries from Miss Caroline's ears, and rolling that young lady, who could make but little resistance, encumbered with the shawl in the mud. At this mistake, the before-mentioned young ladies and gentlemen laughed and jumped about in great ecstacy of delight, and proceeded forthwith to bonnet each other with much good-will and energy ; and several errand-boys, who had been urged to make good speed on their journeys, stopped and laid down their various parcels, as it is the custom and undoubted right of that fraternity to do upon any such occasion, and sitting upon various doorsteps, in total disregard of their worldly prosperity, made many enlivening remarks upon the scene ; and one in particular, who was hastening from a surgeon's with some medicines to a patient whose life depended upon their speedy delivery, laid down his basket, and by an ingenious application of the flat of his hand to the crown of Master Adolphus's hat, effectually prevented, for some moments, the removal of the obstruction to his sight ; and much longer might the experiment on the part of the surgeon's boy have lasted—for it was hailed with renewed raptures on the part of the bystanders—had not an old lady, returning from purchasing some vegetables, saluted him with a blow on the back with some half dozen cabbages and a bunch of turnips, which at once upset that precocious genius and terminated all consideration and uneasiness concerning the medicines by precipitating him upon the basket and smashing it, together with its brittle contents. How changeable is public opinion ! and by what a frail tenure do the greatest men hold popular favour !

No sooner had this feat been accomplished, than an uproarious shoot of ecstacy arose from the crowd, and several boys and several dogs—for the latter animals are as fond of a row as the former—threw themselves on the fallen hero, and forthwith commenced a conflict very common to the locality, during which Master Spangle, having drawn his hat from before his eyes with great violence to his nose, and picked up Miss Caroline, pursued his way.

They walked up Skinner-street, which at that time of the week and at that time of the day, was at its height of bustle. The usually red faces of the butchers were redder than customary, and those who were selling their meat were tolerably quiet, and only occasionally vociferated " buy, buy, buy," in the ears of the startled passengers ; but those who were not selling so quickly as they desired, were rushing from the shop to the pavement and from the pavement to the shop with the most awful rapidity, and shouting their invitations to " buy" in tones resembling the infuriated war-cry of some frantic Indian. And the vendors of vegetables, oysters, calfs'-feet, lucifer matches, &c., were in full cry, and jostled each other, and swore, and bawled, with an energy which, if exerted in a higher cause, must have ensured the plaudits of mankind.

Still onward through the thickening throng (although at an old pace) went Master Adolphus and Miss Caroline Spangle. The young gentleman held in his hand a penny, with the proceeds of which he intended to regale himself; but in what luxury it was to be expended was the question. A tempting array of currants was passed—a pause made at the stall of a dealer in some atrocious compound of treacle, rancid butter, and almonds, facetiously termed black-jack. But no—there might be something still more temptingly luxurious; and Master Spangle's hand still clasped the circulating medium. The pause, however, had enabled Miss Caroline to nearly dislocate her ancle, by thrusting her foot into a plug-hole with much pains, merely as it appeared, for the pleasure of drawing it out again; but in reality, it was an illustration of that commendable spirit of practical inquiry which induces children to risk life and limb on every possible occasion. Adolphus's eyes were now attracted by no less than nine excessively small pears, arranged in a beautiful pyramid, which an old lady, who spoke like a brass trumpet with a violent cold, announced at the price of one penny.

"What's the matter, Ady?" said Miss Caroline Spangle, as shouts of fear arose from the further end of the narrow street, and the whole mass of humanity, with all their wares, set in strong currents to the right and to the left, leaving the carriage-road in a moment in a singular state of peace.

"Oh! Ady—run! run!" But Adolphus Spangle paused for a second, irresolute as to which side of the street he should fly to. Like Lord Brougham, he did not exactly know to which party he belonged.

A strong voice now shouted in stentorian accents, "Stop him! stop him!" and the mob shouted, "Stop him!" but no one stopped him; and while Caroline clung to her brother, shrieking, a horse and chaise plunged upon them at headlong speed.

A cry of horror arose—the horse had fallen, and lay stunted amid the fragments of the chaise.

A hundred arms were outstretched to drag a boy from the ruins. It was Adolphus Spangle, pale, bleeding, and insensible.

A parish beadle, in full costume, had rolled out of the chaise, and, with a loud shriek, had said something about Bung and Bungleum, which the crowd did not understand, and had then fainted away and rolled down a cellar, among a parcel of second-hand boots and shoes.

CHAPTER XX.

THE stranger, who was foremost in dragging Master Spangle from the wreck of the chaise was a man of gentlemanly appearance, and, as he gazed upon the pallid features of the insensible child who lay so passively in his arms, a tear trickled from his eye, and fell on Master Spangle's face."

"Poor child, I fear he is much hurt," he said, as with tenderness and care he parted the clustering hair, which was clotted with blood, from Adolphus's eyes. The action aroused the child to a momentary consciousness of pain, and he screamed once; and although but once, in so piercing and agonizing a tone, that it went to the heart of all who heard it; and a loud cry arose for a surgeon, and each one wondered why each one did not fly to procure one, but no one stirred. Meanwhile, the stranger looked up and down the street to see if there were any signs of a professional man within sight; but none met his view; so he questioned Miss Caroline Spangle, who was sobbing by his side, and learned the address of Mr. Spangle Upon which, beseeching the crowd to allow him a passage, he proceeded with as quick a step as the state of his charge would admit of, towards Camden Town, followed, however, by an immense concourse of persons, as is usual in such cases. In fact, it would seem as if at least one half of the population were determined to escort Master Adolphus Spangle to his home; and half an hour must have elapsed before Somers Town was restored to its wonted composure; and many were the regrets expressed and unexpressed for the poor child, who all feared was hurt past recovery; and each of the population who had met with any accident in his or her existence, proceeded forthwith to relate the same to small knots of attentive auditors, and chaises and chaise-drivers sunk many degrees lower in public opinion in Somers Town.

The stranger meanwhile proceeded with his charge, followed as closely as foot could fall by Caroline, whose grief overpowered all restraint. A gentleman in a moleskin waistcoat, with a bag of rats in his hand, having heard Adolphus's address, suggested to another gentleman in a fur cap and ostler's jacket, and unexceptionable high-lows, the propriety of preparing the minds of Master Spangle's anxious parents for the scene which was to come; for, as he remarked, "He'd be blowed if he'd like to see a young un of hisun all of a heap arter being killed by a hass of a chaise-driver." To which the gentleman with the high-lows having replied by making a handsome and voluntary consignment of his eyes and limbs to the mansion of an elderly gentleman not to be profanely named, at once started upon the benevolent mission, which he ingeniously executed by arriving at the door of Mr. Spangle's house, considerably a head of the procession, and knocking with extraordinary energy and violence an uninterrupted succession of postman's knocks, until the door was opened, by which time the stranger had arrived with his insensible burthen.

Mrs. Spangle, at the moment that the apparent legion of twopenny postmen invaded the knocker, was seated quietly by the fireside, fondly dreaming of her son's future advancement in life—for that he should advance in whatever station he might be placed, was to that good lady's mind a natural deduction—but when Miss Caroline Spangle rushed into the room with a fresh torrent of tears, and hiding her face in her mother's lap, shrieked with heart-rending accents the name of her brother, and the last two blows of the knocker died upon her ears; for even after the door had been opened by Phœbe, the gentleman with the fur cap was told to quit his benevolent intention, Mrs. Spangle might well be supposed to be tolerably prepared for something unusual; and, despite the rheumatism, she sprung from her seat with an alacrity she had not exhibited for at least twenty years, and rushed into the narrow passage, which was now thronged with persons; and the first sight that met her gaze was Adolphus in the arms of the stranger, disfigured, bleeding, and insensible.

The mother saw no more; she stretched forth her arms to clasp her son —tottered, and would have fallen, had it not been for the timely intervention of the rat-catcher, who had pushed in amongst the foremost, and who now, in a very heroic manner, threw away the bag of rats and lent his arm for the support of Mrs. Spangle.

The stranger, by the direction of the alarmed Phœbe, proceeded at once to the back parlour, and deposited his charge upon the bed, and, upon a promise of a reward upon his return, induced a lad to run to the nearest surgeon's, and request his immediate attendance; and by threats and entreaties succeeded in clearing the house of all strangers, excepting the rat-catcher, who was busied in his search for his bag of animals. Mrs. Spangle had been recovered from her fainting-fit, and was seated by the bed-side of Adolphus in an agony of tears, although somewhat calmed by the stranger's repeated assurances that his hurts were but trifling. And here lay the boy, calm and still, as if sleeping, while the st ranger cas

many an impatient glance at the door for the arrival of the surgeon.   There
was something exceedingly annoying in the stillness that prevailed.   Minute
after minute rolled heavily onwards, and still no knock announced the
arrival.

"Poor boy!" said the stranger, as if communing with his own thoughts
rather than addressing Mrs. Spangle, "so young, and, doubtless. so much
loved, now so calm and still, so tranquil—but to awaken but to pain
and misery! Oh! would that in the spring of life I had so slept and
never wakened!"

Mrs. Spangle raised her head to look scrutinisingly at the stranger.   His
hat was removed, and he appeared much younger than before; and there
was upon his face an appearance of such deep melancholy and suffering,
combined with gentleness, that Mrs. Spangle spoke unconsciously with respect and commisseration, when she said,—

"Do you really think, or do you wish, my boy to die, sir?"

"Pardon me, madam," he replied. "God forbid! may he long live.
spoke not with such a thought."

A loud rat-tat at the door interrupted the conversation, and the pompous
step of some gentleman in very creaking boots, announced the approach of
as the stranger rightly conjectured, the surgeon, who at once recommended
Adolphus's removal to an hospital, mildly but firmly urging the impossibility of bestowing upon him proper attention at home.

An uninterrupted silence now ensued for a few moment's duration,
during which the stranger looked earnestly at Master Adolphus Spangle
and Mrs. Spangle looked anxiously at the stranger, as if to read from his
looks what was next to be done; and by the quivering of the lip it might
be seen that the child was in pain, if the half-suppressed moans which he
uttered, had not eloquently said as much.

No. 15

"This will not do," said the stranger. "Have you no relative or friend to send to, madam?"

"My husband, sir, Mr. Spangle, he is in the City."

"Send to him then, by all means."

"Bless you, sir, no one knows where to find him."

"Dear me," said the stranger; and then another pause ensued of some minutes, which was, however, again broken by the stranger.

"Perhaps, madam," he said, "notwithstanding it may not be so agreeable to your feelings, it may be better to send this wounded child to an hospital. He will, most probably, there receive all the attention that skill and kindness can suggest. I perceive that I can be of no further service; I leave you, madam, with heartfelt wishes for your son's recovery."

"You have been very kind, sir," said Mrs. Spangle, as the stranger laid his hand on the door; "will you favour me with your name? Mr. Spangle shall thank you."

The stranger smiled faintly, and placing a card in Mrs. Spangle's hand, closed the street door behind him.

On the card was, "Mr. Smith," and no address. "Mr. Smith," said Mrs. Spangle, "as she turned the card several times over in her hand, in a most unsatisfied manner—"Mr. Smith"—and a little consultation with her memory brought to her recollection so many Mr. Smiths, with none of whom could she identify the stranger, that she eventually gave up conjecturing upon the subject, seating herself by the bed-side of Master Adolphus, who had dropped into an unquiet slumber, the good lady remained anxiously, and weeping, awaiting Mr. Spangle's return.

Minute after minute and hour after hour passed away, and still Mr. Spangle came not; but at length the wished-for rap at the door announced his arrival. Mrs. Spangle met her husband in the passage, and there was something so cold and desolating in the manner in which she took his hand, and so much of the natural language of real grief in her face, that the old gentleman stopped amazed, and dropping the old gingham umbrella, he involuntarily inclined his head to hear what his wife should say.

"Adolphus, my love, has met with an accident," said Mrs. Spangle "but—but not serious, I think—he has been run over!"

"Gone to Dover!" said Mr. Spangle. "He has no business there; that's an undeniable fact."

Mrs. Spangle had not spoken in her usual high key when addressing her husband, for grief had choken her utterance. She now, however, took him by the hand, and led him, silently, to the little back parlour, where slept the object of her solicitude.

Mr. Spangle was struck by the sight of Adolphus lying so still and pale, with his cheek spotted with blood, and he sunk into a chair, paralyzed by the sight; then covering his face with his hands, he burst into tears, exclaiming,—

"He is dead!—he is dead!—he is dead!"

"No, no," said Mrs. Spangle, in a high hysterical tone, "he is not—no, no."

Adolphus here awakened, and slowly opening his eyes, he gazed for, some moments upon Mrs. Spangle; then, by a slight separation of the bloodless lips, he seemed to say something; and Mr. Spangle, who would not have heard the sound had it been uttered with ten times the intensity, seemed to know that it was "father," for he stooped over Adolphus, and kissing his pale cheek, he said:—

"I am here, Ady;—your father is here, my poor boy."

"What is to be done?" said Mrs. Spangle.

"What, indeed," said Mr. Spangle, raising his head, and clasping his hands tightly. "Where is Carry?"

"There," replied Mrs. Spangle; and there she was lying, sleeping on the hearthrug, and looking like a small bundle of clothes, with a light coloured wig thrown upon the top of them.

"I have been advised to send him to an hospital," said Mrs. Spangle, doubtingly.

"Send him where?"

"Hush!" said Mrs. Spangle, pointing to the boy who lay so still that he slept, or seemed to sleep, and the good lady informed Mr. Spangle, close to his ear, of all that had passed with the stranger, and the surgeon's opinion, and then a whispered consultation ensued, which terminated by Mr. Spangle saying, with a sigh, "It must be so;" and Mrs. Spangle wept more than before, and sat down by Adolphus, while Mr. Spangle crept along the passage, and in a few moments the door closed gently, and all was still.

Five minutes might have elapsed when the creaking sound of a hackney-coach stopping, was heard at the door, and Mrs. Spangle rose and listened, and the rustling of a latch-key sounded in the lock of the street door, and Mr. Spangle entered the parlour.

"It is here," he said;—"come in;" and a robust man, enveloped in about eight great coats, entered the room.

"It's very dark, sir," observed the man.

"True, it is," replied Mr. Spangle. "Wait a moment," and he crept softly as foot could fall from the room, and presently returned with a lighted candle, which he gave to Mrs. Spangle.

"Now," said Mr. Spangle, as he gently slid his arm under Master Adolphus's neck.

"Stop!" exclaimed Mrs. Spangle.

"Drop what?" said Mr. Spangle.

Mrs. Spangle kissed Adolphus's lips.

"It may be for the last time in life," she sobbed.

"Never no good in taking on so, marm," said the coachman, speaking as if his head was an empty quart pot.

"No, no, it is not—go, go;" and she sunk on a chair, offering no further interruption.

Mr. Spangle now gently raised the boy, though his arm trembled so much as to be hardly equal to his slight weight, and slowly carried him to the street-door.

Two or three idle passengers had stopped to see who were to be the occupants of the coach, and gazed with surprise at the two men with their burthen. The child was slightly shaken upon being lifted into the coach, and he uttered an exclamation of pain, which caused the bystanders to shrink back upon the coach-door. Mr. Spangle told the coachman where to drive, and entered the coach.

"Water, Jack, your honour," said a voice at the door.

"Water who?" said Mr. Spangle.

"You're a precious hunfeeling hanimal, you are, blow you, to come axing for a copper, arter a haccident; where do you expect to go to? You're worser nor a pelican wort, always lays a hegg on Saturdays for Sunday's dinner;" and the coachman accompanied this reproof to his assistant with a peculiar blow in the region of the ribs, which caused that gentleman to strike several curious and original attitudes.

"Drive slow," said Mr. Spangle.

"He must," your honour, with them ere hosses; vun on um's unkimmun lame, and t'other was bought to match that ere von."

The vehicle, after swinging to the right and to the left for a few moments, slowly advanced up the narrow street towards the New-road.

" Coach !" said a voice in the street.

" Coach !" screamed a boy, who had seated himself behind for a ride, not that the coach was going his road, but because a chance was not to be thrown away.

The coach stopped.

" I will go, too," said Mrs. Spangle.

" Caroline," said Mr. Spangle, in an enquiring tone, " we will all go. Phœbe, mind the house.　Oh, dear !"

Mrs. Spangle returned into the house, and awakened Miss Caroline Spangle, and again proceeded to the coach-door.

" Are you going, ma'am ?"

" Yes," said Mrs. Spangle, as she stepped into the vehicle with Caroline in her arms.

" Werry good," said the coachman, as once more he slammed the door, and mounted the box.

CHAPTER XXI.

THE next morning presented a cheerless scene at the Spangles'.　Breakfast was served, and partaken of in dead silence ; nor was the kind-hearted and compassionate Phœbe untroubled at the accident which had a gloom on the little family circle of which she had now so long been a humble member.

They knew that till later in the morning they could not visit the unfortunate Adolphus according to the regulations of this hospital, and in vain Mrs. Spangle strove to fix her attention for the intervening time upon a book.　The letters danced before her eyes and her tears fell upon the leaves.

Phœbe had cleared away the breakfast things, and Mr. Spangle had just risen from his chair, and was gazing abstractedly from the window upon nothing at all, when a knock sounded on the door."

" My dear," said Mrs. Spangle, " there's a knock at the door."

" Eh !—what ?" cried Mr. Spangle, aroused by his wife's voice.　" Lock the door, did you say ?"

" A knock !" screamed Mrs. Spangle.

" Oh'! perhaps it's somebody from Adolphus," said the anxious father ; " I'll go myself."

He hurried to the street door, and opened it just as Phœbe, whose duty it was to do so, had partially ascended the kitchen stairs, and her head was just about on a level with the passage, as she came up, when Mr. Spangle opened the door.

Poor Phœbe could hardly believe her eyes.　She was transfixed with amazement and terror.　Mr. Bung, the identical Mr. Bung, beadle, &c., of the parish of Bungleum, walked in.

" I wishes you a wery good morning, sir," she heard him say to Mr Spangle.

" You wish to give me warning ?" asked Mr. Spangle—" warning for what ?—I've paid my taxes.

Phœbe, with a sinking at her heart, retired back to the kitchen, and would have fallen, had there not been a chair near the door, into which she sunk.

The orphan girl had conceived a great horror and dread of the workhouse, and being ignorant of such matters, she always imagined that having been once within its walls, its authorities had acquired some sort of power over her, and could drag her back again at their pleasure.

Poor girl, she little imagined how glad they were to get so easily rid of her as they had done, and that the most unwelcome sight to them would be her voluntary return to their tender mercies.

It was, however, a fact that Mr. Bung was in London, with the parish chaise, for the express purpose of finding out Phœbe Grainger, which may be accounted for upon quite separate grounds than any anxiety on the part of the parish authorities to repossess themselves of the person of the orphan child.

Mr. Bung, being unused to driving in London, had, in the New-road, first of all taken fright himself, and then the horse had taken fright sympathetically, and hence the catastrophe in Skinner-street, down which the animal had madly dashed with headlong speed.

Mr. Bung had not escaped altogether scathless in the matter, for he was now adorned by divers oddly-shaped plaisters upon his face, which gave him very much the appearance of some Indian chief prepared for the war path.

Phœbe sat trembling in the kitchen, making sure that the beadle had undertaken a journey to London, upon gaining some private information of her place of residence, for the express purpose of dragging her forthwith back to Bungleum, and she snatched up her bonnet, and opening her little box, which stood under the dresser, took out of it the remainder of Mrs. Greenfield's money, and a few articles of necessary clothing, and stole up the kitchen stairs with the intention of escaping, if possible, and, at all risks, an encounter with Mr. Bung.

In the meantime Mr. Bung had been shewn into the parlour, and making a low bow to Mrs. Spangle, he deposited his cocked-hat on the table, and addressed that lady.

"Look at me, mum," he said. "List; have the kindness to look at me, mum."

"Oh! dear me," replied Mrs. Spangle, "I see you. Oh! dear, you're a beetle, I believe. Mr. Spangle always called a beadle a beetle, and a beetle a beadle."

"A what, mum?" said Mr. Bung.

"A beetle of the parish," replied Mrs. Spangle. "Oh! dear me, what do you want? We never give Easter offerings; besides, you know, bless me, it isn't Easter nor Christmas. Don't ring a bell here, we've had a calamity. Oh! dear me, what is it, beetle?"

Mr. Bung looked very much puzzled at this address, and glanced at Mr. Spangle with the confident expectation of receiving some private information that Mrs. Spangle was not right in her mind; but Mr. Spangle was looking intently at the ceiling, and had forgotten the presence of Mr. Bung altogether.

Forty discount, and still going down," muttered Mr. Spangle, "and granite continually falling.

"Dear me," said Mr. Bung, looking likewise, up to the ceiling, in expectation of an immediate shower of stones.

"Oh! don't mind Mr. Spangle," said the lady; "he's always thinking of some of his nonsense. My dear, don't you see here's the beetle come about something?"

"Ah!—eh!—yes—yes—how are you? Good morning—a fine—eh?—wet—no—dear me—cold day."

"Wery, wery," replied Mr. Bung looking from one to the other, and just faintly surmising that he had got into a private madhouse.

"Your blessed little boy, mum," he continued, addressing Mrs. Spangle, "was runned over, mum, by a chaise, and I was in that ere identical chaise, and I have been obliged, mum, to give security for my wery appearance afore some blessed board in London, on account o' that wery accident, mum."

"Oh! dear me," cried Mrs. Spangle, blowing her nose, "so it was you, you stupid beetle, was it? You ought to have known better, you ought, indeed. You parish people really—oh! dear, you should run over each other, and not the public. How came you to think of such a thing?"

Mr. Bung had in vain attempted to stop the torrent of Mrs. Spangle's eloquence, but that lady never did stop speaking till she was thoroughly exhausted of words.

"Mum," said the beadle, a little infuriated, "I didn't think of it. Do you imagine, mum, as I'd in a woluntary and thoughtful way, throw myself, mum, out of a chaise-cart, mum, and wop down a cellar on the wery top of a—a lot of shoemaker's boots, mum? Do you imagine, mum, as I'd permit myself, mum, the wery support of a unkimmon large parish, to be runned away with in a promiscus and thoughtful manner, mum? Am I a beadle, or isn't I? Am I a pump, mum? I asks you to look at me, mum, and say if you think me a werdent pump, mum?"

"A pump?" said Mrs. Spangle; "Oh, dear me, no. Bless me, really you know you shouldn't run away with the cart; it's wery wrong."

"Never," cried Mr. Bung.

"And I want to know why you run down Skinner-street of all the streets in the world? Why didn't you go along the New-road, and then I shouldn't have minded a bit."

"Never," screamed Mr. Bung.

"People are so wilful, they always run where they shouldn't. I dare say you'll say it's all the same a hundred years hence; but it's no use you're saying that, for what's done can't be undone—it's Hobson's—no, Dobson's no, dear me, it is Hobson's—Hobson's choice, you know. Money's a scarce commodity. Really for a beetle, who ought to know better, to run away with a cart, and trample with his iron heels, upon people, and throw the horse—no, the beetle,—bless me, one or other,—down an arch, or a cellar, or something. It's quite absurd."

"Mum! mum! mum!" roared Mr. Bung.

"Well, dear me, what is it? You go on talking, and yet say nothing to the purpose. I never met such a beetle before, not that I'm aware of ever meeting a beetle in my life. We've lots of beadles in the kitchen."

"Beadles in the kitchen, mum?"

"Oh! dear, yes. Under the hearth it's cracked, you see, and at night up come the beadles, looking as shiny as possible. Mr. Spangle trod on one of their backs one day. It gave me quite a turn to see it laying, smashed."

"So I should think," said Mr. Bung, holding up his hands in horror.

"But what did you come for, Mr. Beetle? Do you want to run over us all? Dear me, I am amazed at your assurance."

"Mum! mum!" cried Mr. Bung, "I've comed here, mum, for to say as I'm wery sorry for the wery melancholy haccident, mum, which was quite a haccident. I'm a affection for little boys, mum; I sees lots of 'em, mum, daily, in the workus, mum. It was a wery mere haccident and nothing else, no how. The hoss, mum, isn't used to Life in London, and he was sneered at by other hosses. A hoss in a hackney coach, mum, actually laughed, mum, at him, and he runned clean slap away, a dragging me and the blessed chaise cart arter him, mum, like nothing.

"Oh, it's all wery well, but what business had you in a cart at all? I never heard of beetles in carts; I thought they always were in churches, or at the doors, with a pewter platter, to prevent the people quitting till they paid again, I assure you that was my impression. I suppose you'll be hung, or transported, or something—oh! dear me.'

"You're wery kind, mum. I come to London, mum ——"

"Oh! you're not a Londoner beetle?"

"No, mum; I belong, mum, or rather, mum ——"

"Then what business had you to come to London at all? Why couldn't you run over the country people you know? that wouldn't have mattered. Oh! dear me, it's very odd you should come to London to injure people in this way."

"I come to London, mum, on a errand, to find out a orphan pauper, mum."

"I dare say, and run over him; but you ought to be careful, and be sure it is him. Really, Mr. Beetle, your conduct is most absurd. You come to London at fifty miles an hour, to run over an orphan child, by your own admission, and then run over some one else. I think, Mr. Beetle ——"

"My name is Bung, mum, not Beetle. Jeremiah Bung, mum, &c. &c. &c., is my name."

"Oh! dear, yes, I dare say it is—just as you please."

"Mum, the reason as brought me to London is this here. There was in our workus, mum, two orphan wicious paupers, mum, as was unkimmon horrid in their behaviour, mum. If you wasn't mum, a female, which you is I could tell you how the female pauper walked down stairs in her thingumy only, but I won't."

"Oh, no—dear me, how odd, what a singular thing—early depravity," said Mrs. Spangle.

"Wery early, mum, wery. The he pauper, mum, was given to wice, and he inwaded the sanctity of the wirtue of fifty paupers, mum, as slept in wirtuous wirgin innocence, and all screamed, mum, when they was told as he was gone away."

"Dear me, it's singular and, rather interesting. Go on, Mr. Beetle; what's in the next volume?—Dear me, I mean what happened next?"

"Well, mum, he absconded, with property, and I was brutally and wiolently assaulted. He runned away with a large ship, and all the crew, and particularly one wretch, as blew impertinence through a trumpet. Then, mum, we gets the female pauper a place, but, mum, she wallops her blessed missus, and leads her a life rather. Then, one night, mum, she makes her master drunk."

"Drunk!" cried Mrs. Spangle; "I never heard of such a thing. Make her master drunk!—oh! dear, me! It's worth a whole chapter itself. What a little wretch! It's the most singular incident I ever read of."

"I expected as you'd stare, mum. Then she wollups her missus again, and bumps her head on the step of the door, and wops her with a pail, and then cuts away unkimmon."

"Does what?—Cuts her?"

"Cuts away unkimmon, mum—runs away, mum, runs away."

"Oh! she murders her mistress, and then elopes in disguise to seek adventures."

"Wery good, mum, She 'lopes, mum, and nobody knows vere she goes, mum no how."

"Perhaps, Mr. Beetle, it's reserved you for the last chapter in the last volume. Oh! dear me, I mean—bless me, what am I thinking of?"

"I don't know, mum—but we always makes the paupers read a chapter, mum; and some on 'em swears dreadfully."

"Well, go on, Mr. Beetle."

"Well, mum, then arter awhile there comes a letter to the female pauper from the boy pauper, enclosed in one to the blessed parson of our parish, and what do you think was in it."

"Why, really I don't know. Perhaps a blood-stained dagger, or an old chest, that he found in some castle."

"A what, mum?—a chestesses? No, mum, it was a fifty pound note, and the latter said as it was to be dewoted to the female pauper what had cut away, mum, so smashing. So the board sat on the letter and the fifty pound note."

"Bless me, to prevent her from getting it, I suppose. What an uncommon thing?"

"No, mum, not at all. The board sits on every letter as comes, and often sits a hour or two on a pauper, mum."

"You don't say so? How can they bear it? It's singular, but not at all romantic."

"Rum antic? Mum, you should see the rum antics as some of our paupers makes; they would astonish you. Well, mum, it was decided as the female pauper should be made to pay out of the money, mum, all the expenses of the parish, for the funeral of the mother of them ere orphans, and there own B. B. W. L. mum, which comed to forty-eight pounds, seventeen shillings, and threepence halfpenny. But that ere person of ourn, mum, was wicious, and he said as the board shouldn't have the money till the female orphan was found to acknowledge the debt, and he's a unkimmon obstinate man; 'and though the board sat on him, mum, he wouldn't give way not a inch."

"A very strong man, I suppose?" said Mrs. Spangle.

"Oh! wery, mum, wery. Well, mum, the board has sent me to enquire for that ere female pauper in London, as it's suspected she's comed here; and here I is, mum."

"And you haven't found her, Mr. Beetle?"

"No, mum, I haven't. I'm ready to hand over to her one pound two shillings and eight-pence halfpenny, mum, whenever I sees her."

"Oh! dear me; and you go running over children in hopes it's her, do you? I think it's wery wrong indeed. You're a bad beetle, a very bad beetle; you really ought to know better at your time of life. Why don't you put in a mysterious advertisement in the 'Times,' to say,—'If A. B. will apply to a beetle, she will hear of something to her advantage.' I'm sure I've seen such things done."

"But A. B. wouldn't do, mum."

"Why not?—I am sure it's A. B. that's generally put—I declare I've seen it often—it's a capital plan. I once knew a lady who lost her reticule, and she advertised it, and got a very singular answer from some gentleman, telling her to 'be blowed,' and signed 'Ax My Eye.' It was a remarkable answer. She didn't get the reticule, but you see she got an answer, which was very satisfactory."

"But I don't see, mum, as A. B. woulld do."

"And why not? I thnk it's your best plan—in the 'Times,' you know."

"But Phœbe's name isn't a A. or a B."

"Phœbe's name. Dear me, how singular," cried Mrs. Spangle.

"Phœbe Grainger, mum, would be a P. and a G. I rather think; but I mean to call at all the warious workuses first, and then—"

"What did you say, Mr. Beetle?—Phœbe Grainger?"

"Yes, mum; Phœbe Grainger is the female pauper orphan, and wery wicious she is."

"Oh! dear—oh! dear. It's a romance in seven volumes. Phœbe Grainger! Mr. Spangle, do you hear what the beetle says?"

"Eh!—ah!—my dear—oh! yes—what was it?" said Mr. Spangle.

"He comes for Phœbe, my dear—our Phœbe."

"What!" cried Mr. Bung, "your Phœbe. Who?—what?—Oh, lauk! oh, lauk!"

"Why, she's here, Mr. Beetle; she let you in."

"Let me in, mum," cried Mr. Bung, looking very hard at Mrs. Spangle. "What a miscovery."

"Yes! oh! dear, yes," said Mr. Spangle, quite forgetting that he himself had opened the door.

"You hardened hussey, you are in disguise!" cried the infuriated Mr. Bung, to Mr. Spangle.

"Disguise!" said Mr. Spangle. "What do you mean?"

"Oh! orphan! orphan! take off them ere spectacles, and weep, your hardened little wretch."

"What do you mean?" cried Mr. Spangle, for Mr. Bung was shaking his head within an inch of his nose.

"Oh! dear me, it's a mistake," said Mrs. Spangle; "that's Mr. Spangle; Phœbe's in the kitchen. Really I don't know whether I'm on my head or my heels, it beats everything."

"Phœbe Grainger in the wery kitchen of this here house," cried Mr. Bung; "oh! impossible."

"Just ring the bell, Mr. Spangle, if you please, my dear, and she'll come up. What did you say she did? Murdered her mistress and master, and made you drunk? Dear me—dear me. I wouldn't slept in the house with her on any account. Do ring the bell, and let her be placed in a dungeon, beneath the moat of the castle."

No. 16

Mr. Bung flew to the bell, and rung it furiously. He then placed himself behind the door, ready for a spring upon poor Phœbe, when she might make her appearance in answer to the loud summons.

Nobody spoke, and Mr. Bung wiped the perspiration from his face with the yellow handkerchief, and looked very much excited.

Five minutes passed away, and still Phœbe came not, and the occupants of the parlour began to get excessively fidgetty and uneasy.

"Oh! dear me, ring again," said Mrs. Spangle; "she sometimes falls asleep."

"I will, mum," said Mr. Bung, rattling some money in his pocket. "Here's one pound ten shillings and eight-pence halfpenny for that ere female orphan pauper, and she won't come and take it."

He rung the bell again as he spoke, and he skipped back to his place at the door.

Again the bell remained unanswered, and Mr. Bung looked at Mrs. Spangle, and Mr. Spangle looked at Mr. Bung, both of them in very great surprise.

"It's very odd," said the lady.

"Very odd, indeed," replied Mr. Spangle.

"Oh! wery, wery," said Mr. Bung. "Suppose we all go down, mum, and see what she's a doing?"

"Why, really, I'm so fatigued myself; but you and Mr. Spangle can go, you know. You musn't mind finding the kitchen a little out of sorts, Mr. Beetle, for really I can't see to it myself, and I dare say it's neglected, while that girl's planning murders and assassinations."

"Wery likely, mum," said Mr. Bung. "Perhaps you'll go first, as you know the blessed way, and I'm rather narvous."

"Oh! yes—yes—yes," said Mr. Spangle; "I hope no harm has come to her, poor thing."

Mr. Spangle, followed by Mr. Bung, descended to the kitchen—it was empty. Mr. Bung sunk upon a seat in an agony of disappointment.

"Where can she be?" he cried.

A little piece of paper was lying on the kitchen table. Mr. Spangle took it up, and read the few words that were written on it aloud.

"'FAREWELL,—kind friends. Thank you for much goodness to a poor orphan. God bless you. I may never see you again, but may you enjoy health and happiness.

"'PHŒBE GRAINGER.'"

"The devil!" cried Mr. Bung.

"It's singular," said Mr. Spangle. "What's to be done?—she's gone."

"And I'm done to a cinder," screamed the discomfitted beadle.

"We always burn the cinders," said Mr. Spangle, catching, as usual, the last word.

"Damn you all," cried Mr. Bung, and he rushed up stairs and out at the street door, in a most frantic and unbeadle-like manner.

CHAPTER XXII.

THE alarmed Phœbe, when she had completed the few arrangements for her flight from Mr. Spangle's house, crept cautiously up the kitchen stairs. She trembled as she passed the parlour door, and heard Mr. Bung's voice within, explaining to Mrs. Spangle her various delinquencies. She heard the words "female orphan," and the shadow of a doubt as to the beadle's errand vanished from Phœbe's mind. She reached the street door in breathless anxiety, opened it, and closing it as softly as possible, again she fled into the street.

Taking the direction which avoided passing by the parlour window, Phœbe hurried onwards, not knowing whither. She had but one object, and that was, to place as great a distance as possible between herself and Mr. Bung, the much-dreaded beadle of Bungleum.

Phœbe relaxed not her speed until she was a full mile from the street in which the Spangles' dwelt, and then she paused, to see what part of the town she was in.

"Drury-lane," she saw written up; and she walked, without any definite object, down the long, narrow, dirty throughfare.

She had deposited in the breast of her dress the money which had been left from the fifteen pounds which Mrs. Greenfield had given her; and, anxious for its safety, as it was now her only hope, she took it out, and counted it in the street.

She walked slowly, for she was in deep thought as to what should be her next proceeding, now that she was fairly clear of the Spangles' and Mr. Bung. After much consideration, she determined to make enquiry for some coach, or other conveyance, to the place where the honest waggoner was; and, risking recognition there, where she had been so well known, she resolved to seek the good old man, and once more be beholden to him for protection.

She walked straight forwards with this idea, and soon found herself in the Strand; and, after a short distance, she saw a coach-office, which she entered, and enquired of a red-faced man at the counter if she could go to Bungleum?

"There ain't nothin' until Friday," said the man; "and then it's the mail."

"Friday!" said Phœbe, "and this is but Wednesday."

"Vy, you can go to Canterbury at the half-arter two coach, and that ain't far off."

"Oh! yes, I will do so," said Phœbe, eagerly; "I know it."

She recollected well the vast cathedral, which the waggoner had pointed out to her, as being at Canterbury, and she felt a sensation of pleasure as she thought she should once more gaze on the sublime and stupendous structure.

"Vill you book your place?" cried the man, fancying she hesitated. "There's nothin' else till Friday."

"Oh! yes—I mean to go—I will go. At half-past two?"

"Half-arter two," replied the man, opening a great book. "Twenty-five shillings, if you please, Miss. What's the name?"

"Phœbe Grainger, sir," she answered, at the same time handing two sovereigns to the man.

In a moment he slapped down fifteen shillings change, and then paid no more attention to Phœbe whatever, but, thrusting his hands into his pocket, commenced humming a popular melody with great composure.

Phœbe walked out of the coach-office much gratified that she had thus so successfully taken the first step towards proceeding in search of the kind-hearted waggoner. She thought she would have such pleasure in walking from Canterbury to Bungleum, and calling upon the kind-hearted landlady by the way, who nearly two years since, had given the little stranger so hearty a welcome. She had some confidence, too, in her changed appearance, that she might not be recognised at Bungleum even if she were to meet the redoubtable Mrs. Marrables face to face.

These were pleasant reflections to poor Phœbe, and she smiled as she took her course back to Drury-lane, where she remembered to have passed an eating house. She had not even breakfasted, and she intended to purchase something to take with her on her journey. She could not immediately find out the place she had seen, and she stood a moment in the street looking about her.

"Are you looking for anything, Miss?" said a man, with a braided frock-coat, out at the elbows, and a shirt front which would have screamed, had it possessed a voice, at the sight of a washing tub.

"I saw a shop where they sell ham," said Phœbe, innocently, "and I don't know where it is now, and yet it was here."

"Oh! dear, Miss, yes," said the man. "This here's the entrance of that ere consarn, Miss."

He pointed up a dark narrow entry as he spoke.

"Thank you," said the simple Phœbe, and she walked up the entry.

In a moment she found her arms seized by the gentleman in the frock coat, who said, with a coarse oath, both at the beginning and end of the speech,—

"The tin, my tulip—the mopuses. Snigger a whisper, and I'll slice your whimy. Here, Bill, my covey, the young un's flush."

Phœbe was too much alarmed to speak, and another man immediately coming up, thrust his hand rudely into her bosom, and dragged out the little purse, which was, as well as its contents, the gift of Mrs. Greenfield.

"Mizzle's the word, my precious," he cried to his companion, and in an instant they both ran off, leaving Phœbe perfectly bewildered.

She rushed from the narrow entry into the open street, and was upon the point of proclaiming her loss, but she stopped, and thought that the publicity she might thus give herself might place her at once in the hands of Mr. Bung; and yet it was sad and cruel to be left thus, without a penny. What could she do? She wept as she once more walked to the Strand, and stood opposite the coach-office; and yet a feeling of rejoicing came across her heart as she thought that she had paid for her conveyance to Canterbury, and that in a few hours she would be free from London—she hoped for ever.

She felt faint and hungry, and she walked into the coach-office, and asked permission to sit down till the coach started.

"Oh! wery good," said the red-faced man. "You'll have to vait a hour and a half, for it's only wun o'clock now. It doesn't start from Oxford-street till a quarter arter two."

Phœbe, however, availed herself of the permission to sit, and she rested herself upon a trunk, which stood on the floor, waiting to go by the same coach.

The time passed very slowly to poor Phœbe in the office, but, at length, the coach did arrive.

There were three other inside passengers, who were in their places when the coach arrived at the Strand, and Phœbe, being assisted in, made the fourth.

The coach did not wait five minutes, but started off through the City, and over London Bridge, at as good a pace as the crowded streets would permit.

For the second time in her life, Phœbe now crossed London Bridge, and she could not help falling into a train of anxious reflection regarding all that had occurred to her since she first caught sight of the great Leviathan —London—from the waggon, to the present time, when she was rattling out of it, with all the speed that four good horses could conveniently accomplish.

The time had been short; but still it appeared to her as if much had happened, of an eventful character, during its brief period. She had witnessed the death of her dear friend, Mrs. Greenfield, and that was the only very calamitous circumstance which bore upon her memory. She thought with kindly feelings of the Spangles, for they had [been, in their strange and unsettled manner, very kind to her. And what was to be her future fate, if she failed in finding the good waggoner? She shuddered to think of it. How, even was she without the means to reach him, or even the inn, on the road between Canterbury and Bungleum, where she doubted not of receiving a kind welcome, and every assistance from the landlady? Already the pangs of hunger began to assail her.

She looked cautiously and timidly at her fellow passengers. One was a bluff-looking old gentleman, with a travelling cap on his head, which left but a very small portion of his face visible, and what it did leave, was very fiery. The others were a pale, sickly-looking female, who was duly wrapped up in shawls and cloaks; and a pert, coarse-looking young man, with hair on his head as stiff as the bristles on a hog's back. There was a self-sufficient expression upon this young man's face, which was peculiarly disagreeable, and his actions were all of the vulgarest and most inelegant description. He had indulged himself with a long stare at Phœbe, with his eyes half shut, as if to see the better, upon her entrance into the coach, and he was several times inclined to address her, but seemed awed by the presence of the old gentleman, who was evidently, from his side-long glances, not at all prepossessed in his favour.

Meantime the coach rattled merrily towards its first stage, and then drew up to the door of a pretty country inn to change horses.

A great deal of bustle always attends the changing of horses. The coachman must have a glass and his chat at the bar of the inn, and the state of the road must be remarked upon, &c. &c.

The disagreeable-looking young man thrust his head, and half his body out of the window, to the great discomposure of the old gentleman, and in a loud, confident voice ordered a pint of ale—"and let it be good," he added.

"And now, sir," growled the old man, "perhaps you'll take your seat again, for I don't like you in my lap at all."

"I believe, sir," said the young man, drawing himself in with a sulky look, "that it's one of the rights of the people, that when they are anywhere whatever, they may do as they please. The working classes, sir, are the sinews of the country. We are ground down by a vile aristocracy, sir—an aristocracy, sir, of wealth and birth."

The old gentleman drew his travelling-cap closer over his ears, and gave an awful grunt, and muttered something, in which the words "damned radical rascal" were very apparent.

"The sovereign people," continued the rapid young man, "are the proper lords of the soil—the—oh! here's my ale. How much?"

"Fourpence, sir," said the waiter.

"It's a gross imposition; but there's nothing but imposition everywhere. The House of Commons is not the people's house. Here, my dear."

These latter words were addressed to Phœbe, as he thrust the ale pot close to her face.

There was nothing particularly objectionable in the words themselves, for Phœbe was but young, but there was an insulting air of assumption and superiority in the tone and manner which even Phœbe recoiled from, and she shook her head in dissent.

The old gentleman glanced towards her, and said, in a tone of great kindness,—

" My dear, have you no refreshment?"

" No, sir," said Phœbe, slightly blushing ; " I—I can do without."

" Let an old man, my dear, invite you to lunch," said he, in a mild, gentle tone. " Here, waiter, bring some nice ham sandwiches, and some port wine and water."

" Yes, sir," said the waiter, and he returned, in an incredibly short space of time, with a tray of sandwiches, and the wine and water.

The old gentleman smiled so kindly, and pressed Phœbe to partake of them so good-naturedly, that she could not find in her heart to refuse ; and, to his great pleasure, she made a hearty meal for her breakfast, which she really was much in need, for she was faint for want of nourishment.

The coachman mounted the box. " All right !" cried somebody. The old gentleman paid for the refreshments, and off they started again with renewed vigour.

The coach took the same route that Phœbe had come in the waggon, and the familiar objects on the road gave her all the pleasure of old acquaintance as she recognised them.

Nothing of particular interest occurred on the journey, save that at a village the independent young man alighted, and was received by a re-spectable-looking farming man, who laid a tolerably stout walking-stick three or four times over his sovereign shoulders, saying at the same time,—

" I'll teach you to rob me, and go to London, you vagabond. Go home, sir, and ask your poor mother's pardon, you scapegrace. Be off with you."

The old gentleman was highly amused at this ; and the young man, with a most sheepish look, and the most crest-fallen manner possible, sneaked off.

It was quite right when they arrived at Canterbury, and the coach drew up at the inn door.

The city was, however, thronged with busy passengers, and all was bustle and animation.

" Have you friends here?" asked the old gentleman of Phœbe, but she did not answer him ; and when a gleam of light from a lamp at the inn door lighted up the coach, he saw that she was weeping.

" Bless me," he cried, " my dear girl, what's the matter?"

" Oh ! sir," said Phœbe, " my only friend is still a long way from here, and—and I have no money—none, none."

" No money ! Dear me, how did you come here, then? Tell me the honest truth, and you shan't want a friend. I go back to London to-morrow, but I'll see you on your right way, my dear, before I go, only tell me the truth."

Phœbe, thus encouraged, related to him the robbery in London, and that she was going to seek her only friend, the honest waggoner at Bun-gleum.

" Well, well," said the old gentleman, " don't fret. You shall stay at this inn to-night, and in the morning we will talk more about it."

He took Phœbe by the hand, and led her into the inn, and summoned the landlady, who soon appeared all smiles and red ribbons.

" You will be so kind," said the old gentleman, " as to take this young lady under your care, ma'am, till the morning. Let her want for nothing, the house affords."

" Oh ! dear me, sweet young thing," said the landlady ; " we have everything here, sir. Come with me, Miss, if you please. Dear me, sir, she's a beauty, surely, and the picture of you, sir."

" Bother !" cried the old gentleman, very much fluttered notwithstanding, for he instantly ordered a roast duck and a bottle of claret for himself.

The landlady was most profuse in her attention to Phœbe; and, at length, upon her intimating that she was fatigued, conducted her to a bedchamber, which poor Phœbe thought the height of magnificence.

In the morning she was conducted to the old gentleman, who greeted her with great kindness.

"My dear," he said, taking her gently by the hand, "there is a chaise going to Bungleum in the morning, in which I have taken a place for you. I have paid for it, and here are two sovereigns for you, my dear, and God bless you and direct you."

Phœbe was much affected at the kindness of the old gentleman, and thanked him.

He waited until the chaise came to the door, and then shaking her cordially by the hand, he watched her, with a tear in his eye, departure from the inn.

The chaise driver showed the greatest possible respect for Phœbe, as he had been most liberally paid by the old gentleman to convey her safely to her place of destination.

They rapidly proceeded on the road between Canterbury and Bungleum, and now the little inn at which the waggoner had stopped came in sight, and Phœbe directed the nothing-loath driver to draw up at it, which he did, wondering very much at the great foresight of the young lady to stop at a place of entertainment for man and beast the moment she saw one, and he remarked to himself that she must be a "wery uncommon trump," and so was her old grandfather, who he guessed the old gentleman to be.

Phœbe sprung from the chaise, and embraced the astonished landlady, who had hurried to the door, after putting on, in a great hurry, her best cap, and did not at all recognize in the occupant of the chaise, the girl who had passed a night in her house so long ago.

"Don't you know me?" said Phœbe. "I am going to Bungleum to meet good father Greenfield."

The landlady now recollected her in a moment, and kissed her heartily, and almost carried her into the house.

"Here, Peter," she cried, "send the man at the chaise a pot of our best."

"Yes, yes, missus," said Peter.

"And now, my dear, tell me all about you, and where you've been since I saw you; but first let me tell you that Robert Greenfield is not at Bungleum."

"Not at Bungleum?" cried Phœbe.

"No—I wonder you don't know—he is gone to Ferrystone."

"And where's that?—oh! where is it?" cried Phœbe, clasping her hands in disappointment.

"Why it's fifty miles off.

Phœbe covered her face with her hands, and burst into tears.

"Dear heart, what's the matter?" cried the landlady. "My dear child, why do you cry?"

"Oh! ma'am," said Phœbe, "I don't know what to do. I must find him. I have no other hope."

She then related to the landlady all that had happened since she saw her last.

"My dear child," said the good woman, "you have nothing to fear from the parish. They have no power whatever over you, my dear; but I think now you had better proceed in your search for poor Robert Greenfield, who don't know of his loss, poor man."

"I wish to see him—I must see him," cried Phœbe, "if I go to the world's end after him."

Hush! hush! my dear, don't fret yourself; we'll find a means of sending you to Ferrystone."

"But see," cried Phœbe, "I have a deal of money—see"—and she produced the two sovereigns which the old gentleman had given her.

"Keep them, my dear," said the landlady, "till some great emergency. I will take care that you get safely to Ferrystone; but the chaise at the door had better be sent back to Canterbury at once."

"Yes," said Phœbe, "I don't want it now. It was very good of the old gentleman."

"It was, indeed," said the landlady, going out of the room; "and you may live, my dear, to thank him for it yet."

"And to thank you," said Phœbe, "for you are as kind as he."

The chaise was dismissed by the landlady, and the man went back to Canterbury, not a little pleased at completing his job so soon.

CHAPTER XXIII.

THE landlady, after a little reflection, advised Phœbe to wait till the next day, when there would be a carrier's cart that was going more than half way to Ferrystone, which was a manufacturing town, surrounded by a rich corn country.

To this Phœbe assented, although it was with a heavy heart, and she passed the remainder of the day in the company of the good-hearted landlady, who did her utmost to cheer her spirits by predictions of future happiness and welfare.

Phœbe retired early to the couch prepared for her, and laid long awake, pondering upon her perverse destiny. She much regretted leaving the Spangle family so precipitately as to that ill-advised step, which was founded on her ignorance of Mr. Bung's powers, she attributed, justly, her loss of the money in the court in Drury-lane, and her present difficulties and troubles. She was, nevertheless, convinced, that her best plan was to proceed onwards in her search for the kind friend, in whose protecting arms she expected before then to have found herself. But if she should again, by some perverse fortune, miss him, what should she do then? Who, then, would pity her?

In these and similar reflections Phœbe fell asleep, to dream as she always did when her mind was oppressed, of her dear mother and George, and the little cottage, where they had all been so happy long ago.

The morning came, fresh and bright, though cold, and Phœbe descended to the bar of the inn to prepare for her departure, in search of him, to whom each misfortune and disappointment that she endured seemed to bind her more closely.

The carrier's cart arrived; and, with many thanks to the good landlady, who repeatedly kissed the fair girl, she departed.

Phœbe was recommended by the landlady to be very careful of the two sovereigns, and on no account to shew them to any one, but to reserve them in case of any unlooked-for disappointment, which might render them of essential service.

The carrier saw that Phœbe's mind was oppressed, and that she was out of spirits, and, with a rough kindness, he strove to interest her about the various objects which they passed on their journey. Phœbe always appreciated kindness, without caring in what garb it was attired, and she strove

to seem interested in what the carrier said, although her thoughts were far away.

The landlady of the little inn had taken care to stock her amply with provisions for the day, and she and the carrier partook of a hearty meal, after they had proceeded about eighteen miles on the road.

"What sort of place is Ferrystone?" asked Phœbe of the man.

"Why, Miss," he replied, "I never was there but once, and it's full of steam-engines, and all sorts of most uncomfortable-looking chimnies, that vomit up ever so much black smoke every minute. Those are factories, where lots of young children work."

"Indeed," said Phœbe; "and—and they would, perhaps, employ any one?"

'I don't know Miss;—they get them mostly from the parishes, but they might for all that."

A sudden thought came across Phœbe's mind that if she failed in finding the waggoner at Ferrystone, she might procure some employment there, that would, at all events, save her from absolute destitution.

The carrier was going no further than a town about sixteen miles from Ferrystone, and there about the middle of the day they arrived.

"Miss," said the man, "there's a village on this side of Ferrystone, and within two miles and a half of it, where, I think, I can get a man to take you in his cart. He's a gardener, Miss, and it's market-day here to-day, so he is sure to be here."

"Oh! thank you," said Phœbe; "I will pay him."

"No, no, Miss, he won't want anything; leave that to me, Miss; I'll speak to him. You stay at this public-house. The landlord knows me, and will take care of you while I go and look for Joe Ormond, the gardener."

No. 17.

Phœbe was seated within the bar of the public-house, and presently the carrier returned, to say that the gardener would call for Phœbe on his way out of the town.

The grateful girl thanked the carrier for his care and attention, and he departed, promising to call at the inn from whence he had taken her, and inform the hostess of her safe arrival so far on her journey.

Presently the gardener drew up his little market cart, and Phœbe was kindly assisted into it, and seated beside him. He was an old man, and so thin and spare, that he seemed almost like a living mummy. There was, however, a bright healthy glow in his cheek, and he was as active as a boy.

Phœbe had the name of the house of entertainment, at which she expected to meet the waggoner at Ferrystone, written upon a piece of paper, and she shewed it to the gardener, asking him if he knew it.

"Oh, yes," he replied, "it's at the beginning of the town; you can't miss it; you'll see a large post, with the sign of the Lamb and Spectacles painted on a swing board at the top of it."

The cart was one of those which forced whoever sat in it to give a sympathetic jump every moment as the horse trotted onwards; and Phœbe was very thankful when, after three hours of such riding, the gardener pointed to a cluster of cottages at some distance off, and told her that was the village where he lived.

It was now about half-past four in the afternoon, and Phœbe felt very much fatigued, although she had ridden all the way.

The gardener drew up at the door of a pretty cottage, and Phœbe could see from her situation in the cart that behind it there were extensive orchards and plantations.

The gardener's wife came out, and seemed very much astonished to see Phœbe in the cart.

"This young lass," said the gardener, "be going to Ferrystone, and I gave her a lift, wife, to here."

"You'll stay, my dear, and take a cup of tea with us," said the woman, kindly.

"In course she will," replied the gardener—"in course, wife. Come, my pretty lass, let me help you down. She be going to meet her friend at the Lamb and Spectacles, at Ferrystone."

Phœbe thanked her homely entertainers, and alighting from the cart, entered the pretty cottage.

The gardener's wife bustled about the preparations for tea, and likewise placed before Phœbe some choice and tempting fruit, of which she partook with much pleasure.

It was the decline of the year, and the fruit was in perfection.

"You will not go to Ferrystone to night, my dear?" said the good woman to Phœbe.

"Oh, yes, I must go to night. It won't be dark till half-past eight, and I have come so far to see my dear friend and father, that I must go," replied Phœbe.

"It's a good two mile and a half," said the gardener, "and I'll walk with thee, my little lass, the greater part of the road, for it be rather lonesome.

"I thank you, sir—kindly thank you," said Phœbe; "but if you will put me in the right path, I shall do very well."

"Oh, my lass, I'll see thee some part of thy way. I'm an old man, but I can trudge a bit with anybody, even now."

The gardener arose, and put on his hat, to escort Phœbe on the road.

She parted with the hospitable wife of her guide with many thanks, and then proceeded with her ancient companion towards Ferrystone.

The road was, indeed, most wretched and lonely. It lay, for the most part, across a wild common, where scarcely a blade of grass could find nourishment sufficient for its existence.

They then entered a long lane, with trees and hedges on each side, and upon again emerging into the open country, the tall chimneys of the factories at Ferrystone were distinctly visible, rising black and grim into the sky.

"That is Ferrystone," said the gardener, "and I will now bid you good-bye, my pretty lass. You cannot miss your way. Here, you see, is a well-trodden path; it will lead you direct to the sign-post I told you of, and it is scarcely half a mile."

"Thank you," said Phœbe; "good-bye; I shall find my way quite well."

The gardener smiled and waved his hand as he turned back, and Phœbe was alone on the road to Ferrystone, where all her hopes were now centered.

She looked towards the town, and the hum of voices and the clanking of machinery came upon her ears. Volumes of smoke rolled from the tall chimneys, and obscured the fair sky; a black cloud seemed to hang over the place, and Phœbe was not at all prepossessed in favour of Ferrystone by the view she had of it from where she stood for a moment to contemplate its aspect in the distance.

She soon, however, hurried on in the direction of the path which had been pointed out to her by the gardener, and after about a quarter of an hour's fast walking, she observed, at some distance before her, the sign-post of the inn she had come so many miles to seek. Her heart beat high with hope and anxious expectation as she neared the door. There was but one thought that cast a gloom upon her spirits, and that was, that she had to be the bearer of the mournful intelligence of his wife's death to the good man, in whose kind protecting arms she hoped so soon to be clasped.

And now the inn-door came in sight, and Phœbe quickened her steps; a flush of expectation came across her face, and she forgot her fatigue, and everything else, in the excitement of the moment.

She reached the step of the door, sprung through the porch, and looked anxiously round her with the hope of seeing the object of her search.

"What do you want?" said a woman.

"Robert Greenfield!" gasped Phœbe. "He—he—is here?"

"No, he ain't," the woman calmly replied. "He went to London the day before yesterday."

Phœbe gazed at her for a moment, as if scarcely comprehending what she heard. She was stupified by the unexpected and unwelcome intelligence.

"I tell you," repeated the woman, "he has gone to London; can't you hear?"

Alas! poor Phœbe heard too well. A deadly paleness overspread her face, she clasped her hands, and repeated the words, "Gone! gone!" and fainted away.

There was a great bustle when it was found that Phœbe had fainted, and she was picked up and carried into the parlour of the inn, and a glass of water applied to her pale lips, and various other restoratives were resorted to on the spur of the moment.

At length she recovered, and opening, languidly, her sweet blue eyes, she looked round upon the group of persons that surrounded her for a moment, and then burst into tears, and wept freely and bitterly.

All her fond hopes were at once crushed. The dear friend she had travelled so many weary miles to see once more was gone, and she was homeless, friendless, with nothing but the two pounds which had been given her by the kind old gentleman at Canterbury on which to depend.

The night was now fast approaching, and one by one the idlers who had crowded round the insensible girl dropped off, and she felt that she must immediately decide upon what to do.

"Can I stay here till to-morrow?" she asked, timidly, of the woman who had given her the melancholy intelligence of the departure of the waggoner.

"Yes, you can," replied the woman. "We let beds, of course."

"I can pay," said Phœbe; "I have money."

"Oh!" said the woman, with a smile, "no doubt—no doubt, Miss. I'm sorry you're disappointed."

"Thank you—thank you," said Phœbe, faintly; "I have come very far."

As poor Phœbe spoke, she felt in her breast for the two sovereigns, which had been carefully wrapped in paper by the hostess at the little inn where she had started with the carrier.

A thrill of alarm came over Phœbe. She could not find the little packet. She was sure she had it safe, for she felt it after she had parted with the gardener. Again, with great alarm, she searched her dress; but no, the money was gone, and Phœbe sunk upon a chair, in utter despair. It needed but that as a crowning misery, and the poor girl's wretchedness was complete.

She felt that she had nothing to hope from the compassion of the woman of the inn. She was not rude, absolutely, in her behaviour, but there was a studied coldness about her words and manner which seemed to say,—

"Now everybody take notice, I've neither sympathy nor feelings, and expect ready money, even for a smile."

"May I ask what's the matter, Miss?" she said, in a calm, cold tone.

"I've lost two sovereigns," said Phœbe; "it's all I had. What shall I do?"

"Oh, indeed. Well, Miss, you've not lost them here. Nobody ever lost anything here. As to what you must do, really you must know best. And now I think of it, we haven't a bed to spare, and this room will be wanted soon by the 'Philanthropic Sons of Charity and Goodness,' and they can't bear beggars at all."

"Beggars!" cried Phœbe, starting up; "I've not begged of you, ma'am, yet. I am going."

She walked to the door with a firm step and a flush of pride upon her cheek, and left the inhospitable mansion.

"Hoity toity!" cried the landlady; "my little madam gives herself airs enough; some artful baggage, I'll warrant. Of all things, I hate people without money."

Phœbe never looked behind her at the Lamb and Spectacles, but walked onwards until she got clear of the town, and than she sat down upon a green bank, and wept in pure loneliness of heart.

A houseless, homeless, destitute wanderer she found herself beneath the canopy of Heaven. What should she do?—where find a place to lay her weary limbs and aching head till morning?

As she sat there and sobbed, she heard, at a short distance, the barking of a dog, and she resolved to follow the sound, and beg for leave to lie down somewhere under cover for the night, for she began to shiver with cold, and feel the want of rest.

She rose, and walked along a meadow, and. creeping through a hedge, she came to a little steep path, which led her to the out-buildings of a farm-house.

It was nearly dark as she approached, and at the door of a barn she could see standing an immense mastiff, who was barking, apparently for amusement, for he did not seem to be regarding anything with a hostile manner.

Phœbe drew back, for she was afraid of the dog ; but the animal had seen her, and bounding over a hedge, to her great alarm, he rushed up to her.

The dog seemed to regard her for a few moments very attentively, as if he were conjecturing who and what she was. He then shook his tail, and bounded two or three times round her, as if inviting her to a game of romps forthwith.

" Poor doggy," said Phœbe, and she patted his huge head, at which the kind animal shook his tail more violently than ever, and whined and barked round her in an ecstasy of delight.

Phœbe walked towards the barn-door, and looked in. The floor was covered with clean straw and hay, and the dog bounded in and rolled over among it a great many times.

Poor Phœbe was very weary, and she walked to the further end of the barn and sat down, and the dog walked up to her, and sat down too.

Sleep came upon her, and she slowly sunk down among the straw in a deep slumber.

The dog looked at her very quietly, and with a great air of understanding ; then he licked her hand, and walking to the door of the barn, he gave one bark, which seemed a sort of general defiance to society at large ; he sat himself down as a sentinel at the entrance, to guard the repose of the gentle Phœbe, who he evidently considered was entirely under his care and protection, for he never closed an eye the whole night long.

The morning sun was streaming brightly through the numerous crevices in the sides of the barn when Phœbe awoke, and upon her slightest movement the dog was at her side, and commenced a series of gambols, which perfectly astonished Phœbe. Her former thoughts occurred to her of seeking for employment at one of the manufactories, and she rose and left the barn, followed for a good distance by the dog, who seemed very much chagrined at her departure, and commenced a barking and whining, that was answered by other dogs at different farm-houses, in all sorts of tones.

Phœbe proceeded to the town to put her determination into practice ; and as she neared it, she saw a miserable-looking troop of ragged children hastening on before her. She followed them until they came to a high wall, in which were two heavy gates, through which they passed.

" This," thought Phœbe, " must be one of the factories."

She advanced to the gates, and looked in. Nothing of a very inviting character presented itself to her eyes. Long high ranges of buildings were all she could see, dotted all over with little windows.

As she stood irresolute for a few minutes, gazing in at the open gates of the factory, a man came to shut them, and observing her, he said,—

" Well, what do you want ? Do you come for Mr. Russet, eh ?"

" No," said Phœbe ; " I—I want some work. I am poor, and have no friends here. I want some employment, if you please, sir."

" The deuce you do ! Where do you come from ?"

" From London. I came to meet a friend, but he is gone, and I know not what to do. I thought I might get employment here."

" There's employment enough here," said the man with an oath. " Come in ; you shall see Mr. Russet ; he may take you on."

Phœbe stepped in, and the gates were closed behind her.

A confused hum of many sounds met her ears; the roaring of furnaces and the clanking of machinery filled the air. The atmosphere was hot and sultry, and Phœbe was a few moments before she could breathe freely in that contaminated medium.

"Follow me," said the man, and he led Phœbe into a kind of office, where he left her, and presently returned with a man of coarse and revolting features, who had but one eye, and glanced at her for a few moments with the other, in a singular disagreeable manner.

"What can you do?" he cried, addressing Phœbe.

"I am willing, sir, to do anything," she replied. "I am friendless and homeless, and have no means of returning to those who would help me."

"Humph!—you don't want any wages, of course?" said the man.

"Food and a home is all I wish for," replied Phœbe, mildly.

"Put her on, Morgan," said Mr. Russet, turning to the man who had spoken to Phœbe at the gates; "let her sleep at Mother Ross's."

"Am I to have employment, sir?" asked Phœbe.

"Why, we've lots of brats here, but we will see if you can do anything. No d—d skulking here, mind—work's work."

The man who was called Morgan signified to Phœbe to follow him, and he conducted her through many rooms, where the clanking and thumping of the machinery was to Phœbe nearly deafening. She was, likewise, greatly alarmed by the rapid revolution of all kinds of shafts and wheels above her head.

She was placed to an employment which, although not difficult, still required the nicest attention, and for the whole day did poor Phœbe fag at it until her fingers became so sore, and ached so fearfully, that she left off in great pain.

"D— you," said a harsh voice behind her; "I suppose you come here to play?" and at the same moment she felt a heavy blow across the shoulders.

Poor Phœbe was astonished at this treatment, and, turning round, she saw the man with the one eye glaring ferociously at her.

A bell now sounded, and the business of the day was over. Phœbe had had a scanty meal given her, and she was now told to inquire for Mother Ross's, where she could sleep.

"And let me catch you outside the gates a minute after five in the morning, and I'll brain you," said the man with the one eye.

Phœbe had made her determination, when she received the blow in the factory: and the moment she was clear of the gates, she hurried off, without speaking to any one, in the direction of the open country, resolving never again to set foot within the hateful walls.

"Better, oh! better," she cried, "to live in the green fields, or die there, than be beaten by that cruel man."

CHAPTER XXIV.

PHŒBE resolved once more to claim the protection of the mastiff dog, and sleep in the barn till the morning, when she could better decide upon what she had best do than now, when she was wearied with a day's slavery.

Again she found the faithful animal at his post, and was welcomed with every demonstration of joy. He frisked about Phœbe, whined, barked, and seemed never tired of testifying his pleasure at seeing her once again.

Phœbe patted and caressed the faithful creature, and shed tears to think that that poor dog was kinder to her than any human being she had seen that day.

Phœbe was about to enter the barn, when she was suddenly interrupted by the voice of a woman, who, in a cracked and termagant voice, cried out,—

"Ay, ay—who's that, I should like to know?—what next?"

The poor girl turned round, and saw a thin, wiry-looking woman, who stood at the door of the barn in an attitude of surprise at Phœbe's assurance.

"I beg your pardon, ma'am," said Phœbe, "but I have nowhere to sleep, and the dog let me into the barn, ma'am. I did not mean any harm, indeed I didn't."

"And pray who may you be that don't mean any harm?" said the woman, a little mollified by Phœbe's humble address and gentle manner.

"I want something to do," said Phœbe; "I have no friends here."

"Something to do, you want?" cried the woman. "Can you nurse children, weed a garden, clean up a place well, and be tidy?"

"I think I can, ma'am," said Phœbe; "I'd do my best, you may be sure."

"Here, Benjamin!" screamed the woman; "Benjamin, come here—come here, I say, this moment!"

"Well, well, missus, I'se coming," said a farming man as he made his appearance.

"You idle good-for-nothing wretch!" cried the mistress; "just look at that girl."

"Yes, missus, I sees her. She bean't a highwayman, missus, be she?"

"You fool!—I mean to let her be here to weed and do odd jobs. Do you hear?"

"Oh! yes, I hears. Isn't there a pond, my dear, at the end of the lane?" said the man, addressing Phœbe.

"Yes," said Phœbe; "I saw it yesterday; what of it?"

"Oh, nothing; on'y you've got a missus now as wouldn't be pleased even if you were to bring it here in tea-spoonfulls."

"You wretch!" cried his mistress, bestowing a score of thumps on his broad back. "You hardened villain! I'll teach you to say I'm exacting and difficult to please. Take that, you rascal. I don't why I keep you."

"Cos nobody else 'll stay with you, missus," said the man with a grin; "and I'm so wery good-natured I doesn't like to desart you, nohow."

"Oh, I'll give it to you to-morrow, you wretch. Come along, little girl—come this way, directly."

Poor Phœbe little knew into whose hands she had fallen when she accepted the post of slave of all work with Mrs. Barnacle, for so the woman was named who surprised her in the barn.

Mrs. Marrables was merciful in comparison to Mrs. Barnacle, who, at the time that Phœbe Grainger took refuge in her barn, was without any female domestic, and had a prosecution hanging over her head for the ill-usage of the last one who had been in her employment.

Mrs. Marrables was vexatious, passionate, and tyrannical; but Mrs. Barnacle was cruel; and Phœbe was not long in discovering the melancholy fact, although she remained for some months in the service.

Mrs. Barnacle had no children of her own, but she kept a kind of boarding-school on her premises for a limited number of young children. She had at the time that poor Phœbe came in her way four of these little unfortunates, who were immediately handed over to Phœbe's entire care—a blessed change for the children.

In addition to the care of the young children, the oldest of whom was not eight years of age, Phœbe was expected by Mrs. Barnacle to work in the garden, wash, feed the poultry, cook, and make herself a perfect slave from morning till night.

All this Phœbe would have borne humbly and meekly, and striven to do her best, but the cruel beatings she received from Mrs. Barnacle, and which that lady seemed to feel a fiendish kind of spirit in inflicting, broke her spirits, and in a month's time the poor orphan girl looked pale, sickly, and languid. The end, however, was rapidly approaching, and the bright sun of the suffering girl's prosperity and joy was near its rising.

The winter was approaching with rapid strides, and an occasional storm of wind and rain had swept round the farm-house, scattering the leaves from the trees, and in a few short hours effecting a greater change upon the vegetable kingdom than a month's calm progress of the season could have accomplished.

Poor Phœbe was scant of clothing, and her mistress would give her nothing to add to her comforts, but met all her gentle remonstrances with blows from the first weapon that came to hand.

The faithful dog was Phœbe's only comfort. At all times that he could possibly get at her he was her delighted companion, and many a time had the persecuted girl crept to his side, and wept bitterly, after some scene of violence with Mrs. Barnacle.

Often and often she thought of flying from the house, but the longer she remained, the weaker her resolution to fly became. The harsh usage had for a time almost succeeded in blunting her feelings and her judgment, and it was evident that it must be some more than ordinary act of oppression that could now nerve the weakened and spirit-subdued child to any measure of active resistance.

Mrs. Barnacle would not have willingly parted with Phœbe, for the poor girl was friendless, and there was no one who would interfere to inquire into her condition.

An action at law had been brought against Mrs. Barnacle for gross ill-usage to a little girl, who had been with her before she encountered Phœbe in the barn; and as the time for its decision drew near, and Mrs. Barnacle began to tremble for its result, her acidity of temper materially increased, and poor Phœbe felt the full measure of her wrath, as being the only living thing, excepting the young children, upon whom she could with impunity vent it.

Benjamin, her only farming servant, laughed at and defied her. The children had parents, such as they were, who might have been stirred up to vengeance. Even the dog might probably have bitten her, so upon Phœbe it all fell. She was alone, and too weak to resent ill-usage. She had no friends, and, therefore, was a safe victim.

The day for the decision of Mrs. Barnacle's lawsuit at length arrived, and she departed to the county town at which it was tried to learn the result.

Numerous were the charges and injunctions she gave to Phœbe before she set out, coupled with awful threats and denunciations regarding household affairs in her absence, and finally, wrapped in many shawls and handkerchiefs, to preserve her sweet person from the cold, Mrs. Barnacle, in a state of fiery and nervous impatience, fairly started.

How quiet and pleasant everything was in the absence of Mrs. Barnacle. The day was fine, and Phœbe and the dog and the children fairly enjoyed themselves for a little time, without fear or restraint.

Mrs. Barnacle had particularly ordered Phœbe to keep in the fire, and have a pair of slippers properly aired, to be ready immediately upon her return, in which she might thrust her victorious or defeated feet, as the case might be.

Now Phœbe, in the joy of her heart at one half day's happiness, forgot both fire and slippers, and, with the dog and the children, wandered about the farm-yard, feeding the ducks, chasing the chickens, and pulling the flowers to adorn their hair.

The evening was approaching, and the clear sky began to lower,—a portentous redness in the west seemed to betoken a coming storm; not a breath of wind stirred a leaf upon a tree, and Nature seemed preparing herself for something unusual.

It was early as to time, but the darkness increased rapidly, and Phœbe and her companions, becoming rather alarmed at the appearance of things in the open air, sought the shelter of the kitchen.

The fire was out, and Phœbe forgot the slippers altogether.

In the meantime matters had gone rather crossly with Mrs. Barnacle. She had been recognised by the mob, which always attends the assizes of a county town, as the defendant in the action for cruelty to a girl, which it was well known was pending, and she had been duly hooted and groaned at as she passed into the court.

Then the case had gone all against her. The judge said she might think herself well off that the prosecution was not a criminal one, and the jury awarded fifty pounds damages against her, accompanied by a strong reprobation of her conduct. Then, as she came out, the mob hooted and groaned again, and, in fact, nothing of a satisfactory nature at all occurred to Mrs. Barnacle, except that she succeeded in seizing one man who hooted, by the hair of his head, and pummelled him well, to the universal delight of the mob.

Was it to be wondered at, then, that Mrs. Barnacle returned home in an unusually irritated frame of mind, which was further heightened and influenced by a shower of rain, which caught her just within sight of her home, and drenched her to the skin?

No. 18

Phœbe had just struck a light, and was hastening to rekindle the fire, with the hope that before Mrs. Barnacle came home she might repair the effects of her forgtefulness, and so escape the certain punishment which she knew would be inflicted, when that lady, wet and furious, bounced into the room.

"What!" she exclaimed, "no fire, and I drenched to the skin! You little wretch!—you reptile!—I'll be the death of you, I will, and they may hang me."

"Oh! ma'am, ma'am," cried Phœbe, "I forgot it, indeed I did, but I'll light it again in a moment. See, please, ma'am, it's all ready laid."

Mrs. Barnacle was not, however, to be thus turned away from her wrath, and she flew at poor Phœbe like an infuriated tigress.

"You little villain!—you hardened little wretch!—I'll see who'll make me pay fifty pounds, and the deuce knows how many lawyer's expenses besides, for you."

The rain was coming down fast, but Phœbe rushed out of the house into garden, pursued by Mrs. Barnacle.

The poor girl fled with all the precipitation of despair; but catching her foot in something on the ground, she fell, and was immediately seized by Mrs. Barnacle.

"Oh! you'd get away, would you?" she cried.

"Mercy! oh, mercy!" cried Phœbe.—"Oh, madam, mercy! mercy!"

Mrs. Barnacle heeded not her cries, but seized a stake from the garden, and commenced beating poor Phœbe with it most unmercifully.

The poor orphan would most probably have met with her death under the blows of her savage assailant, had not Benjamin heard the tumult, and hurried to her assistance.

He rushed headlong at his mistress, and without the least hesitation upset her into a large gooseberry-bush, while the dog, who had likewise, hearing Phœbe's cries, rushed to the scene of action, with a loud bark, grasped her by the ankle, and growled his dissent at her proceedings.

Phœbe in an instant sprung to her feet, and with a loud shriek of pain, flew from the garden, and rushed swiftly from the place for ever.

The night had set in unusual darkness, and the wind blew in fearful gusts across the open country, as Phœbe Grainger fled from the farm-house, where she had experienced such bitter usage.

It was evident that the night would be one of fury and storm. The clouds were careering through the sky at a rapid rate, and the attentive ear might catch the low mutterring of distant thunder. For a moment there would come a gust of wind, which seemed to threaten destruction to everything in its progress; then, again a dead stillness would prevail, as if the wind, from the remotest corners of the earth, was collecting for another exercise of its tremendous power.

Occasionally a wild, dashing deluge of rain would fall, and then subside so suddenly, that the wanderer in that night of storm might well wonder from whence it proceeded.

An inky darkness fell upon the face of the earth, and the trembling Phœbe had not the slightest notion in what direction she was proceeding.

The excitement and hurry of her spirits prevented her from fully appreciating, as she would have done any other time, the terrors of the night.

Wildly the orphan girl hurried forward, unmindful of whither she bent her rapid course. She crossed meadows, crept through hedges, and dashed across roads and footpaths for a full hour, without any relaxation of her speed. Her garments were thoroughly saturated with rain, and they clung to her in a manner greatly to impede her progress.

A flash of lightning was now so vivid and intense, that Phœbe recoiled, before it lit up, for a single instant, with dazzling and unearthly splendour, the whole country for many miles. This was immediately followed by a clap of thunder, which seemed to shake the very earth to its centre, and which was repeated by echoes for many minutes, until it died away in indistinct mutterings in the far distance.

Phœbe now became more alive each moment to her real situation. As the pain of the blows which had been inflicted upon her, and the wild excitement of her feelings gradually subsided, she became conscious of the full horrors of the situation into which she was plunged.

The wind now increased to a fearful gale, and Phœbe crept despairingly under the shelter of a hedge, with the resolution of waiting till the fury of the storm had passed.

Far, however, from such being the case, the anger of the Heavens seemed to increase each moment. Flash succeeded flash of blue lightning, with frightful rapidity, and the fearful thunder kept up a deafening noise.

Phœbe clasped her hands, and sunk upon the ground in terror and despair. She felt as if she must inevitably die in that fearful tempest. She could gain no comfort from a single reflection : there was not the smallest ray of hope to lighten the despair of her mind ; it was the will of Heaven, she thought, that she should die in the midst of that dreadful warfare of the elements.

She covered her eyes with her hands to shut out the glare of the forked lightning, and in that dreadful moment of despair she recalled to mind the different scenes of her short, but varied existence.

The poor persecuted orphan child seemed to have been hurried by fate to that dreary spot, there to render up her pure spirit, after the many trials it had undergone, to Him who, in His wisdom, had appointed its mortal career.

Phœbe was roused from these gloomy meditations by a loud crash, followed by a peal of thunder more formidable than any she had yet heard.

She started to her feet, and gazed wildly around her.

A majestic tree, which stood within a hundred paces of where she had taken refuge, had been struck by the lightning, and splintered to the earth. The remains of its trunk was in a blaze, and looked like some gigantic torch, set up by the hand of Heaven, to guide the wanderer in the wilderness.

Phœbe was much alarmed ; but by the light of the blazing tree she saw well all around her. Nothing she saw was familiar to her eye, but a new hope sprung up in her breast, and she resolved to make one more effort to reach a human habitation.

She struck into a narrow path, which she observed at no great distance, and battling, with what little strength she possessed, the fury of the wind, she slowly struggled onwards.

Poor Phœbe was soon out of reach of the beams of light from the burning tree, but still she walked onwards in the pitchy darkness, determined that as long as she had sufficient strength still to proceed, she would not abandon all hope.

For upwards of a mile the wearied and exhausted girl struggled feebly forward. The lightning now was not so frequent in its flashes, nor so intense in its brilliancy ; but still at intervals, as it lit up the dreary scene, Phœbe would look anxiously round her, but no sight or sound of human habitation rewarded her toils.

The rain now came down in torrents, and with such force and impetu-

osity, that Phœbe could scarcely keep her footing. Large pools of water collected in her path, through which, in the darkness of the night, she waded.

Slowly now she dragged herself forwards—a dimness came across her eyes—her limbs trembled, and seemed about to refuse her further support. Once she fell, and for an instant she thought she would remain on the wet ground, and at once abandon hope, but such was not to be the melancholy fate of the orphan.

The eye of Heaven was upon the friendless girl, and that friend of the afflicted who, in their greatest woe, never deserts the pure and gentle, was guiding the course of the poor child. She rose, and still onwards she urged her way.

Amid the darkness which was upon all things, she could, nevertheless, perceive a little cluster of trees immediately in front of her. To these she hastened, as she thought they might afford her shelter until the heavy rain passed away. She neared them, and plunged into their thickest re- cesses.

Here, again, she was doomed to be disappointed, for the rain had been so heavy and so copious, that the trees had ceased to afford shelter to the ground beneath them, and the branches and leaves kept up a constant dripping of water, which was fully equal to the rain in the open fields. It did not, however, fall with so much violence, and Phœbe preferred to be under the partial protection of the trees.

She waited for some time, but the rain abated not; and as she stood inactive, an icy chillness crept over her frame, and it seemed to her as if a cold hand was laid upon her heart.

In a few moments more she felt she should sink to the earth, never to rise again. There was intense agony now in that idea. The feeling of self-preservation had taken strong possession of her mind, and she clung still to hope.

One more effort—one more, she thought—and she fought her way through the entangled underwood of the little wood in which she was. She was soon clear of the plantation, and again emerged into the open country.

Sleet and hail was now mixed with the rain, and the wind, blowing in fearful gusts, would sometimes send such a mixture of hailstones and rain into Phœbe's face, that she was nearly blinded.

She raised her eyes after one of these attacks, and through the thick mist of hail, rain, and sleet, she thought she saw some large object rearing itself high in the sky.

Phœbe strained her eyes in the direction in which she saw it, with the hope of discovering some house or human habitation of some sort.

As she came nearer and nearer, the huge object assumed a more distinct form. At first sight she thought it was a large tree. A blinding shower of hail now for a few minutes entirely prevented her from seeing distinctly, and she was obliged to screen her face and eyes with her hands. Still, however, she dragged her wearied limbs onwards, and when she could again look forward with any degree of safety, she saw that the large object which rose so high in the Heavens was a mill.

A feeling of hope, stronger than ever, sprung up in the mind of Phœbe Grainger at the sight; and as she stood for an instant gazing at the black mass which the windmill presented to her eyes, she forgot the raging storm, and tears of thankfulness, that she had at last seen some hope of human aid, trickled down her cheeks.

There was one chance of succour which it had not till that moment oc- curred to her mind to try. She might call for assistance, and the wind

might carry her feeble voice to the ears of some one who would be the destitute orphan's friend.

"Help! help!" cried Phœbe, as loudly as she could, but the moaning of the wind seemed to her more than sufficient to drown her voice.

She was now very near the mill, and she thought she could perceive a flickering light from some low building close to it.

"Help! help!" again she cried.

Again and again the dashing hail and sleet impeded sight, voice, and movement of the faint and weary girl.

Onwards she tottered, for she could now plainly perceive a ray of light streaming from the latticed window of a cottage, close to the basement of the mill, against which she could hear the hail wildly beating.

Oh! how in her inmost heart the orphan Phœbe blessed that ray of light! It gilded, with a bright and holy lustre, the dreary melancholy scene. There was blissful hope in its mild, gentle radiance—it spoke eloquently to her heart of warmth, comfort, and happiness—a new vigour seemed, for a moment, imparted to her limbs. Forward she rushed towards the cottage by the mill.

And now she saw the door opened—she heard the bark of a dog—she was nearly at the threshold.

"Help! help!—oh! pity and protect me," she cried, and sunk insensible at the door.

CHAPTER XXV.

How gently and calmly onwards flows the tide of time when the beings who float upon its surface are borne upwards by hope and joy,—when day succeeds day, each rising with its predecessor in the calm happiness of its progress—when the sun rises upon joyful anticipation, and sinks upon content and peace—when happy slumber succeeds cheerful labour, and the joy of the pure heart beams in beauty from sparkling eyes, and life is like a long happy dream of innocence and gentle hope.

Oh! who would exchange cheerful and contented poverty for the fever of ambition ?—the ambition to be what ?—the envied possessor of that wealth which the pallid heart has no longer the capacity to enjoy! the ambition to be feared—for how few of the great and wealthy are truly loved for their own sakes merely! Pure affection is to be sought for where the true heart has nothing to give but its own rich treasures of joy and gushing tenderness, and nothing to expect to wish for in return but the throbbing love of a kindred spirit.

Four years had rolled onwards since the orphan, Phœbe Grainger, fell fainting at the cottage door of Gilbert, the miller ; four happy, happy years. The trials and vicissitudes of the poor girl seemed passed for ever, and she now looked back upon the scenes of her former life as she would have remembered and reflected upon the incidents of a drama or a romance.

The hue of health had returned to her cheeks, and Phœbe Grainger was happy.

It was in the middle of August, and early in the morning, but the golden sun had risen, and was shedding a yellow radiance over every object ; the birds were gaily singing, the dew drops yet trembled on each blade of grass, and the sweet flowers which bloomed in the garden of the cottage of the contented miller were slowly opening their blossoms to the sweet influence of the god of day.

Troops of gaudy butterflies were skimming from flower to flower; the swallows were flitting about in mazy flights, and taking their parting glances at the summer, before they started on their rapid flight to other climes, where they might still be cheered by the sunbeams long after they had, in their prime and beauty, deserted our own sea-girt isle.

It was in sooth a lovely morning as ever shone out of the blue Heavens.

And now a little casement in the cottage opened, and the fairest flower, among all the fair flowers that bloomed in beauty around that spot, appeared.

A girl looked out, and, as she marked the beauty of the awakening day, she smiled, and shook back from her face the long fair ringlets of hair, and burst into a song of joy.

I LOVE THE BIRDS AND FLOWERS.

" There dwelt afar a gentle maid,
   Her home was near the sea ;
She loved the happy birds and flowers,
   Which bloomed so fair and free.
Her father's halls were rich and rare,
   More stately could not be—
And oft sweet sounds of minstrelsy
   Came wafting o'er the lea ;
And suitors wooed the gentle maid,
   While swiftly flew the hours,
And to each ardent swain she said.—
      I love the birds and flowers,
      I love the birds and flowers.

" One boasted of his deeds in war,
   And many a foeman slain ;
Another of his riches rare,
   But ah ! twas all in vain.
A fair youth, on a milk-white steed,
   In tender accents sued her ;
The rose-bud bloomed upon his cheek,
   As whisperingly he wooed her.
Then blushed the happy gentle maid,
   As passed the fleeting hours,
She took the youth who, whispering, said,
      He loved the birds and flowers,
      He loved the birds and flowers.''

She was a lovely girl, who thus, in the pure gladness of her young heart, breathed such pure melody. Sixteen summers could not have more than passed over her head. There was in her face an expression of almost infantine beauty. It was the gentle, guileless heart which shone through every speaking feature.

She possessed that rare charm, a healthful bloom without coarseness ; and, in truth, Phœbe, the Miller's Maid, had more than realized in her more matured loveliness the fair promise of her early years.

The casement at which she appeared was that of her own little bed-chamber, and the clustering roses hung around it in a luxuriant beauty.

Who could have recognised in the charming and happy girl, who, with beaming eyes and pleasing smiles, tended the flowers upon the window-sill of her pretty chamber, singing, in the joy of her young heart, gay snatches of happy songs, the deserted, beaten, and despairing orphan child, who had begged for mercy from a Mrs. Marrables and a Mrs. Barnacle? And yet it was, indeed, the same Phœbe Grainger—the same girl, who, in her state of orphan destitution and despair, had laid down in the little wood, which was now within her sight, and thought it would be happiness to die.

"Ah! Andy, Andy," she cried, as a large dog arrived under her window, and whined and testified in every possible manner his joy at seeing her.

The door of the cottage now opened, and Gilbert, the miller, appeared. He cast his eyes to the mill immediately, and for a moment said nothing. Then, with a variety of nods of the head, he was about to return into the cottage.

Phœbe had watched with laughing eyes his movements, and now, just as he was half within the door, she called to him.

"Father, dear father, won't you speak to Phœbe?"

The miller looked up, and although an appearance of vexation had been upon his face, it gave way at once as he saw the fair face of Phœbe peeping laughingly from the little casement.

"My dear child," he said, "how be'st thee? Bless thee! How long hast thou been up, my Phœbe?"

"Oh! father, not long, indeed. But you know my poor flowers want attention early this dry weather."

"Ah! girl, thee be as good to thee flowers, and thee little pet lamb, and thee kid, as thee be to anybody else. Thee be good to all, thee be, my girl, because thee be good theeself."

"But you gave me the lamb, you know, father."

"Ah! and George he gave thee the kid from his wages."

A slight blush came over Phœbe's cheek as the honest miller spoke, and she was excessively busy tying up a straggling branch of roses.

"But you, dear father," she said, "you gave me most of all! You gave me a kind welcome when I was a poor houseless orphan, without a friend in the wide world. You gave me a dear, happy home, and took the little stranger kindly to your heart. I—I—God bless you, dear father."

Phœbe brushed away a tear from her eye, and smiled sweetly on the miller.

"Hold thee tongue, my girl, will thee?" he cried, rubbing his nose vehemently with the skirt of his coat. "Thee hast given to me and my good old dame more than we can ever give to thee. Thee hast given us, my Phœbe, happiness, my girl. Thy coming was a blessing. We can give thee but little. But thou hast given us what no money or cunning, my dear Phœbe, could give to any one—love and joy. Bless thee, my girl, bless thee! Thee hast been a blessing to Gilbert the miller, and far distant be the day when he shall no longer see thee fair face. I—I—love thee, my girl, better than the dear old mill. Come down, my dear. I will wait here for thee."

Phœbe was in a moment at his side, and the good miller, with a lustrous tear in his eye, kissed the fair brow of the beautiful girl.

"Father, you looked vexed when I first saw you. What's the matter?"

"Why, my girl, isn't it enough to vex any one? I forgot it when I saw thee sweet face peeping out among the roses; but don't thee see, the mill is as close shut up as a church on a week day? And there be George and Giles, and Tim Miggles a-snoring away, I'll be bound, like so many bacon pigs. Oh, I'll be at them! I'll tell 'e what I'll do, my girl. Some morning, I'll fire the old blunderbuss clean off at the mill, and if that doant waken 'em, drat it, I doant know what will. Hey-dey, what here?"

As the miller spoke, a young man breathless with running, and without his hat, arrived, and without appearing to see the miller, he flew to Phœbe with a bunch of flowers in his hand.

"Dear Phœbe," he said, "good morning. My dear Phœbe, I—"

"Well, that's uncommonly cool," said the miller, aside.

"You see, my dear Phœbe, you wanted some of the variegated dahlias, and you know nobody had them but Farmer Hodgson; and—"

"The deuce!" cried the miller, "you don't mean to say you've been to Farmer Hodgson?"

"Oh! sir, good morning, sir; I—I—really—you're looking uncommonly well, sir—a—a good morning, sir. How—are your—"

"Hold thee tongue, will 'e?"

Phœbe smiled and took the flowers.   "Oh," she said, "they are indeed beautiful."

"Dost thee mean to say," cried the miller, "that thee hast been eleven miles and back again, to Farmer Hodgson's?"

"Ye—ye—yes, sir.   I—I gave him your respects, sir,—and—and—you know, my dear—"

"Eh?   Art thee mad?"

"Oh! I beg your pardon.   I—I thought—you see—"

"Thee thought thee was making love to my girl, Phœbe, did thee? George, George, thee art a good lad, and I like thee, as thee knows; but my Phœbe is the pride of my old heart, and I love her dearer—"

"Oh! sir, my kind benefactor," cried George, with much emotion, "you to whom I owe so much.   I do love Phœbe, and I would leave the mill this moment, if—if—"

"Thee hast left the mill too long, deuce take thee," cried the miller; but his kind voice belied the anger of his words.   "And hark, master George, if my little girl wants flowers, and thee knows even where to get them, if thee dare—a—a—hang thee, thee be no true lad if thee wouldn't go a hundred miles for her!"

Phœbe and George both laughed as the honest miller, in the frankness of his heart, expressed a sentiment so very different from what he intended.

"Go thee ways, go thee ways," cried the miller.   "Open the mill, open the mill."

As Gilbert spoke, a door in the mill opened, and there appeared at it an athletic young man, whose coal-black hair and eyes and dark complexion contrasted forcibly with the blue eyes and fair hair of George, who had now nearly reached the mill.

"Giles, Giles," cried the miller, "how art thou so late?   Thee were not used to lie a-bed.   Come, rouse thee, rouse thee."

"Oh, Gilbert, Gilbert!" cried the dame, his wife, coming from the cottage, "thee must make an alteration, I tell thee.   Here's that idle Tim Miggles: he's of no use at all."

"I'm afraid not, I'm afraid not," said the miller, with a sigh and a shake of the head.   "When once people take to making verses, of what use can they be?"

"What, indeed," cried the dame.   "Come in, my dear Phœbe.   Bless you, my love, what a colour thou hast got this morning, to be sure."

"Where is Tim?" asked the miller.

"Where, indeed," cried the dame.   "You may well ask.   I'll be bound he's been up all night with his poetry nonsense."

"And that makes him quite unfit to do his work in the day.   What a thing that poetry is!"

"Oh, a most dreadful thing, Gilbert."

"I never knew but one good poet," said the miller, "and that be he who said,

'When the wind blows,
Then the mill goes.'

Now that is poetry."

"I'll ferret master Tim out, I'll warrant me," cried the dame.   "Bless us and save us!   Thee took the creature for an odd man, Gilbert, and an odd man he be likely to prove.   The mill will be burnt down some of these nights, I'll be bound, for he steals candle-ends and sits up a-nights to read poetry and such-like nonsense."

"The mill burned down!" cried the miller; "the deuce take him."

"He's a foolish fellow, but so good-tempered," said Phœbe.

"Good-tempered, forsooth," cried the dame, "he'd better be ill-tempered and do his work."

As she spoke, she advanced to the mill and called loudly,—
"Tim, Tim, you lazy fellow! Tim Miggles, Tim Miggles!"
But no Tim Miggles answered.
"There's a light in the cow-house," said Giles, from the mill.
The dame immediately rushed to a little barn, which was used as a cow-house, and in a few moments returned, dragging with her Tim Miggles.
In Tim's hand was a small lump of clay, in which was stuck a lighted candle, and in the other was a little book.
"You idle fellow," cried the dame, "what do you mean?"
"I'll go to bed, missus; I'll go to bed," cried Tim. "On my bed I'll lay my head; in sweet repose, shall sink my—my nose."
"Come, come," cried the miller, "to your work, lad, to your work, and leave making verses to those who have got nothing better to do."
"Missus," said Tim, "can you tell me a rhyme?"
"I'll tell thee a clout o' thee ears, thee idle fellow!" cried the dame; and dealing at the same moment a blow upon Tim's back, the candle and book were both jerked from his hands, the latter of which the dame immediately secured.
"What nonsense is this?" she cried, handing the book to the miller who deliberately put on his spectacles to look at it.
"Oh, that's a beautiful work," said Tim; "it's called 'The Kitten's Lament; or, the Lost Tail;' and it begins this here way :—

"There was a kitten,
Who was a sitten
All upon the floor,
When wop fell the knife,
And, on my life,
Cut off her tail clean and it wouldn't grow no more."

"Was there ever such stuff?" cried the dame, tearing the book into fragments, and scattering them over the garden. "Oh! Tim, Tim, you'll come to no good."

"Oh! missus, missus, what have you done? You've tored it. Oh dear! oh, dear!"

"Be off with you," cried the miller, "be off to your work. I don't know why I keep you; but I suppose if I was to turn you off you'd be starved. Ah! wife, wife, we must just make the best use we be able of this poor fellow. But we'll have no more poets, dame, at the mill."

"Poets, indeed!" cried the dame; "I'm sick of 'em—an idle set! They've ruinated that poor foolish fellow, that they have."

"There's the mill, and I'm a standing still. I'll go and work just like a turk. Oh, dear! oh, dear! if I could but find a rhyme for Phœbe, I'd be a happy genius. But it's very difficult—it's impossible. Maybe isn't a good 'un—maybe, Phœbe—Phœbe, maybe."

"What do you say about Phœbe?" asked George.

"Eh?—Does he dare to mention Phœbe?" cried Giles.

"Can either of you tell me a rhyme to Phœbe? I've been a trying at it for five weeks, and I haven't done it yet. It's wery afflicting; oh, dear! oh, dear!"

George laughed; but Giles, who had not George's happy temperament, said,—

"Can you tell me a rhyme for a fool's head?"

"Yes," said Tim. "Giles, the miller's man, who stares at Phœbe's window instead o' going to bed."

"Ha!" cried George, "was this so?"

"And if it was," cried Giles; "what then?"

"Then, Giles," cried George, while his lip quivered with emotion, "we must understand each other. Hear me."

"No," cried Giles; "hear me. I have been at the mill afore thee were known to Phœbe—I loved her afore thee came—I love her now."

"Phœbe's heart," said George, "is at her own disposal. You speak plainly."

"I do speak plainly," cried Giles, with excitement; "I care not who know it. The whole world may. I love the miller's child—I love her, and by my life I'll have her."

"With her free consent only shall you dare so much as look at her with hope," said George. "You never shall have her. Phœbe can never be your's. You dream of improbabilities. I love her, and will win her gentle heart, if it be to be won, by pure devotion and honest love."

"Beware of me, George!—beware!" cried Giles, fiercely. "I will not be crossed, man. I love Phœbe more than thee can. She was kind to me afore you came. I will be revenged."

"Phœbe never gave you any encouragement," said George. "You are disappointed, and I can allow for your passion."

"Liar!" cried Giles; "thee shall never have her while I live."

"Say but that word again," cried George, "and I'll hurl you to the earth!"

"Liar!" cried Giles.

In a moment the two were struggling together, and Tim called loudly for the miller to come and separate them.

"Master! master!—come, be quick—here's a row—bring a stick! George is walloping of Giles like a pussy on the tiles."

The miller hastened to the spot, and at his approach the incensed rivals separated.

"What be the meaning of this?" cried the miller. "George, I thought better of thee. Giles, Giles, thee art ever violent, and I fear thee hast been doing wrong."

"I am sorry, sir," said George, "that I lost my temper, but he called me by a name which no honest man could hear himself called, unmoved."

"And what did thee do?"

"I own I struck him, sir."

"Then," continued the miller, "I cannot interfere for thee. Thee should'st have left me to do my will, and thee should have been protected."

"I called him a liar," said Giles, "because he said I should never call Phœbe mine."

"And what right have you," said the miller, "to call my child thine?"

"I don't care who knows it," said Giles, sullenly; "I love her, and by Heaven——"

"Hold!" cried the miller. "Do thee not bring wickedness upon theeself by talking of Heaven, when thee only thinks to favour thee own designs."

"Sir," said George, "he goaded me out of temper about Phœbe, and I, unfortunately, struck him. It is a subject upon which I never more will talk to him; but it maddened me to hear him say he would have Phœbe, as if she was not all to be consulted in the matter."

"Now listen, both of you," said the miller.

"And mayhap you'll let me listen, too," said Tim, "for I love Phœbe; oh, dear me, don't I. She is like a little mouse, so sleek, and I love her every day of the week; and when she smiles, oh! lawks a daisy, it's enough to make poor Tim go crazy."

"Peace, fool!" cried Giles.

"No, Giles," said the miller, mildly, "thee art the fool theeself. This poor half-witted lad is made by Heaven what he be, and do not let us speak harshly of God's meanest works."

"Poor Tim," said George, "can be nobody's rival; but Giles is angry with him, because he told how he sat up all night to look in at Phœbe's window."

"This is all very bad, lads," said the miller; "I like thee both, but I love my dear child better, and thee must both leave me, I fear."

Giles and George both looked aghast at this unexpected sentence.

"And when they're gone, I'll grow genteel and slim, and then sweet Phœbe, mayhap, will have poor Tim," said Master Miggles.

"I must not," continued the miller, "have my girl annoyed by thee quarrels. If thee stay, thee must shake hands, and I must hear no more of this."

"From me, sir," said George, "you shall hear of no more violence. I would not give Phœbe one moment's uneasiness for the world; I love her too well. If she prefers Giles, I—I can go to sea, or anywhere, but I will bear him no malice. There's my hand, Giles."

A dark cloud was still on Giles's brow, and he seemed unable to control his fierce passions.

"I dcan't see why I should take thee hand, George," he said. "Before thee came I was as happy as the day is long, but now——"

"As you please," said George, coldly.

"For shame, Giles," said the miller. "I cannot deny that I see you both love my dear girl; but Phœbe will never bestow her hand and heart upon one who bears malice."

Giles sullenly and slowly stretched forth his hand to George and took his.

"I be not a going to bear malice, master," he said; "but it do rile me to see Phœbe smile upon George, and have no welcome for Giles."

"It would rile me, as you call it, a great deal more," said the jolly miller, "if Phœbe smiled upon any man with a bad, unforgiving temper. Thee wert once a good lad, Giles, as ever stepped, and I do grieve to see thee give way to thee passion. Come, lads, to work—to work. What with thee quarrels, and thee love-making, the work goes on queerly enough. Drat thee both, thee will bring the old mill to a stop. Get thee gone, too, Tim, and let us hear no more of thee nonsense and poetry. Thee art nearly as bad as these two young hot bloods, with their love and their quarrels. Thee will drive old Gilbert crazy among thee all."

"Oh, lawks! oh, dear!" cried Tim. "They ain't a going, and my mind on warious agonies wriggles, that pretty Phœbe, with her eyes so blue, won't e'er be Mother Miggles."

CHAPTER XXVI.

In the neighbourhood of the mill was the little village of Haredale, consisting of not above three dozen of white-washed cottages, each with their pretty garden in front, and inhabited principally by industrious families. Sir Herbert Foster, who resided on an estate in the immediate vicinity—that is to say, when he was entirely satiated with the routine of London enjoyments, would come to Haredale, and strive to recruit his exhausted mind on his estate. He was a libertine of the most unflinching character, and the trait of his vices had long been the theme of conversation among the humble inhabitants of the pretty village.

In addition to the white-washed cottages of the humble inhabitants of Haredale, there were several pretty villas scattered about, within a short distance, so that altogether the district was tolerably populous.

In one of these villas dwelt Mr. Olinthus Scrimp, who was an attorney, and much beholden for business to Sir Herbert Foster, whom he held, or pretended to hold, in the very highest veneration and most extraordinary and exalted respect.

Mr. Scrimp had brought a clerk with him from London, who, although a rather favourable specimen of clerks in London, to the class of which he considered himself a distinguished ornament, nevertheless boasted not a few of the peculiarities of attorneys.

Mr. Perk—for so the young gentleman was called—had what he thought a proper contempt for yokels, by which epithet he distinguished the whole of the inhabitants of England who lived out of sight of the Inns of Court and Chancery-lane.

A young man had recently come down from London, and set up as a surgeon in the village, to the great astonishment of the inhabitants, who never had such an animal located among them before, and were all, as Mr. Perk remarked upon the stranger's unexpected arrival, so disgustingly healthy, that there was literally nothing to do, in a general way, for a medical man. Mr. Pomander, the surgeon, however, in the course of a little time hit upon an expedient for procuring the means whereby to live himself, as he ran the chance of being the only sick person in the place, for want of bread, which produced a dire feud in the village, and that was by exciting a desire on the part of the population for unheard-of powders, hair oils, pomatums, washes for the complexion, and such like matters. This he accomplished by giving away divers bottles and little neat boxes, containing such wares, and when once in use, the ladies were seen to resort to Mr. Pomander for a fresh supply of "roseate powder," "pearl dentifrice," "the Sultana of Turkey's imperial hair oil," or "Tippoo Saib's wash for the complexion," which was warranted to restore youth and beauty to everybody, remove wrinkles, and restore dimples, &c. &c.

Now, previous to Mr. Pomander's insidious arrival at Haredale, the barber of the village was in the habit of supplying all kinds of simple cosmetics; but he became so overwhelmed by the names of Mr. Pomander's articles, and backed, as they invariably were, by a—"As a medical man, miss," or "madam," as the case might be, "I beg to recommend you this," that he felt that he stood not the least chance of hereafter disposing of scented lard for bear's grease, or brick-dust for tooth-powder.

These rival parties would sometimes meet at the village ale-house, when many very bitter taunts and sarcasms would proceed from both parties.

It was on the evening of the day on which the misunderstanding had arisen between George and Giles respecting Phœbe, that it becomes necessary, in the due course of our narrative, to introduce the reader to the time-blackened parlour of the Golden Lion, in the village, which was kept by a widow, of most ample proportions.

The ceiling of the well-frequented room had become, by the constant ascent of tobacco smoke, of a dull mahogany colour. The tables were indented, and worn by long service, and the seats of the chairs had become highly polished and slippery from the same cause.

Little artful pieces of wood were stuck on to the walls, and in divers corners, for the convenience of the elbows of the smokers, and altogether the parlour of the Golden Lion was rather a comfortable place than otherwise.

There was one chair with elbows, which was always reserved for a Mr. Thorn, who was an old bachelor, and reputed rich, and whose principal peculiarity consisted in contradicting everybody, upon which everybody would say, "Oh! it's only Mr. Thorn," and put up with the contradiction with the most easy manner in the world.

Upon the evening to which we have alluded, there were several persons assembled in the parlour of the Golden Lion, and Mr. Thorn was in his accustomed seat. Mr. Scrimp was likewise there; and it would appear that some observation had been made which called forth some of the legal acumen of our learned personage.

"Mr. Moss," said the attorney, taking the pipe from his mouth, and speaking with great deliberation to the barber, "there are such things as actions, sir—actions for libel, Mr. Moss—and I really should not feel a bit surprised to be engaged in Pomander v. Moss, for really, Mr. Moss, you are so incautious, that if I were put upon my oath——"

"You'd of course swear anything that was most to your advantage," grumbled Mr. Thorn.

"Now, really, Mr. Thorn," said the lawyer, "your observations are very objectionable; to accuse a man of a distinct disposition to commit perjury."

"Oh! it's only Mr. Thorn," said several voices.

"It's no such thing," said Mr. Thorn.

"I'll tell you what it is, Mr. Scrimp," said Mr. Moss, speaking with great rapidity, "that stuff that Mr. Pomander calls the miraculous tooth-powder of the Empress of Japan's, is nothing in the world but baked carrots grated down, and a little lemon-peel to give it a flavour."

"You don't mean that?" said the lawyer.

"Don't I!" cried Mr. Moss. "I'll tell you what it is, that Pomander is a humbug—a humbug, Mr. Scrimp—an abominable humbug."

"That ain't actionable," cried Mr. Scrimp. "Calling a man a humbug is nothing in the eye of the law, because you see, gentlemen, a—a—that is, because——"

"There's nothing else but humbug," said Mr. Thorn, with great emphasis.

"I only hope one thing," said Mr. Moss, "and that is, that Sir Herbert, when he comes down, won't think proper to patronize Mr. Pomander, for I am of opinion that if he does there'll soon be an end of all law in the land, and we shall all be slaves incarnate."

"Why," said Mr. Scrimp, with a knowing sort of look, "you know Sir Herbert does not care much about patronizing anybody down here but the——"

"Oh, yes," replied Mr. Moss, tapping his nose with his finger, "I understand—the wenches."

"I didn't say anything of the sort," said the lawyer. "Bear witness everybody, I meant the poor—the exemplary poor of the parish."

"You didn't—you know you didn't—you scamp of a lawyer," said Mr. Thorn; "you meant just the contrary; and you know Sir Herbert Foster is a vagabond, and he knows——. All the world are thieves, and they know it. Humph!"

"Quite actionable," muttered Mr. Scrimp to the barber. "All the World v. Thorn—Sir Herbert Foster v. Thorn—Scrimp v. Thorn. Dear me, it's grand."

Mr. Perk now entered the room, without the slightest ceremony to his employer, and sat himself down as coolly as possible; then drawing up his shirt collar, and putting his outward man in other respects to rights, he called for a glass of gin and water, and producing a cigar from his pocket, he, with great effrontery, asked his employer for a light.

Mr. Scrimp winced a little at the familiarity of his clerk; but the real fact was, that Mr. Perk knew two or three professional secrets concerning Mr. Scrimp and Sir Herbert Foster, which made it rather imprudent to aggravate that gentleman, so the dignity of the attorney was obliged to be merged in the safety of the man.

A solemn silence ensued after Mr. Perk's entrance, until that gentleman volunteered a remark, to the following effect,—

"I say, governor, that girl at old Gilbert's mill is a rum 'un, ain't she?"

"Ah!—ah!—hem!" answered Mr. Scrimp.

"No, sir, she's no such thing," said Mr. Thorn. "You're the rum 'un, sir."

"Ah! ah!—very good," said Mr. Perk. "I met Tim Miggles to day, and he told me there had been a spree at the mill. I like a spree vastly. We've such lots of sprees in London, you can't think. Always kick up a spree at White Conduit.—Glorious!—Lots of gals! What do you think of that, Mr. Thorn?"

"I think you're a d—d puppy," growled the old gentleman.

"Oh! you're droll—very droll. By the by, governor, I saw Ralph Freegrove as I came here."

"Ralph Freegrove?" said the attorney.

"Aye, to be sure; as big as ever, as large as life, and five times as natural."

"Then Sir Herbert is coming down, you may be sure."

"Well, I shouldn't wonder; but somehow or another he rather seemed to get out of my way than otherwise. I hallooed after him, but he skulked under the park wall, and mizzled. I'd lay a wager he's come on some reconnoitering expedition, he has. He's a downy one, he is."

"Well, you surprise me," said Mr. Scrimp.

"Do I?" answered Mr. Perk, in an incredulous tone. "Really I thought now you'd a sure to have known he was coming."

"I think I must go," said Mr. Scrimp; "it's getting late, rather."

"It isn't, and you know it," said Mr. Thorn. "You are after some roguery or another."

"He! he! he!" said Mr. Scrimp, as he moved to the door. Some one was coming in at the precise moment, and run against the attorney, who exclaimed,—"Dear me, how do you do, my dear sir? How are you, Mr. Pomander?"

Mr. Pomander was a soft, silky gentleman, and he replied, with a bland smile, to Mr. Scrimp,—

"Oh, perfectly well, I thank you. You are leaving early."

"Business, my dear sir—business, you know, must be attended to."

Mr. Pomander was a great favourite with the landlady of the house, and he had been conversing with her in the bar some time previous to Mr. Scrimp's exit.

Mrs. Staples—for so the hostess was named—was immensely fat, and had, withal, a highly inflamed countenance, at which one might easily imagine a lucifer match might be lit instantaneously. She had heard some of the injurious expressions of Mr. Moss against the Empress of Japan's tooth-powder, and duly amplified upon the same to Mr. Pomander.

"Eh?—really—bless me," said that gentleman, in a soft tone, "did he say so?—Humph!—Dear me, I must gain his entire confidence.— Humph!"

"But ain't it abominable, Mr. Pomander? I am sure the lotion you gave me has done me a world of good. What do you think, my dear sir?"

"For my own part, my dear madam," said Mr. Pomander, "I admire as much as I respect the beautiful bloom on your sweet countenance, madam; but if you prefer a more delicate tint, I think I can manage it, my dear madam."

"You are very kind and obliging, Mr. Pomander; but I think as I am otherwise so exceedingly delicate-looking in every particular, I should prefer just a little—a very little, my dear sir—less of the—the—a—a——"

"That of the blushing rose-bud on your cheeks, my dear madam."

"Yes, Mr. Pomander; just so. Dear me, what a thing it is to be able to express oneself so very properly."

"Yes, my dear madam," said Mr. Pomander, graciously bestowing upon the fat landlady the compliment, "you do express yourself most charmingly. But, my dear Mrs. Staples, you are looking rather delicate?"

"Oh!" sighed Mrs. Staples, with a great vibration of a blond cap which she wore on her head, "I feel rather delicate, Mr. Pomander—I ain't at all a robustious person—would you like to take anything, my dear sir?"

"Why, really, my dear madam, you know I so seldom—but just for once in way, a little brandy and water."

"Hot, Mr. Pomander?"

"Rather hot, my dear madam, and—and——"

"Strong, Mr. Pomander?"

"If you please, ma'am; and I think, my dear Mrs. Staples, that considering the extreme delicacy of your fragile structure, you might venture just upon a small tumbler yourself, madam."

"Do you, indeed, sir? I do think you understand my case thoroughly, Mr. Pomander. I often feel, do you know, a kind of—oh! dear me—a sort of——"

"I comprehend, ma'am," said Mr. Pomander, in his most silky tones.

" It's not at all dangerous ; and something a little strong, occasionally, I should think would be about the best thing."

" Well, if you as a medical man, my dear sir, think so, I don't mind just a small drop."

Mrs. Staples suited the action to the word ; but the action far outshone the word, for she tossed off half the contents of one or two streaming tumblers of brandy and water which she had with great expedition prepared.

Mrs. Staples was decidedly on the wrong side of forty-five, but she was a thriving woman, and Mr. Pomander had more than once thought that the proprietor of the Golden Lion might, possibly, be a more comfortable personage than Mr. Pomander, Chemist and Druggist, &c., &c., in the little village of Haredale, where the inhabitants were so dreadfully healthy.

" It's a shame, I declare," said the hostess, " that that Moss, who is nothing but a barber, should dare to presume, Mr. Pomander, to talk about you, my dear sir, otherwise than with the greatest respect. It's frightful !"

" Eh ?—dear me, yes, my dear madam, Mr. Moss, my charming Mrs. Staples, is a man who—but we must be charitable—humph !—bless him."

" Ah ! you are too good, Mr. Pomander, you are, indeed. Some people would be quite in a passion now, but you smile quite kindly."

" Oh, my dear madam, we must not bear malice. Poor Moss may be ill some day, you know, and I may be sent for. Dear me—humph ! There's somebody coming out of the parlour, my dear madam, and I'll just step in and sit down for a few moments."

Mr. Pomander had heard the door opening, and he did not wish exactly to be caught in the act of a vigorous flirtation with the fat landlady, so, hastily finishing his brandy and water, he made a quick movement to the door, and met Mr. Scrimp coming out.

Mr. Pomander looked after the departing Scrimp in deep cogitation for some moments.

" Humph !" he said ; " Scrimp's after something. I may just as well see what it is, if possible. All's fish that comes to net."

Mr. Pomander with this resolve, instead of entering the parlour of the Golden Lion, cautiously followed the footsteps of the departing attorney.

Mr. Perk remained but a short time in the parlour after the sudden exit of his employer, when he, too, rose, and walked out.

" Oh ! oh !" he said ; " Scrimp's trying to keep me in the dark about something, I see. I'll know what he's about, or my name's not Perk, oh, no, by no means whatsoever. We'll see, my dear Mr. Scrimp, we'll see," and away walked Mr. Perk.

The attorney had his own reasons for expecting Ralph Freegrove at Haredale Park, and he hurried off in the direction of Sir Herbert Foster's mansion, in expectation of meeting that person.

Ralph Freegrove had been an inhabitant of the village when a boy, and by his sharpness had attracted the favourable notice of Sir Herbert Foster, who had taken him into his service, and conveyed him to London, where he had soon become fully initiated into all the vices of high life.

Sir Herbert Foster found Ralph Freegrove an unscrupulous assistant in his intrigues, and a ready actor in any project of deceit or villany which might be found necessary in forwarding the views of his dissipated master.

Ralph affected a great deal of the fine gentleman, but Nature had made him a reckless ruffian, and such he looked. His assurance was immense, and a confidence in his own brutal strength induced him to tyrannize, insult

and oppress others whenever he thought he dared. He was as destitute of all honour and honesty as his master; in short, they were a pair well suited to each other in every respect, and, like all rogues, hated each other mortally. Ralph hated his master, because he was forced to truckle and be submissive to him, and Sir Herbert Foster detested and despised, while he used the man, who was the base fool of his passions and the pander to his vices.

Of these worthies we shall have further occasion to speak, for a cloud was hovering in the fair horizon of Phœbe's happiness, which had been called into existence by a man who was much worse than the perpetrator of vice himself, because he occupied the baser and meaner part of suggesting it, and the mode of its commission, while his cowardly nature shrunk from its actual consequences in his own person.

Such a man was Mr. Scrimp, attorney-at-law, and gentleman, by act of parliament, though rogue by nature and practice.

CHAPTER XXVII.

The harvest moon shone with a mild yellow radiance upon the mill, and the fertile fields which surrounded it, on the evening of the day which had witnessed the avowed rivalry of Giles and George, the miller's men, for the affection of the fair Phœbe, whom they both considered to be his daughter.

After a short period from the night of the fearful storm, in which Phœbe had sought shelter and pity at the miller's humble cottage, she had become so endeared to the good man and his worthy dame, by her sweet and grateful disposition, that but one fear cast a shadow across their happiness, and

No. 20

that fear was, that some relation might spring up some day, and claim the orphan girl from them.

So oppressed were they with this idea, that they prevailed upon Phœbe carefully to conceal her name of Grainger, and to adopt their's, and pass in every respect for their own child. She called them respectively father and mother, and no tender parents could exceed them in pure love and kindness to the orphan girl.

The good dame and her husband would often, when sitting by their contented, though humble fire-side, recal the events of the night of storm which brought the persecuted child to their dwelling, and vie with each other in thankfulness to Heaven for bestowing upon them so great a blessing.

From the moment of Phœbe's arrival, the old mill, the cottage, and all around, seemed to the old couple to have assumed a brighter aspect. A spirit of joy and beauty seemed to pervade everything; and as the old man would sit in his arm-chair, pretending to be reading, but in reality watching the fairy form of his darling Phœbe, flitting about the neat little cottage, and singing, with her sweet voice, snatches of old songs, his heart would expand with joy, and he would drop his book, and call her to him, and with a tear of fondness in his eye, pray God to bless her who had brought such a blessing upon his heart in his old age, when his connection with the young and beautiful seemed to have been long at an end, and quiet content-ment his only portion.

The good miller's mind was, however, now sorely troubled by the con-tention of George and Giles, which he had witnessed, and been forced to interpose to quell in the morning, and he thought, with painful feelings, over the probable consequences of the rivalship of the two young men.

But we must leave the honest miller for a time to his meditations to fol-low the light footsteps of Phœbe, the Miller's Maid.

The yellow disc of the full round harvest-moon had scarcely risen above the horizon, when Phœbe tripped lightly and gaily through the pretty little flower garden, which she had herself attended, and brought to its present beauty since her arrival at the mill, and commenced her evening labour of watering the plants, for no rain had fallen for many days, and the tender flowrets hung faintly their drooping heads after the extreme heat of the day.

By that mild moonlight, the fair girl might well have been taken for some aerial spirit—some nymph of the woods and sylvan groves, who had come to shelter from destruction the fair flowers.

Her step was light and elastic, and she flitted among the drooping flowers, with her fair long wringlets dancing on her neck and shoulders, with that true grace which is Nature's own, and which she so rarely be-stows even upon her most favoured children. When, however, this pure natural grace—this poetry of motion—is really found, it is always in some young girl, at that sweet age when the infantine graces of the child still hang round the girl—some fair innocent creature, who has never seen a dancing-master in her life, and who has not been the victim of any of the atrocious contrivances for improving upon nature, which have ever been, and are now, considered as perfectly indispensable to fine ladies.

Phœbe's attire was by no means fashionable; it was only becoming and graceful. She neither walked erect as a kitchen poker, and with a a jolt at each step, which some ladies consider to be the height of dignity and ease, nor did she attempt the swimming movement of others, who fancy grace of action to consist in a series of bends and doubles, and swings of the skirts of their garments, but she moved without a thought, and nature, who, notwithstanding the general opinion to the contrary, understands a little about grace and elegance, supplied the rest; and

Phœbe, the Miller's Maid, was a purely natural, graceful, and beautiful girl.

There was one person who gazed at the fair girl, as she flitted from flower to flower, with the most enthusiastic approbation, and that was Tim Miggles, who, with his chin resting upon the top bar of the little garden-gate, was admiring Phœbe, while she was totally unconscious of his proximity.

"She's prettier than all the flowers put together," sighed Tim, "and I could look at her in any sort of weather. It's all very fine of Master George to say to me, 'Tim, Tim, my good fellow, just tell Phœbe, will you, that I want to say a word to her in the meadow about the chantilly violets.' Oh, dear! oh, lauks! I loves her far more better nor him, and I wouldn't call the king my mother if she'd be Missus Tim."

Tim accompanied this impromptu by a slap on his waistcoat, and then another upon his forehead, which startled Phœbe, and caused her to turn round quickly.

"Who is that?" she said: "is it you—a—George?"

"Don't be alarmed; it's only me," said Tim Miggles. "Oh! Phœbe, dear—oh! Phœbe, dear, my heart is in a fluster, and if you won't consent to wed, I'm afeard 'twill be a buster."

Phœbe laughed a happy, merry laugh, for she always laughed at Tim.

"Why Tim," she said, "I declare you improve, indeed you do; that was capital."

"Oh, dear, Miss Phœbe, do you really think so? You haven't happened to think of a rhyme for Phœbe, have you? I've thought of another besides, maybe, but it isn't a good 'un either."

"And what is it, Tim?" asked the laughing Phœbe.

"Why, you've heard of Alonzo the Brave and the fair Imogene?"

"Oh, yes; but what has that to do with it?"

"Oh, everything in the world, Miss Phœbe. Now you shall hear.

> 'Fair Imogene was so pretty that she be
> Very nigh as beautiful as my charming Phœbe.

What do you think of that?"

"Why, I think that's very good indeed, Tim, but much too flattering. So now good morning."

"Oh! Miss Phœbe, don't go, pray, I've got something to say.

> 'The moon upon a bank of clouds reposes,
> And shines like a good 'un on our lovely noses'"

"Well, what have you got to say?" asked Phœbe. "You know, Tim, dear father will be vexed to find you loitering here."

"Missus has vexed me.

> "She took away a book,
> And did bacon with it cook.

Oh, dear! oh, dear! I hadn't read but the first twelve pages; oh, lauk, oh, dear!"

"What was it about?" said Phœbe, restraining with difficulty her laughter. "You know mother would not take a good and useful book from you."

"It was a poetical conversation atween a elephant and a mouse. Oh, it was wery good, Miss Phœbe; it was beautiful. This here's the way it begun:—

> ' Once upon a time,
> An elephant sublime,
>   With a mouse went out to fetch a walk.
> Says the mouse, says he,
> If I doesn't make too free,
>   We'll have some very serious talk.
> There's birds and there's fishes,
> And hedges and ditches,
>   And lots of other things, good lauk.'

"Oh! I see, that'll do," cried Phœbe, fearful that Tim's memory might oblige her with the whole of the composition. "Good evening Tim—good evening."

"As Shakspere says, Miss Phœbe, I wishes as I was a pair of gloves if I haven't nearly forgot what George asked me to say to you."

"What!" cried Phœbe; "George, did you say?"

"Yes, Miss, yes; let me think. He wants to see you in the meadow, and it's something about violets; but really I—let me see. 'Tim, my good fellow,' said he—dear me, what was it? A warrior so bold and a maiden so fair, conversed as they sat on the green. No, no, that wasn't it at all. 'Tim,' said he—eh?—dear me, where are you, Miss Phœbe? Well, I declare, now she's gone—how very odd. That strongly reminds me of the tragical poem of 'The Death of the Brave Baron of Fitzfuddleumboski-wobble,' where it says,—

> "'Then at her feet he was going for to fall,
> But he didn't, 'cause he saw she wasn't there at all.'"

Phœbe, while Tim Miggles was puzzling himself to recollect George's precise message, had tripped lightly across the garden, and opened a little wicket-gate, which led her direct to the meadow.

George Andrews, the miller's man, had not been above two months at the mill, but that short time had still been sufficiently long to make an indelible impression upon the young heart of the Miller's Maid. When first she saw him she had felt an unusual flutter at her heart. His form was manly and prepossessing, and there was, likewise, a mild, melancholy expression upon his handsome face, which had an irresistible charm for Phœbe.

Nor was the strange youth less struck with the innocent beauty of the fair Phœbe. He felt, after he had once seen her, that henceforth with her was wound up his very existence,—that upon her depended his every hope of earthly happiness. Each succeeding day heightened the impression which the gentle girl had made upon his heart, and his love for Phœbe became the ruling passion of his existence.

The feelings which began to agitate the breast of the fair orphan were to her new and inexplicable, and yet they were delightful. She watched George as he worked at the mill, and each hour added to the dangerous feelings which were excluding all other thoughts in the pure young heart of the Miller's Maid. She would have started had any one said, Phœbe, you love George Andrews; and yet, without knowing it, she had given to him her gentle heart.

No declaration of mutual attachment had passed their lips, and yet by that mute language of the eyes, which is a thousand times more eloquent than words, they knew that they loved each other, and were happy in the blest feeling that the first affections of their hearts were reciprocal.

George was never happy but when he was contriving some means of testifying his affections for Phœbe. If she expressed in his hearing the slightest wish, he rested not till he had gratified it; and Phœbe's wishes seldom extended beyond the desire to possess some rare plant or flower.

Giles's violence in the morning had furnished George with ample food for most anxious reflection. Well he knew, from a thousand little circumstances, the wild, ungovernable temper of his now avowed rival, and he trembled to think it possible that the impetuous passion of Giles, now that it had once thrown off disguise and declared itself, might prompt him to the commission of some act inimical to the peace of the gentle Phœbe.

He passed the whole day in these gloomy reflections, and finally resolved to seek a private interview with Phœbe, and, at the same time that he would declare, in fervent language, his own dear affections for her, warn her against falling into any snare that might be laid for her by the vindictive spirit of Giles.

George felt the truce between him and his rival was but a hollow one, and that Giles would not remain long an inactive spectator of the obvious preference of Phœbe for his raval. How truly could he have said, " the course of true love never yet ran smooth ;" for even now, with the conviction upon his mind that he was beloved by her, without whom life would be but a dreary waste, without one green spot to redeem the monotony of the wilderness, yet he was tortured by a thousand fears and anxieties, which clouded his brow, and converted the gladness of his heart into fearful forebodings of coming misfortunes.

He had asked the good-tempered Tim to be the bearer of his message to Phœbe, as he knew that on account of his harmless peculiarities, he was allowed to wander freely about the cottage and the garden without question or molestation ; and Tim, incited by the promise of George, that he would give his serious attention to finding a good rhyme to Phœbe, and let him know the result on the morrow, had freely undertaken the errand, which he executed in the manner we have recorded.

With light bounding steps and a fluttering heart Phœbe sought the meadow, which had been by Tim mentioned as the place where George wished to see her.

The fair Miller's Maid never for a moment hesitated about going. Her innocent and artless soul never hinted to her the slightest scruple or impropriety in thus so freely according a private meeting to one who was nearly a stranger to her.

Phœbe had been so accustomed to act from the immediate dictates of her own pure, guileless heart, that she would have been shocked exceedingly had any one, hacknied in the word's ways, told her she was doing wrong.

It so happened, however, that the orphan girl had not bestowed her young affections upon one who would misconstrue the innocent actions cf her pure spirits. George Andrews loved her for her gentleness and innocence, and he would not have exchanged her simple, unsuspecting heart for a diadem.

There had been a time in the life of the orphan girl when she was surrounded by those who reviled and ill-used her, that she shrunk from her fellow-creatures with suspicion and apprehension ; but that time had passed away, and the oppressed spirit had regained its tone. Human nature had become redeemed in Phœbe's eyes ; and happy, oh ! how happy was it, that at that dangerous period of life, when the young susceptible heart is too apt to be led astray by the glitter of mere outward virtue and excellence, she encountered a pure heart, in which dwelt feelings kindred to her own, and which was the blest abode of sterling virtue.

George was waiting, with anxious expectation, the approach of her who was so dear to him. Fears and hopes, alternately predominating, agitated his mind. He would sometimes think that he might have misconstrued the actions of the fair girl, and that she would refuse to meet him, or, if she did come, come but to destroy, with a breath, all his air-built castles and dreams of joy and love.

Then, again, gentle hope would whisper to his soul that the Miller's Maid was to be wooed and won by a true heart ; and her looks and smiles, which he had treasured up in his memory, would bid him not despair, for she should yet be his.

He looked anxiously in the direction which she must come in, if she came at all, and each minute seemed an hour of anxious expectation to the impatient lover, who thus waited for his dear love, upon the first occasion that he had thought proper to venture to solicit the favour of a secret interview with her.

Now he could see the flutter of her garments, as she advanced to meet him, and his heart beat with delightful emotion. His doubts and fears vanished, and in another instant he was at the dear one's side.

"Dear Phœebe," he cried, "how kind of you to meet me here."

"But you had something to say to me, George," said Phœbe, "so you know I was sure to come."

"Phœbe, you—you are an angel. Your noble nature knows no stain, and suspects nothing bad in others. Oh! dear Phœbe, if all were like you, what a happy world would this be."

"Father and mother, and—and you, George, are all good; but why have you sent for me? I trust that you have no bad news to tell me, George?"

"I hope—I trust not, dear Phœbe; and yet——"

"Yet what? Do not keep me in suspense. Is it anything about dear father or mother? Oh! speak if it is;—you make me fear some calamity by your silence."

"No, Phœbe, it is not about them; God bless them both. They have been kind to me, and that, too, at a time when I most required the hand of kindness and pity to be held out to me, for I was friendless and destitute."

"God bless them," echoed Phœbe; "they are always kind and good. Heaven will, indeed, bless them."

"Phœbe," continued George, while a slight flush came across his cheek; "Phœbe, do you know——"

"What, George—oh! what? Your manner is disturbed. Of what would you tell me? Am I to be torn from my happy home?"

"Dear Phœbe, why this agitation?—no one can injure you—you are, I fondly hope, free from all peril. What I wished to tell you was, that there had been a little quarrel at the old mill this morning."

"A quarrel, George?—between whom? Who could quarrel at the mill?"

"It was, Phœbe, between Giles and myself."

"Indeed!" cried Phœbe. "Oh! George, why did you—you——"

"What would you say, dear Phœbe?" cried George, with animation. "Oh! finish the dear sentence, and let me hope."

"Nothing, George—nothing. Why—why did you quarrel?"

"About you, Phœbe; it was all about you."

"About me, George? Impossible! Quarrel about me! That was very cruel of both you and Giles. How vexed my dear father would be. Oh! George, George, you should not—indeed you should not."

"Dear Phœbe, hear me; and, however you may blame me, you will acknowledge that, at the worst, I was guilty but of indiscretion. If you, then, will be offended with me, Phœbe, I—I can but go away, and—and—and never see you more."

"Oh! no, no," cried Phœbe. "George! dear——"

"Dear Phœbe, speak but that word again, and then drive me for ever from you, if you will. Oh! I would die with that sweet sound in my ears."

"Tell me, oh, tell me," said the blushing Phœbe; "why you quarrelled with Giles. Tell me at once, George. I—I know not what I said."

"Phœbe, I will tell you; but, dear girl, you have bestowed more happiness upon me by one word than my whole life has ever felt. Bless you, dear, dear Phœbe; bless you!"

Phœbe did not speak, but she hung down her head, and a pleasureable flutter at her heart told her how happy she was, with the fervent words of him whom she dearly loved quietly breathing in her ears.

"Giles, Phœbe, declared that he loved you."

"Loved me?" cried Phœbe.

"Yes, dearest; he said that he loved you, and that he had sworn a vow that you should be his, or he would perish in the attempt."

"Is this possible," cried Phœbe, clasping her hands. "And, George, what—what did you do?"

"I am ashamed to tell you, Phœbe, that my passion got the better of my judgment, and when he called me a name which no honest man can bear, I struck him."

"Oh! George, George; and I am the unhappy cause of this quarrel? Unfortunate that I am!"

"No, Phœbe, you are not the cause, dearest; it's Giles's own ungovernable temper that is the cause. I thought, dear Phœbe, that I had better tell you this myself, than risk your hearing it from any one else. And—and——"

"And what, George? what more is there for me to hear?"

"Phœbe, I—I thought to have taken this opportunity. Dear Phœbe, I—I——"

"I think I had better go in," said Phœbe, faintly, and feeling her limbs almost unable to support her as the conviction flashed across her mind that George was about to make a declaration of his own attachment to her.

"Dear Phœbe, stay but a moment, and hear me; then—then, Phœbe, leave me, if you please, to despair, and I shall never offend you by my presence again."

"What—what would you say?" gasped Phœbe.

"I would say, dear Phœbe, what my tell-tale eyes may long since have led you to surmise—I would say that I love you."

Phœbe turned very faint, and leaned on a wicket-gate, close to where they were standing.

"Phœbe—dear Phœbe—will you listen to me now? You have the fond cherished secret of my heart—I love you—dearly love you."

Phœbe said something, but so faintly, that George could not catch the sound.

"Dear, dear, Phœbe," he cried; "speak to me—oh! speak to me but one word, to say you do not hate me, and cast me for ever from you."

"I—I—I hear, George," said Phœbe, and her words fell upon his enraptured ears like the notes of some sweet melody.

"Dear, kind girl," he cried, snatching her hand and covering it with kisses, "from the first moment that I saw you, your dear image took possession of my heart. I loved you then—dearly loved you, Phœbe. Since that happy hour my life has been a dream of joy, for I saw Phœbe. My daily toil was sweet, for its dear reward was in the evening time to listen to the voice of Phœbe. I lived but for thy dear sake. The air you breathed was fraught to me with Heavenly sweets; the verdant sod around your dwelling to my eyes boasted a richer green—the pure spirit of my Phœbe was around me—and I saw everything adorned by the reflected beams of loveliness and goodness. Condemn me to despair—tell me that I may not even hope, and I will leave you for ever. My heart may break, but your pure happy spirit shall not be oppressed by witnessing its sufferings. You shall think of me sometimes as one who dearly loved you, and in deep sorrow passed away a wanderer from his native land."

"Oh, George! George!" cried Phœbe, sobbing, "you—you will not go."

"Again, dearest, again breathe to me those sweet words of hope and joy. Let me again hear thee speak."

"George, dear George!" said Phœbe, faintly.

"Oh, Phœbe, Phœbe, dearest heart, this is too much happiness. Heaven,

I thank thee. Oh, dear, ever dear Phœbe, you have made me happy, indeed."

He clasped her for one moment in his arms, and the first kiss of pure affection rested upon her glowing cheek.

"And, Phœbe," he cried, " dear Phœbe, are you not happy?"

She looked up to his face with a sweet smile, while a pearly drop trembled upon her eyelid.

"Dear George," she said, "I feel as if the sun was shining on my heart."

CHAPTER XXVIII.

HAREDALE PARK was an old substantial mansion of the Elizabethan era. It had been in the family of the Fosters for many years, and the present Sir Herbert was the fifth baronet of his house.

At the present time the house was unoccupied, except by such servants as were absolutely necessary to keep its suites of splendid apartments in a fit state for the residence of its owner, whenever he might choose to visit the ancient abode of his family.

It was customary with Sir Herbert Foster to send down Ralph Freegrove to Haredale Park a day or two always before he purposed visiting it himself; and about the close of the evening that, in his own estimation, important personage arrived at the mansion, and with all the consequence in the world, ordered a dinner to be prepared for himself, and intimated his intention of sleeping there that night; and what astonished the domestics much more than Mr. Freegrove's assumption of authority, for that they were used to, was his threat, that if any one of the household so much as hinted in the village at the fact of his arrival, Sir Herbert should be informed of it, and they would be instantly dismissed.

Ralph Freegrove then tarried till the night had fairly set in, which he was evidently waiting for with much impatience, and then he sallied forth from the mansion to perform a mission, with which he had been entrusted by his master, and which might be the immediate precursor of the latter's arrival.

The whole of the village was on the estate of Sir Herbert Foster, as was, likewise, the old mill, which had been so many years in the family of Gilbert the miller.

The baronet, however, had no power over the land on which the mill and the cottage of the honest miller stood, for it had not formed a portion of the original property, but had been purchased by an ancestor of Sir Herbert's, and bestowed upon the great-grandfather of the present miller, for him and his family in perpetuity, upon payment of a merely nominal rental, in consideration of an important service rendered by a daughter of the then miller to the noble family, by snatching the infant heir of the Fosters from the blazing ruins of a wing of the mansion which had caught fire, and which was the lodging of the infant and its courageous and faithful nurse.

Gilbert the miller was, therefore, the most, and in fact, the only true independant man on the estate of Sir Herbert Foster—a fact which he frequently congratulated himself upon when he had occasion to observe the cruel and tyrannical conduct of the baronet to some of the humble tenantry who had displeased him.

We left the honest miller sitting by his fire-side in deep meditation on the occurrence of the morning, between George and Giles in the mill.

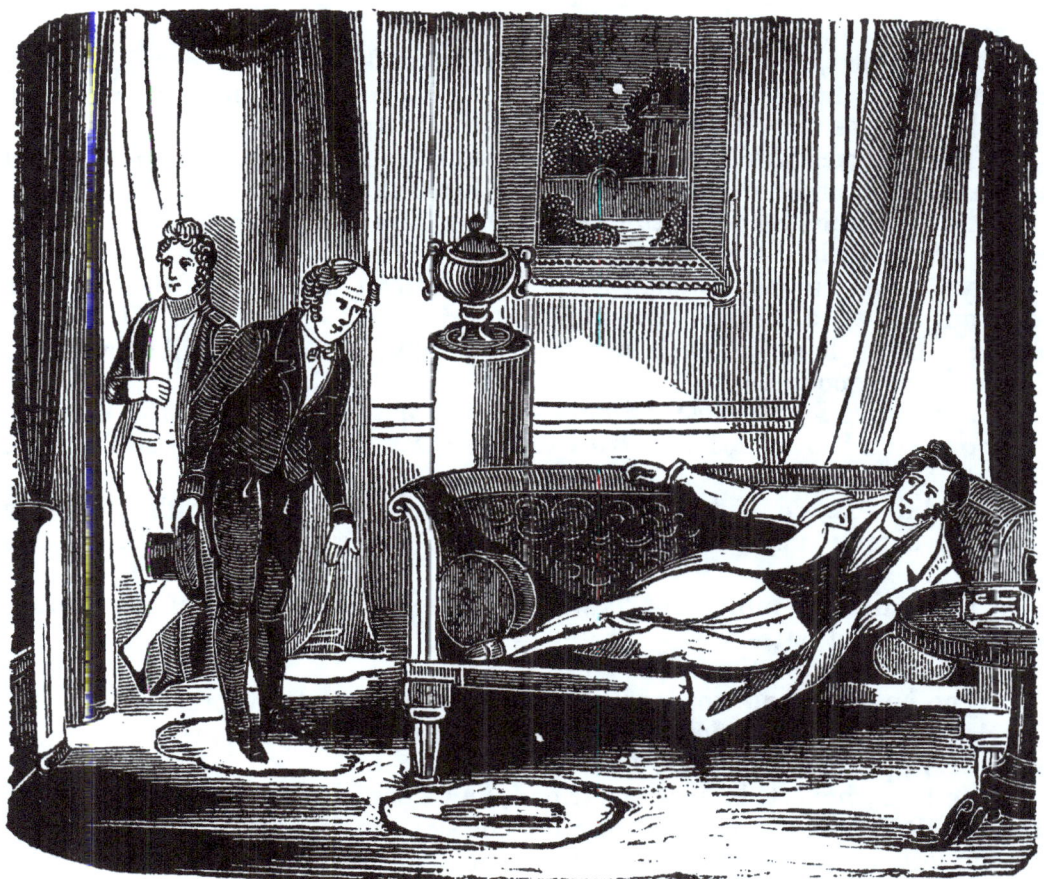

"I tell 'e what it be, dame," he said to his honest helpmate, to whom he had related the circumstance as it had happened, "we be beginning trouble, dame. That poor child will be plagued by they two young men till she will not know what to do, and the old mill will come to a stop with their quarrels and love-making."

"No, no Gilbert," cried the dame; "Phœbe be a good girl, and she will soon let them know what she be thinking about them both."

"They be both good lads in the main," replied the miller; "but when love do come into a lad's head, the wit do fly out, dame. Giles be main ugly when he be crossed."

"I tell 'e what, Gilbert," said the dame, "thee must speak to Phœbe thee-self. She be a good girl, and thee must ask her if she be going to have either of the lads, and then thee must tell them what she do say, and they must be content."

"Dost thee think, wife, she do like either of them?"

"In truth, Gilbert, I be sometimes thinking that she be glad when George do come into the cottage, and she do sometimes make a mortal mistake when he be by. She gave me some pepper, Gilbert, instead of ginger, to put in the ale, and I see she be looking at George all the time. Oh! Gilbert, I do re-member when I was a young lass, and thee used to come——"

"Don't thee be foolish, old wife, with thee recollections. I am troubled, I tell thee, about these lads, and our dear child, bless her."

"Oh! bless her, indeed, sweet thing. She be a dear child to me, and I tell 'e, Gilbert, no lad shall take her from me."

The dame sat down as she spoke, and wiped a tear away with the corner of her apron.

"Thee be foolish, wife," said the miller. "I tell 'e, whoever she be
No. 21

mind to have shall live here, and have the old mill and the cottage when we be gone."

"But, Gilbert, thee talkest what thee don't know if thee can do, for Sir Herbert Foster he be a bad man, and when we be gone it be in his power to take the land, as there be no children of our own to claim it."

"That is true, wife," said the miller, with a sigh ; "but he be rich to his heart's content, and he could not have the heart to do it."

"The next heir, Gilbert—the sweet young lady who came to the mill once would be main kind, I'll warrant."

"Aye, he be the last baronet, for he be childless, and his younger brother be dead, as we all know, and the estates do pass to dear sweet Miss Adele Foster. Bless her, she be a sweet young lady, and mortal like our dear Phœbe in her goodness."

"Let us hope for the best, Gilbert—let us hope for the best. Sir Herbert, we know, be a bad man, for he tried to take away the garden ground from the dear cottage."

"He did—dang'd if he didn't," said the miller, in great wrath ; "but he couldn't, dame ; no, no. He may try, but Gilbert, the miller, knows his own."

As the indignant miller spoke, a knock sounded at the door of the cottage, and a voice cried out,—

"Halloo !—within there."

"Who be that, I do wonder ?" said the dame, in some surprise.

"Somebody, perhaps, lost their way, wife," said the miller, rising, and immediately opening the door.

"Well, my honest, industrious friend, how goes the world with you, eh ?" said Mr. Ralph Freegrove, entering the cottage.

The miller knew the character of the man well, who now invaded his humble dwelling, and spoke in such a tone of patronizing superiority.

"Ralph Freegrove," he said, continuing standing, "what be thy business with me ?"

"Why it's partly business and partly pleasure," said Freegrove, with a swaggering, although uneasy manner, under the gaze of the miller.

"Then tell me thee business quickly, and thee may take thee pleasure somewhere else. Ralph Freegrove, we are pleasant enough without thee."

"Oh ! you are ill-tempered to an old friend," cried Freegrove. "I suppose something has gone wrong about the mill, eh ?"

"No, there be nothing wrong about the mill ; it be sounder now at the heart than some folks. As for thee being an old friend to me, Ralph Freegrove, thee know thee art no such thing. I told thee once I never wished to see thee face again, and yet thee comes and knocks at my door. Now I ask thee, what dost thee want ?—for I will not sit down in my own dwelling till I see its door shut upon thee."

"Thee art a bad man, Ralph Freegrove," said the dame, "and thee knows thee art. Thee hast the death of poor Nancy Groves at thee door. Thee and thee master did carry the poor child—for little more than a child she was —from her poor blind mother, and thee didst bring her to shame and death, while the poor mother did go out of her mind through thee."

"Oh ! pho, pho !" cried Freegrove, with a forced laugh, "it's no such thing—an idle tale. Come, my good woman, shake paws and be friends. Ha ! ha !"

"Now, hear me, Ralph Freegrove," said the miller, his wrath rising as he spoke ; "if thee speak one more word to my good dame, big as thee art, and old as I be, I'll knock thee down, as sure as thee and thy master are two rogues."

"Ha ! ha ! ha !" laughed Ralph Freegrove, "you are out of humour, both of you. Why, I thought, just for old acquaintance sake, you'd have made a fellow welcome to a glass of ale and a crust of bread and cheese; but it's no matter. To business, then."

"Thee shall not eat or drink in my house," said the miller, emphatically. "I will not break bread with thee; I have known thee long, Freegrove—I knew thee before thee robbed the poor widowed mother, but I never knew any good of thee."

"D—n you, then," said Freegrove, rising in a rage, "you and your dame and your mill be hanged, you bull-headed old brute."

The miller sprang at once upon his sturdy antagonist; and so sudden was the attack, and so utterly unexpected, that Ralph Freegrove staggered under it, and his head came with an alarming bump against the wall.

The athletic ruffian, however, recovered himself in a moment, and entwining his arms round the miller, he made a prodigious effort to throw him.

"Murder! murder! help!" cried the terrified dame, and in an instant the cottage door was thrown wide open, and Phœbe and George appeared upon the threshold.

"Ha!" cried George, and he threw himself in a moment upon Ralph Freegrove, and threw him so heavily that the little cottage shook to its foundation.

Phœbe screamed, and clung to the miller, who was much flushed by the encounter.

"Father! dear father! what's the matter?—oh, what is it?—who is that man?" cried Phœbe, in great terror.

"A villain!" cried the miller, "who, for some bad purpose of his own, or his bad master, has dared to come beneath a honest man's roof."

Ralph Freegrove now slowly rose, and looked round the cottage with a scowl of malignant vengeance. His eye rested upon Phœbe. For a moment he gazed fixedly at her; then, with a smile of hatred and revenge, he rushed from the cottage.

"Dear father," said Phœbe, "what is this about?—who is that bad man who scowled upon us all so as he left the cottage?"

"He be a bad man, Phœbe—he be, indeed," said the miller. "George, thee came in time, my good lad, for I do believe the rascal would have murdered me."

"I rejoice," cried George, "that I was sufficiently near at hand to hear the tumult. I trust, sir, you will not allow this outrage to pass unnoticed."

"Let him go, George; let him go," said the miller. "I did strike the first blow, but the villain did revile me under my own roof."

"Who is he, dear father," asked Phœbe.

"He be called Ralph Freegrove," said the miller, "and he be—I don't know what exactly—to Sir Herbert Foster, who be as great a rogue as he."

"Indeed they be a bad pair," cried the dame, "and I be sure he came here for no good."

"What he be wanting here, I don't know," said Gilbert, "but I could not bear to see Ralph Freegrove standing or sitting in a house of mine, even if it were the meanest cottage in the world. I be main afeard he be bent upon some evil doing. Take care of theeself, George, my lad, for he be a bad man, and will try to be revenged on thee."

Phœbe turned very pale as the miller gave thus free utterance to his thoughts, and she sunk into a chair in great distress of mind.

"Why, my girl, my dear," cried the miller, "what be the matter with thee? thee be looking quite pale."

"Oh, nothing—nothing," said Phœbe, faintly, "only—only the looks of that man alarmed me."

"He be ill-looking enough, surely, to frighten a horse; but don't thee be afeared, my dear, he cannot harm thee."

"He dare not," cried George; "I'd tear his worthless heart out were he to attempt anything against—that is—against any of my dear friends."

"Thou art a brave lad, George," said the miller, "and I respect thee; but how came thee and Phœbe so nigh at hand?"

George and Phœbe glanced at each other in confusion at this question, and the dame screwed up her lips, and looked very frigid and solemn at poor Phœbe.

"Why, sir," replied George, "I—I—you see, sir—Phœbe—I—come, you see——"

"Why, what does the lad mean?—I know thee come."

"Ye—yes," cried Phœbe. "We—we—you see, father—I—I—George, you know—a—a——"

"Art thee both mad? I see thee both. What dost 'e mean by I—I—I—I—and we—we—we?"

"Thee had best get thee to thy rest, George," interposed the dame, who was much more clear-sighted than the miller as to the cause of the mutual confusion of the young lovers.

George thankfully availed himself of the suggestion, and was out of the cottage in an instant.

"And thee, my dear child," she said, addressing Phœbe, "thee hast been frightened, and thee will be better when thee hast had some sleep. Go to thee room, my dear, and compose thyself."

"Good night, dear father and mother," said Phœbe, as she glided from the room.

"Gilbert, Gilbert," said the dame, when she was alone with her husband, "thee sees that George be the man."

"Yes, dame, I did see that he be. That were a main clever back fall he did give to that rascal, Ralph Freegrove, surely."

"Don't thee be foolish in thee old age, Gilbert," cried the dame. "Did thee not see that Phœbe and George be very thick like, and great lovers?"

"Why, dame," said the miller, "I did think as much. George be a very good lad, as far as we do know, but he be still but a stranger nearly to us, and our dear Phœbe be all the world."

"That be very true, Gilbert, but she be giving her young heart to George, and let us hope that he be deserving of it, for Phœbe, indeed, be a good girl."

"After some further discourse, the miller and his dame retired for the night, and deep silence reigned in the humble but happy dwelling.

How happy had that evening made George. His heart was light, and his bounding footsteps seemed to spurn the very earth on which he trod, as he took his way along the short space between the cottage which contained her who was to him the sweet chain which bound him to existence—the one loved being that cast a halo of glory around his path, and made in his eyes the world look beautiful and bright. Oh! if there be one moment of bliss, which, in its pure ecstasy, gives mortals a foretaste of the joys of Heaven, it is that moment when the murmuring accents of the dearly-loved object, for whom all toil and sacrifices would seem pleasures, breathe the soft confession of mutual love. It is a rapture, a delirium of joy; it is one moment of pure happiness, which we can never taste again. Man may pursue ambition, wealth, distinction. He may gain all that his warmest fancy can paint to him as desirable. But, truly,—

> "He'll never meet
> A joy so sweet,
>   In all his noon of fame,
> As when first he sang to woman's ear,
>   His soul-felt flame."

That ecstasy of pure affection—that capacity to love and be beloved so devotedly—is the one dear remnant of man's divine origin. The "trail of the serpent" is over all the rest of man's nature, but at those moments he is himself again, the high pure being fresh from the hands of his glorious Creator, and the melody is in his heart.

That one happy moment, when we feel that the gentle and beautiful being whom we love, worship, is truly our own, and doubts and fears have vanished before the full completion of our dreams of joy, when the soft voice, like some blessed angel's sweetest whisper, tells us we are loved or enshrined in the pure young heart; and the velvet lips, with shrinking, modest grace, scarcely give, and yet do not refuse the kiss, making joy more requisite by its gentle dalliance. Oh! then, these are the green spots in memory's waste —these are the moments in human existence which, in the dreams of after years, come pleasantly across the soul, and yet ever leave a sigh behind. These are the things that make the morning of life a delight, and a happy advent of hope and joy; and when they are past, when—

> " The days are gone when beauty bright
> The heart's chains wove—''

we may look around on the deepening gloom, and say with a sigh, " The sun of youth and joy is setting—I see the shadows of evening approach. Where is the grave? for sweet hope is already dead."

George stood again in the meadow, in which, but a few short minutes since, he had told his tale of love to the gentle Phœbe. The beautiful moon shone upon the verdant sod, and touched with silver each blade of grass and closed flowret and humble weed. The shadow of the old mill fell, large and black, across the ground, a holy stillness reigned around, and in that calm moment, unseen by mortal eye, George breathed a prayer to the High Throne of Mercy for happiness to the fair child of nature, whose fate was irrevocably mixed up with his, and there he vowed to love her well and truly, and blessed God for the pure happiness of his heart.

He looked towards the cottage, and he saw a light at the window of Phœbe's bed-room. It shone but faintly through the drawn curtains, but he could mark the shadow of the loved one as she flitted across the room, before retiring to rest.

George watched the window till the light disappeared, for it was a pleasure even to know that she was so near. He then walked towards the mill, in which he, Giles, and Tim Miggles slept. As he approached it, he thought he could hear the voice of some one muttering something. He looked carefully about him, and could presently perceive in the dim light, for the moon shone from the other side of the mill, a window was open, and some one was looking from it, with a fixed and steady gaze, at the cottage.

George walked slowly up, although he well guessed who it was who thus wasted the hours which should have been devoted to repose, in gazing hopelessly at the little casement of Phœbe's room.

He arrived under the window; but so absorbed was Giles, for it was him, in his own reflections, that he did not notice that any one was near him.

George heard him sigh heavily, as he still gazed at the now darkened window of Phœbe's room, and he was about to call to him to signify his presence, when Giles spoke, and, by a natural impulse, George remained still and silent.

"She be beautiful," said Giles, in a mournful tone; "she be beautiful as the sun, but she do despise me. There be no flowers like her—there be no music—but she do despise me. Phœbe, Phœbe, I do love thee, better than all the world. I would live for thee, or I would die for thee—but thou dost not love me."

George heard him, then, after a pause, sobbing bitterly; and he would fain have left the spot, if he could have done so without noise, for he felt that it was unworthy of him to listen to the reflections even of his rival; but again Giles spoke, and his voice trembled with emotion, and a deep sob would occasionally choke his utterance.

"She be an angel—she be more beautiful than a dew-drop in the morning, when it be shining, with a world of colours, from Heaven—she be like a young dove, she be so gentle and so good—she loves the birds—the trees—and flowers—but she do not love me."

Heavy sighs seemed now to prevent Giles from further speech, and George felt that this, indeed, was a drawback to his new-born felicity.

"Even poor Andy," continued Giles, "she be kind to, and old Bardam, and every living thing she do speak kindly to but me. No, she has no kind word for me—none—none; and I do love her better than all."

A silence now ensued of some minutes, and George felt the peculiar awkwardness of his situation. He thought, however, he might creep away unobserved, and was about to do so, when Giles again spoke in a raised voice.

"I will not cry for thee, Phœbe," he said, "but—but I will have thee. George shall never call thee his while I live; I will die for thee, but I will have thee."

George now stepped forward and said, "Giles!"

"Ha!" cried Giles, "beest thee here?"

"I am," said George, "but quite accidentally, and not with any purpose of listening to you. Giles, I would fain be friends with you; you are too honest-hearted to be unjust."

"Friends with me," cried Giles; "friends with me? No, no. Thee can never be friends with me, thee love Phœbe!"

"As I love truth, life, and Heaven," cried George.

"Thee shall not have her, though. Thee cannot love her as I do. I—I would die for her; I would do murder for her; I would—I would. I tell thee, thee shall not have her."

"You do not love her truly," cried George; "it is yourself you love, not Phœbe. True love seeks the happiness of the loved object above all other things, and you do not——"

"Not love her?" answered Giles; "I love her as much as I hate thee."

"Giles," replied George, sorrowfully, for he saw what havoc disappointed passion had made in the mind of his rival. "I would be glad to take thee by the hand in fellowship. If Phœbe, much as I love her, gave the preference to you, I would leave her to-morrow with a heartfelt prayer for her and your happiness."

"But I tell thee she shall be mine, and thee can, therefore, leave when thee like, and my curse go with thee."

"Phœbe's own lips have power only to decide between us," said George, "and God alone has power to curse. It is in vain to reason with you, so good night; I shall retire to rest."

"I wish thee no good night," cried Giles, as George entered the mill. "I—I—I could tear thee heart out of thee breast. I will have her—I will have her. Devils! devils! she shall be mine—she she shall—I say she shall."

CHAPTER XXIX.

THE discomfitted Ralph Freegrove left the cottage of the miller, breathing threats of bitter vengeance against the whole of its inhabitants, and particularly the miller's man, who had overcome him so signally. He had not been at all aware that there was such a person as George at the mill; but he had seen enough in his short visit to feel assured that George would be a great stumbling-block in the way of the schemes of both himself and his master. What those schemes were will appear very shortly.

When the first ebullition of his passion was over, the polite Ralph Freegrove blamed himself very much for his rashness in thus for ever shutting the miller's door against him, when he had such cogent reasons for wishing to become a visiter there, if possible; and, on his road back to Haredale Park, he strove to arrange some plan of operations, which should repair what he considered his unfortunate blunder, which had arisen from his too hasty disposition.

He immediately ordered lights when he arrived at the hall, and taking from his pocket a letter, he commenced reading it with great attention, taking no heed whatever of the servant's announcement that Mr. Scrimp had been patiently waiting an hour to see him.

The letter was addressed to himself, and ran thus:—

"MY DEAR SIR,—

"Knowing your kind wish to become acquainted with anything that is stirring at Haredale, I take up my pen just to say that the crops are very good. A Mr. Pomander, a young medical man, has settled here, and, I think, is rather an acquisition, as he seems quite a man of the world.

"The cattle have been rather unhealthy, and Farmers Maywood and Hodges are in arrear, and must be seen to. We sincerely hope to see you and Sir Herbert, to whom I beg to tender, through you, my grateful service and most profound acknowledgments, soon amongst us again.

"Believe me to be, my dear sir,
"With the greatest esteem,
"Your very grateful servant,
"OLIVER SCRIMP."

"P.S.—By the by, the miller has a daughter—the miller Gilbert, I mean, who I should like you to see, as you are a judge of exquisite beauty."

"Humph!" said Mr. Freegrove, when he finished this epistle. "And upon this, Sir Herbert has sent me down here to take a look at this 'exquisite beauty,' and by all that's lovely, she is an extraordinary girl; I never saw her equal. Ha! ha! Scrimp's a good-pointer—he'll find the game. I am expected to run it down, and Sir Herbert to come in at the death. Humph! we shall see—I rather like the girl myself. By Heavens! who would have thought there was such a rare piece of goods rusticating down here? It'll be a devil of a troublesome job though, I'll be sworn, for the old miller, with his cursed morality and his nonsense, is enough to drive anybody frantic."

Mr. Scrimp at this moment gently opened the room door, and, with a servile smile, stepped into the room. Mr. Scrimp worshipped anybody who had money and power; and he knew very well that Ralph Freegrove had been so long with Sir Herbert Foster, and had become so necessary to him, that he was nearly as important a person as the baronet himself. It was, therefore, with a cringing manner that Mr. Scrimp, attorney-at-law, entered the presence of Mr. Freegrove, and said,—

"My dear sir—my very dear sir—how do you do? What an unexpected pleasure to see you at Haredale; dear me, I hope Sir Herbert is well?"

"Bother," cried Mr. Freegrove, in reply to this address. "You expected me directly I could get down here, after receiving your note."

"Oh! oh!—dear me, yes—about Maywood and Hodgson; they owe two quarters. Really they ——"

"Now will you be reasonable? What's the use of pretending to be virtuous, and all that sort of humbug here?—I know you—I've seen the girl."

" Why, my dear sir," said Mr. Scrimp, " you must be aware that there's a way of conducting these little matters, you understand, which is more favourable to—to the feelings, you know, of a gentleman, you see—a sort of moral varnish——"

" A moral fiddlestick," cried Fregrove. " Come, to business. I've seen the girl you wrote about, the miller's daughter, you know."

" Well ?" said Mr. Scrimp.

" She's an out and outer," cried Mr. Freegrove. " Scrimp, you're a famous fellow; you've got the best nose in the county. Sir Herbert, I feel sure, will stand any sum we please for current expenses in the business."

" No doubt, no doubt," cried the lawyer. " He is a most liberal gentleman ; it's a pleasure to do any little service for him ; he's a perfect gem, and—and so charitable. I dare say he'll provide for the girl. It's uncommon pleasant, Mr. Freegrove, to see persons who have the means, like Sir Herbert Foster, of casting an eye to the wants of the poor."

" Now, d—— it, Scrimp," cried Ralph, " don't let us have any more moral varnish. The girl's a fine girl, and Sir Herbert will spare no expense, I know, to get hold of her. How comes it we never heard of her before ?"

" Why, from all I can learn," said Mr. Scrimp, " she was not at the mill in early life ; but the miller and his wife say, she was at nurse with a distant relative, who, dying suddenly, they had to take her home about five years ago."

" Humph !—and who is the fellow there who looks so jaunty, and not like a miller's man—not Giles, but another !"

" Oh, his name is George Andrews. The miller has only engaged him lately ; and who he is, nobody knows."

" D—— him," cried Mr. Freegrove, to Mr. Scrimp's surprise, " I'll let him know soon exactly who I am, or I know a good reason why."

" Oh ! you saw him, too, then ?"

" Saw him, yes, and felt him, too. I'll tell you how it was : I called at the mill, and old Gilbert and his ranting old dame became abusive, and I got out of temper, and had a bit of a tustle with the old man, when in comes this George Andrews—the devil seize him—and gave me a fall."

" Dear me, Mr. Freegrove, gave you a fall ! Bless me, I really thought nobody could do that."

" D—— what you thought. I was entangled among the whole lot of them ; that's how it was. " But I'll give Master George Andrews a fall before I leave Haredale again, that he shan't get up from so easy quite, as I did. I'll——"

" Now really," cried Mr. Scrimp, in a flurried manner, " excuse me, my dear sir, but these threats, you know, are very injudicious. Suppose any little accident should happen, and in the high generous feelings of your mind you were to meet the man, and he was to die, you know, don't you see ?"

" Why, you mean to say you'd give evidence that I said I'd do it ?"

" Oh, no—oh, dear, no—you didn't say you'd do it—you only joked about a fall—he ! he ! a mere joke—a—a passing jest—friendly—merely friendly."

" I suppose that's some more moral varnish !" said Freegrove, with a sneer.

" Mr. Freegrove" replied Mr. Scrimp, slightly irritated, " that's legal varnish, which might save you from being hanged some fine day."

" Well, well," said Mr. Freegrove, flinching slightly, " there's an end of it. I can't go to the cottage of the miller again, and, therefore, you must. Sir Herbert told me to see the girl, and, if she suited, to offer to repair the mill, and so on, so as to be on decent visiting terms with old Gilbert."

" Humph !" said Mr. Scrimp ; " really I don't think I should be very wel-

come, for don't you recollect I served the processes, to try and turn them out of the garden grounds ; but rather than take a third party in, I think I'll try what can be done."

"If nothing else will do," said Freegrove, "we must get some men from London, who are not known here, and fairly carry her off."

"Now, really you are cruel and indiscreet, Mr. Freegrove. I did not hear your last remark, but I fear it was something illegal. I've often taken the liberty of advising Sir Herbert, but he's a most straightforward, fine character, and he always said,—'Pho! pho! Scrimp, there's no harm.'"

"And what kind of varnish used you to recommend to him?" sneered Ralph.

"Why," said the lawyer, who generally retorted upon Mr. Freegrove whenever he said anything particularly sneering or unpleasant, "I said to him, 'Sir Herbert, seduce who you like, but get rid of the violent blackguards who urge you to strong measures, or some of these days—he—dear me, I mean they will drive you into a criminal court.'"

"Ha! ha! ha!" laughed Ralph, "you can be bitter when you like, Scrimp ; it's tit for tat, however, we're never the worse friends."

"My dear sir, you do me great honour."

"Well, well, you'll undertake the job? You'll call on the miller, and write to Sir Herbert that matters have begun, and are in a good train."

"I shall," said Mr. Scrimp ; "the first thing in the morning it shall be done. Sir Herbert is very kind, indeed, and deserves great praise."

"Very good," grinned Freegrove. "I shall sleep here, and wait in for you to-morrow morning."

"Mr. Scrimp left Haredale Park, and proceeded homewards. He had not, however, got far before he thought he saw some one slinking before him, and his eyes deceived him, or it was his clerk, Mr. Perk. He quickened his pace, and called—

No. 22

"Mr. Perk!—Perk! I say."

That gentleman, finding himself thus discovered, immediately turned and walked, with a confident air, up to his master, to whom he said,—

"I have been for some time watching for you, Mr. Scrimp. Your very footsteps are dogged, sir."

"So it seems," said the attorney, drily.

"Mr. Pomander," continued Perk, "has been dodging about the park, evidently on the look-out for somebody or something."

"Mr. Pomander!" said Scrimp, "what can he want? Humph. That is a man who will either be a friend or a foe, as he is made one or the other."

"Is Sir Herbert arrived?" asked Perk, in an indifferent tone.

"No," said his master; "Ralph Freegrove is there. He came down about Maywood and Hodgson's arrears—they must be seen to in the morning—don't neglect it, Mr. Perk."

"Oh, dear no, not at all. It's all very fine," thought Perk, "but there's something in the wind, that I don't know nothing about, but will soon, or else my name isn't Perk—oh, no, by no means—not at all."

The morning arrived, serene and beautiful, and the inhabitants of the cottage and the mill rose to their daily labour; but how different were the feelings with which they severally hailed the coming day. George had risen early, and again sought the meadow, which would be henceforward ever associated in his mind with the happiness he had enjoyed in it. There, with his eyes fixed upon the window at which Phœbe was wont to appear in the morning, he waited, with a heart beating with love and joy, the moment when he should see her smiling face among the roses, which nearly obscured the latticed window.

Her first thought, too, as she awoke, was of George, and how happy would he have been could he have seen the sweet smile that dimpled her glowing cheeks as she, whispering, pronounced his name.

At length the window opened—George waved his hand—their eyes met, and they needed not words to express to each other the feelings of their kindred hearts.

Not long had this sweet interchange of love taken place, when Giles, with a slow and measured step, came forth from the mill.

Sleep had evidently been a stranger to his eyes, and his face was pale and haggard, so much so, that George started as he saw him, and could hardly believe that it was really Giles who stood before him.

Slowly he walked onwards, without appearing to notice George, and placed himself opposite to the window of Phœbe's room, and he looked so wretched and truly miserable, that George could not find in his heart to interfere with him, but allowed him to place himself so as to complerely intercept his view of Phœbe.

Phœbe was much startled at the pale and haggard appearance of Giles, as he there stood, profoundly still with his arms folded across his breast, and glaring at her with his blood-shot eyes, while his whole frame seemed to tremble with emotion.

"Giles," she said, "speak; what is the matter?—shall I call father?—you look ill, Giles."

"I am not ill," said Giles, and the sound of his voice startled George and Phœbe, it was so strange and unearthly. "I am not ill," he repeated; "I am well and happy."

"Well and happy!" echoed George.

"Yes," cried Giles, turning fiercely; "well and happy—ha! ha!—I am looking upon my bride—my wife that is to be; I've sworn it I will have her—she be mine—she be mine."

Phœbe was much alarmed at the excited tone in which Giles spoke, and immediately retired from the window to seek the miller.

"Giles, Giles," said George, "this is madness—sheer madness—I pity you from my soul."

"Away," cried Giles, "away! I hate thee sight of thee. Thee hast sent her away—my Phœbe, where be she gone?—I loved her afore thee came—I loved her when she was a little thing and sat upon my knee—I loved her then—I love her now—ha! ha!—we shall be happy—happy as the day be long, for she be mine—my Phœbe—mine, mine."

The miller now emerged from his cottage, and was astonished to see Giles looking so unlike his usual appearance, and speaking in so frenzied a manner.

"Phœbe, my Phœbe," cried the infuriated Giles, approaching the miller; "I want my Phœbe. You know I do love her—five years I have loved her; she be mine—she be mine; you know she be mine."

"Why, Giles, lad," said the miller, "be thee mad? She be mine, and thee hast no right to claim my child. Get thee to thee work, lad; thee looks like a ghost. What does all this mean, George? Is thee lad moon-stricken?"

"It means this," cried Giles, suddenly turning, and clutching George by the breast. "This it means, that Phœbe shall be his—never, never—I'll have his heart out first—she be mine, I tell e'—my Phœbe."

George was unprepared for this attack, and Giles's strength was so much increased by the excitement of his mind, that he for a moment staggered under it. In an instant or two, however, he recovered himself, and a fearful contest would most likely have ensued, even supposing George to have maintained sufficient strength to have acted only in self-defence, had not Phœbe suddenly rushed from the cottage, and placed her hand full upon the breast of the infuriated Giles.

The effect of this simple and unpremeditated action of Phœbe's seemed magical. He loosened his hold of George, and his hands dropped listlessly to his side as he faintly said,—

"Phœbe! Phœbe!"

A stillness, as of the grave, succeeded for several moments, and Phœbe continued looking fixedly in Giles's face, and her hand was still pressed upon his breast.

"You have said you loved me, Giles?" she said firmly.

Giles seemed to try to speak, but was unable.

"If you would have me look upon you as I never yet looked upon living thing—if you would have me not hate you, as I hate strife and contention, you will never let me again see your hand raised against George Andrews. Giles," she continued, and her voice softened down to sweet tones of mild entreaty —"Giles, you have known me long, you have been kind to me, and I have ever loved you as a brother; you do not want to kill Phœbe? Oh! Giles, Giles, be yourself again."

Neither the miller nor George spoke or moved during this scene, and Giles, for a few seconds after she had done speaking, continued gazing in her face, as if he would still drink in the magic of her words, or fain linger still, while the tones of her voice yet lived and lingered in his ears. Then he tried to speak, but his lips only moved, and clasping his hands over his face to hide his deep emotion, he rushed into the mill.

"What be all this about, George, my lad?" cried the miller in great bewilderment.

"Indeed sir," said George, "I can hardly tell you. Giles suddenly came from the mill in the state you have seen him, and he had not been here more than a moment or two when you came from the cottage."

"Dear me! dear me!" cried the miller. "The lad's gone clean mad for love. What can we do with him? George, my lad, don't thee catch the disorder, or I shall have to work the mill by myself, with nobody to lend a hand but poor Tim Miggles, who, I be thinking, is the most sensible of the whole of thee. Go to thee work, George, and don't 'e stand there pulling faces at Phœbe, and she pulling faces at thee. Get thee in, lass, and I will see what be the matter with poor Giles, who really seems to have lost the few wits he be blessed with. Here comes Tim, I'll warrant, by his hurry, with some news."

Tim Miggles, as the miller spoke, might have been observed hurrying towards them from the mill, and ever and anon looking behind him with the most ludicrous terror.

"Well, Tim, lad, what be it now?" asked the miller. "Hast seen a ghost, boy, that thee stares so?"

Tim looked from one to the other, and produced from his pocket a dirty greasy bit of paper, from which he commenced reading,—

> "There's rats in the mill,
> And be sure they will,
> Unless you kill
> Them, continue still
> Their insides to fill,
> From the grist just now in the brave old mill."

"Don't be a fool," cried the miller. "Come, give me that paper. Where did you get it?"

"What do you think of it, master?" said Tim, with a smile. "I sat up last night to write it. Don't tell missus. I think it's rather the thing, I do."

"You sat up all night, did you, to write such rubbish? Ah! that's how it is you're lolloping about and falling asleep every minute of the day. What the dickens are you winking at?"

Tim had commenced a vigorous course of winking at George, and then approaching close to him, he said,—

"Have you found it?—tell it us, do. Is it a real good one?"

"What is he talking about?" cried the miller.

"It's merely some silly rhyme, sir," said George, "that Tim has been teazing me to think of for him."

"Silly, indeed," cried Tim, as "'The Despairing Lobster and the Bandit Crab,' commence with—no, let me see, it ain't that; it's 'The Castle of Humphumooblaidin, or the Cream turned Sour,' where it says,—

> "'Them as forgets the wery next day,
> All them ere promises as they guved away,
> Is just like the snail what plumped in, they say,
> To the cream which the baron had caused to be laid in
> The elegant dairy of Humphumooblaid n.'"

"Stuff, stuff," cried the miller. "Where's Giles? Did thee see him in the mill, thee simpleton?"

"I came to tell you o' purpose," replied Tim.

"Then why did thee put off time with thee nonsense and poetry. What hast thee got to say?"

"Why, master, in comes Giles, in a wery great rage, and he says she shall be mine, he says, I've swored that ere—she shall me mine—'Who,' says I, 'who?' Then he looks just like the 'Unhappy Perriwinkle,' as no doubt you're read on, and he says 'Phœbe.' Then I says, 'Maybe she be.' Can you find anything better than that? Then round he turns, and he catches me a wipe on the head, and then he kicks me out of the mill. Oh, dear! oh, lauks! oh, everything. Egad! I can't help thinking as that ere black Giles is mad."

"And so I think, too," said the miller. "Poor lad, he be a good lad in the main, and he have been with me so long, that I be loath to part with him."

"Dear father," said Phœbe, "he will be better. Forgive him now, and he may not thus vex you again. Poor Giles! I am so sorry for him."

" Well, well, my lass, get thee in, will 'e, and go to thee work, George. I do see what all this be about; it be thy pretty face, Phœbe, that be the cause of all this mischief. Thee will have to take one of the lads to make peace, my child. Bless thee, thee need not blush so. We will talk about all that by and by. Drab it, George, art thee going to thee work? What dost thee mean by kissing thee hand, and making such antics? Go to thee work. Who be that coming along the meadow?"

CHAPTER XXX.

THE miller looked earnestly in the direction of the meadow as he spoke, and a cloud came across his usually serene and jovial face, as he saw who his visiter was.

" More trouble, more trouble," he said. " That be Lawyer Scrimp, and be sure he be come on some knave's errand. Get thee in, Phœbe; he shall not come within my door if I can help it."

Mr. Scrimp came trippingly along, with a smirk and a smile, in the most amiable manner imaginable to where the miller stood, but he met with no answering politeness, for the miller, with a look of dogged obstinacy, stood upon the threshold of the door, determined to defend the sanctity of his humble dwelling against what he considered the contaminating presence of the man of law.

Mr. Scrimp did not seem exactly to like the posture of affairs, for he several times stole a glance behind him, as if to see that his retreat was by no means cut off, but was perfectly clear and safe. Then, with an immense expenditure of smiles, he approached the miller.

" Ha! my good friend, how are you?" said Mr. Scrimp, laying, as was his custom, a great emphasis upon the word " how."

" I be very well, Lawyer Scrimp," said the miller; " but there be one who came here last night, and called me his dear friend first, and then an old bull-headed wretch. Now, I'd rather, you see, that thee would say at once what thee hast got to say."

" Ah! very good, very good," cried Mr. Scrimp, pretending to take the miller's bluntness in good part. " You are a plain-speaking honest man, Master Gilbert. Candour and plain dealing for me all the world over. Ha! there's nothing like it—nothing."

The miller made a great many wry faces at Mr. Scrimp's professions, but he contented himself with a grunt of disapproval, not of the sentiments, but of the man who uttered them, and Mr. Scrimp continued,

" I come here, my good sir, with feelings of great, I may say, intense satisfaction."

" Thee be very easily pleased then," said the miller, gruffly.

" Sir Herbert Foster, my dear sir, is now thoroughly convinced that you were right in that little friendly piece of business about the garden-ground."

" And so be I," said the miller; " but the jury at Devonport convinced Sir Herbert, you know, lawyer, and it be my own conscience as convinced me."

" Very true, very true. Sir Herbert says, just lately, in a conversation with a friend, ' Now,' says he, ' there's the miller, Gilbert, an honester man never lived; he has my warm esteem—my warm esteem. I was very wrong about the garden-ground; it was an error of the head, though not of the heart."

" Lawyer Scrimp, come to the point. What does thee want with me?"

" In a moment, my good sir, in a moment. Then he said, ' I must make him some amends ; I don't feel easy about that business.' "

" I should wonder if he did," interrupted the miller.

" Then he thought for a little, and said, ' I'll repair that mill for him, I will indeed ; it shall be done, and that good creature, Scrimp, shall see it all done.'"

The miller looked very hard for some minutes in the lawyer's face before he replied, and the habitual effrontery even of Mr. Scrimp shrunk from the steady gaze of the old man.

" Thee said thee liked plain dealing, lawyer. Now what do Sir Herbert expect in return for repairing the old mill ? What be his scheme ?"

Mr. Scrimp flushed in the face very slightly as he replied,

" Expect ! my good sir, oh nothing—nothing but the pleasant feeling of a good action. Good deeds, my dear sir, are their own reward."

" They be," said the miller ; " thee hath spoke truth there ; and I can tell thee, too, that bad deeds be their own punishment. Thee art at something, thee and Sir Herbert, but d— thee both, thee shall not touch so much as an old nail in the mill while I, Gilbert the miller, own it."

" Oh, very well," cried the lawyer, somewhat staggered at this unexpected opposition to an offer which he thought a master stroke of policy ; " if you don't wish it repaired, that's another thing. I merely called to state Sir Herbert's kind intentions ; nothing else in the world."

" Then, perhaps, thee will go now," said the miller, with great coolness.

" Why, ah ! yes—oh, dear, yes—you're busy, of course—your time is always valuable, I'm aware. This is a sweet place—oh ! dear me, a most sweet place—a little earthly paradise—I never saw your garden look so well before, my dear sir ; it really looks as if some presiding genius honoured it by —by—oh ! dear me, Miss. I wish you very good morning. How do you do ?"

These latter remarks were addressed to Phœbe, who at the moment walked from the door of the cottage to enter the garden.

Phœbe merely bowed slightly, and looked at the miller, as if to see what he would wish her to do. He slightly waved his hand, and she returned to the house.

" A most charming girl ! oh, dear me," said Mr. Scrimp, " you may well be proud of her, my dear sir, and keep her secluded from all female society. I almost think I should myself, if I was blest with such a really——"

" I will shut the gate after thee, if thee please," said the miller, moving to the gate which led to the meadow, and holding it open.

" Oh ! dear, thank you. You are so kind—so friendly—so—so hospitable, really you must not press me to stay any longer. Business, you know, miller, must be attended to. Some other time, when I've an hour or two to spare, I'll just pop in and take pot luck."

" Perhaps thee'll wait till thee are asked ?"

" No, no," said the audacious Mr. Scrimp, who was resolved to take no offence short of a kick. " No, no, you'd be making preparations, and putting yourself out of the way, as well as your good dame, and your charming daughter."

The miller's wrath was rising as he held the gate, and Mr. Scrimp thus defied his indignation.

" Thee may be d—d," said Gilbert, at length ; " and I hope never to see thy rascally face again. Dost thee understand that, drat thee ?"

This was rather plain, and Mr. Scrimp felt that he ought to have gone before things went so far. He was, however, relieved from his perplexity by a cry from the mill, and Tim Miggles came rushing and calling loud for the miller.

" Master, master, they're at it again. There they go—they're at it again,

" Poker and tongs,
Shovels and prongs.

It's the old story, master.

> " George is a kicking up a shindy;
> 'Cause Giles says he'll throw him out at the windy.

So I runs atween 'em, and they both rolls over me ;

> " And by the whales and little fishes,
> Don't you see master they have tore my br——."

"Peace, peace," cried the miller, much vexed that Scrimp should have been there, and heard of these dissensions at the mill. " Now, Mr. Scrimp——"

"Oh, dear me, my good sir, these little domestic fracas will happen in the best regulated houses. Don't mind me a bit. Perhaps, as a friend of the family, I may be of some assistance. Assault and battery, I think you mentioned, young man ?"

At this moment Giles rushed from the mill, followed by George. He was in an instant by the side of the miller, and holding aloft a blue silken ribbon, with something attached to it.

"He shall not have it," he cried, " never—never. I'd a torn it from the middle o' his heart, I would. She be mine—she be. She did place her hand upon my breast, and it did calm my heart, and I knew she would be mine—my Phœbe—my little Phœbe. I have nursed her on my knee, and she be mine—mine."

"Eh ?—ah !—oh, dear me. Lunatico inquirendo," said Mr. Scrimp, smiling. " Dear, dear, who would have thought it ? How vexed dear Sir Herbert will be."

"Giles, Giles," said the miller, " I must part with thee. Thee will bring disgrace upon us and upon theeself. What hast thee got there ?"

Before, however, anybody could reply, Phœbe came from the cottage, and took the piece of ribbon from the hand of Giles, and, with a face suffused with crimson, rushed back again, before the miller could interfere to prevent her.

George's face had burst into a radiant smile as Phœbe appeared ; and now that she was gone again, he stood gazing abstractedly at the cottage door, through which she had passed.

The miller seemed about to address George ; but, recollecting himself, he turned to Mr. Scrimp, who stood muttering all sorts of unintelligible offers of service, as a dear friend of the lovely family.

"Mr. Scrimp," said the miller, " we wish thee to go."

"Oh, dear, yes ; private family business, I suppose, coming on. Really your charming daughter seems to have done some mischief. I wish you a very good morning, indeed."

"We must take the morning as we find it," replied the miller. " I am pleased to see the last of thee, and hope never to be troubled with thee again."

"Oh, dear, it's a pleasure," muttered Mr. Scrimp, as he walked towards the gate, in which progress he took occasion to pass close to Giles, to whom he whispered,—

"Be calm—meet me at nine at Foyle's Hollow."

Giles started back, but the lawyer had passed on, and he could hardly believe that it was, indeed, he who had spoken to him.

"The time be come," said the miller, " when we must have an end of all this. George and Giles, now both of thee hear me, lads. It be very likely that Phœbe will have one of thee ; and whichever she do have, I will see if I cannot leave them the mill."

George was about to speak, but the miller, with a wave of his hand, commanded silence, and continued,—

"Thee shall both come into the cottage, and we shall see who Phœbe do prefer, if so she be inclined to either of thee: but thee must promise me that whoever she do refuse shall be quiet, and put up with the decision."

"I am perfectly willing," cried George, "and happy to accede to such a course; and here I solemnly promise, that should Phœbe prefer Giles, I will be content."

"Thee may easily promise that," said Giles; "thee knows thee has had good hopes that thee be chosen; but I tell 'e Phœbe be mine—she be—be mine afore thee saw her."

"Well, well," cried the miller, "enough of this. Do you consent, Giles, to the matter I have mentioned?"

Giles had been much struck by Mr. Scrimp's manner when he desired him to meet him at Foyle's Hollow, which was an unfrequented and romantic dale, about a quarter of a mile from the mill, and he thought, that before submitting to the ordeal which the miller proposed, he had much better hear what his new friend, the lawyer, had to say upon the subject. He, therefore, replied,—

"Give me till to-morrow, master—I be not in spirits to-day—give me till to-morrow."

"Certainly," said the miller; "and now, lads, to your work, and do not let me hear any more noise or quarrelling. Thee ought to be ashamed of theeselves. Away with thee both."

Mr. Scrimp was tolerably well satisfied with his visit to the miller's, although he had certainly most signally failed in his main object, which was to induce a feeling of obligation to Sir Herbert Foster in the mind of the miller, which should pave the way to visit, and a degree of intimacy, which would materially forward the views of the vicious and unscrupulous baronet.

The discovery, however, that there was dissension at the mill, he seemed to regard as of great importance to his interests, and he fully believed that the disappointment of Giles, the miller's man, would prompt him to be a ready tool in the hands of Sir Herbert Foster and his agents.

It was, therefore, with great exultation that Mr. Scrimp hastened to Haredale Park, to disclose to Ralph Freegrove the result of his proceedings at the miller's cottage.

"Well," said Freegrove, "what news?"

"Glorious news," replied the lawyer. "There's a division in the enemy's camp. We have a spy at head quarters."

"What do you mean?" demanded Freegrove. "Have you bribed the miller's dame with a new cloak, or a gown, or what?"

"Neither, my good sir. But this girl,—this Phœbe, seems to have turned the heads of the miller's men; and Giles, who, you know, has been a long time at the mill, seems to be a disappointed suitor."

"Humph!—Well."

"Why, don't you see, my dear sir? This Giles, while his anger and rage is on him, will be the very man to assist Sir Herbert in—in his charitable purposes."

Ralph replied by a broad grin, and nodded his head.

"We shall, at least," continued the lawyer, "get every information from him, in case of—of being obliged, by the obstinacy of these people, to— to——"

"Use a little violence—ha! ha!—a little rough varnish," said Ralph.

"Oh! dear me, no—nowhere—that is illegal—nothing of the sort—nothing but the most gentle persuasion in the world."

"Well, well, have it your own way—just as you like—it shall be moral violence, if you please, Mr. Scrimp, and no other."

"You had better, I think," said Mr. Scrimp, "come with me to Foyle's Hollow. You can keep out of sight, you know, as two might alarm the

fellow; but I should like you to know immediately what I am able to effect with him."

"I will," said Ralph. "What time do you go?"

"At nine; and now, when do you expect Sir Herbert Foster?"

"I have written to him, and make no doubt he will be down here to-morrow some time in the day. This will prove a troublesome job, lawyer, I am thinking."

"No, no, it must be done legally. I cannot sanction any other mode; and if it fail, then I am out of it, you know. No violence."

As they spoke, the rattling of wheels were heard in the avenue which approached the house, and Freegrove, springing to the window, exclaimed,—

"By everything that's Sir Herbert's travelling carriage, and he's inside of it, I'll wager my head!"

Mr. Scrimp immediately assumed an air of the most bland humility when he heard of the close proximity of Sir Herbert, and seemed at once ready to attack him with a legion of bows and smiles.

The sound of the wheels rapidly increased on the ear, and presently Mr. Scrimp could see from the window the handsome travelling chariot of Sir Herbert Foster dashing across the lawn, and rattling among the loose gravel.

The carriage now drew up to the hall door—the steps were lowered—and, to the utter astonishment of the bewildered Mr. Scrimp, there stepped out Mr. Pomander, with a face wreathed in smiles, and then Sir Herbert Foster, who seemed on the very best possible terms with his companion.

Ralph Freegrove had hurried to the door to receive his master, and the lawyer was alone. After ascertaining this fact, he exclaimed,—

"D—n you!" as he shook his clenched fist in the direction of Mr. Pomander.

In about a quarter of an hour Ralph Freegrove entered the room.

No. 23

"Mr. Scrimp," he said, "how the devil did that fellow, who I hear is the Mr. Pomander you spoke of in your letter, get hold of Sir Herbert?"

"Upon my word," said Mr. Scrimp, "I'm astonished. The thing is perfectly inexplicable to me. He's a clever man—a remarkably clever man."

"Confound his cleverness!" cried Ralph; "I can tell you he seems all in all with Sir Herbert, and they are talking now about different sorts of physics."

"Did Sir Herbert ask for me?" said Mr. Scrimp.

"No, indeed, he didn't," replied Ralph; "he hardly spoke at all; but I think I'll tell him you are here. We must not be done by that infernal doctor, if he were as clever as the devil himself."

"Dear me, no—by no means," said Mr. Scrimp. "My dear Mr. Freegrove, you know we share and share alike in these little matters."

"To be sure," replied Ralph; "I'll just go directly."

Mr. Scrimp waited for some time in great impatience for the return of Ralph Freegrove, and at last he appeared.

"Pomander is gone," he said, "and Sir Herbert is taking a bath, after which, he says, he should like to see you if you can wait."

"Oh, dear me, yes, by all means. I'll wait, my dear sir, with great pleasure."

In about half an hour a servant entered to announce that Sir Herbert Foster would see Mr. Scrimp, and that gentleman arose with great alacrity and followed the domestic.

He was conducted to a dressing-room, where Sir Herbert reclined upon a couch with an appearance of great langour and indolence.

Sir Herbert Foster's income was enormous, for the two baronets who had preceded him had happened both to be exceedingly frugal men, and the property had, under their management, greatly increased, so that even the extravagances of the present holder of the estates for nearly twenty years, although it had greatly encumbered his property and reduced his annual income, had failed materially to effect him, and between twenty and thirty thousand pounds per annum were still at the disposal of the heartless and profligate Sir Herbert Foster.

The room was magnificently furnished and adorned. It was replete with every luxury which the imagination could conceive. Costly mirrors—superb hangings—rare plants—pictures, in short, everything that could add to the enjoyment of a refined voluptuary and educated libertine was there to be found.

Reclining upon a sofa of flowered crimson velvet, and seemingly thinking of nothing, and gazing upon the ceiling, was Sir Herbert Foster. His age at this period was thirty-eight, and but for his dissolute habits, and the years of excess in all kinds of animal indulgences which had passed over him, he might have been called a handsome man.

His eyes, however, were sunken and dim, his hand trembled, and his frame was altogether weakened by his vicious mode of life.

He was one of the most selfish of men. He had but one principle of action, and that was to decide whether a proceeding was pleasant or unpleasant to himself. The consequences to others never entered into his imagination. Those who were his most ready tools in procuring for him gratification, could have found no sure claim upon his gratitude thereby. With the price that they received for their services terminated all Sir Herbert's thoughts on the matter. He would not have changed an easy posture on his couch for a doubtful one to ensure the happiness and prosperity of one half the human race.

Such was Sir Herbert Foster; and yet he was followed, admired, deferred to, and applauded. He was the rich—the great—the fashionable—the elegant Sir Herbert Foster.

Mr. Scrimp almost held his breath as he entered the room, and kept up a succession of bows, which were entirely lost upon Sir Herbert, whose eyes happened to be turned in another direction; and had he been told that a thunderbolt was at the door waiting his pleasure, he would certainly not have exerted himself so far as to turn round.

Standing in the recess of a window, was Sir Herbert's valet, a young man of supercilious aspect; but a close observer might well have shrunk from an examination of the face of that man, for sneaking villany was stamped on every feature.

Mr. Scrimp waited for some few minutes, but Sir Herbert Foster did not betray the least symptom of being aware of his presence.

The silence was very embarrassing, and Mr. Scrimp at length broke it by saying,—

"Sir Herbert, your very humble servant. I rejoice to see you, Sir Herbert, at Haredale."

"Eh—ah," said Sir Herbert, after a long pause, "Cury!"

"Sir Herbert," said the valet, stepping forward.

"Who?" said his master.

"Mr. Scrimp, Sir Herbert."

"Oh!—ah!—Scrimp—how do?"

"You are very kind, Sir Herbert," said Mr. Scrimp; "I have the honour to be very well, Sir Herbert, if you please."

"Cury!"

"Sir Herbert."

"Go."

The valet immediatly left the room.

"Eh—ah!—Scrimp—I—I—draw the blinds, there's a—a—disgusting vulgar light down here."

Mr. Scrimp immediately drew down the blinds as he remarked,—

"Oh, dear me, yes! it's very wrong, there's a great deal too much light in the country."

"Scrimp," said Sir Herbert again, after a pause, "the female—ah! ah!—the young female!"

"The Miller's Maid, Sir Herbert?" said the lawyer.

"I—I—ah—don't know nor care whose maid she is!—ah—ah!"

"No, certainly not,—oh, dear, certainly not! It's merely accidental, Sir Herbert. She happens to be the Miller's Maid, if you please."

"Very well. Was—ah!—that the man—ah!—about the pigstye?"

"The gardener, Sir Herbert, he's a bad man,—a very wrong-headed, obstinate man. He wouldn't give up his garden, if you recollect, Sir Herbert, —oh, dear, no!"

"Let him—ah— ah—keep it."

"Exactly. I am sure you are very good, Sir Herbert—most kind indeed. You are——"

"Stuff! Fetch the girl."

"Why, my dear sir, we have not just yet, you see, Sir Herbert — She don't exactly know the honour. There are, Sir Herbert, vulgar prejudices."

"How much money do they—ah—require for their prejudices?"

"Why, I think, Sir Herbert, that I can put things to a proper train—for—for—I should say a couple of hundred or so."

"Oh—ah! I forget. A man wrote me a letter. He's a physical fellow—a—ah!"

"Pomander?" said Mr. Scrimp, inquiringly.

"Oh—ah! I think it was Pomander, or something of that kind."

"He took the liberty of writing to you, Sir Herbert?"

"Ah—yes—he did. Cury, read the letter, and then put me—ah—into the travelling carriage, and I saw him."

"Yes, Sir Herbert," said Scrimp, eagerly.

"Ah!—he says he knows the female, and she is—charming—charming!"

"She is indeed, Sir Herbert, most charming. Her beauty is most rare. I never saw her equal, and I think you will agree with me when you see her, Sir Herbert."

"Yes—I—am going to see her to-morrow."

"To-morrow!" cried Mr. Scrimp, amazed.

"Yes—I—am going with the man—the Pomgranate—or Pomagrantum—whatever is his name."

"Pomander, Sir Herbert."

"Oh—ah! he's going to let me see her."

"But how?—dear me, how, Sir Herbert?"

"Ah! don't know."

"There will be great difficulty—dear me, great difficulty."

"Ah! don't care. Cury!"

"He's not here, Sir Herbert; shall I ring?"

"Yes—ah!"

The obsequeous valet immediately answered the summons.

"Ah—eh! show Scrimp out—ah!"

"But, my good Sir Herbert," cried Mr. Scrimp, much alarmed at the turn things had taken, "I really thought this little affair was committed to my management. Dear me! oh, bless me! My dear Sir Herbert, this man Pomander—really unjustifiable. Oh, dear me!"

"Cury."

"Sir Herbert."

"My pistols."

"Yes, Sir Herbert."

"The devil!" cried Mr. Scrimp, as he rushed from the room.

In the passage he met Ralph Freegrove, who exclaimed in surprise,—

"Well, what now?—what's the matter?"

"The matter!" cried the discomfited lawyer, "matter enough. That rascal Pomander has got the ear of Sir Herbert, and ruined us both."

"Let him look to himself!" cried Ralph Freegrove, "I will not be crossed by him."

CHAPTER XXXI.

It had so happened that Mr. Perk, Mr. Scrimp's clerk, and Mr. Pomander, had met on the evening, when they both formed the resolution of watching the proceedings of Mr. Scrimp, when he left the Golden Lion so abruptly.

The result of the meeting had been a mutual compact, or agreement, between these worthies, offensive and defensive, which was founded on the well-known fact that Sir Herbert Foster was a very wealthy man, who liberally rewarded those who were instrumental in his gratifications, and they might just as well slip into the profitable trade of panderers to the vices of the baronet as Scrimp and Ralph Freegrove.

They had together watched Ralph Freegrove to the miller's, and in part, as far as consistent with their care to conceal themselves, they had been witnesses to the ejectment of Ralph from the cottage.

By a consideration of all the circumstances, coupled with a few stray expressions, which they overheard from Freegrove, in the heat of his passion, they had no difficulty in fully comprehending the nature of the business upon which the lawyer and Freegrove were engaged.

Mr. Pomander had taken the bold step of writing to Sir Herbert, offering his services, and even going so far as to arrange an interview for him with the Miller's Maid, if he would hasten to Haredale, and he had met the travelling chariot some two miles from Haredale Park, when, making himself known to the indolent baronet, he had been indulged with a drive homewards, while he expatiated, in glowing terms, on the beauty of Phœbe, whom he had occasionally seen during his residence in the village.

Mr. Pomander, after his interview with Sir Herbert, had hurried homewards to meet Mr. Perk, by appointment, so that those two scoundrels should consult upon the means of redeeming the bold pledge of securing to Sir Herbert an interview with Phœbe.

It was finally agreed between them that Mr. Pomander should write a note to Phœbe, in which he should affect much candour and good feeling, and request to see her upon some business of importance, which could only be disclosed to her at a private interview, and that if she kept the appointment therein requested, he, Mr. Pomander, should break it, and leave Sir Herbert to make the most of his opportunity.

The principal difficulty now arose as to the delivery of the note, but that was one which did not long exist; for by one of those accidental circumstances which sometimes lend their unexpected assistance in bad as well as good projects, they secured a messenger, upon whom they thought they could implicitly rely.

In the midst of their conversation Tim Miggles entered the little shop of Mr. Pomander.

Tim's air and manner were uncommonly mysterious as he entered the shop, and Mr. Perk immediately retired to the little back parlour, where he could overhear what passed, without himself being seen.

"Mr. Pomander," said Tim, "did you ever happen to read ' The Maid and the Mulberry ?' "

"Never, Mr. Tim," said the delighted Pomander, "but I dare say it's uncommonly good."

"You may say that," replied Tim; "it just is, I can tell you. Oh, it's uncommon good. But oh, dear! oh, lauks! were you ever in love ?"

"Why, really Tim, I can hardly say."

"Because I am—George is—Giles is—oh, dear! oh, dear!—oh, Phœbe, Phœbe. Hope pats my back, upon my life. She yet may be Tim Miggles's wife."

"Why, what do you mean, Tim ?"

"I'll tell you. You're a doctor, and know about these things. Oh, what a fool I was not to think of it afore, but it's the 'Maid and the Mulberry' as has put me up to it."

"And what is it ?"

"It's a love powder—oh, dear! it's the very thing. I do love Phœbe so as never was. Couldn't you now just let me have a love powder?—a wopper, you know. I should like her to love me uncommon hard."

"Why, Tim," said Mr. Pomander, "if you'll keep it a great secret, I don't mind serving you."

"Oh, honour bright, won't I keep it snug. Bless your heart, I wouldn't tell any one for the world—oh, no, not I. But how shall I get her to take it ?—oh, lauks! 'oh, dear! Master and missus wouldn't let me hold her nose and make her, oh, dear no. What shall I do? I never thought of that."

"Did you never hear," said the pleased Mr. Pomander, " of the great magician, Abner Snapallhecanup ?"

"No, never. Dear me, who was he ?"

"Why, he could write something, that when it was read would do just as well as a love powder. I know what it was."

"Do you?—oh, dear, oh, dear. Will you write it for me?"

"Why, it's what I never would do yet for anybody, and you must consider it a very great favour. Now, if you could do me any good turn some day, I should not mind letting you have it."

Tim seemed to think for a moment, and then said, in a mysterious whisper, across the little counter,—

"Mr. Pomander, I'll tell you the only secret I know, if you will write the words for me; it's a wery uncommon secret."

"Well, then, if you let me know it, I'll write the charm for you."

"It's this, then," said Tim, leaning over to Mr. Pomander as he spoke. "Phœbe ain't Phœbe at all, oh, dear, no—quite another thing."

"Why, what do you mean?"

"She's a princess in disguise, she is—I know it."

"A what in disguise?"

"A princess—an enchanted princess. She ain't the miller's daughter— oh, no."

"Indeed!—how do you know that?"

"Why, you see I came to the mill about a year after Phœbe had been there, and they said as she'd been out at nurse somewhere; but one night as I was a creeping into the cow-house to see if I couldn't find a bit of candle, and I heard the dame say to the miller, says she, 'Everybody will believe as she's our own child, if we don't say ourselves to the contrary.' And then he, the miller, says, says he, 'I wouldn't lose her now for the king of England.'"

Mr. Pomander was, in truth, deeply interested by what Tim Miggles had related, although at the same time it caused him some embarrassment as to his future proceedings.

"Tim," he said, at last, "you shall have the writing, but you must promise me not to tell any one else that the Miller's Maid is not his own daughter."

"Oh, yes, I'll promise—I want to have Phœbe—I'd have her any how; but if she should turn out to be a princess, which I am pretty sure, oh, dear, won't I come it then.

"Saddle my steed,
With uncommon speed.

Slaves, attend, and be sure you never fail
To bring Prince Miggles in the morning a pot of the best ale.
Hurrah! hurrah! blow trumpets blow, sound the drums so rare,
The fair princess, Mrs. Miggles, is a curling up her hair."

Tim threw himself into so many extraordinary attitudes, while he was thus speculating upon his future greatness, that even Mr. Pomander looked at him with astonishment, and thought the small quantity of brains poor Tim did possess had become suddenly awfully deranged.

"What do you think o' that?" said Tim. "I can come it, I believe you. Missus and Master thinks I be a fool, but I know better; I've read too much for that. Oh, lauk, I could be an emperor, I could; I knows how emperors come it, as well as most folks, I believe you. Doesn't it say in 'The King of Tartary's Ball,'—

"The slave who doesn't attend to the bells,
Shall have his back scooped with oyster shells.

Oh, I could come it."

"Well, I think you could, indeed," said Mr. Pomander. "If you will wait a moment, I'll give you the writing, which you must be sure to place secretly into Phœbe's hand, and you'll soon see its good effect."

"Capital," cried Tim ; "that'll do. I'll give it to her to-night, I will."

Mr. Pomander retired to the back parlour, from whence he soon issued with the letter to Phœbe, which he had agreed with Mr. Perk to write.

"Here," he said to Tim, who took it with great reverence ; "here is the proper thing. You must let no one see it, or it will spoil the charm."

"I won't," cried Tim. "Thank you—thank you.

> "Bundle sorrow, toddle pain.
> Tim Miggles is himself again.
> Master he will stare to see the precious rig,
> Of Tim being a king yet afore he hops the twig."

Tim Miggles departed in great exultation of spirits to the mill, and Mr. Pomander remained in earnest consultation with his ally, Perk, upon this new complexion which the matter had assumed.

"We must be above a bit careful, Pomander," said Mr. Perk, "and not commit ourselves in any way, for if it does turn out that the Miller's Maid is the child of any people of importance and wealth, it's better to be with her than against her."

"It's rather perplexing," said Mr. Pomander ; "but should anything happen in consequence of the letter which I have written, I can, of course, deny it's authenticity."

"Oh, dear, yes ; nothing more easy—a vile forgery, and all that sort of thing ; don't you see ?"

"Oh, certain. But I think I saw Scrimp just pass the window."

"Did you ? Then I must be off, for he'll look for me the first thing. He may become confidential yet, but I'll be hanged if I do."

Mr. Perk now departed, and Mr. Pomander remained in deep reflection upon the unexpected information he had received from Tim, which, upon consideration, many little circumstances seemed to confirm—at least, that part of it which established the fact, that Phœbe was not the child of the miller and his dame, but that she had been placed in their hands for some particular purpose, which he, Mr. Pomander, would have given a great deal to fathom.

Meantime the day was passing on tolerably quietly at the mill, the inhabitants of which, and of the cottage near it, little imagining that they were the subjects of so much conversation and conjecture.

Tim Miggles had been sent by the miller to the village on a message, and he was so accustomed to take no account of the flight of time, especially if he met with any poetry on his road by any means, that the delay he had made at Mr. Pomander's passed quite unnoticed, and he went to the mill, with the letter in his poket, unquestioned by any one.

Giles was in a state of considerable agitation the whole of the day, and he kept incessantly revolving in his mind the words of Mr. Scrimp, with the hope of abstracting from them some slender ray of hope upon which he could contrive to build a superstructure of happiness in the possession of Phœbe. He was resolved, that let the effort cost him what it would, he would reserve himself completely until after the evening interview.

How warped and turned from a right mode of thought and just conclusions does the mind become when under the sole dominion of some one feeling, which absorbs every other faculty of the soul, and exerts an universal influence upon every action. Giles was not of an unjust or wicked nature ; but he had become so enraged, and his passions so influenced by his bitter disappointment in securing the affection of Phœbe, that he could not think calmly ; and although she was dearer to him than anything else in the world, yet he never seemed to consider into what unhappiness she would necessarily be plunged by any violent act of his for securing possession of her, nor how utterly worthless to him that heart would be, even could he call it his own, which he felt well aware (for hence her better feelings) beat only for another.

Again the sun sunk, and the mill and the cottage were wrapt in the mantle of night. Phœbe was again in the little garden, attending the flowers, and not without a hope that George might be able to embrace some opportunity to see and speak to her, even if it were but a few moments. And now she saw a figure approaching; but the quick eye of love immediately detected that it was not he whom she would have welcomed with joy.

It was Tim; and never, perhaps, was Phœbe, gentle and kind as was her beautiful nature, in a worse frame of mind for giving an ear to his poetic rhapsodies as upon the present occasion, for she well knew that while he remained George would avoid the spot, as, although she never suspected they had anything to fear from Tim's observation, yet, as is usually the case with fervent heart-felt love, they both shrunk from any manifestation, by look or word, of their affection before another person, even although that person might be the good-tempered and half-witted Tim Miggles.

Poor Phœbe was little aware of the flame which she had lit up in Tim's breast; and by her kind indulgence to him—an indulgence which arose from her pity for his mental infirmity, for his poetic frenzy almost amounted to a harmless insanity—had been fanned into a flame, which, in Tim's mind, almost smothered the sacred fire of poesy.

She was not a little astonished, therefore, at the peculiar amorous look which Tim put on as he, as was his custom, rested his chin upon the top bar of the little garden gate, while he addressed her. Nor was this surprise likely to be lessened, when he said,—

"Phœbe, empress, queen, and princess of the Pearl Islands, I come to share the diadem. Slaves, avaunt!—bury yourselves in the deepest dungeon under the castle moat."

"Why, Tim," said Phœbe, "what do you mean? What is the matter with you?"

"The matter, Miss Phœbe—princess. Did you ever hear of the magician, Snapallhecanup?"

"No," said Phœbe, with a smile; "I confess, Tim, I never have. What of him?"

"Ha! he was a rum 'un."

"A what?"

"He knowed a thing or two, he did. I can't find a rhyme for his name though, it's such an unusually long one. Just turn it over in your mind, my queen."

"Why, Tim, I really think you are unusually wild to-night. I beg you won't call me other than my real name."

"What uncommon diffidence," cried Tim. "It puts me in mind of 'The Grasshopper's Reproof,' when it says,—

> " ' There was once a grasshopper,
> Who came across a chopper,
> Which proved quite a stopper
> To that same grasshopper,
> For it cut off his hind leg clean.' "

"Well, I don't exactly see what that has to do with the subject of diffidence, Tim, so I'll bid you good evening."

"Oh, dear, don't go; I've got something for you, my princess of the stars of Arabia."

"What is it?" said Phœbe, slightly blushing, as she thought the poor simpleton might be the bearer of some token or message from George.

Tim looked carefully around him for some time; and then, when he seemed satisfied that no one but Phœbe was within sight or hearing, he produced the letter, which had been given him by the artful and designing Pomander.

"What is that, Tim?" cried Phœbe, eagerly. "From whom is it? Give it to me, quick."

"It's a working already," said Tim, as he thrust the letter carefully into Phœbe's hands, and then resting his chin again on the top of the gate, he gently moved his head to and fro, in most anxious expectation of the happy effects of the magician Snapallhecanup's wonderful words.

The letter was addressed "To Phœbe, the Miller's Maid," and ran thus :—

"A friend has something of the greatest importance to communicate to the fair Phœbe, if she will meet him at the back of the meadow adjoining the mill, at eight o'clock to-morrow evening. It is a matter of importance to her and her family—lives may be sacrificed if she fail to come.

"A FRIEND."

"Can this be true?" said Phœbe, when she had finished the epistle, "Tim! Tim!"

"Yes," cried Tim, "I'm here. Enslaver—princess, behold me!"

"Where did you get this letter? It may be some idle jest, and yet it makes a strange impression upon my mind, for am I not the child of misfortune—and my dear brother, too."

Phœbe spoke in a low voice, and Tim could only see that she was much agitated. She clasped her hands together.

"Oh!" she cried, "if it be news of him! Could I once hold his dear hand in mine, and share with him my happiness! Oh, it would be too much oy—too much happiness."

"No, it wouldn't," shouted Tim, "not at all. Here I am, my princess— my queen.

"Oh lauks, oh lauks—oh dear;
Tim is not small beer."

As Tim spoke in the certainty of his full acceptance by Phœbe, he sprung, No. 24.

with great agility, over the gate, and dropping upon one knee at Phœbe's feet, he exclaimed,—

"I'm yours—yours, and not no others.   We'll be king and queen.

> "My milk-white steed,
> Give him a feed.

Slaves, avaunt !—Behold the emperor !"

Phœbe now fully believed that Tim had taken leave of his senses, and she would have escaped from him, but he held her by the skirt of her dress, and, in her terror, she screamed for help, and the miller rushed from his cottage at the same moment that George, who was in the immediate vicinity, rushed to the garden gate.

"What be the matter, my lass ?" cried the miller, who did not for a moment observe Tim, who, in making a snatch at Phœbe as she sprang from him, had fallen on the ground.

"Tim is really out of his mind, I think, father," said Phœbe ; "for he has jumped over the garden-gate, and keeps calling me a princess."

"How dare you ?" said George, saluting Tim with a kick on an ignoble part of his person.

"Why what the deuce do you mean ?" said the miller, seizing Tim by the collar, and dragging him to his feet.

"Mean, eh ?" cried Tim, quite astonished at the turn things had taken. "Mean ?

> " The cricket sings upon the hearth,
> The fly sleeps on the wall ;
> It's beautiful to be a king,
> For that's above them all."

"Get along with you to the mill," cried the miller, giving him a good shake. "And hark'ee, lad ; if I see thee ever out of it again after troubling my little girl, I'll give thee over to my good dame, and she will teach thee how to behave theeself, thee natural."

George was as much amazed at the state of affairs as the miller, for he never could have imagined for a moment that Tim Miggles too was smitten with Phœbe's loveliness.

"I wish you good-night, sir," he said to the miller, and was walking away after an expressive interchange of glances with Phœbe, when the miller called him back, saying—

"George, my lad, my mind do misgive me that that rascal Freegrove will do thee a-harm ; take care of theeself, and do not wander out o' nights."

"I thank you kindly, sir," replied George ; "but I fear him not ; he must be a coward, or he would not have behaved in the way he did."

"It be because I know Ralph Freegrove to be a coward, George, that I bid thee beware of him.   If he were an honourable man, and a brave one, thee would have nought to fear.   Come in, my lass, come in ;   thee shall tell me how this simpleton, Tim, came to frighten thee."

"And—and," said Phœbe, lingering, "George will be careful."

"For your,"—began George, but he stopped short, and with a flushed cheek, hurried from the spot, for he saw that the miller was steadfastly regarding him, although it was rather with a kind than an angry glance.

Phœbe held the letter crumpled up in her hand that had been given her by Tim Miggles, and she had held it for the last few minutes mechanically, quite forgetting in the excitement of the moment, and her awakened fears for George's safety, that she even possessed such a document.   Now, however, when she entered the cottage with the miller, she recollected it, and turning to him, said, at the same time appealing to the dame :—

"Dear father and mother, poor Tim has, I truly believe, been made the idle sport of some one. See what he brought me," and she laid the note before the miller.

Mr. Pomander and Mr. Perk, entirely miscalculated when they thought to raise the curiosity or the vanity of Phœbe by the epistle which they had penned to her. They never imagined for a moment that it would find its way into the hands of the sturdy miller; but they knew not that innocent, guileless heart of the gentle girl, whose happiness in life they were, with all their wicked cunning, so basely endeavouring to undermine and destroy.

It was no effort for Phœbe to lay the mission before her dear friends and protectors; but it would have been at effort to have kept it from them.

The miller put on his spectacles, and read the note slowly aloud, and then he shook his head, and looked with a scornful expression across the fire-place at his good dame, who had listened to each word of it with breathless attention.

"What shall I do, dear father?" said Phœbe, looking in his face with an innocent smile. "Suppose it should be news of my dear long lost brother."

The miller shook his head again.

"Phœbe, my dear child," he said, "I would not destroy thee hope of seeing thee dear brother once more in this world; but thee knows that three years ago we were surely informed of the loss of the vessel in which I ascertained he had sailed from Buugleum."

"It is too true," added Phœbe. "Poor George!"

"Now, my lass, go thee to thee bed, and we will think about this letter, and tell thee what we advise thee in the morning. God bless thee, my dear; good night."

"Dry thee eyes, my dear child," said the dame, "and go to thee rest; thee art good and innocent as an infant; bless thee. Go thy ways; good-night to thee my dear."

Phœbe smiled through her tears, and imprinted a sweet kiss on the furrowed cheek of the miller, and then threw herself into the arms of the dame.

"You are both—both," she said, "too good to me; but I cannot help weeping when—when anything recals a hope, however slight, of once more seeing dear George, who loved me so well. Good-night, dear father and mother, good-night."

Phœbe left the room, and the miller continued to gaze upon the door through which she had passed, totally unconscious of the presence of his good dame. He then brought his hand down upon the little table with a thump, which made her start, and exclaimed—

"Dang'd if they shall, that's flat!"

"Why, what dost 'e mean, Gilbert?" cried the dame; "art ye out of 'e senses, like?"

"Eh—ah—dear heart alive; bless me," said the miller, as if suddenly awakening from sleep; "I be thinking of our dear little girl; and I tell 'e dame, I do not like to let either of them lads have her. She be too good for all of 'em put together."

"Why, thee can't have her theeself, Gilbert?"

"But I tell 'e I will, dang'd if I don't. The cottage would never more be a happy home without the dear child."

CHAPTER XXXII.

Phœbe, after commending to the care of that all-seeing Being who is the orphan's father, the dear friends who had made her life for more than five years one long happy summer's day, and mingling in her prayers a blessing upon him who had sworn to love her, and for whom her young and innocent heart beat with so pure an affection, laid her head tranquilly upon her pillow, and was soon wrapt in profound repose.

The miller and his wife, however, still sat with the letter before them, which Phœbe had received, and that simple piece of paper, their knowledge of human nature, although they were not prone to evil thinking of their fellow-creatures, led them to suspect some wicked project, which aimed to destroy the peace of their dear adopted child.

"Dame," said the miller, "there be many things that make me think that some one has seen our darling, and would wrongfully take her from us. There was that Ralph Freegrove's visit here, for some purpose which I don't know, but do now suspect; then that rascal Scrimp's coming here this morning; and, lastly, this letter, to tempt my poor girl to meet some stranger; all these things do grieve me, dame."

"There be but one man, Gilbert," said his wife, "that I be afeard have cast his eyes upon our lamb, and that be——"

"Sir Herbert Foster. Dame, I see it all. The villain—it be he. They would repair the old mill, would they, to stop the mouth of the old miller, the villains. The little finger of my poor Phœbe be worth all the mills in the world. This letter be a scheme to entrap the poor child."

"I do think it be, Gilbert, although I say it with sorrow. What art thee about, Gilbert?"

The miller had risen, and taken an old blunderbuss from a cupboard, and was peering, with a curious eye, down the barrel.

"We used, in old grandfather's time, dame, to call the old gun, 'Kate,' and I be thinking that 'Kate' mayhap will do better to meet Sir Herbert than Phœbe."

"No, Gilbert, no; put thee gun away; we will think of something better. I tell thee what, old man, Phœbe must have a good husband, who will stand between her and all harm, and then she be safe."

"Then George be the man, dame; for, drat it, he will throw that big Ralph Freegrove clever, surely. He be a brave and a good lad; and it be my wish that Sir Herbert Foster may come within reach of the right arm of George Andrews."

"But hast thee not found out, Gilbert, who gave the letter to poor simple Tim Miggles?"

"I'faith, no, dame; but I be not inclined to sleep, and I will just step to the mill, and know the rights of the matter at once."

"Thee will not be long, Gilbert?"

"No, no, dame, I will not; but I could not sleep, and know that my Phœbe—my own pretty lass—was in danger."

The night was cloudy, but not dark, and the miller soon traversed the short distance between the cottage and the mill.

He rapped with his hand at the little door, and was immediately answered by George, who asked loudly,—

"Who's there?"

"It be I, George," said the miller. "I wish to speak with thee, my lad."

George opened the door in a moment, and betrayed by his looks his great surprise at a visit of the miller to the mill at that time in the evening.

"I be come to speak to thee, George,' said the miller, "about something which thee will, perhaps, think a great trouble."

There was a lurking smile as he spoke.

"Sir, I can think nothing a trouble that I do for you," aid George. "I never can do enough to repay you for your kindness."

"But it be not for me; it be only for my little lass."

"Phœbe, sir—for Phœbe—oh, tell me, and see me fly to do anything for her."

"Listen to me, George," said the miller, seriously. "I be bound by promises to Giles to give neither of thee any more encouragement than the other as to Phœbe, till she be pleased to decide herself to one of thee. But it be at my own discretion to employ either of thee, as I think fit, and I now tell you that Phœbe be in danger."

"Phœbe in danger!" cried George, his eyes flashing fire.

"Stop!" said the miller; "thee must not go to her just now, for I dare say she be asleep. But there be evil-minded persons, who—who would lead my poor dear girl astray. God forgive them, they would. They—they—George, I can tell thee, but my heart be full—they would take from me my girl—my—my darling—they would, George, they would."

The miller leaned heavily upon George's shoulder, and could not speak for a few moments, and George was much affected, although burning with indignation.

"Thee art a good lad," continued the old man, "and—and I have deep faith in thee—I be an old man—that thee will save and protect my poor girl—my treasure—my—my—my——" The old miller dropped upon a seat, and George could see the tears trickling through his fingers, as he covered his face with his hands.

"My kind, dear friend," said George, in deep, but broken tones,—"my generous master—I have bright hopes of joy here, and a pure reliance of mercy hereafter; but if I fail in one single instance—if, in word or action, I renounce the confidence you now place in me—may just Heaven so fail me at my utmost need, and God renounce me for ever!"

The miller grasped his hand, and wrung it heartily.

"No more, George, lad—no more," he cried, firmly. "Read this letter."

George took the epistle; and when he had perused it, he looked for a few moments at the miller, without speaking; then he said,—

"This is the weak scheme of some villain to procure a clandestine interview with Phœbe. Some one, who knew not her confiding nature and her dear love for the best parents, has thought, by this means, to involve her innocent heart in trouble and vice. By Heaven! I will meet the villain myself, and he shall see, be he who he may, that the fair Miller's Maid is not without a protector."

"I think with thee, George," said the miller, "that this be a scheme of some one to lead our poor little girl astray, and so do my dame. There be no man but Sir Herbert Foster who would do it."

"Sir Herbert Foster?" said George. "I have heard talk of him since I came to the mill."

"He be my landlord—that is, it be to him I have to pay the small sum by which the ground on which the mill and the cottage stand is secured to me and mine."

"I have heard," said George, with deep indignation in his tone, "of the rich, the great, and the noble, casting their eyes upon the humble cottage where peace, the pure offspring of honest labour, dwelt serenely, and blasting for ever the happiness they themselves could never taste, because some child of nature was in their eyes lovely, but I almost doubted it till now."

"It be too true," said the miller; "thee had heard right. There be instances in Haredale which would bear thee out in what thee says. I have seen the bereaved mother implore from Heaven justice against the seducer of her child, and name Sir Herbert Foster as the monster who had wrought her woe."

George paused for a time, and then said,—

"My kind master, along with such tales as these I have sometimes heard that there has arisen some one who would not—could not sit calmly, and see the despoiler triumph in his base arts, and that the hand of such an one has been raised in defence of suffering innocence and virtue, and levelled with the dust the haughty libertine who dared, by word or action, to assault the pure and gentle innocence of those he loved. Let Sir Herbert Foster look to it. He knows me not ; but when he does, the knowledge may cost him much."

"What would thee advise, George, that we do about this letter, my lad?"

"How came it in Phœbe's possession?"

"Tim Miggles brought it to Phœbe, I understand, and I come now to the mill, before I could rest, as well to question him as to talk with thee, George."

"He's asleep, I believe," said George ; "but I'll have him here directly."

So saying, he left the miller, and took his way to the part of the mill in which Tim Miggles slept, but he was much mistaken in the supposition that Tim had retired for the night, for since, by the dame's orders, he had been routed out of the cow-house, which he had much preferred, because it was so situated with regard to the cottage that the light which he burned could not from it be observed, Tim had fallen upon the contrivance of hanging up his bed clothes before the little window of his sleeping-room in the mill, and then lighting a bit of purloined candle end, he luxuriated in poetic aspirations for half the night usually.

George hammered at his door, and was answered by Tim with an exclamation of surprise, for he made sure that the mill was on fire.

He unfastened the door in an instant, and would have rushed out, had not George caught him fast, and ordered him immediately to put out his light and attend the miller, who wanted to speak to him upon something of importance.

"Something of importance!" said Tim, looking very solemn. "Do you think it's anything about Snapallhecanup?"

"About who?" cried George.

"Or Phœbe? Perhaps she can't sleep, and wishes to know if I really mean it."

"Are you asleep?" cried George, shaking him to and fro in a style that would effectually have awakened him had he been in the soundest slumber imaginable.

"Asleep? oh, dear, no. Bless us, don't shake so—don't be alarmed—I'll keep you on at the mill, only you must not wink at Phœbe, you know. Giles, I shall give him the sack.

"No longer shall he fix his eyes on Phœbe's window-sill,
When she is Princess Miggles, and I'm master of the mill."

"Idiot!" cried George, "what are you raving at now?"

"Raving, indeed! Mind I don't give you the sack, too. Didn't I hear old Gilbert say he would leave the mill to Phœbe and her husband? You'd better behave yourself—no nonsense, or else you'll be in for it."

"It's useless to ask you your meaning," said George, "for you have none. Come along, master wants to see you immediately."

"Does he!—I thought he would.

"Poor soul, before she lays herself down to rest,
She's sent the old man to see the individual as reigns triumphant in her breast.

Oh, Snapallhecanup, you is a rum 'un."

"Come along, I tell you," cried George, seizing him by the collar, and dragging him before the miller.

"Tim," said the miller, "I want to ask you a question."

"I tell you what, Master George," said Tim, arranging his collar, "you may just as well purwide yourself with another place ; I give you notice."

"What does the lad mean?" said the miller.

"I really can't tell," said George ; "he seems entirely bereft of his senses."

"Come hither, Tim," continued the miller. "You brought a note, my lad, to Phœbe."

"I believe you," cried Tim, then suddenly recollecting the injunctions of the wily Mr. Pomander, not to tell from whom he got the charm, or it would lose its efficacy, he said, "No, I didn't—I know nothing about it.

"There's nothing like magic,
Either comic or tragic,
    And Snapalihecanup's the man ;
He's a wizard so bold,
And a thousand years old,
    But for Miggles he'll do what he can.
He has got an old dragon,
With never a rag on,
    But armour made fast with a rivet ;
I'll leave it to him
To look after poor Tim,
    And make all as right as a trivet."

"Tim, my lad," cried the miller, "I be sorry for thee ; thee will lose the little wit thee has by thee poetry and thee nonsense. I be main sorry for thee. But now tell me who gave thee the letter, will 'e, like a good lad? I have always known thee to be an honest boy, and to speak the truth. Who gave you the letter to my lass, Phœbe?"

"I don't know," said Tim, with a troubled look. "I don't know anything about it, master.

"His breath is a flame,
Or, at least, all the same,
    For it burns every thing it attaches ;
His step's like a rammer,
He's down as a hammer,
    And he feeds upon lucifer matches.
Whenever he sneezes,
The houses and treeses,
    They totter and nod at each other,
As if they would say
It's a queer time of day,
    Can you tell me, pray, how is your mother ?"

"He be worse and worse, George," cried the miller.

"Really," said George, "I think he has gone clean mad. I fear we shall get no information from him."

"We will try in the morning," said the miller. "Go thee ways, Tim—to bed with thee. George, my lad, I wish to see thee and Giles to-morrow at the cottage ; thee can both come when thee leave the work. I will speak to Giles, as I be here."

George went to Giles's room, and called to him, but received no answer. Then trying the door, he found it open, but there was no one in the little apartment.

"Giles is not in the mill," he said, returning to the miller.

"Ah! he be nearly as bad as Tim Miggles, in a different way. He be wandering about to catch a glance at my lass."

"I have not seen him," said George, "since the early part of the evening, and then he was walking towards Foyle's Hollow, apparently lost in deep thought."

"George, thee must try to keep thee temper to Giles. He be in the main a good lad, although he be now well-nigh mad. But to-morrow we'll settle all, and I hope we shall have the old times of peace and fellowship back again at the old mill."

"I trust, sir," said George, "that I have your permission to meet the person who wrote that note to Phœbe. I would fain do so."

"Thee shall," said the miller; "but thee blood be hot, and thee be main hasty, so I will go with thee, and if a word be said about my lass that may be not right, I will knock the rascal down to the earth."

George could not help smiling at the idea of the miller going with him to keep him cool, and then bursting out with such a threat.

"I thank you, sir," he said, "and shall ever be proud of the confidence you have placed in me."

"Good night to thee, lad," said the miller; "it be getting late, and I be wrong to keep thee from thee bed so long."

"Good night, sir," said George, and the miller and his man shook hands cordially, and separated for the night.

George had been too much interested by the communication which had been made to him by the miller to permit him immediately to seek repose, and he opened the casement of his chamber, and remained for a long time wrapped in meditation, looking out upon the quiet, rural scene around, but really observing it not.

He saw the difficulties in the way of his union with the fair Miller's Maid vanishing away. The miller, it was evident, considered him as the chosen lover of his daughter, and he dwelt with much pleasure upon the expressions of confidence and esteem which the old man had used so frequently towards him during their recent interview. But the morrow, which was now so near at hand, would at once establish his claim to the hand of the beautiful Phœbe, by the decision which her father was going to call upon her to pronounce in favour of one or other of the candidates for her love.

There seemed to him but one dark spot in the otherwise cloudless Heaven of his joy, and that was Giles. George had seen enough of his stormy and outrageous temper to dread everything from his insane violence. For himself he did not entertain the shadow of a fear, but he dreaded some explosion of feeling or passion on the part of Giles, when he should see that there was no hope for him, which would, he knew, be a lasting grief to the gentle Phœbe.

Then again he would forget all but Phœbe's gentle whispered words of true affection. Over and over again he would picture to himself the sweet interview in the meadow, when the confiding unblushing girl had softly owned the secret of her heart. It was, indeed, a moment to dream of again and again. It was a dear reminiscence, well worthy of being enshrined in memory's deepest recesses, for it was a rapture which was past never to recur again. The sunlight throughout the day is beautiful and bright, but it is it's first golden beam, as it rises from the far off horizon, which is hailed with the greatest delight. The first moment of all joys is the sweetest, and the first kiss of love is the sweetest of them all.

Nearly two hours must have passed in these reflections, when George was aroused to the consciousness of where he was, by hearing a step approaching the mill.

He looked earnestly in the direction of the sound, and by the general appearance of the figure that was approaching, he could guess that it was Giles, who at that late hour was returning to the mill.

He passed with a hurried step, close under George's window, and the latter muttering incoherently, as he walked towards the door of the mill, of which each had a key. He seemed much excited; and by the partial glance which George caught of him as he passed, he could see that his whole appearance betokened unusual agitation and passion.

For a moment George thought he would call to him, and make one more effort to reason with him on the violence of his resentment to Phœbe, who must be both annoyed and alarmed at his repeated outbreaks of ungovernable rage. He, however, allowed him to pass on ; for, in addition to reflecting how hopeless it was to combat with the wrathful and violent disposition of Giles, he thought that by forcing him into a conference at that hour, and when he was evidently in a state of extreme excitement, he might be defeating his own object.

Giles entered the mill, and George was about to retire from the window, and endeavour himself to seek repose, when he thought he observed a dark object moving between him and the cottage.

George strained his eyes to the utmost in order to discover who it could be that seemed to be thus slinking about the cottage.

Danger to Phœbe was George's uppermost thought, and without waiting to go the door, he clambered from the little window, and quietly dropped upon the green turf.

Stooping almost to the ground, he cautiously approached the cottage, and occasionally he could see the figure flitting carefully along, at some distance before him.

Nearer—nearer he came, and now he could see some one standing exactly opposite Phœbe's window, and gazing intently at it.

George was determined to ascertain who the intruder was, and he advanced most carefully towards him.

The figure seemed totally unaware of its danger, or if he knew it, despised it, for it never moved, but still appeared curiously to reconnoitre the whole tenement, but particularly the window of Phœbe's room.

The figure was quite unknown to George, but he could not see the face, and even the figure was indistinct, for it was enveloped in a cloak, which reached to the ground.

No. 25

Now he was within twenty yards of the intruder, but still he moved not, and George paused for a moment to see what would be its next movement.

The stranger at length, however, seemed satisfied with his scrutiny, and he turned slowly from the house. George did not move, for the figure was walking in the direction in which he was.

Nearer and nearer it came, and George waited but the moment of its arriving to where he lay crouching to spring upon it and demand its business there at that unseasonable hour, and accordingly, as the figure was about to pass him, he sprung to his feet, and grasping the cloak, cried,—

"Hold ! you pass not here. Who and what are you ?"

The figure slowly turned and faced George. He shuddered, and dropped his hold of the cloak ; large drops of perspiration broke out upon his brow, and he glanced wildly at the figure, which slowly passed onwards, and was in a few moments lost in the gloom.

"Gracious Heavens !" cried George, "what can this mean ? Am I awake ; or is this some frightful dream ?—some horrible creation of the imagination ? It was"—he shuddered as he spoke—"a skeleton !"

CHAPTER XXXIII.

Giles had kept the whispered appointment with Mr. Scrimp. A full hour before the appointed time he had hurried to Foyle's Hollow, in great anxiety, to know what the attorney could possibly have so secretly to communicate to him. That it was something that concerned his hopes of Phœbe he did not doubt ; and although conscience whispered to him that whatever it was it would be most likely subversive of Phœbe's peace and happiness in some way, yet he stifled the low admonitions of the secret monitor, and proceeded to his appointment with a wild determination of acceding to any plan which should promise the completion of his wishes in the possession of the hand of the Miller's Maid.

Foyle's Hollow was a desolate little valley. It appeared as if it had either been at one time the bed of a sheet of water, or that some convulsion of nature had occurred at a distant period, and thrown up the earth in mounds around it.

It was surrounded by masses of earth and high trees, whose gnarled and tangled roots spread themselves down the sides of the Hollow.

For some reason or another the place was disliked by the surrounding peasantry, probably from some old legend connected with it, which was now forgotten, for no other information was ever given by the rustics concerning it to any curious tourists than that it was Foyle's Hollow, and main unlucky like. Why, or wherefore, they neither knew not, nor particularly cared.

No spot could be better calculated for holding a secret conference, for no one in the neighbourhood had sufficient hardihood to venture even near it, far less into the Hollow, after nightfall.

To this place, however, Giles took his way, although fully aware of its bad reputation, for he was possessed by feelings which overpowered all others which custom and habit had imprinted on his mind. It is, however, probable that the wily attorney had purposely fixed upon the suspicious and shunned Hollow as well to affect the mind of Giles, and render him more fit for his purposes, as for concealment of their interview.

The night, as we have said, was cloudy, and the Hollow was involved in the deepest gloom, for it was only in the brightest weather that even a glimmering of light succeeded in illumining its deepest recesses.

Now, however, the shadows of the trees cast over it a black mantle, and even Giles, highly strung as his mind was to encounter anything in the pursuit of the one object of his existence—the possession of Phœbe—hesitated for a moment before he plunged into the yawning Hollow.

There were various paths, which led to the very bottom of the place, by serpentine courses, but Giles descended from the spot at which he had happened to arrive, and clutching at the roots of the trees, he flung himself over the brink, and amid a rattling shower of stones, earth, and gravel, he made good his descent into the place.

The noise occasioned by his violent descent died away. Now and then a loosened stone would roll and bound from ledge to ledge, until it reached his feet, and then all would be still again as the grave.

"I be here," cried Giles, but his own voice only broke the wrapt repose of the place, and that sounded hollow and unearthly, as it was echoed by the earthy banks around him.

He now heard the village church clock strike eight, but Mr. Scrimp came not.

Again Giles cried, "I am here." The owl hooted in reply, and his voice again died away in the echoes of the Hollow, without an answering sound.

A long tedious quarter of an hour passed, and Giles was about to give utterance to a torrent of invectives against the lawyer who had so deceived him, when he heard a voice, in a low tone, on the brink of the Hollow, cry to him by name.

"Here," answered Giles.

"'Tis dark," said Scrimp. "Where is the footpath?"

"Thee can scramble down by the roots of the trees," said Giles; "I did so—it be the shorter way."

"Thank you," said Mr. Scrimp: "I'd rather not, if you please; I'll find the path and be with you in a moment."

Mr. Scrimp now took from the breast of his coat a dark lantern, and casting a gleam from it upon the ground, he walked slowly along till he came to the path.

It so happened that an owl was perched upon a branch of a tree, which exactly overhung the little irregular path for which Mr. Scrimp was diligently hunting.

As he approached, the full glare from his lantern came upon the eyes of the owl, who immediately, with a cry, flew straight forwards, and came in Mr. Scrimp's face with great force.

"The devil!" cried the attorney, half smothered—"what's this?"

"It be an owl," said Giles, who could see clearly the cause of Mr. Scrimp's alarm. "Thee mayest catch it if thee hold up thee hand."

"One owl!" cried the attorney; "d—— it, I thought it was a dozen owls. It's gone now, though, and here's the path."

So saying, he descended cautiously the winding way, and was in a few moments by the side of Giles.

"Well, lawyer," cried Giles, "I be come, thee sees."

"So I perceive," answered Mr. Scrimp; "and you see I am here true to my appointment."

"What dost thee want with me? I be come to meet thee according to thee words."

"Giles," said the attorney mildly, and laying his hand upon his sleeve, "George Andrews will marry the Miller's Maid."

"He shall not," cried Giles fiercely—"he dare not. I—I will have the heart's blood of him afore he do make a wife of my Phœbe."

The attorney had succeeded in his object, which was that Giles should put himself into a rage early in the interview, for he came to play upon his passions, and make him, through their instrumentality, subservient to the purposes of Sir Herbert Foster, who, he was assured by Ralph Freegrove, must ultimately place the whole matter concerning the seduction or abduction of Phœbe, the Miller's fair Maid, in his hands, notwithstanding Mr. Pomander's insidious interference, who had certainly, for the purpose of at once establishing himself with Sir Herbert, promised what he would find it very difficult to perform—namely, the meeting with Phœbe, to which he had pledged himself on the morrow, and which Mr. Scrimp was determined should never take place.

He had placed his lantern again in his breast, and in the darkness he was not afraid to smile, as Giles uttered his impassioned words.

"But he will do so, my good fellow," said Scrimp, "unless——"

"Unless what? Lawyer, if thee be come to help me, I will take the hand of thee, were thee the devil even himself; but if thee come to jeer at me, I will leave thee dead in the Hollow."

"I do come to help you," said Mr. Scrimp, not much flattered by Giles's speech. "You are not well used at the mill?"

"No, that is true, I am not. Master be a kind master, but he be taken up with George, and he do forget me."

"Hem!" said Mr. Scrimp, "I don't like to see any injustice; it's agony to me."

"I do love Phœbe," continued Giles; "she be beautiful; the day be beautiful, and so be the night; but Phœbe, oh, she be more beautiful than they."

"Why, certainly," said Mr. Scrimp, "she is a fine girl, and I admire your taste."

"She be like a star," continued Giles, "for she be set by Heaven in the world as a star be set in the evening sky."

"Well, but my good fellow," interrupted Mr. Scrimp, who by no means wished Giles to proceed in such a mood, "you must take active measures, or your rival will have the wench."

Giles, however, seemed not to hear him. He stood, with his hands clasped, as in mental contemplation of the charms of Phœbe.

"George Andrews!" cried the lawyer, in his ears,

Giles started at the sound, and he clenched his hands tightly, as he cried,— "What of he?"

"He will have your Phœbe—your star, you know," said Scrimp, calmly.

"And dost thee ask me here but to tell me so? Thee hadst better have whispered that thee would kill me, for I would then laugh at thee."

"No, no," cried Mr. Scrimp, retreating a step or two, as Giles put on a menacing look. "I really, my good friend, wish to serve you. You are so violent. If you will but listen a little calmly——"

"Say thee say—I will listen to thee."

"Well, then, I just wished to tell you that Phœbe is going to meet some one to-morrow, and unless you look sharply after her, you'll lose her."

"Meet who?"

"I don't know—nor where—nor at what time. But, Giles, never lose sight of her all day to-morrow. Watch her every moment."

"I—I will—I will—meet some one. I—I will kill—kill!"

"No, no, my good friend, that is not at all necessary. You need only prevent her from meeting any one to-morrow."

"To-morrow?" repeated Giles; "to-morrow she is to decide."

"Decide what?"

"Whether she be going to have George or me; but she will have him —I do well know it—and yet she be my Phœbe. She was mine before he came."

"But they are not to be married to-morrow; and something may arise that will entirely put an end to George's hopes, if you would be guided by me."

"How?—in what way?—what can I do?—and yet—yet he shall not have her."

"I'll tell you what you must do, you must run away with her; then she will marry you, and all will be well."

"Run away with Phœbe! If she would come, I would go with her to the furthest corner of the earth. But, no, she would not—no—no."

"But you don't understand me. You must run away with her, whether she likes it or not."

"Run away with Phœbe? Drag her from the little cottage? No—no, I cannot."

"Then you will have tamely to stand by, and see her wedded to George, and all your life you will repent your want of spirit and courage."

"I—I cannot—no—no—and yet——"

"Yet what?"

"She shall not be George's wife. I will fight—kill—do anything, but she shall not be his. No—no, she be mine, and mine only. What right has he to my Phœbe—my—my beautiful Phœbe."

"None whatever, of course; in fact you have the most right. Now, if I thought I could fully rely upon you, I could tell you something."

"What be it?—be it about Phœbe?"

"Will you swear not to mention it to any one?"

"I will, so help me —— I—I—what is it?—I cannot say the word."

"Never mind, another time will do as well. Meet me to-morrow night here, and I will tell you something that shall place Phœbe within your reach."

"To-morrow, then. Be it so. Lawyer, I will meet thee."

"But, Giles, remember, never let Phœbe, if possible, out of your sight to-morrow, or you lose her at once and for ever."

"I will not. She shall meet no one. Day and night I will watch."

"Good-night, then, and depend upon it Phœbe shall be yours."

Giles looked after the retreating form of the lawyer for a time, and then muttering the words "To-morrow, to-morrow," he slowly slunk from the Hollow, and departed for the mill, where he arrived, as it will be recollected, while George was absorbed in meditation at the window of his chamber.

Hardly, however, had Giles left Foyle's Hollow, when a figure slowly emerged from a deep hole, which had been effectually concealed from observation by a furze bush, which grew at its brink, and standing up in the Hollow, looked earnestly after him.

"Humph!" said Mr. Pomander, for it was he; "I have watched good, worshipful Master Scrimp, to some purpose, I think. Run away with Phœbe, the Miller's Maid? Humph! You advise that, do you? Oh, dear me— we shall see—we shall see."

As he spoke, he drew a whistle from his pocket, and produced a low sound, which in a moment was answered by another, and then the cautious tread of some one descending into the Hollow might be heard, and Mr. Perk emerged from the gloom.

"This is really an odd place, Pomander," said Mr. Perk; "it's enough to give anybody the infernal blues. I wonder Scrimp liked to come here; but he don't sport a conscience. He's a clever man in his way; but I think, with all due deference to him, that we have been just one too many for him to-night."

"What do you think, Perk? He has found out, d—— him, by some means, the projected appointment with Phœbe, and has set that hot-headed ruffian, Giles, the miller's man, to watch her. I fear she will not be able to come."

"That's ugly," replied Mr. Perk; "but some means must be thought of of appeasing Sir Herbert Foster, for you say he fully expects to meet her, and has promised——"

"A hundred pounds if he likes her, and an unlimited command of money
till she is lodged in her town-house. Upon my soul, it must not be lightly
given up."

"A cool hundred," said Mr. Perk ; "fifty a-piece."

"Exactly. We work together, and share the proceeds, you know."

"What did you gather from the conversation between my worthy governor
and the yokel?"

"Why, it seems," said Mr. Pomander, "that there is a great deal of rivalry
betwixt the two bumpkins, the miller's men, about this same girl, and this one,
Giles, as they call him, being the ugliest of the two, is the rejected swain, for
which he vows vengeance on the other. Old Scrimp has found it out, and is
practising upon the ignorant fellow's feelings of disappointment, evidently
with the hope of still working his way with Sir Herbert, and cutting us clean
out."

"Upon my honour it's ingenious," replied Mr. Perk ; "I respect Mr.
Scrimp very much indeed. He's an uncommon clever man for a country
practitioner; but we do come such rigs in town. Lord bless you, Flickins,
Robinson, and Mucks, would have eaten him up."

"Who were they?"

"The uncommon fine firm that I was with in the lane four years. Bless
your heart, we used to have a fellow there who was always kept about the
door to irritate clients, and particularly those who came to compound actions."

"Irritate clients!—what do you mean, Perk? Why I should have thought
the best thing would have been to keep clients in good humour."

"Ah, that's your sweet simplicity. I'll tell you how we managed it. There
are two sorts of people who may get notice of action. Some are all fire and
bounce, and come to blow up the attorney, and make a row in the office. Now
that's all very well. But others, they get funky, and come running down to
compromise. Now, you see, that wouldn't do at all, so we used to make
inquiries before hand, you know, and if we thought the fellow would come it
mild, and compromise, you see, we were forced to irritate him."

"Oh, I begin to perceive ; but how did you manage it?"

"Why, I'll tell you exactly. There was once an old gentleman, a very respectable old cove, he came to compromise an action about a water-pipe of his
that projected three-eights of an inch into his neighbour's property, who was
an uncommon good client of ours. Well, the old gentleman was advised to
offer costs, and stay proceedings, which we pretty soon heard of, and down he
comes next morning to our office. He knocked at the door in a very gentle
sort of way ; we knew it was a compromising knock, so we didn't open the
door ; then he knocked again another compromising knock, and I went in to
Flickins, who was acting partner then, and says I, 'Sir, here's a compromiser at
the outer door. He's knocked twice.' 'Humph!' says Flickins, 'have you
laughed through the key-hole?' 'No,' says I in great admiration, for it was
very clever that. Then back I goes, and says, 'Ha! ha! ha!' through the
key-hole. Then the old gentleman he knocks again, not nigh so compromising a knock, and I went into Flickins again, and I says, 'Sir, he's a coming
round.' 'Humph!' says Flickins, 'have you squirted some dirty water
through the key-hole?' 'No,' says I, and back I went and squirted a jolly
lot of dirty water slap through the key-hole. Then the old gentleman he
knocks a most uncompromising knock, and stamps dreadfully. So I goes in
to Flickins, and I says, 'He'll do, I think, now, sir.' 'Humph!' says Flickins,
as grave as the chancellor ; 'open the door suddenly, with the paste-pot in
your hand.' So away I goes, and takes the paste-pot, and getting a jolly lot
on the brush, I opens the door, and the old gentleman he rushes his face slap
against the brush, and I lathers him well. 'D— you all,' cries the old gentleman, 'you d—d pettifogging scoundrels—you d—d infernal pickpockets!'—

and he whacks an office stool with his stick till there's such a cloud of dust you can't see a bit. Then out comes Flickins, and he says in a mild way, 'Humph! turn out this old maniac.' Then the old gentleman says, 'You're a scoundrel, sir—you're a rascal, and be d—d to you! I came here to compromise—Flabby versus Gutter—but I'll be d—d if I do now. If it costs me my last shilling, I'll see myself righted, d— you!' Then the old gentleman gives his hat a whop on the crown, and rushes out in desperation, swearing like one o'clock; and Flickins says, 'Humph! that will do. You can get on, Mr. Perk, with Flabby v. Gutter.'"

"Well, I must confess," cried Mr. Pomander, laughing, "that that was a well managed scheme."

"Oh, bless your heart," said Mr. Perk, "that's nothing to the practice I've seen."

"What would you advise to be done in our present circumstances concerning this girl, who seems inclined to give us more trouble than enough?"

"What time did you promise Sir Herbert he should see her?" asked Mr. Perk.

"At eight to-morrow evening," replied Mr. Pomander; "but I much fear that Scrimp, although a country practitioner, has been clever enough to foil us."

"Oh dear, no, not at all; he has made his move, and we have the advantage of knowing what it is."

"It is quite clear," interrupted Mr. Pomander, "that to-morrow's proceedings must decide whether you and I, or Scrimp and Freegrove, are to manage this little matter for Sir Herbert Foster."

"And manage it we will," replied Mr. Perk. "Nothing is impossible if you are determined to do it. Sir Herbert Foster must have this meeting, only it would be more convenient if he would have it in the morning instead of the evening."

"Why, what do you mean, Perk? It is the shortness of the time that makes the difficulty."

"Not at all, my good sir. Do you really think Sir Herbert Foster would consent to meet the Miller's Maid by eight to-morrow morning?"

"Upon my soul I do; I wish I had it in my power to make the proposition to him."

"I'll tell you the means. Write a note in the name of the favoured lover, and I'll contrive that she has it soon enough. Let it be earnestly soliciting a private meeting at eight o'clock to-morrow morning on this spot. She will be sure to come, and Sir Herbert may meet her. The fellow's name is George Andrews."

"Upon my word," cried Mr. Pomander, "that seems a likely scheme enough: it is the only thing we can do. Come home with me, Perk, and we will write the letter immediately."

"I'd wager my hat, with my head in it, that it will succeed."

"I must then," continued Mr. Pomander, "proceed immediately to obtain an audience of Sir Herbert Foster."

"Then you had better proceed at once," cried Perk. "I'll manage the letter if you will manage the baronet, and between us, if we don't astonish Scrimp, the deuce is in it."

CHAPTER XXXIV.

THE morning was anxiously welcomed by almost every one of the inhabitants of the mill and the cottage, and they each rose with the expectation that something would happen in the course of the day which would influence, probably, the remainder of their various existences.

A September sun shone cheerfully upon the smiling landscape, and Phœbe, as usual, opened her chamber window to look forth upon the young morning.

She cast her eyes towards the mill, and there was George smiling from his little chamber window, and making signs to Phœbe.

The colour deepened on the cheek of the fair girl as she bent her head among the flowers that screened the little casement, and plucked a rose, which she kissed, and then threw towards the mill.

George sprung from the window in an instant; but he had but just time to pick up the flower and press it to his lips, when Tim Miggles, an unusual thing for him, emerged from the mill, apparently in deep thought, and ran full against George.

George did not like to approach Phœbe's window in sight of Tim, so he slowly turned to the mill, ever and anon turning his eyes upon Phœbe, who still smiled from the little casement.

And now George had disappeared from her sight into the old mill, and Phœbe turned away her eyes with a sigh.

She then commenced her morning's task of attending her flowers; but hardly had her attention rested upon them before she observed, tied round the stem of one of the plants, a small slip of paper. The innocent girl untied it, and read the following words :—

"My dear Phœbe,—Let me beg of you, as you love me, to meet me in Foyle's Hollow, by eight o'clock at the latest. My adorable angel, do not fail.

"Yours eternally,
"GEORGE ANDREWS."

"George Andrews!" repeated Phœbe, in a tone of doubt, for there was something about the short epistle, a tone, a manner, which she shrunk from. Again and again she read it, but it did not awaken in her breast any of those delightful sensations which usually accompany the reception of the first epistle from a dear object. On the contrary, Phœbe seemed to shrink from the brief note. The expressions, although they did not actually offend, yet in some measure surprised and annoyed her. That was not the style in which George spoke to her.

"My adorable angel" could never have passed his lips, she felt assured. Phœbe did not at all like the brief note, and she felt a pang of uneasiness as she re-read it for the twentieth time. "And yet," she thought, "something may have happened which dear George wishes to tell me of, and why should I make exceptions to the mere wording of a hurried note? 'George Andrews!' that is sufficient; that name is there, and all else is nothing."

As Phœbe thus stood at the little window, wrapped in meditation, Giles was not unmindful of his interview with Mr. Scrimp, and the strong injunctions of the latter not to lose sight of Phœbe for the whole of the day. He had risen early, and now stationed himself in the meadow in such a position that he could watch the cottage, and see if Phœbe came forth.

Phœbe knew Foyle's Hollow well; she had often visited it, both with the miller and his dame, and Giles, shortly after she first came to the

mill, and hers was not a disposition to entertain idle fears in connection with any particular spot, however lonely it might appear, or gloomy its aspect.

The fair girl did not hesitate long upon the subject of the note. Had she not, she thought, already bestowed her best affections upon George? and had she not an undivided faith in his pure love and honour? She felt that she would rather he had not asked for so deliberate a clandestine interview, or that, having asked it, his manner had been different; but these reasons did not appear to her sufficiently cogent to justify her in refusing to meet him, and she hurriedly hid the note in her bosom, and descended to the ground floor of the cottage to see the hour.

It was half-past seven, and the note mentioned eight at the latest. She once more sought her little chamber, and throwing a light scarf across her shoulders, she put on her straw hat, and with a hurried step descended again to leave the cottage.

"Why, child," cried the dame, "what a main hurry thee be in. Gilbert says we had rain in the night, and the flowers will not need thee care this morning."

"I shall be soon back," said Phœbe, blushing as she spoke, for she did not feel quite satisfied in her own mind that she was doing exactly right.

She hurried from the cottage, fearful each moment of meeting with the miller himself, who might question her more closely with respect to her early errand.

Opening the little gate which led through the meadow, she flew over the ground with great rapidity. She passed the spot on which George had first breathed to her willing ear the tale of his true love, and a tear rose to her eye as she thought again of the far different language of the note which she had in her bosom.

No. 26

It never occurred to Phœbe for a moment to doubt the authenticity of the summons to Foyle's Hollow. Had such a thought crossed her mind, she might have hesitated ere she so freely acceded to the invitation; but the name of George Andrews could not be resisted. She was invoked by that name to be at Foyle's Hollow by eight o'clock; and although, certainly, the language of the note shocked her high sense of delicate feeling, yet—yet it was his note, and she must go.

The morning air was cold, and a fresh breeze skimmed along the surface of the ground—a slight indication of the waning season.

Phœbe walked, however, quickly; and by the time she came in sight of Foyle's Hollow she no longer felt the coldness of the morning air. Its freshness was grateful to her feelings. A rich glow of health and beauty suffused her cheeks; and as she at length stood upon the brink of the Hollow, with her village hat in her hand, and her long fair hair floating in beautiful freedom in the light breeze, while she slightly panted, from the haste with which she had come, she might well have been taken for some sylvan nymph, who had risen from her leafy bower, in some deep recess of nature, to greet the bright-eyed morning.

She looked carefully down in the Hollow, but she saw no one, and a pang of disappointment shot across her heart, as she said, faintly,—

"He is not here."

Not a sound met her ears in that deep solitude; Nature seemed sleeping, and deep in the Hollow were black shadows, which looked like yawning pits of fearful depth.

Phœbe clasped her hands as she looked around her, and once more she repeated,—

"He is not here."

She felt confident, however, that it was not yet eight o'clock, and she determined upon descending to the Hollow, and resting herself upon some one of the disjointed masses of earth and rock that formed the irregular and wild basement of the little valley.

She walked along until she came to the winding path which Mr. Srimp had with such caution descended the previous evening, and with careful steps she followed its serpentine course until she found herself at the bottom of the Hollow.

The universal stillness around her produced in her mind an uneasy feeling, which she could neither shake off nor define. She had never visited Foyle's Hollow alone, and the feelings which now oppressed her, as she there stood, apparently the only living thing within sight or sound, were of as novel as they were disagreeable a character.

She seated herself upon a mound of earth, which was covered with short velvet-looking grass, and eagerly listening for the slightest sound which should proclaim the approach of her lover, the fair confiding girl sat like a fair statue in the wilderness of nature.

Suddenly she started—a sound met her ears—it seemed like a low whisper. Was it imagination?—No. Then again, from behind a thick mass of stunted trees, there arose a low whispering sound, and in a moment more she heard the rustling of the branches and the crackling of the dry twigs under the tread of some one.

Phœbe rose, and looked eagerly in the direction from whence the sounds proceeded.

"George! George!" she said; and as she spoke a figure emerged from behind the leafy screen to which she was an entire stranger.

For a moment Phœbe could neither speak nor move, and for the first time a suspicion darted across her mind that she had been deceived, and that the note was not really from George. A feeling of intense satisfaction and thankfulness filled her heart at the thought, and notwithstanding her present perplexing situation, she felt no sensation of great relief in the supposition.

"No, no," she thought, "he did not write it. My heart ought to have told me he did not. I am deceived—but not in George. No, no; he did not write it."

The stranger advanced very slowly, and Phœbe had fully time to examine his figure and appearance before he arrived near to where she stood.

He was a tall, gentlemanly-looking man, elegantly attired. A handsome cloak hung from his shoulder in graceful folds; but still there was something about his appearance that Phœbe shrunk from, and felt she could not trust.

Before he arrived close to her, which seemed to be his intention, Phœbe turned quickly to seek the path by which she had ascended, but she was repelled by seeing the face of a man peering over the extreme edge of the bank below which she was, with a self-satisfied grin upon the countenance.

She could not fail to understand her situation in a moment. She had been entrapped, and was now constrained to an interview with the man who was in the Hollow, who was, she thought, most probably the person who had first sent her the note which had been given to her by Tim Miggles the day before.

Phœbe was not a fine, sentimental young lady, or she might have screamed, or, perhaps, fainted; but as she was bold, and secure in her own conscious innocence and guileless heart, she turned to confront the advancing stranger, not, certainly, entirely without alarm, but still with a composed air, although her heart fluttered, and she slightly trembled as she faced him.

The stranger paused when he arrived within about half-a-dozen paces of where she stood, and placing an eye-glass to his eye, where he fixed it with great expertness by a contraction of the eye-brow, he seemed quite lost in a long contemplation of Phœbe.

Again the frightened girl looked towards the path, but the same sneering, smiling face was there, and she felt certain that it was there to prevent her from escaping from her companion in the Hollow, who now spoke in drawling accents. He rather seemed, however, to be making remarks to himself than addressing her.

"Ah! ah! divine!—charming—quite an air. Ah! ah! a tone—ah! a torment, eh?—ah, my little angel. You, ah!—are rather uncommon. How came you to—ah!—ah!—monopolise all the beauty in the county? ah! By God, you're a fine creature!"

"I do not know you, sir," said Phœbe, drawing back. "If that person who is keeping the path will permit me, I wish to go home."

"Oh—ah, he's an uncommon clever fellow. My rustic Venus—you, ah!—you can't think of going home just yet."

"I came here to meet—a—a dear friend," cried Phœbe. "He is not here. Let me go home, sir, I beg of you."

"Yes—oh, yes—ah!—the dear friend is here. Ah! ah! I am the individual."

"You may be the person," said Phœbe, "who has deceived me, and lured me from my home by an untruth; but I do not know you, nor do I wish. George! George! where are you now?"

Phœbe clasped her hands as she spoke, in great distress, for the air and manner of the man was becoming more insolent each moment.

"Oh, ah—charming, quite a village coquette. Ah! ah! it adds a zest do the matter. Like—like a rich sauce to—ah! ah!—a luxurious dish. My charmer, I'll make your fortune."

"Do not approach me, sir!" cried Phœbe. "If there be anything that you wish to say to me, say it now, and quickly. I must be gone."

"Oh! ah!—yes! I have something uncommonly particular to say, my charmer. I—I—ah! will remove you from a humble sphere—ah! unsuited to your charms—ah! I'll give you a *carte blanche*, as to expense. Ah! by G—d, you'll make—ah—ah—quite a sensation."

"I do not understand you," cried Phœbe.

"No?—dear me; innocent simplicity. Hah, ha! you shall have your own box at the opera."

Again Phœbe looked anxiously towards the path. The man's face was no longer there, and with the fleetness of a fawn, she sprung up it.

"Ha! ha!—the devil! stop her!" cried the person who had been speaking to her in the Hollow.

Before she could ascend half-way, she saw that she should be opposed, for a figure started up on the edge of the Hollow, and extended his arms so as completely to block up the way.

"Ha! ha!" he cried; "my nymph—I, ah, must really see if—ah—ah, that bloom on your cheeks is natural. Ah, I never, 'pon my soul, saw anything like it. Never—ah, 'pon honour."

As he spoke, he slowly ascended the pathway after Phœbe.

"Help! help!" cried the now thoroughly-alarmed girl. "Help! help! George, save me—save me!"

A cry from the man above now caused her suddenly to turn her eyes in that direction, and she saw him rolling headlong down the precipitous sides of the Hollow, which was close to the path.

"Giles!" she cried, with a tone of pleasure, and she instantly bounded up the pathway, and stood by his side.

It was Giles, and there he stood glaring fiercely into the Hollow. His eyes hollow and blood-shot—his face pale and haggard—even his very lips blanched, he looked like some spectre risen from the grave to defend the orphan girl.

"Giles! Giles!" cried Phœbe, clinging to him, "take me home—oh, take me home."

He did not, however, seem to hear her. His whole attention was directed to the Hollow, and upon the man in the cloak, who had very leisurely fixed the glass in his eye, and was scrutinizing Giles through it with great deliberation.

"Wretch!" cried Giles, in a voice of thunder.

"Eh!—ah!—my verdant young man—ah! ah!—do you mean yourself? Ah! I never saw such a bad smock-frock in my life. Ah! why, man, it's like a sack—ah! eh! Are you—ah!—the rustic lover of the—the charmer, eh?"

"Home, home, Giles—oh, take me home," cried Phœbe.

"Ha!" he cried, shaking her from him, "art thee here? What dost thee do here? Oh, Phœbe, Phœbe, I did not think this of thee."

"Think what of me, Giles?—what have I done? I have been deceived, but I am innocent of all thought of evil. Oh, take me home now. What will dear father and mother think?"

"Think, Phœbe? What be my thoughts? I tell thee, my brain be turned to melted iron. I be surely mad—mad; but thee—thee shall not escape."

These latter words were addressed to the man with the cloak, who still regarded Giles with the utmost composure—a composure which was soon to be ruffled, for, with one bound, Giles sprung to the spot on which he stood, and seizing him fiercely by the throat with a wild yell of triumph, he rolled with him from the path into the deepest part of the Hollow.

Phœbe screamed loudly as she saw them dashing downwards from mound to mound, rolling over each other, and crashing away roots and branches of trees and shrubs as they proceeded.

"Revenge!" shouted Giles, "revenge!—I will have revenge on thee!"

"Hold, Giles," cried a loud voice, which rung through the Hollow.

Phœbe uttered a cry of joy; she knew the tone well—it was the miller's.

"Father, father," she cried.

"I be here, my lass, I be here," said the miller, and in the next moment she was in his arms. "That's it, my lad, George. Part them, part them, there will be murder else."

Phœbe looked towards the Hollow, and she saw George descending, with the rapidity of lightning into it. From crag to crag he bounded until he reached the bottom, and then he rushed between Giles and his opponent.

"Hold!—forbear!" he cried; "what would you do?—madmen both of you—what is this?"

The man with the cloak held a pistol in his grasp, and his dress was torn and deranged, and Giles was covered with gravel, and his face streaked with blood from the stones and branches catching him as he descended.

The voice of the miller had, in all probability, saved the lives of one, if not of both, of the combatants, for, upon hearing it, Giles had instinctively given way a little, and his antagonist had risen to his feet, and drawn the pistol from his pocket, just as George dashed in between them.

"Revenge!" cried Giles; "I will have my revenge."

"On whom, and for what?" cried George, loudly. "I am the enemy of the first who stirs, and by Heavens you'll find me no mean one!"

"Hold! I tell thee, Giles—hold!" cried the miller, again; "art thee mad?"

The man who had had the cloak, but who had it no longer, for it had been torn from him by the shrubs and branches in his rapid descent into the Hollow, and now lay upon the propitious bank, made a strong effort evidently to recover his composure and usual indifferent manner, although there was an expression of unutterable passion upon his fine features.

"Ah! what the devil is all this?" he said; "is this man a maniac, and are you his keeper?"

"I tell thee, George," said Giles, with a wild laugh of exultation; "Phœbe did come here to meet this man. She be neither thine nor mine— ha! ha! D—n thee all. She be his—his. Thee mayest have her now, George; she be worthless."

George's arms dropped powerless to his side as he heard Giles speak; and if a thunderbolt had fallen at his feet he could not have looked more petrified with consternation.

He tried to speak for a moment, but could not; then turning to the man, who, despite his scratched and bleeding face, had assumed a careless air, and fitted the eye-glass to his eye, he said, in a tone struggling with deep emotion,—

"I ask you, sir, is this true?"

"Ah—ah—yes—oh, yes, uncommonly true. The little charmer came here to meet me, and this maniac interfered—ah! ah!"

George hesitated apparently for a moment, and the man did not know the danger he stood in, for George's first thought was to tear him to the earth. With a strong effort, however, he subdued his feelings. A deep sigh burst from him, and he turned away.

"It is over," he said, in a low voice; "the dream is past; it is morning."

"Ha! ha! ha!" shouted Giles; "dost thou feel it now?—dost thee feel the heart beat and the brain turn? If thee do, I—I pity thee. George, I, even I, do pity thee."

George heard him not, but slowly ascended the winding pathway. His steps were weak and unsteady. All energy seemed to have departed from him. In one moment the elasticity of youth seemed to have fled, and the bold, brave George, who, a few moments before, in all the pride of his manly strength and power, had plunged fearlessly into the Hollow, now walked from it with a tottering step, as if half a century had been suddenly added to his age in that brief time, and he had become an old man.

The occurences in Foyle's Hollow had not taken half the time in their actual transaction that we have necessarily taken to relate them, and Phœbe was still clasped in the arms of the miller when George slowly reached the spot on which they were.

"Mind Phœbe, my lad," cried the miller, "while I be gone into the Hollow."

As he spoke, he released himself from Phœbe's grasp, and walked quickly down the path. George shuddered as he looked at Phœbe, but he drew back.

"No, no—never again—never again," he said. "It was a beautiful vision, but 'tis gone, gone— gone for ever."

He walked slowly and mournfully on, to the astonishment of Phœbe, who passed her hands several times across her eyes, to be sure that she was in waking existence.

"George, George," she said. "Ah—a—what? who am I?—dear George. You—you spurn me from you. Oh, Heavens, this is the end!"

She dropped upon the verdant sod as she spoke; a film came across her eyes, and she knew no more; she had fainted on the spot.

The miller had not allowed himself time even to look at George as he arrived at the summit of the bank, and he was far down in the Hollow before Phœbe fainted on its brink.

He hurried up to the two who had so recently appeared to be bent upon each other's destruction, and who now stood face to face, presenting so great a contrast to each other, both in appearance and manner.

Giles was flushed with passion and excitement—an excitement which had only for the moment given way at the deep distress of George, which, wild and furious as he was, had had more effect upon Giles than could possibly have been imagined.

His antagonist assumed an attitude and manner of indifference as he there stood, with one hand concealed in the breast of his coat, grasping the hilt of the pistol, which he was devoutly wishing the other would, by a renewed attack, give him an opportunity of using. He was deadly pale, and it was evident that he was a man who, sooner or later, would have his revenge, and that, as far as in him lay, it would be full and ample.

"Sir Herbert Foster!" exclaimed the miller, as he approached near enough to note his countenance.

"Yes, man, Sir Herbert Foster," said the baronet, drawing himself up to his full height, and looking the miller undauntedly in the face.

"Then," cried the miller, clasping his hands tightly across his breast, "I do begin to understand this business. There can be no good where thee be."

"I claim your assistance to arrest this man," said Sir Herbert, pointing to Giles. "He has made an attack upon my life, and by my hand he shall pay the penalty."

"Sir Herbert Foster," replied the miller, calmly, "what did thee come here for?"

"I do not see that I am bound to explain my motives and actions to every base-born peasant who chooses to question them."

"I will tell thee myself, then," replied the miller; "but first let me tell thee I be not base-born, for my father was an honest man, which thee art not; thee life is base; thee actions are all base; and if thee had a child, which it be the mercy of God thee hast not, it would be base-born, because it was thine. Thee art a bad man, Sir Herbert Foster."

"You shall bitterly repent this language, miller," said the baronet.

"I shall not," cried Gilbert; "thee may do me harm, but I never can repent telling thee the truth. Thee came here to—to seduce my dear child; thee knows thee did. D—n thee, thee art a black villain."

"Ha! ha! miller, you're a fool. But mark me, I will not be abused with impunity even by such as thee. Sir Herbert Foster would pluck the tongue out of a dog that yelped at him."

"I know thee would," cried the miller, "but thee cannot pluck mine out. I will denounce thee as thee art, an enemy to innocence and virtue. Go thee ways. Thee hast been punished."

"Master," said Giles, "hear me. This man be speaking to Phœbe, and she be trying to leave him when I came here. I could not bear it, and I grappled with him."

"Get thee home, Giles, get thee home."

"Your man may escape me now, miller, but he shall not long. Let him beware; I will not be crossed by peasant or noble."

"Thee shall be crossed. I—I, Gilbert the miller, will cross thee. And there be another, a younger and stouter arm than mine, that will cross thee, powerful and rich though thee be. Thee would tear from me my child, but I will tear from thee thy heart first."

"You make—ah! ah!—fuss enough about your girl—ah! ah! I must ascertain really whose girl she is—ah."

The miller nearly fell to the ground as Sir Herbert spoke.

"Ah—eh? Oh, you don't like that, my friend," continued the baronet, who in a moment saw that he had pitched upon the right track. "You know—ah—that you have no right to the wench."

"I will not tell an untruth," cried the miller; "but I will speak no more to thee further than to say that I will protect the innocent and virtuous against the wicked and designing, and by the blessing of God I feel I shall succeed."

"Ah, ah—good day, my dear fellow. I dare say—ah—in your way you are a mighty honest fellow—ah. I would make a lady of the charmer; I told her so, but she is wofully ignorant; rust—rust of simplicity—ah, quite verdant. I—I would not mind settling an annuity on you. Oh, I shall hang the— ah—rustic lover. The charmer would make quite a sensation in—in town—ah, ah."

The baronet, as he spoke, slowly and carelessly left Foyle's Hollow, and never once looked at the honest miller, who was much disturbed at what had transpired.

"The secret, then, he knows," he said. "That bad man do know that poor Phœbe be not my child. She must have a protector, who can claim a right to do so. Poor Phœbe, I be old and this bad, rich man may crush me. God help thee, my dear girl; my heart be nigh broken to think of thee; yet there be George, he be brave, and a good lad, he shall be thee husband, he shall—he shall; and thee shall both stay with me and my old dame, and a hundred Sir Herberts cannot then harm thee: and yet, meeting with him, will George, after this, take the poor girl to his heart?"

He ascended the path, expecting to find Phœbe and George where he had left them ; but when the old man saw that George was not there, and Phœbe was lying, to all appearance, dead upon the ground, for a moment he stood bereft of reason ; then falling to the ground, he called Phœbe frantically by her name.

"My child ! my child !" he shrieked, "they have killed thee."

Phœbe was recovering. She gently opened her eyes, and murmured "Father."

The miller heard the sound. He clasped his aged hands to Heaven.

"Thank God !" he cried, "all be joy—she be alive—there be no sorrow now."

He raised her gently from the ground, and forbearing to question her in her weak state about the events of the morning, he quickly led her towards the cottage.

CHAPTER XXXV.

WHAT desolation was in the heart of George as he reached the mill, and threw himself upon the humble couch where he had enjoyed such blissful dreams of future happiness with her who, henceforward, he thought, must be to him as nothing. Oh! could he but blot from his memory the remembrance of having dearly loved. The remembrance? Did he not fondly, madly love still? He had heard that she was faithless ; but how, oh, how could he tear her image from his heart? He and Phœbe he felt, in the words of the poet, must—

> —————"Stand apart,
> Like rocks that had been rent asunder;
> A dreary sea now flows between;
> But neither heat, nor frost, nor thunder,
> Shall wholly do away, I ween,
> The marks of that which once hath been."

His heart might be seared thus early in life, and never again expand to love and joy ; but could he forget? As well might he attempt to forget his being as to forget his love for the Miller's Maid.

Again and again he revolved the circumstances in his mind. There was no hope to cling to ; all was darkness and despair. Foyle's Hollow was some distance from the mill, and Phœbe could not possibly be there accidentally, and at an hour when the morning meal was commonly partaken of in the cottage.

Giles had proclaimed that he had detected her in a clandestine interview with a stranger, and that stranger himself had owned the fact. Was there room for doubt?

He abandoned himself to despair. His dream of happiness was over, and he was alone in the wide world, without even hope to cling to.

Meanwhile the miller had conducted the trembling Phœbe to the cottage.

"Dame," said he, and his voice shook as he spoke, "dame, here is our dear girl. Still, dame, she be dear to us, though by some means she has been induced to meet a bad man. God forgive us, even our enemies, and God forbid that we should not forgive our dear child her follies."

The good old woman shook her head and wept as she kissed Phœbe, who had hardly strength to speak, and scarcely heard what the miller said.

"Hast thee seen George, dame ?" asked the miller.

"No, Gilbert, he be not come back, I believe. He will be sore grieved.

He be a good lad, but he will never get over Phœbe going to meet another."

"And that other, dame, was Sir Herbert Foster. He has sworn to take our dear child from us."

"Sir Herbert Foster?" cried the dame. "Alas! poor child, has he cast his eyes upon thee? Oh, woe the day."

"Father—mother," softly whispered Phœbe, "what—what mean you? I—I George—what is it? Dear George—oh—now I recollect, he shuddered and passed me. He—he did—George."

"Oh, Phœbe, my dear child, why did thee go to meet the bad man? Thee hast brought sorrow to poor George, who loved thee, my child."

Phœbe looked earnestly at the miller.

"Tell me, father—mother, tell me—both of you, why did he shudder as he passed me and—and weep! I think I saw him weep,"

"Because, my Phœbe, my dear child, for thee art still dear to the old miller—"

"Still," cried Phœbe; "still. What, oh! what have I done?"

"Thee did meet Sir Herbert Foster in Foyle's Hollow."

"Meet Sir Herbert Foster in Foyle's Hollow?" repeated Phœbe, and her face brightened as she spoke! "oh, say, is—is that why George passed me so."

"I believe it be, my child."

"Oh, I am happy—happy again—so happy!" She burst into tears as she spoke; and as she wept she became calmer, and the fever of her mind gradually subsided. Suddenly she looked up. "Where is he?" she cried; "where is George?"

As she spoke, a knock was heard at the door of the cottage, and in a moment Tim Miggles put his head into the room.

"Master," he said—

No. 27

" Master and missus, alack, alack,
   There's George laying on his back.
He really does seem of his reason bereft,
   And wants Snapallhecanup to give him a lift."

" George in the mill ?" cried Phœbe.

" Yes, my princess, he is in the mill, and seems rather ill. I'll just tell
you all about it."

" Quick, Tim, quick," said Phœbe.

" Well, I'm glad to find you want to hear it.

" He's got some hot coals,
   Which serve him for rolls,
      And he eats them without any gammon ;
   Were a river at hand,
   He could stand on the land,
      Pop his nose in and cook all the salmon."

Phœbe was gone long before Tim Miggles had got to the last line of the
verse.

" She be gone to George at the mill, Gilbert," cried the dame.

" Let her go, dame, answered the miller. " My mind do seem to tell me
that all will be right. Perhaps we have been too hasty, and blamed the
dear child wrongfully. God send it be so ; but let her go to George.
He be a good lad, and he loves her."

" I wish I saw her fairly married to him, Gilbert."

" Amen," said the miller. " Thee may, perhaps, have thee wish soon,
dame. They be worthy of each other ; they be, indeed."

" Eh ? what ?" cried Tim.

" Is this the way, while time onward creeps,
   Tim Miggles is to be done up in heaps."

" Hold thee tongue, will thee, and go to thee work," cried the dame.

" Where shall I find another princess in country or in town,
   Oh, Miggles, Miggles, you'll be done a most particularly fine brown."

" This poor fellow be gone clean foolish," said the miller, taking Tim by
the arm, and leading him to the door. " I'll turn them from the mill,
and thee'll then be full of cares, if thee interferes with other folks affairs."

Tim was so taken aback and astounded by this poetic effort of the miller's,
that he could not say another word, but slunk back to the mill, thoroughly
defeated.

Phœbe proceeded direct to the mill, and entering it, she never hesitated
till she reached the room which led into that occupied by George. Here
she paused a moment, as if to recover composure sufficient to speak. Then
gently knocking at the door, she called him by name, and stood waiting,
with a sweet smile upon her face—that voice which to him had ever been
the sweetest music. He started and listened.

" No," he said, " it is the memory of joy, it is the sweet remembrance
of tones I never more may hear, which are still ringing in my distracted
ears. This place—the old cottage—the meadow, where she said—oh,
Heavens, let me not think of it—'tis madness—I must leave this place—
every object must remind me of her. In other scenes I may sometimes
snatch one bright moment of forgetfulness. On the sea—the deep blue sea
—I will strive, amid the roaring of the billows, to forget and to fancy that
I have only dreamed of so fair—so—no, no, I must not think thus of her ;
she is false, false.

He rose as he spoke to pass out of the mill, intending at once to put the
project of leaving the place for ever in execution. Oh, if he had done so,
what years of misery and regret might have been his. The possession of a
young pure heart's love should make us pause ere we voluntarily take a
step which may for ever sever us from the dear possession ; and this—this
love, for which men will toil, slave, entreat, nay, commit crime upon crime

for, is, of all possessions, that which, upon the slightest pretext, we cast from us. The very pure intensity of the feeling is its own bane. It is a pure, holy thing, which we value so highly that we can never feel fully assured that we really possess; and the least incident which favours the mind's dread suspicion of faithfulness, is caught at by the fancy, and inflated to a monstrous size.

George opened the door and recoiled as if it had been an apparition. Phœbe stood upon its threshold.

"George, dear George," she said.

"Phœbe! you here?" he cried. "What—why—oh, Phœbe, Phœbe."

He walked into the room, and sunk upon a chair, unable to express himself.

"George," she said, "you said you loved me once. Say you do not now, and I will leave you. You will never hear murmur or complaint from me."

"Phœbe, Phœbe, do not—oh, do not torture me."

"Torture you, George. What have I done that you should look thus at me?"

"Done, Phœbe! I—I cannot speak it. You smiled to me from your little window—you—you looked so like an angel—a bright inhabitant of Heaven—I—I could not dream that you——"

"What—of what do you accuse me?"

"One short hour after this, Phœbe, I found you—you whom I fondly believed was something more than mortal——"

"Well, George, where did you find me? It was at Foyle's Hollow, with strangers. You were summoned by my cries."

"No, Phœbe, your absence was alarming. I know not by what chance the miller and I sought you at Foyle's Hollow; suffice it we did."

"And then, George?" said Phœbe, mournfully.

"And then, Phœbe, I was told that you had been there to meet a stranger."

"And you believed it, George?"

George looked for a moment confounded at the fair girl before him, who had ever been associated in his mind with all that was gentle and endearing; but now, as she stood before him, with a slight flush upon her cheek of wounded feeling, and regarding him with a glance, half tender and half reproachful, he hesitated to reply.

"I did believe it, Phœbe," he at length said. "Everything conspired to convince me of it—the man owned it—Giles asserted it—I saw you there—yes, I—I did believe it."

Phœbe regarded him with an expression of mournful interest for a moment, and then said, in a voice of deep emotion, as she moved to the door,—

"Is it indeed so? George, George, you—you do not know me. I had a thought—an idle thought—that I was loved, and—and trusted——"

"And so you were—are now," cried George, whose conviction had been much staggered by Phœbe's manner. "Give me but one word, Phœbe. Tell me you are——"

"What?" cried Phœbe, turning fully upon him, while the tears started to her eyes.

"Innocent."

"Tell you, George Andrews, that I am innocent? No, no; it needed but that. I thought you knew me innocent. George, farewell—we part for——"

"Oh, do not say that word," cried George, frantically; "in mercy stop. The scales are off my eyes—it was some hideous phantasy—oh, Phœbe, forgive me!"

She hesitated for a moment, then sunk upon his breast, sobbing.

"Forgive you, George?—as I hope to be forgiven."

"My Phœbe—my own dear love."

"Now, George," she cried, disengaging herself from his embrace, and smiling through her tears, "question me as you will—ask me the minutest circumstances of my actions—anything—everything—I will answer all, George, now; but do, oh do not suspect me."

"Never, oh never, Phœbe. I have nothing to ask—I desire to hear nothing; I see you and love you, that is all the world to me"

"Then," replied Phœbe, "dear George, I will tell. I did not go to Foyle's Hollow to meet any of the persons you saw there."

"I ought to have sworn you did not, Phœbe."

"I went to meet George Andrews."

"Meet me, Phœbe?"

"Yes, George, meet you. Much against my judgment, I went to meet you. Look at this letter."

As she spoke, the smiling girl placed the epistle in George's hands which she had found in the morning when at her chamber window.

"Phœbe, dear Phœbe, I never saw this before."

"I ought to have sworn you did not, George," she said, with a winning smile, "and yet I went."

"My own kind girl, oh, how much have I wronged you."

"Hush!" she said, placing her hand upon his mouth, which he instantly covered with kisses. "No more doubts or fears, dear George. I ought to have known you better."

"And I you better, dear Phœbe. This has been the device of the villain whom I saw with Giles in the Hollow. Oh, had I but known this much then."

George clenched his hands as he spoke, and his flashing eyes bespoke his anger at the vile author of the note, which, in his name, had induced the confiding girl to leave her home, and incur so much risk and censure.

"This, George," said Phœbe, "should be a lesson to us both not to come to judgment too hastily."

"It should, indeed, to me, dear Phœbe. Bless you, my sweet girl, I must have been too much maddened and excited to think clearly, or I never could have acted as I have done. Dearest, I shall ever think of this morning with a grateful feeling. I was about to leave the mill for ever, when your kind spirit prompted you to save me from a destructiou which I was madly bringing upon myself."

"Now, George, I will go to my dear father, who, I fear, thinks his child is still to blame."

"Shall I come with you, Phœbe?" said George.

She shook her head.

"No, George, stay here, now. I—I will see you in the meadow at sun set. Till then——"

"Till then, my dearest, best of beings, farewell! and may kind Heaven guard you from all ill."

Phœbe smiled and waved her hand, and then hurried to the cottage.

She was about to enter the little garden which would lead by a shorter way to the cottage door than going round its low fence, when some one started up from the side of the gate suddenly, and stood before her.

It was Giles; but he was so altered from the Gilles of the few weeks previous, that had not Phœbe seen him daily, and marked the change gradually, she would not have known him. As it was, she at first started back, but instantly recovering herself, she held out her hand to him with a smile, and said,—

" Giles, I owe you many thanks for your kind service this morning. You rescued me from violence."

He had washed from his face and dress the marks of the recent conflict in which he had been engaged, and save that he was scratched and torn by his fall with Sir Herbert Foster, but little traces remained of the strife in which he had been engaged. On the contrary, a flush, as of awakened hopes, seemed to hang upon his face, and the ghastly paleness which had of late given an almost unearthly appearance to him, was for the time conquered.

" Phœbe," he said, " 1 wish to speak to thee."

" Now, Giles ?" asked Phœbe.

" Yes, Phœbe, it be now I wish to speak to thee. If thee really thinks 1 have done thee a service, all 1 be going to ask in return is, that thee will let me say my say to thee now."

" I am anxious to seek my dear father," said Phœbe, mildly, " but I will not deny you, Giles."

" Will thee come to the meadow ?"

Phœbe turned reluctantly from the gate, and was soon in the meadow, with Giles at her side. When there, he seemed so oppressed by his feelings as to be unable to speak, but when he did, his voice, which at first had trembled, soon gained firmness, and he spoke in a tone of exultation, which betrayed the excited state of his feelings.

" Phœbe," he said, " thee knows that, day and night, in summer and in winter, I have loved thee—watched over thee—would have died for thee."

" You have been ever kind to me, Giles, and, believe me, 1 can never forget it."

" 1 would work—toil for thee, Phœbe. 1 would watch over thee as a bird does its young. Thee art dear to my heart, and, Phœbe, I still do love thee dearer than the whole world."

" Alas! Giles," cried Phœbe, " I do, indeed, thank you for all your kindness and care, and ever as a dear, dear brother, will 1 esteem you. Such love, such dear love, as I would give to so near and dear a relative, shall ever be yours."

" No, Phœbe, no ; that be not it—no, no. 1 saw George pass thee, and——"

" And what, Giles ? What did you see ?"

" He did cast thee from him, he did. He did possess a dear treasure, and he did cast it from him, because he did see that it was not all gold. Oh, Phœbe, I have loved thee longer—better than he ever could ; I loved thee from the first ; I thought best of thee. Oh, say that thee will be mine, my Phœbe. I will wait upon thee and cherish thee ; thee shall have no sorrow—no tear shall come from thee eye ; thee shall not feel the winter's cold—the summer's sun shall not offend thee. Say thee will be mine—oh, Phœbe, say thee will be mine."

No language could describe the impassioned vehemence with which Giles spoke. Sometimes his voice would sink into the tones of the mildest tenderness, then it would rise to entreaty, and then be choked with sobs.

Phœbe trembled and wept as she witnessed the sad effects of his passion—a passion which she could not bid even hope, far less reciprocate.

" Giles," she said, " it grieves me to see you thus. Be what you have always been, my kind dear friend, and I will ever esteem you as such ; but——"

" Oh, Phœbe, Phœbe, thee must not say thee will not be my Phœbe. I be rough and rude, but to thee I will not be so. I will love thee, Phœbe, dearer than life itself. The eyes with which I do see the fields, and the flowers, and the morning light, be not so precious to me as thee. I would give all—all for thee. There be sweet sunshine where thee dost go. The winter be not about thee, for thee beauty do make make all things beautiful."

"Oh, cease, cease, Giles," said Phœbe, "you distress me much. I would that I could love you as you wish, but I cannot."

"I will be thee slave, Phœbe—thee shall do what thee please—thee may tread upon me; say but that thee shall be mine—I do love thee more than I do love Heaven."

"Giles, Giles," cried Phœbe, "this is wickedness. Let me hear this no more. You cannot mean what you say; and if you do, I grieve much for you. Oh, Giles, think more calmly."

"I cannot—I cannot. My head do throb, and my heart do bleed in my breast. I do not want to see the sun again; I only do want to look at thee."

"Giles, I cannot listen to you any more. This talking will distress us both."

Phœbe wept as she spoke, and her tears seemed to give the despairing man some fresh hopes.

"George will despise thee," he cried, "the miller will despise thee, but I will love thee—love thee, Phœbe, better than them all."

She moved towards the gate, but he dropped on his knees, and clung, with the energy of deep despair, to her garments.

"Mercy, mercy," he cried, "thee will think of me. Say thee will be my Phœbe in many years. I will do much for thee, I—I will kill. Say but one word. I be nearly mad."

Phœbe was now much alarmed at the vehemence of his voice and gestures, and rushing from the meadow, she left him, shrieking in a frenzy of depair after her, and sunk upon a seat in the cottage, quite exhausted by her feelings.

"My dear child," cried the dame, "what be the matter? Has George——"

"No, mother, oh, no; Giles has alarmed me. I—I—"

Phœbe leant upon the dame's shoulder and wept, for her heart was wrung to see the agony of distress which Giles's hopeless passion had driven him to.

"Alack, alack," cried the dame, "what a thing this love be now-a-days. Aye, it was not so in my young day; but now I do think the young folks be all gone mad, and I believe it be main owing to poetry and such like."

"What dost thee say, dame, about poetry?" said the miller, descending from an upper room.

"Why here be Giles have frightened Phœbe."

"The deuce take Giles; he be worse than Tim Miggles, for Tim be harmless mad, and Giles be main furious, I think."

"Father and mother," said Phœbe, slightly blushing as she spoke, "I—I have seen—George, and he knows I am not to blame in going to Foyle's Hollow; that is, dear friends, I ought to have told you both first, but—but it was so sudden I had not time to think; and, perhaps, you will forgive me when you read this, which I found upon my window. I know I ought not to have gone, but I—I—"

She hid her face on the dame's breast and could say no more, while the honest miller adjusted his spectacles upon his nose, and proceeded to read the note which had seduced Phœbe so early in the morning from her dear home to Foyle's Hollow.

He threw down the spectacles when he had read it on to the floor, and in a fit of absence of mind thrust the note into his spectacle case.

"Come to me, my darling," he cried, "my dear child. God forgive me for suspecting that thee could be induced to meet a stranger, unknown to me; but thee should not have gone even to meet George. But never thee mind, say no more about it. Dame, dame, dost thee recollect climbing out of window to meet me, and catching thee dress in a mulberry tree?"

"Gilbert, Gilbert," cried the dame, "what art thou saying?"

"Well, well, dame, it be ended. Say no more," cried the smiling miller, clasping Phœbe in his arms, and kissing her tenderly.

CHAPTER XXXVI.

IT was Mr. Perk who kept so smiling a watch at the top of the little winding pathway from Foyle's Hollow, and prevented Phœbe from escaping the importunities of Sir Herbert Foster.

The evening before Mr. Pomander had obtained an interview with the licentious baronet, and easily induced him to be at Foyle's Hollw by the hour in in the morning at which, in the forged epistle to Phœbe, it was appointed that she should be there.

The baronet was by no means accustomed to be stirring at so early an hour; but he looked upon the pursuit of his pleasure as he would have done upon a shooting, hunting, or a fishing excursion, which required early rising to fully enjoy.

Before eight, therefore, without acquainting either the complaisant valet, Cury, or Ralph Freegrove, with the nature of his expedition, from indolence, rather than mistrust or caution, Sir Herbert Foster, accompanied by Mr. Perk, who had been introduced to him as a subordinate agent in the matter by Mr. Pomander, arrived, and by that gentleman's suggestion, secreted himself in the Hollow.

Whatever expectations Sir Herbert might have formed or indulged in respecting the personal beauty of the Miller's Maid from the description which had been given him of her exceeding loveliness, fell far, very far short of his impression when he first saw her from his hiding-place, standing for a moment on the brink of the Hollow, before she sought the winding pathway which led into the depth of its recesses.

He mentally determined to spare neither expense nor trouble to secure the possession of so surpassingly fair a prize; and, considering the indolence of Sir Herbert's disposition, he really exerted himself wonderfully in the interview with Phœbe which succeeded.

He was astonished at the rapid and unexpected descent of Perk from his elevated position by the hands of Giles; and his rage, although he suppressed much outward exhibition of it, knew no bounds after the attack upon himself, which had forced him to use more personal exertion than he had done for the last twenty-five years of his life.

Mr. Perk, upon the principle that the better part of valour was discretion, no sooner recovered from the effects of the stunning fall he had received, than he looked carefully about him, without deeming it essential to make his presence particularly striking and public, by rising from the bed of weeds and brushwood into which he had fallen.

He saw that Sir Herbert Foster was hotly engaged in strife with some one, and he heard the voice of the miller; so without more ado, Mr. Perk most prudently quitted the scene of action, by crawling along, screened by the bushes till he came to a part of the Hollow at some distance from the contending parties, up which he climbed, and without observation, made good his retreat to Haredale, and arrived, dirty, jaded, torn, and bruised at the shop of Mr. Pomander, where that latter gentleman was waiting in anxious expectation of his (Mr. Perk's) arrival, with news of the full success of the interview between Sir Herbert Foster and his intended victim.

Mr. Perk sunk into a chair, and surveyed, with a rueful air, his new suit of black, which he had that morning put on in honour of the introduction to the baronet, and Mr. Pomander looked no less astonished at the plight of his copartner.

"Dear me, Mr. Perk," said the son of Esculapius, "you really—upon my honour you have been much ill-used by some one—beaten, I may say— scratched—your clothes torn.—Humph !—Dear me, they have punished you, my good friend, and how charmingly patient you are, too. Not a frown—not an oath. Oh, bless me, you are an example."

"Mr. Pomander," said Perk, "you be d—d !"

"Oh, dear me, I can make allowance for wounded feeling and—and wounded body. Really that serious scratch on your nose will, I very much fear, leave a permanent cloatrix."

"None of your humbug, Pomander," cried Mr. Perk, who saw that his dear friend was coolly practising a little of the much admired science of tormenting. "You be d—d up in little heaps; nobody has beaten nor scratched me. Some infernal yokel came behind me and pushed me clean neck over nothing into the Hollow, confound him !"

"Did he, indeed ? Rash, very rash. Are you sure there's no fracture, luxation, or serious strain. Perhaps there's some inward bruise, eh ?"

"Nothing of the sort, thank you all the same ; but I'm pretty sure—and when I'm tolerably sure I always take my oath—that the rascal who as- saulted me was that Giles, the miller's man, who we overheard so prettily planning matters with Scrimp."

"Then the appointment was discovered probably ?"

"No, I think not ; but the d—d yokel watched the little chit, no doubt, according to Scrimp's advice, and followed her to the Hollow. I tell you what it is, Pomander, but for my advice Sir Herbert would never have met the girl at all to-day, for I tell you she's an out and-outer ; but owing to my fixing the appointment so early, you see she hadn't time to think, but came at once on the impulse of the moment."

"And, Sir Herbert," asked Pomander ; "what has become of him ?"

"Oh, I left him, having the jolliest, rough and tumble mill that ever you saw in your life. It was beautiful. No business of mine, though, thought I, so, you see, I mizzled."

"Humph ! all this is rather unfortunate than otherwise. I must go to Haredale Park immediately. You've got leave of absence from Scrimp for to-day."

"Yes, and ha !—ha !—I do believe he was very glad to get rid of me."

"Well, my good fellow, you'll find soap and water in the next room. You can put yourself a little to rights while I am gone ; and if anybody should come for anything ——"

"Oh, I'll manage the doctoring business. Just tell me where you keep the laudanum and white arsenic, that's all."

Mr. Pomander smiled and left the shop, in some tribulation of spirit with respect to his reward, towards Haredale Park.

Ralph Freegrove was not a little surprised at the early departure of Sir Herbert Foster, but he dared not run the risk of offending him by following him, and he remained lost in conjecture, until he was still more astonished at the return of his master, covered with dirt, his clothes torn, and his hands and face smeered with blood.

Sir Herbert Foster passed through the hall of his mansion with a scowl- ing brow, and no domestic, not even the favoured Ralph Freegrove, dared

to utter even an exclamation of surprise at the unusual appearance of the baronet.

He walked silently up the marble staircase, and hurried to his dressing-room, where he imperatively commanded the obsequibus Cury to commence assisting in his toilet.

In a short time nearly all traces of his recent disaster had vanished from the person of Sir Herbert Foster, and, save an unusual paleness upon his cheek, and a few unsightly scratches across his face and hands, no one would have supposed that anything remarkable had occurred to disturb the serenity of the accomplished roue.

A domestic now entered, and announced that Mr. Pomander begged the honour of an interview with the baronet.

"Humph! Pomander!" said Sir Herbert, with a sneering smile. "Ah, ah!—admit him."

In a few moments Mr. Pomander was ushered into the presence of the incensed Sir Herbert, who bit his lips as the obsequious medical man approached, to conceal the deep vexation he was suffering.

"Cury," said Sir Herbert.

"Sir Herbert," simpered Cury.

"Go."

Cury disappeared in a moment, and Mr. Pomander was alone with the baronet, upon whose countenance there sat an expression which was anything but pleasing to the former.

"I extremely regret," began Mr. Pomander, "that you should have been subjected to any inconvenience, Sir Herbert, arising from the obstinacy and stupidity of a clown, who ——"

"Ah! ah! the girl did not come to meet me."

"Why, Sir Herbert, she did meet you. I believe that was all that was

No. 28

required.   There could not exist any reasonable doubt then, but the—grace—the ineffable charm of manner —"

"The girl came to meet some one else ?"

"Why, to tell the truth, she did ; but she met you, Sir Herbert; that was the thing to be most desired.   I truly regret that any unfortunate accident should have occurred to produce an inconvenient result to the interview, which ought, really, my dear sir, to have been crowned with the most—really —"

"Ah! ah!   Then you deceived me by telling me that—ah, ah—you had made an appointment for me with the—the girl."

"Not deceived, Sir Herbert ; oh, dear, no.   I really thought you were quite aware that some little pardonable stratagem must be employed to procure the presence of the rustic beauty at the time appointed, and I had the honour of succeeding in a little ruse, which it appeared really had the desired effect, although one of those unfortunate accidents, to which we must all bow and submit, occurred to cast a—a gloom—a kind of —"

"Trash!   You have done nothing, sir.   Any idle tale will bring a village girl to a meeting.   Tell her that her grandmother, father, or brother, or some other infernal relation is—ah, ah —"

"Mr. Scrimp, Sir Herbert," announced Cury, "at the door."

"Ah !—shew him in."

Mr. Pomander looked astonished at the order of Sir Herbert to shew in Mr. Scrimp while he was there, and a slight flush passed across his usually imperturbable face as the bowing and smiling attorney appeared at the door.

If Mr. Pomander was annoyed at the visit of Mr. Scrimp, that latter gentleman was no less taken aback, as the saying is, at the appearance of Mr. Pomander, apparently in close consultation with Sir Herbert Foster, and he paused when about two or three paces in the room to stare at the man of drugs, who had risen from his seat with a bland smile, determined to put a good face on the matter, and, if he could accomplish nothing by staying, to make a masterly retreat.

Sir Herbert Foster fixed his glass in his eye, and steadily regarded the two, although he did not betray, by the slightest movement, any interest in their proceedings.

"My dear sir, this is an unexpected pleasure," said Mr. Pomander, extending his hand to the attorney, and smiling in the most amiable manner in the world.

"Oh, my dear sir," replied Mr. Scrimp, "you are really too good.   I hope you are better than when I last saw you.   You are looking now a little feverish and heated."

"I thank you," replied the doctor, "You know I must be well. Gentlemen of my profession dare not to be indisposed.   How do you find business ?"

"Scrimp, ah, ah," said Sir Herbert.

"Yes, Sir Herbert.   Your most obedient and very humble servant, Sir Herbert."

"Ah, ah—ring."

"With the extremest pleasure, Sir Herbert.   Your slightest command is, I may say, to a feeling mind, quite a—a sort—oh, yes."

"Ah, ah, Pomander—eh ?—good morning."

Mr. Pomander could at the moment have twisted Mr. Scrimp's head off with the most sincere and heartfelt gratification, if time and circumstances had empowered him to do the deed ; and as it was, he glanced at him as he tripped smilingly across the room to ring the bell, with the vague hope that at some future period Mr. Scrimp might be suddenly taken ill, and be compelled to call him in, which would be most delicious.

"Sir Herbert," said the discomfited disciple of Galen, "if you will allow me the honour of five minutes private conversation, I believe I can communicate to you some particulars which —"

"Ha! ha! Cury, shew the medical individual out."

"But, Sir Herbert —'

"Good morning, Mr.—ha—a—a—I forget your name."

"Good morning, Mr. Pomander," said Mr. Scrimp, with a diabolical sneer.

Mr. Pomander was determined not to be outdone, if possible. He saw that all hope of doing anything further with Sir Herbert Foster was past, but revenge was in his power.

"My dear Sir Herbert," he said, with rather an air of insolence, "if you follow my advice, you will endeavour, by a judicious course of the medicine I have recommended, to restore your most awfully shattered constitution. I shall be, I am sure, most happy at any time to render to you my professional advice and assistance."

"Ah! ah! Cury. Is the medical individual gone?"

"Good morning, sir," said Cury, bowing Mr. Pomander out of the room, and closing the door.

"Scrimp," said Sir Herbert.

"Sir Herbert, I fear you have been misled by the—the person who has just had the honour to—to leave your honourable presence, Sir Herbert."

Sir Herbert dropped the glass from his eye, and with a vehemence which quite startled the cringing attorney, cried,—

"Scrimp, how much money will it take to hang a few men—two—of course I mean two of the lower classes—the scum—the *canaille*?"

"Why, really, Sir Herbert," stammered Mr. Scrimp, somewhat confounded by so curious and original an inquiry from his patron, "I—I— indeed, Sir Herbert, if it be your wish, they really—I should say ought— to be hung very cheap indeed. May I be humbly permitted to ask who, Sir Herbert, you have done the honour of wishing—a—a—suspended?"

"The miller, and a scoundrel of his who attacked me this morning."

"Humph!" said Mr. Scrimp. "There might be some little 'difficulty, Sir Herbert, May I be humbly permitted to inquire if you have seen the —the young woman who —"

"I have seen her. She is an angel; and, by God, I will have her if it cost me Hardale Park—every acre."

Mr. Scrimp gave a great jump in his chair as Sir Herbert spoke, with a loud voice, and accompanied his words with a gesture of rage and impatience.

"Sir Herbert," said the attorney, after a pause, "I know these people at the mill well. Threats, entreaties, supplications, all will fail."

"But—but there are other means. Damnation! do not tell me. There are other means, I say. I neither supplicate nor entreat. I am determined, and I will have her, I tell you, cost what it may."

"Not a doubt, Sir Herbert, but the means are the thing to be considered. Now, Sir Herbert, this man—this Pomander —"

"D—n him, he has led me into trouble and difficulty."

"As might be expected, Sir Herbert. I knew he would when you did me the honour of telling your very humble and devoted servant that he had promised you an interview with the damsel."

"Well, well, let that pass. What do you advise? Quick."

"Why, in the first place, Sir Herbert, I advise you to forget everything but the attainment of the principal object—the possession of the girl—hem! legally, of course."

"What do you mean?"

"Why, I mean, Sir Herbert, that Pomander should be forgiven and employed, or he may do much mischief. The individual who was, I have ascertained, with him—my clerk, Perk, d—n him—I beg your pardon, Sir Herbert,—must likewise be employed."

"Well, proceed."

"The hand who assaulted your honourable person must be made useful."

"How is that possible?"

"He is mad—raving, Sir Herbert, because this very girl will not condescend to bestow her charms upon him. He has a favoured rival at the mill."

"Humph!" said the baronet, after a pause. "Be it so. Act as you please in those matters. Love and delight for the first course, and revenge for the second. Be it so. What do you propose to do?"

"I have had the honour of stating that entreaty, persuasion, and brilliant offers, will be useless with these pig-headed rustics."

"Well."

"Therefore, Sir Herbert, there is only one alternative, and that, Sir Herbert —"

"Is force."

"Oh dear, no; only just a little mild—a—a—a kind of gentle abduction. You see we must be very careful, Sir Herbert. All who know anything of this little a—a—amiable transaction, must, if possible, be engaged in it, so far that—that—"

"Their own safety will keep them silent, you mean. D— you, you cringing slave, why don't you speak out?"

"Why, really—ah, ah!—you have so pleasant and jocular a manner. Dear me—"

"Now, Scrimp, let me understand you. This girl I must and will have, by fair means or foul. You and Freegrove, with what other assistance you please, must manage the business. And, mark me, if I live another month, I'll have that miller out of the cottage and the mill if I am forced to burn it down with my own hand. I tell you out he shall go, and I will have the girl."

"Oh, certainly, certainly. A gentleman with your means, Sir Herbert, ought really to be allowed to do these little things without hindrance; but there are people who take a malicious delight in crossing the little frolics and inclinations of their superiors."

"You know my villa at Brompton, in the neighbourhood of London?"

"I have that distinguished honour, Sir Herbert."

"Let her be taken there. I will remain here at the d—d dull place till all is accomplished, and you can let me know when it is so."

"Certainly—oh, dear me, yes, Sir Herbert. You see we shall require in this matter the assistance of the most potent auxiliary, a—a—"

"Money, you mean?"

"Why, yes, Sir Herbert; money will do wonders."

Sir Herbert looked languidly about him, and pointing to a desk which laid on an inlaid table near him, he said—

"Bring me that desk."

Mr. Scrimp obeyed with the greatest alacrity; and Sir Herbert opening it, took from it a pocket-book, which he handed to Scrimp.

"There — ah, ah — are two hundred pounds," he said, listlessly. "When the girl is at the villa, come to me for as much more as will make five hundred."

The pocket-book was out of sight in a moment, and in Mr. Scrimp's pocket.

"Ah! ah! ring."

The satisfied attorney rang the bell, which was immediately answered by Cury.

"Cury."

"Sir Herbert."

"Is Freegrove in the—ah—house?"

"Yes, Sir Herbert."

"Scrimp, you will—ah, ah—see Freegrove. When next shall I have —ah!—the pleasure of your company?"

"You will hear, Sir Herbert, that your commands are obeyed."

"Ah—good-morning."

Mr. Scrimp bowed his way out, inwardly congratulating himself upon the issue of the interview. The wily attorney felt the necessity of immediately taking Mr. Pomander into his councils, for he knew that in the iniquitous transaction in which he was engaged, an enemy who already knew so much as Mr. Pomander did upon the subject, would very likely take active measures to know more, and probably, if not instantly employed on the one side, would bestow his services, from revenge and disappointment, gratuitously upon the other. Mr. Perk, too, he was determined to conciliate; for, besides having the highest opinion of, and admiration for, that young gentleman's talents in intrigue, Mr. Scrimp felt that he came under the same category as Mr. Pomander, for he had not been so short-sighted as not to perceive that an unusual degree of intimacy obtained between the learned doctor and his clerk.

Mr. Freegrove and Mr. Scrimp heartily congratulated each other upon the turn things had taken, and laid their heads together, for upwards of an hour, over some choice claret of Sir Herbert's, debating upon the most practical scheme of carrying into effect the wishes of the baronet.

"By the devil and everything d—able," cried Freegrove; "I'm glad, Sir Herbert has himself got some private scores of revenge to settle at the mill, for in the scramble I may chance to pay off my little debt to the scoundrel who made my back acquainted with the floor of the miller's cottage. Hang the whole canting lot of them! If Sir Herbert don't burn them out, I will."

"Hush, my dear sir, hush," said Mr. Scrimp; "the subject is rather a delicate one. It's all very well, you know, for Sir Herbert Foster to threaten a little, because a—a—hem!—he has, you know, somewhere about five-and-twenty thousands a-year."

"Well, well, lawyer, just you settle how the job about the girl is to be done, and let me know. My own little private concerns I'll find a proper time for."

"Exactly, my good sir. To-night, if you please, I will do myself the extreme pleasure of seeing you, if you please."

"Very good. I shall expect you. Ah, lawyer, I thought you'd be one too many yet for the doctor. Ha! ha! ha!"

"The doctor, however, is a clever man, Freegrove, and can help us if we like. D— him, I would be glad to do without him, and Perk, too, the villain, but we must make use of the tools that come to our hands, though we may not like them."

"But the money, lawyer, you don't mean to share with those rascals, unless you have a good opportunity of robbing them afterwards."

"No, no. Five hundred is the sum Herbert has promised. We can, by a little harmless mistake, just call it two to them, eh?"

Ralph Freegrove grinned and nodded his head, and Mr. Scrimp, with a gratified smile, left Haredale Park, with the immediate intention of coming to an explanation and satisfactory arrangement and league with Mr. Pomander and Mr. Perk.

CHAPTER XXXVII.

THE occurrences of the morning, although they had not obliterated from George's mind the recollection of the singular being he had encountered on the preceding evening under Phœbe's window, had been, notwithstanding, of sufficiently engrossing importance to chase from his memory his intention of communicating the circumstance to the miller, and hearing what would be his solution of the seemingly supernatural and truly horrible appearance.

When he came, however, to hear from Phœbe how and in what a situation she had found the note which invited her, in his name, to Foyle's Hollow, a ready solution of the mystery occurred to him, namely, that the appearance which at the moment had really somewhat unnerved him, had been, by some trickery, assumed by the person who had placed the note in the position from which his gentle Phœbe had taken it.

Acting upon this supposition, which was really the true one, for Mr. Perk, among his other accomplishments, was no despicable actor, George resolved not to mention the circumstance, as it might possibly create needless alarm in the breasts of the inhabitants of the cottage.

Mr. Perk calculated that there would be some little danger in so placing the note that Phœbe would see it if she looked from her window, and he selected, from a variety of miscellaneous property which he possessed, a dress of black velvet, upon which was painted the form of a skeleton, and which at night, upon a momentary glance, might very well impose upon any one.

Private theatricals had engaged much of Mr. Perk's attention while resident in the metropolis, and hence his possession of the means of disguising his skin and unremarkable person almost at pleasure.

Although George felt that his solution of the mystery must be the correct one, the circumstance gave him a great deal of uneasiness on several grounds.

It induced, in the first place, a strong belief in his mind—a belief which occasioned him the acutest uneasiness, that no slight efforts were being employed to wound for ever the peace of all he held dear ; but that the most violent exertions, directed by ample means, might well be expected to be made, for the poor triumph of seducing from her home, and leading to destruction, a simple-minded and innocent girl, and for what ?—because it had pleased Heaven to bestow upon her the perilous gift of rare beauty.

Then, again, from the appearance which for a moment had paralysed his own energies, he feared that some atrocious attempt might be concocted to work upon the fears of poor Phœbe—those fears of the supernatural, which, however they may be scouted and laughed to scorn, still lurk in some secret corner of the heart even of the most sceptical or the most philosophical.

These were not pleasant reflections for the ardent and devoted lover, but they obtruded themselves upon his mind during the whole morning ; and had it not been that the sunshine of joy was in his heart, and that he felt happy—irrisistibly happy—in the consciousness of being beloved by the fair girl whose happiness and wellfare dwelt so near his heart, he would have given way to despondency ; but as it was, he strove to shake the uneasy thoughts which crowded to his brain, and to dream those soft, beautiful waking dreams of early life, when the young imagination takes its course through years to come, and paints to the delighted soul, in all the rich colouring of hope and joy, the coming time.

Oh, if but one tithe, one tithe of a tithe of those bright visions which adorn the morning of life could be realised, life would be a dream of bliss—a sojourn in a happy valley—an Elysium upon earth.

How sad is the moment when we feel that we have grown wise in the world's wisdom, and can dream no more. Who is there that would give the bright glorious fancies, fragile though they be, of youth, for the cold realities of after years? The philosopher may sneer at the brilliant anticipations which live but in the sunny fancy, and smile in derision at the airy castle, which a breath will scatter to the winds, and oppose the cold truth of bitter experience to all that is beautiful and good,—he may tell us that all that we have dreamt of—sighed for—hugged to our best of hearts—

> ——— "Will dissolve,
> And like an unsubstantial pageant,
> Leave not a wreck behind—"

but if he dared to say it, he would give his love and learning—his experience of evil—his indifference—his knowledge—all—all—he would give for one bright ray of such anticipations and hopes—hopes that rob Time of his pinions, and lift humanity above the skies.

The day wore on in dreams of bliss to George. Phœbe, too, looked to the happy future as if through some magic glass, which lent a glow and beauty to each varied scene.

Giles had gloomily sought the mill, and mechanically proceeded with the labours of the day. His manner was listless, though, and it seemed as if all feeling, all hope were crushed and dead within his breast.

His eye was bent as coldly upon George as upon poor Tim Miggles, and his mind appeared as if it had received some sudden blow, which had deprived it of all sensation—all capacity of thought.

The faith of Tim Miggles in Snapallhecanup was considerably lessened, unless, as he thought, Phœbe was at that present moment really almost dying in love of him, and the matter was kept a secret by the old people till the effect of the wonderful note had subsided.

He went about his work in the mill, shaking his head from time to time as doubts arose in his mind with regard to the magical powers of Snapallhecanup, and occasionally breaking into snatches of rough, and in many instances ludicrous verse.

George could not but notice the pitiable state of Giles's mind, and he could not help picturing to himself what would have been his own feelings had Phœbe preferred any one to him. The very thought was agony, and his heart warmed to poor Giles, whose love for Phœbe he fully believed was most sincere and heartfelt.

He was resolved once more to attempt conciliation and kindness to him, and watched for an opportunity which should enable him to make some remark soothing to his feelings, without it appearing to be premeditated.

"Giles," he at length said, "I know not why we should be enemies. You conferred a great service upon Phœbe this morning. From my heart I thank you for it, and would fain take by the hand him who saved her whom——"

"Thee does love her still?" cried Giles.

"Giles, you were mistaken this morning. It is necessary, for Phœbe's sake, that I should tell you she did not voluntarily go to meet the man in Foyle's Hollow, from whose importunities you so nobly and gallantly rescued her. She went——"

"Why did she go?—I ask thee why did she go? It be a mad thought, and I be mad ; but I did think because the meeting with a strange man would be a spot upon the beauty of thee dear—but no—no——"

"She was deceived, Giles, basely deceived. She received a note, which acted strangely on her mind, and upon its impulse she she——"

"Note!" cried Tim Miggles, triumphantly.

> "Oh, Snapallhecanup's a codger,
> Who really has made me a lodger
>   In the heart of the miller's fair maid;
> I thought he had proved but a dodger,
> And I should have gone for a sodger,
>   If I hadn't been rather afraid.

Oh, it's wonderful, glorious. Slaves, you may have the mill.

> "Why the deuce didn't I go to Foyle's Hollow?
> I seed her, but didn't think proper to follow.

Oh lauks."

"I will not speak to thee, George," said Giles, "but just to tell thee that thee will not have Phœbe for thee wife. Thee may smile and shake thee head, but thee will be heart-stricken; and I, who be nearly mad, will—will laugh—aye, laugh at thee and thee misery."

"No, Giles. Come what misery may by the decree of Heaven, you will not laugh at my misery. I know you better, Giles. You would not,—could not."

"Hurrah!" cried Tim, quite unheedful of the meaning of his companion's conversation,—

> "I'll sit upon a throne,
> But not all alone,
>   For Phœbe shall sit by my side;
> At fortune we'll rail,
> And drink rather strong ale.
>   When we quite connubial is tied.

Laugh, did you say? I believe you will laugh.

> "Care to our coffin adds a nail, no doubt,
> While every grin so merry draws one out.

George, my boy, how do you feel?

> "Don't your fancy, with many wriggles,
> Confess there's no one like Tim Miggles?"

"Peace, fool!" cried Giles, as Tim thrust his head between him and George; "peace. Thee will get thee fool's head broken."

Tim in a moment jumped up to the further end of the loft in which they were, contenting himself by muttering,—

> "Slaves, who wait upon my every tread,
> Attend, and off with that ere Giles's head."

"George, listen," said Giles, and a wild gleam-like insanity darted from his eyes, as he placed his hand upon George's arm,—

"Last night, I did dream of thee and Phœbe. I did dream that thee were walking in the meadow, and that the sun did shine and the birds were singing, and thee looked happy, and smiled, while the heart within me was as cold as stone. I saw thee as plainly as I see thee now. Thee were talking to Phœbe and she were smiling, as she do sometimes smile, like one of God's dear angels. I did hear her voice, and it was sweet, and sounded like music, soft music. I did see the flowers as she did pass, and they did spread their leaves, and seemed to smile upon Phœbe, because she be like the fairest and sweetest among them. On, on thee went, and I followed thee, for my heart, though it were cold and chill, would still follow Phœbe. I heard thee speak to her, and as thee spoke I did see that it was growing dark, and I heard thee say that she should be thine; and as thee spoke the ground did open betwixt thee and she, and thee stretched out thee arms, but—but the could not reach her, and she was mine—mine—my Phœbe, my own."

"This is more folly," said George. ' Giles, Giles, rouse yourself, and do not give way to these feverish creations of your brain. Your disordered fancy will prove dangerous to your health. How can you be thus strangely moved by an idle dream?"

"I held her in my arms, and she was mine; but—but it was not for long, for I did hear sweet music, and I thought it was Phœbe speaking, but she did not move her lips; and the ground did fill up again, and I saw thee coming, and heard thee say again that she was thee Phœbe; but thee had her not, for thee fell, with a groan, to the ground; and—and—George, listen. I—I did look upon my hands and they were red—red—blood-red."

Giles sank his head upon his hands in apparent exhaustion as he finished the recital of the vision which his distempered fancy had conjured up in the silence of the night. His frame shook with the intensity of his feelings, and deep groans burst from his labouring breast.

"Giles, rouse yourself," said George, much affected at the agony of mind of the desolate man. Heaven knows I would do much to rescue you from the thraldom of the dark feeling with which you seem to be oppressed. This dream you speak of is nothing. Why should it appear to you so frightful when to me it wears no such shape? Am I not equally interested in it?—nay, more; for me it threatens, while it leaves you scathless."

"Blood! blood!" cried the agitated Giles. "There has been on my hands all day a blood-red colour. Now, I tell thee, now they be red."

"Nay, Giles, you are wrong, indeed, for there is no such thing," said George; "it is your fancy misleads you. It may please Heaven to place a barrier betwixt me and my dear love—to open some chasm which I cannot, or dare not, leap—but I will hope otherwise, and as my love is just true, and pure, in God's mercy will I trust that it may be lasting and most happy."

No. 29

"See! see!" cried Giles, starting up and holding his hand to George, vehemently. See, there be blood. Will thee believe now?"

George started, for there was, indeed, a stream of blood trickling down his hand, and a drop fell upon the floor with an ominous and sullen sound. In a moment, however, George recovered his presence of mind and composure, for he recollected to have noticed that Giles had a wound in his hand when in Foyle's Hollow, which he had, doubtless, received in his struggle with Sir Herbert Foster, and he instantly said,—

"Nonsense, Giles—nonsense, man. In your defence of Phœbe this morning you received that wound. It has now, most probably, bled afresh, from some accidental strain or pressure. Come, come, Giles, give up those fancies, they are unworthy of you."

"No, no," repeated Giles; "there is blood—blood; and—and God help us all, there will be more."

As he spoke, he rushed wildly from the mill, and George watched him cross the meadow, and he soon became lost in the plantation, which was at hand.

George, although he might put no faith in the visions of Giles's disordered fancy, yet was not without some apprehensions, more on Giles's account than his own, that the excitation and frenzy of the poor fellow's mind might lead him to attempt the commission of some act of desperation, which might, at all events, involve himself, if others escaped the consequences, of his partial insanity, in the most disastrous and ruinous of consequences.

"Well, I declare," said Tim Miggles, advancing to George. "I think that Giles is uncommonly violent. I suppose he means to kill you, George, get hung himself, and leave Phœbe to me. What a wery uncommon decree of fate. I shouldn't a bit wonder now that old Snapallhecanup means to settle the thing that way. I'm very sorry for you, George, for you're a very good sort of fellow in your way."

"Cease, Tim, cease; I cannot attend to your folly."

"Folly! Well, I'm sure; I wonder who is the most foolishest, you or me. Why, it was but the other day I seed you a walking about the loft, and a whacking the side of your head, and a saying, 'Ha!—will she—does she love?—ah!' and all that sort of thing, while I—I was composing a piece of poetry, which, if Phœbe would but read, she'd say, Miggles, Miggles, I'm yours."

"Psha! psha!—nonsense, Tim. Go to your work, my good fellow."

"Perhaps you'd like to hear it; don't you go passing it off as yours, though. Fair play, you know. I'm going to try its effect myself upon Phœbe and the miller and the old dame. Ah! she's the worst of the lot. She has no kindred soul for poetry, not she. She'd think nothing of boiling the kettle with a whole bundle of poetry. She'd light a candle with 'Alonzo the Brave,' and stuff the fair 'Imogine' into a crack in the door to keep out the wind, that she would. What do you really think she did with 'The Dark-eyed Maiden; or, the Lord of Bumblepuppy?' Why, she actually wrapped 'em round a candle, 'cos it was too big for the stick, and said as how she was glad they'd come to a good end. Then she singed a precious duck as she had on the old man's birthday, with 'Love's First Home,' and pinned 'The Forsaken One' on its breast to keep it from burning."

"Ah!—yes—ah!" said George, who answered Tim mechanically, without knowing what he was saying.

"Yes, indeed, I can tell you she did; but, perhaps, you would like to hear the beginning of the poem. I mean to come it strong with—

> " Old Bordons loves a mouse,
> And Andy loves a souse
>   In the mill stream, when he's thirsty.
> The rats love the grist,
> But only list,
>   They won't touch that that's musty.
>
> The calf loves the cow,
> And Giles loves a row,
>   While George makes a fuss about a letter.
> He loves Phœbe,
> But I know she be
>   Loved by him much better' ''

" Yes, I should do so immediately," said George, suddenly rising from his reverie. " I pity, but I must, at the same time, not blind myself to the possible, if not probable, consequences of his rash passion. I must warn the honest miller, and—and my dear, dear Phœbe."

" The deuce you must," said Tim, as George left the mill, without bestowing upon him the least notice whatever. " You may warn them as much as you please, but she shall hear the verses, whether you like it or not, old fellow."

George proceeded at once to the cottage, with a determination of imparting to the miller the singular behaviour of Giles, and his fears lest his excited feelings should drive him into the commission of some act, which, while it would bring destruction upon himself, might go far to destroy the peace and serenity of the inhabitants of the mill and the cottage.

George knocked timidly at the cottage door, and his heart fluttered with a hope that Phœbe might be visible to him; but he was doomed to disappointment, for when he opened it, in obedience to the honest miller's cry of "Come in," and entered the neat and prettily arranged sitting room of the cottage, a single glance sufficed to tell him that the dear object of his ever anxious and fond solicitude was not there.

" Well, George, my lad," cried the miller, " dost thee want me?"

" I thought it my duty, sir," said George, " to tell you, that since the morning poor Giles has appeared to be in an unusual state of agitation."

" George," said the old miller, shaking his head thoughtfully, " I be main afraid the poor lad's wits be leaving him, and all for love of Phœbe. I did think to have had thee both in the cottage to-night, and to have asked the dear child before thee both if she did mean to make choice between thee, or have neither of thee."

George turned away his head to prevent the miller's seeing the confusion in his face.

" The poor old mill," continued the miller, with a sigh, " do come bad off among thee all. One of thee do nothing but quarrel, and that be Giles."

" Alas! sir," cried George, " it is, indeed, so; I see it with pain."

" Another of thee do nothing but make poetry, which be nearly as bad, although it be not so noisy."

" Indeed, sir," replied George, " poor Tim's brains seem to be so infected with verse making, that he can think of nothing else."

" And another of thee," continued the miller, drily, and looking in George's face, " be always love-making."

" Sir!" said George, with a start.

" I say another of thee be always love-making," cried the miller. " And now get thee gone to thy work, for, what with the worry and the fighting in the morning, poor Phœbe be not very well, and my dame do say she be not to be plagued by any of thee to-day."

George departed to the mill again, and left the old miller in serious contemplation on the many events which had been crowded into the last few days. He sighed as he thought of the happy years which had flown so fleetly by since that night when Phœbe, a poor houseless wanderer, came to his cottage door. The words of Sir Herbert Foster, which intimated a knowledge of the fact that the fair girl was not his own child, except by adoption, had given the old man the greatest uneasiness, and he looked forward to her union with George as an event which would at once ensure her a protector, whose right to do so could not be disputed by the proudest noble in the land.

The miller had fully intended that that very evening should settle the question with regard to the disposal of Phœbe's hand; and although it was a subject upon which he had never discoursed or mentioned, save very incidentally, he could not but be well aware of the obvious preference of the gentle girl for George Andrews, at which the old man was much pleased, for there was much in the manly, open character of George which he admired

It was true that the events of the morning had produced some effects upon Phœbe, and by the advice of the dame, the miller had suspended his intention of holding, as might be termed, a high court of love in his little cottage, upon the state of Phœbe's affections.

"Dame," said the miller, "I shall not be happy till our dear child be married to George, who, I believe, she do love, then she will be out of the power of even Sir Herbert Foster."

"Ah, Gilbert, Gilbert, he be a main bad man, and my mind do much misgive me about him."

"Don't thee give way to fear, dame. George be a good lad, a main good lad, and better than e'er a baronet of them all."

"The dear child, Gilbert, has asked me to tell her how you met with George, and I did say that you would do so."

"Gadzooks!" cried the miller, "here she be. Phœbe, my lass, my darling, why did thee come down?"

"I could not sleep, dear father and mother," said Phœbe, "and I thought I should be happier sitting here by you, than up stairs by myself."

"Come, then, my dear child, and sit thee down by me. Thee mother has been saying, Phœbe, that thee wished to hear how so be as I did meet with George."

Phœbe blushed as she replied,—

"Yes, yes, dear father, if—if you will tell me."

"Listen then, my darling, and I will tell to thee what he did tell to me."

Phœbe almost held her very breath, in order that no one word of the narration which concerned one so dear to her should escape her, and the honest miller commenced his narrative.

CHAPTER XXXVIII.

"THEE knowest, Phœbe," began the miller, "that Sir Herbert Foster, the man who thee saw this morning at the Hollow, did try to take from me the garden ground which thee hast made so beautiful, and which I did love for thee sake?"

"Yes, dear father, I recollect; it was just before George came."

"Well, thee must know I did go a far way to see a main clever lawyer, who I was told would tell me if Sir Herbert be right or be wrong; and surely he be a clever man, for all he did say came to pass."

"Ah! that it did, Gilbert," cried the dame. "He said we should gain the day, and so we did."

"We did, dame. Well, my child, it was many miles from home, and many days it did take me to go backwards and forwards on the journey, and, after all, a sore journey it was ; for the errand, although it was to right myself, was not to my mind, for it be mian uncomfortable to me to be at strife with anybody, and an ancestor of Sir Herbert had been good to those from whom I came."

" But it was wicked, dear father, to wish to take away our dear little garden. Sir Herbert has many fine gardens, and a park, and fields that would make a hundred gardens. You have often shewn them all to me from the high loft in the dear old mill. Oh ! it was wicked."

" It was wicked, my dear child, but it be the way of the world. They that have plenty wish for more, and they that have little do most often have that little taken from them."

The miller sighed as he spoke, and the dame said,—

" Ah, my dear child, the world be a sad world, and the less thee knows of it the better for thee peace and thee happiness."

" Will 'e stir the fire, dame ?" said the miller, " for the after part of the days do begin to be chilly, and the fire be pleasant."

The dame coaxed the wood into a cheerful blaze, and the bright light shone upon the cottage walls with a comfortable lustre.

An aged cat sat by the fire-side, and perpetually nodded, in dozing unconsciousness, upon the hearth. It was old Bordons, who was an old cat when Phœbe, cold and shivering, had kissed her on the night of the storm, when she had taken refuge at the cottage. The creature's life had been prolonged beyond the usual lot of her race, which was mainly owing to the kind care of Phœbe, who cherished, fondly, each record of her arrival at the miller's happy home. Andy, the dog, was most commonly Phœbe's companion on her walks, and old Bordons, the cat, would welcome her return with a staid and serious joy.

" As I did come home I did come by the sea-port town of Inderdown, and when I got there I was told that there had been a fearsome wreck, and that but one of all the poor souls that had been in the large ship that had been lost, had, by God's mercy, reached the shore."

" Alas !" cried Phœbe, the tears rushing to her eyes, " it must have been a fearful scene. I have often told you, dear father and mother, that my poor brother went to sea, and——"

Phœbe wept bitterly.

" Do not take on, my dear child," cried the dame. " Thee dost recollect that Gilbert did go to Bungleum, and did hear that the ship in which thee brother was, was lost, far—far away ; but thee should keep a good heart, for if he was like thee he has been blessed by God, and be happy."

" I know it—I feel it must be so," cried Phœbe. " Poor, poor George. Forgive me, dear, dear friends, but—but when you spoke of the ship, I—I could not help but weep."

" That one brave sailor, my child, who, they said, had swam to the shore, had left the town to look for some friends, and on the day that I was there he did come back, and he did stand, with the tear of hope in his disappointed eye, in the market place, and did ask for work, by which he might earn an honest living, for he had lost all he had on board the ship, and he had not even the means to go to sea again."

Phœbe knew that it was of George, her own dear George, that the honest miller was speaking, and she could not hide the tears of sympathy which the recital forced from her eyes.

" Many did pass the poor lad by, for his clothes were torn, and he was poor and wasted."

" But you—you, dear father," cried Phœbe, throwing herself into his arms, and sobbing upon his breast, " you did not pass by the poor sailor ?"

"No, my dear child, I did not, bless thee.   God had not passd me by, but had given me many days of happiness.   He had given me my old dame when she was young, and—and, to my eyes, nearly as beautiful as thee be theeself, my dear child ; and in my old age he brought thee, with his blessing, to my cottage door, and gave thee to me.   No, my child, God has not passed me by, and—and I did not pass by the poor forsaken lad who stood in the market place.   He did look at me," said the miller, after a pause ; "he did look at me, as I came up to him, and I could see that hope did flush the cheek of the lad, and I did say to him,—

"'Come, and I will employ thee ; be good and honest, and as God has helped me, I will strive to help thee.'"

"Bless you—Heaven bless you, dear father," cried Phœbe ; "both, you have saved—both he and I.   May we both live but to bless your kindness."

"Thee hast blessed me, my child.   Thee hast brought joy to the old man's heart, and thee hast made the cottage happier than the hall.   Well, my child, he did come with me, and he did tell me that there was but one person in the whole world who he did believe could claim to be related to him, and that—that person was lost.   I did not press the lad to tell me his story, for it did seem painful to him, and from that day to this I have found him a honest and a faithful lad as ever breathed, and I be much rejoiced that I did meet with him."

"Poor George," exclaimed Phœbe, "he, too, like myself, has known misfortune.   Like me, perhaps, he was left alone and desolate until this friendly roof received him."

"I do sometimes fancy," continued the miller, "that there be a something which does prey upon the poor lad's spirits, but it be not right to question him ; and as long as he be a good lad to me, I will believe that whatever he do think proper to keep secret be nothing to his disadvantage, but be like some bitter sorrowful matter which he cannot bear to talk of."

Phœbe had been previously aware that the honest and benevolent miller had rescued George Andrews from some unhappy circumstances, but what they were exactly she had not before known ; for with native delicacy she had shrunk from even trusting to her lover her natural curiosity and interest in every matter of circumstance in any way connected with him or his fortunes.   If such a thing were possible where already the purest and truest affection existed, George was still more endeared to the artless Phœbe by the miller's narration.   Like herself, she found that he had been the child of misfortune ; and the melancholy circumstances from which the miller had rescued him, presented themselves vividly in her imagination, and carried her memory back to the time when she, too, was the victim of misfortune, and suffering the bitter pangs of unmerited poverty and hard usage. The similarity of the circumstances affecting both her and the chosen of her heart, seemed to Phœbe to form a new bond of union between them, and she could not but reflect upon the singular train of circumstances which had made her kind and indulgent friends at the mill the means of bringing her in association with him, whose equal she fondly thought she could never in this wide world have met with.

"And now, my dear child," said the miller, when he had finished his little tale respecting George, "thee must be upon thee guard, for I do not doubt but Sir Herbert Foster will not rest until he be convinced that he can have no hope of deceiving you, Phœbe.   This morning's work will be a lesson to thee, Phœbe, not to put thee trust in letters."

"It will, indeed, dear father, but I did not doubt it came from poor George, and—and —"

"And thee could not help going ?   Well, well, my child, thee hast done

no great wrong, although thee might have done wiser. Thee art so innocent, that thee suspects no evil, and God forbid that thee innocence of heart
should ever depart from thee, for it will be the best protection in this world,
and the truest friend in the next."

"Ah! Gilbert," cried the dame, "Phœbe will do well enough, poor
thing; but there be one thing that do vex me in this quarrel with Sir Herbert, and that be that he do have it in his power when we be gone to lay
his bad hands on the old mill and the cottage, and the sweet little garden
that Phœbe do love so, and take them all from the dear children, because
they be not of our name."

"What you say be true, dame," replied the miller, "and it be a dark
spot in my heart to think that such may be the case. But we will not
plague ourselves about what may not happen, but hope for the best, and
trust to Heaven that our dear young friends will be happy."

"And that they will be, Gilbert; for George, he be a fine lad, and he be
able to put his hand to a mortal many things, by which he may keep the
hearth warm and the wolf from the door of his home."

"That be true," replied the miller. "He be young and hearty; and
there be always some good to be done when the heart do go with the
purpose."

As the miller spoke, a knock came to the door of the cottage, and
without waiting for an answer, it opened, Tim Miggles popped in his head.

"Well," cried the miller, "what dost thee want?"

Tim threw his body into a curious attitude, and commenced a set of
smiles and smirks, which he had practised before a little bit of broken
looking-glass in the mill, and which he thought could not fail of fascinat-
ing, and at once capturing, without more ado, the heart of the fair Phœbe,
who looked at him with mute wonder, for the smiles were evidently directed
towards her.

"Why, what the dickens dost thee mean?" shouted the miller. "Thee
get ssillier every day. Why dost thee make such faces for, thee foolish
fellow?"

Tim replied not to the miller, but addressing Phœbe, he commenced the
poem, which, together with his personal exertions in the way of smiles and
winks and amatory glances, he felt convinced no female heart could possibly
resist.

> "The calf loves a cow,
> Giles loves a row,
> While George makes a fuss about a letter."

"Hold thee nonsense!" cried the miller, interrupting him; "what dost
thee come here for? If thee can't tell, get thee back again, thee thick head.
I wonder why I keep thee."

"Master," replied Tim, condescending at last to answer Gilbert, who he
saw was getting a little angry—"master, I've got a letter."

"What another letter?"

"Yes, master; it's for Phœbe. Oh, lauks! I dare say it's a teaser, this
is. Oh!—aye—this will do the business."

The miller rose, and going to the door, he locked it, and put the key in
his pocket; then taking Tim by the arm, he led him to the middle of the
room, and said gravely,—

"Give me the letter."

Tim was rather alarmed at the miller's serious manner, and after a good
deal of fumbling about his pockets, he at length produced it.

"Who gave it thee?" asked the miller, in an authoritative voice.

"Who?" replied Tim, looking much confounded; "who—I—a—a.
Oh, lauks!"

"Who gave this letter to thee?" thundered the miller.

Tim looked up at the ceiling, and then on the floor, and took a survey of the walls of the cottage, and seemed counting the pots and pans that hung around.   At length his eyes seemed to rest upon a bright copper tea-kettle, and he said, as if addressing it,—

> "There's nobody knows
> How a mill goes."

"Cease thee folly, Tim Miggles, and answer me, if thee can.   Where did thee get the letter?"

"Oh, lauks! oh, lauks! you mustn't ask, indeed; it's a uncommon secret.   I couldn't tell, oh, dear, no, not on any account.   I've no objection to let you see.   You shall be our miller when you are on the throne of the realms of —"

"Dame," cried the miller, "will thee get together what thee will give to Tim?   He be going to leave us.   There be no secret letters come here.   Good-bye to thee, Tim.   I wish thee success, lad, but we two must part.   Thee will go in the morning."

Tim looked amazed at this sudden determination on the part of the miller, and seemed unable to speak, but allowed his master to finish entirely what he wished to say before he could recover sufficiently to protest against his dismissal.

"What!" he cried, "leave the mill?—leave the—the uncommon blessed mill?   Oh, dear! oh, dear.   Oh, master, master, I'll tell—I will, indeed."

"Well, then, where did thee get the letter?"

"Oh, dear! oh, lauks!   Do you know, master, what's to become of me, if I tell?"

"No, I do not; but I do know what be going to become of thee if thee do not tell."

"Oh, dear! you hard-hearted individual."

"Come, come, no nonsense.   Say thee say at once.   Dame, thee can give the lad what thee can spare, as he be going, and he be not over bright."

"Oh, dear me! oh, lauks!   Don't say anything more about sending me away, and I'll tell—indeed I will.   I'll consent to be broiled in oil, and stirred with a five-pronged fork."

"You'll what?"

"Oh, master, master, that's what I'm to be done to, if I tell where the letter came from."

"You foolish fellow, can you believe such nonsense?"

"Nonsense!   Oh, I can tell you it's no joke.   There was a fellow once as told where he got a letter, and what do you think came of him?"

"I can't say.   Perhaps he was allowed to stay in his situation, which he might have lost, if so be he hadn't told."

"No, not at all; nothing like that.   He was found scraped to death with oyster-shells, and a little bit of him put into each shell, and it took eighteen dozen to hold him; and then he was peppered, and wine gard, and bolted.   Oh, dear! oh, dear! if I should come to that ere melancholy end!"

"Thee'll come to a fool's cap and bells," said the miller, "that thee will.   Come, who gave it thee?"

"Oh, dear! oh, dear!   Oh, crikey—oh, everything!

> "In a great can of oil
> I surely shall boil.
>   And bob up and down in the greases;
> And when I am done,
> For fear I should run,
>   They'll cut me up in small pieces.

"Oh, lauks! You see, master, I was forced to say *greases* to make it rhyme to pieces. I'm settled—I'm hashed—I'm an unfortunate monarch."

"Art thee ready, dame? Hast thee got his things?"

"Yes, Gilbert, they be all ready. Good-bye to thee, Tim. I wish thee may do well."

"Oh, no, no," it was—it was—"

"Who? Quick—who was it?"

"Snap—"

"Who?"

"All—he—can—up. Oh, dear! I've done it now."

"Who dost thee say? I never did hear of such a one. Who did thee say it was?"

Tim groaned as he replied,—

"Snapallhecanup!"

"Snapall—dang'd if I can recollect the name. And who be he?"

"Oh, he's a magician. He's here, there, everywhere, and no where."

"Old Snapallhecanup
On my carcase will soon sup;
  My tears they now fall in a drizzle;
Poor Tim is undone,
He'll see no more fun,
  To the oil-can he quickly must mizzle."

"None of thee nonsense. Who gave thee the letter? Thee silly talk about the magicians be all nonsense. Who gave it to thee?"

"It came from Snapallhecanup. Oh, dear! It would have done the business."

"But who gave it to thee hands?" said the dame.

"Oh! Perk—Perk. He's a uncommon good fellow. Perk's the individual."

No. 30

"Perk ?" said the miller, "be not that Master Scrimp's man ?"

"It be Gilbert," said the dame, "it be ; and the lawyer be at the bottom of the whole matter, and that be the reason why he did come here to speak to thee about the mill."

"No doubt, dame, no doubt. He be capable of anything that be bad. I tell thee what, Tim, if thee dare to bring any more letters here, thee shall surely leave the mill. Thee may take my word for it thee shall. Now get thee gone, and take thee foolish brains to bed."

Tim departed, looking very much crestfallen at the result of his scheme to charm Phœbe, and the miller took up the letter which had been left on the table, and read the superscription, which was "To Phœbe Hawthorn."

"Phœbe Hawthorn !" cried the miller. "What do this mean ? Phœbe Hawthorn !"

The dame was as much surprised as the miller at the address on the letter, and Phœbe herself looked at it with the utmost astonishment.

"This be some scheme," said the miller. "There be something more in this than be here seen. They who be wicked inclined be always trying some artful scheme. Never fear thee, however, my dear child. With the blessing of Providence we will take care of thee. 'Phœbe Hawthorn,'— what can it mean ? 'Phœbe Hawthorn, at Gilbert Mark's, miller, &c.' Dang them and their &c."

"Dear father," said Phœbe, "open it yourself. I know not what this may mean. It surely must be some mistake."

"No, no, my dear, it be meant for thee, although they have thought fit to give thee a name that does not belong to thee. But we will see what it is in the inside."

The miller opened the letter, and to his great surprise and bewilderment read the following most unaccountable, and to all the party, unexpected communication :—

"My Dear Niece,—How do you do ? I'm dying to clasp you round in my arms. Your dear mother is in Heaven—poor dear Mrs. Hawthorn that was—the wife of Gilbert Hawthorn. Bless me, how time has flown ! So you are boarding at the mill ? Who would have thought it ? Oh, what good people they must be. I long to embrace them all for hours. I am your dear mother's youngest sister. I am very rich—uncommon. Oh, my love, my dear niece, I have been told where you are. You shall live with me ; you shall indeed. I'll call for you to-morrow in my carriage. God bless you ! Oh, dear, who would have thought how things have turned out ? My dear niece, your dear aunt, (very rich.)

"Martha Dovetail."

"P. S.—Give my respects to the worthy people, and tell them to pack up the things. Oh, dear ! I shall do nothing but embrace. I am weeping on the paper—you'll see the blisters. Farewell !"

The miller, his wife, and Phœbe looked at each other in silence and amazement.

CHAPTER XXXIX.

In order, in some measure, to explain the extraordinary epistle which had been addressed to Phœbe, we must leave the astonished party in the cottage, for a time, to follow the footsteps of Mr. Scrimp, after he had made so satisfactory an arrangement with Sir Herbert Foster.

When the wily attorney parted from Mr. Freegrove, he lost no time in proceeding at once to the shop of Mr. Pomander, which he entered with an innocent and bland smile.

Mr. Pomander had gone home in a great rage, and recounted to the expectant Perk the unfortunate light in which the incensed Sir Herbert had chosen to consider the meeting which they had with such great trouble arranged for him with the maid of the mill.

"Upon my soul," said Perk, "that's unlucky. By the by, a boy came for some medicine for his aunt, a Mrs. Smiffings."

"Bless me, I forgot," said Mr. Pomander; "I ought to have left it out for him before I went. What did he say, Perk?"

"Oh, dear me, nothing particular. He said the old un was rather worse."

"Well, did he say he'd come again?"

"No. I just gave him whatever came to hand. I opened one of your little drawers, and seeing some pills, I gave them to the fellow, along with four bottles of soda water, and told him to be sure, by all means, to tell the old woman to take one of the pills every half hour, and the four bottles of soda water directly she got them. That was the drawer."

"Dear me," said Mr. Pomander, "you have been rather rash; but it can't be helped. How long ago was it do you think?"

"Upwards of an hour, I am sure."

"Then she's taken two of the pills, that's for certain; and if they don't settle her business, the deuce is in it. Bless me, she couldn't stand the shaking of one of them."

"Well, but you know, Pomander, there is such a load of old women in the parish, it's quite horrid."

"Why, that's true—so to business. Who do you think came in while I was at Sir Herbert's?"

"Scrimp, or the devil, of course."

"The former, although I would, for my own part, as soon it had been the other gentleman. I tell you what—Perk has got the upper hand of us. I was hurried out, and was forced to leave him there, closeted with Sir Herbert—damn him!"

"Upon my soul, it's clever," said Mr. Perk, "I really didn't give Scrimp credit for half the wit he has shown lately. I begin quite to respect the man. By the by, your ginger beer ain't bad, Pomander."

"How do you know, Perk? I don't recollect—"

"Oh! I've been amusing myself with a few bottles while you were gone. I saved the corks; they may be useful."

"And how many?"

"How many? Let me see. About ten or twelve, I think. I feel, do you know, ready to burst. Why don't you put a little brandy in it?"

"But really, Perk, my dear sir, ginger-beer, you know, comes to something."

"Well, well, make Sir Herbert Foster pay for it. Put down in the bill, 'ginger-beer for Mr. Perk,' so much; or say the girl dropped in and drank it?"

"Well, but Perk, what is to be done to recover lost ground? I tell you I was bowled out at Haredale Park by Sir Herbert's dammed valet."

"Not kicked out. Are you quite sure?"

"Damn it, no! Kicked out, indeed! No, no, not quite so bad as that, either."

"Why," said Mr. Perk, with much earnestness of manner, "my own opinion is, that we are now a vast deal too dangerous to be dispensed with.

We know too much, and Scrimp will assuredly advise Sir Herbert better than to quarrel with us. Scrimp, after all, has talents."

" So far, so good; but we shall have, in working with him, to divide the proceeds."

"Not exactly, Pomander, for you may depend Scrimp will take good care that we do not divide the proceeds with him if he has the management."

" What! will he cheat us ?"

" Certainly; and uncommonly right, too. I honour him for it. Principle, Pomander, principle is everything. Scrimp is not quite green."

" By everything, here he comes," said Mr. Pomander, as Mr. Scrimp's face appeared, looking through the half glass-door, which led into the little shop.

" How do you do, Mr. Pomander ?" said the attorney, smiling. " Allow me the pleasure of a few—just a few—short moments' conversation, if you please ?"

" Certainly, my dear sir, ' said Mr. Pomander. " You do me too much honour."

" Oh, no, no, my dear sir. Allow me to call myself your very humble and most obedient——"

" Really, excuse me, Mr. Scrimp. Pray be seated—pray, now, I beg."

" How do, governor ?" said Mr. Perk.

" Ha ! Perk, my right hand, my most amiable and exemplary fellow, are you here ?"

" Yes, governor, I'm here, you see. Got a little complaint in my liver or lights, or some of those things—a pain in my chitterlins—so I've just dropped in for advice."

" Oh ! dear yes," said Mr. Scrimp, " I—I, too, came for—a—little advice."

" Shall I notch my timber, eh ?" inquired Perk.

" Why, Mr. Perk, I rather think you may as well stay," said the attorney. " I wish to put a merely hypothetical case, as to whether Pomander, Scrimp,' Freegrove, and Perk, as a firm, you understand, doing business upon mutual profits, don't sound better than Pomander and Perk versus Scrimp and Freegrove,—a mere hypothetical case, gentlemen."

Mr. Scrimp, as he spoke, looked from Mr. Perk to Mr. Pomander, and back again, repeatedly, from the man of physic to his clerk.

A silence of a few moments ensued, during which Mr. Perk scratched his nose with a paper-knife, and Mr. Pomander seemed attentively regarding a large bottle on one of his shelves, which was labelled in gilt letters, " Aqua pura."

" A compromise," said Perk.

" I agree with you," said Mr. Pomander. " Union is strength, Mr. Scrimp."

" We understand each other then ?" said the attorney. " We work together for the future."

" I believe you," said Perk. " Governor, I honour and respect you. Give us your fist, old cock."

They thenh sook hands in silence.

" There can be no doubt now," said Mr. Pomander; " that we shall be able to arrange everything to Sir Herbert's satisfation."

" Legally, of course," said Mr. Scrimp.

" Oh, yes, legally always," cried Perk.

" Of course, legally," said Pomander. " Hem ! we divide proceeds."

" We do," replied the attorney. Here are one hundred pounds to begin with. As a pledge of my good faith, I willingly deposit it in your most worthy hands, my dear Mr. Pomander,—of course, subject to draughts for necessary expenses."

"Humph!" thought Perk; "he must have had three hundred, at least."

"Who can doubt you, my dear sir?" said Mr. Pomander, taking, however, the hundred pounds, and immediately placing them out of sight.

"Now, governor," said Perk; "what is to be done? You are senior partner, you know."

"Why, Sir Herbert Foster, you see, gentlemen, is so anxious for the—the welfare of the young girl, that he wishes her to be sent to his villa near London immediately, and he don't mind if it cost him not far short of two hundred and fifty pounds."

"It must be done," said Pomander; "but the *how* is the thing to be considered. She never comes into the village but to go to church."

"Finesse, finesse, my dear fellows," cried Mr. Perk. "No violence. That will never do. I've thought of a scheme; and as we are among friends, if Pomander will tap a dozen bottles of his ginger-beer, and put a little something strong in the glasses, I don't mind if I just tell you how I came by the means of making the uncommon fine proposition that I have thought of."

Mr. Pomander winced a little at the destruction of his stock in trade; but the thought of the hundred pounds recurred to him, and silenced his scruples.

"I'll tell you how it was. When I was in the Inn—you know when, governor—in Lincoln's Inn, with 'Snuffles and Dewemal——'"

"Yes," said Mr. Scrimp, "I recollect. They were against me in 'Swaggles v. Sidebotham.'"

"Exactly. Well, you must know, that in the lane there was a grocer's shop, in which one day a bill was stuck, saying, 'FOUND. A gold watch, chain, and seals. Whoever will accurately describe the same, may have them upon payment of expenses.'"

"Well, gentlemen, every time I went up and down the lane, for about a month, I saw this bill sticking in the infernal ass of a grocer's window, and nobody seemed to own the watch. It's an uncommon hard thing, thought I, that a watch, chain, and seals, should go a begging in this way. But there was the bill, day after day, staring me in the face, till at last it drove me quite frantic."

"A species of monomania," said Mr. Pomander.

"Watch-seals-and-chainomania, I should think," said Mr. Scrimp, with a grin.

"Well," continued Perk, unheedful of the interruption, "I said one day to our common-law, says I, 'Richards did you ever see that bill in the grocer's window about the watch?'

"'See the bill,' says he, 'damme, if I have seen anything but the bill for six months, I dream of the bill—think of it all day. Hang it,' says he, 'it will be my death, and a coroner's inquest will bring in a verdict of, Died of a bill in the damned grocer's window!'

"Well my boy—'Richards, I've thought of a scheme,' says I, 'that I think will take the bill down.'

"'So have I,' said he, 'I'm thinking of burning down the house, in the hope that the bill may go with it, and the watch too.'

"No, no, my boy,' says I, 'I'll tell you a better rig than that. Nobody seems to come and claim the watch, and it's most likely the owner's dead or gone abroad. Now, Richards, I've made up my mind that we will have it.'

"So Richards he ups with his fingers and makes a double sight, and asks me to describe the watch.

"'So I will,' says I, 'when you tell me all about it.'

"'I tell you,' says he, 'how should I know? I wish I did. The bill wouldn't be long there, I can tell you.'

"'Why,' says I, 'if you be guided by me, I'll wager you a new hat and a lobster supper, that I'll have the watch in my pocket the day after to-morrow.'

"'Done,' says he. 'Done,' says I.

"'Well, then,' I said, 'you go to-morrow to the grocer's, and say you've lost a gold watch, chain and seals.'

"'Well,' says Richards, 'I can tell a lie with any one in the profession : but what's the good of one going there, when I can't describe the watch?'

"'That's the very thing,' says I. 'When the grocer asks you the maker's name and the number, you say, Smith, of Manchester—No. 3420.'

"'Well, what of that?'

"'Why, the grocer will tell you that isn't it. Then you must hang on a little, and ask to see the watch, to be convinced it isn't yours.'

"'Oh, by G—!' says Richards, 'I see.' And out he flings from the office in a minute.

"Well, in a little time, back comes Richards, and down he flops on his stool.

"'Perk,' says he, 'you're a rum un. The maker's name is West. The number is 240, and all the seals are plain but one, and that's got an arrow on it.'"

"'That'll do,' said I, 'but what did the grocer say?'

"'Why, when I went in,' says Richards, 'I told him I'd lost a watch, and had called to see if the one he had was mine. So the old file pops on his spectacles, and says, 'Describe it.' Smith, maker, Manchester—No. 3420,' says I.

"The old fellow then takes off his spectacles, and he lugs the watch out of his fob with a grin, and says,—

"'Young man, I am sorry to say this is not your watch—see.' And he opened it, and showed me the name and number. Then he winked, as much as to say, 'You're done, young'un, and popped it in his fob again.'

"'That'll do,' says I. So away I went to an aunt's of mine, where I had the run of the house, and I got together a tolerable lot of female tog-gery—a black dress, bonnet and veil, a false front, and so on. These I took to chambers.

"Well, next morning, as I went back to chambers at six, there was the bill in the infernal window, as usual, and the old fellow of a grocer was standing at the door, rubbing his hands together.

"When I got to the office Richards says, 'Perk, recollect the wager. The bill is still up.'

"'Never mind,' says I; 'you may order the lobster.'

"So as I didn't expect the governor till eight or nearly, I popped into his room, and put on the woman's things. Then out I came, and I'll be hanged if Richard's wasn't taken in, and stared at me as if he had been stuck.

"Well, out I went, and going into Holborn, got into a coach and told Jarvey to drive me to the grocer's. When we got there and the coach stopped, out bundled the old man, and helped me into the shop.

"'May I beg to know your commands, mum?' says he, for I can tell you I looked most uncommonly respectable.

"'You've a watch, sir,' says I, 'that's been found? My son has lost one, and he has written to me to say, that a friend of his, about a week ago, saw a bill in your window that one had been found?'

"Then the old grocer he gives his spectacles a push, and he rubs his hands together, and says,—

"'Yes, mum, a watch has been found. Perhaps you'll have the kindness, mum, to describe the one your son lost, mum?'

"With that the old fellow gives a sort of chuckle, as much as to say, 'I have you there; I'm up to a thing or two, rather.'

"'Describe it?' says I. 'Oh, dear me, yes.' Then I fumbled about in my pocket, and produced a letter that I had prepared. 'West, maker, No. 240.'

"The old fellow gave a jump as he heard this, and he stammered out,—

"'Th—the—there are seals, mum,—a—seals.'

"I pretended to be reading the letter, and went on. 'The seals are all plain.'

"'All plain, eh? All plain?' cried the old man, whipping off his spectacles—

"'But one—and that has an arrow on it.'

"The grocer gave a deep groan, and he slowly pulled the watch out of his fob, and he says, says he, 'It's rather singular!' And he turned rather pale.

"'Madam,' says he, 'there must be some mistake.'

"'West, maker,' says I, 'No. 240. Oh, dear, no—no mistake! I'll read you all the letter:—

"'My dear and honoured mamma,—I trust your dear back is better. I——'

"'Oh, no, no,' said the old man. 'By no means. Take the watch, mum; but d— me if I know how it can be yours.'

"'What do you mean, sir?' says I.

"'Why, if you must know,' says he, looking carefully round him, 'I—I accidentally altered the number to 240.'

"'Oh! did you?' says I. 'Good evening,' and out I went with the watch, leaving the old man standing clean on the top of his silver spectacles, that he had dropped in his fright.'

"That wasn't so bad," cried Mr. Scrimp.

"No," said Mr. Pomander; "it was not, indeed. But how does it apply to our present position, my dear fellow?"

"This way," said Perk; "I've got the woman's togs by me, and I advise, that as we know, or, at least, shrewdly suspect, this girl is really not the miller's daughter, that we write a note, as from a female relation who has found out her place of concealment, and offer to take charge of her at once."

"Humph!" said Mr. Scrimp. "Such a thing might succeed with ignorant and poor people; but there is a difficulty about the name. The girl passes by the miller's name."

"That, indeed, is a difficulty," said Mr. Pomander.

"But not an insurmountable one," said Mr. Perk. "Let us use any name. I will represent myself as Phœbe's aunt, who has been abroad, and only heard of the marriage of the girl's mother by hearsay, and has mistaken the name."

"It may succeed in one way," said Scrimp. "That is, the thing may be bounced through. If the pretended aunt goes to the cottage in a carriage, the old people may be overawed, and the girl bewildered. The result may be, that she may be induced, at least, to take a drive with her new relative, and then——"

"Then," said Mr. Pomander, "of course she can be taken to London at once, and a letter to the miller will prevent any outcry on his part. Upon my soul, I think the thing very feasible, if Perk can act the old lady."

"Leave me alone for that," said Perk; "I'll do it to perfection. Scrimp, my governor, you must get a loan of a private carriage of Sir Herbert's, without arms, or anything that might lead to a suspicion of whose it was, and the thing is safe of success."

"It's well worth trying," said the attorney, "and—and it has a more legal appearance than an attempt to carry her off by force."

"It certainly has," said Perk, "and now for the letter."

Thus was the letter concocted, which had so surprised the miller and his dame, and filled Phœbe with a thousand anxieties and fears.

Mr. Scrimp once more proceeded to Haredale Park, when this scheme was thoroughly digested and resolved upon for the purpose of explaining it to Freegrove, and securing the proper accessories on the morrow in the shape of a carriage, horses, and servants.

Ralph Freegrove rubbed his hands, and appeared quite delighted with the plan, and would fain have accompanied the expedition on the coach-box, or behind, but that he feared his person was so well known to the inhabitants of the mill, that he should run a risk of involving the whole scheme in discovery.

"I will take care, lawyer," said he, "that the coachman and footman shall have top coats, which will effectually conceal their liveries, and if you'll wait, I will get Sir Herbert's word for the carriage. There's quite a plain one in the coach-house that Sir Herbert sometimes uses himself when he don't wish to be known altogether."

The required permission was easily obtained from the baronet, and Mr. Scrimp returned to the shop of Mr. Pomander more than ever convinced of the practicability of the scheme, always provided the execution of it was well managed, and he had the greatest confidence in Perk's ability to enact whatever he undertook heartily.

The evening was drawing in, and Mr. Pomander graciously invited his coadjutors to supper, which invitation was accepted, with many oily protestations from Mr. Scrimp, and with great glee by Mr. Perk, who hinted the propriety of forthwith making a night of it, and sallying out into the village after supper for a spree.

CHAPTER XL.

IT was some time before the miller could sufficiently arrange his thoughts as to determine what to do in regard to the singular epistle which Tim Miggles had been made the innocent bearer of. At length he said,—

"There be but one thing that we do need to care about, or say, and that be, that Phœbe shall not be taken from him by any one, without she be willing herself, and I be quite sure she be not willing to leave her dear home."

"Leave it!" cried Phœbe; "oh, no, never, not for the wealth of the world. Dear father and mother, it is all a wicked fabrication; I have no aunt. My mother never spoke to me of such a relative. It is not true, indeed it is not."

"I believe thee, my child, and they shall not take thee from me. Before twelve o'clock to-morrow I hope that something may have occured to prevent even the visit of the brazen-faced woman who do dare to lay claim to thee."

"You will protect me from her. She shall not take me from home when I have been so happy. Were she to prove herself over and over

again a relation, I know her not—love her not. What can she be to me?
Nothing."

"Go to thee rest, my dear child, and don't 'e fear. Thee shall come to
no harm while the old miller has an arm to protect thee, and if I should
want help, mayhap there be a younger arm that be not disinclined to do
thee a service. Thee art safe, Phœbe, quite safe. No one can touch thee
or harm thee."

Phœbe smiled in confidence of heart, and with a firm reliance upon the
protection of Heaven, and the dear friends who so long had stood between
her and harm, she retired to her little chamber, and was soon wrapped in
gentle and dreamless slumber.

The night advanced rapidly, and ere long there was no light gleaming
from the casement of the miller's cottage, and all was rest and peace, save
in one tortured breast, and that one was the unhappy Giles's.

The night was dark and lowering; no moon lit up the scene, and the old
mill seemed to repose amid the black shadows which it cast around it. The
wind had risen since sunset, and new moaned in fitful gusts around both
mill and cottage, as if presaging some coming evil, so wild and mournful
were the sounds.

George had retired early to rest, and to dream of her who was to him
the embodied spirit of his young imagination.

Tim Miggles, too, for a wonder, had actually gone to rest, or it might be
that a bit of candle was not to be had, and so the worship of the muses
was forced to be suspended for a time, and Tim had to go to bed, like vulgar mortals, without poetic imaginations or pretensions to enrol themselves
in the bright list of the tuneful Nine.

Giles, too, slept, if sleep it might be called, which consisted of a succession of startling dreams and fearful visions, which ever swept across the

soul of man. Fiends, demons of all grotesque and horrible shapes, aspects, and hues, appeared to him in his feverish slumber. Gibbering, mouthing, chattering, and shrieking they came. In vain he tried to fly from them. He imagined himself chained down by massive chains, whose links were twisted, in endless convolutions, around his burning limbs. ,

Then there came one fearful vision—a slimy, gabbering demon, who sat upon his head, and held a hand over each eye, a hand dripping with human gore, and the words "blood! blood! blood!" rung in his ears. Another and another came, and assuming each the same position, they each raised the same shout of "blood!" and the hands of all were dripping with the ensanguined fluid. He could see the clotted blood rolling from the hands, along the long crooked nails; it slowly coursed, and then fell, with a sullen splash, upon his heart. He tried to scream, but a weight was on his chest, and he could not even gasp. The chain was wound tighter and tighter round.

Now came a demon, and with an iron instrument, heated to whiteness, bored through his skull into his very brain; hissing and crackling it went. He felt it touch his brain—horrible! horrible!—yet he could not move; and then again arose the cry of "blood! blood!" Suddenly he seemed endowed with supernatural force, and he strained against the chain, and struggled with one fiend who was scooping out his heart. Fearful was that imaginary struggle. Over and over each they rolled and panted; the chain was broken, but the demon remained unconquered. Some unseen hand had placed a knife in his hand; once, twice, thrice he plunged it into the heart of the demon; a wild shriek answered each thrust, and the black blood followed the avenging blade. Now he was dead, and Giles fancied that he looked upon the face, and form of his face, and saw that it was George Andrews. He did not sicken at the thought of the deed he had done, but he breathed more freely, and looked round him. He was then in the meadow at the back of the old mill, and Phœbe was near him. He pursued her, but ever as he stretched out his hands to clasp her, the murdered George interposed, and he dabbed his hands against the bleeding body. The low moans struck his ear, and he thought his foe was not yet dead. He searched for the knife again; again it came to his hand, and again he plunged it into the heart of his rival.

"Blood! blood!" he cried, and his own voice awakened him from that dream of horrors, and starting from his couch, he stood erect in the middle of the floor, with his hands clasped.

The moaning still sounded in his ears; and although his slowly awakening reason told him it was the wind sighing round the old mill, still he could fancy that, amidst the blast, the words "blood! blood!" were faintly uttered.

He passed his hands several times across his brow, as if to clear his mental vision, but still the words, which were rife in his imagination, seemed uttered by the moaning blast.

"Blood!" he cried; "who says blood? The blood of George—George Andrews? No, no; and yet I—I be not able to think. Be it a dream? Oh, they did sit upon me, and the blood did drop upon my heart like falling water. I be not mad, and yet I did see them. Oh, horrible!—it be dreadful. And the knife, too. Phœbe, Phœbe, thee dost not know how I do love thee, nor what I do suffer for thee. I—I do not wish—I cannot kill—George—Andrews."

He sunk upon a chair, and rocked backwards and forwards for some minutes, and moaned, as if struggling with the most fearful thoughts.

Then he rose, and striking his breast, he paced his small chamber, and spoke incoherently, and with great wildness, for the fearful visions of the night, produced, as they were, by the fever of his mind, had greatly aggravated his excitement, and he still raved, like one under the influence of some awful vision of the distempered soul.

"I be not wishing to kill thee, George," he said; "I—I cannot kill thee, and yet I do hear the cry in my ears of blood. Thee hast killed me, for thee hast taken from me all that I do love. Where dost thee suppose that I can find another Phœbe? Thee had no right to take her from me. I did love her before thee. A knife—yes, it was a knife they put into my hands. What knife?—what for? There be some one that do whisper to me it be to kill —to kill George. I—I cannot—no, no. Phœbe, Phœbe, thee would then love me if thee saw him no more! and how could thee see him more if he was dead—dead. Thee would no more hear him speak. He could not smile upon thee, and thee would love Giles. A knife!—where be there such a knife? Ha! I do know well. It be the knife that I did buy of the wandering pedlar. I do remember it now. There be no blood upon my hands, and yet, even in the dark, they do seem to shine and to be red. How soon I might do it. Phœbe would then be mine. Ha! did I hear a voice again, and it did say, 'Do it.' Do what?—kill?—murder?—I—I do not know. I be called to, and—and my head be hot, because I do recollect there be a hole into my brain."

Giles now slowly groped about the room till he found a small lantern, which was usually kept in the mill, and having at hand the means of procuring a light, he lit the little lantern, and without any determined purpose, but as if hurried on by some fearful impulse, which he could not withstand, he went to a chest in the room, and searching among its contents, he laid his hand upon a large knife, with a dirk blade of about six inches in length.

He set the lantern on the table, and laying the knife down before him, he sat for a long time looking at it as if lost in deep thought.

Suddenly a chill run through his frame, and he said, in a low, husky voice,—

"I do hear thee—I do hear thee. Blood! blood! I do see it now on my hands. Phœbe, thee shall have only me to love thee and protect thee. Peace, I say; I hear thee—he shall die. I cannot help it—no, no—I cannot, George. Thee should not have taken my Phœbe, and I should have loved thee; but now—yes, yes—soon, soon——"

He rose, and lifting the lamp high above his head, he looked carefully round the room, as if he expected to see some one.

"Thee art not here," he said; "if thee were, I would ask thee to take the hot, burning hot iron from my brain, and not let them knaw at my heart so; but thee says they will leave off when George be dead."

He walked to the door, and, opening it, listened attentively. All was fearful repose. Not a sound, but his own hard breathing, broke the solemn stillness that reigned in the old mill.

Any one who at that fearful moment could have seen Giles might well have started, and supposed that he looked upon an apparition. His eyes were dilated and bloodshot—his hair hung in wild disorder about his blanched face, and he trembled as if under the influence of some mortal terror.

"Thee be sleeping," he said; "it be better while he do sleep. I must— George, George, I cannot save thee. Thee should have left me my Phœbe. I have been told to kill thee for many nights; I told thee I had dreamed of thee. Thee must know I cannot but kill thee. My hands be red now with blood. Whose, I do not know; but they will be red with thine. Sometimes I do think thee be something that be not a man; but such things as do come to me in my sleep, and do mock at me, and tell me that Phœbe do not love me. Sleep, sleep, George; I—I be now coming to thee—I must kill thee. Thee hast taken my Phœbe, and thee must die. Hush, hush; thee must n o awake. The knife—the knife. It be the same that was put into my hand. George, I be coming to thee, and Phœbe will be mine, as she was before thee come."

He returned to the room, and lifted the knife from the table; then taking again the dim lantern in his hand, he left the chamber.

Cold drops of perspiration stood upon his brow, and he trembled excessively as he pursued his route to the room in which he knew George reposed. His own shadow appalled him as it flitted along the walls, but still he fancied that there came, on each howling gust of wind, which swept around the mill, the fearful words, "blood! blood!"

Onward he took his way, as if impelled by fate. Shuddering at the deed he contemplated, and yet trembling to consummate it, he took his way through the mill, on the dreadful errand of death.

Still his brain burned, and it appeared to him as if some beast of prey was feeding on his living heart, and that the death of his rival could alone assuage his mortal agony. And now he neared the room where slept, in calm contentment and fancied security, the being, whose existence had sapped and undermined the happiness of the wild and disordered Giles.

The lantern cast but a feeble light around; but Giles, as he glanced at the shadows of the various working parts of the mill as they seemed to dance, and advance and retrograde, like living things, fancied that he was not alone on his dread expedition, but that he was accompanied by all the fearful beings who had haunted his slumbers, and urged him to the deed.

"They be come," he said, "to see me do it. When it be done, they will go far away, and I shall see them no more. Phœbe will be mine, and all will be happy. Hark! I do hear them. There be more outside, and they do all cry 'blood—blood!' The light from the lantern I do see be red. Yes, yes; thee need say nothing more. Thee tell me that he did take Phœbe from me—I know, I know—he did bewitch her. She did look kindly upon me, and—and I was happy; but he did come, and a blackness did come upon my heart, for my Phœbe did go to him. Thee need not tell me. I do know, I do know. I did shew her all the wild places that she did love, and the sweet shady walks. I did pluck for her the wild flowers, and lift her over the hedges and the rivulets. I did wander with her to many sweet places, and she did smile upon me, and I did think she loved me; but—but he did come, and she did leave me, and did love him. I did see it from the first; and then when I did lay down to sleep, the dreadful shapes did come and tell me to kill him. Now the time it be come, I would not harm a hair of thee head, George; but thee hast taken my Phœbe, and thee hast made the shapes come to me in sleep, and I have no peace, but must kill thee."

He now laid his hand upon the handle of the door of the room in which George slept, and then, after a pause of some moments, he turned the latch and entered the room. When within the door he stopped, and holding up the lantern, glanced wildly round him upon the various articles in the little chamber.

He then slowly approached the bed, and hung over the sleeping George.

The repose of the sleeper seemed sound and serene, and the wrapt composure of the features were singularly at variance with the countenance of the man who leaned over him, and whose face betrayed, by a thousand distortions, the fearful conflicts of his mind.

"Thee art asleep," muttered Giles, "and thee seem happy. Thee dost not know that I be forced to kill thee. Sleep thee on; thee will not wake. Thee blood will be upon my hands, as I have seen it so many nights in my dreams, and yet I do not think that all were dreams; for the shapes which do come to me and whisper to me to kill thee, be in the room now, and be crowding round thee bed. I do see them all about. They do press upon my arm, and they do tell me to kill thee now that thee beest sleeping; but I do tremble; yet thee must die. Hush, hush! I do know it all; hush!"

It might be that the faint light from the lantern, as it shed its slight dim beams on the sleeper's face, slightly disturbed him, or it might be that he was dreaming of happiness and joy, for he slightly stirred, and a smile played for a moment upon the handsome and manly face of George Andrews.

Giles held his breath as he there stood in momentary expectation that the eyes of his slumbering rival would open, and that a struggle, such as he had passed through in his fearful dream, would ensue. But no. The smile died away, like a sun beam gently retiring behind a fleecy cloud, which still but half obscures its radiant beauty, and the deep regular breathing proclaimed that George was again in sound repose.

Giles wanted, long before he felt that he could again trust himself, to speak, and then it was only in a faint whisper, that he said, as he gently waved his arm,—

"Hush! hush! Peace, all of thee. Thee see I be going to do it."

The wind had been increasing in violence all the evening, and now blew in fitful gusts round the mill, moaning, sighing, and straining the old timbers of the ancient edifice. These sounds, to the disturbed fancy of Giles, were so many fearful incitements to pursue his dreadful purpose, and ever, as a more fearful blast of wind swept by, and moaned and whistled among the crevices in the old mill, he looked wildly round and round, and cried,—

"Hush! hush! I being going to do it. Blood! blood! blood!"

Now his face became more deathly pale, and the slight remnant of colour forsook his lips as he touched a spring, by which the long two-edged blade of the knife which he held in his trembling grasp flew open.

"Phœbe, Phœbe," he gasped, in a husky whisper, "'tis for thee—for thee that I be going to do this. He—he cannot love thee as I do. He—he would not kill, slay, murder for thee. No, no. He can smile upon thee, and sing to thee, and fetch thee flowers, and talk to thee of foreign parts, and—and win thee to be his; but he would not feel the drops of blood upon his heart —he would not do for thee what I be going to do—and—and then how can he love thee as I love thee? No, no; he do not. The old mill will miss thee, George, and I shall miss thee; but Phœbe—she shall not miss thee— for thee love her, and I will love her better than thee can. She was a small, little fair thing when she did come here first; and many a time have I held her in my arms. Oh, God! I have held her to my heart, and I did love her then as I do love her now; but—but—thee—thee, George, came, and the sky did turn black, and the pure blood did congeal in my heart."

Giles now placed the lamp upon a chair, which stood by the bed-side, and with his hands clasped with fearful violence round his head, he said,—

"Quiet—quiet. Peace—I tell thee, peace. Will thee drive me more mad by telling these things to me? I do not forget; but I will not think. No, no. Away with thee!—away! I feel thee hot breath upon my face. Now—now."

He leaned over George, and, with a trembling hand, removed the clothing from his breast. The movements of Giles were very slow and cautious, but slight as the disturbance was, it seemed sufficient almost to break the slumber of the sleeper. He moved and muttered something, and, with the rapidity of thought, Giles hid the lantern in his breast.

The little couch upon which George reposed, creaked as he turned, a black darkness was in the chamber, and Giles stood motionless as a statue, although the cold dank perspiration of intense agony trickled down his cheeks.

George seemed half awake, for he spoke.

"Phœbe—dear—dear Phœbe—I—ah—a—the wind—the moaning wind—the moan—moan—"

He ceased, with a heavy sigh. For many weary minutes Giles waited ere he dared again to cast the light from his lantern on the countenance of the sleeper; but when he did so, it was with the expression of a fiend that he bent over him, and seemed to gloat upon the thoughts of the destruction he was about to bring upon the handsome and manly form which lay before him so entirely at his mercy.

"Thee hast spoke the word," he said; "thee hast said 'Phœbe;' and by that word thee shall bleed. Thee shall lie and soak in the blood."

He laid down the lantern once more, and raising the gleaming knife high above the unconscious George, he was about to bring it down, with an unerring aim to his heart, when he caught sight of a blue ribbon, which was round the neck of his victim, and which George's providential change of position had brought into view.

He paused, with the uplifted instrument of death in his hands, and a strong convulsion shook his frame. He stooped till his hot breath almost fanned the cheek of him who slumbered so serenely, and glared like a wild and infuriated animal upon a small silken bag which hung by the ribbon, and which now reposed upon the heart of George, for it was slightly moved at each perceptible pulsation.

"This be worse than all," said Giles, in a hissing whisper; "it be a gift from Phœbe; it be mine—mine, now; but it be not right that it should soak in his blood. No, no—mine—mine; it be by right mine. Ha! what noise be that?"

It seemed to Giles that he heard a rattling sound at the window of the chamber, and he turned his eyes in the direction with the rapidity of lightning. Nothing, however, was visible.

"It be those that come with me." he said. "They be waiting to see it done. I do see their eyes, but naught else. They do glare upon me, and do ask me to shed the heart's blood of him who do lie there."

He now slightly raised the ribbon that was about George's neck, and severing it with the knife, he drew the love token quietly and cautiously from his breast.

"Now—now," he said; "the whole world could not save thee. Thee took from me my Phœbe, who I do love more than life, and I do take her back by killing thee."

Once more the gleaming knife was raised in the air; nay, it was in the very act of descending, when the room door opened slowly, and Phœbe glided into the apartment.

At the same instant there was a loud crash at the window, and a man bounded into the room.

"George! George!" shrieked Phœbe. "Awake! awake!"

"Damnation!" cried a hoarse, strange voice.

"George! George!" again screamed Phœbe, rushing to the bedside. "Awake! awake."

George started up, with a loud exclamation, and Phœbe fell senseless on the floor of the apartment.

CHAPTER XLI.

WHEN Phœbe retired for the night to her own little chamber, she felt her mind to be in too anxious and disordered a state to seek repose. Again and again she called to mind every conversation that she had heard her mother engage in with respect to her relatives, but she could not recollect the most indistinct allusion to an aunt, either at home or abroad. She felt, nevertheless, much vexed and annoyed at the receipt of the singular letter, which, with all its vulgarity, seemed evidently to be the commencement of some scheme, which had for its object to tear her from her home, and those dear and fondly attached friends who made that home so happy and delightful.

She would fain that George had been consulted upon the mysterious epistle, but she had shrunk from suggesting such a course to the miller. Phœbe's whole thoughts and feelings were now so wrought up in George and his fervid protestations of affection, that in any doubt or difficulty her mind naturally reverted to him as one who could best, of all human beings, solve it, and pluck from it its danger.

Her faith in the affection and unchanging kindness of the miller was unbounded; but it is a principle of the young heart, when first it feels the delicious throbs of pure affection, to invest the image of its fond idolatry with the most exalted virtues, and the greatest powers of action.

The night, as we have before remarked, was dark and gloomy, and the sternness of nature, as it generally does upon sensitive minds, added much to the anxiety which oppressed the mind of the gentle girl. The wind, as it swept by her latticed window, seemed by its sigh to presage to her coming misfortune, and to tell her that her days of calm, peaceful enjoyment were drawing to a close. A hundred times she asked herself who could be the person who had threatened to come on the morrow, and, at least, make the attempt to take her from her home; an attempt which was to be resisted; and what would be the result of such resistance?

Phœbe was as innocent and unsuspecting of evil as an infant; but the scene at Foyle's Hollow had been, as it were, her first introduction to the knowledge that there were those who lay in wait, like beasts of prey, to destroy the peace of the innocent and happy. The extreme beauty which had so attracted Sir Herbert Foster had never been a subject of reflection with the unassuming girl. She had always been pleased when the miller and his dame would call her their dear, beautiful child; but it was the pleasure of pleasing them which delighted her, not the tribute to her own charms of person. George, too, he had told her she was beautiful, and she had listened with delight to his words, because, when translated by her heart, they meant but that he loved her. In fact, no one of God's creature's, possessing the rare gift of almost faultless beauty, could be more unconscious of the dangerous, and, alas! too often fatal gift, or assume less upon it than did the fair and humble Phœbe, the admired Miller's Maid.

An hour or more she passed in her chamber a prey to the most uneasy reflections, and she felt that to retire to rest would be but a mockery of repose, for the anxiety of her mind appeared to increase rather than to diminish.

She opened the latticed window of her room, and extinguishing the light, she leaned upon the window-sill, and strove to pierce with her eyes the intense darkness, and to catch a glimpse at the window of the apartment, which she knew George occupied in the mill which rose before her, huge and black, into the gloomy sky.

The wind was gathering strength, and as it passed her window, and caught on its wing the waving tresses of her flowing hair, and spread them to the night, she felt that the anxious fever of her mind was abating, and hope again whispered to her heart that all would be well; that the clouds which now obscured the clear sunshine of her happiness would pass away like the night she now gazed upon, and a dawn of renewed happiness and joy was approaching.

Phœbe remained for some time at the open window, but the wind was increasing in power each moment, and she began to feel cold and chilled. She was about to withdraw, and close the little casement, when a light for an instant flitted across her eyes, and caused her heart to start suddenly, as if it had been a flash of lightning, and yet she felt convinced that it was not lightning, for it had not the character of that phenomenon. It came from the earth, and not from the sky, and glanced across her window in a distinct ray.

Phœbe looked anxiously all around as well as the darkness would permit her, but for some moments she could see nothing, and was about again to close her window, attributing the light to some accidental cause, when she saw between her and the mill a light, not larger than a star, slowly moving along at some feet above the surface of the earth.

Onward—onward it went towards the mill and Phœbe's eyes were rivetted upon it without the power to withdraw them.

Suddenly the light stopped, and Phœbe fancied that it was returning towards the cottage. She stooped down very low by the window, but kept her eyes still fixed upon the movements of the mysterious light. Slowly it advanced, and she could see it higher and higher as it came to the little gate which led from the meadow to the garden, as if it were climbing over it. She never, of course, doubted that it was carried by some one, who, in the darkness of the night she could not distinguish; but why, or with what intent, any one could be thus prowling at such an hour, for it was past midnight, about the mill and the cottage, she could not divine. The idea of robbery never entered her mind, for the temptation to plunder never was so slight in the purely agricultural district in which the mill stood, that it had been the custom for years for the inhabitants of the village to leave their doors the whole night on the latch merely, and it is probable that in the whole neighbourhood, excepting Haredale Park, half-a-dozen door locks could not have been mustered.

The mill, it is true, was always locked at night-fall, and the miller and each of his men had keys, so that in case of any alarm of fire, or otherwise, there need be no unnecessary delay.

Nearer and nearer the light approached, until it came sufficiently close to the cottage for her to perceive that it was carried by a tall man, who seemed to tread with the greatest caution.

He examined, apparently with the greatest care, every part of the garden and exterior of the house, and finally holding the light close to the ground, he followed the direction of the little gravel walk, which led from the door of the cottage to the gate which opened upon the largest garden, which was at the back; he then came close to the window, which was not above twelve feet from the ground, and holding his light up as high as possible, he looked up at it, and Phœbe being low down, and with her eyes just above the window-sill, could see clearly, by the dim rays of the lamp, his upturned face, and in a moment she recognised who it was that was thus making midnight observations.

It was Ralph Freogrove—he who had uttered such dark threats against George.

In a moment all the miller's repeated cautions to George to beware of that man, rushed across her mind, and she came at once to the conclusion that his object in this secret enterprise was connected with some scheme of revenge upon George, who, for his gallantry in defending his master and friend, had incurred the hatred of the ruffian Freegrove.

From the moment that this idea crossed her mind, Phœbe had but one thought, and that was to warn George of his danger.

The man with the light seemed satisfied with his scrutiny of the cottage,

and its surrounding paths and fences, and once more the light moved rapidly towards the mill, at once confirming to Phœbe her suspicions of the object of Ralph Freegrove in his midnight intrusion.

For a few moments she continued at the window, gazing after the light as if paralyzed, and then she rushed from the window, and gained the door of her little apartment. Her first thought was to awaken the miller, and apprise him of what she had seen ; but was there time? Was not the light now close to the mill?—and what awful deed of violence might be committed before she could effectually arouse the honest miller, and explain to him the circumstances which had aroused her suspicions. No, there was no time ; each moment was of importance. These thoughts flashed across Phœbe's mind with the rapidity of lightning, and before she had scarcely made her resolution to be herself the messenger of warning to George, she had opened her door, quickly descended the stairs, and passed from the cottage.

Phœbe trembled and shivered with the cold as she went forth into the night air, but she paused not a moment in the execution of her intention.

She looked towards the mill, and she saw the light still rapidly approaching it. She flew forwards along the familiar paths with the fleetness of a fawn, and was soon at the door of the mill. She had been unobserved, for Ralph's back was towards the cottage, and he was holding up his light, and gazing intently at the window which Phœbe well knew belonged to the chamber occupied by George.

As she, too, looked from the crouching position she had taken under the little alcove which was above the mill door, she was surprised to observe that there was a light in George's chamber. For a moment her heart fluttered with the anxious hope that, like herself, he had not retired to rest, and the ruffian, who sought his room in the silence of the night to do him, perchance, some deadly injury, would be disappointed.

How different would have been Phœbe's feelings at that moment had she

No. 32

known that Giles, with the fire of insanity in his eye, was at that instant brandishing a knife above the sleeping form of him whom she had come to warn of another, and, to her thinking, his only danger.

Freegrove now laid his lantern on the ground, and commenced climbing, slowly and cautiously, by the assistance of innumerable projections in the wall of the mill, towards George's window, and Phœbe felt that not another moment was to be lost in warning George, whether up or not, of his approaching danger.

The door of the mill, she knew, was locked, but she recollected that the window of the room occupied by Tim Miggles was within a few feet from the ground on the other side of the mill, and to that she instantly flew, and knocking with her hand on the glass, she called to him in as loud a voice as she thought prudent, to arise, and open the door instantly.

Tim, as we have said, for a wonder, had retired to rest ; and the head of his bed being near the window, he was soon awakened in great alarm and consternation.

His imagination had been haunted, since his disclosure to the miller of where he had procured the letter, by a dread of the consequences of the violation of the secret of which he had been urged to keep so religiously, and his slumbers had been haunted by visions of boiling cans of oil, into which he was continually being pitchforked by a dreadful looking being, who could be no other than Snapallhecanup himself. When, therefore, Tim was awakened at that dreadful hour of the night by a knocking at his window, and a voice, which in the confusion he did not recognise, commanded him to rise immediately, and open the door, he burst into a torrent of groans and wailings of his unhappy fate.

"I tell you I couldn't help it by no manner of means," he cried, "Master would have it.

> " I feel all in a broil
>   At the thought of the oil.
> Oh, Snapallhecanup ! have pity on Tim,
> Put George or Giles in the oil-can, and don't think of him."

"Tim! Tim!" cried Phœbe; "hasten, oh! hasten, 'Tis I—Phœbe; undo the door of the mill."

"Eh—ah—what?" cried Tim, rubbing his eyes. "Phœbe! Oh, lauks, that's the caper is it? Well, who would a thought it. That letter must have been a uncommon good love charm to bring her out of her bed at this time of night; but, then, I am rather handsome than otherwise."

"Oh, hasten, Tim, hasten; you don't know the consequences of delay."

"God bless me," said Tim; "I'm almost alarmed."

He jumped up, however, and huddling on some of his clothes, made his way quickly to the door of the mill, and Phœbe hastening round to it the moment Tim opened it, rushed in, and to his great astonishment, passed him without bestowing the slightest notice upon the amourous look and attitude which he had assumed.

The narrow staircase which led to George's apartment, which was on the first story of the mill, was immediately before her, and she bounded up, without a moment's hesitation. She had then a great part of a loft to traverse before she could reach his chamber; and when at last she stood at the door, the impulse which had sustained her so far seemed all at once to desert her, and her heart beat with wild agitation and alarm at the step she had taken.

She placed her hand upon the door; it yielded to a slight pressure, and Phœbe stood in the apartment.

The first glance she cast round the room nearly deprived her of sensation, and curdled her blood with horror. Giles was leaning over the sleeping object of her most anxious cares with his gleaming knife.

When George rose from his bed, as we have recorded at the conclusion of the last chapter, he was for a time perfectly bewildered by the scene which presented itself to his eyes. Phœbe was lying insensible on the floor. Giles stood trembling as if he had suddenly been confronted with an apparition, and the glittering knife, still in his hand, held aloft in the attitude to strike. And lastly, Ralph Freegrove, who little expected to find the apartment into which he had so recklessly plunged so full of persons, stood for a moment, with his hand upon the window-sill, undetermined what to do in the emergency.

"Villain!" cried George, springing towards Freegrove; but the latter anticipated the movement, and, before George could get at him, he sprung through the window again, with a bitter oath of disappointed malice.

"Good Heavens!" cried George, as he seized upon some of his clothes, and hastily began dressing, "what is the meaning of all this? Giles, speak! Why stand you thus motionless?"

A loud cry of "Help! help!—murder! murder!"—was now heard in the voice of Tim Miggles, who had observed from the door, where he had stood transfixed with surprise, the descent of Freegrove from the window.

Giles started as the voice reached him, and, with a wild laugh, he pointed to Phœbe, who lay motionless on the floor.

"Blood! blood!" he cried. "Ha! ha! ha! Blood!"

He glared fiercely at George, and brandishing the knife above his head, he slowly walked backwards from the room.

George had partially dressed himself, and he raised Phœbe from the ground.

"Gracious Heavens!" he cried, "is it possible that any harm can have befallen her? Phœbe, Phœbe, speak to me. Phœbe—dear Phœbe—but one word, to tell me you are safe. What can be the meaning of this most inexplicable scene!"

"Help, help—miller—fire—murder!"—cried Tim Miggles, from below.

"Oh! Phœbe, Phœbe," cried George, in an ecstasy of grief, "can I see thee thus, and live? This silence is dreadful."

He tenderly supported her in his arms, and gazed upon her pale face and closed eyes in a perfect agony of apprehension.

As he thus gazed, half blinded by his tears, which fell upon the cheek of the fair girl whom he loved so tenderly, so devotedly, the colour began to deepen on her face, and, with a deep sigh, she opened her mild blue eyes, and fixed them upon George's face.

"George, dear George," she said, faintly, "save—save yourself; he comes —he comes! oh, dreadful! dreadful! It was Giles—I—I saw the knife— the knife!"

"Nay, dearest, be calm," said George. "There is no one here but myself. Dear Phœbe, think not of such horrors."

"Oh, George, George, I saw him come. The light—the small light, no bigger than a star—directed me. I—I came to save you, or—is it all a dream?"

"No, Phœbe, it was no dream. You have, dear girl, saved me, probably, from much harm. I begin now to see somewhat more clearly into the affair. Dear, dear Phœbe, you came to warn me of some danger."

"Yes, George, yes; Freegrove, it was Freegrove. I saw him from my window; he came, George, to kill you; and—and I surely have dreamt it, or I mix reality with some feverish vision; but there was one standing over you, dear George, with a knife; I saw it glitter—and that one was Giles; it was—it was Giles!"

"Dear Phœbe, quiet yourself; it was Giles you saw; but, dearest, he may have come here for my protection. He would not do me an injury."

"Heaven in its mercy grant it may be so. I will think so. Oh, yes, let us think so. Dear George, we will tell him so; and yet —"

"Yet what, dear Phœbe?"

The door of the room now opened again, and the miller rushed into the apartment. Phœbe rose, with a cry of joy, and sunk into his arms.

"George—Phœbe," cried the miller, "what be all this? Don't 'e cry, my child. How came thee here? That poor fool, Tim, did cry help and murder! but thee be not hurt."

"No, dear father, oh, no; and George, too, is saved!"

"Saved, Phœbe! What dost 'e mean? What is all this, George! and how be the dear child in the mill at this hour?"

"Sir," replied George, "I hardly know; but I was suddenly awakened by Phœbe crying to me to rise; and when I sprung from the bed, she was lying fainting on the floor, and the ruffian, Freegrove, had just jumped into the room, through the window."

"Yes, dear father," said Phœbe. "I saw Freegrove from my window going towards the mill, and—and I thought George was in danger. There was no time to give an alarm, and I am here to warn him of his danger. Thank Heaven I came in time."

"The rascal!" cried the miller; "and where is he now?"

"Before I could seize him, he sprung back again through the window," replied George, "and I could not leave Phœbe."

"And down he came nearly upon my back," said Tim, who had followed the miller into the room, "and then off he cut like twelve lamplighters. Don't I wish I'd had your blunderbuss, master, wouldn't I have given him notice to quit."

"I did truly expect," said the miller, "from my knowledge of that bad man, that he would try to be revenged on thee, George; but I did not suspect that he would be so daring as to seek thee in the old mill. Phœbe, my lass, thee should have wakened me."

Phœbe hung her head on the miller's shoulder, as she said,—

"I—I only thought, dear father, of —"

"Thee only thought of George, thee would say. Well, well, my girl, thee hast not done so much amiss. Thee hast more courage than I thought thee had, and I warrant thee hast a stouter heart now than the scoundrel who has caused us all so much alarm. But where be Giles all this while?"

"Here," said Giles, who had returned to the room, and was standing at the door.

"Giles," said George, "give me your hand. You were in my room, and armed with a knife. I cannot doubt that you came to assist me against that ruffian, Freegrove, who, for aught I know, aimed at my life."

"Oh, yes, yes, it was so, Giles," cried Phœbe, rushing to him, and grasping him by the arm; "it was so. You came to save—to protect George, you did. You would not harm him for worlds. You flew to his aid. Giles, Giles, tell me that you did this, and I will bless you."

She looked imploringly in Giles's face as she spoke, and seemed to await his answer as the fiat of life or death.

He gazed in her face, beaming with beauty and gentleness as it was, and his mind seemed tortured with many contending emotions. His breast heaved, and his whole frame shook with the violence of his feelings. He tried to speak, but for some moments utterance seemed denied him. Nature at length asserted her better sway, and he burst into a passion of hysterical weeping.

"Bless thee, Phœbe," he faintly articulated, after his tears had flowed for some minutes, "bless thee, thee hast saved me, too. Heaven bless thee."

He covered his face with his hands and hurried from the room.

CHAPTER XLII.

THE miller and Phœbe retired to the cottage, and by the advice of the dame the latter proceeded to her room, to endeavour, now that the alarm of the night had subsided, and the danger was averted, to snatch some few hours repose before the morning arrived. Long streaks of grey light were beginning to appear in the east, and the miller determined to remain up for the remainder of the night.

When Phœbe had retired to seek repose, he once more proceeded to the mill, and brought George with him to the cottage.

"George," said the miller, "I will not disguise from thee, my lad, that I do see that Phœbe has a preference for thee, and I be getting old, and the poor child, it is the wish of my heart, may find a protector in thee."

"With your approval," said the highly gratified George, "it should be the duty of my life to love and protect Phœbe, for whom I entertain the most sincere affection."

"I do believe thee, George," replied the miller, "and thee hast my good wishes and my good word, lad, and there be no one that I should be more glad to see the husband of my dear child than theeself. But now about this Ralph Freegrove?"

"This proceeding of his cannot and shall not," answered George, "be passed over in silence. What would you, sir, advise should be done in this matter?"

"It be main difficult to know what to do, George. Sir Herbert Foster be himself a county magistrate, and the matter do lie in his jurisdiction; and thee knows, George, what kind of justice we be likely to expect from him."

"No doubt he would attempt to screen the villain, who is but too faithful a counterfeit of himself in the pursuit of vice and crime."

"He has not scrupled to do so on other occasions, George, within the memory of myself and many others in these parts; but we will let this matter of Ralph Freegrove's bide till to-morrow, if thee please, and I will show thee something that will surprise thee more than Ralph Freegrove making an attempt to do thee an injury, if thee will come here to-morrow morning, and bring Giles to me, for I be determined that there shall be no more doubt and jealousy about who Phœbe do prefer."

In this, and conversation of much the same import, the miller and George spent the intervening hours between that time and the morning.

The night vanished slowly away, and the morning's light became more and more pure and intense. The light in the cottage burned more and more dimly in its languid struggles with the coming day. The sun at length showed the tip of its golden disc above the far-off horizon, and a sweet radiant beam of light shot in an instant over the whole face of Nature.

"See, George," said the miller, extinguishing the candle, "it be full morning. The birds be singing, and all the cocks in the village be crowing right merrily."

They both walked from the cottage and stood in the sun-light.

The veil of night was rent asunder,
And the young day looked forth from out the orient east,
Smiling in beauty like a child of Heaven.
And new-born blossoms shook the cold night's dew,
Which like a mother's tears of joy upon her darling's cheek,
But half concealed, and yet increased their loveliness
From off their rainbow-tinted breasts.
And welcomed, with a thousand fragrant odours,
The glorious sun, which, like a smile from God,
Brings fruitfulness and blessing upon all;"

The night wind had dropped and died away, as if in obedience to the sweet influence of light and warmth, and the morning was serenely lovely.

George proceeded to the mill, and the miller, hurrying to the mill stream, commenced the business of the day.

The first meal of the day was soon dispatched, and Giles and George had risen from the table to retire to their labour at the mill, when Gilbert the miller rose, and, with a serious air, addressed them.

"My lads," he said, "I do want thee both to stay here awhile, for I be going to make an inquiry this morning which I do think, for the happiness and the peace of all, it be necessary should be made by me."

Both George and Giles guessed well to what the miller alluded; and while the former crimsoned to the very temples, the latter grew as pale as death, and leaned upon the back of his chair for support.

Phœbe made towards the door, and would have left the room, but the miller called to her.

"Phœbe, my dear child, I wish thee to stay, for it do concern thee much what I be going to say to the young men, and I think it be for thee welfare as well as for theirs that I should say it at once."

Phœbe's heart fluttered, and she felt so faint, that she was compelled to sink into a chair as the miller spoke.

The good dame hastened to her side, and sitting down by her, affectionately took her hands between hers and said,—

"My dear child, don't be afeard. We do love thee better than we do love ourselves, and what Gilbert be a going to say, be for thee happiness, my dear child."

"You have both been always too kind and good to me," replied Phœbe.

"I suppose, master, I may stay?" said Tim Miggles.

> "Like a snail that's lost his shell,
> My hopes were high, and then down they fell."

"Thee may stay," said the miller; "but if thee do, thee must keep thee foolish tongue quiet,

> "Oh, Snapallheeanup! I'm greatly afraid,
> You've chisseled poor Tim, and he'll lose the fair maid."

muttered Mr. Miggles with a deep sigh.

"Now, all of thee attend to me," said the miller. "Thee all knows how dear to my heart and to my good dame's is our dear child Phœbe. She has been to us a blessing and a comfort in our old age, and thee will not wonder that we do look upon her future happiness as the first wish of our hearts. She be a good girl, although I do say it before her face, and I do believe that he who she do incline to may be happy with our dear Phœbe as the day be long."

"The world," cried George, fervently; "could not prevent him——"

"Will 'e hold thee tongue?" interrupted the miller. "If one of thee do have a say, each of thee must have a say, and I do not intend that any of thee should have anything to say but my own dear girl."

"Oh, father!" cried Phœbe; "what would you have me say?"

"Hold thee tongue, too. I be coming to what I would have thee say. Now, lads, I need not tell thee that all be going wrong at the mill."

"All going wrong at the mill?" cried George.

"All going wrong at the mill?" said Giles.

"What a crammer," muttered Tim Miggles.

> "There's water in the mill-dam,
> And sure I am
> That that's a cram,
> And all a flam."

"Silence, will 'e, with thee nonsense," cried the miller. "How dare thee all interrupt me? I say there be something wrong at the mill, and what be wrong be this, that thee be all plaguing each other, and fighting and quarrelling about my Phœbe instead of minding your work and attending to the mill."

George felt a little conscience-stricken at this charge, but he said nothing.

"Now," continued the miller, "I do not altogether blame thee; but I do believe thee be both in love with Phœbe."

"Oh, dear father!" cried Phœbe.

"Both—both," said Tim Miggles. "Do you mean by that, master, that I—I—Timothy Miggles, Esq., &c. &c.——"

"If thee open thee foolish mouth once more," said the miller, "I will send thee out as sure as my name be Gilbert. Now, George and Giles, I will not take upon myself to say that Phœbe will have either of thee, but I be determined that if she do prefer one of thee, that if the other do make any more bickering and jealous quarrelling that he and I shall part, be it which of thee it may. I do esteem thee both, lads. Now will thee consent to this bargain? and I will ask Phœbe to say if she do incline to either or neither of thee."

"My kind master," said George, "all here at present know, or, at least, I hope they know, the deep obligations I am under to you. You rescued me from poverty and want. I had by the violence of the ocean lost all that I possessed upon earth. The only being for whom I had long toiled, and the dear thought of whom lightened every labour, and made my duty a pleasure, had flown no one knew whither. I fear death has—has—taken from me the only one who I believe bore my own name in the wide world, and to whom I could claim dear kindred. I was alone, a wanderer on the face of the earth. You, sir, brought me here. I saw Phœbe—and—and how could I else? I loved her from that moment. I love her, sir, dearly love her. Gladly—most gladly do I consent to this day's trial. I have not words in which to plead my suit, but my heart beats but for her. True love cannot be told; it is like the blessed sunlight—it——"

"That be enough, George," interrupted the miller, most unseasonably, as Phœbe thought, for she was drinking in with her whole soul every word which was uttered by George, and had nearly forgotten the presence of all besides while his voice was ringing like music in her ears.

He now, however, ceased, and Phœbe, with a sigh of pleasure, looked up to the miller's face to note the impression which the words had made upon him. She fancied she saw a glistening moisture in his eye, and that his voice was more low and broken as he continued speaking.

"Now, Giles, what say thee, lad; will thee abide by what Phœbe shall say?"

A deep dejection seemed to have hung over the spirits of Giles during the whole time he had been in the room, and he now spoke but faintly.

"I do love Phœbe," he said, clasping his hands, "but she do love me not; she be to me the whole world, but I be to her nothing: she be music and sunshine to me, but I be hateful to her, and she do not look kindly upon me."

Deep sighs burst from his heaving breast as he ceased speaking, and he dropped his face upon his hands as he sunk into the chair.

There was a dead silence for some minutes, for no one liked to intrude upon, though all were inexpressibly pained at the mental agony of the unfortunate Giles.

Phœbe at length, with tears streaming down her cheek, arose from beside the dame, and approached the sorrow-stricken man. She gently removed his hands from before his face, and in mild and pitying accents, addressed him:—

"Giles, dear Giles, will you not be the friend—the dear friend of the little Phœbe who used to ramble with you in the sweet summer evenings? Giles, I had a dear brother once, but he is gone—gone. Will you supply the lost one's place, and be to me what he would have now been, the best—the truest friend? You have done a thousand kindnesses for poor Phœbe; do one more and let her see you smile as in old times. I've heard you say a hundred times my happiness was a dear wish. Oh! say so once again, and let me not mourn the loss of a dear friend who will make the happiest moments happier by his sympathetic pleasure. Speak to me, Giles, as you used to speak, and do not —oh! do not plant in the heart of Phœbe, whom you love, a thorn of anguish which, amid her sunniest, happiest hours, will cast over her spirits a shadow of grief. Your arm saved me from insult in Foyle's Hollow. Do you think I can forget it? No—no; you, that would risk your life to save me from persecution—the persecution of a miscreant there—will not force from my eyes the tears of sorrow and bitterness here in my dear father's happy home—your home, Giles, as well as mine."

The storm of passion gradually subsided in the breast of Giles as Phœbe spoke; and, although his face wore still the traces of his deep mental agony, and his very lips were bloodless, he gazed up into her eloquent and beautiful face, and for the moment a calm joy lit up his features,—but it was but for one fleeting moment,—like a gleam of sunshine o'er a wintry heath, which for an instant lights up all that his chilling and dreary with a momentary splendour, and then dying away, leaves the gloom of Nature more gloomy than before, did that faint radiation of joy and peace light up Giles's face, and then went from it, leaving a deepened cloud behind it.

"Phœbe," said the miller, in a low tone, "dost thee decide for Giles?"

Phœbe started, and Giles sprang upon his feet in an instant.

George stood immoveable, but the rapidly varying colour in his cheek showed how deeply interested he felt himself in the question of the miller.

"Why, Gilbert," cried the dame, "what dost thee mean?—what hast thee got in thee head now, man?"

"Phœbe," continued the miller, "thee reserve is natural; but thee see these two young men. They be both unhappy on thee account. Thee can make one of them happy, and the other ought to have the good sense to prefer certainty to doubt. Now, my dear child, place thee hand in the hand of the one that thee do choose, and be he which he may, he shall have my good word and the mill when I be gone if it be in my power to give it to him and to thee."

The utmost excitement and attention now pervaded the group in the little cottage, and Phœbe hung down her head and seemed afraid to meet the earnest looks which she felt convinced were bent upon her.

"It be Giles, then," cried the miller.

Phœbe started.

"No, no," she exclaimed, stretching forth her hand,—"no, no, I——"

George sprung forward and clasped her hand in his, then with a voice which made the cottage ring again, he cried,—

"Mine—mine!—she's mine!—for ever mine!"

Phœbe did not withdraw her hand, but covering her face with the other, she wept freely.

"Then it be decided," exclaimed the miller, drawing a long breath.

"No!" cried Giles, furiously, "it be not decided,—no, while I be alone, —no, no, it be not decided while Giles be alive!"

"A Miggles—a Miggles!" shouted Tim, jumping upon a chair, off which he instantly fell again, by overbalancing the back, with a great crash.

"Peace all of thee," cried the miller; "peace, peace, Giles! I will make one offer in thee name. Phœbe, will thee consent that if anything should cause thee not to marry George that thee will take Giles."

Phœbe hesitated a moment, and then said faintly,—

"I promise if—if I marry to—to take George or Giles."

"That be enough," cried the miller, "Giles that even be more than thee ought to expect."

"She's mine—she's mine!" muttered Giles to himself, as he rushed from the cottage.

"Hush! hush!—silence," said Tim Miggles. "Phœbe promise, if you don't marry somebody else, will you marry me?"

"Certainly, Tim," said Phœbe smiling.

"I give you my free consent to that, Tim," said George. "After everybody else, you have certainly a fair claim."

"There be one more thing to say, Gilbert," said the dame.

"There be—there be," cried the miller. "George, come here again in the evening, and bring Giles with thee. I—ha!—what sound is that?"

"It seems like a carriage," said George, "stopping in the cross road that runs by the back of the meadow."

"A carriage?" said Phœbe, turning very pale. "Heaven protect me."

"George," said the miller, "there be something to tell thee about our dear Phœbe, which be nothing to the disparagement of the dear child, but I cannot tell thee now. She must be protected against those who are now coming here, who pretend to lay claim to our dear child, and to take her from us. They be people of Sir Herbert Foster's, without a doubt. Do thee stay here, my lad, and assist me to protect the dear girl."

Phœbe clung to George's arm in great terror, and the latter looked astonished both at what the miller had said and the evident apprehension of Phœbe.

"Dear Phœbe," he said, "be not alarmed; am I not here? and what evil can you fear? I will protect you with my life."

"Secrets, George," said the miller, "be bad things in any house, but there be few without them, and it be Heaven's mercy when they be such as bring neither disgrace nor dishonour when they be known."

"I am convinced, sir, and will uphold it with my last drop of blood,

No. 33

that neither of those terms can be, with justice, applied to Phœbe, or anything concerning her."

"Thee art right ; I tell thee before God that thee art right, lad. Thee hast taken to thee heart the best and most blameless of Heaven's creatures."

"Dear Phœbe," said George, " you have this day given me greater happiness than I ever thought the world could present to me."

"Dame," said the miller, "thee will take Phœbe up stairs with thee, and don't come down either of thee, let 'e hear what 'e will. Go !—quick—quick."

Phœbe, with one silent pressure of the hand to George, and a glance, which said more to his enraptured heart than could possibly have been put into words, departed, with the dame, to the upper story of the cottage.

"Tim," said the miller, to the self-satisfied Miggles, who still lingered in the cottage, " go, thee, and see if any one be asking for me, and if there be, bring them in here."

"Very well," said Tim. "I love a mystery, I do. I shouldn't wonder," he muttered, as he left the cottage, "that the emperor of somewhere has come, in his second-best coach, to claim Phœbe as his daughter, in which case I shall certainly say a word for myself, and I'll just mention, as a proof of attachment, the little circumstance of her nearly pulling me out of bed last night."

"George," said the miller, "I have told thee that this be an attempt to take our dear child from us, under the pretence that she be the niece of some woman. Here, thee had better at once read this letter, and then thee will know better what to think of the person who I do suspect be now coming."

The miller handed the letter to George, who rapidly run his eye over it.

"It is not possible, sir," he said, "that such an evident fabrication as this can give you any uneasiness ? This letter is not even written by a woman ; the language and general style is that of a flippant, uneducated man."

"It was brought, George, by Tim Miggles, and he did confess to me that he got it from one Perk, who is the clerk of Scrimp, the attorney."

"I cannot," said George, " but think it some idle jest. Mr. Perk had better not carry the joke too far."

"But—but, George, my lad, I may tell thee as well now as at any other time."

"Tell me what, sir ?" cried George, alarmed at the miller's manner.

"Phœbe be not my daughter."

George turned very pale, and sunk into a seat, with a groan of anguish.

"And—and,"—he said, faintly—" Is it possible that the writer of this letter is——"

"No, no," cried the miller ; "no. Phœbe has no such relation. It be a plot to take the child from us."

How quickly were all George's airy fabrics of future happiness levelled with the dust by this most unexpected communication. Where all was prosperous love and joy, unclouded, but a few moments previously, he now saw perils innumerable. Phœbe was still the bright pure being that had enthralled his youthful fancy ; but what undreamt-of obstacles might now intervene to prevent their union. Relations, friends, might arise, who would give their determined opposition to his love. She might belong to a class of society which would look down with scorn upon the true love of the humble miller's man. Well might he have said, in the language of the poet of all ages,—Shakspeare,—

This is the state of man. To day he puts forth
The tender leaves of hope ; to-morrow blossoms.
And tears his blushing honours thick upon him.

The third day comes a frost—a killing frost ;
And when he thinks, good easy man, full surely,
His greatness is a ripening—nips his root,
And then he falls as I do.' '

Tim returned in a few moments, breathless.

"There's a carriage, master," he said, "and there's a most magnificent female a-coming this way. Oh, lauk, she's a creature."

CHAPTER XLIII.

THE words had scarcely escaped Tim's mouth when the cottage door opened, and a tall, bulky-looking lady rushed in, exclaiming, with great rapidity, and in a shrill vixenish voice,—

"My dear—my darling niece, come to my arms. Where is she ?—where is she? Let me embrace her instantly. I dare say she's the picture of her dear mother ; I long to see her. Mr. a—a—what's your name ?—how do you do? Bless me, where is she, my dear darling Phœbe?—I haven't seen her since she was a blessed baby. How time does cut along, to be sure. I've had three husbands since then, and they each left me handsome fortunes. Where—oh, where is she ? Come to my bosom, my love ; come to my bosom. Oh, dear me, my feelings quite overpower me. Young man, a chair if you please. Fetch the dear child directly. Don't lose a moment. Fetch her down. Is she up stairs, poor dear thing ? It will be a trying moment when I hold her to my dear heart."

All this was said with such amazing volubility that it was perfectly hopeless to attempt to stem the current of the lady's eloquence, and George and the miller both stared aghast at the female, who seemed thus determined to take the cottage by storm, and confound their faculties by torrents of words.

She was very elegantly attired in black silk ; and were it not for a certain stiffness and singular manner about her movements, she might have been considered an exceedingly lady-like personage.

She now sat down, and commenced fanning herself furiously with a large Indian fan, which hung by a silken cord to her wrist.

The miller looked at George, and George looked at the miller, but neither seemed for a few moments to know what to say to the rather imposing looking female who sat before them. She did not, however, give them long time for reflection, for she broke out again into another storm of words, which came from her mouth with the most wonderful rapidity, and were highly calculated thoroughly to confound her hearers.

"This is a sweet cottage—dear me, a desirable little dwelling ; it puts me in mind of love in a cottage. Oh, dear me, yes. I always admire cottages, though I keep a large establishment ; twenty-three servants, a travelling carriage, town chariot, two pony pheatons, and a park chair. Mr. Thingummy, you are looking entremely well, and you, too, young man ; but the dear child—where is the dear child ? What a person you are to talk, to be sure ; there's no such thing as getting in a word edgeways ; but then, dear me, what you say is so very uncommonly sensible. Go and fetch the darling ; I am all impatience ; or, oh, dear me, just tell me the way up stairs. Perhaps the dear child is not yet up. I never was up so early in my life ; but I'm told you country folks always rise before twelve, so as to have a long day before you. Bless me, it must be terrible. That I do call slavery. I hope you are doing uncommonly well."

"Madam," said the miller, "I——"

"You know," continued the lady, "we are always tormented in town about agricultural distress, or some such thing. I hope Swing and those kind of low people don't live down this way. Dear me, it would be quite shocking."

The miller looked at George in despair, and nodded to him to speak.

George Andrews had seen more of the world than the worthy miller, although he was not much above one third of his age, and he listened to the voluble speeches of the would-be fine lady with great suspicion; for although he was well aware that in proportion there was quite as many vulgar rich as vulgar poor, yet there was, to his thinking, such an evident strained manner about the lady, that he could not help coming at once to the conclusion, that whoever she was, she was there and then acting a part, with some sinister object in view, detrimental to the peace and happiness of his 'dear Phœbe and the inhabitants of the cottage. He was, therefore, pleased that the miller had deputed him to conduct the conversation with the strange lady, and he immediately broke in upon the torrent of her eloquence, by saying,—

"Madam, it is the desire of those you have obliged with this visit that you would be pleased to favour them with your name, and make known your business."

This was said in so calm and determined a tone, that a slight shade of uneasiness passed over the lady's countenance, and she plied the fan vigourously before she replied.

"Oh, bless me, yes. Didn't either of my footmen bring in a card? How very remiss; I must lecture them well. Mrs. Martha Dovetail, late Mrs. General Popham. Where's the dear girl? Oh, dear, oh, dear! I can't bear suspense. Call her directly, and let me fold to my bosom the dear child of my only sister."

"General Popham!" cried Tim. "Well, I never."

"Are we to understand, madam, that you claim the young lady who—who resides here, as your niece?" said George, his voice slightly faltering as he spoke.

"Oh, dear me, yes, you are quite right, and really seem a most sensible young man. I intend to make her my heiress. I have all the Popham jewels; they are worth twelve thousand pounds at least. Oh, dear me, you are remarkably like my first husband, Mr. Plenipotentiary Jones. He was Ambassador Extraordinary and Charge d'Affaires from—dear me, some place I can't recollect; but he was remarkably like you. I declare I've taken quite an affection for you on that account. I've got a little interest at court; for, as his late majesty used often to say, Mrs. Penipotentiary Jones can do more for a young man than I can. Oh, dear me, old times make one forget everything. The Plenipotentiary died, and I married General Popham, and became possessed of the Popham jewels. You really must go with me to town, young man, or—let me see—I'll send for you in a few days, when I'm a little settled with my dear niece."

"You wrote a letter yesterday, I believe, madam?" said George.

"A letter?—Oh dear, yes, very likely. I write so many letters. I've an immense correspondence. Now if you'd like to push your fortune in India, I could send you out on General Funkie's staff; but really I am determined to do something handsome for you."

George detested the woman, and could not bring his mind to give even a civil refusal to her profuse offers of services.

The miller looked very much confounded, and Tim gazed at Mrs. Martha Dovetail, late Mrs. General Popham, late Mrs. Plenipotentiary Jones, in speechless wonder and intense admiration.

"Tim," said the miller, "get thee gone about thee business."

Tim Miggles most reluctantly quitted the cottage.

"Mr. Gilbert Marks, madam," replied George firmly, indicating the miller with his hand as he spoke, "refuses to deliver to you the young lady who you say is your niece. If you can legally claim a right to her guardianship, you will be put to the trouble of doing so."

"And I tell 'e, Mrs. What's-'e-name," cried the miller, now that the ice was fairly broken, "thee dost not even know the name of her who thee say is thee niece, and she do not acknowledge thee. Thee shall not have her if thee were fifty generals."

"Eh? what?" exclaimed the lady, "do I hear right, or do I dream? Not have my own dear niece that I have travelled post from London, with four horses and two outriders to pay toll-bars, to see? It can't be possible. Oh, dear me, the Lord Chanceller is my most particular friend, and he said to me, and shook his dear old wig as he spoke, 'Mrs. Dovetail,' says he, 'late Mrs. General Popham, late Mrs. Plenipotentiary Jones, I beg you won't scruple to make use of my name in case of any legal difficulty.'"

"This," said George, "is too ridiculous. Madam, you are deceived. You appear to imagine that you have to deal with the most ignorant rustics. I can tell you that such is not the case. How do you account for the ignorance you are in with regard even to the name of her whom you claim as your niece?"

"Oh, dear me, names I never could recollect. Her poor dear mother married while I was in India, and I really thought it was Hawthorne. What did you say it really was?"

"I gave her no name," replied George, "and I advise Mr. Marks to be equally cautious."

The lady bit her lips, and plied her fan for a few moments; then taking up a pocket handerchief, she held it to her eyes, and sobbed, or appeared to sob bitterly.

"Oh, dear, oh, dear," she cried, in the intervals of her grief, "that I should live to see this day!—my own poor dear niece to be denied to me— I, that have thought of her day and night, and meant to make a lady of her and leave her all I possess. Cruel, cruel men, you cannot know my feelings. I—I would have enriched you all."

"Madam," said George, quietly, "your tears cannot place this matter in any different light. Even if you prove yourself the aunt of the young lady who is here, I doubt if you will be able to exercise any legal control over her; but should you really prove your near relationship, I am well convinced that she would be the first dearly to welcome you to her heart."

"Well, well," said Mrs. Dovetail, "I believe you are right, and I respect and honour you both for your caution. I have my carriage at the lane by the meadow there, and I will just take the dear child half an hour's drive to talk to her about her dear mother. Pray send for her if you—Mr. a—a —Parks. I long to see her. She is, I dare say, the very image of her dear mother."

"At the risk, madam, of appearing unnecessarily harsh and suspicious," said George, mildly, "we beg to decline your kind offer, or even allowing you to see the young lady at all."

"Yes, we do decline thee altogether," said the miller. "She be not going with thee, so I tell 'e. It be no use thee staying here."

Again the lady hid her face with her handkerchief, and seemed absorbed in deep grief or reflection.

"Now listen to me," she said. "A lady of my fortune is not to be browbeat by such as you. You are bringing destruction upon your own heads. I warn you. Give up my niece instantly, or if it costs me twenty thousand pounds, I'll ruin you, and you shall both of you rot in gaol."

"Threats, madam," said George, smiling, "will not not succeed here."

"Threats!" cried the lady. "You'll find me a good friend, or a terrible enemy. I ask but to take my own niece half an hour's drive in my own carriage, and you refuse me. Are you aware that I could call in my servants, and enforce my wishes?"

"No," cried the miller, "we be not aware of any such thing; but we be aware that if one of the rascals do dare so much as set a foot in this cottage, he will have a scramble to get out of the mill stream, for in there, as sure as my name be Gilbert, will I throw him."

"Oh, you'll repent this, both of you," cried the lady. "I would have done wonders for you, but your own obstinacy stands in your way. You may have been kind to my dear niece, and I'll forgive you if you'll let me have a little talk with her. Come, where is she? Call her directly, for my time is precious."

"Madam, I tell you once more," said George, "you will see no one hear but ourselves, no, not for one single instant."

"Wretches!" screamed the lady. "Monsters!—has it come to this? Oh, dear, oh, dear, I shall faint—I shall faint."

"Thee had better faint in thee carriage, ma'am," said the miller, "for the floor be main hard here if thee should fall down."

"Brute! wretches!" cried Mrs. Dovetail; "oh, you shall repent of this, you shall, indeed. I'll have you out of the cottage, and the mill too. You sha'n't, you wretches, have a bed to lie upon, as sure as I'm born."

"You have used the language of threats to us, madam," said George, "but we have been civil to you. I think, now, you had better leave this place, for your further presence here, I beg to tell you, is most disagreeable."

"You beg to tell me, you scum of the earth—you vile puppy! I've no doubt you've among you seduced my poor dear niece, and you are all now afraid to let her see me, for fear she should tell her kind and affectionate aunt."

George's face flushed with resentment at this base insinuation, and he replied in a tone of suppressed passion,—

"If you were not a female, I would cram the foul lie down your throat."

"Get thee gone," cried the miller, "thee female devil; get thee gone. I will not have thee under my roof."

"Oh, yes," cried the lady, rising, "do threaten; bully and threaten an unprotected female. Oh, dear, yes, it's very manly. If the General was alive he'd soon settle this business; but we shall see. I'll apply to the Secretary of State. Why don't you strike me? Two men bullying one woman."

"When a woman," said George, "forgets her sex, and deals in language and insinuations that a man should blush for, it is not to be wondered at that men for a moment join her in forgetfulness. You, madam, remember that you are a female, and be assured that we shall never forget it."

"You shall never forget this morning, I promise you," said the lady, moving in a very dignified manner towards the door. "You have brought destruction upon your own head. You don't know, you ignorant scum, what you've done. I'll have you out of house and home, and I'll have my niece before another week. Poor thing, she is kept here a prisoner. I'll go to the nearest magistrate, and have warrants against you all. Shake in your shoes, you vile wretches, or give me up my niece. I'd forgive you, even now. I'll give you fifty pounds on account of what her dear board and lodging has come to, if you will but be reasonable, and let me take her with me."

"No, madam, no; once more, no," said George, "not for fifty thousand pounds."

"Then curses on you!" said the lady, hastening to the door.

Her dress, however, caught against a chair as she was going out, and the lady was thrown down on her knees. "Damnation!" cried she.

George and the miller stood for one moment bewildered, and then the conviction, from both the voice and the nature of the exclamation, rushed across George's mind that the pretended aunt was not a woman.

With one bound he caught her at the door with one hand, and with the other he tore off the whole of her head-dress, and exposed the close crop of Mr. Perk.

The lawyer's clerk felt the full danger of his situation, and made the most energetic struggles to get away from George's gripe, but as well might he have writhed under an iron chain.

"You reckless fool!" cried George, "what could tempt thee to place thy worthless life in such fearful jeopardy? You contemptible idiot! I don't know why I don't close my hand upon your throat, and rid society of such a shallow knave."

"A man!" cried the miller, "a man! Now, by everything, I be glad on't. You—you—I do not know what to call thee, thee hardened wretch."

"I—I was sent by others," said Mr. Perk, trembling in the grasp of George. "Oh! for mercy sake, spare my life!"

"Your life, you reptile," said George, "is not worth taking. Who are thy employers in this vile transaction? Answer instantly, or I'll shake the truth from you."

"I—I—you—you hold my neck too tight. My good, dear sir, I—I can't speak."

"Now, then," replied George, slightly relaxing his grasp, "who set you on this despicable errand?"

"Sir—Herbert—Foster—and—and Scrimp."

"Sir Herbert Foster and Scrimp, eh?" cried the miller. "I did think as much; and I do wish that either of them had come in thee place, thee poor wretch."

"Gentlemen," stammered Mr. Perk, "you—you won't hurt a poor fellow, who—who only does what he is told, you know. I couldn't help it. I—I——"

"The tools with which men work," said George, "must put up with the rubs they get. What shall we do with this mean-spirited scoundrel?"

"Boil him in a can of train oil," said Tim, popping his head in at the door.

"What do you want, Tim?" asked the miller.

"Why, master, the servants at the slap-up female's carriage wants to know if they are to wait."

"No," said George; "tell them to go; and tell them also to report to Sir Herbert Foster that his shallow emissary is discovered, and that we regret he did not enact the part himself."

"What!" said Tim, starting at Mr. Perk, "can that be you? Oh, lauks.

> There's nothing like magic,
> Whether comic or tragic.

Oh lauks, oh lauks—here's a rum go."

"And hark'e, Tim," said the miller, "send Giles here."

Tim departed on his errand; and Mr. Perk, casting an implcring look on the miller, said, in a whining tone,—

"Oh, sir, let me go—I—I never will engage in such a thing again, upon my soul I won't. I'll be with you in this matter. I'll put you in the way of transporting Scrimp, I will, indeed. Do but let me go, and I'll betray them all. Pomander's in it, too, and Freegrove. Don't do me any harm, and I'll work for you night and day."

Giles and Tim now returned to the cottage, and the former was not a little surprised at the singular scene which was taking place.

"Pens, ink, and paper," said George. "Let's have them instantly. Now, you scoundrel, if you don't sit down at that table, and write a confession of who employed you, and your purpose in coming here this morning, I'll throttle you, as sure as you are a sneaking cowardly villain."

"Oh, dear, yes—yes—I—I'll write anything—anything, gentlemen, you please—a—a full confession—a most full confession—I'll tell you all about it. You shall be revenged on Scrimp, and on Pomander—he's a great rascal —and on Sir Herbert, even. You see, gentlemen, I am your most humble servant—yours to command. I honour and respect ——"

"Peace!" cried George. "Your disgusting protestations increase your danger. Your base services we despise as we do you and your employer's. Write."

"Oh, certainly. What shall I say? I will say anything you please. Shall I say anything about myself? I—I——"

"I do not dictate to you except the first words."

"Yes—oh, dear yes—the first words. Anything, everything you like, my good gentlemen. You are a most charming, united family, bless you all. I—I feel quite happy and—and comfortable. The first words; yes, my dear sir."

"What is your name?"

"Perk, my good sir. Stephen Perk at your most humble service."

"Then begin thus:—I, Stephen Perk, being a most contemptible and cowardly villain, did conspire with certain other vile scoundrels, hereinafter mentioned——"

Mr. Perk winced a little at this, and looked in George's face to see if there were any signs of relenting; then he looked at the miller who stood by, with knitted brows, but all was stern determination, and he actually wrote the words.

"Now follows your confession," said George. "Let it be brief, and to the purpose."

"Oh yes—yes—I—I will state all—and—and you will let me go—you will?"

"I make no promise," replied George. "Act as you think proper."

"Oh, dear, yes, you are very kind. You—you wouldn't hurt a poor fellow."

"What a insignificant wretch," said Tim. "I despises him."

"Giles," said the miller, "this man has made an attempt to carry off Phœbe, and to convert her into a mistress for Sir Herbert Foster."

Giles clenched his fists, and made a forward movement towards Mr. Perk.

"Forbear, forbear," said George; "he is doing us a good service."

This passed in an under tone while Mr. Perk was writing. In a few minutes he ceased his occupation, and looking up, said, with a servile grin :—

"Now, gentlemen, I think you will admit that I have done you justice. Your kindness is not misplaced, I assure you. I am your most devoted slave for ever. Do but let me go, which I see by your kind looks you will, and I will at all times do anything you please. If you have an enemy, and want to do him a queer turn, I'm your man. I'm bound to you for life. I——"

"Silence," said George, "silence. You and your offered services are alike despised. Read the paper. Let all present listen to it, that it may be properly witnessed."

"Witnessed—ah! no need. Surely you don't think I would deny it? I——"

"I am sure you would whenever it was convenient or safe for you to do so. Read."

Mr. Perk, with a trembling voice, read as follows :—

"I, Stephen Perk, being a most contemptible and cowardly villain, did conspire with certain other vile scoundrels hereinafter mentioned, namely, Sir Herbert Foster, baronet, Mr. Scrimp, attorney-at-law, Mr. Pomander, chemist, and Ralph Freegrove, servant to the aforesaid Sir Herbert Foster, baronet, to force away by unlawful means, a certain young girl, known by the name of Phœbe Marks, for the purpose of her seduction, by force or fraud, by the aforesaid baronet, for which he was to pay certain sums of money. Dated this twenty-eighth day of September, one thousand eight hundred and fourteen.

(Signed)   "STEPHEN PERK,
"Clerk to the aforesaid Scrimp, attorney-at-law."

George took the pen, and witnessed the document, as likewise did the miller, Giles, and Miggles.

"Now," said George, folding the paper, and carefully placing it in his pocket, "I believe, there is a pump on the premises."

"A—a—what, gentlemen?" shrieked Mr. Perk; "a—a pump!"

"Yes, a pump," replied George. "You look heated, Mr. Perk, and a shower bath would do you a little good."

"Aye," cried the miller, "that do break no bones, and the warmint might drown in the mill-stream: it be main deep. Pump upon him well, my lads."

"Oh, we will," cried Tim; "uncommonly we will.

' We'll hold his head under the pump with a jerk;
Up and down goes the handle as we pump upon Perk,' "

No. 34

" Just add," said George, " on the back of this paper, a few words."

"Oh yes, yes, anything, but have mercy, gentlemen—spare me, oh, spare me the pumping. I'm of a delicate constitution; it may give me my death of cold. Mercy, mercy. You will catch Scrimp some day, or Pomander, or even the baronet. They are all strong men. For Heaven's sake pump upon them, but spare me. I am weak and delicate. Oh, mercy, good kind gentlemen, mercy."

" Just add," said George, " these words to the paper. 'I hereby agree to accept a pumping upon as a just reward for my rascality to-day.'"

"Oh, you won't ask me to be pumped upon! My dear sir, pray consider my weakness—my nerves."

"Very well. Then Giles and Tim what do you propose to do?"

. "To the mill-stream with him," cried Giles. "I will throw him in myself, and thee all may keep theeselves quiet here. To the mill-stream."

"Oh, no, no, no," shrieked Perk, "I—I will be pumped upon. Don't give me to him you call Giles. He's a madman. Oh, dear! oh, dear! what shall I do? I'll give you money—I'll do anything you please, but don't hurt me, pray don't hurt me. Where—where is the dear young lady? Miss Phœbe. She will beg me off."

"You scoundrel," cried George, "if you dare so much as to mention her name again, I will, indeed, show you no mercy. Will you write what I ask you?"

"Yes—yes—I will not mention her; oh, no, never while I live. You know I can refuse you nothing. You will be my friend. I'll write it."

Mr. Perk wrote the words, and George again put the paper away.

"Take him away, lads," said the miller; "take him away. I be sick of the sight of him. My dear child be saved, and I wish to see the last of him."

"Won't you come and see the jolly pumping, master?" asked Tim.

"Oh, my dear friend Miggles," cried Perk, catching like a drowning man at any straw which promised him the least hope. "How do you do? You know we are friends, my dear Miggles—friends, you know."

"Yes," said Tim; " but I believe Snapallecanup's a dodger. He's done me brown, quite to crackling. I've got the promise of Phœbe, though, and I don't care for him now.

> ' All in a lump
> You'll go under the pump,
>   And my eye! won't there be a good smother;
> You'll spit and you'll splutter,
> Like a duck in a gutter,
>   And wish you were rather more t'other.' "

Giles seized Perk by the collar, and commenced hauling him from the cottage.

" Mercy! mercy!" cried the alarmed clerk; " mercy! Can't you throw a pail of water over me, if it's ever so dirty, or—or kick me? I've been kicked. Oh, mercy! don't hold me under a pump. I was pumped upon once. Oh, dear! oh, dear! Help! help!"

" If thee don't hold thee tongue," said Giles, " I will drag it out of thee mouth."

Notwithstanding his urgent cries and entreaties, Mr. Perk, in his disordered female apparel, was dragged to the pump, which was close to the mill.

Giles held him by the neck, and placed his head exactly under the spout of the pump, while Tim laid hold of the handle.

" Murder! murder!" cried Perk.

" Hurrah!" shouted Tim, and a torrent of water drowned Mr. Perk's vociferations.

When he was throughly drenched from head to foot, Giles let him go, and he tottered from the pump gasping and shivering.

"Now, be gone from this place," said George, "and know that the innocent girl who you and your employers would have brought to ruin and hopeless misery, is not so unprotected as you and they imagined."

Mr. Perk said not another word, but upon hearing Giles ask Tim to fetch a horsewhip, he started off at great speed for the village.

CHAPTER XLIV.

"Giles," said George, "the miller wishes to see us both again in the cottage."

"I will follow thee, George," replied Giles.

George then proceeded back to the cottage, where he found assembled the miller, his dame, and Phœbe.

"Dear Phœbe," said George, "the danger you dreaded is past, and I trust I am now in possession of a document which will prevent a repetition of all such attempts for the future."

"Oh, George," replied Phœbe, "I know not what to fear. I am an orphan, and indebted to my dear friends who you see before you for a kind and happy home, and the truest affection."

"The affection that we have rendered to thee," said the miller, "thee hast, my dear child, more than returned. The blessing of Heaven has been upon my humble home since thee come to it, and I do hope that I shall never live to see that day when thee shall depart from it."

"That day be not a-going to come," said the dame; "for George, if thee do marry our dear Phœbe, as it do seem likely thee may, thee must still live here, for we cannot part with the dear child."

"This place, and all around it," replied George, "is endeared to me by the sweetest of recollections. Here I first found rest after a life of hardship and toil and bitter disappointment. This was my haven of peace. From the moment I beheld the dear old mill, the cottage, and the blooming garden, a feeling of calm enjoyment came across my mind, and I was happier than I had yet been amid the turbulent scenes of the world. Here, too, I first saw my dear Phœbe. Each shady brake, each murmuring rivulet, will remind me of some dear moment passed with her. Oh, best, my kindest friends, believe me I have no thought to stray from these loved, happy, and peaceful haunts. Here I could live with her who will make life one sweet summer's day; here die calmly at its close, and rest in peace."

Giles now entered the room, and Tim Miggles in a few moments after made his appearance.

"My good lads," said the miller, and he now spoke with hesitation and reluctance, "the secret which my good dame and I have cherished so long I be now about to disclose to thee. Thee need not feel jealous, Giles, that George has known partly what I be going to say before thee, for it was for the protection of Phœbe that I told him what I now tell thee, that Phœbe be no child of mine."

Giles started as if a serpent had stung him, and rushing to the miller, he grasped his arm, exclaiming wildly,—

"Not thee child?—not a child of thine? Whose—whose be she then?"

"Be calm," said the miller, "and you shall know all that can be told of Phœbe, who though she not be my own flesh and blood, be still as dear to my heart as any dear child could in the whole world be to its own parent."

"Now, Phœbe," said the dame, "there should be no further conceal-ment. Tell them, my dear child, what thee told us the morning after the storm when thee sought shelter here, and when we determined to call thee by our own name, and to forget that thee were other than a dear child of our own."

"And dear father and mother," said Phœbe, "I might well forget that I was other than your own dear child, for—for never child received greater kindness and affection from its parents than I have from you. I had nothing to give in return but my true heart's love and my prayers, but yet the poor friendless orphan was taken to your hearts, and her life has now passed away for more than five years like one happy dream of peace and joy."

"I do believe thee hast been happy, my child," said the miller, "and if thee had not been, it would not have been our faults. As thee hast been the good and kind daughter, so it be my fervent prayer that thee become the valued and happy wife."

"It shall be my anxious hope," said he, "to render her union with me but as a new tie to bind her to a world which to her shall ever be radiant and beautiful, because the sunshine of her pure heart shall ever gild the winter's gloom."

"Who be she?—who be she?" gasped Giles, evidently in great emotion.

"A princess, to be sure. I knew it—I always knew it," exclaimed Tim Miggles, in a tone of great triumph.

"Phœbe," said the miller, "tell us all now, my girl, what of thee history thee please, that no one can say that we kept anything concerning thee secret."

Phœbe cast a glance at George, and the colour deepened in her cheek as she spoke.

All that were in the cottage listened with the most eager attention for the sound of her voice, and betrayed, by their several attitudes, the deep interest they severally felt in each word that might fall from her lips.

"I am an orphan," said Phœbe, gently. "My father I never saw, and my poor dear mother died when I was very young."

"Dear, dear Phœbe," said George, seeing that her eyes were filled with tears, and that she could not proceed, "our fates in life were strangely similar. I, too, have neither father nor mother, and can truly sympathize with your grief."

"It be easy," said Giles, "to say that thee fates be the same, but we have only thee bare word for that, and love will make a man deny father and mother, all the world, and—and even the hopes he do have of Heaven."

"Giles," said George, mildly, "I forgive your doubts of my veracity, for I know they proceed not from your heart, but from your disappointed affection."

"Now, lads," cried the miller, "don't 'e begin quarrelling, but remember the agreement of this morning. Phœbe, my dear, do thee go on."

"My dear mother's death," continued Phœbe, "was the first event in my young life that made a serious impression upon my memory. The cir-cumstances are, even at this moment, as fresh in my memory as when they first happened. I and a young brother were her only children; and—and scarcely was she dead, when the brutal persons, who had embittered her last moments, forced from the orphan children all the little that she had left behind her, and they were thrown upon the compassion of a heartless world."

"You had a brother, Phœbe? Surely Heaven, has decreed that our fates should so far be nearly allied, for I had one dear sister, who—who, I be-lieve, is now an angel in her native skies."

"We were," continued Phœbe, "consigned to the parish workhouse."

"The workhouse?" cried George.

"Yes," said Phœbe, hanging down her head. "You will blush, perhaps, for your Phœbe, when—when you know——"

"Oh, no, no—go on, go on."

"The cruelty we experienced there drove my poor brother to abscond, and try his fortune on the sea."

"Great Heaven!" cried George.

"With many tears poor George and I parted. He escaped the pursuit of those who would, for some reason, have kept him in the workhouse. I was soon after sent to service. My mistress cruelly drove me from her, and by the humanity of a poor waggoner I was taken to London, where I passed through various scenes. At length, upon the death of a dear friend, I left London again, and went into service not far from here, where I was treated with frightful cruelty. Nature could not bear the harshness I was subjected longer, and I fled."

"Thee did," cried the miller, "and in the midst of such a storm as I never before saw, and hope I may never see again. My dame and I were sitting in this room, by the fire-side, when we thought we heard a wailing cry of deep distress. At first we thought it was the wind, but soon we became convinced that it was a human voice that sounded in the storm."

"It was Heaven that led me to your door," said Phœbe. "That night I slept in peace and happiness, and the morning dawned in joy."

"And—and your father, Phœbe?" said George.

"I've heard my mother say he was a soldier, and died in India."

All eyes were now directed upon George, who stood in the centre of the cottage, gazing upon Phœbe like one possessed.

"What be the matter with thee, George?" cried the miller, but he heeded nothing.

His eyes were fixed intently upon Phœbe. He spoke in a choked, husky voice,—

"Phe—Phe—Phœbe, answer me. Your mother died, and left you with an only brother?"

"She did, George; a dear brother, named as you are—'George.'"

"And—and the workhouse? You said the workhouse, or I dream?"

"We were sent there, for we had no home."

"And he—he, the boy—sought your—his sister's couch before he left—"

"He did; but the ship in which I afterwards learned he sailed was lost. It was called, I recollect well, the——"

"The Flame!" cried George.

"It was," said Phœbe, surprised.

"I had a dear sister," cried George; "her name was Phœbe. I—I left her in the dismal workhouse. I went to sea. My name is——"

"Grainger!—Grainger!" shrieked Phœbe.

"It is—it is—my long lost—my own sister!"

"George—dear George," cried Phœbe. "Are you?—can it be that you are——"

"Your brother, Phœbe. I am he who parted with you on the workhouse stairs, and held you in my arms one moment, while those who would have stayed me were hot in pursuit of the poor fugitive boy."

"Once more," cried Phœbe; "oh, once more in those arms let me rest."

She rushed forward as she spoke; but at the instant Giles rushed between them, and in a voice of thunder, cried,—

"Hold! She be mine. Ha! ha! ha! Mine—mine—she be mine—my wife—my bride—my own Phœbe. Touch her not—she be mine. Ha! ha! ha! The time be come at last, and I do claim my bride."

George sank backwards into a chair with a deep groan, and a deadly paleness came over Phœbe, and she fainted in the arms of the miller, who was just in time to prevent her from falling to the ground.

The greatest confusion and consternation now reigned in the cottage. Giles still stood erect in the middle of the room, with a flush of triumph upon his otherwise habitual pale and haggard face, while Tim Miggles had slunk into a corner, thoroughly bewildered with the scene which had just taken place.

The good dame, with tears streaming from her aged eyes, bustled herself in procuring restoratives for the insensible Phœbe, who still lay in the arms of the astonished miller.

"Dame, dame," he said, "the hand of Providence be in this matter. Here be these two young things brought under our roof in a strange manner, after being separated so many years, and it be the great mercy of God that the discovery be made that they be brother and sister, in time to prevent their everlasting misery."

"Gilbert, Gilbert," cried the dame, sobbing, "I do not know if I be on my head or my heels, for I be quite bewildered like."

"The time be come," still muttered Giles, in a tone of exultation. "She be mine—mine—mine; no one can take her from me. She be promised to me. My own Phœbe, that I have loved so long be mine at last. Ha! ha! I be happy now—I be happy now."

"How, Giles, can you be happy," cried the miller, "when you see the unhappiness that be all around thee? Think thee, what must be the feelings of these two—George and Phœbe."

"She be his sister, and he cannot marry her. She may be his sister, but she be my Phœbe—my own wife—I will have her. I tell you, master, she be mine—mine only, and not all the world shall take her from me."

"Stay, Giles," said George, rising, and speaking very faintly; "and you, my honoured master and dear friend, think not that I am unthankful to kind Heaven for restoring to me her who I had mourned as dead. No, there is still joy in my heart. If I have lost a wife—one who would have been the dear companion of my life—I have gained one who has ever held a sacred place in my heart."

"Thee art a good lad, George," said the miller, with a deep emotion, "and I honour thee feelings much."

"Still—still," said George, gaining animation as he spoke, "there is something whispers to my heart that Phœbe shall even yet become my wife."

"What!" cried the miller, "art thee mad boy? Hast thee lost thee wits? She be thee sister; how can she be thee wife?"

"Ha! ha!" sneered Giles. "She be mine, George, not thine. She never can be thine—mine—my Phœbe—my own bride."

"Hold!" cried George. "Triumph not. Phœbe has not pledged herself to you if I am her brother. I have a right to defend her against solicitations which she may not approve of. She promised her hand to you only conditionally. I marked well the reservation which her words conveyed, although, in the excitement of your feelings, you may have only understood their import according to your own wild wishes."

"She did promise to have me if she did not have you," cried Giles fiercely.

"No," said George; "she said, that if she married, it should be one or other of us, but she cannot be forced to wed at all by such words as those."

Giles glared fiercely at George for a moment, and then cried in a voice of rage and indignation,—

"She did promise to wed you or me."

"Yes, my good lad," said the miller; "but suppose Phœbe choose to remain single?"

"No—no—she cannot—dare not—she is mine—mine only."

"Surely—surely, Giles, thee would be unhappy with her if thee could force her into a marriage with thee contrary to her own inclinations."

"Say what thee will, she be mine, I tell thee both. I do live but for her. No power on the whole earth shall take her from me. She be promised. Ha! ha! ha! George, thee knows she be my own bride."

"The very circumstance," said George, "which deprives me of the dear cherished hope of being the husband of my Phœbe by proclaiming me her brother, and which I call Heaven to witness I do not repine at, gives me a right, as her nearest, and, I believe, only relative, to guard her from all evil. Giles, with her own free consent, which I deny she has yet given, she shall be yours, but not otherwise. I will not have her even importuned beyond a certain point. If she be not my bride, she is my sister, and, believe me, I will do a brother's duty by her."

"Spoken like theeself, George," cried the miller. "Thee own passions have blinded thee, Giles. Thee must be mad to suppose that any one can be forced into a marriage to which they are reluctant; and thee would not, I be sure, wish to wed Phœbe, if thee thought she did not love thee?"

"Let her be mine—let me but call her mine. She—she may hate me, but only let me call her mine—the—the love would come—yes—yes, it would come."

"Tush! tush, boy, these be dreams, ; thee brains be disordered."

Phœbe had now somewhat recovered from her swoon, and was gazing intently in George's face, as if endeavouring to trace in the manly features a resemblance to the fair-haired boy who had wept with her over their dear mother's grave. George cast his eyes towards her, and smiled. She clasped her hands, and springing from her seat, rushed into his arms.

"George, dear George, I know you now. That old well-remembered smile; I always, dear George, loved you for that smile. It ever seemed to bring back pleasant fancies and happy scenes to my heart. I know it well. It was like the reality of some vision of my slumbers. In the sunshine of its beauty I fondly basked, without a thought as to where i had before seen it. I only felt that I was happy."

"Dear, dear Phœbe, this is a happy meeting. Do you remember the little cottage and the garden where, with our dear mother, we passed such happy hours?"

"Oh, yes, George, well do I remember all. Your presence seems to have awakened slumbering memory; and events, which before floated but dimly in my mind, have now started forth, bold and distinct."

Giles looked with bitter and jaundiced eyes upon the brother and sister, as, linked arm in arm, they indulged in the pleasant reflections and retrospections of days gone by. He had been so accustomed to look upon George as his rival in the affections of the fair Phœbe, that even with the fact upon his mind of the near relationship between them, it was wormwood to his spirit to see their affection. He was turning, with a face expressive of the bitterness of his feelings, when he was called back by George.

"Stay, Giles," he cried; "yet another moment, stay. There is something still untold yet concerning this matter, a something which I have always cherished in my inmost heart as a dear hope, and should it be Heaven's mercy to confirm my supposition, I may yet, in the dear sister of my happy childhood, find the wife of my maturer years."

Giles stood aghast, and trembled violently as he stood by the cottage door.

"Dear George," cried Phœbe, "what can you mean? Am I not your own sister?—your little Phœbe, whom you always loved so fondly? Did we not together attend our dear mother's couch of death? Did she not bless us with her dying breath?"

"And what more, Phœbe? You were young at that time; but does nothing yet cling to your memory of what my mother spoke with her last breath?"

"I—I—there was. 'Tis like a confused dream. She did say something, which I have tried in vain to remember. Yes, George, she did; you are right. I cannot recollect, but I feel 'twas something that was worth remembering. What could it be?"

"You were young, Phœbe, and well nigh dead with bitter grief."

"I was—I was; and yet my memory tells me something was said that made a transient impression on my mind. I would to Heaven that I could recollect it."

"I recollect it, Phœbe," continued George. "I was but a boy; nevertheless the words sunk deep into my heart, and they still live freshly in my memory."

"What were they, George?—oh! what were they?—my mother's last words?"

"They were her last, and they were unfinished. Ere she could say all she wished——"

George dashed a tear from his eye, and Phœbe sobbed aloud.

Giles drew his breath hard and thick, and awaited, with great apprehension of he knew not what, the communication he was about to make.

"My mother," continued George, in a voice which betrayed his deep emotion,—"my mother raised herself in the bed, and while with horror I saw the film of death was gathering on her eyes, she said,—'*Do not part the children; they are not both mine, but——*' Here nature failed her, and —and the kindest mother that ever breathed was—was an angel in Heaven."

Phœbe grasped George's arm when he had ceased speaking, and, with the tears streaming down her cheeks at the vivid recollection of the sad scene, she exclaimed,—

"'Tis true—'tis true—these were the words—I recollect them now. They seem at this moment to be ringing in my ears in the voice of my dear mother. George—dear George—my—my—my husband."

"Never! never!" cried Giles, with his face awfully distorted by the agony of his mind; "never. It be not true; it be a lie."

"Beware!" cried George, proudly. "Beware, Giles; you may goad me too far. I have treated you with the greatest forbearance; but there is a limit to human patience. Do not tempt me to do what in my cooler moments I might regret."

"Peace, Giles! peace!" cried the miller. "Thee conduct this day has proved how unworthy thee be to wed anybody but some one as wild as thee-self. With my consent thee never should call the dear child Phœbe thee wife."

"Revenge!—revenge!—damnation!—revenge!" shouted Giles, and he rushed wildly from the cottage.

CHAPTER XLV.

Mr. Perk, leaving a stream of water behind him, fled with the greatest precipitation, towards the village, intending to shelter himself in Mr. Pomander's shop. His appearance was sufficiently grotesque. Without anything on his head, and attired in female garments, which were torn and dishevelled, and saturated with water, and with but one shoe, he arrived at the outskirts of the village. Human beings are like other animals always ready to hunt the hunted, and oppress the oppressed. Raise but the hue

and cry that some one, no matter who, or for what, is not in a state to offer resistance, and the whole human pack is at once at the unfortunate's heels, ready and willing to run him to death.

So was it with the unfortunate, though criminal, Perk. His appearance in the outskirts of the village of Haredale was hailed by a shout of anticipated enjoyment by all the idle and worthless inhabitants of the little hamlet.

Mr. Pomander's shop was at the further extremity of the village, and the unhappy Perk had to run the gauntlet through the whole length of it before he could reach the haven of shelter.

"Hoora! hoora!" shouted the bipeds. "Bow-wow," barked the dogs. But we may excuse the latter, as they did not possess the immortal and godlike power of reason.

It was soon seen that Mr. Perk was dripping with water, and so entangled in his female apparel, that he could not make any effectual resistance, and "the sovereign people," who exhibit much the same general characteristics in a quiet country village as they do in London, commenced immediately saluting him with showers of mud, dead cats, and other missiles.

One lad, in the extasy of his enjoyment, danced an extemporaneous dance, which would have made his fortune at a minor theatre, such as Drury-lane, when under the dominion of foreign fiddlers and buffons. The young gentleman, however, reckoned too much on the fallen greatness of his victim, for Mr. Perk, goaded to desperation by an indifferent egg hitting him exactly with a swash in the left eye, darted suddenly forward, and seizing the facetious youth, stopped his performance in a twinkling, and popping his head into a peculiar position, called chancery, on account of the uncommon difficulty that any one so situated always experiences in extri-

No. 35

cating it again, he rained such a shower of blows upon his "human face divine," that the crowd were struck with involuntary respect; and when the young gentleman was released, by way of proving to him how unstable was human greatness, they transferred their future favour to him, and pelted and hooted him well. He was a new victim, and human nature, God bless its beauty, is fond of variety

Exhausted, sick, and covered with mud and filth, Mr. Perk reeled into Mr. Pomander's shop, to the intense surprise of that gentleman and Mr. Scrimp, who were both waiting eagerly with some intelligence confirmatory of the success of the brilliant scheme which had been conceived in so happy a moment by Perk for carrying off, with an appearance of legality, the Miller's fair Maid.

"Why, Perk—the devil!" cried Mr. Scrimp.

"Done, by G—d!" shouted Pomander.

"Curse you both," said Perk. "Give me something to drink. I'm parched."

"Parched!" said Scrimp. "You seem anything but dry, my dear Perk. Why, in the name of everything uncomfortable came you in this abominable mess?"

"Drink, I tell you, drink. Some drink," cried Perk.

"Would you like a black draught?" said Mr. Pomander, calmly.

"Damn you!" said Perk, seizing a great blue bottle, and hurling it at the head of the sneering doctor, who just ducked in time to allow it to pass over him, and create unheard-of havoc among a legion of small phials.

"The deuce!" exclaimed Pomander, "what do you mean? Are you mad?"

"Oh," said Perk, greatly soothed by the destruction he saw he had perpetrated, "oh, you are serious now, are you. Don't joke another time with a man that's just been pumped upon and pelted with mud and unwholesome eggs, that's all. Roll that up in a cigar and smoke it, old fellow."

"Then you have entirely failed," said Scrimp, "and been found out into the bargain?"

"Exactly," replied Perk, with an assumption of awful calmness. "Entirely failed, and found out into the bargain; pumped upon, laughed at, abused, pelted, and made the bearer of a kind message to you, Pomander, and Sir Herbert, that the pump is always ready, on the very shortest possible notice, to accommodate any one of you."

"Humph!" said Scrimp; "upon my word this is rather an unpleasant announcement. What the devil is to be done?"

"There's nothing to be done," replied Perk, "but to burn down the cottage and the mill, and stand at the doors to prevent any one from getting out."

"That's an extreme measure," said Mr. Pomander. "I shall pay myself for the broken bottles out of the money in my hands on account of this business."

"And pray how am I to be paid?" asked Perk. "Curse your broken bottles, look at me—look at me, I say, my best bombazine dress ruined for ever."

Neither Scrimp nor Pomander could forbear laughing, as Mr. Perk turned himself round to fully exhibit his woful plight.

"Now," said Scrimp, "in sober seriousness, tell us how you came to be so desperately taken in?"

"Sober seriousness," cried Perk; "you may well say sober seriousness. I have taken in water enough to have lasted a teetotal society for a month."

"Come, tell us what passed, and we will see if we cannot hit upon some scheme to procure some revenge for you, at the same time that we further the general object."

Mr. Perk, thus urged, related what had occurred at the cottage, with the exception of the written confession, which he could not bring himself to mention, for he well knew that it was an entire knock-up to the whole scheme, and would have brought down upon his head the bitterest reproaches from companions and coadjutors in crime.

"This is most unfortunate," said Mr. Scrimp; "but, after all, we can but revert to the original plan of using a little gentle violence."

"You are quite sure," said Mr. Pomander, who had noticed some little hesitation in Perk's manner during his narration, "that you made no mention of our names?"

"Oh, yes," replied Perk, undauntedly, "quite sure—not the least; but permit me to say one thing. I—I am tired of the business, and would rather not have anything more to do with it."

"What!" said Scrimp, "and forego your hopes of revenge on those who have used you so very scurvily?"

"Why, yes," said Perk, faintly, "I—I am sick of it. I begin to think that these affairs with women are quite out of my line."

"As you please, of course," remarked Mr. Pomander; "but you will assist us with your advice, I suppose?"

"Why, yes; but upon my soul, my dear fellows, I'd advise you both to give it up; leave Sir Herbert Foster and his bully, Freegrove, to do the business between them. I tell you, my opinion is now that there is more danger in it than you suppose."

Mr. Scrimp looked rather uneasy as Perk spoke, and then rising, he said :—

"I will go at once to Haredale Park, and try to talk Sir Herbert out of his rage at this disappointment. You had better change your dress, Perk."

"Your proposition to work on the jealousy of one of the clodpoles who aspire to the girl," said Pomander, addressing Scrimp, "seems to be now the only chance."

"I shall advise that course," replied Scrimp, "in preference to all others. Did the one they call Giles, Perk, assist in—in—"

"In the pumping, you mean," said Perk; "say it out. Yes, he did, d—him. He held me while that idiot (Miggles, I think, is his name) worked the handle as if the parish was on fire, and it depended upon his personal exertions to pump up water enough to put it out."

"He may be made useful likewise," said Scrimp.

Sir Herbert Foster had been waiting in anxious expectation for an announcement of the success of the plans for gaining peaceable possession of Phœbe.

Mr. Scrimp had great confidence in the talents of Perk; and he had, on his last visit, flattered Freegrove with great hopes of success, who, in his turn, had communicated to Sir Herbert the sanguine hopes of the whole party.

The baronet was, as usual, in a reclining attitude when Mr. Scrimp was announced, for he held it to be excessively plebeian to sit upright, and, withal, very troublesome to a man of his wealth and rank.

With an appearance of something like vitality and energy, Sir Herbert Foster started from his couch when Mr. Scrimp's name was uttered in dulcet accents by the obsequious Cury. He, however, as if ashamed of his momentary excitement, immediately sunk back again, and resumed his listless attitude.

"Ah! ah!—Cury."

" Sir Herbert."

" Ah! ah! — bring me some — ah! ah! — eau de millefleurs, and—ah! ah!—show the—the legal individual in—ah!—and retire."

Mr. Scrimp entered the room with a cast of countenance expressive of deep veneration, mingled with regret. Sir Herbert Foster was no fool, although he affected to be one, and he saw in a moment that the scheme had been unsuccessful.

" My dear Sir Herbert," simpered Mr. Scrimp, " I deeply regret — most deeply———"

" You have failed," said the baronet, biting his lip with intense vexation.

" Why, if you please, Sir Herbert, in a manner of speaking, a slight accident has occurred which has—a—a—just for the present, my dear sir———"

" Cease this jargon; you have not got the girl? By Heavens! each new difficulty that presents itself in the prosecution of this matter but inflames my passion. I tell you, Scrimp, I will have her—aye, if it cost me my life. What do you stare at, you shallow-witted fool? Where are all your promises and prognostications of success? Is it possible that you, the most politic and unfathomable rascal in the neighbourhood, can suffer yourself to be outdone by a parcel of clowns?"

" Excuse me, my dear Sir Herbert," replied Scrimp; " it is because they are a parcel of clowns that we have failed in this matter. The scheme was a little too good, too refined, Sir Herbert. Vulgar nature must be presented with vulgar motives, or the result will be disappointment."

" Oh, you have found out that point of moral philosophy, have you?" sneered Sir Herbert. " It is strange so admirable a piece of ethics never struck you before, my most polite and deep-thinking Scrimp."

" If you please, Sir Herbert," continued Scrimp, in a tone of vexation, " I think something very much to [the furtherance—of — your kind intentions with respect to the Miller's Maid may be accomplished through the medium of the disappointed lover — Giles is his name. He, Sir Herbert, who———"

" Who attacked me," cried the baronet. " Why don't you speak out, you d—, cringing piece of humanity. He shall hang for it yet."

" The same, Sir Herbert. I was about to say so, when you did me the honour to interrupt me. He who rolled you down the side of Foyle's Hollow, covered you with clay and gravel, and scratched your face, my dear Sir Herbert; that is the man I mean. Oh, dear me, I will speak out whenever you please, Sir Herbert."

" Sir Herbert Foster writhed under the circumstantial account of his conflict with Giles, but he merely said, gloomily,—

" Go on."

" Well, then, Sir Herbert, this fellow. This Giles, smarting as he is under all the feeling of disappointment and jealousy, for the fair Phœbe does not favour his suit, is ready to become a tool in the hands of any person who may wish to fashion a few events at the mill to his own use."

" Make what use of the peasant you will, Scrimp; I care not, so that my purpose be soon accomplished. I will not be baulked in this matter. By force or fraud—by foul means or by fair—I tell you, if I live another week I will have that shrinking piece of rustic modesty on her knees before me. I am determined, Scrimp, no difficulties shall deter me; nay, they shall rather spur me forward. I live now but for the accomplishment of this matter, and by Heaven and hell it shall be accomplished, aye, even if the bloody hand of my order should in its prosecution acquire a deeper dye. I swear it, I will have her. Burn, destroy, slay, do what you will, but give me possession of the girl I saw in the damnable place you call somebody's Hollow, quickly, and I will enrich you."

"Oh, dear me, yes," said Mr. Scrimp, casting an eye to the door, for the unwonted vehemence of Sir Herbert rather terrified him. "Oh, certainly, certainly—hem!—most reasonable."

"Am I," continued the incensed Sir Herbert, "the descendant of a long line of illustrious ancestors, am I to be bearded by a gang of hinds?"

"Oh, dear, no, Sir Herbert. Bless me, no."

"I, the representative of a family celebrated in the annals of the country?"

"Oh, it's too bad, indeed, Sir Herbert."

"With an ancient title, not a mushroom dignity."

"Oh, monstrous! The ingratitude of the lower orders is shocking, my dear sir——"

"I, the possessor of unbounded wealth, to be defied by—by——"

"Low-minded wretches."

"Low-minded wretches, and actually threatened. Where are the privileges of my high rank? Where the all-pervading influence of station?"

"Dear me, yes, very good; very true, indeed."

"There was a time when the hot blood would have boiled through the veins of a Foster at one tithe of such—such——"

"Such rural impertinence."

"Such rural impertinence. It's enough to make a saint swear."

"It is, indeed, Sir Herbert. A moral revolution is very much wanted. The good old times are past and gone when a nobleman had but to say I will it, and the thing was done. Oh, dear me, quite gone."

"By G—, it appears so."

"It's all owing, Sir Herbert, to reform bills and marches of intellect, and so on."

"D— this intellect. What right have the lower classes to intellect, I should like to know?"

"None—oh, dear, none in the least, Sir Herbert."

"An infernal set of vile——"

"Thick-headed——"

"Puddle-blooded——"

"D——d sneaking——"

"Low-minded wretches——"

"Who set up for morality, oh dear, and interrupt a gentleman's private pleasures, and talk of pumping on a baronet."

"What!"

"Oh, dear, Sir Herbert, I didn't mean to tell you, but they sent word by Perk, my clerk, you know—the young fellow who——"

"D— him. What did they say?"

"Why, they said, they should like to pump upon you, Sir Herbert."

"Pump upon me? Ha! ha! ha! Very good, very good.'

"Ha! ha! Oh dear, yes. Ha! ha! Good—good."

"D— you, if I see so much as another smile upon your face, you infernal scoundrel, I will blow your brains out."

"Smile?—I smile—oh, no—oh, dear, no. I'm—I'm burning with indignation. Pump on a baronet! Oh——"

"Peace, miscreant! peace. Another word, and I'll do one good deed in my life, by ridding society of you."

"You are quite—quite, as one may say, facetious, Sir Herbert."

"Now, hear me, Scrimp. Once for all I tell you, that I am determined upon this affair. Follow what course you like. Do whatever the occasion calls for, I will bear you harmless, and carry you safely through. I must and will have the girl at the villa immediately. Carry her off at once. Surely that may be done. You are cunning enough, and that rascal, Freegrove, is strong enough.   Settle the matter somehow among you.   I hate plotting and manœuvring.   There's nothing like straightforward—a—ah !——"

"Abduction," mildly suggested Mr. Scrimp.

"Well, an abduction, if you please.   Bring her to me, that's all.   Now, begone."

"But Sir Herbert, there are a few trifling difficulties."

"Cury !"

"Sir Herbert," said the valet, popping his head into the room so suddenly as to give rise to a suspicion on the part of the attorney that he must have been airing his ear at the key-hole.

"Shew Mr. Scrimp out."

"But, Sir Herbert, just allow me to say——"

"Good day,"

Mr. Scrimp found it was useless to attempt to prolong the conversation, and he backed out of the room with a profusion of bows, while Sir Herbert Foster lay upon his back on an ottoman, gazing, apparently intently, on the ceiling.

"D— it all," muttered Scrimp, "there's no resource.   She must be carried off, and that's a matter that don't exactly suit me.   I am in rather a ticklish situation with respect to one or two little matters already, and some busybody some of these days may call the attention of the Lord Chancellor to so humble an individual as Mr. Scrimp, attorney-at-law, and that disagreeable functionary may take a rather awkward view of the matter, and strike me off the rolls.   Humph! an abduction.   It's getting serious, upon my word.   I must manage it somehow so as to be not personally concerned.   Scrimp, Scrimp, be wary."

CHAPTER XLVI.

The evening of the day upon which so many important events had occurred at the cottage of the miller, saw a happy little party assembled in the humble abode.

George and Phœbe sat side by side, and opposite to them were the honest miller and his dame.   A cheerful fire blazed and crackled in the grate, and never could four human beings be found who regarded each other with kindlier emotions than did those who there sat in sweet discourse in that rural home.

The recollection, in moments of peace and happiness, of bygone troubles, provided there be no character about them materially to effect the mind, is always delightful, and for several hours had Phœbe and George indulged in their reminiscences of the past, while the happy miller and his dame listened with eager and delighted attention to everything which in any way concerned those who they looked upon as their own children.

"Dear Phœbe," said George, "you remember the beadle ?"

"Oh, yes," said Phœbe ; "Bung.   He gave me a sad fright when I was in London, as I have before narrated to you.   How singularly does Providence work out its own purposes.   That which I then thought a great misfortune, namely, my being forced to leave the family of the Spangles, turned out to be the means of introducing me to much happiness."

"Thee hast not, George, told us one thing," said the miller, "and that be, why thee did change thee name from thee proper one of Grainger to Andrews."

"I will tell you," replied George.   "It was done upon a most slight motive, and then continued through habit. When I went on board the 'Flame,' I gave my proper name of Grainger to the mate and captain; but after the fracas with Mr. Bung on the quay, the captain came up to me, and said, kindly,—

"'My lad, you see there has been some contention on your account which may give us some trouble when we come to this port again; but you are now so young, that a twelvemonth at sea will alter you so much that no one could possibly know you. Take my advice, and call yourself by a new name.'

"I thanked the captain, and asked him to call me what he pleased.

"'Well, then,' said he, 'be George Andrews instead of George Grainger.'

"I got so used in a little time to the name of Andrews, that I should hardly have answered to my proper one; and when you, my dear sir, asked me my name in the market place, I answered, without the slightest thought or wish to deceive you, 'George Andrews,' and afterwards I did not like to risk your friendship by contradicting myself, which might, probably, have induced you to believe that I intended intentionally to deceive you with respect to who I was."

"And that ship, dear George, was lost," said Phœbe.

"It was," replied George; "but I had left it before that melancholy event. Our captain died at a port in the West Indies, and the ship was then committed to the command of a man who was as choleric and tyrannical as the former one was mild and gentlemanly. I left the vessel, and drew what money I had to take, which amounted to fifty pounds, in consequence of our capturing a vessel engaged in the illegal and detestable slave trade. That fifty pounds I sent to Bungleum, Phœbe, with directions that it should be devoted to your use."

"Dear George," said Phœbe, "you thought of your poor Phœbe?"

"I should not have deserved any good in life if I had ceased to think of you," replied George.

"But tell us—oh, tell us, George—how you came to be so badly situated when dear father found you in the market place, and brought you here?"

"When I left the 'Flame,'" said George, "I shipped myself in a vessel that was proceeding to China. From there I went to New Zealand; and it was not until I had traversed almost every ocean, and touched at every port of consequence, that I took a berth in a vessel bound for England, called the 'Emerald.' Oh! with what rapture, after a tedious voyage—a voyage of eight weary months—I at last saw the white cliffs of Old England once again. I had ever sighed for home, and the picture of happiness we had indulged in when the world to us was as an untrodden canty of a dear cottage, and a smiling garden was ever present to my imagination. My heart bounded with delight as I gazed upon the dim outline of that shore, on which was, I fondly imagined, everything that could make life happy. I could not turn my eyes from the land. Let me be doing what I would, I continued to look in that direction. Oh! no one but he who has been long—long a stranger to his country—the land of his birth and childhood, can imagine the sensations of the wanderer when in the distant horizon he first catches a glimpse of the dear place which in many dreary days and long nights he has sighed once more to have the deep pleasure of beholding. I have met in different climes those who have voluntarily left their native land, their own sea-girt isle, and I have ever found, that let their position in life be what it might, they had left their hearts behind them."

"Thee speak true, my lad," cried the miller, "and I do well remember a poor lad, who did leave Haredale when I was a boy—his name was Angus —and he did return after many years. It was a Sunday when he did come back, and he walked into the church, and no one knew him. He was put into a seat, and the people round about did hear him sobbing, and when the service was over they did find that he was dead. He had come many hundred miles to die in his dear native place."

" I can well believe such things may happen," continued George.

" But, dear George," said Phœbe, " you were wrecked, were you not? Tell us how so cruel a misfortune overtook the brave ship when so near home."

" I will, Phœbe. We had been, as I told you, many months at sea, and when we neared the shore, the crew were almost mad with joy. That ship had been to many places before I gained it; and those who had left England with her had seen but strange lands, and heard but strange tongues, for five weary years. Imagine, then, their delight, their delirium of joy, as the white cliffs of Britain came in sight. I saw the captain; he was a hard and weather-beaten sailor. I had seen him amid tempests, which might well appal the stoutest heart. I had seen him in dangers which made the hardiest tremble, but he flinched not his eagle eye, nor quailed for one moment. But now—now, when the man who was aloft sung out in a clear voice, ' Land,' and he knew it was his own dear native land, I saw him stretch forth his hand, and the tears fell from his eyes like rain. Then arose the joyous shout from every mouth of ' Land! land! Old England on our lee.' He tried to speak, but could not; and till the shades of evening deepened on the sea, and the line of white in the far horizon could no longer be observed, he stood there on the same spot, with the tears of joy, hope, and expectation, coursing each other down his furrowed cheek."

" Go on, dear George ; go on," said Phœbe.

" Alas ! Phœbe, he never set his foot upon that shore that he had wished for so long. Another sunset, and he was sleeping calmly beneath the waves."

Phœbe wept, and grasped the hand of George, as she mentally breathed a prayer of deep thanksgiving to Heaven that he was spared to her.

" And the ship, George, was lost, my lad ?" said the miller.

" Poor souls !" ejaculated the dame.

" It was," continued George, " of one hundred and twenty human beings, in the pride of manly health and strength, with hope fluttering at their hearts—the dear hope of seeing again those who were dear to them— fathers, mothers, sisters, of all that number, of as gallant a crew as ever trod a vessel, there escaped but one !"

" And that one, dear, dear George—"

" That one, my Phœbe, by the judgment of Heaven, was myself."

" It was God's will," said the miller; " but we may give a tear to the brave men who were lost, while we do thank Heaven that he who was dear to us was saved."

" How was it George ?" asked Phœbe ; " oh ! tell us how it happened."

" I will, Phœbe. The whole crew were so elated at the prospect of getting soon to shore, that they begged the captain to make for the first port, and that was one about fifty miles southward of Bungleum. The wind was fair, the ship went gallantly on ; no clouds of danger seemed to lower in the horizon of our joy ; and now the night set in, and the mate suggested to the captain to lie by till morning, as we were not a dozen miles from the shore. The sight of his native land, however, seemed to have deprived him of his reason, and his only answer was, ' Oh, all's safe; creep in—creep in shore.'

" ' There are shoals and breakers for miles along the coast,' said the mate.

"'Creep in, creep in shore,' answered the captain; 'it's a light night. They may see us, and send out a pilot when the moon rises.'

"All was mirth and jollity on board the vessel that night, and no one thought of retiring to rest; to-morrow would see them on shore. The old ship rung again with shouts of laughter, and the song and the jest flew merrily round."

"Oh, horrible! horrible!" said Phœbe, "and they so near death."

"It is horrible to think of, Phœbe. One hour more, and they had ceased to breathe. There never was so total a wreck as the loss of the 'Emerald.'"

"Go on, George, oh, go on."

"Slowly onwards drifted the fated ship. Nearer and nearer she approached the shore which had been so longed for, but which was to be seen at last but for so brief a period, and never trodden by the inhabitants of that ship. The mate took me to the side; he was an old man, and his hand trembled as he laid it upon my arm :—

"'Andrews,' he said, 'do you see anything?'

"I looked shorewards, and there indeed, I saw, not half a mile ahead, amid the dim obscurity of the night, a long ridge of white foam. 'Breakers ahead!' I shouted, and so loudly that my voice drowned the sounds of mirth from below.

"'Put her about!' cried the mate.

"The captain sprung to my side, and looked anxiously towards the shore; then he spoke, and my impression at the time was, that he was insane. I still think so. His brain was evidently affected.

"'Land! land!' he said; 'let her creep in shore. Old England's on our lee. Hurrah! lads.'

"'Let go everything,' cried the mate.

No. 36

" ' Aye, aye, sir,' cried the seamen, who had crowded upon deck.

" We were not carrying much sail, and were making but little way. The canvass was cast loose, and flapped idly against the cordage. Slowly the ship obeyed the helm, and I thought we should clear the danger.

" ' Hurrah !' shouted the crew.

" Hardly, however, had the cheer of exultation passed their lips when the ship struck, once, twice, thrice ; and had I not held firmly by a rope, I should have been dashed to the deck, as many were. The captain leaped upon the poop, and while his thin white hair was tossed by the breeze which blew in shore, he waved his hand, and cried,—

" ' Land ! land !—Old England's on our lee.'

" I saw no more of him ; the ship was settling fast. A shriek arose, which even now, in the silence of the night, often rings in my ears, such an impression did it make upon my memory, and in another moment the devoted vessel heeled over on her beam ends. Then arose a wild cry for the boats, mingled with shrieks, prayers, and oaths. Short was the scene of confusion. The ship rapidly filled, and within ten minutes of the moment when she first struck, with a heavy plunge, like a leaden weight, she went to the bottom."

" And you—you, George ?" said Phœbe.

" I was so bewildered that I hardly know what I did. I felt myself sucked under the water by the ship, and I thought, in my fear and agony, that I seemed to go down, down, down miles and miles."

" Oh, that must have been most dreadful."

" It was, indeed ; I must have lost consciousness, for the next thing that I can recollect was, finding myself on the surface of the water. I swam immediately in the direction in which I happened to find myself, and striking against something, I found myself close to an empty cask. This I seized instantly, and it saved my life. The sea was calm, and a dead stillness reigned around. Most of the crew that had sunk with the vessel had been, doubtless, entangled among the rigging ; others had been stunned by the heeling over of the vessel ; but I saw but one besides myself at the surface, and before I could approach him, with a wild cry, he sank to rise no more. It was the captain, I knew his voice ; and if I had not recognized him by that, the cry would have told me who it was.

" ' Land ! land !' he shrieked, and the bubbling waters drowned his voice."

" Oh, George, George," said Phœbe, " how dreadful to think that such a fearful scene was enacting, and you in such peril, while I lay calmly sleeping."

" It be, indeed, a fearsome story," said the miller. " Poor fellow, it be a hard case, after so many dangers on the far-off seas, to come so near home, and then to perish."

" Oh," cried the dame, " no doubt there be many an aching heart that will hear the story of the loss of that ship."

" Well, dear George," said Phœbe, " what did you then do ? How did you reach the shore which you alone were permitted to tread ?"

" I felt so stunned and bewildered," continued George, " by what had happened, that, still holding by the cask, I swam with one hand for some time, without knowing in what direction I was going. After a time I heard a voice hailing, and as well as I could see for the water, which kept dashing over me, I looked in the direction from whence it came, and thought I saw a boat.

" ' Ahoy ! ahoy !' cried a rough voice.

" ' Boat, ahoy !' I shouted as loudly as I could. My strength was nearly exhausted, and the barrel slipped from my grasp. I recollected nothing more till I found myself in a small boat, and a weather-beaten fisherman trying to pour some brandy down my throat. I quickly recovered, and the man was perfectly panic-stricken when I informed him of the catastrophe of the loss of the 'Emerald.' In an hour more I was on shore, but I had, of course, lost everything that I possessed in the world. My savings of years went down in that fated ship, and I was a wanderer in my native land, without means of procuring a meal's victuals, or knowing where to lie down for the night."

"But you were saved, dear George," said Phœbe. "You were saved from the fate which overcame the crew of the lost ship."

"I was, Phœbe, and that was all I could say. I was, it is true, in my native country; but my prospects, you must confess, were none of the brightest."

"The prospects, George," said the honest miller, "of an honest man be never entirely without something that be pleasing."

"I determined," continued George, "to make my way to Bungleum to inquire concerning you, dear Phœbe; and a long weary march I had of it before I arrived within sight of the odious workhouse. I thought by applying there first I should learn where you had gone to, and so be enabled to trace you. Of course, I did not expect to find you an inmate of that place, and I hoped that the money I had sent had been the means under Heaven of bettering your condition."

"Alas! George, I never heard of your kindness to me."

"I know it Phœbe: but still I do not regret sending it; for the thought that I had done you a service beguiled many hours of tediousness and suffering."

"They be great thieves at that workhouse," said the miller; "and I do not doubt that they did keep the money, George."

"It is more than probable," replied George.

"Go on with the story through, and don't 'e mind about the money."

"When I arrived at the door of the workhouse, my heart throbbed with emotion; for I fondly hoped that I should procure sufficient information to trace your place of abode, dear Phœbe. The door was opened by a man whom I did not recollect; but I saw one crossing the yard who I knew well, although he had grown immensely fat."

"Bung the beadle, you mean," said Phœbe.

"Yes," replied George, "it was Bung himself; and how I smiled to myself as I recollected what an important person we used to think him in our young days, and how innoxious he now was. I immediately hailed him, and asked him what had become of Phœbe Grainger, who had been an inmate of that workhouse. He recollected the name at once, and, in his peculiar jargon, said 'that he was wery unkimmon sorry, all of a blessed heap, for to say as that ere female orphan had assaulted a wery great number of respectable people and then absconded.'

"In vain I tried to procure some further information from him concerning you, and then I asked him after myself, when he replied,—

"'Why, that ere unkimmon boy orphan laid wiolent hands on a ship; and, arter getting me wolloped by an immense crowd, off he went, and we never no more heard on him.'

"'What,' said I, 'you old sinner, 'didn't he send some money to his sister? He told me in the West Indies that he sent her fifty pounds.'

"'Eh?' said Mr. Bung,—'fifty pounds! Upon my wery unkimmon word I don't recollect. Them ere orphans was both very wicious.'

"I did not make myself known to him, but with a heavy heart left the place; and as I had no further business at Bungleum, I took my way back to the port close to which I had been wrecked. There, by the intervention of Providence, I arrived on the very day that you, sir, my best of friends—the kind protector of my Phœbe — happened to be there. You know the rest. Your generous kindness rescued me from misery and want, and made me what I am."

"Don't 'e say anything more about that George," cried the miller. "I be none the poorer for trying to be kind to thee and Phœbe, and I be much the happier."

"Dear George," said Phœbe, "let us think now that our adventures and our sorrows are one. We will live by our own labour in calm retirement, and the vision,—the sweet airy fabric of our early years respecting the cottage and its clustering roses,—may yet be realised in all its loveliness and peace."

"Alas, Phœbe !" replied George ; "you forget the mystery which still hangs over us, you forget that still we know not how to feel towards each other. I put great faith in our dear mother's last words, and believe from my heart, that could we penetrate the mystery in which those words are shrouded, that I might still think of you as the dear reward of all my toils and dangers, and call you by the sacred name of wife."

"Think not of it, dear George," replied Phœbe. "As a dear brother and sister let us be happy and content with the blessings that kind Heaven has bestowed upon us."

"No, my child," said the miller, seriously, and shaking his head ; "thee will neither of thee ever be happy while this mystery do hang over thee. Thee will both be oppressed with many hopes and many fears, and thee days will be embittered by the uncertainty of thee feeling towards each other. I and my good dame will consult about what thee had best do, and what advice we can offer thee we will freely give thee, with a hope that it may make thee happier."

"Whatever that advice be, my dear friends," said George, " I here pledge myself to follow it ; for in my heart I feel that it will be for the best."

"And I too," said Phœbe. "We will both, dear father and mother, be guided by you, and then I am sure we shall do right and be happy."

"Heaven may give us all good counsel," said the miller ; "and if we do what we believe to be right in its eyes, the whole world cannot prevent us from being as happy as the day be long."

CHAPTER LXVII.

WHILE these matters were being transacted at the cottage of the miller, there was a grand cabinet council held at Mr. Scrimp's, to decide upon the next step to be pursued in the accomplishment of Sir Herbert Foster's unholy and vicious wishes.

There were present Mr. Scrimp, as a sort of president of the council, and Mr. Pomander, and Ralph Freegrove, and Perk.

"I tell you what it is, gentlemen," said Scrimp, "Sir Herbert seems quite determined upon this business ; and, having settled with ourselves that we will by some means or another manage it for him, we have only to consider some safe way of proceeding as regards ourselves ; for I can inform you that the consequences of the whole affair may be anything but pleasant or soothing to our various feelings."

"I could say something, governor, upon that head," said Perk. "My feelings, I can assure you, were not much soothed this morning when under that infernal machine called a pump ; and I swear eternal enmity against a great chuckle-headed fellow who shied an egg whack in my eye as I came home. D— him, I hadn't done anything to him !"

"The dear people," said Mr. Pomander, "saw you were game."

"Well, gentleman, we must pocket for a little while our private wrongs," said Mr. Scrimp; "they will keep, you know."

"That's all very well," muttered Perk; "but they happen to be all in my pocket."

"No, hang the whole lot of them!" exclaimed Freegrove; "I will have revenge somehow or another, and you and I, Perk, can work it out together."

"I propose," said Scrimp, "that you, Freegrove, that you get hold of this Giles—this discontented, rejected swain,—and try what you can make of him."

"Thank you," growled Freegrove; "you know I can't go near the mill."

"Nor I," said Perk.

"Nor I," said Scrimp.

"Really, gentlemen," said Mr. Pomander, "unless some of them were ill, I really don't know how, with any decent or good face, I could go to the infernal mill."

"Oh, your own face will do," said Perk, "instead of one or either of the sorts you mention."

"Thank you, Perk," said Mr. Pomander; "I will set that down to the pumpkin."

"You'd better set it down among the broken bottles."

"Now, really, gentlemen," said Scrimp, "we waste time. I think, my dear Pomander, that with address—manner—and—and ——"

"Brass," suggested Perk.

"And easy assurance," continued Mr. Scrimp, "you could manage better than any of us to see how the land lies."

"Perhaps," said Pomander, with a grin, "they might ask me, as they have done Perk, to see how the water lies—eh?"

"Done again," said Perk. "Go it, doctor. I've got the shivers, and you are too many for me to-night. Go on—joke away—make a handle of me, do."

"A pump-handle, do you mean?"

"Bravo!—bravissimo!—encore!"

"No, Perk, I've done for the present; and what's more, I'll go to the mill in the morning and try my luck. You are quite sure, all of you, that my name has not been mentioned in this little affair?"

Mr. Perk winced a little as he thought of the "confession," which perfectly haunted him.

"Not to my knowledge," said Scrimp. "All I want you to do is, to make an appointment, if possible, with this Giles, and then I will see him."

"Don't let it be in Foyle's Hollow, then, I advise you," said Perk; "and I rather think that I could manage the clod-pole as well as any one. I will see him, if you like."

Mr. Perk was induced to make this handsome offer from a dread that the "confession" might be mentioned by Giles to Scrimp or Pomander.

"Well, then, you can manage it this way," said Scrimp; "you can tell him that the pumping has made a great impression on your mind."

"And d— me if it hasn't too!"

"Then you can go on to say that it is George Andrews you want to be revenged upon, and you can propose to him to run away with the girl himself, in which you will kindly assist him."

"Oh, dear, yes, in a most engaging manner."

"Just for the sake of being revenged upon George, you know."

"Oh, certainly; and if he nibbles and decoys the girl from home, which I dare say he could do if he liked, for I'll warrant the little baggage looks upon him as the second string to her bow ——"

"Why, then, Perk, you know we can have him arrested, or some such thing."

"Or Pomander can give him a blue pill in some bread and milk."

"Or a pumping," said Pomander.

"Anything you please, gentlemen," continued Scrimp, "provided you get him out of the way, and keep me harmless, for I risk more than any of you."

"And you'll take good care," muttered Perk, "to gain more than any of us, or I don't know you, old governor."

"You know, Perk," said Scrimp, "as you are a single man, and an admirer of the fair sex, you might strike up a match with the Maid of the Mill eventually."

"Oh, thank you, governor, thank you. Your kindness brings tears into my eyes. You are quite paternal, I declare."

"There's no doubt when Sir Herbert is tired of the damsel, that some one might make a good thing of taking her off his hands," said Pomander.

"Oh, gentlemen, you overpower me," cried Perk. "I happen to be not connubial, I assure you; thank you both all the same. Now I should have thought you, Pomander, might have thought of such a thing for yourself. As a medical man, you know, old Camomile Flowers, you want a wife. Now, for me, who have no particular use for one, being merely a ——"

"Rogue," said Pomander.

"Exactly," continued Perk. "I leave the matter to one who caps me in all things, roguery included."

"Dear me, gentlemen," said Scrimp, "allow me to remark that the censorious world is always ready enough to call people rogues without their being at the trouble of bestowing that unenviable title upon themselves."

"A truce—a truce, Pomander," cried Perk.

"Agreed," said Pomander." "It's only sparring for practice, Scrimp. I bear no malice; and to convince you of my faith in you, I tell you candidly, that I intend to be mine host of the Golden Lion, if I can persuade Mrs. Staples to that effect."

"Bravo!" cried Perk; "I wish you success. You'll get fat, Pomander."

"I live in hope, Perk."

"Now, gentlemen," said Scrimp, "you'll do me the honour of supping with me."

"Ha!" cried Freegrove; "let's have something to eat. Hang your wit, all of you; there's no making head or tail of it. Let's be sensible, and eat and drink."

"You're right, Freegrove," said Perk. "there are only six things worth attention in the world."

"And what may they be Mr. Perk?"

"Eating and drinking—eating and drinking— eating and drinking."

"D— it all," said Freegrove, "that's uncommon true. I honour you, Perk, I do."

"Thank you; but the next time you honour me, don't knock all the breath out of my body by such a blow on the back."

"It was suiting the action to the word," said Scrimp.

"As if one should say 'pump,' and then work the handle," muttered Pomander.

"Or 'poison,' and run to Pomander," cried Perk.

"There you go," exclaimed Freegrove; "at it again—at it again."

"Gentlemen, gentlemen," said Scrimp, "you are too keen; it's enough to set one's teeth on edge to hear you both. You must have swallowed a few brad-awls, and washed them down with vinegar before you came here."

"Hip—hip—hip—hurrah!" cried Perk. "The governor has broken out in a new place. He has sprung a leak."

"Please, sir, supper's ready," said the dirty-looking charity boy, whom Scrimp made a housemaid of, popping his head in at the door.

"So are we," said Perk. "I knew a fellow once, gentlemen, in Lincoln's-inn, who had an oath that always lasted twenty-three minutes and a half."

"D— it," said Freegrove.

"No, that wasn't it. That charity splinter put me in mind of it. He used to practise it on one."

"Well, Perk, you shall tell it us after supper," said Scrimp.

"I will, my Congreve light," replied Perk.

Mr. Scrimp's invitation to supper was not entirely an act of disinterested hospitality. From certain pauses and fidgettings of Mr. Perk during the recital of what had occurred to him at the miller's cottage, Mr. Scrimp was inclined to believe that something was kept back from him by his worthy clerk, and if his suspicions were correct, he (Mr. Scrimp) felt perfectly sure that something was a great deal more important than anything that had been communicated. Mr. Scrimp was, therefore, not without a sanguine hope that certain strong liquors, with which he intended to ply Mr. Perk, might have the not uncommon effect of inducing a fit of extraordinary confidence, during the continuance of which the concealed matter might be revealed.

"What have you got for supper, governor?" asked Perk.

"A couple of ducks and a leg of pork," replied Scrimp, graciously.

"That'll do," said Freegrove. "That's the smartest thing I've heard said since I've been here."

The party sat down to supper, and for a time the business of the table superseded every other consideration.

"You're a clever fellow, Perk," said Scrimp, when the cloth was removed, "and I'm very sorry your very talented scheme failed this morning."

Mr. Perk made no answer to this further than looking very hard at Scrimp, and deliberately buttoning up all his pockets.

"It was a good idea," I repeat," said Scrimp; "upon my word it was; and I am heartily sorry that anything should have occurred to spoil it."

"Oh, thank you," said Perk, "you are very kind. What would you like to take after that? You are at home, you know. Order just what you please, governor."

"Suppose we have a bowl of punch," said Freegrove.

"With all my heart," replied Scrimp. "Crumples! Crumples!"

The charity boy popped his head in at the door.

"Go down," said Mr. Scrimp, "to Mrs. Staples, and give my compliments, and ask her to be so kind as to make me a bowl of punch, and send it here under a cover."

The punch was brought according to order; and before it was half consumed the party grew tolerably jovial.

"Come, Perk," said Pomander, "sing us a song, like a good fellow. You know you're quite a nightingale."

"Well," said Perk, filling his glass again, "here's luck in a bag, and shake it out as you want it. What will you have?—sentimental, tragical, comical, or dramatical?"

"Oh, let's have something about eating and drinking," said Freegrove.

"You must give me a chorus, then, gentlemen," said Perk, and here goes for the pic-nic party.

  "'There never was yet a party planned,
   Whether in sea, or air, or land,
   But with misfortune it was crammed,
   And in the end 'twas surely d——d,
     Oh, dear, rumti foddle!

   Buggins, and Grubbins, Trump, and Brown,
   And Miggs, who kept the Rose and Crown,
   And Snicks, who lived in Somers' Town,
   To Richmond thought they would go down,
     With cheer, rumti foddle!

> They thought they well could do the trick,
> And called their frolic a pic-nic;
> There was lots of children, well and sick,
> Nine, Master Sniggs, from Candlewick,
>   So queer, rumti foddle!

(Spoken.)—" ' Sniggs, Sniggs, I say Sniggs, *do* you hear?'

" ' Yes, my lollypop.'

" ' Have you brought the umbrella, pattens, parasols, baskets, knives and forks?'

" ' Yes, my lollypop.'

" ' Sniggs, just pop this one in your pocket. Here's Juliana Adelaide Victoria. Nonpareil Sniggs has ——'

" ' Oh, dear me.'

" Chorus, gentlemen.

> Tiddledum toddled um dol li ti,
>   Oh, rumti toddle."

" Here's to all unfortunate monarchs," said Mr. Perk, draining his glass. " Upon my word I really forget the rest. Dear me, I must try another."

> ' The coat of other days is faded,
>   And all its glories past ;
> The front was so nicely braided,
>   But that's all cut at last.
> The tailor he won't make another.
>   'Cos I'm one wot never pays ;
> I sing my sad despair to smother,
>   For the coat of other days.

" Chorus, gentlemen.

> ' The coat of other days.'

" D— me, my memory wants clear-starching. You must take the will for the deed, gentlemen, as the boa constrictor remarked to the large billy goat, when he swallowed him all but his horns."

" Bravo! bravo!" cried Scrimp and Pomander. " That'll do, Perk."

The last echo of chorus to Mr. Perk's song had hardly died away, when a loud knocking was heard at the door of the house.

" Who the deuce can that be?" said Scrimp, rising.

" Perhaps the old gentleman who lodges down below," said Pomander.

Again came the knocking, louder than before.

" Crumples, Crumples," cried Scrimp. " Go to the door, you villain, will you?"

Crumples was heard shuffling slowly to the street door, and those at the supper sat looking at each other in silent surprise and meditation as to who it could be who at that time knocked so furiously at the door.

They heard the street door opened, and a heavy step sounded in the passage.

They all rose instinctively, and looked earnestly towards the door. In a few moments it opened, and a man, enveloped in a cloak, entered the room. He walked with an unsteady step, and dropped into the first chair which presented itself.

The cloak slipped to the ground ; and those who were in the room could hardly believe their eyes as they recognised Sir Herbert Foster.

" Sir Herbert?" cried Scrimp.

" Is it you?" exclaimed Freegrove.

" Silence," said Sir Herbert, faintly. " Wine—wine—anything—I—I am faint."

Mr. Scrimp officiously filled a tumbler with punch, and handed it to Sir Herbert, which the latter drank off at a draught.

" May I be permitted, my dear sir," said Scrimp, " to humbly inquire——"

"No, no," said the baronet, shuddering. "Inquire nothing. Can I sleep here to-night?"

"Certainly, if you please, Sir Herbert," replied Scrimp, much astonished at the request. "I shall feel but too much honoured."

"Show me a chamber, then, at once."

Mr. Scrimp took a candle, and walked to the door of the room, followed by Sir Herbert Foster, who was observed to tremble violently. His head was uncovered, and he wore a dressing-gown, and had slippers on his feet. It seemed as if he had suddenly rushed from home, without any preparation whatever.

It was a full hour before Scrimp returned to the room where the confederates sat, and he looked serious and thoughtful as he took his place by the table.

"Gentlemen," he said, "Sir Herbert seems much disturbed in his mind; I think we had better separate for the night."

"What's it all about, governor?" asked Perk. "No secrets among friends, you know."

"I hope not," said Scrimp, looking hard at Perk. "Sir Herbert has certainly told me the cause of his present uneasiness, but it was in strict confidence. He has charged me to tell no one."

"But we are three, you know," said Perk, " so you may as well let us know something about it."

"No, I cannot. I am sorry to throw cold water on your mirth, gentlemen, but Sir Herbert is in the room above, and he is really in a state of mind not to be disturbed."

Mr. Scrimp winked at Mr. Pomander as he spoke, and pointed to Freegrove.

Mr. Pomander rose and said :—

"Well, then, we will bid you good night, Scrimp."

No. 37

"D— me," said Freegrove, " if I ain't fairly bothered. I'd as soon have thought of seeing my grandmother, who has been dead these dozen years, walk in as Sir Herbert at this time of night."

The party all together walked to the door, and Mr. Pomander made a feint of going.

"Good night all of you," said Freegrove.

"Good night—good night," said the others.

"Now come in both of you," said Scrimp. " That clod of humanity has no discretion. I could not speak before him."

"What the devil has happened ?" said Pomander.

"Upon my word, something that I consider is uncommonly foolish," replied Scrimp. "Sir Herbert is very much scared."

"At what ?" asked Perk.

"An apparition, he says."

"An apparition !"

"Yes ; I'll just tell it to you in his own words as nearly as I can. But first of all, do either of you recollect hearing anything of a girl called Ellen Wade ?"

"Helen Wade ?" said Pomander. "Now I recollect Mrs. Staples mentioned some story about a person of that name."

"About forty years ago," said Scrimp, "Sir Herbert Forster came down to Haredale Park very unexpectedly, and with him was a young girl, in a riding habit and a hat. I saw her as she alighted at the hall, for I happened to be there."

"I recollect all about it," said Perk.

"Well," continued Scrimp, " it appears that Sir Herbert had made a mock marriage with her in the morning in London, and then brought her direct to Haredale. The girl firmly believed herself the wife of Sir Herbert. Some few days afterwards, however, she found out the truth ; how I don't know, but certainly she did find it out. Well, it appears she put on the riding habit and hat, which were her own, and tried to leave the house, in which she was impeded by Sir Herbert, who chased her through some of the rooms into a closet, which opens into the old armoury, and in which closet the plate and jewels of the family were kept. What happened then nobody knows exactly, but in a few minutes Sir Herbert rushed out, calling loudly for help."

"And the girl ?" said Pomander.

"The girl was found dead, with the riding habit and hat on her. It appears she had broken a blood-vessel, for she was lying in a pool of blood."

"I remember the inquest," said Perk. "No one came forward to own the body, and Sir Herbert gave evidence that she was without any relatives to his knowledge."

"At all events," continued Scrimp, "Sir Herbert had some trouble to get out of the scrape. There was no doubt about her death being from the cause I have mentioned, and a verdict was returned accordingly."

"It was rather an awkward affair," said Mr. Pomander.

"It was, indeed."

"But how about the apparition ?" said Perk.

"Why, Sir Herbert knowing that I knew all about this Helen Wade, made no scruple of telling me the cause of his visit here to-night. His words were these :—

" ' I was walking,' he said, ' from the supper-room to my chamber, when, as I passed the door of the armoury, I thought I heard a noise within that apartment. I opened the door carefully, and distinctly saw some one make a rush from the room into the jewel closet. Without a thought, I walked through the armoury to the closet to see who it could be who was trying to elude me. When I opened the closet-door, I saw Helen Wade standing in the middle of the floor.'"

"Upon my word," said Pomander, "that's a most singular story."

"It is," said Scrimp, "and I cannot attempt any solution of it. Sir Herbert declares he was thinking on quite other matters, and that when he opened the closet door, the thought of Helen Wade never crossed his mind."

"Then I suppose he left the house?" said Perk.

"So he says. He tells me that he was so horrified by what he saw, that he gave but one look, and rushed from the house, stopping but for one moment in the hall to take the cloak which you saw he had on."

"It's a most uncomfortable story," said Perk. "Upon my word I never heard a thing of the kind that was more difficult to get over."

"I tried in vain to shake Sir Herbert's belief in the supernatural character of the figure, but he sticks to it that it was Helen Wade, and no other."

"Has it shaken his resolution, do you think, about the miller's fair lass?" said Pomander.

"He never mentioned her. Wait till the morning, and the impression of this unaccountable appearance will be much weakened. Sir Herbert Forster is not exactly the man to be frightened at the laws, and I dare say he will be the first to profess his conviction that the figure was a trick of the imagination."

"A very disagreeable trick," said Pomander. "These things, however, frequently occur in diseased states of the brain, and such disorders are most commonly first indicated by such things as the present."

"I do not," said Scrimp, "see the least occasion for altering our plans for to-morrow. Late as it is, I must go to Haredale Park, and account for Sir Herbert's absence in some way. Perhaps you won't mind walking with me, gentlemen?"

"Certainly not," replied Pomander. "Come, Perk."

The three rose, and donning their hats, proceeded towards Haredale Park.

"The more," said Perk, "I think of what you have just told me, the more I'm puzzled. I can give but one solitary solution of the matter, and that is, that the appearance was the trick of some one to rob the jewel room."

"If it be so," said Scrimp, "it must be some one who knows Sir Herbert's history; but it will be soon ascertained if anything is missed."

CHAPTER XLVIII.

"With the morning comes reflection," saith the proverb; and the reflection that crossed Mr. Pomander's mind was none of the pleasantest on the morning after the supper at Mr. Scrimp's. The wily Pomander had no objection to being a participator in the profits likely to arise from the abduction of the Miller's Maid, but he had many objections to compromising his personal safety at all in the matter.

He would have helped from a distance to make a practicable breach in the walls of a fortress, but then he would have liked some one else first to put his head through it.

With these highly prudent feelings and opinions, it is not to be wondered at that Mr. Pomander, when busy memory reminded him of his promise to visit the mill, felt some uncomfortable foreboding of what might be the consequences of thus, as it were, putting his head into the lion's jaws. Visions of pumps came across his imagination as he was dressing, and altogether Mr. Pomander certainly disliked the job.

After some thought, an idea struck him which he thought might, at all events, secure him a safe retreat. He wrote a note, and addressed it to himself, requesting his attendance at the cottage of the miller, by ten o'clock.

"At least," he said, "they will think I have been imposed upon by some one, and they will consider me not as an intruder, but the victim of low malice."

Now it happened rather singularly, that at the time that Mr. Pomander was concocting this scheme at his own proper abode, Tim Miggles was taxing his ingenuity to the utmost to devise some means of getting the learned doctor to the mill.

Tim on the preceding evening had had a long conversation with George, who pitied the delusions under which the harmless and half-witted lad was labouring.

In this conversation George, with a view, likewise, of stopping any further communications from reaching the mill through Tim's means, had succeeded in thoroughly convincing him how much he had been duped by Mr. Pomander, who, under the pretence of serving him, had made him the bearer of letters which had caused so much anxiety and disturbance. By talking to him in a kindly manner, George had made a great impression upon his simple mind, which, when withdrawn from the romance with which it was encumbered, was not altogether incapable of drawing very shrewd conclusions.

George shewed him the letters that he had been the unconsious bearer of, and explained fully to him the nefarious scheme which had been so signally defeated for carrying off Phœbe.

"Well, I never read anything like that," said Tim.

> "It's much worse than robbery, murder, or treason;
> I'd have them all crimped, like cod when in season.
> Pomander, the flame of my love tried to fan up,
> But there ain't no such person as Snapallthecanup!

"Just let me catch him here, that's all. Wouldn't I roll him just a few in the flour bin—oh, dear, yes. I'd make him free of the mill."

"He certainly deserves something at your hands, Tim," said George, laughing; "but I advise you to leave him alone. It is not very likely he will ever shew himself here."

"If he does, I'd serve him as the Baron Bombigometer served the slave who cut his nose in shaving him—I would, indeed.

> "I'd laugh to see his curious wriggles,
> And make him recollect a Miggles."

"How was that, Tim?"
"Oh, I'll tell you. It's a beautiful poem."

> "The Lord Bombigometer,
> Looked at the barometer,
>   And saw it would be a fine day;
> He called to the slave,
> Who always did shave
>   Him, and told him to lather away.
>
> "The slave came, all trembling,
> It was not dissembling,
>   For he'd over night not been quite sobe
> As the story then goes,
> He took hold of the nose

> " Bombigometer swore,
> The slave flew to the door,
>   But he couldn't by no means get through ;
> And the baron sat down
> In a study, called brown,
>   To bethink him of what he should do.

> " He called for a knife,
> Which with notches was rife,
>   And two men held the slave in one place,
> Then this baron of power
> Took a whole hour,
>   To scrape the nose off the slave's face."

" I must think," pursued Tim, " upon some uncommonly artful way of getting Pomander here. I'd burn six candle ends over it to-night."

Under these circumstances Tim's surprise was immense, when, from a window of the mill, he saw Mr. Pomander himself crossing the meadow, evidently with the intention of proceeding to the cottage.

" George—George !" he cried, tell him I'm ill and confined to the mill, there' a good fellow, do now."

" George replied, laughing,—

" I can't think what brings him here, except it be to make some other attempt against our peace. If you tell me you are ill, Tim, and want to see him, I will deliver your message."

" Oh, yes," said Tim, " I'm very bad. Oh, dear! oh, dear! my poor head !"

George hastily left the mill, and reached the cottage before Mr. Pomander.

" Phœbe, dear," he said, " one of these rascals is coming here to renew, doubtless, the attempts to bring unhappiness among us. Do not give him the satisfaction even of seeing you."

" Who be coming ?" asked the miller.

" Pomander is crossing the meadow," said George.

" Now, by all——" began the miller; but before he could finish the sentence, Mr. Pomander opened the door of the cottage, and nodded and smiled in a very amiable and easy sort of manner.

" My dear sir," he said, " Mr. Marks, how do you do ? I hope nothing particular, eh ?"

" What does 'e mean ?" said the indignant miller.

" Oh, dear! mean ?—why, I assure you I have lost no time in attending to you. I hope your good lady is quite well—and—your charming daughter, Miss,—really I forget her name."

" To what, sir," said George, " are we indebted for the honour of this visit ?"

" What ?—oh, dear me ! A medical man, you know, is a sort of privileged person. We and the clergy just go and come, you see, in a desultory sort of manner."

" Well, sir," replied George, " now that you have availed yourself of your fancied professional privilege and visited here, I tell you that, as far as your professional safety is concerned, you had better not come again in your desultory manner; nor will I answer for the consequences if you remain here much longer."

" My dear sir," said Pomander, who was much disappointed at not seeing Giles anywhere, " you speak in a most singular manner. I am not aware what offence I have given to Mr. Marks, that you should take upon yourself to command my absence from his house, in which you can be but a servant."

" I tell you to your face, sir," said George, " that you are a sneaking villain; and if you don't quickly get out at the door, I shall be under the necessity of throwing you through the window."

"Mr. Marks," said Mr. Pomander, in an affected rage, "is this the way, sir, that a medical man is to be spoken to after being called in?"

"Called in?" said the miller, "who called thee in?"

"Why, you yourself, sir."

"Now hang thee impudence. I would as soon think of calling in lawyer Scrimp as thee, thee rascal."

Mr. Pomander now felt that to effect a judicious retreat and trust to his chance of encountering Giles before he got quite clear of the premises, was the best and most prudent course he could adopt.

"I have your kind and complimentary note, sir," he said, "which was left with me by some one very early this morning."

"My note!" roared the miller.

"Yes, your note," replied Pomander, with unblushing effrontery, producing the letter he had himself fabricated. "Here it is."

"'Mr. Marks presents his best compliments to Mr. Pomander, and begs to request that he will favour him with a call before ten this morning. Mr. M. begs to apologise for troubling Mr. P. so early, but trusts to his kindness to call by the time herein mentioned.'"

"There it is, sir," said Pomander, "your own invitation, sir."

The miller looked perfectly staggered at the production of this epistle in his name.

"This is too flimsy a contrivance," said George, "to impose upon any one."

"Well, gentleman," said Mr. Pomander, "if I have been imposed upon, it is no fault of mine. We medical gentlemen are peculiarly liable to such impertinencies. You will permit me to wish you a very good morning."

"Don't 'e come here any more," said the miller.

"And, hark ye," said George, "you are known, sir. The pump is not dry, and there are willing hands to use it."

Mr. Pomander started at the word pump, and hurried from the cottage, congratulating himself upon being allowed to leave unscathed, and cursing Perk in his heart, who he now felt certain must have implicated him in some way.

Giles he could see nowhere, although he looked for him most anxiously, and he was upon the point of passing through the little wicket which led to the meadow, when he happened to cast his eyes towards the mill and he saw Tim Miggles at a window beckoning to him.

George had quite forgotten, in his indignation, the message with which Tim had charged him, and which he had promised to deliver to Pomander. When the latter now saw Tim beckoning to him from the window, he hesitated a moment, for he thought it might not be quite safe to go to the mill; but then he thought he was sure to see Giles there, and he did not like the thought of failing in his mission, now that he had fairly undertaken it, so, in an evil moment for him, he turned his face to the mill, and nodding at Tim, to signify his acceptance of the invitation, he entered the building.

Tim met him at the door, and, with an air of great mystery and seeming friendship, beckoned him forward.

"Come along," he said. "Follow me. I want you uncommon particular."

"Where is Giles?" asked Pomander.

"This way," said Tim.

Now, every one who has been in a mill must be well aware how very slippery a place it is. The finest slide in the world is not more slippery than the flooring and staircases of a mill. The finest particles of the flour are continually settling upon everything; and one unaccustomed to walking in such a place, unless he or she hold very fast to something, will infallibly fall down with great velocity and violence. The mill was quite a novelty to Mr. Pomander, and his first achievement was to throw up his heels, and fall down upon his back with great force.

"Never mind," said Tim. "I forgot you, perhaps, didn't know how slippery the floor of a mill is. It's no matter—get up—you haven't hurt the old mill a bit."

"D— the old mill!" said Mr. Pomander, making a great many singular flourishes with his feet in attempting to rise.

"Oh! it's uncommon strong," said Tim. "You might fall down here ever so many times, and do no mischief here at all. Come on."

"Might I!" said Mr. Pomander; "I've nearly broken my back, though, at the first attempt. It's all very well to say 'come on.' What am I to hold by? Do you think I can climb up these perpendicular stairs?"

"There's a rope," said Tim, "you can hold on by. Come on."

Mr. Pomander shook his head as, with fear and trembling, he ascended the steep glassy staircase.

"This is the loft," said Tim, when they arrived at the top of the flight.

"Oh, is it," said Mr. Pomander; "that's very satisfactory. But where's Giles?"

"Giles?—Do you want Giles?"

"Why, yes, Tim; I should like to see him a moment."

"Oh! then, I don't know when he'll come back."

"Come back! Why, where is he?"

"He has gone to Farmer Hodgson's on a message for master. Look here; this is the great bin."

"D— the great bin what do I care about it?"

"No; but Mr. Pomander, if you just hold this rope, and lean forwards, you'll see it so well."

"Which rope? That one that goes over the pulley concern?"

"Yes; it's quite fast."

Mr. Pomander took hold of the rope, and leaning forward to look into the great bin, which was really a novelty to him, he trusted his whole weight to its support. The pulley round which it wound could be stopped, or set in action, in a moment. Tim watched his opportunity, when Mr. Pomander was leaning very far forward, and gazing into the flour-bin.

"What a quantity of flour, Tim," said he. "How much should you think there was there, eh?"

"I don't know," said Tim, releasing the pulley. "Perhaps you'd like to go and see for yourself?"

Round flew the rope, and Mr. Pomander descended upwards of twelve feet, with a soft flop, into the flour-bin, from whence there immediately issued a dense white cloud, and half-smothered cried of "Murder! murder!"

The more Mr. Pomander floundered about the deeper he got, and every time that he opened his mouth such a quantity of flour flew in that he could hardly speak at all.

"Murder! murder! Tim—help!—murder!" he shouted as well as he could.

Tim ran to the window of the mill, and looking out, he cried, with all his might,—

"Master! master!—George!—master!—missus!—here's such a wopping rat in the great bin."

"What be the boy making such a noise about?" said the miller from the door of his cottage.

"I'd wager my life," cried George, "Tim Miggles has been playing Pomander some trick. I saw him beckon him to the mill."

"Do 'e think so?" said the miller, with a grin. "Tim be not such a fool sometimes."

When Tim saw George and the miller coming towards the mill he ran back to the bin, and looking down upon Mr. Pomander, who could hardly be distinguished from the flour, he gave a kind of Miggles war-whoop over the unfortunate medical man, and repeated innumerable scraps of poetry in great derision and utter defiance of him, Pomander, and the imaginary Snapallhecanup.

"Oh, Tim, Tim—my dear Mr. Miggles," cried Pomander, "for God's sake help me out, I shall be smothered. It's God knows how many feet deep of flour. I know it was quite an accident. Miggles, Miggles, help me out. It's worse—d— it—oh, Lord, my mouth is full—it's worse than the fluff—fluff—fluff—than the pump."

"That's the time o' day," said Tim, resting his elbows very composedly on the side of the bin.

> " ' You may stay there an hour
>   Fighting the flour,
>   And then call on Snapallhecanup ;
>   Who must be a screw
>   Not to help you,
>   And from the bin fish a white man up.'

"How are you? Here comes Master and George to throw in some water. You'll make a neat pudding, then, you know."

"What's the matter, Tim?" said the miller, arriving in the loft. "What's amiss with the great bin?"

"Help! help!—murder! murder!" cried Mr. Pomander.

"It's a rat, sir," said Tim; "he fell into the bin. He came to eat us out of house and home, master, and now, you see, he's caught in the bin."

George cast his eyes into the bin, and could not refrain from laughing at the singular appearance of Mr. Pomander, who seemed to have changed "his customary suit of solemn black" for a miller's costume.

The miller placed a ladder into the bin, and Mr. Pomander, after a great deal more floundering, succeeded in crawling out.

"Now get thee gone," said the miller; "thee had no business here."

"The devil and all his imps," muttered Pomander, as he clutched the rope that hung by the stairs, and slowly descended. He shook himself repeatedly, and created as often a cloud of flour around him.

"By all the devils," he said, "I will have some infernal revenge. To be outwitted in this manner by that idiot—that—oh, the devil!"

CHAPTER XLIX.

HAD Mr. Pomander been exactly aware of the state of affairs at the mill, he might have saved himself the trouble of visiting it, and would, consequently, have avoided the little unpleasant adventure in the flour-bin; for it so happened that Giles had determined upon seeking an interview with Mr. Scrimp; and at the very moment that Mr. Pomander was whitening his outward man, he, Giles, was arranging an interview, in the evening, with the attorney.

Tim had stated nothing but the truth when he said that Giles had gone some distance on a message for the miller; and it was the opportunity he thus had of passing through the village which enabled him to call upon

Scrimp, in the first heat of his resolve, and commit himself to another inter-view with that gentleman.

Giles was returning homewards, in deep thought and abstraction, when, upon turning the corner of a lane which led direct to the meadow, he sud-denly confronted a figure all in white, which was rushing forwards with great violence, and ran against him, covering him from head to foot with loose flour.

Giles was rather confounded at this apparition, but when his first sur-prise was over, he saw, notwithstanding his singular disguise, that it was, in truth, Mr. Pomander who stood before him.

"Giles," said Pomander, "I've been to seek you at the mill; and d—r, this is the state I've got in through trying to serve you."

"And what be you wanting with me?" said Giles.

"Oh, Mr. Scrimp wants to see you particularly."

"I know it," said Giles, in a surly tone; "I have seen him. Go thee ways, and let me go mine."

"What a pig-headed brute that is," said Pomander, as Giles, without another word, passed onwards.

Giles felt himself now, as he fancied, in a different position with regard to Phœbe to any he had before occupied. He had fancied that her promise to wed, if she did wed at all, either George or himself, fully amounted to a positive engagement to unite herself to him, if any circumstances should occur to prevent her union with George. He acquiesced in such an arrange-ment with a floating, indistinct idea in his mind that he might be able to throw some insurmountable obstacle in the way of Phœbe's marriage with George, although he had no notion whatever of what that obstacle was to consist of, and he almost shrunk from the inquiry.

Passion, although it had taken almost entire possession of the mind of

No. 38

Giles, had still not quite succeeded in quenching every spark of virtuous reflection, and the struggle in his mind was fearful between his conviction of the unworthy part he was contriving, and the fierce and outrageous passion which was hurrying him to premature destruction.

His nature was not bad; his faults were almost all those of temper alone. Before George came to the mill he had himself hardly been aware of the nature of his feelings for Phœbe; but when he saw her delight in George's presence, which she was too artless to conceal, and became convinced that a mutual passion had sprung up between the shipwrecked sailor and the fair girl, the flame of passion, which was burning in his breast, and which till then had shed but a faint glow upon his mind,—a glow which was only sufficient to give warmth to his words and energy, to his actions,—now burst forth, like the lurid light from a volcano, and his reason " tottered on its throne." Still, however, there came moments of calm reflection, when, with convulsive sobs, and the tears streaming from his eyes, the voice of conscience would speak out, and tell him that he was wrong, perfectly wrong. Then some word or look of Phœbe's would rouse the demon, Jealousy; and in some sequestered spot he would rave and storm, and vow revenge upon him who had embittered his existence by depriving him of her whom he loved with so turbulent a passion.

Racked with these contending feelings, Giles, from a robust young man, had become thin and unhealthy. A settled gloom was on his brow, the colour fled from his cheeks, and he seemed fast hurrying to the tomb, where, alone, his passions and his sighs, his hopes and his fears, might find repose.

He had stormed, raved, threatened, but hitherto he had actually done nothing. A latent sense of rectitude kept him from the commission of any decided act which would bring unhappiness upon Phœbe. He still could not entirely smother the conviction that he had nothing to complain of either from Phœbe or George, and that his only real antagonists were his own unbridled passions.

Hope, however, had at once sprung up in his breast on the discovery of the relationship between George and Phœbe. Now at last he saw the prize for which he had panted within his grasp, and we are aware with what a burst of exultation he hailed the discovery of the circumstances which at one fell swoop destroyed all George's dearest hopes.

The explanation given to him that Phœbe's promise was by no means binding in the way he had thought, he looked upon as a subterfuge invented by George to get rid of his claims, and for the first time in the whole business he told himself that he was ill-used, and had something to complain of.

The greatest obstacle, however, was removed. His rival—the only one whom he believed could rival him in the affections of Phœbe—was virtually dead. The lover was gone, and was replaced by himself. He was for a few hours restored to partial tranquillity. Phœbe would still be his. Who else could claim her?

When, however, he heard George's subsequent declaration, that he believed he was not the brother of Phœbe, his rage knew no bounds. He looked upon George's statement, and Phœbe's corroboration of the dying words of her mother, as one of the most awful and gross impositions that had ever been practised or attempted, and he rushed from the cottage in a frenzy of indignation.

Now his scruples had vanished. Revenge!—revenge!—he would have revenge; and he determined to see Scrimp again, and see if he still professed the same interest in the matter that he appeared formerly to have.

With this object in view he called upon the attorney, who was as much pleased as surprised to see him. A meeting in the evening was at once arranged, without entering into any particulars, and with a gloomy feeling of satisfaction that he had commenced the work he had so long meditated, Giles returned to the mill.

The morning had found Sir Herbert Foster much more composed, and he lent a more attentive ear to Mr. Scrimp's repeated suggestions of the evening efore, that his vision must have been imaginary.

"My dear Sir Herbert," said Scrimp, "permit me to remark, that in all these appearances we generally omit to notice the remarkable fact, that, in addition to the ghost of the individual, there are, generally, the ghosts of various articles of clothing, which seems most certainly rather ridiculous."

"It must have been a waking dream," said Sir Herbert.

"Certainly, Sir Herbert. Now, if Miss Wade had appeared in—in a state a little more natural, why ——"

"Cease, cease, say no more about it. I saw her as plainly as I now see you. I knew the hat, veil, and riding-habit in a moment. I did not see her face; but I knew—I felt in my heart that the face was there."

"I would advise you to institute a search, Sir Herbert, in the jewel-closet. I much suspect that plunder is at the bottom of this business, if we acquit imagination of any share in it."

"I wish to God," cried Sir Herbert, "that I may find everything taken."

"Why, in one way, Sir Herbert, it would relieve your mind; but, nevertheless, my dear sir, such a robbery would, I conjecture, be no trifle."

"I tell you, Scrimp, I would give Haredale Park to be sure—mind you, quite sure—that what I saw last night was a form of flesh and blood."

"Or the work of the imagination."

"No, Scrimp, no. What matters it whether these things be really supernatural visitants, or produced by a diseased brain? The latter supposition, if anything, I think is the more horrible of the two. If these appearances be supernatural, they come for some object: when that is accomplished, they come no more. If they be the produce of a teeming fancy, where shall he who is so persecuted find peace? He carries with a host of horrors—a legion of spirits who come but to appal the soul, and cease but with death. No, no, let it be a trick—a robbery."

"And, Sir Herbert," said Scrimp, "with respect to the Miller's Maid?"

"Well, sir, I will not be turned from my course by shadows."

"Then you still desire your humble servant, Sir Herbert, to ——"

"To do my bidding. I shall stay at Haredale just so long as will complete this rural intrigue, and then for London; and I will never cross the threshold of Haredale again. Has Cury arrived?"

"He has, Sir Herbert, and waits your pleasure with your clothes."

"You did not tell him the cause of my sudden absence last night?"

"No, Sir Herbert, I merely said you would sleep here, and told him to be with you in the morning. He said he would bring your travelling toilette, and ——"

"Well, well, send him up."

Cury attended upon his master with his usual calm indifference. A remark about his absence from home he knew he dared not make, and he assisted in the various operations of dressing with an appearance of great *sang froid*.

Sir Herbert once, as Cury was behind him, chanced to glance at the dressing-glass, and he saw in it the reflected face of his valet. It bore so singular an expression, that the baronet started and exclaimed,—

"Cury!"

"Yes, Sir Herbert," replied Cury, and the face was immediately calm and composed as usual.

"Nothing, nothing," said Sir Herbert.

But he could not forget the perfectly demoniac face which he had seen peeping over his shoulder.

Sir Herbert Foster and Cury shortly departed for Haredale Park. The baronet turned a shade or two paler as he entered the house. He sat down in his private apartment for some time, and appeared lost in thought. Suddenly he rung a small silver hand-bell, and Cury appeared at the door.

"Cury," said Sir Herbert, "have you been in the jewel-closet lately?"

Sir Herbert was not looking at Cury, or he might have observed a slight flush pass over the valet's face as he answered,—

"No, Sir Herbert, not for months."

Sir Herbert Foster rose, and opening a cabinet, he took out a bunch of keys; then turning to Cury, he said,—

"Follow me," and left the room.

The baronet proceeded through many rooms of his splendid mansion till he came to the armory, which, in the days of chivalry, when a man's claim to distinction rested upon his reputation as a hard hitter, was an apartment of very great importance. Latterly, however, it had been neglected, and for a long time was kept locked. There were rusted suits of armour hanging on the walls, and weapons of defence of all kinds hung in fantastical groups. These things had no charms for the voluptuous and effeminate Sir Herbert; and the dust and decay of years had been allowed to quietly accumulate upon those suits of mail and weapons which had been the chief care and pride of his ancestors.

He paused for a moment at the door, and Cury advancing, threw it wide open.

Sir Herbert Foster saw nothing which the armory contained. From the moment of his entrance his eyes were intently fixed upon the door of the jewel room. He seemed afraid to take them off for one instant.

"Is that door locked, Cury?" he asked.

"I will see, Sir Herbert."

Cury advanced and turned the handle, when the door immediately opened.

"Remain here, Cury," said the baronet: and he passed into the jewel-closet and closed the door behind him.

The room which was called the jewel-closet was small, and Sir Herbert Foster felt quite sure that there was no other entrance to it than that through which he had just passed. When he stood alone in that room, he could not help feeling a sickening sensation of fear at his heart. He drew his breath short and quick, and a cold perspiration broke out upon his brow.

He always avoided the room since the catastrophe which Mr. Scrimp had alluded to, and which, coupled with his startling vision of the proceeding evening, now invested the place to his mind with a horrible gloom, which seemed to hang over everything that it contained.

There were several cabinets in the room which contained massive silver plate that had been accumulated by the family during many years. There were, likewise, jewels of value in secret recesses in the cabinets.

Sir Herbert Foster had but rarely looked at these riches of his house. He took no pride in the possession of such family heirlooms; but, at the same time, he would have been highly offended at any proposition to dispose of them. They formed in the eyes of the world and his servants a part of his rank and station, and as such, they performed their office by administering to his personal vanity.

He well knew where every article of value was kept; for he had in early life been conducted by his father to this depository of antiquated magnificence frequently, and had had described to him the value of each article, together with the history of its admission among the collection of the Fosters.

Cabinet after cabinet was unlocked by him; but everything was there as some years previously he had seen them.

The search was over,—the cherished idea that he had been duped and robbed was at once dispelled. Oh, how gladly would he have hailed the disappearance of some of the costly gems which met his eyes! But no; nothing was touched. It was no disguised robber who had so scared him. Then it was—Sir Herbert shuddered as the conviction came across his mind, that he might henceforward be subjected to such awful visitations.

"It cannot be," he said. "I will not think it possible."

He, nevertheless, looked round the room with terror; the slightest noise alarmed him. He seemed scarcely to dare to breathe in the atmosphere of that room.

The sun now suddenly streamed through one of the narrow casements, and fell in a long, light, glittering streak upon the floor. He cast his eyes downwards, and a convulsive shudder shook his frame.

There was a dark patch on the floor just where the sunbeams had fallen. Sir Herbert knew well what it was;—it was the blood of Helen Wade!

"Cury! Cury!" he called.

The valet, who had remained in the armory, opened the door of the closet, and stood in the entrance.

"Cury," said Sir Herbert, "see that this room is—is fresh boarded."

"Yes, Sir Herbert," said Cury. He saw by the direction of his master's eyes what had given rise to the order. "Everything has been tried, Sir Herbert," he said, "but the—the stain won't come out."

Sir Herbert Foster appeared to be in deep reflection. At length he said,—

"Let it be—let it be; it would only raise a new clamour."

He walked to the door, and passing through the armory, again sought his own private sitting-room, followed by Cury.

"Stay," said Sir Herbert, as the valet was about to retire; "have you ever seen—or—or—" The baronet paused for some moments, and then continued,—"Have you heard many tales among the servants of—any—any supernatural appearances in this house?"

"No, Sir Herbert; but ——"

"But what?"

"Last night, Sir Herbert, after you had left ——"

"Ha! last night? Well, go on, Cury, go on."

"I was passing through the west corridor ——"

"Well, what—did you? Go on, go on."

"Something came past me, Sir Herbert, very quickly, and went to the head of the great staircase."

"And—and who?—what was it?"

"It wore a hat and veil, and riding-habit."

Sir Herbert groaned heavily, and sunk back on the couch on which he was sitting.

"Well, Cury—well."

"It was at the head of the stairs, Sir Herbert, in a moment, but the figure was gone."

"Gone! gone where?"

"I don't know, Sir Herbert. I looked down the staircase, and I am quite sure no one could have thrown themselves down in time to get away, for I was not three seconds."

"Go on, go on."

"Then, Sir Herbert, I felt rather alarmed, and thought it might be ——"

"Be who?—what?"

"Some appearance, not in the world—some apparition."

"It made no noise?"

"None, Sir Herbert."

"And—and uttered no sound?"

"None, none."

"In a hat, veil, and riding-habit?"

"Yes, Sir Herbert; I saw the habit trailing on the ground."

"You—you are, Cury—on your life you are quite sure?"

"As sure as that I see you, Sir Herbert."

"Who," said the baronet, speaking slowly, and in a husky voice, "think you, it was, Cury? On your soul, tell me truly."

"I hope you won't be offended, Sir Herbert, but I could almost swear ——"

"Swear what?—what? Speak instantly."

"That it was Miss Wade!"

"Yes, yes. I know it; I know it," said Sir Herbert, faintly. "Mention this to know one, Cury. I—I know it was she. Go—go —"

Cury was about to depart, and had reached the door, when Sir Herbert again spoke.

"Cury, what's to-day?"

"Wednesday, Sir Herbert."

"I shall leave here on Saturday morning, never—never to return. See that everything be in readiness. Go —"

Cury was again at the door, when he was recalled by his master.

"Cury, come here. Upon your soul's salvation, man, did you see that thing?"

"I did, Sir Herbert."

"And you are sure it was —"

"Miss Helen Wade, Sir Herbert, who —"

"Peace! peace! You may go."

Cury left the room, and Sir Herbert threw himself back upon his couch.

"This is horrible! horrible!" he said. "I must leave this place. I must chase the impression of this visitation from my mind. I—I did not kill the girl. No, no; 'twas a ruptured blood-vessel. I—I must lose myself in pleasure. The vortex of dissipation shall again receive me. I will shun memory by the sounds of music and festivity. If I must remember it, it shall be in the midst of brilliant crowds. I—I will seldom be alone."

CHAPTER L.

Sir Herbert Foster had scarcely quitted Mr. Scrimp's house in the morning, when Mr. Pomander shot past the door, with the hope of reaching his own dwelling, and cleansing himself from the effects of his immersion into the flower-bin, before he met either Scrimp or Perk.

He had rushed with such rapidity along, that the good folks of the village had no time to salute him, as they had done Mr. Perk, after his mishap. They had, as they stood at their door, only time to wonder for a moment who the white apparition could be ere it was gone.

Personal identity was out of the question; for who would have recognized, in the white figure which flitted through the village, the respectable and serious Mr. Pomander.

Mr. Scrimp saw the singular-looking white apparition rush past his window, but he never suspected who it was, although he went to the door to take a look after it.

Mr. Pomander would have got clear off, and might have reached his own home, and then put what complexion he pleased upon the business, had it not been that, unluckily, he was so intent upon getting past Mr. Scrimp's house, that he did not see the village bell-man, who was standing in full costume, gaping at the approach of so very white a man.

The consequence was, that Mr. Pomander, having his head turned towards Mr. Scrimp's, ran exactly into the arms of the bellman, and they both rolled into the kennel together.

"The devil!" cried Mr. Pomander.

"Murder!" shrieked the bellman; "murder! murder!" and getting one arm at liberty, he elevated his bell, and rung a peal that brought all the inhabitants of the village to the spot.

"Let me go, curse you," cried Mr. Pomander.

"Murder! murder!" screamed the man. "Let me get up."

"Leave hold of my coat."

"Don't touch my bell."

"You won't? Then take that," said Mr. Pomander, dealing a blow upon the bellman's nose, which drew first claret.

"Hurrah! hurrah!" shouted the people. "A fight! a fight!"

"It's Pomander," said Scrimp.

"It's the devil!" said the bellman.

Scrimp's door was open, and Mr. Pomander burst through the crowd, and rushed in like a maniac, as the only place of refuge that presented itself.

Mr. Scrimp followed, and closed the door.

"Why, Pomander," said Perk, "by everything that is white and wonderful, where did you get so much chalk?"

"It's flour, and be d—d to you all," said Pomander, giving himself two or three flaps with his hands, which immediately filled the room with a dense white cloud.

"Mercy! mercy! Pomander," cried Scrimp, opening the window.

"Why, you are a walking dredger," said Perk.

"Go on, go on, both of you," cried Pomander. "Take it out. I fell into the d—d flour-bin at the infernal mill. There, now you have it. Laugh your fill."

"You've brought a precious lot away with you," said Perk;—"it must be valuable."

"It's drier than pump water," said Pomander.

"But not so good-looking," replied Perk. "Come, tell us all about it. Make a clean breast, Pomander. Could you save a lot of it, and pass it off for magnesia?"

"No, I couldn't. By the by, I saw the pump. It has a famous spout."

"Come, come, gentlemen," said Scrimp, "be merciful."

"The joke is going round, at all events," said Pomander. "Scrimp, it will be your turn next, you know."

"Thank you," said Scrimp; "I waive my right."

"Come, Pomander," said Perk; "tell us—tell us. They popped you into a sack of flour, did they, eh!"

"No, they did not, Mr. Perk. I overballanced myself, and fell into the great bin."

"With the assistance of a push behind, eh?"

"Not at all," said Mr. Pomander, beginning again to flap himself with great vigour.

"Come, my portable dredger, own it."

Mr. Pomander deigned no reply, but flapped more furiously than ever.

"A truce—a truce," cried Scrimp, "I'm nearly smothered. For God's sake, Pomander, go into the paddock."

"A truce, then," cried Perk, "for I've swallowed enough flour to make a dozen dumplings."

"Then, gentlemen," said Mr. Pomander, "I've no objection in the world to say that I was, I think, pushed into the bin, and by Tim Miggles, for a bit of private revenge at my humbugging about the love charms. D— him."

"D— him," said Perk.

"D— him," said Scrimp.

"You did not see Giles, Pomander," said Scrimp; "for he has been here."

"And you have settled a meeting with him, I suppose?"

"I have. He is as furious as a baited bull."

"Perk," said Pomander, "you and I are fellow sufferers. We must pump on the people at the mill, and then tip them into the flour-bin, to ease our consciences."

We must now leave Mr. Pomander to cleanse himself from his flour-bath, to return to the mill.

Phœbe had been much alarmed by Tim's cries; but she could not preserve her gravity when George and the miller returned, and reported the disaster of Mr. Pomander.

"I be not sorry that that rascal be well frightened," said the miller. "I do believe he came here with some motive that was bad."

"There can be no doubt of it," said George. "The letter he produced was, without doubt, fabricated by himself."

"It be rather odd," said the miller, "that after the confession which thou did get from the lawyer's clerk, any of them will venture here at all."

"Unless, as I much suspect," replied George, "he has kept the confession, for his own credit's sake, a secret, which I am inclined to think he has. In the event of any desperate attempt being made to molest us, I am convinced I could use that document with great effect."

"No doubt, George, my lad," said the miller; "but sit thee down both of thee. I have been talking over the matters with my good dame."

"Whatever you shall advise, sir," said George, "I will do. To say that I am not much concerned at the mystery which surrounds myself and Phœbe, would be to say that which was untrue, but at the same time I do not look forward with a repining spirit to whatever may befal Phœbe will be ever ever dear to me."

"And," said Phœbe, looking with winning sweetness in George's face, "at least you, dear George, were the loved companion of my childhood, and either as a dear brother, or—or——"

"Or a husband, you would say, Phœbe."

"Or anything; you will always, dear George, be first in Phœbe's heart."

"What dost 'e say?" cried the miller, with a smile. "Dost 'e forget me?"

"Forget thee, my dear friend and father? Oh! never, never, I never can love you enough."

"Thee hast made me quite foolish like in my old days by thee pretty ways," said the old man. "When I ought to be wise and steady, I be wanting to fight with doctors and lawyers. But sit thee down, my children; sit thee down."

Phœbe and George seated themselves next to each other, and opposite the old couple, who had acted the parts of parents to them both.

"I do think," said the miller, "and my dame do think so too, that thee

will never be happy till thee have both tried all in thee power to find out the meaning of what thee mother did say upon her death bed."

"Thee will both of thee be ever anxious," said the dame.

"I would, indeed," said George, "fain penetrate the mystery. I am convinced that if we do not penetrate it, we shall, occasionally at all events, feel a degree of unhappiness and constraint."

"But how, dear father," said Phœbe, "how can we possibly discover the truth?"

"If it be the will of Heaven," said the miller, "that thee should discover it, thee will be shewn the way. Now listen to what I advise thee."

"We will listen," said George, "with a resolution to obey you."

"Anything," said Phœbe, "but a separation from——"

"No, Phœbe, I do not wish to separate thee from George; but thee theeself do see thee know not what to call him. I have faith in thee mother's words and do yet believe I shall still have the pleasure of seeing thee wedded."

George sighed as the miller spoke.

"What," continued the miller, "be the utmost that thee did ever hear of thee father?"

"The story is this," said George, "as I have heard my mother tell it. It appears that my father's friends were averse to the match, and he was so much persecuted on account of his attachment to my mother, that he enlisted as a soldier, and was away from his native place two years with his regiment. My mother preserved her attachment to him, and when the regiment returned, it happened to be quartered in the vicinity of her abode. The intimacy was renewed, and they married. There was then every prospect of a long peace throughout Europe, and for nearly three years they lived together in uninterrupted happiness. My father, as I have heard, was

No. 39

much esteemed by his officers, and was permitted frequently to absent himself from his regiment.

"Suddenly, however, it was rumoured that war had broken out in India, and my father's regiment was ordered off at four-and-twenty hours' notice. My mother never saw him more. The war terminated, but no news could my mother get of him but that he was missing, and, consequently, killed; but where, or under what particular circumstances, she never could learn."

"And what was thee father and mother's native place?" said the miller.

"Lanstock, as I have heard," said George; "about twenty miles from Bungleum."

"Then, my dear children, my advice to thee be this," said the miller:— "That thee should go together to Lanstock, and make inquiry concerning thee parents. Thee may, mayhap, light on some one who may be able to clear up the mystery which does now surround thee both, and embitters the happiness which thee do so well both deserve."

"I will go with pleasure," said George; "but Phœbe is delicate, and I fear the fatigue of such a journey would be too much for her."

"Hark thee, George. Neither thee nor my dear child, Phœbe, shall be fatigued at all. Old Gilbert, the miller, has not been so long at the mill without laying by a little something in case of need or old age."

"Shall I bring the old desk, Gilbert?" said the dame.

"Aye, aye, dame, do. We be not without a friend in the old desk."

The dame proceeded up stairs, and presently returned with an old-fashioned desk, which the miller had possessed since he was a mere boy.

Old Gilbert produced the key, and opening it, he took out a small bag, from which he emptied a number of old guineas, mingled with their more modern golden companions—sovereigns.

"Here be the saving of forty years or more," said the miller; "and as my dame and I did, since our dear Phœbe did come to us, always consider them as for her, why thee shall provide theeselves with what thee may call thee own money, with the means of making inquiry for thee father and thee mother, in a manner which will get thee attention and respect."

Phœbe and George looked at each other, but neither of them could speak; and Phœbe's feelings quite overcoming her, she threw herself into the miller's arms, and wept aloud in the fullness of her heart.

George, too, was much affected, and he just managed to say,—

"You—you are too good, sir; God bless you."

"Why, thee two foolish things," said the miller, "what be the matter with thee? I would not make thee cry, my Phœbe, for the world. What have I done?"

"You—you have done nothing, dear father, but what you have always done—been a great deal too good and kind to your poor Phœbe."

"Don't 'e say anything more about that, my dear. I and my dame be so used to look upon the old desk, and what be in it, as thine, that I did not give a thought of hurting thee kind heart by offering it to thee."

"Dear, sir," said George, "if I could ever hope to be able to feel properly grateful to you for all your kindness, I should be happy."

"Now don't 'e say anything more. Thee shall both go, if thee please, in a few days, and I will take care, with the help of my dame, to get things ready for thee both, so that thee may go comfortable. All I ask of thee is to come back as soon as thee can, for I be getting main old, and I do not like the cottage without my dear child Phœbe."

"And, dear father and mother," said Phœbe; "believe me, I shall be unhappy every hour that I am away from you."

"And when we do come back," said George, "whatever be our tidings, we will leave this dear spot no more."

" My dear children, I do thank thee both for thee consideration for the old miller. I shall be happy in thee happiness."

" There be only one thing that do give me a fearsome uneasy feel," said the dame, who was wiping some tears from her eyes.

" I know what thee means," said the miller. " Thee be afraid that Giles, in his passion, may do something to give us all trouble."

" Indeed, Gilbert, I be. I did see him this morning, when he did not think that any one did see him, and he did look like mad."

" I am truly sorry for Giles," said George, " and have done all in my power to bring him to a state of serenity and calm reason."

" I do not like to part with the lad," said the miller, gravely, " for we be all liable to be foolish when we are bitterly disappointed. He be more an object of pity to me than dislike; but still there be a duty which we do owe to ourselves which will force me to try to get him a situation elsewhere, and he may then, in time, forget the unhappy passion which does now deprive him of his reason."

" I don't think," said George, " that poor Tim will be the bearer of any more epistles. I have taken some pains to open his eyes to the villany of those who were making him the tool of their own base purposes; and I attribute Mr. Pomander's sad mishap altogether to Tim's conviction of the scandalous manner in which he had been taken in."

" If Tim would have a little common sense, and give up poetry," said the miller, " which be no good to anybody, he would be a likely lad enough, for he be mortal strong."

" I would rather," said George, " have assaulted Mr. Pomander myself, for poor Tim may be exposed to some danger from the revenge of the doctor."

" Be that Giles ?" said the miller, as a shadow of some one passed the window of the cottage.

" Yes," said George, looking out; " he is going to the mill. He appears sullen and gloomy."

" Poor lad, poor lad," said the miller. " I did send him to Farmer Hodgson's, to keep him a little out of harm's way."

" Here is Tim coming for something," said George.

" What do thee want?" said the miller, popping his head out of the window as Tim Miggles approached.

" Want?" said Tim; " I wants nothing; but there's Giles just come back, and saying,—' I'll do it! I'll do it!' and when I told him I wouldn't if I was him, he hit me this dab in the eye. Only look, master, and you, too, Miss Phœbe.

> " For you, my love, I'd be a rose,
> To bloom beneath thy lovely nose.

I'm not going to be wopped, you know, master, for nothing,"

" Well, well," said the miller; " nor shall thee either, foolish fellow though thee be. Come with me; I will go back with thee."

" Oh! I'll give him a sender," said Tim. " I'll walk clean into him if he touches me. Oh, lauks, to be sure, won't I.

> " I'll double my fistesses, and pitch into him,
> Till he'll wish he had never seen nothing of Tim."

" Patience ! patience !" cried the miller; " Giles is mad, and you, Tim— but no matter. Come along—come along."

CHAPTER LI.

GILES felt that he was now at war with the inhabitants of the cottage and the mill, and he shunned communion with any of them. He had leagued with their worst enemies, and he could not conceal from himself the fact, that villainous as was Mr. Scrimp in his practice, that he, Giles, was acting an unworthy part by eating the miller's bread at the same time that he was making common cause with those who would bring ruin and destruction upon his humble home.

The deep strong sense of his supposed injuries urged him onwards; and whenever reflection for a moment pointed out to him his iniquitous situation as a spy in the household of the miller, he stifled the thought by a re-capitulation of his injuries, and crowned all by his detestation of what he conceived to be George's fabrication concerning the last words of his mother, which he fully believed to be invented for the purpose of thwarting him in his just claims to the hand of Phœbe.

Giles had promised, as soon as his day's work at the mill was over, that he would proceed to the house of Mr. Scrimp.

Sunset always terminated the labours at the mill, and Giles impatiently waited the approach of that time. It came at last, and he departed to the village.

The depression of his spirits was dreadful as he pursued his route between the mill and Haredale. He felt that he was taking a step which could never be recalled. Many times he looked back to the mill, but most frequently to the cottage. He thought he saw some one in the little garden. It was—yes, it was Phœbe—she for whom he had suffered so much—she who was the guiding star of his existence.

For a moment the thought recurred to him to return, throw himself at her feet, and implore her forgiveness for all the uneasiness he had occasioned her, bless her! and then leave the mill for ever. But no; passion pre-vailed over principle and feeling—Giles's better nature was crushed, over-powered; he walked on, breathing vengeance upon George.

"She would scorn me again," he muttered, "as she has scorned me be-fore. Revenge! revenge!—I must have revenge. I will leave the mill, but not till this George be well aware of who the man be whom he has outraged and so bitterly wronged. He—he did take Phœbe from me; and I—ha! ha!—I, Giles, who be hated and scorned, will take her from him."

With these reflections in his mind, Giles arrived at Mr. Scrimp's, who was most impatiently awaiting his arrival.

"Ha! my good fellow," said Mr. Scrimp, "I'm delighted to see you. You look uncommonly well. Where can be the eyes of that maid of your master's?"

Giles scowled at Mr. Scrimp, and replied,—

"I do not like thee to speak of her name."

"Oh, certainly not—certainly not, my good Giles. If you please I will abstain. Now, upon my word from all I can hear, you seem to have been very much ill-used by these people of yours at the mill."

"Lawyer," said Giles, "I did come to thee because thee did once say that thee would help me. Will thee do so now?"

"Certainly I will, my good fellow. With the greatest pleasure in life I will assist you. You are clearly in the right; and it's a duty, as well as a pleasure, to assist suffering virtue, and—and—hem—"

"I will have faith in thee," said Giles, "because thee has something to revenge."

"Why, certainly," replied Mr. Scrimp, "that miller of yours did not behave to me with that degree of kindness and cordiality which is grateful to a man's feeling, and I really feel a little kind of a—a—hem. You understand, my good fellow, Giles?"

"I do understand thee. Thee will help me to revenge theeself?"

"Oh, dear, no; not exactly. Suffering innocence and virtue always has a claim upon a susceptible heart like mine."

"Well, well, lawyer, as thee please—as thee please. I have news to tell thee."

"What is it, my good friend?"

"George Andrews be Phœbe's brother."

"Her brother?"

"Yes, her brother; and still—still he do wish to marry her."

"But, my good fellow, he can't. In the eye of the law, you know, that would be a kind of a—a—you know."

"I do know that while I live he do not have Phœbe."

"Her brother?" repeated Mr. Scrimp. "Well, that is, indeed, a piece of most unexpected news. Why, how did this discovery come about?"

"It do appear," said Giles, "that they be brother and sister. I cannot tell thee how it did come about; I did not hear all that they did say; I did only hear that Phœbe could never be his."

"And a very pleasant thing to hear, I dare say you thought it."

"I did, lawyer. It was sunshine to my heart. She be mine, I did say—she be mine; but then George did bethink him of how she should be kept from me."

"Did he, indeed? That was uncommonly wrong."

"He said that his mother, with her last breath, did declare that he and Phœbe were not both her children."

"The deuce he did. And did Phœbe believe it?"

"She did pretend to recollect it, too; but I know it be not true. My heart had grown calm and still before they did say that. I did feel happy—happier than I had felt for many, many months, and I did think that Phœbe might be mine. I did begin to feel kindly to—to George, and to the old miller, and to every one. It did seem to me as if I had had a bad dream, and had awakened, and found myself with dear friends about me. The old mill did look as it used to look long, long ago. I did see the happy fish in the mill stream, and I had not seen them for many a day. The flowers did look fresher in the garden, and—and old happy times had come back again. I—I could have loved them all then. There was a throbbing at my heart; and—and lawyer, I tell thee, I did go to the mill, and I did weep."

Mr. Scrimp was quite out of his element, and did not seem to know very well what to say, so he merely shook his head very sagely, and said,—

"Yes, yes—oh, dear, yes—certainly—of course—a—a—hem!"

"I tell thee, lawyer, how happy I was that thee may know how I did feel the change."

"Oh—ah—yes— dear me—yes."

"Well, I did go again to the cottage, and—and then George did tell me the tale which did scorch my brain like hot iron, and from that moment I did feel as if a snake did lie coiled up at the bottom of my heart. I do now feel the cold weight."

"Dear, dear, that's uncommonly uncomfortable; but you did not believe this absurd tale about the mother?"

"No, I did not—I do not. It be made because—because I was too happy. They could not see me smile again. They could not bear to think there was a little sunshine in my heart. No, no. They did make up the tale, and they did look at me to see if it did drive me mad."

" Eh !—mad !" said Mr. Scrimp, moving his chair a little further from Giles, who spoke with vehemence.

"Yes, lawyer, mad ; and—and it nearly did, but I would not let them see it."

" And what did you do ?"

" I cannot tell thee ; I do not quite know."

" Really, my friend, this is an uncommonly bad piece of business. Why, this idle tale of the old woman's last words that they have trumped up, don't you see, will for ever keep you from getting the girl ?"

" I see it—I do know it—I—I will be revenged."

"You know my good Giles, as this story of George Andrews, or whatever his name is, is a fiction, there never can be any explanation of it. We have some fictions in the law which nobody ever attempts to explain, and there's the beauty of them. When you press your suit to the wench——"

"Who do thee call wench ?" cried Giles. " Phœbe be—be an angel."

"Oh, dear me, yes, if you please. Well, when you press your suit to the—the angel, you know, she'll just say,—' Wait till I hear about mamma's last words,' and then George and the angel will laugh at you when your back's turned, and consider that they have done you uncommonly, don't you see ?"

" I do know it—I do know it. When I did feel bitterness in my heart, and that I was scorned, I did think to come to thee."

" Certainly, a very good resolution."

" I thought thee would give me revenge. I knew thee had no heart, and I become to thee because—I—I be nearly mad."

"Oh, dear, you are very complimentary ; but among friends that's nothing."

"What will thee do to help me ?—what will thee do ? Thee hast been aggrieved theeself at the mill. What dost thee mean to do ?"

" Why, really," said Mr. Scrimp, " it requires a little consideration. I quite feel for you, Giles—upon my word, I do."

" I will have Phœbe. Tell me how to do that, and I will help thee to thee revenge. I be done with the miller, and the mill, and George ; but Phœbe, Phœbe, I do love her still, and still I would die for her, but she must be mine."

" Certainly. Highly proper, Mr. Giles. Your feeling seems very correct on this occasion. Now pluck up some spirit, man. Carry your head a little higher."

" What dost thee mean ?"

" Why, now, if I were in your place ——"

" What—what would thee do ? Would thee fire—destroy—murder ?"

" God bless me, my good friend, you are really quite alarming. You talk of incendiarism, wilful damage, and murder, quite coolly. Recollect I am a member of the legal profession, and such uncommon expressions are quite a—a-hem !"

" What, then, would thee do ?"

" Why, you are a likely young fellow, and I dare say the girl has—I beg your pardon—the angel has a sneaking kindness for you."

" I did think she loved me once ; but it was a dream—a dream."

" A dream !—oh, dear me. Sometimes, you know, Giles, dreams come true. I once dreamed I was retained in a remarkable case of breach of promise, Wiggins v. Hogsflesh, and sure enough the next morning the papers were sent to my office."

Mr. Scrimp was playing with the unfortunate Giles as an angler does with an unhappy fish, which he feels conscious has swallowed his bait, but which might still, without extreme caution on his part, snap his line, and escape.

The little remains of reason and reflection which Giles's passion had left him, Mr. Scrimp looked upon in the same light that the angler might view the struggles and plunges of his prey. Each moment the victim gets weaker and weaker, until at length he is triumphantly drawn to the fatal shore.

So it was with Giles. Mr. Scrimp feared he was hardly in a fit state to receive, as he would wish, the proposition which he had determined to make to him, and he resolved to play with his feelings a little longer.

Giles listened with great and visible impatience to Mr. Scrimp's digression about dreams.

"It was not a dream; no, no," he cried. "I did mean it seemed like one, for I do think she did love me once."

"How long have you been at the mill, my good friend?" said Mr. Scrimp.

"I had been there one year before Phœbe did come. I was a boy; but —but even then I loved her."

"And she was quite young, too."

"I saw her," said Giles, speaking as if to himself—"I saw her in the morning after she had come. There had been a storm, which had shaken even the old mill, but the morning was beautiful. The birds were singing, the sun was shining, and the flowers which had been beaten down by the hail and rain were looking up, and smiling upon the daylight. I—I saw all this. I did bless them all in my heart. I was happy, oh! so happy. My heart was as light as a young bird's."

"I recollect the storm," said Scrimp.

"Then," continued Giles, "I did see her—Phœbe. I was going to the cottage, and I did see her standing by the door, holding the hand of the miller. I did not hear the birds any more. I did not see the flowers. I only saw Phœbe, and I did love her from that time. I did think of nothing but of her. I brought her wild flowers. I listened to her voice. I loved her—I loved her."

Giles clasped his hands, and seemed about to give way to a passion of tears; but Mr. Scrimp did not think a scene of such a nature would advance his views, so he said abruptly,—

"And then this George came, and she fell in love with him?"

An immediate change came over the countenance of Giles. His remembrance of his early love for Phœbe had for a moment obliterated from his mind all recollection of the subsequent events which had given him such exquisite torture; but the name of George recalled him in an instant from his vision of the past, and he was again the wild, infuriated, disappointed man.

"Death! death!" he cried. "He must die—he be killing me—he has taken from me my Phœbe, and I be destroyed—lost—lost."

"Oh, no, by no means; and yet it is provoking to see a girl that one loves in the arms of another, and that other a mere interloper, too. Upon my word, I think, considering all the circumstances you are wonderfully quiet and patient, Master Giles."

"Yes, yes, I have been patient. I have seen her look from the window in the morning, and smile upon him as if—as if he was the daylight."

"And you bore it with patience?"

"I—I—did not kill him—I did not kill him. I have sometimes thought to do so."

"I beg you won't mention anything so decidedly illegal," said Mr. Scrimp, looking rather alarmed, and fearing he was goading Giles just a little too far.

"No, no, I will let him be; but I will have Phœbe to myself."

"Yes, certainly, that's more sensible. Now, if you were inclined to a little sort of frolic—a mere ebullition of youth and hot blood—a little illegal, certainly, but still to be winked at."

"What dost 'e mean, lawyer?"

"Why, if I were in your place, upon my word, I think — But you are pretty sure she looked kindly upon you before this George came?"

"Yes, yes, she did. We rambled together by the murmuring streams. I took her everywhere. I shewed her the quiet, deep places in the woods. She—she must have loved me."

"No doubt—no doubt. Well, presuming a little upon that, I certainly would—not that I would advise you to do so —"

"Would what? Speak, lawyer. Do not drive me mad. What would you do?"

"Run away with her!" said Mr. Scrimp, quickly.

Giles rose, and looked fixedly in the face of the attorney for a few moments, without speaking, then he said, slowly, as if hardly comprehending the full signification of the words,—

"Run away with her?"

"Yes," replied Scrimp, "run away with her. Get her out of the house —pop her into a vehicle—be off with her, and marry her."

"I—I will think," said Giles; "and I will either take thee advice, or—or I think I shall kill thee for wishing a harm to Phœbe."

"Oh, you are joking," said Scrimp; "you are joking, man. There is no great harm done if you were to run off with her. A girl likes ardent affection. She would esteem you for your courage, man, and ten to one she would marry you the first opportunity."

"Run away with Phœbe?" said Giles.

"Aye, man; take her from George."

Giles started at the name of George, and clenched his hands violently.

"Shew him and all the rest of them that you have spirit and resolution. Take her away from them all, and leave George Andrews—ha! ha! ha!— it would be capital—leave George Andrews in despair—such despair, you know, as he left you in."

"That was, indeed, despair," said Giles. "I—I know not what to think."

"Think only of the means of carrying your project into effect."

"I be without means. It be not in my power."

"But if it were—if it were, Giles? You—"

"Yes—yes, if it were—I think—I—I—yes, I would—"

"Take Phœbe from George Andrews?"

"Yes, from a hundred George's. I—I would take her through pools of blood. I would carry her over their dead bodies. I will have her—I will have her."

"Bravely spoken, Giles—bravely spoken. That Phœbe has a winning smile. I suppose she gives George sisterly embraces, and—"

"Hell! hell!" cried Giles.

"And sweet kisses from her dear pouting lips."

Giles sprang at Mr. Scrimp; and before the latter could get out of his way, he had fixed his fingers like a vice in his cravat.

"Fiend! devil!" he screamed; "I—I must kill some one, and it may as well be thee. Thee hast driven me mad. I tell thee I will take her if it be from the old miller's fireside. I will drag her from before their eyes. I will take her—I will have her—if there be a heaven or a hell."

"My—dear—sir," said the half-throttled attorney, "I—I—oh!—assault —battery. For God's sake, let me go—oh!—ah!"

Giles released his hold ; and Mr. Scrimp, looking very pale and fright-ened, said—

"My good fellow, really now, I—a—a-hem.   You are violent to an ex-treme."

"The means—the means, lawyer?" cried Giles ; "the means to take her away?"

"That's the question," replied Mr. Scrimp.

"Shall I sell myself to thee?   Do thee buy men's souls?"

"Not exactly," muttered Mr. Scrimp.   "D— their souls, I prefer their bodies and personal estates, and so on."

"The means !—the means !" shouted Giles,

"Why, as you really have been hardly dealt with," said Scrimp, "I don't mind if I lend you a helping hand in this scheme of yours of running off with the girl."

"It be your scheme," said Giles.

"My scheme?" said Mr. Scrimp ; "I beg your pardon.   Didn't you say you would take the girl from the old miller's fireside, and drag her over a hundred dead bodies?   No, no, it's no scheme of mine.   I don't say any-thing against the scheme, but you know it's yours, my good friend. I could not think of anything half so illegal."

"Well, well," said Giles, "as thee please, lawyer, as thee please, but I thought thee had mentioned it?"

"Yes, after you, certainly.   Then you asked me for the means.   Now, as I have just said to you, I don't mind helping you to the means, but you must just sign a little memorandum of the transaction."

"Anything—anything."

"What is your other name, Giles?"

"Dawson."

No. 40

"Mr. Scrimp drew a sheet of paper towards him, and wrote a few lines, which he read over hurriedly to Giles. They were as follow :—

"I, Giles Dawson, having agreed with Phœbe Marks, commonly known as the daughter of Gilbert Marks, miller, that, under my direction, she shall leave the house of the said Gilbert Marks, with her free will and consent, have applied to Olinthus Scrimp, attorney-at-law, of Haredale, for certain means to carry the wishes of the aforesaid Phœbe Marks into effect, which he, Scrimp, upon this my solemn declaration, that Phœbe Marks is free and willing so to act, has kindly agreed to."

"A mere matter of form to smother difficulties," said Mr. Scrimp, pushing the paper towards Giles, and handing him the pen.

"But," said Giles, "I—I—Mr. Scrimp—Phœbe has not ——"

"Oh, you mean that she has not actually spoken to you on the subject. Oh, that's nothing. A mere legal fiction, rendered necessary by the state of the law, and the determination of George Andrews that you shall never wed Phœbe, you see."

Giles took up the pen and wrote his name.

"Thank you," said Scrimp. "Look upon the business as finished."

"But—but how?"

"Come to me to-morrow evening, and you will find everything satisfactorily arranged. Phœbe shall be yours in spite of them all."

CHAPTER LII.

It is now imperative upon us, in the due progress of this narrative, to take leave, for a very short space, of the inhabitants of the mill and the cottage, to direct the reader's attention to an occurrence which took place at Bungleum.

The day had scarcely dawned upon which Mr. Pomander paid his unlucky visit to the mill, when a number of persons might have been observed on the little jetty close to the harbour of Bungleum. Some were provided with glasses and telescopes of all kinds and descriptions; but all, whether so assisted or not, were looking with the greatest attention, seawards, at a large vessel, which was lying about two miles only off the port.

Those who were provided with glasses could perceive an unusual bustle upon her deck, and presently a boat was lowered, and rowed rapidly towards the shore.

"That be an Indiaman," said a weather-worn fisherman, as he shaded his eyes with his hands, and took a long look at the vessel.

"If so be as how it be an Indiaman," said another, "it's very uncommon, for I never yet heard of one putting in here."

"They're a going only to put ashore some nob or another," said the first speaker, "and here he comes, with twelve oars, too. I say he's somebody, he is."

"Aye, aye, I see him," replied the other man. "He's a lying in the stern, wrapped up in a ocean o'cloth and shawls, he is. Lord bless me, those ere Inde fellows they never feels hot enough, they don't.

The boat now rapidly reached the shore, and when its keel grated upon the stony beach, the person who had been described as enveloped in so much clothing, rose and stepped from it.

He was still a handsome man, although much past the prime of life, and his appearance was weak and sickly, which arose principally from his long residence in the enervating climate of India.

He was in an undress military uniform; and although his rank could not be accurately guessed at from his apparel, yet it was evident from the respect which was shown to him by the owner of the boat, and the naval officer who commanded them, that either personally, or on account of his station, he was no ordinary man.

He stood on the beach as the boat pushed off, and lifted the travelling-cap from his head with a courteous action.

" Your captain will hear from me on his arrival in London," he said.

The officer in the boat bowed, and the men, with a cheer, took to their oars again, and made for the ship.

The gentleman—for gentleman he evidently was—who had landed, stood for a few moments irresolute upon the jetty. He then turned to a man near him, and said,—

" Can I get a conveyance of any kind to Lanstock?"

" Yes, your honour," answered the man. " Your honour can get a chaise at the 'Albion.'"

" Thank you, thank you," said the stranger.

" Shall I show your honour the way?" said the man, touching his hat.

" No, I know it well," said the stranger, as he handed a piece of money to the man.

" God bless your honour!" said the fisherman, as he saw what had been given him was gold.

The stranger cautiously inclined his head and smiled as he passed onwards, like one familiar with the place.

" That's a gemman, he is," said the fisherman, " and no mistake whatsomdever. He's come here not for nothing."

" I shouldn't wonder but he's some great soldier officer," said another.

Meantime the stranger walked slowly towards the town. He looked frequently around him, and sighed deeply.

" There is but little hope," he said, as he entered the 'Albion;' " but upon that hope I have lived long."

He walked into the coffee-room of the hotel, and sat down in the recess of a window. Here he appeared to give himself up entirely to his own reflections, and to be quite unconscious where he was.

This sort of abstraction in a guest after he had given his orders, would not have been considered as of any consequence at the "Albion;" but as the strange gentleman had ordered nothing, it filled the whole establishment with uneasiness.

A waiter was accordingly directed to awaken the guest to a sense of his great impropriety, which he attempted to do by fetching a napkin, and diligently dry-rubbing a table, on the corner of which the stranger's elbow was resting.

This produced no effect whatever, and the waiter flourished the napkin close to his face, but still he moved not.

" Dear me," said the waiter to himself, " it's very singular; he's in a wery uncommon brown study, he is. I'll get master to come."

Off trotted the waiter accordingly.

" He won't move, sir, nor do nothing whatsomdever, sir," said the waiter to his master.

" Dear me, Sam—dear me," said the landlord. " He may, poor gentleman, be thinking of something uncomfortable, in which case it is a duty to disturb him."

" Yes, sir," said Sam.

" Does he look—a—like a kind of hot, hasty sort of man, eh, Sam?"

" No, sir. Mild-looking gentleman, sir. Sighs like a bottle of ginger-beer, with little hole in cork, sir."

"You don't think he'll fly in a rage, Sam?"

"No, sir. Quiet-looking gentleman, sir. Put up with a good deal, sir."

"Then just go in and upset all the fire-irons, Sam."

"Yes, sir."

Sam departed, and executed his master's order with most startling effect, but the strange gentleman never so much as winced.

Then Sam took up a water-jug that was on the table, and placed it down again with a thump, which threatened its immediate fracture. But no; the stranger was evidently proof against all noises.

The waiter went back to his master with the intelligence that he couldn't make the gentleman order nothing no how.

"It's uncommon strange, Sam. You think he's a mild sort of gentleman?"

"Yes, sir; but you recollect, sir, the mild-looking gentleman once, sir, as comed here and broke the looking-glasses, and walloped you, sir?"

"Yes, I do—I do, Sam. Those mild-looking gentleman ain't always to be depended on—oh, dear, no."

"I can't do nothing with him, sir."

"Well, I'll just go in promiscuous like myself, Sam, and see what I can do."

The landlord himself, with all the dignity of the "Albion" in every step, walked into the coffee-room.

"A—a—hem! hem! hem!" he cried, but the stranger took no heed of him whatever. "Sir—sir—a—a—hem!—sir ——"

"Their long silence," said the stranger, in a low, mournful voice.

"Sir! sir!—we—we forgot what you ordered sir—hem!"

"No answer to my letters. Have I not everything to fear? and what to prove?"

The landlord could stand it no longer, and he laid his hand upon the stranger's arm.

"Sir! sir!—a—a—hem!"

The stranger started in an instant, and said, mildly, but firmly,—

"Well!—what is it?"

This quiet answer rather posed the landlord, and he only glared with his little round eyes at the gentleman, without making any reply.

"What do you want?" said the stranger. Then smiling, he added :— "Let me have some claret, and get me a chaise ready."

The landlord flourished his napkin, and bowed to the ground.

"Yes, sir—oh, dear, yes, sir—beg pardon, sir—claret, sir—directly—Sam! Sam!—claret! claret!—chaise for gentleman!"

"Claret! claret!" shouted Sam. "Chaise for quiet gentleman. Coming—coming—coming."

The stranger waited till the chaise was announced as ready, and then, leaving the wine untasted on the table, he stepped into the vehicle.

"To where sir?" said the postillion, touching his hat.

"To Lanstock."

Crack went the whip, and away rattled the chaise from the door of the "Albion" with the strange gentleman.

It was late in the evening when the chaise again stopped at the door of the inn.

The landlord ran out and assisted the gentleman to alight.

When the stranger had departed in the morning he had looked pale and sickly, but it now appeared as if years had elapsed since that time, for his hand shook, and his whole appearance indicated debility and mental suffering.

He walked with a tottering step into the inn, and called for wine. When it came he drank four or five glasses in succession, and then rising, he drew his cloak about him, and walked more firmly to the door.

The landlord saw by the general appearance of his guest that he was a gentleman, and, probably, of some high rank, who was prosecuting some secret business. He had, likewise, caught sight of a well-filled purse; and as the strange gentleman paid for everything without a question, and appeared never to see his change, mine host concluded in his own mind that the "Albion" ought to rejoice exceedingly in his presence, and he accordingly determined to leave no stone unturned to keep the strange gentleman.

Mine host followed him to the door with a vast profusion of bows, and flourishes of a white damask napkin.

"Will your honour sleep here to-night, sir?" he said. "Good beds, sir; well-aired—quiet—comfortable, sir—best inn."

"Possibly, that is, most probably," said the stranger. "You will keep a bed for me?"

"Certainly, sir—yes, sir. Sam, Sam, best bed-room for gentleman. Light a fire, sir? Getting chilly in evenings, sir."

"Yes; a fire by all means."

"Sam, Sam."

"Coming—coming—coming."

"Fire for gentlemen in best bed-room, di—rectly."

"Yes, sir. Best bed-room for mild-looking gentleman, and fire. Coming —coming, sir."

The stranger walked from the inn-door, and then paused in the street, as if uncertain of his course.

"Of whom can I inquire," he said, "This place has greatly increased in size since my absence. Formerly each inhabitant knew, at the least, the names, if not the very concerns, of all the rest. Some shop will be the most likely place."

As the stranger spoke he looked up and down the street, and observing a little chandler's shop at some distance from him, he proceeded to it.

Upon entering the shop he was confronted by an old woman, of a sharp and vinegary aspect, who, with her mouth screwed so close as hardly to permit her words to escape, said,—

"What may you want, sir?"

"I wish to make an inquiry," said the stranger.

"Oh, you'd better go to the baker's, or the public-house; they know everybody."

"Very well," said the stranger, restoring to his pocket a sovereign, which the old woman had not observed he had laid gently on her dirty counter.

"Oh, godness gracious!" she exclaimed. "Pray, sir, sit down a moment. You wanted to inquire, sir?"

The stranger, however, calmly left the shop, and the infuriated elderly female rushed, in a state bordering on frenzy, into her parlour, and seizing upon a poor little girl, who she called her servant, allayed her wretched feelings by bestowing her an unmerciful chastisement.

The gentleman proceeded onwards till he came to a baker's shop, which was at the corner of the street.

There was a woman in the shop with an infant in her arms. The stranger entered, and preferred his inquiry.

"I wish to know, madam," he said, "if you recollect the name of— of——"

"What name, sir," said the woman, respectfully, and then observing that the stranger seemed much affected, she added,—" Will you take a seat, sir ?"

" I—I thank you," he said ; " the name is—is Grainger."

" Grainger ?—Grainger ?" repeated the woman.

" Yes, it was long ago. Did a person of that name, to your knowledge, live in this town ? or—does she still ?"

" Now I do recollect," said the woman ; " you must mean the Widow Grainger."

" Widow !"

" Yes, 'poor woman. Her husband was a soldier, I've heard, and was killed, poor man, somewhere."

" She—she had a child—a little girl."

" Oh, yes ; a little girl and a boy ; and beautiful children they were, too."

The stranger seemed quite overcome by his emotions, and sank into the chair which the woman had placed for him.

" Grainger," he said, after a psuse ; " you—you are quite sure? Her name is Grainger ?"

" Oh, yes ; I have seen her often."

" She was fair, was she not, with blue eyes, and—and—long auburn hair ?"

The woman shook her head doubtingly.

" You must mean a younger person, sir, than the Widow Grainger ?"

" No, no—I had forgotten—years have flown by—yes, yes—I only remember her as she was."

" She might have been, sir, as you describe ; for when I last saw her I recollect thinking she must have been very handsome. The little girl was very like her."

" Yes—yes, the little girl—Phœbe—Phœbe."

" Yes, sir, that was her name. She has often been here, and used always to speak so affectionately of her poor mother, that I quite loved the dear child."

" Tell me—oh, tell me—do they reside here now ?"

" Alas ! no, sir."

" Where—where, then ? Where shall I seek them ?"

" Perhaps, sir, you are some relation ?"

" I am ; I have come many miles to seek them. I have traversed half the world to hold that dear infant in my arms again, and hear her lisping voice."

" Infant, sir ?—lisping voice ? Why, I haven't seen Phœbe Grainger for six or seven years—oh, dear me, more than that, and then she was quite a fine girl, although rather delicate-looking."

" Tru—true. I forget time. It must be so. I only think of her as she was."

" And the boy, sir, was quite a fine lad as could be seen."

" The boy ! Oh, yes, yes—I recollect. But tell me where to find them ?"

" Sir, you seem much interested in them, and——"

" And what ? Oh, do not keep me in suspense. Tell me, I conjure you, tell me all you know about them. Your looks alarm me."

" They are not here now, sir."

" Not here ! Well, well, it matters not ; I can seek them anywhere. I'll travel to the furthest corner of the earth to find them. Give me but the least clue to where they are, and I shall be much indebted to you."

" Sir, I grieve to tell you bad news."

" Bad news ! Wh—what !—Speak, oh, speak ?"

" Why, sir, the Widow Grainger, poor woman——"

"She is poor—very poor, you would say. Well, well, that is past—it is now over—she is poor no longer."

"Indeed, that is true ; she is poor no longer, for she is——"

The stranger rose, and seemed struggling for utterance. He shrieked, rather than said,—

"What!—what is she?"

"Dead!" replied the alarmed woman.

With a heavy groan the stranger fell on the floor in a state of insensibility.

"Help! help! help!" cried the compassionate woman, running to the door.

Several neighbours, alarmed by her cries, rushed in, and raised the fallen man.

"The poor gentleman has fainted," said the baker's wife. "I'll get a light, for it's getting quite dark."

"Some water," said one—"some water."

"A little vinegar," said another.

"Here's a card case has dropped from his pocket," said a neighbour.

"Give it me," cried the baker's wife. "We shall see who the gentleman is."

She took a card from the case, and held it to the light.

Every one pressed eagerly forward to hear the name.

"Colonel Grainger!" said the woman.

"Colonel Grainger!" repeated everybody.

A deep sigh now burst from the insensible man, and he opened his eyes, and looked inquiringly about him.

"Forward! forward! my lads!" he cried; I'm wounded. Charge! charge!—Hurrah! hurrah!—Forward! forward!"

"His mind is wandering," said the baker's wife. "Alas! poor gentleman, what shall we do?"

CHAPTER LIII.

GEORGE now spent most of his time in the company of Phœbe, and the happy hours passed in her society seemed to him but as moments. It is in pain only that we can pause to note the existence of, and calculate upon its presence. Pleasure flits past us on fleet pinions; and, as with the forked lightning, which for one instant dazzles the eyes, ere we can say "behold!" 'tis gone.

But all too short and fleeting as they were, those were delightful hours that George and Phœbe spent together. All was confidence—all affection. The time of their childood seemed to be restored, and they talked of the various incidents of their lives, and the adventures they had passed through, as they would have talked of some interesting romance that they had read.

Arm in arm they wandered about the green lanes and among the majestic trees. They saw beauty in everything, for the alchemy of the happy heart turns everything to gold.

The union of their pure heart was perfect. If they were not tied to each other by blood, they were by affection—an affection began in early life, and never—never for one moment forgotten.

How many subjects of conversation they had in which each were equally interested. They would recal with pleasure each trivial incident connected with their happy home, when their poor mother was the whole world to them. They could name to each other each particular flower which bloomed in the garden of the cottage in which their dear parent breathed her last sigh. Then how much had they to tell each other of what had occurred during their long separation—of hopes, fears, kindness received from some, and unfeeling harshness from others. They could have listened to each other's narratives, as well as the dear love for the narrator, which lent a glow to each circumstance, however trivial.

When the evening deepened into night, they would repair to the cottage, and there, by the honest miller's fireside, they would listen to him, as he would again and again tell how on the night of the fearful storm he had heard the wailing cry for help in the blast, and rescued her who had become so dear to his heart from want and misery; and then in quaint and homely, but still eloquent, because sincere language, he would say how largely he had been repaid by the dear love Phœbe had given in return, and how happy had been his humble home since it had been illumined by her sweet face.

He had arranged that they were to depart for Bungleum, and thence to Lanstock, on the next Monday, and the good dame was busying herself for their departure.

To George, who had been so great a wanderer in the world, the little journey was nothing; but poor Phœbe, who had hardly since childhood known a day's happiness till she came to the mill, looked upon the preparations for leaving it, even for a short period, with great sorrow, if not alarm.

"Oh, George," she would say, "let us stay here and be happy, as brother and sister. We always believed ourselves such;—let us think so still."

"Dear Phœbe," said George, "we must take the advice of our best friend —the good miller. I feel a kind of presentiment that there will something occur shortly to put an end to the doubt and uncertainty in which we are now. I do not, dear Phœbe, say that I am not happy, but if there be a thin cloud which dims the sunshine of my heart, it is created by the mystery which has been produced by our dear mother's last words. Would to Heaven she had been granted time to tell us more, or had told us nothing."

"It is for the best, George," said Phœbe, "no doubt. The designs of Heaven are always good. I will go, dear George, and go without anxiety, for we will be happy either as a brother and sister, or as——"

"Husband and wife, dear Phœbe. In either case you will ever be to me the dearest object on the earth. My wandering life, I hope, is over, and if it please Heaven, I would fain pass the remainder of my existence on this quiet, happy spot."

"We will, George. This journey shall be our last. We have no ties to bind us to the world. Here we will live in peace and happiness."

Such were the anticipations of future happiness which were indulged in by Phœbe and George. Early in life they had seen quite sufficient of the world to make them long for a peaceful home. Wealth they courted not. They had passed through the ordeal of society uncontaminated by any of the vices, and with hearts as pure and innocent as when they wept together over their mother's grave in the village churchyard. They possessed the advantage of a knowledge of what to shun as destructive of that peace and serenity of mind, without which the pursuit of happiness is but chasing a shadow, and with which there need be no pursuit.

Giles, on the morning after his interview and compact with Mr. Scrimp, was gloomy and sullen. He went to his work in silence, and he avoided any conversation whatever with the inhabitants of the cottage. His mind was highly wrought to the purpose which had been so cunningly suggested to him by the attorney, but still he formed his own resolution; and it was only by keeping up an appearance of warfare and ill-will between himself and those against whose peace he was so recklessly conspiring, that he could keep his mind fixed to its purpose.

"I say, Giles," said Tim, "what do you think?"

"Peace! peace! Don't trouble me."

"Well, but really I thought you'd like to know, and you might have *knowed*, too, only you look so queer nobody likes to speak to you."

"Queer!—ha! ha! ha! So my looks are watched, are they?"

"I don't know what you mean by watched, old fellow; but you look like the enchanter, Flurrycumfodde, who had an immense scaly tail, and one day——"

"Tush! tush! Don't trouble me with your nonsense."

"Nonsense, indeed. How would you like, if you had a magnificent tail, all over shining green scales, to have it all of a sudden——"

"Peace! peace! I say;—thee art a fool!"

"A fool am I? I know which side my bread's buttered on for all that."

"Away, away. Carry your folly elsewhere."

"I wish you'd send off your black looks, Master Giles. Oh, you needn't frown; I don't care. I haven't come to the time of life that I has to care about you. Oh, come on—come on."

"Thee will get thee foolish head broke for thee folly."

"No, I sha'n't, oh, dear, no."

"Well, well, leave me—leave me, Tim."

"Oh, you've come down a peg, have you? Well, I'll try to amuse you a little. Did you ever hear of the tragical poem of the 'Fate of Ingratitude; or, the Lord Cramanguzzleal?'"

"No, no, I don't want;—go thee ways."

"Then I'll tell it to you. Here goes.

   " 'Cramanguzzleal was a lord,
    Who couldn t very well afford
     To drink such a lot of Rhenish wine;
    Yet he would never stint a drop,
    And slept as sound as any top,
     With his vassals on the floor, like swine,

He run such queer uncommon rigs,
And was so very fond of pigs,
  Till they couldn't be had for any money;
Cramanguzzleal then groaned,
For a leg of pork he moaned,
  For without it he felt quite funny;
Then the steward who was big,
Said my lord, there's a pig,
  Who's a whopper, aye, as large as any moke,
He's in the finest herd, by——' "

"Peace! peace!" cried Giles. "What news did thee say thee had?"

"Why, don't you know that Phœbe is George's brother—no, dear me, his mother—his sister, I mean?"

"Well, well."

"And he says he isn't no such thing as a brother to nobody not no how, you know."

"I know—I know."

"Well, what do you think?"

"I don't know—what is it?"

"Why, there's George and Phœbe going away on Monday."

"What?—going away?" cried Giles, vehemently.

"Yes, they are. They say it's to find out who they really are."

"So soon," said Giles—"humph!—Monday. Art thee sure it be Monday?"

"Master said Monday."

"It must be done—yes—yes—quickly. Oh, Phœbe, Phœbe."

"Dear me, Giles, ain't you well?"

"Don't talk to me. I be not able to talk to thee. Monday—Monday, and this is Thursday."

"Yes, Thursday, and no mistake."

"We shall see—we shall see."

"In course we shall."

"The time be short. I—I know not what to think. My brain be hot —hot."

"I don't wonder at it, for you've just hit your head a deuce of a punch."

"The die be cast—there be no hope—all be black—black."

"Well, that is a good 'un. Black, indeed, why, it's all white here, Giles. You must be a little mad, or so."

"Yes—mad—mad. I—I shall be mad. Perhaps I be mad now."

"You may depend you are."

"To be gone on Monday—Monday—this being Thursday. Yes, it shall be done—there be no other hope—no other."

Giles leant his head upon his hands, and appeared lost in deep meditation.

The day crept slowly by, and the evening had hardly began to usurp the place of the bright daylight, when Giles left the mill, and with a hurried step, which betrayed the agitation of his mind, walked to the village, to hold, according to arrangement, another meeting with Mr. Scrimp.

The attorney had considered his last interview with Giles so important, that on the evening he had lost no time in proceeding to Haredale Park, to communicate to Sir Herbert Foster the auspicious state of affairs.

A confederate at the mill was certainly all that could be desired for the furtherance of the villanous scheme of Mr. Scrimp and his associates.

About making the unhappy Giles a mere tool and victim in the business the wily attorney made not the least scruple, and one object of his visit to Sir Herbert Foster was to procure a warrant for the assault in Foyle's Hollow against Giles, which might be put in force immediately that he had been of all the assistance he could in decoying Phœbe some distance from her home, after which Giles would have become a serious encumbrance to the further progress of the abduction.

Mr. Scrimp, when he arrived at Haredale Park, first asked to see Freegrove, and was directed into a small parlour, which was used as a waiting-room for visiters.

Mr. Scrimp opened the door, and walked in without ceremony. Both Freegrove and the valet Cury were in the room, and Mr. Scrimp was astonished at the sudden start that they both gave when he appeared, and the confusion which was manifest in both their countenances.

"Oh, Mr. Scrimp," said Freegrove, "how are you? I was just chatting a little to Cury, and——"

"And," said Cury, "as we were talking of rather a startling subject, your appearance rather took us by surprise."

"Oh, gentlemen," said Scrimp, "I can but apologize."

"Oh, don't name it," said Cury in his softest and silkiest tones. "You are an old friend, Mr. Scrimp, and we may mention to you what we would not to everybody. I'll tell you a little plan we were arranging."

"Cury," said Freegrove, turning very pale.

Cury went on, however, without heeding him.

"You know the jewel-room, Mr. Scrimp?"

"I do," said Scrimp. "Among the family papers I have an inventory of its contents."

"Well, Freegrove and I were——"

"The devil!" said Freegrove.

"We were talking of this ghost which Sir Herbert says he has seen in the jewel-room, and as he seems greatly alarmed at it, we were trying to think of some means of easing his mind upon the subject."

"It's a singular circumstance," said Scrimp. "Is Sir Herbert within?"

"He is," said Freegrove.

"I will do myself the pleasure of announcing you, Mr. Scrimp," said Cury, leaving the room for that purpose.

"We shall manage this matter of ours, Freegrove," said Scrimp, "for I've got the swain whose affections—ha! ha! ha!—are blighted."

"But you did not think fit, Mr. Scrimp, to tell me about this ghost affair?"

"Oh! pho! pho! my dear fellow, don't think of it. Sir Herbert made such a point of none of his household knowing anything about it, you see."

"Well, he told it all to Cury."

"Oh, then, you know all about it?"

"Yes, it's uncommonly queer; I'm afraid it's a bad business."

"Why, you don't mean to say you believe it?"

"Yes, I do. How could it happen else?"

"Sir Herbert will see you, Mr. Scrimp," said Cury, opening the door. "He's in the yellow drawing-room. He has changed his dressing-room since the—the——"

"The ghost business you mean?"

"Yes, Mr. Scrimp. Do you know the way?"

"Oh, yes, perfectly."

Mr. Scrimp left the room; and as he proceeded to the magnificent apartment in which he was told he should find Sir Herbert, he muttered to himself,—

"Humph!—There's something going on between those two rascals—Freegrove and Cury. I saw it in their looks. They are 'shallow knaves. I'll find it out, or my name is not Scrimp. We shall see—we shall see."

The room in which Sir Herbert Foster sat, or rather reclined, may well deserve a passing notice. It was one of those drawing-rooms which occupied the front and two sides of the mansion. They had been fitted up by the predecessor in the family wealth and honours of the present baronet.

The furniture and ornaments of one were all of rich crimson and gold; of the other, blue and silver; and of the third, in which was Sir Herbert, pale yellow and gold.

This yellow drawing-room was the largest, and, if any difference, the most costly of the three.

The walls were hung in the old style, with rich yellow satin. The various articles of furniture were of the finest maple wood, inlaid with plates of metal, and gilded in the most elegant style.

Mr. Scrimp had frequently been in the superb apartment, and he now gave but a tribute of a glance to its magnificence.

Sir Herbert Foster was, as usual, reclining on a couch, as if mere exist-ence was a vile trouble to one of his great refinement and courtly taste.

It might have been partly the tint given to his countenance by the colour of everything in the room, but Mr. Scrimp absolutely started as his eye fell upon the face of the baronet, so ghastly pale and wan did it appear.

"May I presume to hope," said the attorney, "that you are well, my dear Sir Herbert?"

"Oh, Scrimp?" said Sir Herbert.

Again Mr. Scrimp started, for the very voice was altered.

"Yes, Sir Herbert. Scrimp your very humble servant."

"Oh—oh—oh, very well, thank you. Shut the door. You did not see anything uncommon, did you, as you came here?"

"Uncommon, Sir Herbert!—no nothing."

"Because, Scrimp, I—I have seen it again!"

"What, Sir Herbert? The—the——"

"Helen Wade—the apparition. Oh, it is too horrible. I—I have been obliged to change my apartments."

"May I be permitted, Sir Herbert, to ask any particulars?"

"Yes, yes; I will tell you." The baronet cast an anxious glance round the magnificent apartment as he spoke, as if in search of something.

"Can I get you anything, Sir Herbert?" asked Scrimp. "Pray com-mand me. I shall be most proud and happy——"

"No, no. I sometimes fancy she is here. There is a kind of shadow flits across my eyes. But about this girl, Scrimp—this miller's girl?"

"Why, Sir Herbert, I came to tell you that everything was going on well; and one of the young fellows at the mill, from feelings of disappoint-ment and fancied ill usage, will very materially assist us."

"Well, well. I only wait down here for the completion of that matter. My mind is stagnant. I require something to arouse me from this state of mind. Can I sell this property, Scrimp?"

"Why, no, Sir Herbert; Haredale is entailed."

"Well, well, let it go. I shall never see it after Saturday, or Sunday at the latest. When do you expect the matter to be settled?"

"Why, Sir Herbert, I want two things of you, if you please."

"What are they?"

"One is an order for your plain posting chariot."

"You shall have it."

"The other is a warrant, Sir Herbert, in your capacity as a magistrate, for the apprehension of the rascal who assaulted you in Foyle's Hollow."

"In whose Hollow?"

"Foyle's Hollow, Sir Herbert, where you did the girl the honour to meet her."

"Oh, yes, yes. Tell my clerk to prepare it, or you can do it yourself, and I will sign it. Scrimp, just look outside the door."

"Outside this door, Sir Herbert?"

"Yes, yes;—just cast your eye along the corridor."

Mr. Scrimp walked to the door, and did as he was directed, and then returned.

"Did you see anything?" said Sir Herbert Foster.

"No, Sir Herbert—nothing."

"I—I have not seen it here, Scrimp. There was no robbery. All was safe."

"You mean in the the jewel-room, Sir Herbert?"

"Yes, in the jewel-room. I examined everything. Cury has seen her as well as myself. It can be no delusion."

"Humph!" thought Mr. Scrimp—"so, so. This is some fine-drawn scheme of Master Cury's, is it?"

"Last evening," continued Sir Herbert, "I was coming from my dressing-room, and I saw the figure standing at the head of the marble staircase. Cury saw it there."

"And did you follow it, Sir Herbert?"

"No—I—I could not; I think it disappeared. A mist came over my eyes, and it was gone. Horrible! horrible!"

"I should strongly advise you, Sir Herbert, when next this apparition appears to you to follow it, and not lose sight of it by any means."

"I—I cannot, Scrimp—I cannot. It would lead me to that room—the jewel-room—which witnessed her death. No, no; I cannot follow it."

"Then I fear, Sir Herbert, you will never solve the mystery of the appearance."

"Mystery, Scrimp. There is no mystery. Who can doubt the supernatural character of the visitation?"

"I doubt it, with all due submission, Sir Herbert."

"No, no. Do not say you doubt. Suppose—suppose even now your doubts were to be resolved by—ha! what is that?"

The door slowly opened as Sir Herbert spoke until it was quite wide, and even Mr. Scrimp looked towards it with some degree of nervousness.

For about five minutes they neither spoke nor moved; but as nothing was to be seen, Mr. Scrimp recovered from his first sensation, which certainly partook, in some degree, of alarm and uneasiness.

"This is merely accidental, Sir Herbert," said Scrimp. "I must have omitted to fasten the latch of the door."

"Did you hear nothing?"

"No, I heard nothing. It might be that the wind, which, doubtless, opened the door, might make some slight sighing noise."

"You—you heard a sigh, then?"

"There was certainly a something," said Scrimp.

"There was—there was; and I could see a light shadow steal across the tapestry."

"Eh?" said Scrimp, starting;—"a shadow, Sir Herbert!"

"Yes, Scrimp. There is now in the room an inhabitant of another world."

"The deuce there is," said the attorney, jumping up, and placing his back against the wall.

Mr. Scrimp was not aware, from the walls being covered by drapery, that he had placed his back against the door of a small closet; but he was soon made aware of the fact, for his weight opened the door, and he fell backwards with a great crash, carrying with him a long strip of the satin hangings.

"Help! help! murder!" roared Scrimp.

Cury entered the room instantly.

"Bless me," said the attorney, scrambling out of the closet. "Really, Sir Herbert, I beg ten thousand pardons. I really, my dear Sir Herbert— I feel ——"

"Never mind—never mind," said the baronet, who had never moved from his couch.

"Cury."

"Sir Herbert."

"Where did you come from?"

"I, Sir Herbert. I—I came from the drawing-room, Sir Herbert."

Mr. Scrimp marked the hesitation with which the answer was given, and he said,—

"If I might presume a remark, Sir Herbert feels somewhat surprised at your very quick and sudden appearance, Mr. Cury."

"Sir Herbert's servants are taught to attend him quickly, Mr. Scrimp," said Cury, softly.

"You may say what you like," thought Scrimp, rubbing his back, which had been rather hurt from coming in contact with a pair of steps which were in the closet, "but I feel pretty sure, Master Cury, that you were just outside the door."

"Did you see anything?" said Sir Herbert.

"No, Sir Herbert;—and yet ——"

"Yet what? What would you say, Cury? Speak freely."

"I thought something seemed to leave the room like a shadow as I came towards the door. I am not sure what it was, Sir Herbert."

"You may go."

Cury bowed himself out.

"Scrimp," said Sir Herbert,—"Scrimp, what do you say now? Where are your doubts?"

"My doubts," thought Scrimp, "are removed, and I feel convinced that Master Cury knows more about the ghost than anybody; but it ain't exactly prudent to say so just now. I really, Sir Herbert, don't know what to think exactly. I cannot say I saw anything."

"No, no; but you are conscious—you feel that there was a something uncommon present—you must have felt it—I saw it in your looks."

"Why, Sir Herbert, I was rather astonished at falling into the closet, for which I beg again most earnestly to apologize; but I would rather suspend my judgment about the matter for the present. I repeat, with all deference, my former advice. When you see anything of the figure again, follow it, Sir Herbert, or keep it in view till you call for assistance."

"You are sceptical, Scrimp. Pray ring the bell."

Mr. Scrimp rung, and Cury again appeared.

"Cury, see that the crimson drawing-room is immediately got ready for me. I will sit there."

"Yes, Sir Herbert," said the obsequious valet.

Mr. Scrimp shortly left Haredale Park, perfectly convinced in his own mind that something was going on in which Cury thought it expedient to play upon the imagination of his master.

"I will, I must find it out," said Scrimp. "D—n him, what business has he to be hatching schemes, and with that thick-skulled wretch, Freegrove, too. I dare say there's a pretty plan of plunder at the bottom of it. I must think it over. Beware, Master Cury, beware! I must not have poor dear Sir Herbert frightened out of his wits by you—oh, dear, no. That would not answer at all. Master Cury, Master Cury, I must be down upon you."

CHAPTER LIV.

THE incoherent expressions which fell from Colonel Grainger in the baker's shop filled the good woman and her neighbours with the greatest alarm and consternation, and the nearest medical man was immediately summoned to attend upon the afflicted gentleman.

Before his arrival, however, Colonel Grainger had greatly recovered from the shock he had sustained.

"The Albion—the Albion!" he said, faintly, by which they surmised that he desired to be taken to that house of entertainment for man and beast.

"You had better not attempt to walk, sir," said the medical man.

"I thank you—I thank you all," said the colonel, who we shall no longer call a stranger, now that our readers are well aware of who he is, and the nature of his errand to Bungleum.

"Will you, then, take my arm, sir?" said the surgeon.

"With great pleasure," he replied. "Madam," turning to the baker's wife, "if you or your husband will favour me with a call at the 'Albion' the first thing in the morning, and tell me all you know of—of—you know who I mean ——"

"Yes, sir; certainly, sir," said the woman.

The colonel laid a five pound note upon the counter, and then left the shop with the medical gentleman.

In a few moments they were at the door of the "Albion," to the great surprise of the landlord, who did not at all expect to see his guest back so soon."

"Sam, Sam!" he cried, "the gentleman has come back again. Sleep here, now, sir, I suppose. Best bed-room, sir, well-aired."

"Colonel Grainger will retire to rest at once," said the surgeon; "at least, I advise him to do so."

"Colonel—Colonel—Colonel Grainger?" said the landlord. "Here, Sam, Sam. Colonel Grainger's bed-room directly."

"Yes, sir," replied Sam; "colonel's bed-room—colonel's bed-room. Coming, sir, coming."

"I will do myself the honour, sir, of calling upon you in the morning," said the medical man, into whose hands the colonel had been placed at the baker's.

"I shall be happy to see you," said Colonel Grainger.

It was evident that everything that the colonel said was merely mechanical, and that his thoughts were otherwise occupied. He looked wretchedly ill, and sighed deeply as he was shown into the chamber, which had been put hurriedly into a state of readiness to receive him.

When he was there, left alone, he covered his face with his hands, and a copious flood of tears came to his relief.

"Gone! gone!" he said. "Dead! That awful word—dead! dead! How many have I seen dead upon the field of battle, and how lightly have I then thought of death? But now with what terrors is that word clothed! Dead! dead!—gone from me, and I shall never see her more. Why do I live?—and yet is there not the child—the dear young thing, who they tell me has now grown a dear resemblance of her sainted mother? Yes—yes—still let me cherish life. For her sake, let me cling to existence. Yes—for her—for her—my child—for my dear child!"

Colonel Grainger descended to the coffee-room of the "Albion," at a very early hour, and waited with great impatience the appearance of the baker, or his wife.

It was not long before the woman herself arrived, and the colonel motioning her to a seat, turned himself in such a position that she could not see his face, for he feared his feelings would overcome his firmness.

"I thank you, madam," he said, "for the kindness of this visit. Any particulars which can tell me of—the—Mrs. Grainger I shall hear with grateful feelings."

"Sir," said the woman, "I can tell you but little further than that she was a most amiable and kind-hearted creature, and much esteemed by all who knew her."

"Yes, yes, she was that—she was—she was," cried the colonel, in a voice struggling with deep emotion.

I think it is about seven years ago she died."

"Seven years. Go on—go on."

"And I believe that, although she kept a cheerful countenance, and her dear children were always as neat and clean and handsome-looking as possible, she was in very great poverty before her death."

"Go on—go on," was all that the colonel could utter.

"Well, sir, she died, poor thing, and was buried in the churchyard of the church here."

"And—and the child?"

"The children, sir. Oh, poor things—poor things."

"What! They—they did not die?"

"No, sir; but there was nobody to befriend them. Those who knew the dear young creatures, and would gladly have helped them, had not the means. There was a poor, a very poor woman, who attended, from motives of kindness, upon their poor mother at her death, who did all she could for them."

"God bless her," cried Colonel Grainger. "It is great and noble when abundance gives part of its store to poverty; but when poverty gives to want, it is sublime."

"Ah! sir, poor Mrs. Lee is now herself in great want."

The colonel took out his pocket-book, and wrote down the name.

"Where," he said "does she reside?"

"Alas! sir, she's in the workhouse, poor old creature."

"Such," said the colonel, "is the fate of humble virtue, while vice and crime riot in extravagance and dissipation. I thank you, madam. Go on —go on."

"The children, sir, were forced to be sent to the workhouse. Mrs. Lee went with them, and begged the board to be kind to them, for they were orphans."

"The workhouse? And—and are they now?" said Colonel Grainger, rising hastily.

"No, sir; no one knows very well what has become of them. The boy, I heard, ran away, and went to sea. The girl ——"

"Yes, the girl?—the girl?"

"The little girl, then, was, I understand, put to service; but, I fear, with an unkind mistress, for she left suddenly, and has not been heard of since."

A deep groan burst from the colonel, and he covered his face with his hands, and appeared lost in an ecstasy of woe.

"That is all I can tell you, sir," said the compassionate woman.

"And that all has seared my heart."

"Perhaps, sir, if you were to call at the workhouse, you might hear something of them?"

"Yes, yes, I thank you; if they live, they shall be found. There is no spot on earth, be it ever so lonely, can hide them from—from a father."

"You are Mrs. Grainger's husband, sir?"

"I am. I wrote often to England, but received no reply to my letters. For several years I was a prisoner of war, and carried far into the interior of India. I live now but for my dear, dear child."

"There are two children, sir."

"Yes, yes; I know—I know. I thank you sincerely, madam, for the kind interest you have taken in those who were and are so dear to me."

The woman shortly withdrew, and Colonel Grainger rung the bell.

"Where is the workhouse situated?" asked the colonel, when Sam, the waiter, appeared in obedience to his summons.

"Workhouse, sir?—workhouse?"

"Yes, the parish workhouse."

"Top of street, sir—turn to left—down hill—pass pond—through fields, sir—large house—wall, sir, paddock behind."

"Get some one to show me the nearest way. It appears to be out of the town?"

"Yes, sir; quite out of town, sir. Get a boy to run before you."

Away scamped Sam to his master.

"Please, master, colonel wants workhouse."

"Wants what, Sam?"

"Workhouse, sir. Boy to show way, sir."

"Get him one directly, then."

"Yes, sir, workhouse, workhouse. Colonel wants workhouse and boy. Coming—coming—coming."

Colonel Grainger was soon on his road to the workhouse of Bungleum, which the reader is aware was situated some distance from the town.

No. 42

Guided by a boy, who had been procured by Sam, he soon, however, stood before the very gate upon which Mr. Bung had posted the notice of George's elopement.

"There be the gate," said the boy.

"I see," said the colonel, handing him a shilling.

"I beant got no change," said the boy, clawing his head in great perplexity.

"Change?—oh, it's all for you."

The boy looked astonished, and walked off backwards, as if the colonel was some most astonishing animal that he desired to have a long look at.

Colonel Grainger paused for a few moments at the door of the workhouse to collect his spirits, and then he rung the bell.

The door was quickly opened, and when the porter saw his visiter, he flung it very wide, and bowed most profoundly.

"I wish," said Colonel Grainger, "to make some inquiries respecting some—some young persons who were inmates of this place some time since?"

"Mr. Bung, sir, 's the man what knows them 'em all, sir. He's been beadle here, sir, for a matter of fifteen years, sir."

"Very well. Tell him a gentleman wishes to see him."

The visiter was shewn into a room, while the porter went himself in search of Mr. Bung.

"A uncommon-looking swell gentleman, did you say?" said Mr. Bung to the porter.

"Yes; he looks like a officer."

"A millentary man? What can he want? I dare say it's arter some young ooman. Them ere millentary men is wery devils. I was once a millentary man myself."

"You, Mr. Bung?"

"Yes; I was a corporal in the County Militia, I was. I know what it is. Gals is very much taken with the millentary—oh, wery."

"I dare say they is, Mr. Bung; but the gentleman's waiting."

"Beadles and millentary," continued Mr. Bung, "is attractive individuals."

With this remark our old acquaintance, who preserved all his peculiarities in full force, and had, in fact, added, in the progress of time, a few for the old stock, proceeded to the room into which Colonel Grainger had been shewn.

Mr. Bung saw in a moment that his visiter was a man of some rank and consequence, and he immediately assumed the humble tone and manner which invariably characterizes petty tyrants in the presence of those above them.

"Your name is Bung!" said the colonel.

"Yes, your washup," said Mr. Bung, bestowing upon the colonel the highest title in his idea in the world, for the beadle always considered that the title of washup, as he called it, comprehended all other dignities, and was a sort of general epitome of human greatness and glory.

"I am told, Mr. Bung, that from your long connection with the parish, you have a knowledge of whoever has been an inmate of this house for many years."

"I has, your worshup—I has—I know 'em all—oh, wery uncommon. There's some on 'em, your worshup, as is hardly fit to be knowed by nobody, 'specially a beadle. There's wice of all sorts, your worship."

"About seven years ago," said the colonel, with a faltering voice, "I am told you had two children of the name of—of ——"

"'Grammet, your worship?—Mugs?—or was it Slikerins?"

"No, they were orphans."

"Orphans?—orphans?—orphans, your worshup, is the wery devil. They gives more trouble than nothing. I've had my blessed shirt torn off my parochial back by orphans, your worshup. We had two orphans, here as was called 'Grainger,' your washup, and ——"

"They are the children I have come to inquire about."

Mr. Bung started, and looked very hard at the colonel, and he saw by the mute expression of his features that he came as a friend to the villified children. The politic beadle took his cue in an instant. Here was evidently a gentleman, with the tears almost in his eyes, and, to all appearance, very rich, come to make inquiries about two pauper children. "They have, perhaps, come into a fortune," thought Mr. Bung, "and are two washups at this present moment."

The beadle immediately produced a yellow handkerchief, the counterpart of the one he had seven years since, and sitting down upon a chair, in defiance even of his official hat, which he had laid upon it, and which was immediately crushed alarmingly flat, he began weeping with great force.

"What—what is the matter?" cried the colonel.

"Oh, dear, oh, dear," said Mr. Bung; "I always does it—I always does ——"

"Always do what?"

"I always goes nearly into highstricks whenever them ere dear unkimmon —oh, oh, oh, oh ——"

"Calm yourself," said the colonel. "Tell me what you know of the children who are so dear to me."

This speech of the colonel's settled the business in Mr. Bung's mind, and he would have fainted and fallen flat on the floor immediately, had it not been that then assistance would have been summoned, and Mr. Bung wanted the visiter all to himself.

"Them blessed orphans—them loves—them angels—I wery much doated on them ere—I could have gobbled 'em up, the unkimmon, dear, precious— oh—oh ——"

"I understand they have both left this place some time since?"

"Oh, dear, yes, they is gone. They carried away clean all my affections. I could have given that boy—that ere dear sweet orphan boy—my wery laced coat, and my cocked hat, I could. 'Here,' I could a said, with the wery tears in my blessed eyes, 'take 'em. Be the beadle, and I'll be a blessed pauper.'"

"I trust they were kindly treated. No one shall lose by having been a friend to those deserted children."

"Kindly treated!" said Mr. Bung. "Oh—oh—oh. They was my study—they was my dreams—I got up in the wery night to see arter them —I washupped them—I admitted them ere children. They was unkimmon. 'Mr. Bung,' they would say to me, 'we remembers you in our blessed prayers, we does. You're a blessed ornament in society. We looks up to you wery paternal. You are a mother to us, you is. We loves you, Mr. Bung.'"

"And they are gone?"

"They is—they is. Which, sir, did you think was the most affecting?"

"The most affecting? What do you mean?"

"Nobody couldn't have no preference atween them ere orphans," said the beadle, fishing to discover, if possible, about which of the children the gentleman cared most.

"The little girl," said the colonel, "when last I saw her was a sweet smiling child."

"Oh, it's the female orphan, is it?" thought the beadle; "it's that little horrid wixen."

"That little angel of a gal, sir, was the apple in both o' my precious eyes, sir. They used to call me 'Father Bung—dear Father Bung.' I thinks as I hears her now. 'Father Bung,' she says, 'father'—oh, oh, Bung—father—oh, dear—oh, dear—oh—oh ——"

Mr. Bung's feelings here quite overpowered him, and he blew his nose very loudly in the yellow handkerchief.

"It gives me great pleasure," said Colonel Grainger, "to hear that you were so kind to them. I trust I shall not offend you by offering you a small testimony of my gratitude for your care of the friendless children."

"Oh, dear—oh, oh. The blessed world turns round. The stars is a winking in their spears. Feeling says, Bung, refuse that ere grateful offering; but then conscience says, recollect what you sacrificed for them ere children, and—and take whatever his washup chooses for to give you. Take it, Bung; take it, and do good with it."

Colonel Grainger placed in Mr. Bung's hand a twenty pound note, which that functionary immediately pocketed, amid a profusion of groans and sobs.

"Now, tell me," says the colonel, "how did they leave this place?"

"Oh, dear me, yes, your washup. One day, your washup, it striked me as that ere blessed female orphan was rather dull, and I thought a change of scene would be very unkimmon beneficial."

"You were very kind and thoughtful."

"Then your washup, I looked about, and got her a place as genteel companion to a most amiable lady."

"Under the circumstances, nothing could be better devised."

"Then, your washup, I takes the female orphan by the blessed hand, and I goes afore the board, and I says,—

"'Your washups, look at this here picture o' innocence. Look at this juvenile wirgin.'

"Then the board looked at her. Then I says:—

"'She's rather dull, and I wants her to go as genteel companion to Mrs. Marrables, as lives in Bungleum.'

"Then the board gets clean up on end, and says,—

"'Mr. Bung, you're a honour to beadles and parishes, Mr. Bung.'

"Then the female orphan weeps, and the board shed abundance of tears, and then the blessed wirgin goes, and be's a companion to the amiable female."

"And she is still there?"

"No, your washup. One day the female orphan disappeared."

"Disappeared? Good Heavens!"

"Yes, your washup. It was a wery great affliction to me. Let me see, it was a Friday I heard on it, and I went to bed, and never got up till that day fortnight. My feelings was hurt."

"And is there no clue—no means of finding her?"

"Your washup, I went to London on purpose for to look arter her. There was a pain in my bosom, your washup, concerning that ere orphan."

"And—and you—you found her?"

"No, your washup, I didn't. I thought as I'd found her, but I thinks now as I was gammoned, your washup."

"You were what?"

"Regularly tooked in, and done brown. There was a old 'ooman, as called herself Spangles, as pretended that blessed little cherub was in her kitchen, but she wasn't, not by no means—oh, dear, no. That ere was a do."

"This is a singular story."

"Oh, wery—wery."

"And since then you have heard nothing of her?"

"Never a blessed word, your washup. My heart has been a bleeding all this ere time, and my feelings is comflusticated. I isn't the beadle as I was; and I dreams I hears that ere female orphan say, 'Father Bung, you're a rum one.'"

Mr. Bung again put the yellow handkerchief to his eyes, and appeared quite overcome by the emotions of his tender heart.

"Where did this lady live with whom you first placed the child?"

"Live!—oh!—oh! She's moved away, your washup, and nobody knows."

"And the boy? What became of him?"

"He went away, sir, one fine evening, and tooked a ship, and went a apprentice to a admiral."

"Why, what do you mean?"

"He went to sea, your washup. I goved him my blessing, and told him to make his fortin."

"And him you have not seen since?"

"No, your worship, I haven't. I loved that ere boy, your washup; but it were the female orphan as brought a chair, and sot down slap in my busum. There's the chair there now, your washup, but the female orphan has mizzled."

Mr. Bung waved the yellow handkerchief as he gave utterance to this happy and highly figurative idea, and Colonel Grainger sighed deeply as he thought what misery his dear children might have been doomed to go through, and might still be suffering."

A feeling of suspicion had been creeping over Colonel Grainger's mind as the conversation proceeded with Mr. Bung, that if the beadle was not entirely fabricating all that he was communicating to him, he was, at the least, grossly exaggerating everything.

The non-production of the address of Mrs. Marrables tended greatly to strengthen his opinion, and he said,—

"I am determined that no circumstance connected with the children about whom I have questioned you, shall remain unknown. I have the power of arriving at the truth, and have ample means, both to reward and punish."

Mr. Bung looked a little alarmed as the colonel spoke, and said,—

"Will your washup leave your washup's name, and then if we hears anything, we can let your washup know?"

"I am Colonel Grainger."

Mr. Bung had some indistinct idea that a colonel was some awful military rank, and he turned rather pale.

"You have," said the colonel, "a poor woman here of the name of Lee?"

"We has, your washup."

"Can I see her?"

"Oh, dear, yes, your washup. I'll just tell Mrs. Bung as is—as was Mrs. Fungus afore—to bring her here. Mrs. Bung, sir, doats upon poor Mrs. Lee."

The beadle was not long gone; and when he returned, he brought with him the late Mrs. Fungus, and an old woman, who seemed more worn down by want and misery, than any other causes.

The colonel, the moment Mrs. Bung entered the room, turned abruptly to her, and drawing himself to his full height, he said, in a tone of authority—

"The address of Mrs. Marrables instantly, madam, if you please?"

Mrs. Bung was taken completely by surprise, and answered,—

"Number 10, Pleasant-row," before Mr. Bung could produce the slightest cough of warning.

"Thank you," said Colonel Grainger, with a glance at Mr. Bung. "You have a short memory, my friend. You see this Mrs. Marrables has come back again."

Mr. Bung was thoroughly confounded, and shrunk beneath the searching eye of the colonel, who, to his great relief, turned immediately to Mrs. Lee, and said, in a softened and kind tone, as he took her hand,—

"Colonel Grainger begs to thank you from his heart for your kindness some years since to Mrs. Grainger and her children."

"Colonel Grainger!" said the poor woman, in surprise.

"Yes, madam, Colonel Grainger. The husband of Mrs. Grainger is most happy to make your acquaintance."

"The husband of Mrs. Grainger! God bless you, sir. Where are the dear children?"

"They shall be found; and in the meantime I cannot allow you to remain in this place. Name a yearly sum that will make your old age comfortable, and I will see that it is secured to you. I do not say that by so doing, I can repay you for what you have done; I only give what I can well spare. You shared with my children, I understand, what you required for yourself."

The poor woman sunk upon a chair, and burst into tears.

Mr. Bung flourished his yellow handkerchief, and affected the most extravagant grief and sensibility, while the late Mrs. Fungus looked on, perfectly amazed at the whole scene.

After a great deal of trouble, Mrs. Lee was prevailed upon to name a sum.

"I may as well," she said, "end my days here; but twenty pounds a-year would be quite a fortune."

"You will hear from me before the day is past," said the colonel. "I will arrange with some respectable gentleman at Bungleum to pay you forty pounds a-year. I cannot consent to only twenty. I will see you again soon, madam, for I would fain hear from your lips the particulars respecting the death of—of her you were so kind to, but not now—not now."

The colonel, without even another glance at the discomfited beadle, took up his hat and departed from the room, and left the workhouse.

CHAPTER LV.

Giles was true to his appointment with Mr. Scrimp.

The intelligence which had been given to him by Tim Miggles, and which, indeed, was no secret at the mill and the cottage, of George and Phœbe's departure, tended to confirm him still more in his determination to adopt some desperate means of possessing himself of Phœbe.

The ulterior consequences of such a step did not strike his heated imagination. To take her from George, and to have her in his power, were all that his mind reflected upon. How the matter was to end he left to chance.

Mr. Scrimp was, of course, not aware of the circumstance that had occurred at the mill to strengthen the resolution of Giles, and he had resolved, even at the risk of again being half choked by the infuriated lover, to continue his system of ingeniously tormenting until the unhappy rustic was too far committed to the enterprise to retreat.

"Ha! my dear fellow," he said, as Giles entered, "how are you? The very man I was just thinking of. You are looking rather poorly."

"Never thee mind my looks. The means, lawyer, the means?"

"Oh, yes, certainly. You are impatient, my friend, rather impatient, but I haven't forgot your business—oh, dear, no."

"They be going from the cottage."

"Going from the cottage? Who is going from the cottage? Not the old miller?"

"No; but Phœbe be going, and George be going."

"Going where?"

"I cannot tell thee; but I hear that they be going."

"Upon my life it's uncommonly cool of them. I'd lay any wager they are going to be married at some distance off to be out of your way."

"I do think so, and yet I do not know hardly what to think."

"Why, now, I'll tell you what I think, my good fellow. They are trying to humbug you throughout the whole business."

"What does thee think, then?"

"Why, I really think they are afraid of you. They all know you have the best right to the girl, and they just want to fob you off."

"I will be revenged. They do not know me. I will have revenge."

"All this concern about the brother is very doubtful."

"Phœbe shall be mine, lawyer."

"Of course she shall; she ought to be; and it's your own fault if she don't."

"Thee said thee would find the means. Where be they?"

"Why, I dare say when once you get her fairly from the mill she will consent to marry you. Girls usually do under such circumstances."

"Where—where be I to take her?"

"Oh, take her anywhere, so that it is far enough. Take her at least twenty miles."

"But thee hast not told me how."

"Well, then, I will tell you. Early on Saturday morning try if you can, on some pretence or another, get the girl to come from the cottage across the meadow, and as near to the high road as possible."

"I—I will—I will."

"Well, you will find a carriage there, which I will provide."

"Yes, yes—a carriage. Thee will not fail me?"

"Certainly not. Well, you must pop her in."

"But—but if she should scream, I—I——"

"Why, if she should you must not mind that; they all scream, just to keep up appearances. My dear fellow, there's nothing in the world they like so well as to be run away with. Oh, you must not mind a little scream-ing. Why, George will be quite frantic."

"I will do it—I will do it."

"Then, you know, then you jump into the carriage beside her, and tell the driver, who I will see is the right sort of person, to drive wherever you please."

"Yes—yes. You do, then, think she will consent to marry?"

"Not a doubt—not a doubt of it. She will admire you still more than she does for your spirit and determination. You'll have everything your own way, and George Andrews, or whatever the fellow's real name is, may whistle for his bride."

"Yes, lawyer, George did take her from me, and now I will take her from him. She shall be mine. She did love me once."

"No doubt; and will love you again if you mind what you are about. I dare say she likes you even now as well as this George. He has only got a little the start of you, man. Show a proper spirit, and you get the start of him."

"She will then see that I do love her better that he."

"Of course she will. The idea of her becoming his wife is ridiculous, you knew her first."

"I did—I did."

"She was as kind as possible to you till this interloper comes with his smooth tongue and courtly speeches, and bewilders the girl completely."

"It be true—it be true. If he do cross me——"

"No violence, you know; no violence."

"I will have his blood. I tell thee, lawyer, I will tear his heart out if he do cross me. She shall be mine—mine."

"Well, you'll recollect. On Saturday morning you will be ready to do your part in this really trifling affair, and do not doubt I shall be ready to perform all that I have promised to you."

"If she will not come?"

"Oh, she'll come. She can't very well refuse you an interview. Let me see. Tell her you think of leaving, and would like to say a few words to her before you went away for ever."

"Yes, yes; I will—I will say so. She—she will be happy at last."

"Happy! aye, to be sure; happy as possible. You wouldn't be happy yourself to see her in the arms of that George."

"In his arms? Never—no, no—never."

"You would have to leave the mill at any rate, for it wouldn't be very pleasant to you to see her hanging about his neck."

"Don't thee say more; I be resolved. He shall never see her again; never while I do live."

"Oh, you'll think of all this in after life when you are settled and comfortable with Phœbe, and tremble to think how you might, by a little faint-heartedness, have actually thrown her into the very arms of your rival."

"Yes, yes, I shall. True—true—that be true."

"Of course it's true. These things happen every day."

"On Saturday morning?"

"Yes, Saturday morning. The carriage shall wait for you from eight o'clock till you make your appearance. My good fellow, I shall rejoice in your success. I think you have been most shamefully ill-used, and this rascally attempt to jilt you out of your bride deserves to be defeated."

"It be true—it be true, lawyer, what thee do say. Thee be a good friend to me."

"Oh, don't mention it. I don't like to see any one downright imposed upon. Some of these days, perhaps, you may be able to do me a favour."

"I shall be willing. I be thankful to thee. I—I could not live without Phœbe; and thee be a true friend to help me to have her."

"Well, I have no doubt it will all go off swimmingly; and in case, you know, I should not see you again till your happiness is completed, you'd better have some money of me now."

"Thee be very kind."

"Oh, don't say a word about it. Here—here's a ten pound note. You'll want it, you know, to fee the parson, eh?"

"I thank thee," said Giles. "I—I will pay it to thee again."

"At your leisure. Don't put yourself out of the way about it. We lawyers, you know, sometimes make money easy, and we can afford sometimes to spend it as we please."

"On Saturday morning?" repeated Giles, as if bewildered.

"Yes, Saturday morning, as soon after eight as possible. Permit me, my good fellow, to wish you a very good evening."

"Good evening to thee. I be beholden to thee, lawyer."

"So far, so good," said Mr. Scrimp, rubbing his hands together. "These yokels are uncommonly green, to be sure, absolutely verdant. He is fixed—fixed as fate. And now to see Pomander and Perk, to settle a few details."

Mr. Scrimp then walked to Mr. Pomander's, where he found Perk,

"Well, gentlemen," he said, "I think I've arranged matters satisfactorily with that violent yokel."

"The Giles creature you mean?" said Perk.

"Yes; he nibbles bravely; he's ripe for anything. Now, Perk, I shall want you just to run up to Sir Herbert's with this warrant to sign, so that we may make a legal caption of Master Giles at the very proper moment. We must have too active constables, who will stick at nothing, and do what they are told, and no more."

"I'll put the constables up to their business," said Perk. "Leave me alone for that, governor. I've known constables afore to-day."

"You, certainly, Scrimp," said Pomander, "have managed this thing uncommonly well. I think we can't now fail of success. What sort of mind is Sir Herbert in?"

"Why, he is awfully disturbed about this ghost business."

"So he can't account for it yet?"

"Not he; but my own suspicions are awakened."

"Are they, governor?" said Perk. "Then you know something about it. Whenever you say there's smoke, I make up my mind you've seen the fire."

"You are complimentary, Perk; but really I believe there is a something going on at Haredale Park that we know nothing about."

"Very likely," said Perk. "Perhaps the d—d old clock in the hall that leads everybody astray is going on at last."

"No, no; but, joking apart," said Pomander, "what is your opinion of the business, Scrimp? You have evidently some strong opinion on the subject. Come, tell us what it is?"

"Why, among friends, I have no hesitation in saying that Cury and Ralph Freegrove have got up this ghost concern for some private object of their own."

No. 43

"Indeed!" said Pomander.

"No doubt," cried Perk. "The governor's got a nose."

"Have you mentioned your suspicions to Sir Herbert?" said Pomander.

"Why, not exactly," replied Scrimp. "1 thought I'd try and find out what Master Cury was aiming at first, and then——"

"I see, governor," replied Perk. "If there was anything to be got by going shares, eh?"

"Why, a—a—hem!" said Mr. Scrimp.

Mr Perk nodded at Mr. Pomander, as much as to say, there's a genius for you. Don't you admire that man?

"Well, how is this matter of the girl's to be managed?"

"Why, Giles, the disappointed swain——"

"The verdant yokel," said Perk.

"The romantic chawbacon," said Pomander.

"Exactly so, gentlemen. Under the pretence of a leave taking, he will decoy the miller's wench, who seems to have turned so many heads, to the high road. There will be Sir Herbert's private posting chariot. In goes the girl——"

"With a little kicking," said Perk.

"And hysterics," said Pomander.

"Exactly, and away goes the swain in custody of the officers, which we will leave you to procure, Perk."

"You may, governor. I recollect getting an officer once to arrest an old gentleman for debt. There was a young fellow, the son of a governor of mine once, and he came up to London, unknown to the governor, to look after a little wench. Well, the governor thought he was in the country, where he'd articled him, to keep him out of bad company in London."

"Such company principally consisting of Perk," said Scrimp.

"As you please, governor. Well, the governor never used to come to chambers till nearly eleven, and the young spark used to make an appointment with the young lady at the chambers at ten. They always used to be off before the old gentleman came. But somehow or other the governor found it out, and he went prowling about till he found a fellow as the young one owed something to, and he got him to get an execution against the young one, intending to punish him by popping him into quod for a week or two. Well, one evening, just as the office was closing, the governor comes up to me, and he says :—

"'Take this writ the first thing in the morning, and have an officer on the stairs by ten o'clock.'

"Well, I saw by the writ that it was against the young 'un, and I smoked the whole affair in a minute. Well, in the morning I got the officer, and I says to him,—

"'Now, mind you wait here, and ask everybody that goes up the stairs if his name is Nathaniel Pumpkin, and whoever says yes, is your man. Away with him at once, for he has as many doubles as a hare.'

"I couldn't leave the office, but I kept looking out of window, and presently I saw young Nat Pumpkin coming as usual. Now here goes, thought I, and if Nat is the clever fellow I take him to be, he'll take a hint.

"'Halloo! halloo, Smith,' says I; 'Smith, how are you?'

"He looked up, and saw me wink, and said,—

"Pretty well, thank you.'

"'Come up, Smith,' says I; 'come up.'

"Well, the officer on the stairs looks very hard at him, and says he,—

"'Is your name Pumpkin, sir?'

"'No,' says Nat, 'Smith,' and up stairs he came.

"'Don't say a word,' says I. "Get in the cupboard directly.'

"In he popped, and I listened at the head of the stairs. Presently old Nat Pumpkin comes puffing along, and the officer says,—

"'Is your name Pumpkin, sir?'

"'Yes,' says the old governor.

"'Nathaniel, sir?'

"'Yes, my man.'

"'Then, sir, you are my prisoner.'

"'Oh! pho! pho! my man, you mistake; it's my son you mean.'

"'Walker,' says the bailiff. 'How's your mother?'

"'The devil!' said the old man. 'Come up to my chambers.'"

"'Hookey!' says the bailiff. 'I've heard you're a rum 'un, sir. Will you come to a lock up?'

"'But d— you, I don't owe a person a sixpence.'

"'In course. Come along, if you please, sir. You won't double upon me. Oh, no. Come along my old buffer.'

"Well, the fellow dragged off the old man, who was swearing like mad."

"Well, that was not so bad, either," said Pomander.

"And I escaped all blame too," said Perk, "for the old man, when he got cool, praised me very much for warning the bailiff."

"Well, then," said Scrimp, "we perfectly understand each other about Saturday?"

"Yes," said Pomander. "I suppose we need not show ourselves."

"Certainly not; but some one must go to town with the girl."

"Then Freegrove had better do that part of the business. He is fit for nothing else."

"And hardly for that, the brute," said Perk.

"It's rather dangerous and uncomfortable, however," said Scrimp; "so let him do it. Sir Herbert will, I suppose, start immediately after. I shall give him personal notice of how the thing gets on."

"Well, I am sanguine of success," said Pomander.

"And so am I," said Perk.

"It can hardly fail," said Scrimp.

CHAPTER LVI.

Giles walked home from Mr. Scrimp's almost in a state of stupor. He felt like one in a fearful dream, who was hurried by an irresistible fate towards a yawning precipice, down which he felt that he must madly plunge.

From step to step he had proceeded in the execution of the unhallowed suggestions of his disappointed passion, until now he found himself committed and compromised to a degree of guilt which a few short weeks previously he would have shuddered to contemplate.

In no respect are the pliancy of the human mind and the power of habit better exemplified than in the progress of crime.

From the first weak suggestion of the wandering fancy to the commission of the blackest deed which has ever disgraced human nature, there is commonly so gradual a graduation of feeling, that the perpetrator beholds the consequences of this act, and wonders how he came to dream of its commission.

The first step in guilt is the parent of a hundred others, and each one of the numerous offspring of, perchance, a puny crime, is more athletic and vigorous than his predecessor, until at last some monstrous iniquity arises, and men shudder at their own acts.

Notwithstanding Giles's expressed determination to proceed in the course which had been pointed out to him by Mr. Scrimp, there were still moments when he felt, in full force, the horrors of the situation in which he would soon place himself, and all that he held dear; and what torments could equal the bitter agony of such moments? Truly might Giles, in the figurative languange of his heated imagination, say, "that a snake lay coiled up at the bottom of his heart;" and at those dread moments of remorse and agony it might well appear to him as if the slimy monster had reared its head, and fixed its envenomed fangs in his breast. Still he had no power to resist the fatal destiny which hurried him onwards. He was in the meshes of a web, from which extrication was impossible, and he made but feeble struggles to escape.

His greatest dread now was to meet some of the inhabitants of the mill and the cottage. He dreaded the observation of any one, for he fancied that any eye could read in his countenance the dread purpose of his soul.

The usual time for retiring to rest had arrived as Giles reached the meadow, on his return from Mr. Scrimp's, but he feared to approach the mill. He might meet George, or even the simple-hearted Tim Miggles, and what could he say or do? How comport himself to those he was plotting to betray?

He then thought he would wait till all should have retired to rest, both at the mill and the cottage, before he ventured to approach.

Already had the consequences of crime began to oppress his actions. He dreaded the sight of his fellows.

Moving cautiously along, under the shadow of the hedge which skirted the meadow, Giles watched the lights in the cottage windows. The night was cold, and damp exhalations arose from the earth, but Giles felt nothing but the consciousness that for worlds he would not see Phœbe, or hear her utter a word.

All was still around him, and a confusion of images in his brain usurped the place of reason.

"Will she," he thought, "be happy? Will she, indeed, consent to an union with me? The lawyer do say so, and—and surely he do know these things. I—I fear, and my heart trembles. Oh, Phœbe, Phœbe, thee might have spared me all this, but thee cast me from thee, and thee took to thee heart George—George Andrews. Curses! curses! I will have thee—I will take thee from him; and then, if thee still despise me, I—I can die—yes, yes, I can die. That be in my power. Then thee will see that I loved thee, and what I did do I did for love of thee; and thee may ask him, George, if he would die for thee?"

Now as he gazed towards the cottage, he saw a light in the chamber of Phœbe, and his whole attention became rivetted to the latticed window.

"She be there—there," he said. "Her beauty do make the light dim. I see her shadow and even that be beautiful. Oh, Phœbe, Phœbe, who loves thee as I love thee? I did love father, mother—dear friends I did once love. I—I did love Heaven; but now—now, Phœbe, I have forgotten all, and I love but thee. There be no place in my heart for others. Thee, thee—it be only thee that I do think of and love. Where be there one like thee? Where be the music that be like thee voice? All do love thee, but I love thee most of all, and—and thee love me least. Oh, no, no, no; thee must love me. I—will think thee so, and thee shall be mine. And now I see thee shadow flitting by the window like a young bird. Bless thee, Phœbe—bless thee. Heaven! I feel as if I ought not to say Heaven—what have I none? I only love—love truly, and—madly. Well—it be as well —Phœbe, we will talk of Heaven when we be happy in our home together. Thee must be mine!"

Still he watched the latticed window of Phœbe's chamber, from whence gleamed a calm and steady light. Suddenly, however, it disappeared; and as Giles still gazed in the direction of the cottage, he saw, by the broad gleam of light which suddenly appeared, that the door was opened. A figure came forth, and made towards that gate which opened into the meadow.

Giles had scarcely time to observe so much, when he heard some one hastily approaching from the direction of the mill. The step was that of a man, and there was a springing lightness in it which betokened a heart at ease. Within a few paces of the spot where Giles lay crouching in the shadow of the hedge the person passed him. He saw that it was George, and a deadly sickness came over his heart as he watched his receding figure.

An agonizing thought came across Giles's brain. George, he felt convinced, had left the mill to keep an assignation with Phœbe, and she it was who now waited for her favoured lover at the little gate leading to the meadow.

Giles was quite right in the fact, but he was wrong in supposing the interview was a stolen one, for there was now no occasion for secret assignations between Phœbe and George, as their intercourse was unrestricted.

They loved, however, to wander after nightfall about the garden and the meadow, and on that evening they had arranged to meet, and together watch the rising of the moon, and see it cast its silver beauty upon the familiar objects that were so dear to them both. It was no lover's meeting, for although George still addressed Phœbe in the language of romantic tenderness, yet the doubt of the nature of their relative situations toward each other imposed an honourable silence upon his feelings.

With a beating heart and a reeling brain Giles crept along the hedge in the direction of the gate, and using as much expedition as was consistent with concealment, he arrived sufficiently close to hear George's first salutation to Phœbe.

"Phœbe," he cried, as he approached her, "dear Phœbe, I have seen the moon from the topmost loft in the mill. The silver rim is just breaking the line of the distant horizon, and see dear Phœbe—see, even now—you may note a silvery hue upon the tree tops. Look, dearest, look; is it not beautiful?"

"It is, indeed," said Phœbe. "This was worth the coming to see, George. 'Tis like magic. How altered everything appears."

The moon as they were speaking, slowly and majestically rose above the horizon. There was not a cloud to shroud its beauty. The before black and sombre landscape was shortly bathed in floods of mild white radiance. It seemed as if, by the touch of some enchanter's wand, the meadows and the fields had been converted into lakes of molten silver.

Phœbe and George stood close together, in silence, looking with pleasure upon the fair scene. Higher and higher the queen of the night climbed the steep ascent of Heaven, and the shadows of the tall trees slowly lessened, as if they shrunk from obtruding upon the chastened glory of the mild light.

"I have been, dear Phœbe," said George, speaking softly, as if he regretted to break the sweet stillness of nature, "in distant climes, where the night was more like the shadow of a passing cloud before the sun than the departure of light; but never, oh, never, in all my wanderings, and in all my admiration of those sunny climes, which seem so favoured of Heaven, have I seen anything to equal in beauty the dear moonlight as it sleeps upon the verdant sod of happy and free England. The suns of other lands may be brighter, but they shine upon slavery and bondage, and man is almost crowded from the face of the teeming earth by the rankness of its vegetation, and the redundancy of animal and insect life. The nights may be but faint reflections of the glories of the days, but disease stalks abroad in all its horrors beneath the soft influence of its balmy and spice-laden winds. Oh, Phœbe, there is no place like our native land—England! dear England!—the land of equal laws—the land whose very air breathes freedom to the most abject slave the moment he inhales it. England! England! There is no place in the beautiful world that is like thee!"

"Dear George," said Phœbe, "you will never more wander from your native land?"

"Never, Phœbe, never. I am rather of a stay-at-home disposition than otherwise; I had a powerful motive for my wanderings."

"And that, George, was to procure the means of succouring your poor Phœbe."

"It was, Phœbe; but in so doing you know I succoured myself, for, dear Phœbe, our hearts were then as they are now—in union."

"And they will ever be so, dear George."

"I do well believe they will, Phœbe. Life were otherwise valueless in my eyes."

"They be pouring melted lead upon my brain," muttered Giles.

"I have been thinking, George," said Phœbe, "upon our journey."

"It is ever present to my mind, dearest Phœbe. I trust that it will promote our happiness. I quite agree with our best friend, the miller, in the necessity of our taking such a step. It may end all anxieties, all doubts, all fears, and clear for us the flowery path of happiness which we may together tread through life."

"It may, dear George—it may. Possibly the thoughts of leaving a home where I have tasted so much happiness, and which is endeared to me by so many sweet incidents, may have cast a shadow across my mind, but I feel a presentiment of some evil hanging over us."

"What evil can assail us, Phœbe? We are truly independent. We depend for our happiness only upon ourselves. While we are true to each other, the storms of fate may assail us in vain. Wealth we cannot be deprived of, for we are dependants only upon that property which never fails, and can rarely, if ever, suffer deterioration—honest industry."

"But still, dear George, have we not been made the subjects of persecution? May not the same bad men who have visited our dear father's peaceful cottage be even now contriving some plot to disturb our happiness, and, perhaps, involves us in distress? Alas! that I should be the innocent cause of so much wickedness! Why am I singled out for persecution by these men, to whom truth and honour appear so strange?"

"Phœbe, your wondrous beauty; your beauty and your innocence, which shed a heavenly light around this humble spot, are the dear gifts of Heaven, which have bred this mischief."

"Oh, George, dear George, you tell me that I have this fatal gift. Oh, would that I had it not!"

"Say not so, Phœbe—oh, do not say so, dearest. To me you would ever be dear, were you far other than what you are. Beauty is an accident. It is but the casket in which the pure gem, the mind is enshrined. If there be spots upon the jewel which is placed in a costly case, who values case or jewel? But the pure gem, which sparkles with undimmed lustre, is beautiful, although enshrined but in the humblest covering."

"Beauty, George, should be esteemed, because all the gifts of Heaven should be dear to us, but how often is it the fatal delusion—the glittering *ignus fatuus*, which leads to ruin and despair?"

"Beauty, Phœbe, is like gold—powerful for either good or evil. The possession of the bright metal which is so courted by all, involves its possessor in a thousand dangers, while at the same time it casts upon him and around him the dazzling lustre of its own rare excellence. It is a price we seem to pay in this world for all that is excellent and beautiful, that those who possess not such gifts, will, with maddened jealousy, disturb the serenity of those who do."

"How happy is a humble lot, dear George, which none can envy, none disturb."

"You need fear nothing, Phœbe. There are hearts and hands devoted to you, that will secure you from all harm."

"Yes, dear George, I know it well; but we are more wounded through the hearts of those that love us, than when the shafts of nature strike our own breasts."

"Nay, fear not, dearest Phœbe. These shallow tricksters, who, to gratify the wild and ungovernable passions of a bad rich man, are all harmless——"

"That lawyer, George," said Phœbe, with a shudder, "always reminds me of some serpent, insidiously trying to crawl round his prey."

"He is such, Phœbe, and he may have bad fangs, but 1 have drawn them, and he is now a harmless reptile."

"Dear George, we will talk of them no more. See the moon is high in the clear Heavens, and with its pure bright lustre has put out the small lights of the stars which else were beautifully bright."

"It is even so, dear Phœbe. The greater ever obscures the less; and where that greatness is—the greatness of beauty and purity—who can repine? So dear, dear Phœbe, does thy rare beauty and innocence, like yon moon, obscure all lesser stores, and shine alone, the queen of all."

"Oh, George, your heart speaks for your poor Phœbe, not your reason."

"Nay, not so. As Heaven is my judge, I would not flatter you, Phœbe, for the world's wealth. What the imagination of the boy, far, far at sea, amid the roaring of the angry billows, painted you, the judgment of the man has confirmed. I love you, Phœbe, dearly love you, and I speak to you and of you in simple honesty of heart and purpose."

"It seems that I am doomed, however, to create unhappiness, George. There is Giles. Oh, I would give much to rescue him from the state of mind in which he has been for some weeks past."

"Passion, Phœbe," said George, with a sigh—"wild and ungovernable passion—has, in the case of Giles, obtained its usual victory over a strong but ill-regulated mind. Giles has capacity that would have lifted him far above his present melancholy state, if it had been properly matured and exercised."

"But can nothing be done, George, for him?"

"Nothing, now, Phœbe. There is but one thing that will save him from himself, for he is his own enemy."

"And what is that?"

"Time, Phœbe, time. It may take years entirely to soften the excited feelings that now possess him, but the great enchanter, Time, will at length accomplish it, and Giles will look back upon the proceedings of the present time as upon the dimly remembered raving of some wild delirium."

"Poor Giles," said Phœbe, sorrowfully.

"Nay, dearest; you are not accountable for the wrongs of mad-brained jealousy. You may pity, as I know you do, his state."

"I do—I do, indeed."

"And so do I. I sincerely pity——"

"Hold!" cried Giles, suddenly springing forward, and standing fully revealed in the broad moonlight. "Say that word again, and it will be thee last."

The moonlight fell clear and bright upon the pale haggard face of Giles as he there stood, and it imparted to his countenance a fearfully livid hue.

Phœbe clung to George in great alarm, and the two young men stood silently confronting each other, presenting, probably as remarkable a contrast as could possibly exist.

There was the ruddy hue of health upon the cheek of George, which even the cold pale moonbeams could not altogether quench. He stood erect, and his bearing and appearance was manly and noble. His figure was thin, but sinewy, and many who might have been greatly superior to him in mere animal strength, might well have shrunk from an encounter with him. There was but little passion in the clear blue eye, but there was a world of calm determination in the unflinching gaze with which he could confront any one when he pleased.

Giles was of a robust frame naturally, and his appearance denoted great personal power. Now, however, he looked more like a large skeleton arrayed in garments. The mind had preyed upon the body, and he was but the framework, as it were, of his former self. His bloodless lips were slightly apart, and his arms were uplifted, as if in the act to call down vengeance from Heaven on the head of an enemy. His hair, which was as black as the raven's wing, hung in wild disorder about his face, and his dark eyes flashed, like those of some wild animal, from their hollow sockets.

"Giles," said George, calmly, "you mistake if you imagine that what I said of you I said in ill-will or derision."

"I tell thee," shouted Giles, "Phœbe shall be mine—mine—mine only. I will take her from thee. Look—look at the moon that be shining on us now; it be at the full. I tell thee, before thee shall be able to say, 'that moon be a crescent,' thee shall weep for thee love, and—and thee shall feel as I have felt. Thee shall feel thee heart gnawed by creeping things—thee shall be mocked in thee sleep by gibbering phantoms—thee shall see thee hands like blood—thee shall feel thee brain scorching—thee shall feel all this, George Andrews, as I have felt it all—as I have—as I have."

Before George could reply to this wild and incoherent speech, Giles darted across the meadow towards the mill, and as he sped wildly along, he might still be heard shouting wildly his curses on the head of George, mingled with hints of his own approaching triumph.

"Oh, George! George!" said Phœbe, "this is terrible!"

"He is worse and worse. This, indeed, is the very ecstacy of jealousy. Something must be done with him."

"My mind misgives me," said Phœbe, "that all this will end in some act of frantic violence."

"Fear not, fear not," said George; "the fiercest fire burns out the soonest. This rage of Giles's is like a storm, it cannot last. There must be soon a reaction in his mind. This tumult of passion will most likely subdue into a gloomy despondency."

"And is not such a state more dangerous still?"

"With some it is, but let us hope the best, Phœbe. Come, dearest, come; let me lead you home. Be of good cheer. Nay, dear Phœbe, do not weep. I would fain be calm and considerate with the hot-headed Giles, but your tears will steel my heart. Come, dearest, come. Home—home."

CHAPTER LVII.

As Colonel Grainger left the workhouse of Bungleum, he felt the first glow of consolation in his heart, which had found a place there since he had heard the dismal tidings of the death of her he had so fondly cherished the idea of meeting.

In relieving the distress of Mrs. Lee, he had done something which had partially relieved his heart. It was a propitiatory offering to the memory of the deceased being who had ever occupied the first place in his affections.

His next object was to proceed immediately to No. 10, Pleasant-row, and personally procure all the information he could of "the amiable lady to whom Phœbe had been a genteel companion."

Colonel Grainger, as we have said, was not without some misgivings with respect to the accuracy of Mr. Bung's statements, but he never imagined the extent to which that politic and worthy parish functionary had thought it consistent with his interests to deceive him.

The colonel walked at a rapid pace from the workhouse, and he presently came in sight of the boy who had acted as his guide. He quickened his steps in order to overtake him, and inquire from him the locality of Pleasant-row.

When sufficiently near, he called to him.

The boy turned, and the moment he saw the colonel making towards him quickly, he set off at full speed, never doubting for a moment but the strange gentleman had repented of his extreme liberality in regard to the shilling, and intended to redeem the same.

"It's very odd," said Colonel Grainger. "What can possess the boy?"

He resolved to make the necessary inquiries at his hotel, and he was soon once more in the coffee-room of the "Albion," in which establishment his proceedings excited quite a sensation. There was but one opinion, however, about his willingness and capability to pay whatever the conscience of the landlord thought proper to demand; and as that conscience was highly elastic, and stretched according to circumstances, it is very likely that had Colonel Grainger remained there many days longer, he would have been charged such unheard of prices for what he wanted, that even his at-

No. 44

tention would have been aroused to the system of extortion which was being practised upon him.

"Can you direct me to Pleasant-row?" he said to Sam, the waiter.

"Pleasant-row, sir? Direct you to Pleasant-row, sir? Certainly. Fetch a boy, sir—run before your honour like a lamp-lighter, sir."

Away ran Sam, vociferating through the house,—

"Pleasant row—Pleasant-row for colonel—boy to run before colonel to Pleasant-row. Coming, sir!—coming! coming!"

The juvenile guide was soon procured, and preceded by him, Colonel Grainger started for the residence of the redoubtable Mrs. Marrables.

"Do you know a Mrs. Marrables?" said the colonel, handing to the boy the same amount of gratuity that he had bestowed upon his workhouse guide.

"Does I know Mussus Marrables, sir?"

"Yes, at No. 10, Pleasant-row."

"Be you a gawing to Mussus Marrables, sir?"

"Yes, I am,—why not?"

"Then I won't go not no furder."

"Not go any further? Why, what object can you have?"

"She frowed some hot water over I and another boy, yesterday was a week, 'cos we rattled a stick agin the hairy rails, and she says as how she's blowed if she won't score our backs with a carving knife, if so be she catches either of us."

"Humph!" thought the colonel. "This is the amiable female! Can you tell me what Mrs. Marrables is?"

"What she be, sir?"

"Yes; I wish to know who and what she is."

"She's a out-and-outer, sir."

"A what?"

"A out-and-outer, sir. Didn't you never hear of an out-and-outer?"

The colonel smiled as he guessed the boy's meaning, and thought he certainly had met before with out-and-outers.

"You mean she's a disagreeable woman, boy!"

"You may say that, sir. She wallops everybody, she does."

"But how does she live?"

"She takes in young men, and does for 'em."

"Has she a husband?"

"She had, sir, but he's happy now."

"Dead, I suppose you mean. Well, that will do. Just shew the house, and you may go."

"I'll go on the opposite side o' the way, and make a noise when you gets to the door."

Colonel Grainger walked on, and when he arrived at Mrs. Marrables' door, the boy gave a kind of war-woop in signification of the fact, and then set off at great speed.

"This is but a poor account," thought Colonel Grainger, "of the woman into whose care my poor little Phœbe fell. The poor child's disappearance, I fear, is but too well accounted for. If I was to choose between the narrations of the beadle and the boy, I shall certainly incline to the latter."

The colonel knocked at Mrs. Marrables' door, and wiated patiently for several minutes, but no one appeared, although he thought several times he heard voices in the passage. Again he knocked, and now he felt certain some one was close to the street-door, and he heard a great shuffling of feet and confusion of tongues.

Just as he had his hand on the knocker to make a third appeal for admittance, the door was suddenly opened, and before he could say a word, or move out of the way, some one was thrown completely into his arms, and he saw, standing in the passage, a tall, wiry-looking female, with a gridiron in her hand.

"The wiry-looking female was evidently in the middle of a speech, which the opening of the door did not at all interrupt.

"You wretch!" she exclaimed; "you ungrateful, miserable, dirty, idle, filthy hussey—you slutting, ignorant, vile, wretched beast—you —"

"I thought, ma'am, you liked it over done," said the person who had been caught by, or who had caught the colonel. She was a good-looking servant girl.

"Liked it over done?" screamed Mrs. Marrables, for it was no less a personage than herself who stood in the passage; "liked it overdone, you brazen-faced wretch. It's because I am a lone widow, you monster, you venomous reptile, that you impose upon me. You know I've nobody to take my part, and am a lone, weak, delicate female, you baggage. You know that poor dear Marrables, who had a spirit, is in his grave, you trollop—you hussey—you cat—you wretch—you jade—you porpoise—you thief."

Colonel Grainger looked aghast at this torrent of abuse, which transcended anything that he had ever heard before.

The poor girl sat down upon the step, and applied her apron to her eyes, and wept bitterly.

"What!" shouted Mrs. Marrables, "you crocodile of the Nile, what do you mean? This is the way I'm served, because I've nobody to say a single word for me. A poor, delicate, weak woman, and a widow, is easily ridden over, you sanguinary piece of vile corruption."

"My good lady," said Colonel Grainger, mildly, seeing that he was not likely to receive any attention if he remained quiet. "You are too severe upon this poor girl. What has she done?"

"What's that to you, I should like to know? What do you want, mar-plot? There's nothing to let, and there's nobody at home. There, now, you've got your answer. Your hash is cooked, I hope."

"My name is Colonel Grainger," said the colonel, walking deliberately into the passage. "Let me have no insolence, woman. I come to ask you some questions, and I do not leave this house till they are answered."

"You come to ask questions of me? You won't go away till you please?" screamed Mrs. Marrables. "How dare ——"

"Peace, woman! peace!" said the colonel, in a commanding tone, that made Mrs. Marrables actually drop the gridiron.

"Do you wish," continued Colonel Grainger, "the conversation that we *must* have to take place in the passage?"

"No, no—I really—I don't feel well," said Mrs. Marrables. "If you'll just say what you come about, and then call another time —"

"No, the present is the time;—no consideration is required."

Mrs. Marrables looked rather alarmed; for now that she had had time and opportunity to take a good look at her visiter, she fancied there was something in his appearance that seemed to say he was not exactly the person to be bullied out of a purpose by her, or anybody else.

"Oh, dear," said Mrs. Marrables, debating in her own mind the propriety of fainting forthwith, and so getting rid of the stranger, a scheme which her curiosity to know his business alone prevented her from putting into immediate execution;—"oh, dear! oh, dear! I feel quite faint and poorly. I'm exceedingly delicate, sir. The slightest exertion quite overpowers me. Here, you Emily, come in, come in, I say. Will you —"

The girl rose from the step, and walked in.

"You wouldn't believe, sir," continued Mrs. Marrables, "what a handful I have with that girl. I am forced continually to be turning her out of doors, and then my good nature induces me to take the ungrateful hussey in again."

Mrs. Marrables forgot to add, that the girl was poor and friendless, and being of a quiet, patient spirit, submitted to the violent caprices of Mrs. Marrables, who had not at all improved in temper as she advanced in years.

The poor lone woman and tender-hearted lady now led the way to a little back parlour, followed by Colonel Grainger, who she requested, with a bland smile, to be seated.

" You had a young girl living with you, madam," said the colonel, " some six or seven, or may be more, years since?"

Mrs. Marrables looked up to the ceiling, and pretended to be trying very hard to recollect.

" Her name," continued the colonel, " was Grainger—Phœbe Grainger."

" And you are," said Mrs. Marrables, " the—the——"

" The father of that child, for child she must have been at the period I mention."

Mrs. Marrables considered for a moment or two whether it would not be the best plan to deny all knowledge of the transaction ; but Mrs. Marrables was rather a clever woman than otherwise, and she thought she had better first of all admit the fact, and then be guided by circumstances as to what complexion she should give to the whole affair connected with Phœbe.

" Oh, dear, yes," she said ; " I recollect. Out of compassion, I took a little girl of that name from the parish workhouse about the time you mention."

" I am glad you recollect it, madam," replied the colonel ; " and what became of her ?"

" Why, really it's impossible for me to say. She went away of her own accord."

" Pray, madam, in what capacity did you take the girl into your house ?"

" As servant, of course."

" I was told at the workhouse that you took the child in a somewhat higher capacity than a mere domestic, which her extreme youth must have unfitted her for."

" Oh, that's it," thought Mrs. Marrables ; " there's to be some flattery, is there, about the little charity wretch."

" Why, sir, when I say servant, I don't mean exactly that in every sense of the word. She was quite a companion to me."

" Then she was, I presume, tolerably comfortable with you ?"

" She'd no reason to be otherwise. Pray, sir, do you intend making any stay in this town ?"

" I must be guided by circumstances. My business here is to find that child."

" Because if you do, I shall have my first floor empty in a week."

" You are very kind, madam."

" It's thirty shillings a-week, without extras."

" If I should require it, I will let you know ; but how did it happen that this child having no reason to complain of you or your home, came to leave it ?"

" How can I tell ? She chose to go away one morning."

" What ! a young thing like that go away from where she was happy and comfortable, without the least notice to her indulgent mistress ?"

" Just so," said Mrs. Marrables.

" You will pardon me, madam, but the whole affair seems very mysterious, and grossly improbable."

" Exactly so, sir. Very mysterious and improbable, as you say."

"Can you give me no further satisfaction upon this matter?"

"None, but that I missed a silver spoon after she was gone."

The colonel's face flushed with anger as he replied,—

"Madam, I would much rather believe and think, that in one of your fits of insane passion, such as I witnessed but a short time since, you had swallowed the spoon, than that that child had bestowed a thought upon it."

"My passion?" cried Mrs. Marrables; "my insane passion?"

"Yes, madam, your insane passion. The woman who could behave in the manner I saw you but now, may well have driven from her roof—perhaps to destruction—the orphan child whom she had taken for a household drudge."

Mrs. Marrables, for once in her life, was thoroughly cowed. Colonel Grainger had that rare tact of at once asserting his superiority over such spirits as hers, and each word that he spoke seemed to come like a cannon-shot against Mrs. Marrables, and all her defences were in an instant levelled with the dust.

"Now, madam," he continued, "tell me the truth. I have the power both to reward and punish. I have this morning placed above the reach of want one who I ascertained was, to the utmost of her means, kind to that child for a space of but four days, and I will exact a bitter account from those who have dared to lift a finger against her, dreaming in their bad hearts that she was unprotected, save by Heaven."

Mrs. Marrables groaned as she thought what a golden opportunity she had lost by her conduct to Phœbe of receiving some of the colonel's bounty. It was a harrowing thought to lay up in the store-house of her memory, as a fit companion to another reflection which had occasioned Mrs. Marrables much suffering and vain regrets, which was, that Mr. Marrables, but a week before his sudden death, had asked her for the money to ensure his life in her favour, and she had refused it, with the idea that it was an useless waste of money while he was in good health.

"I'm sure I—I—I was uncommonly good to her. Perhaps you—you are very rich, sir?"

"I set no greater value on riches," replied the colonel, "than simply as a means to an end, and that end the producing as much happiness as I can around me. Since, however, you may be influenced by my answer to give me information, which I would pay a high price for, I will tell you that I have returned from India with what may well be called a large fortune."

Mrs. Marrables groaned again more loudly than before.

"Now, tell me the truth. Why did the orphan girl, Phœbe Grainger, leave your house?"

"I—I had a few words with poor dear departed Marrables, and—and——"

"Well, madam, go on. What had this to do with Phœbe?"

"She interfered for Mr. Marrables."

"She interfere? A child like that interfere?"

"No—yes—I—that is, she—she let him in—and——"

"And what, madam?"

"Oh, dear, sir," said Mrs. Marrables, falling on her knees, "have mercy on me."

"Please, ma'am," said the girl Emily, opening the door at that critical moment, "here's Mr. Sniffles says as he gives you warning, ma'am, as he ain't a going to stay in the two pair back beyond to-night, and he——, Lor, ma'am, is it possible to see you a kneeling?"

"Go away," cried Mrs. Marrables. "Go away, you—you—go away."

"Well, madam, go on."

"Then I—I just touched her."

" You struck her?"

" Ye—ye—yes—oh, dear, oh, dear, I did."

Colonel Grainger walked backwards and forwards in the little parlour with great agitation.

" And have you not heard of her since?"

" Mr. Bung thought she was in—in London."

" Enough, madam. If in your own heart you feel no pang of regret for ill-using that poor child, I can inflict none by anything I can say."

As he spoke he turned from the room, and opening the street-door himself, he left the house.

" More misery—more misery," he said, as he walked from Pleasant-row. " My poor child—my innocent Phœbe—what wretchedness you must have endured. I will never, so help me, Heaven! relinquish my search for thee till I am either convinced thy poor spirit has joined its Maker, or clasp thee in my arms never more to part from thee."

As he spoke he walked rapidly to the " Albion," and sat down in the solitary coffee-room, a prey to the bitterest anguish.

After a time he rung the bell.

Sam instantly appeared in answer to the summons.

" This is Friday?" said the colonel.

" Yes, sir, Friday, sir, if you please, sir. Yesterday Thursday, sir, if you please, sir."

" To-morrow morning, early, let me have a post-chaise and four horses for London."

" Post-chaise and four for London, sir? What hour, sir?"

" At eight precisely."

" Yes, sir. Post-chaise and four for mild-looking colonel at eight in the morning. Coming, sir; coming—coming."

CHAPTER LVIII.

To say that George felt no uneasiness at the obscure threats of Giles would be to say what was not true, although the uneasiness was not altogether on account of what he might attempt to do, and the consequences which must result from any attempt to put his threats into execution.

Phœbe, however, was really alarmed. There was something about Giles's manner when he spoke so wildly in the meadow which had taken powerful hold of her imagination. She fancied she could detect, in the incoherent expressions of Giles, indications of a formed purpose, and that any attempt of his would result in danger to George she firmly belived. Who could have imagined that such a source of disquiet as now deprived Phœbe of repose would possibly have arisen? But so it was. Although she was blessed in her affections by the worth of the object upon whom she had bestowed them, and in the approval of those whose good opinions were of so much importance to her peace, yet here had arisen an evil of magnitude and terror, and one which threatened to become more terrible than any one's imagination seemed to believe possible.

What, she thought, mightn't Giles attempt to do? or what even might he succeed in doing under the impulse of the fearful state of mental excitement in which he was plunged?

The safety of George, nay, even his life, might be at any unguarded moment sacrificed to the insane fury of his rival! She had heard and read of such awful domestic tragedies, and she trembled at the thought that her dream of happy love might be but the prelude to some scene of horror which would for ever sear her heart.

These were not the feelings which were calculated to render the repose of Phœbe either sound or refreshing. Many a time in the course of the night, when exhausted nature sunk into a quite slumber, she would, at the slightest noise, start from her couch, and fancy that she could hear George's voice uttering a cry for help. She would listen, then, with agonized attention for a repetition of the sound, and when it came not again, and she was forced to admit that some accidental noise had been, by her own excited imagination, converted into the sounds of terror, she would, weeping, lie down once again to try to court repose.

Full of these fancies, and as unhappy as her dread of great evil could make her, Phœbe passed the weary hours of the night.

She resolved that with the first dawn of day she would end such torments and fears, if possible, by seeking or meeting with Giles, and procuring from him a solemn promise that he would attempt nothing to the injury of George. She thought she might have sufficient influence over him to extort such a promise, and she had a sanguine hope that if once given freely, it would be held sacred even by the jealous and half-distracted Giles. This project she determined to put into execution, if possible, without acquainting either with the attempt or its result. She felt that, could she obtain such a promise, she should be happy, and George might never know to whom he had, perhaps, owed the preservation of his life. She knew that his high spirit would revolt from giving consent to any such solicitation on her part, and that no danger to which he might be exposed would induce him to listen with patience to any scheme which appeared in the slightest humiliating to her. But his safety was concerned; and, banishing all scruples, Phœbe resolved to make the effort to save him, let it cost her what tears and supplications it might.

Phœbe's mind became somewhat tranquillized after she had made this resolve; and were it not that she was determined to put her purpose into instant execution, she might have enjoyed some hours' refreshing repose. She, however, resisted the soft influence of the drowsy feeling that was stealing over her, and as soon as she observed the first symptoms of the coming day by the increased light in her little chamber, she rose, and enveloping herself in a thick cloak, to keep out the chill morning air, she opened her chamber-door, and descended to the lower apartments of the cottage. All was profoundly still, and with trembling eager hands, Phœbe opened the door, and went forth upon her expedition of peace and love.

The air was excessively cold, and Phœbe shivered under its keen influence notwithstanding the warm clothing in which she was enveloped.

"Oh," she said, "if I can but prevent what I so much dread, and save George from Giles, and poor Giles from himself, for he is, indeed, his own worst enemy, how amply shall I be rewarded for the step which I am taking! If violence was to occur, let the issue be what it might, it could bring but one result, and that would be unhappiness."

She walked forwards quickly, in the hope of overcoming the cold, which sensibly affected her delicate frame, and before many minutes had passed she was standing by the side of the old mill.

But a dim and uncertain light reigned around, and a cold piercing wind swept round the old building, with a sighing sound, as if seeking in vain for some entrance to its interior.

Phœbe had resolved upon her particular course of action, and she now walked slowly round the mill till she came to the shutter of the room which she knew was occupied by Tim Miggles. Here she knocked gently, and waited for some time patiently for an answer.

As no notice was taken by Tim of Phœbe's summons, she again knocked louder than before. Still there was no answer; and Phœbe, placing her ear close to the shutter, thought she could hear a low murmuring sound as of persons conversing in a subdued tone.

The shutter closed from without, and Phœbe, upon trying it with her hand, found that it was only pulled close, but was not fastened.

She pulled it cautiously open, and a feeble light gleamed from the window. She looked into the little chamber, and there she saw Tim Miggles sitting by the light of a very small piece of candle, which was stuck upon the end of a saveall.

Some paper lay before Tim, and he held a pen in his hand. Now and then he would shake his head as if in profound doubt, and then, with a great many successive taps on the forehead, attempt a solution of some apparent difficulty.

Phœbe did not disturb him for some time, for she was too much surprised at his singular movements not to feel some curiosity to know how they would end. Tim seemed to take no notice whatever of the opening of the shutter, and was evidently so entirely wrapped up in his occupation, whatever it was, that no ordinary disturbance was at all likely to attract his attention.

Phœbe was just about, by rattling upon the window, to make an attempt to attract his attention, when, with a great deal of head shaking and rapping on the forehead, Tim Miggles spoke, and sufficiently loud, too, for Phœbe to hear him.

"It's no go," said Tim, with a deep sigh,—"it's no go. Here's eight bits of candle been wasted in trying to find out a good rhyme for George, and it's no go not by no means."

He then took up a paper which lay before him, and commenced reading, with great emphasis :—

> "A maiden so fair, and a sailor so bold,
>   They both fell in love at a mill ;
> They didn't know then what they afterwards knew,
>   And made their tears flow like a rill.
> The maiden was fair, and Phœbe her name,
>   The lover was called happy George ;
> He was a good fellow, which no one can doubt,
>   And——

"There it is. No rhyme for George. It's a perfectly dreadful name is George. Who invented such a wretched name, I wonder? Some blacksmith I suppose, and then he had a rhyme in his *forge*. Oh, dear, oh, dear, it's no go—not a shadow of a go—not a indistnct long way of a smell of a go."

Phœbe now tapped rather loudly on the glass, and Tim gave a jump of alarm, and upset the piece of candle and the saveall in his terror.

"Wh—wh—what's that?" he said.

"Tim," cried Phœbe; "Tim Miggles."

"Oh, lauks," said Tim, "it's the apparition of the fair Imogine a coming to blow me up for making so unkimmon good a imitation of her poem. Oh, dear, what shall I do?—mum—ma'am—Missus Imogine—I won't no more."

"Tim Miggles," said Phœbe; "Tim Miggles, it's I."

"I know it's you; you needn't tell me. 'She shrieks as he whirls her around.' She's come to whirl me around."

"Tim, Tim, don't you know me?"

"Oh, yes; I does, I does. 'The worms they crept in, and the worms they crept out.' Oh, oh——"

"It's I—Phœbe. Make no noise, Tim; I want you directly."

"Eh?—what?—you, Phœbe? Bless me, is it possible? Dear me, what a striking incident."

"Tim, I wish you to tell Giles that I am waiting for him in the meadow, and that I desire most particularly to see him immediately."

"See Giles in the meadow?"

"Yes. Be quick, Tim;—there is but little time to spare."

"Well, I never," cried Tim, who was much amused at the request "I hope, Phœbe, the next indiwidual as you comes to see here will be Tim Miggles. One time you comes and says, says you,—'Get up, Tim, I wants to see George in a minute.' Then you comes and says, says you,—'Tim, I wants to see Giles; come, be quick.'"

"Well, my good Tim, do me this favour, and I will trouble you no more," said Phœbe.

"Oh, but I likes it. You've been now to them, so you must come some time, and make one of them get up, and say :—'Miggles, Miggles,—fetch me Miggles.'"

"Perhaps I may," said Phœbe; "nay, Tim, you are sure I would if it was to do you any real service."

Tim shook his head rather doubtingly.

"Very well, Miss Phœbe; I'll go. You know the uncommon state of my affections."

"Yes, yes; I know all. Tell Giles I shall wait for him in the meadow."

As Phœbe spoke she left the window, and proceeded towards the meadow, where, with a beating heart, she waited the appearance of Giles, who, she doubted not, would at once obey her summons.

She had not waited above six or seven minutes, when, as she looked towards the mill, she could perceive some one approaching towards the meadow with great speed. As the figure neared, she could perceive that it

was Giles, and, for the first time, the extreme difficulty of opening the conversation which she had resolved to have with him occurred to her, and she
almost regretted that she had been so precipitate in carrying her determination into effect.

A pang shot across her heart as she likewise thought that poor Giles
might misconstrue her motive in seeking a meeting with him, and fancy, in
his excited imagination, that something favourable to his suit had actuated
her in her present course of action. This last consideration was to Phœbe's
mind the worst of all; and the moment Giles came sufficiently near to
hear her, she said,—

"Giles, pardon me for sending for you, but I wish to speak to you of
George."

Giles had been in a troubled slumber when Tim Miggles awakened him
with the information that Phœbe herself had been to the mill to ask an interview with him in the meadow.

He sprung from his couch, and hurrying on his apparel, was out in the
open air, and rushing towards the meadow before he was scarcely sufficiently
awake to think upon what could be the cause of Phœbe seeking an interview at such an hour with him.

He arrived, panting and excited, to the place of meeting, and for a few
moments he glared at Phœbe, without speaking, and with an expression
cf countenance which alarmed her, and caused her to regret in her heart
that she had risked a private meeting with one who was in no condition of
mind to hear, or be affected by reason.

"Thee sent for me," he said, at length; "thee—even thee—sent for me?"

"I did, Giles," said Phœbe;—"I did send for you, in the sanguine hope
that the memory of your former kindness to me would induce you to hear
me calmly and do me the favour I come to ask at your hands."

"By the memory of former kindness, Phœbe?—former kindness? Is
the kindness all passed? Do I not love thee even now, now that thee hast
scorned me—better than I do love the world, and even Heaven?"

"Oh, Giles. Love me as you loved the orphan child, whose prattle
amused you, and whose helplessness looked up to you for support as to a
dear brother."

"No, no, that be past. I did ever love thee, Phœbe, for theeself; but
—but thee hast sent for me?"

"I have," said Phœbe; "and, as I said, it is to ask you a favour."

"Thee ask a favour of me? No, no. Unless thee wish me to plunge
into a mill-stream, and so thee will be rid of me."

"Oh, speak not so, Giles."

"And why?—why, Phœbe Marks, or Phœbe Grainger, or whatever thee
be, why be I not to speak so? Dost thee recollect what I was, and dost thee
see what I be now?"

"You are sadly altered, Giles."

"I be altered, I know I be altered; and when I did feel the alteration, I
did go into the deep dark woods, and I did ask my heart why I was so
altered, and the answer was, George Andrews. The trees did say George
Andrews, the little brook did murmur the name—the birds did mock me
with it; George Andrews, George Andrews, nothing but George Andrews;
and in that hour I did swear ——"

"Giles, Giles," cried Phœbe, "if your oath was one at which reason and
justice would shrink, repeat it not. Heaven records not such oaths."

"I did swear ——"

"Hold, Giles, hold! You dreamt—you were not yourself."

"I was, Phœbe, I was, and—and I will keep my oath. It was enmity
to that man."

"To George?" said Phœbe.

"Yes, to George Andrews!" replied Giles. "While I live—"

"Cease, cease, Giles. It is of George I come to speak to you."

"Curses!" cried Giles.

"Curse him not, Giles, oh, curse him not."

"Be it so. It be no use cursing. No, no, but the time will come when he—but no matter—no matter."

"Giles, you must make me a solemn promise."

"Speak; I do hear thee."

"You—you have used threats, Giles."

"I hear thee."

"You have said dark things. My sleep has been haunted, Giles, by your words."

"Has thee sleep been haunted?—haunted, did thee say?"

"Yes, Giles. Your words were foes to rest and happiness."

"Did thee, Phœbe," said Giles, speaking in a low tone, and looking anxiously round him, "did thee see great crawling things? Did they come and sit on thee breast, and laugh at thee, and mock thee?"

"Oh, Giles, do not talk so, and with that look," said Phœbe.

"Did they hiss at thee? Did one, then, whose eyes were coals of fire, fix his fangs in thee very heart? and did thee then try to scream, and find thee breath congealed, and thee could make no sound?"

"Do not think of these things, Giles. These are the creations of your imagination."

"Did thee lie then hopeless in agony, while the blood went hissing hot from thee quivering heart through the veins of the monster?"

"Oh, no, no. Horrible! horrible!"

"Did thee feel theeself dabbling in the gore?"

"Oh, cease, cease; you horrify me."

"Did thee lie, then, hopeless, in agony to scream, and—"

"Oh, no, oh, no. These are dreadful images."

"Don't thee talk of thee sleep being haunted."

"But Giles, oh, promise me one thing."

"What be it, Phœbe?"

"It is about George."

"About George, be it? George Andrews? Do not, Phœbe, oh, do not name him. It be madness to me. Do not, do not."

"Wherefore, Giles? George has ever felt kindly towards you."

"I will tell thee why not, Phœbe," replied Giles. "When I have been tormented, as I have told thee, and when hot lead was poured into my brain, I have shrieked to know why I was so treated, and the answer has been always George Andrews. I was once happy, and when I do ask myself when that was, the reply be before George Andrews did step his foot in th mill."

"But Giles," said Phœbe, "do you not know that all the evils you have endured are not at all attributed to George?"

"Phœbe, I do know nothing, but that I do love thee."

"Then by that love, Giles, I ask you to grant me my request?"

Giles clasped his hands, and looking with an expression of anguish at Phœbe, he said,—

"—I will—I must."

"I knew you would, Giles," said Phœbe; "I knew you would; and, Giles the day may come when you yourself will thank me for seeking this meeting."

"I do thank thee now, I do thank thee, Phœbe," replied Giles, speaking more mildly than he had hitherto done.

"Then, Giles," she said, "what I wish you solemnly to promise is this. That you will not, by word or action, contrive anything against George."

"Against George, Phœbe? How dost thee mean?"

"Oh, Giles, you know my meaning. You uttered dark threats against him. I fear your violence, and fear his resistance."

"Thee do wish me to promise that I will not quarrel with him?"

"Yes. Say you will not, Giles. Harsh words have passed between you, and harsh words are but the forerunners of harsh deeds."

"Phœbe," said Giles, "I do promise thee that I will never lift my hand against George if he do never lift his against me."

"And that, Giles," replied Phœbe, "he never will—oh, no. He would fain be your friend, Giles. He would live with you in good fellowship and love."

"I hear thee, Phœbe," said Giles, "but—no matter. I have something to ask of thee."

"And it is granted, Giles," replied Phœbe, "before you ask it."

"It be this," said Giles, with an agitated manner. "Will thee meet me on this spot?"

"For what object, Giles?"

"I have something to—to tell thee."

"I will, Giles. It is but a slight request, and I see not why I should refuse it."

"Will thee," said Giles, averting his head, and making a strong effort to speak with composure, "will thee trust theeself?"

"And why not, Giles?" said Phœbe. "You have ever been my friend."

"This—this, Phœbe, be Saturday."

"Yes, Giles."

"Will thee meet me here at—at eight o'clock?"

"I will."

"And—and thee will come freely?"

"Most freely, Giles."

"Fearing nothing, Phœbe?"

"Fearing nothing, Giles; for what can I fear from you who have been my friend and protector from wrong."

Giles covered his face with his hands and groaned.

"I—I did not wish this," he said. "If thee will come reluctantly, or—or refuse —"

"What mean you, Giles?" said Phœbe. "Why is this sudden agitation? Ha! I see George looking from the mill."

An instantaneous change came over Giles's manner as Phœbe mentioned the name of George, and he turned suddenly, facing her, and said, with wild vehemence,—

"Thee will come?—thee hast promised?—thee will come?"

"I have promised," she replied, "and I will come."

"Enough, enough, it be enough," he said, and he darted from her side.

CHAPTER LIX.

WE must now conduct the reader to Haredale Park, and we would fain shrink from recording the transactions of the Friday night at that place

As we have seen, the mind of Sir Herbert Foster had been sadly shattered by his belief in the supernatural nature of the figure which haunted his mansion. So firm a hold of his fancy had the idea taken, that, admitting that the first and second appearances of the figure were really no delusion, nothing more was required, for the imagination of the baronet presented it continually to his eyes, and in every slight sound which disturbed the aristocratic repose of his house, he fancied he could detect the voice or the footstep of the apparition which had so fearfully disturbed his repose.

From room to room of his splendid abode he had shifted, but he could find peace in none. The cracking of a door, the rattling of a widow frame, or any incidental noise, was sufficient to awaken all his terrors, and the cool, determined Sir Herbert Foster, the accomplished *roue*—the man who lent even a grace—a charm to vice, was fast subsiding into a state of mental imbecility.

The whole of Friday he had spent in a small room, which was far removed from the apartments he ordinarily occupied. There he had sat in hopeless misery and agitation. Each time that the door was opened by any of his domestics, he would start, and gaze upon the person who entered with a wild expression of inquiry in his eyes, from which all but the wily Master Cury shrunk appalled.

The apparition had never actually met Sir Herbert's gaze since he had seen it on the landing of the great staircase, and it is probable that his mind would have preserved its tone better, and been in a more calm and collected state, had he repeatedly been visited by the appearance, for now the mere dread of its visitation had grown so monstrous in his mind, that it far exceeded anything that he could possibly have felt at the reality.

As the evening drew near Sir Herbert's anxiety increased, and, long before they were actually necessary, he ordered lights to be brought into the room.

"Cury," he said,—"Cury, you—you will be within call?"

"Yes, Sir Herbert. I have been sitting in the next room. I should be sure to hear your hand-bell in a moment, Sir Herbert."

"Yes—true—very true, Cury," replied the baronet. "You have been, I suppose, about the house, and—and in all the rooms? The whole day has passed?—eh, Cury?—the whole day has passed without ——"

"All has been quiet, Sir Herbert," replied Cury ;—"I have seen nothing."

"Cury, I leave here to-morrow morning. You will see that everything is in readiness. I—I shall never see this place again."

A peculiar expression came over Cury's face as Sir Herbert spoke, but he merely bowed, and said nothing.

"And Cury," continued the baronet, who seemed to wish to prolong the conversation, "you will be careful in town never to allude to what has occurred here. Never mention it even to me. I am going to forget it, Cury."

"Yes, Sir Herbert; certainly, Sir Herbert."

"And—and, Cury, let me have more lights."

The room was already brilliantly lighted ; but, in obedience to the baronet's order, more lights were brought, and every corner of the apartment was perfectly dazzling.

"Now, Cury, you—you may go. If I should not ring, you can come in about a quarter of an hour."

"Yes, Sir Herbert."

"Cury, you—you won't be longer absent than a quarter of an hour?"

"Certainly not, Sir Herbert."

"Well, then, go—go."

Cury bowed, and left the room ; and Sir Herbert Foster, placing a chair with its back against the wall, sat down, after drawing a table towards him, upon which lay some books, and tried to read.

The attempt, however, was fruitless. His eyes were continually leaving the page to wander round the room, and to satisfy himself that he was alone.

"To London—to London," he said, in a faint voice; "I will lose myself there, and never be alone. This place is gloomy and melancholy; it ever was so; but now—now it is hateful, awfully hateful. I—I am very cold."

There was a large fire blazing in the grate, which, with the numerous lights, made the temperature of the apartment unusually high. Sir Herbert Foster, however, shivered, and his blood seemed to flow like cold water through his veins.

He rested his elbow upon the open book, and supported his head with his hand for some moments in silence, but he could not remain in one position long, and he rose and paced the room, carefully avoiding going near the door.

"Oh, if I could believe," he said, "that these appearances which so frighten men's souls, and cloud their reasons, were only imaginary, I might be happy; I should then only be suffering from a disease, which art might subdue. But I saw it plainly. I could not—no, no—I could not be deceived—I saw Helen Wade. And how many great, good, and wise men have believed in such appearances? They are not impossible. How close is probability to possibility; and yet what object could supernatural appearances be supposed to exist for? We know not. There are many things that we know not, the uses of which are matters of daily observation, and yet I will not, must not, believe that the human mind is at the mercy of a world of disembodied spirits, who may torture humanity, and render life a grievous burthen. No, no, it cannot be; and Helen Wade, too. I—I did not compass her death."

A piece of furniture in the room, owing to the extreme heat of the air at this moment, as is very usual under circumstances of increased temperature, gave a loud crack.

The sound, had it been that of the last trumpet, could not have affected Sir Herbert more than it did. He glanced wildly round the apartment; his limbs trembled, and a cold clammy perspiration burst from every pore of his skin.

"What was that?" he said, in a husky whisper. "What noise was that? Am—am I alone? What a fearful question. Am I alone?"

He stretched out his hand to the table, and rung a silver bell, which was on it.

In a moment Cury appeared at the door.

"Oh, Cury," cried Sir Herbert, drawing a long breath, "I—I am glad you have come. You should have come as I told you, Cury."

"You have been scarcely ten minutes alone, Sir Herbert," answered Cury.

"Ten minutes! How much misery may ten short minutes hold! Ten minutes of pleasure, what are they? Cury, did you hear anything?"

"I thought I heard a noise, Sir Herbert, just before you rung."

"A noise. Yes, yes; I could not be mistaken; there was a noise. I—I must remove from this room, Cury."

"If you please, Sir Herbert."

"And yet I have seen nothing, Cury. Don't you think I might stay here?"

"I think you might, Sir Herbert. The noise might have been merely accidental."

"You think it might? Oh, yes—yes—surely it might," said the baronet. "Of course it might be accidental; I did not think of that. I will remain here. I—I feel rather better. I think, Cury, I—I will have some more lights."

"More lights, Sir Herbert?"

"Yes, there is a kind of gloom, Cury, in the room. Don't you observe it?"

"I cannot say I do, Sir Herbert," replied Cury.

"Yes, yes, you must—you must," said Sir Herbert Foster, hurriedly. "Why should I see things that other people do not? Why should I? Tell me why, Cury?"

"I really can't say, Sir Herbert, but I'll order more lights."

"Yes—do. What is the time?"

"It is now near nine, Sir Herbert. Will you please to sleep in your old room, Sir Herbert?"

"Sleep, Cury—sleep? I—I don't know. I think, Cury, as this is my last night here, I will sit up, and you and Freegrove shall sit up with me."

Cury looked rather uneasy at this proposal, but he said nothing.

"Now, Cury," continued the baronet, "you can go. Remember the lights."

Cury bowed, and left the room. He had no sooner shut the door upon Sir Herbert Foster than he hurried through a number of apartments, till he came to the same small parlour in which Mr. Scrimp had surprised the valet and Mr. Freegrove in such close council. There was a solitary candle burning upon the table, and Freegrove sat by it. His face was flushed with drink, and several bottles and glasses upon the table betrayed the nature of his occupation.

Cury entered, with his usual quiet stealthy step, and cautiously closed the door behind him ere he advanced to the table.

"Well, what now?" said Freegrove.

"I tell you what, now," answered Cury, "if you go on drinking at this rate you will be fit for nothing."

"Pshaw! Master Cury, you don't know me," said Freegrove. "I'm ripe and ready now. Say the word, and here's Ralph Freegrove ripe and ready."

"Yes," answered Cury, "and as drunk as a pig."

"No, no," said Freegrove; "no, no—no such thing. Steady as a rock. Look here."

As he spoke he poured out a bumper of wine, and raised it to his lips.

"Now, by everything damnable, you are not going to drink any more?" said Cury.

"Here's better luck still," said Freegrove, tossing off the wine.

"You will ruin us both," cried Cury, with an air of deep vexation.

"No, no, not at all. What inspires us and fires us?"

Cury walked to the sideboard, and, filling a large glass with vinegar, he presented it to Freegrove.

"Drink that," he said, "to the success of our business. Drain it to the last drop."

"Oh, yes, Master Cury," replied Freegrove; "I am not apt to leave much in my glass. Ha! ha! ha! What is it?—some of the old bucellas, eh?"

"Drink it, drink it, and I'll speak to you afterwards," said Cury.

"Well, then, here goes," continued Freegrove, with a drunken hiccup. "Here's to the success of our business. There's nothing in the world like eating and drinking."

Freegrove swallowed a deep draught of the vinegar before he could stop himself and throw down the glass, which he did, on to the floor, exclaiming,—

"D——n! Cury, what's that?"

"The old bucellas, Freegrove," replied the valet.

"The old devil!—It's vinegar!"

"Well, suppose it is; it will sober you. Come, now, listen to me. I must go back to Sir Herbert in a few minutes."

"I hear," replied Freegrove, in a sober tone, and making a wry face.

"He wants to sit up to-night, and says we shall sit with him."

"The devil he does," answered Freegrove. "That won't answer, you know, Master Cury?"

"I know it won't, and there is but one way of preventing it."

"What may that be, Master Cury?"

"Why, he must be frightened out of it somehow. I'll tell him, you are not in the house, and he must see Helen Wade again, you understand, when he will most likely leave the house himself, and we can have it all our own way."

"D— that ghost business," said Freegrove.

"How could we have got on without it?" replied Cury. "In my visit to the jewel-room, you know, I have always worn the riding-habit and hat."

"And is it really the riding-habit that belonged to Helen Wade?" asked Freegrove.

"Yes," said Cury; "she died in it; and, after the inquest, I put it and the hat and veil in an old box in the jewel-room."

"You are a clever fellow, Cury," said Freegrove, "though you have no real notion of what is, and what is not, good eating and drinking."

"We have done very well hitherto," continued Cury. "We have already netted four thousand pounds, by getting the real jewels, with our friend the Jew's assistance, replaced by imitation stones. Sir Herbert has missed nothing, although his family jewels are not worth a hundred pounds."

"But the plate," said Freegrove; "the gold and silver plate?"

"That must be carried off to-night, for Sir Herbert leaves in the morning. I hope before sunrise to be many miles from here."

"And if Sir Herbert should place himself in the way by any means, Cury?"

"Why, if he should," replied Cury, ferociously, "we must put him out of the way at all risks."

Freegrove looked at Cury, and drew his finger across his throat.

"Please yourself about the mode," said Cury.

"Oh, you expect me to do that part of the business, do you?" said Freegrove.

"I do, if the necessity arises," replied Cury; "it's more your province than mine. I plan, and you execute. I must now return to Sir Herbert. Keep yourself out of sight, Freegrove."

While this conversation was taking place between the confederates in crime, Sir Herbert Foster sat in his apartment, still a prey to feelings of the most painful nature. His mind was completely shattered, and he found it impossible to withdraw his thoughts for a single moment from the harassing and distressing idea that he was not alone, but that there was present, invisibly in the room with him, some supernatural being.

Cury's depredations in the jewel-room of Haredale Park had been carried on for some years. He had become acquainted in London with a Jewish lapidary, who, upon hearing from him an account of the value and number of the family jewels at Haredale, had suggested to him the idea of stealing some few at each of his country visits, and replacing the real stones by false ones, when next he accompanied his master to Haredale.

The scheme had been completely successful. Three or four jewels had been abstracted at each visit, and taken out of their setting by a Jew, and replaced with imitation stones of so good a quality, that they might well deceive even the most curious eye. The mock jewels were then replaced, and the real stones were sold by the Jew for their mutual advantage.

Freegrove would never have been associated with Cury in the matter but for an accident.

It happened one day that Freegrove, being in the armoury, heard a noise in the jewel-room, and, putting his eye to the key-hole, he saw enough of the proceedings of the valet to place him completely in his power.

Freegrove, not being troubled with any conscientious scruples, made, what he conceeved to be, the most prudent use of his accidental discovery. He sought Cury alone, and told him of it.

Cury felt in a moment that he was in the hands of Freegrove, and he immediately offered to make him a sharer in all future plunder. As this was the very thing which Freegrove himself intended to propose as the price of his concealment, he acceded to it at once, and became of much assistance in the nefarious scheme.

The jewels were at length exhausted, but the insatiable desire for plunder still remained, and the accomplices in guilt formed the determination of stealing the whole of the gold and silver plate, and at once decamping to some other country, to live upon the fruits of their crime.

America was their destination, where they were well aware that money, let it come from ever so polluted a source, would always ensure its possessors a cordial welcome.

Cury was determined, if he could not persuade Sir Herbert Foster to retire to bed, to alarm him sufficiently to prevent him leaving his room.

The quarter of an hour, at the end of which period of time the baronet had commanded him to seek his presence, had expired, and Cury softly entered his master's room.

"I am here, Sir Herbert," he said.

"Oh, yes. Well, Cury," said his master, "have you found all quiet?"

"Why, Sir Herbert, I have heard nothing, but——"

"But what, Cury? What?" cried Sir Herbert glancing uneasily around him.

"You know the painted window, Sir Herbert, that leads to the conservatory?"

"Yes—yes, Cury The painted window——"

No. 46

"The night," continued Cury, "is rather dark, Sir Herbert; but as I came across the long picture gallery I thought something passed by me like a rush of wind."

"And you—you saw——"

"Nothing just then, Sir Herbert; but when I left the gallery I happened to cast my eyes to the painted window, and as I did so, I saw——"

"You saw what? Speak, Cury; for the love of Heaven, speak."

"I saw the shadow of a form pass the window slowly."

"And, Cury, the form was——"

"Was Helen Wade's, Sir Herbert."

The baronet sank in his chair, and groaned heavily.

"'Tis in the house," he said, faintly. "It haunts me everywhere. No peace—no peace. Oh, Cury, you need not envy wealth, titles, estates, distinctions. Look at me—look at me, and thank Heaven you are not Sir Herbert Foster, the courted, the admired, the envied baronet."

"The figure then disappeared," continued Cury; "I saw it no more. A cold feeling came over me as if I was in a vault."

"You are sure, Cury—quite sure?" said Sir Herbert.

"Quite, Sir Herbert. The riding-habit—the hat and veil——"

"God help me!" cried the baronet.

"Will you not retire to rest, Sir Herbert?" said Cury.

"Rest, Cury? Where shall I find rest, except in the tomb?—and, perhaps not there. No, I will remain here."

"Would you please to have a bed at the village, Sir Herbert?"

"No, Cury, no. I have thought of that, but something seems to bind me to the house to-night. I would fain leave it, but I cannot."

Cury bowed.

"Be within call," continued Sir Herbert. "You and Freegrove sit in the next room. Say nothing to the servants. I will sit here till early dawn. Order the travelling carriage to be ready by day-break."

CHAPTER LX.

Cury, when he left Sir Herbert, stood for a few moments outside the door in deep thought; then, with a sneering smile, he muttered:—

"Yes, it must be so. In Sir Herbert's present state of mind the sudden appearance of what he supposes to be the apparition of Helen Wade may put him out of the way altogether."

The valet then proceeded quickly towards the armoury. When there he set down the lamp, which he carried in his hand, and thrusting his hand within the casque of a suit of mail, which hung upon the wall, he drew out a bunch of keys.

"Old friends," he said, as he looked at the keys, "you have done me some service. Sir Herbert little thinks that these are the real keys of his family treasures, and those he takes such care of a set that I had made. Ha! ha! It was of more importance to me that the locks should go easy than to him."

Cury took up his lamp and walked with his usual stealthy step, into the the jewel-room. He held the light above his head, and looked round him with a sneering expression of face.

"Humph!" he said. "Why don't the old Fosters rise up in arms against the daring plunderer of their family treasures? Cury, Cury, you have a mind, but not an imagination. This room has no terrors for me. I saw Helen Wade fall on this spot—I saw the warm blood trickle from her mouth—but what was that to me? Nothing, except—ha! ha!—that it has furnished me with a means of enriching myself securely."

He selected a key from the bunch, and approaching an old chest, which stood in one corner of the small room, he took from it a riding-habit of faded velvet, and a beaver hat, to which was appended a lace veil.

"These," he said, "are my best friends and most trusty confederates. They keep all secrets, work when they are wanted, and require no share of the proceeds. I would that I could use Freegrove in the same manner; but there may yet be an opportunity found of preventing him from becoming either a charge or an enemy. Humph! We shall see, Master Freegrove. My confidence is apt to be dangerous. Humph! There was a man once before who would know a little secret of mine, and he—he was found one day dead. Humph!"

As he spoke, he adjusted the riding-habit around him, and put on the hat.

"Now," he said, "poor dear Sir Herbert, I will give you a little shock. I'm afraid your nervous system is not altogether in the most vigorous state, and this little interlude may put you effectually out of the way."

He took up the lamp, and left the jewel-room, with a quiet and noiseless step.

Hiding the lamp under his habit, Cury proceeded some distance through the house until he came to a door, within which he could distinctly hear sounds of laughter. He extinguished the lamp, and having placed it in a corner, he stood listening at the door.

"I have taken care," he muttered, "to spread an alarm among the servants about this ghost story. This is their hall. They seem merry enough, d— them. I hate anybody to be merry. It would not be amiss just to damp their mirth a little by showing them the ghost. And, besides, if anything should happen to Sir Herbert, there will be plenty of evidence, then, about the ghost; and, who knows, I might even stay and brave inquiry. Humph! We shall see. Laugh away—laugh away."

The assemblage in the servants' hall was evidently a very jovial and contented one, for roars of laughter arose every minute, and the domestics seemed to be enjoying themselves amazingly.

Cury laid his hand on the lock of the heavy oaken door, and slowly opened it far enough to obtain a view of the interior of the large hall, in which the numerous servants were wont to assemble before retiring to rest.

Some rustic game was going on, which seemed equally to amuse young and old.

Cury watched his opportunity, when all eyes were turned from the door, to glide cautiously into the apartment, and there he stood for a moment or two unnoticed.

At length a country-looking fellow, with an immense red face, happened in the middle of his glee, to cast his eyes upon the figure of Cury, who stood still as a statue, within a few paces of the door.

The man's face seemed actually to fix itself in the position it happened to be in at the precise moment he cast his eyes upon Cury. There were all the features distorted by a grin, while the glaring eyes and bristling hair betokened the very extremity of terror. In a moment all eyes were turned in the same direction, and a scream of horror and dismay immediately arose, while the affrighted domestics rolled over each other, and produced a scene of indescribable confusion in their separate attempts to get each as far from the hall-door as possible.

Cury's object was accomplished. He had been seen and that was enough. Every one in the servants' hall was in a condition to swear to the appearance of the apparition in the riding-habit and hat. Before the confusion subsided, he made a hasty retreat, and quickly pursued his route towards Sir Herbert's room, to carry out his more important purpose of acting upon the imagination of the baronet.

The hour of eleven was at hand, and Sir Herbert calculated that in about five more hours there would be light enough for him to pursue his journey to London.

His mind had become a little tranquillized as the time passed, and nothing occurred to disturb the silence of his room. He was sitting gazing at the bright embers which glared in the grate, and a feeling of mental repose was stealing over him, when he heard the door of the room opened, and raising his head suddenly to see who it was, he uttered a loud shriek, and fell insensible on the floor.

"Good," said Cury, as he advanced into the room in his disguise, and bent over the prostrate form of his master. "This is beyond my hopes. This trance may be that of death. I must off with this disguise, and assume a more mortal appearance."

Leaving Sir Herbert Foster still lying insensible on the floor of the room, Cury hurried back to the jewel-room, and deposited the habit and hat again in the chest from which he had taken them.

He then made what haste he could to the servants' hall, which he immediately entered boldly.

The domestics, although they had partially recovered from the personal confusion into which they had been thrown, were still fully under the influence of excessive terror. Not one of them had dared to stir from the room, and when Cury opened the door, and appeared in his own proper person, it was a moment or two before they recognised him, so great was their terror.

"Oh, Mr. Cury—Mr. Cury," said a dozen voices, "we've seen it—we've seen it."

"I don't know what you may have seen," answered Cury; "but you must come with me directly some of you, for I've just found Sir Herbert lying insensible on the floor of his own room."

"Sir Herbert insensible?" exclaimed all, with emphasis. "Then it must have gone to him straight from here. Oh, Mr. Cury, didn't you meet anything?"

"No," said Cury, "I saw nothing. But come along, some of you."

Four or five of the stoutest-hearted among the servants now rose and followed Cury, not, however, without sundry misgivings and secret fears.

Sir Herbert Foster still lay insensible on the floor. They raised him, and placed him on a couch, and in a few moments he opened his eyes, and looked wildly around him.

"What?" he said; "what has happened? I—I dream now—or—or I did dream some time since that I saw Helen Wade."

"Will you retire to your chamber, Sir Herbert?" said Cury.

"Oh, Cury," replied his master, "you are here? My faithful Cury and friends,—good friends all of you, I have now three times seen what a man in his mortal state may not see often and live."

"My honoured master," said the hypocritical Cury, "do not speak thus."

"Listen, all of you," said Sir Herbert; "my hours are numbered—I shall never see another sunrise."

The servants looked at each other in astonishment, and one or two of them pointed significantly to their foreheads, to signify their doubts of their master's sanity.

"Cury—Cury," continued the baronet, "I will retire to my old chamber; that chamber in which the Fosters for so many generations have breathed their last. Let me have there the means of writing."

Leaning upon the arm of Cury, the baronet slowly left the room, and followed by the wondering domestics, he took the way to the chamber, which he had not occupied since the first appearance of the apparition which had worked so strangely upon his brain.

They had to pass the door of the armoury on their way, and just as they came opposite, even Cury's face blanched with fear as a loud crash from within the armoury smote their ears.

Sir Herbert Foster alone seemed not to be startled at the noise. He paused, and said,—

"I know it—I know it. Go in, some of you, and see if there is a suit of chain armour lying on the floor."

Two of the servants entered the armoury, and upon their return, reported that a suit of splendid chain armour, which they knew had been fastened to the wall by rings and stanchions of iron, appeared to have been wrenched with great force from its place, and was lying on the floor.

"There are blood-red feathers in the helmet?" said Sir Herbert.

"Yes, Sir Herbert," replied the servants, "three long red feathers."

"I know it! I know it!" exclaimed the baronet; then, turning to the servants who were following, he said in a firm but melancholy tone,—

"When that suit of chain mail falls to the ground without visible agency, the head of the house of Foster has not twelve hours to live. It has been fixed in its place by each baronet in succession since the first, and so strongly, that it would require workmen to remove it; but it has invariably fallen within twelve hours of the then holder of the family estates and honours. Farewell to you all!—farewell! My time has come. God help me—God help me—God help me!"

Sir Herbert walked slowly onward till he came to his chamber-door, then waving his hand to the servants, he entered the room alone, and they heard him lock the door in the inside. Cury turned to the servants and said,—

"You will do well, all of you, to take no notice of this matter. Sir Herbert is only a little scared at the ghost, I dare say. He will be well in the morning, no doubt; but at all events, I charge you, all of you, to keep this matter secret, and not to spread any alarm."

The servants promised obedience, and retired to their own hall.

Cury prided himself particularly upon his inflexibility to all superstitious tendencies, yet the fall of the suit of mail in the armoury had greatly shaken his mind; and it was with unsteady and trembling steps that he turned towards the parlour where Ralph Freegrove was waiting for him.

Again he had to pass the door of the armoury, and he could not resist the impulse of his curiosity to take a glance at the armour which had so singular and incredible a superstition attached to it.

He had taken a light from one of the servants, and he held it as high as he could as he entered the armoury. He saw at once the object of his search. Lying in a confused heap on the floor, was a splendid suit of chain mail, which was of great value, from the numerous rings of gold and silver with which it was adorned.

Cury examined the wall carefully against which it had hung, and he saw the main staples to which the armour had been strongly linked by bars of metal, had been torn from their holds in the wall, dragging along with them masses of the solid oak, of which the walls of that formerly most important chamber were formed.

"This is, indeed, most strange," he exclaimed. "If Sir Herbert does die in accordance with this prophetic superstition, it will be by Freegrove's hand. There may be more to do to-night than I am aware of; but it must be done. I am not one to shrink from what I undertake because the danger thickens."

He left the armoury, and with a more hurried step than he customarily used, proceeded to the parlour.

"Sir Herbert is in bed, Freegrove," said Cury, "by this time. At all events, he is in his own chamber, and has locked himself in."

"Very well," said Freegrove. "Here am I, Ralph Freegrove, quite ready."

"You have provided the cart for the plate?" inquired Cury.

"Trust me for that," said Freegrove.

"Well, then, let us lose no time. Hark!—that's twelve o'clock."

"So it is," replied Ralph. "What a deuced long time you've been, Cury, with your d——d long-winded ghost concern."

"Come—come," said Cury, impatiently, "be quick; the sooner we are out of the house now, the better. Each five minutes is a mile lost in getting clear."

"You are in a plaguy hurry," said Freegrove; "but I'm ready, so come on as soon as you like. Won't you take a drop of something? I never saw you look so queer before."

"Never mind my looks,—let's to business."

They left the parlour, and walked rapidly towards the armoury, through which they must of necessity pass to get to the jewel-room.

"Hallo!" cried Freegrove, when he saw the armour on the floor; "what's the meaning of this?"

"Nay, never mind it," said Cury; "come on—come on."

"But I tell you what it is, Master Cury," said Freegrove; "I heard Sir Herbert once over his cups in London tell a story about that suit of old mail."

"Well—well, never mind it, it will amuse us another time."

"As you please, Master Cury," said Freegrove. "As you please; but if all that Sir Herbert say, is true, he's as good as a dead man. Howsomdever, it's not much matter to me or you, Cury, for we're going to give him warning old boy, ain't we?—Ha! ha!"

Cury now entered the jewel-room, and beckoned to Freegrove to advance.

"Come," he said, "stow in the pockets of your hunting-jacket all the small articles of value that you can, and help me to pack the others."

"Aye—aye, that's the way," said Freegrove; "open the locks."

Cury, with his keys, opened every lock in the cabinet, and the depredators commenced loading themselves with the spoil.

"I would not leave the mock jewels," said Cury, "if we could conveniently take them, for the gold settings are very valuable."

"Never mind the nut-shell," said Freegrove; "we've had the kernel. Ha! ha! ha!"

Cury had previously provided himself with a number of cloths in which to wrap the plate to prevent any ringing or jingling. Massive gold and silver plates, candelabra, goblets, and vases, tarnished by age and long disuse, were dragged from where they had laid long because they were unfashionable, and enveloped in cloth, for removal. Cury filled his pockets with every small article of jewellery he could lay his hands on; and thus, for a full hour were the two engaged in packing up their rich spoil.

We must now for a brief space leave Cury and Freegrove to gloat over their fancied plunder, and return to Sir Herbert Foster, who had, as we have seen, shut himself up in gloomy despair in his chamber, as he thought, never again to come out of it in life.

He had taken with his own hand a branch candlestick from one of the servants, and he placed it on the table; then, sitting down, he shaded his face with his hands, and remained for some time in deep thought.

At length a violent emotion seemed to shake his whole frame, and he burst into a passion of tears.

Slowly this subsided, and he rose more calmly, and drawing to his side writing materials, he, for a space of half an hour, wrote something, which he then carefully folded and sealed with his own signet ring. He then addressed the packet to "The Lady Elizabeth Foster, Haredale Park."

"Haredale Park will be her's," he said, "before she receives this last memoranda of my wishes. Those that I have injured in life, may rejoice in my death, for they will find that Sir Herbert Foster, when his hours—nay, his very minutes were numbered, thought of them more than of himself."

He took two or three turns up and down the chamber, and then, sitting down again by the table, he said,—

"Poor deluded, sacrificed Helen Wade, I can make no reparation to thee. I have trembled before thy pure spirit; but methinks now, I must be half way in the land of immortal things myself, for my fear has passed away like a shadow. Helen Wade, if it be possible for thee to appear to me once more, I charge thee to appear now. I would talk to thee, for as thou art a disembodied spirit, so shall I be soon."

He looked round the room as he spoke, with the full expectation of seeing the appearance he invoked; but his look was calm and fearless, and it was with a feeling of disappointment that he said, after a pause of some minutes,—

"Well, be it so. I am not to see thee more until I am even as yourself, an inhabitant of another world. The fiat has gone forth. There will be no more baronets of the house of Foster. I am the last."

Sir Herbert now walked to a large mirror which hung from the ceiling to the floor on one side of the apartment. He looked at the reflection of himself for one moment, and then with a shudder turned from it, and grasped the back of a chair for support. The once gay and handsome baronet might well start at the picture which the faithful glass presented to him. The mental agony of the last few days had done the work of many years upon his form and countenance, and he was but the shadow of his former self. The conviction that his hours were numbered, and his existance so near its close, had given a peculiar expression to his countenance. His cheeks had fallen—his lips were thin and bloodless, and an unearthly fire seemed to glare from his sunken eyes.

"The time," he said, faintly, "the time is drawing to a close. Already I feel scarcely human. The blood,—the rich warm current of life flows languidly through my veins. The pulsation of my heart is slow and wearied. I am fast—fast approaching extinction. How shall I endure the last dread pangs that rends the soul from the body? Death is even now stealing over my frame. I feel but strange to the world. There is an icy coldness at my heart, and my brain grows dizzy and confused. The step from mortality to immortality is a fearful one, and the soul may well sicken at its near approach to the confines of that world beyond the tomb to which I feel myself hastening."

With clasped hands and compressed lips he paced the room, striving to calm the excessive agitation of his mind, and subdue the trembling of his frame.

Here he again said, "How am I to die? A fearful question. Is death to steal slowly upon me with his icy fingers here in this room? or am I to become the subject of some catastrophe which shall suddenly deprive me of existence ? There is one thing I should still like to do while strength is left me. I—I feel an impulse—an irresistible impulse to visit once more that chamber in which died Helen Wade. Her blood is upon its flooring. I—I must look at it once more. And yet, why should I ?—I know not—I am a puppet in the hands of Providence ; and I feel that I must go—yes— yes—to the jewel-room—to the jewel-room !"

CHAPTER LXI.

Sir Herbert Foster lit a large lamp, and with a deep sigh walked to the door of his room. When there, he paused for a moment, and cast an anxious glance around him. His eye rested upon the familiar articles which the room contained, and he seemed impressed with the conviction that he was looking upon them for the last time.

"It is fitting," he said, "that I—I, who never truly attached to me one living thing in life, should mourn to separate from the inanimate objects which have been so long familiar to my sight. I may never see this room again."

Slowly he passed through the doorway, and found himself at the end of a long gallery, which terminated at the top of the grand staircase, where once he had seen the pretended apparition of Helen Wade.

The gallery was hung with portraits of the different branches of the Foster family, commencing with the portrait of that one of the race who first attained the title. As Sir Herbert paced slowly along, he held the lamp which he carried near to each of the mute likenesses of the family, and to his excited imagination it appeared as if the eyes of the portraits fixed themselves upon him, and followed him as he proceeded onwards. Sir Herbert Foster, however, was in that state of mind, which, while it left imagination still free to conjure up phantasies of its own which had no real existence, carried him far past any feeling of superstitious fear. He had ceased to consider himself as one of the inhabitants of the earth. He felt convinced he was so near the confines of another world, that he had as much, if not more to do with it and its denizens, than he had to do with the mortal things which were around him.

Slowly, and with many deep and involuntary sighs, he paced along the gallery, which was of very considerable extent. He arrived at the top of the great marble staircase, and he paused upon the spot where he had seen the apparition in the riding-habit, and seemed to expect that probably some similar appearance would be presented to his sight ; and it is surprising that his excited fancy did not succeed in presenting to him the vision he expected. But such was not the case, and he slowly descended the staircase without interruption.

He was now in a passage which led directly to the door of the armoury ; and as if impelled by some irresistible impulse, he quickened his pace, and soon gained the door of the ancient apartment.

He paused for a moment, but opening it gently, he glided into the armoury, and closed the door behind him.

Holding the lamp as high as he could above his head, he glanced round the room, and upon the arms and warlike accoutrements of all ages which were then collected. Rude weapons of warfare were there of an age long anterior to the conquest of England by the hardy Normans. There were the heavy axes and maces, and the long cross-hilted swords of the middle ages, together with the suits of plate and chain armour, of every device and fashion. Then came the cumbrous musket; which, unwieldy and inefficient

as it was when first introduced, still succeeded in giving the death stroke to that mode of warfare which altogether depended for its success upon personal courage and personal strength. To these weapons succeeded the refinements upon fire-arms, which, in our own times, have rendered such weapons so universal in their use.

"Here," said Sir Herbert, as his eye fell upon the various contents of the armoury,—"here is the history of my race. What was acquired by brute force was retained by finesse and complicated ingenuity. My ancestors accomplish their objects by the aid of stout hearts and large muscles. I—I, by chicanery, and such tools as Scrimp and Freegrove. Oh, how little does my life appear now that it is passing from me."

He now cast his eyes on the floor, and saw the suit of chain armour which had fallen from the wall. For some time he gazed at it in silence; then heaving a long drawn sigh, he said,—

"How much more is there in Heaven and on earth than is dreamt of in our philosophy? Lie thou there, senseless, yet awful steel—lie there. No baronet of the house of Foster will ever lift thee from the ground again. Your work is done. I am the last—the last who shall ever bear that name."

He turned from the armoury, and walking across the room, he said, in a low voice, or rather whisper,—

"Now to the jewel-room—the jewel-room."

He was within a few yards of the door which led from the armoury to the jewel-room, when it was suddenly thrown wide open, and a figure, in a riding-habit and hat, with a veil closely drawn over its face, stood in the entrance.

Cury and Freegrove had found the packing of their spoil a work which occupied a longer period of time than they had calculated upon, and yet their cupidity and insatiable desire for plunder would not suffer them to be contented with what could be quickly and conveniently carried from the pre-

No. 47

mises, and they still lingered in the jewel-room while an article of value remained to be enveloped in cloths and prepared for removal.

They had nearly, however, completed their work, when Cury suddenly laid his hand upon Freegrove's arm, and, in a low voice of alarm, said,—

"Listen!—listen, Freegrove. By G—, there's some one in the armoury!"

"The devil there is," said Freegrove, diving his hand into the pocket of the hunting jacket which he wore, and producing a large clasp knife, the blade of which sprung out upon touching a spring.

"Hush! hush!" said Cury. "Silence, or we are lost! The least noise would alarm the house. Hush! leave it to me."

Cury placed his ear to the door, and listened intently for several moments, then turning to Freegrove, with his usual pale face, of a perfect livid hue, he said,—

"It is Sir Herbert!"

"Sir Herbert," cried Freegrove. "Then by h— we're in for it."

Cury took a small pistol from his pocket, and raised the lock to see if the percussion cap was in its place.

"Freegrove," he said, "it's our lives, or his."

"Yes, to be sure," answered Freegrove; "and it's our plunder too. The question is, whether we shall continue to eat and drink, or Sir Herbert continue to eat and drink?"

"Yes, Freegrove," replied Cury, "you are right. He will come here and raise the alarm, and then we are lost."

"There are two words to that bargain," said Freegrove, significantly drawing the knife across his throat.

"True, Freegrove—most true," said Cury. "A knife makes no noise, but a pistol, you see, does, and—and—so——"

"So I'm to do it, you mean?" replied Freegrove. "Well, damme, who cares? In for a penny, in for a pound."

"You are a brave fellow, Freegrove," said Cury. "I have a pair of pistols; and should there be any difficulty, you know, of course, I will assist."

"You needn't trouble yourself," growled Freegrove, whose savage nature was now thoroughly awakened.

"Yet, stay," cried Cury; "there is one chance left. We may get rid of him quietly."

"What do you mean?" said Freegrove; "there isn't time to poison him."

"No, no, I don't mean that. I will try the ghost trick again, I may scare him back to his room again while we get clear.

As he spoke Cury unlocked the chest, and took out the riding-habit and hat, and hastily put them on. He drew the veil over his face, and walked to the door.

"Hush!" he said to Freegrove. "Conceal yourself behind the door as it opens. Do not stir for your life. Make no noise, and all will be well."

"D——n!" said Freegrove, "if ever I like hiding when I've got a knife in my hand."

"Hush! hush! For my sake be quiet," whispered Cury.

"Well, well, have it your own way," replied Freegrove, as he slunk to the side of the door, so that when it opened, which it did, inwards, he would be effectually hidden from observation.

Cury then immediately threw open the door, and stood, in his disguise, exactly on the threshold.

The intriguing valet had, however, quite miscalculated the effect of his appearance upon his master, for, as we have before observed, Sir Herbert Foster's mind was not in its usual state, and his fear of the spirit of Helen Wade had passed from him.

When the baronet first saw what it was that obstructed his entrance into the jewel-room, a convulsive tremor ran through his limbs, and for a moment a deadly faintness came over him ; but he quickly recovered, and without stiring from the spot on which he had suddenly been arrested by the sighr of the apparition, he raised his lamp high above his head, and looked at it fixedly.

There was an awful silence of some minutes' duration, during which it is probable that Cury suffered more agony and fear than his master.

Sir Herbert at length spoke in a hollow and solemn voice.

"Spirit," he said, " I know thee. Thou hast come to warn me that my life is ebbing fast. Speak to me—oh ! speak."

Cury had expected that Sir Herbert Foster would have flown with precipitation from the armoury the moment he caught sight of the supposed ghost, and the idea of anything like a conversation with his master in his assumed character of an apparition had never occurred to the valet's mind. One word from him, he felt convinced, would destroy the delusion under which Sir Herbert laboured, and he dreaded the personal conflict and danger of alarming the house, which must then ensue. Mr. Cury's feelings were, therefore, not of an enviable character, as he saw that his master kept his ground, and showed rather a disposition to court communication with his supposed supernatural visitant than to avoid it.

"Speak! speak !" cried Sir Herbert. "Pure and holy spirit—for such thou must be, for thou wert pure and holy in life—oh ! speak to me !"

Cury slowly shook his head, and raising his arm, pointed to the door of the armoury.

"That solemn gesture," said Sir Herbert, " seems to imply that I should leave this place."

Again Cury, with renewed hope, pointed to the door.

"This—this can be no trick of fancy," said the baronet ; " Helen Wade, I see thee palpably. Too well I know the outline of thy form. I—I see thee now, dear injured being, as I have seen thee often when thy young heart was beaming with delight. Oh, let me once more look upon thy face. If it be, which I believe it would be, the last likeness of a human face which I shall see on earth, let me gaze upon it."

Cury again shook his head and clutched the veil closer.

The clock, which was situated in one of the highest turrets of the mansion, now struck two, and, amid the dead silence which reigned throughout the large building, the sound was loud and distinct.

"I do not dream," said Sir Herbert. "No vision haunts my brain. All is reality."

Again Cury pointed to the door of the armoury, and waved his hand.

"Spirit," said Sir Herbert, " I will obey thee."

"This will do," thought Cury, " but I must follow it up."

Sir Herbert, with the lamp in his hand, and his eyes fixed upon the ghost, walked slowly to the door of the armoury, and Cury followed him, with a gliding step, intending to secure the door after him, in case he might feel a disposition to return.

Cury, in his agitation, did not perceive the chain armour lying exactly in his way, and coming against it suddenly, he stumbled and fell, and the hat and veil dropped from his head to the ground.

For an instant Sir Herbert Foster stood motionless, as if converted into a statue, then with a wild yell, which sounded through the house in awful reverberation, he sprung, with one bound, upon Cury, and clutched him by the throat. The lamp rolled upon the ground and was extinguished, and Cury had but just time to give one cry of terror before Sir Herbert was upon him.

"Monster!" cried Sir Herbert. "Villain! God has mercy upon me now. I see it all—I see it all. Your life, wretch, is too poor an atonement."

"Help! help!" cried Cury. "Murder!—Freegrove!—help!"

Freegrove heard the scuffle between his confederate and Sir Herbert, and, with a deep oath, he rushed from the jewel-room, with a dark lantern in his hand.

Sir Herbert Foster had completely overcome Cury, who was gasping for breath, while his master held him by the throat with the strength of a vice. He tried to cry for help, but all the sound he could produce was a gurgling in his throat, indicative of strangulation.

"D——n!" cried Freegrove, springing forward, and plunging his knife into Sir Herbert's back.

The baronet uttered a shriek, and relaxing his hold of Cury, he sprung to his feet, and closed with Freegrove.

A deadly struggle ensued, and the two rolled over each other on the floor.

Cury lay for a few moments incapable of motion, but then partially recovering, he rose, and with an expression in his face of the most demoniac passion, he cried,—

"Hold him, Freegrove!—hold him! For one moment hold him still."

Freegrove had lost his knife in the struggle, but he was uppermost, and his knee was firmly fixed upon Sir Herbert Foster's breast.

"Mercy! mercy!" cried the baronet. "Help!—murder!"

"D——n! Cury," said Freegrove, "what are you fumbling about?"

Cury's hand trembled so excessively that he could hardly draw a pistol from his pocket.

"Help!—help!—mercy!" cried Sir Herbert. "I will not die; no, no—not yet. Mercy! mercy!"

Cury placed the pistol to his master's ear, and fired.

Sir Herbert Foster sprung from the floor with such force that he threw Freegrove from him. He then staggered a step, wildly swung his arms in the air, and fell dead upon the suit of chain armour which lay upon the floor.

These occurrences, although they have taken some time to describe, took but a few moments in their acting; and two minutes had not elapsed from Freegrove's entrance before Sir Herbert Foster was a corpse.

Cury knelt upon the floor in the same attitude he had assumed to shoot his master, and, with the discharged pistol in his hand, gazing at the corpse, as if he had lost the power of action.

Suddenly, however, he sprung to his feet, and listened attentively.

"Hark, Freegrove," he cried; "the house is alarmed. I can hear footsteps and voices. The servants are assembling."

"D— them," cried Freegrove, "what shall we do?"

"We must be content with what property we have in our pockets, and be off. Our personal safety now is the first consideration."

"Now," replied Freegrove, "if you could frighten those fools who will be here in a crowd directly, by your ghost concern, you would be doing some good."

"It can be tried," said Cury.

He immediately picked up the hat, and placed it on his head again.

"You keep in the background a little," he continued, "and it may be done. Hark! they are coming this way."

Cury stationed himself at the door of the armoury, and directed Freegrove to put the lantern on the floor exactly behind him, so that his figure and dress was in strong relief.

The shuffling noise of the feet of the servants along the passage could now be plainly heard. They were approaching but slowly, and with evident reluctance, and from the sudden stoppage at the door of the armoury, and the murmur of voices, it would seem that they lacked the courage to enter.

Cury waited for a few moments, and then finding that the consultation still continued, and feeling convinced from the sound of the voices that most of the domestics of the establishment were congregated round the door, he suddenly opened it, and appeared before them.

A shout of terror immediately proclaimed the success of his scheme, and in another minute not a single domestic was to be seen.

"Now, Freegrove," cried Cury, dashing down the hat and riding-habit, our only chance of safety is in immediate flight. These frightened fools will not return here for many hours, and the—the body will be undiscovered till we are far off."

"And so we are to leave the plate?" said Freegrove.

"We can take nothing," replied Cury, "but what we have about us. Our lives, man, hang upon a thread. We are both of us spotted with blood. The servants cannot find us. We are lost if we remain."

"D——n!" said Freegrove; "there are some gold plates packed up small; surely we can take them. Come, Cury, come."

"No, no," replied Cury, shuddering, as he cast his eyes upon the body of Sir Herbert Foster; "no, no, we cannot take them. I—I cannot pass that—that which lies there. Let us leave this place."

"Come on, then," said Freegrove. "How infernal unlucky we are!"

"Another time, Freegrove," said Cury, "we may come and take all. Who knows these premises so well as ourselves? We will consider the plate of the Fosters as ours. Another time we will come for it when this affair is blown over."

Cury trembled excessively as he left the armoury, followed by Freegrove.

"What—what," he whispered, "if we should meet some one before we can get clear of the house?"

"Well," replied Freegrove, "if we should? I fancy it isn't some one, or some two or three can stop us."

"Oh, no, certainly; but let us hasten—let us be quick. We shall breathe more freely when we are free of Haredale."

They walked rapidly through the house till they came to the back part of it, and then opening the window of the drawing-room, which communicated by a short flight of steps to the pleasure grounds, they passed from the house.

The moon had risen, and the scene which lay before them was most beautiful. Every means had been used to render the appearance of the pleasure grounds, both by day and night, picturesque and lovely. Trees of different descriptions had been skillfully blended, in order to impart a pleasing variety to the landscape. There were artificial fountains and statues, and every art had been brought into requisition to adorn the grounds of Haredale.

"Well, Freegrove," said Cury, feeling much relieved now that he was in the open air; "there is no baronet now to call these extensive domains his own."

"No," replied Freegrove. "I think the Lady Elizabeth, who comes to the ownership of the estates, ought to be very much obliged to us."

"So she ought," said Cury, "but we will not put her gratitude to the test."

"Now, what do you think of doing?" said Freegrove, suddenly.

"London," replied Cury;—"to London—let us haste to London. There we shall be lost in the crowd."

"That's all very well as far as you are concerned, Master Cury," said Freegrove, "but I tell you what it is,—I have made up my mind to leave this part of the country for good; but before I go, d—me, if I don't burn down the cursed mill belonging to that hoary-headed ruffian, Marks."

"What?" cried Cury, "are you mad?"

"No, Master Cury, I'm not mad; I haven't done it yet; but you know I've been busy with our mutual affairs. But, now, if I don't set that old rascal's mill in a blaze, my name is not Ralph Freegrove."

"Good God! Freegrove," cried Cury, in an imploring voice, "do think better of it. You will compromise both our safetys for this idle scheme of being revenged upon an old fool, who you can be down upon at any time."

"You may say what you like, Cury," replied Freegrove; "it's now or never. I shall never see this part of the country again, and I must do it before I go, you see. When that's settled I shall be easy."

"You will ruin us—you will ruin us," cried Cury, wringing his hands. "See, the morning is now beginning to show itself. Look to the east; see, it's actually getting light. Oh, my dear Freegrove, give it up—give it up."

"I tell you I can't give it up. I'd as soon give up—aye, as soon give up my victuals and drink."

Cury groaned.

"What the devil," continued Freegrove, "are you making such ugly noises about? Go to London youself, and I'll meet you there."

"No, no, I—I will not leave you," said Cury. "You are dreadfully incautious. If this most absurd thing must be done at all, I had better assist you, for both our sakes."

"Now that's reasonable," said Freegrove. "Come along, man. I've got the means in my pocket to get a light. The old mill is as rotten as touchwood.—Ha! ha! ha!—It will light us across the country."

"Well, well," replied Cury, gloomily; "come on—come on. Let us lose no time."

CHAPTER LXII.

THE day had scarcely dawned on Saturday morning, when Mr. Scrimp rose, pursuant to arrangement, and dressed himself hurriedly, in order to meet Mr. Pomander and Perk, both of whom had decided eventually upon accompanying the carriage in which Phœbe was to be whirled off to the metropolis.

The evening before the private travelling chariot had been fetched by Mr. Scrimp, and put up at the Golden Lion, as being the most convenient place for it to remain until it was wanted, and the coachman and footman, who were quite well used to such matters, slept at the inn, after spending a long evening of jollity and mirth, which lasted with them till just about the moment that their master, Sir Herbert Foster, was breathing his last, under the merciless hands of his assassins, Freegrove and Cury.

Mr. Scrimp little dreamt of what had occurred at Haredare Park, and, as yet, no alarm had reached the village, for no discovery had been made of Sir Herbert's body by the frightened domestics, who, hearing all quiet after the first cries which had been heard from the armoury, retired again to rest, attributing all their disturbance and alarm to the tricks of the ghost of Helen Wade.

Thus, notwithstanding the awful event which had happened, everything, both at the village and at Haredale Park, wore a quiet appearance.

Mr. Scrimp crept softly to the chamber of Perk, and awakened him. Perk immediately rose, and very shortly completed his toilette.

"I say, governor," he cried, "these up-early-in-the-morning expeditions are none of the most pleasant."

"Why, I can't say they are," replied Scrimp; "but needs must, you know, Perk, when —"

"The devil drives," said Perk. "I know it. Well, I'm ready. Come on, governor."

"Now, Perk, respecting those constables?"

"It's all right, governor," replied Perk. "They are to meet us in the road. They are just the proper sort of fellows for us; fellows who always do what the strongest party tell them to do, and fellows, too, who have a proper notion of respectability. Now, you see, governor, as we shall be the strongest and the most respectable —"

"Hem!" said Scrimp.

"Well, well," continued Perk, "have that as you like. Success, you know, governor, is virtue, and that's morality, you know, and all that sort of thing."

"That will do," said Scrimp.

They were soon in the street, if the straggling, unpaved thoroughfares of the village could be called such, and making the best of their way to Mr. Pomander's.

"Freegrove is to meet us near the mill," said Scrimp.

"He's a lazy hound," replied Perk, "and I dare say will oversleep himself. He is always doing something over much. He either over eats himself or over drinks himself, or something of the kind. The fellow is a mere beast."

"He is an old servant of Sir Herbert's," said Scrimp, "but he certainly is a ferocious fellow, and would quite as soon, I do believe, cut his master's throat as anybody else's."

They soon arrived at Mr. Pomander's; and, in answer to their summons at the door, that gentleman popped his head out of his bed-room window, and signified by various pantomimic gestures, that he would be down instantly.

The man of drugs soon appeared, and invited the party to walk in. It had been agreed that the three should take a hasty breakfast at Mr. Pomander's, and then proceed to the scene of action, after ascertaining that the chariot was in readiness.

"How are you both?" said Mr. Pomander.

"Why," replied Perk, "we are tolerably well, thank you. I can't give you the least hopes of any indisposition as far as I am concerned."

"Ah!" said Pomander, "you, Perk, have an iron constitution. I know a man who was once pumped upon, and it made him nervous and hypochondriac for ever. He used to fancy himself a pump, and stick one of his arms out for the spout, and work the other by way of a handle; a most singular case."

"So I should think," replied Perk. "Flour don't produce those effects, does it?"

"Not exactly," said Mr. Pomander; "you see it's dry."

"Like some people's wit," replied Perk.

"Now, really," said Scrimp, "gentlemen—gentlemen."

"To breakfast, then," cried Pomander. "Come, gentlemen."

"You are quite sure," observed Perk, "that you are not going to give us anything out of the front shop?"

"Thank you," said Pomander. "The front shop, to tell the truth, is not overstocked. I was forced yesterday to serve out a little hair oil in pepper-water for caster oil."

"The devil you were," said Perk.

"Oh, it's usual," said Pomander, "quite usual. We never say we have not got anything."

"To prevent disappointment, of course," said Scrimp.

"Exactly," replied Pomander. "Imagination goes a great way in medical matters."

"All the way, I should think," said Perk, "except when people are downright poisoned."

"Well, here's your breakfast, gentlemen," said Pomander.

"Broiled ham, eggs, chocolate, and rolls," cried Perk. "That'll do. Upon your soul, now, Pomander, there's no adulteration?"

"Ha! ha! ha!" laughed Pomander. "I tell you I can't afford it, Perk."

"I say," continued the pertinacious Perk, "these rolls, Pomander, are not made of *the* flour, you know, that—that you were so kindly presented with at the mill, eh? You didn't shake yourself in a tub of water, and then make the rolls, eh?"

"Now don't bring up old grievances," said Scrimp. "Perk, you'll give Pomander a handle against you, and he'll throw cold water upon your wit."

"Well, I'll say no more," cried Perk. "Your ham is beautiful, my *flour* of the village."

The breakfast was quickly despatched; and as it was now near seven o'clock, the whole three departed for the Golden Lion, in order to see that the carriage was in readiness.

Mrs. Staples, the portly landlady of the Golden Lion, had so far arranged matters with Mr. Pomander, that that gentleman might well consider himself the presumptive landlord of the thriving house of entertainment for man and beast, and hence a community of feelings and interests had arisen between the medical man and Mrs. Staples, which had induced Mr. Pomander to urge the propriety of having the chariot taken the over night to the Golden Lion stables, in order that in the morning it might not be seen coming from Haredale Park, at the chance of compromising, in some manner, the noble owner of that mansion, who, however unblushingly he might carry on his intrigues in London, had ever been careful that none but subordinate tools should be detected in the country in any act of positive illegality or violence.

"Oh, dear me, gentlemen," said Mrs. Staples, "I'm sure I wishes you all manner of luck."

"Hush! my dear Mrs. Staples," said Pomander. "My dear madam, my—my enlarged angel, don't say a single word. We have done nothing, we are doing nothing, and we are going to do nothing; so you see, my dear madam, the—a-hem! the exceeding propriety of not even hinting, or, in a manner of speaking, you see—a-hem?"

"Oh, dear me, yes," replied Mrs. Staples. "What will you take, gentlemen?"

"Something short," replied Mr. Perk, "for me, ma'am, if you please."

"And you, Mr. Scrimp?" said Mrs. Staples, in an insinuating manner.

"You are very kind," said Mr. Scrimp. "I perceive Mr. Pomander has chosen cold brandy and water, and I can't do better than follow the example of a medical man."

"He! he! he!" said Mrs. Staples. "Ah! Mr. Scrimp, medical men are very artful."

"And they have a singular partiality for flour, ma'am," said Perk, gravely.

"Have they, indeed," said Mrs. Staples; "you don't say so."

"Yes, I do, Mrs. Staples. Now there's our friend, I believe I may say our mutual friend, Mr. Pomander; I have seen him, ma'am, walking about like a portable flour dredger."

Mr. Pomander had departed to the rear of the premises to make personal inquiries with respect to the chariot, so that Mr. Perk was allowed to libel

him without reproof. He, however, very soon returned, and reported that the carriage would be ready in a few moments.

"Well, then," said Perk, "we may as well all go in it ty the place where it is to stop, and then we can be guided as to future operations by circumstances as they may happen to fall out."

"Very well," said Scrimp, "we can do so; but keep a sharp look out for your constables, Perk, for we must not miss them, as what they have to do may be very essential towards preserving the peace; for that fellow, Giles, if he suspects for a moment we are not playing fairly by him, he will be among us like a steam engine. He is, without exception, the most violent fellow ever I came across."

"We can't miss the constables," replied Perk. "This Giles must be laid hold of directly, for he is an ugly customer."

"Was he," said Pomander, "the one that pumped, or the one that held you under the spout?"

"Never mind," said Perk; "it's quite immaterial, my dear sir."

"Oh, quite—quite," cried Pomander. "I merely asked for curiosity."

The chariot now appeared at the door; and with many smiles and bows, and complementary speeches from Mrs. Staples, the party got in, and in another moment were rapidly nearing the mill.

As we have before noticed, the meadow, which was near the mill, was bounded on one side by the high road; on the opposite side was the little wicket-gate, which communicated to the garden of the cottage of the miller, and at the side of the meadow furthest from the cottage and the mill, was the commencement of a thick plantation, or wood, which extended for nearly half a mile across the surrounding country.

The chariot, in which were seated Mr. Scrimp and his confederates, now rapidly approached that part of the road which skirted the meadow.

No. 48

By the attorney's direction, the coachman drove the carriage quite close to the hedge, next to the meadow, which, being high and thick, acted as a very complete screen to the equipage, and effectually prevented it from being observed from the cottage of the miller, who little dreamed of the formidable preparations which were being made for the purpose of disturbing his domestic tranquillity.

"You know your orders?" said Scrimp, to the coachman.

"Yes," the man replied. "To drive to London as quick as possible."

"Exactly," said Perk;—"that's the very thing."

"Who are these?" said Mr. Pomander, as two rough-looking men came up to the carriage-door.

"Oh, they are my constables," said Perk. "Now, hark ye, my men, I'll point out the man you are to take. He is rather a desperate fellow, and you must throw yourselves upon him in a moment, and remember you get a couple of guineas each of you for the job."

"Yes, your honour," said one of the constables. "Never fear, but we'll have him, sir. I say, Jem," addressing his companion, "have you got the bracelets?"

"Yes, you fool," said the other man. "You take the fellow round the waist when the gentleman points him out, and I'll pop them on him in a moment."

"Well, now," said Perk, "you'd better for the present make yourselves scarce."

"We'll hide close to the hedge, your honour," said one of them.

"Well, do, then. Anywhere, so as you don't scare the game; and remember, as you do your duty, so you make a friend, or otherwise, of Sir Herbert Foster."

"Leave it to us, sir—leave it to us," said the man. "His worship won't complain of us, I'll be bound."

"Well, then, gentlemen," said Perk, addressing Scrimp and Pomander, "I think I may conclude we are all ready."

"Yes," replied Pomander, "we are all ready enough. The only question which remains to be satisfactorily settled now is, whether the girl can be induced by the bumpkin lover to come at all."

"And these d—d yokels," said Perk, "are, after all, never to be entirely depended upon. They are all fury and determination one minute, and the next as milk and watery as the very deuce."

"He will not, cannot fail us," cried Scrimp. "He has gone to far to recede now. I have him in my power."

"Don't be too sure of that, old governor," said Perk; "but never mind all that now. Here we wait, of course."

"Then you had better," said Pomander, "get into the carriage, as you are to escort the lady to London, and Scrimp and I can, by getting over this farthest hedge, be out of sight, but not out of reach, if required."

"Very well," said Perk, springing into the carriage; "it's rather cold than otherwise, and I think the chariot is the pleasantest place just for the present. I hope, by all that's beautiful and mild, that that same Miller's Maid has short nails, for she might take it into her head to use them on our route, and a chariot is rather close quarters."

"You can threaten her with the first pump you come near," said Pomander.

"Or flour-bin," roared Perk.

"Hang you both," said Scrimp; "will you never have done?"

Mr. Perk slammed the door of the chariot, and settled himself in its interior as comfortably as he could, while Scrimp and Pomander got over a stile into the field, which was on the other side of the road from the meadow, and sat down, completely hidden from view, except some one had been on a very elevated position.

"Have you," said Pomander to Scrimp, "ascertained anything further with respect to this strange matter of the ghost at Haredale Park?"

"No, I have not been able actually to detect anything of a positive nature," replied Scrimp, "but between ourselves, I don't entertain the least doubt upon the subject."

"You think that Cury is playing the ghost?"

"I do, unquestionably. Cury is a man who will stop at nothing practicable where he has an end in view. He is an amazing clever fellow in his way, and I much suspect that he has some very important object in view in this apparition business. Sir Herbert has certainly received a very severe mental shock in consequence of it, and, between us, I expected that this little affair of the Miller's Maid would have been abandoned, for when I last saw Sir Herbert there was a very peculiar manner about him which I could not at all account for."

"Time," said Pomander, "will let us see what the conscientious valet is about."

"Oh, it's plunder," replied Scrimp, "of course, and, probably, to no insignificant amount."

While Mr. Scrimp and Mr. Pomander were conversing, and the two constables were hiding themselves in what they considered perfect security from observation, they were, nevertheless, all most especially overlooked and observed by no less a personage than Tim Miggies.

It was not yet eight o'clock; and George, who had risen very early to go some distance on an errand of importance to the miller, had not returned.

Giles was skulking beneath the hedge which divided the meadow, on the side nearest the cottage, from a little kitchen garden, and was waiting anxiously for the appearance of Phœbe, to meet him according to appointment.

Tim had not been yet summoned to breakfast, and he had been sauntering, in pure vacancy of mind, about the interior of the mill for some time, when, happening to look out from a little loophole in the lower loft, he saw the roof of the carriage just peering over the top of the hedge, which divided, as he well knew, the meadow from the high road.

Tim's curiosity, of which he had always a large ungratified portion on hand, was at once thoroughly awakened, and he ascended very quickly to the topmost apartment of the mill, in which was nothing but some old stores, and which was very rarely visited. When he arrived there he had a very good view of the whole scene of action, for the old mill was of very great height itself, and was, moreover, built on a kind of mound, or eminence, which made it quite a landmark to the surrounding country.

From this elevated station Tim Miggies could plainly see all the parties in their relative situations, and he could recognize both Mr. Scrimp and Mr. Pomander easily, although he in vain tried to recollect if he had ever before seen either of the other men who were lying so close under the meadow hedge.

"Well, I never," said Tim. "Here's a go. What's all this about?

"'Here's a carriage and horses, and five or six people,
All standing as still as the parish church steeple.'

What can they want here? As the Baron Bombigometer did when the domestic slave notched his nose all over,—

"'I'd better sit down,
In a study, called brown,'

and just think over it a bit. Now, George ain't at home, and if I go and tell Giles, he'll say, 'Peace, fool! peace!' or something equally poetical.

and polite. Well, there's the old miller, if I was to go and tell him, he'd most likely tell me to mind my own business. Ah! he's a foe to the muses, he is, and yet he showed some taste once, for he liked the verses I once made about the old mill.

> " 'The mill, the mill, is a brave old mill,
>   It cares not for wind or weather,
> For a hundred years it has braved the storms,
>   And still holds fast together.
> It groans and sighs in the midnight wind,
>   But the blast sweeps on its way,
> And the brave old mill is standing still
>   At the dawning of the day.
> Tradition says, 'tis a hundred years
>   Since the old m ll reared its crown,
> And may many a hundred years go by,
>   Ere the brave old mill sinks down.'

Now old Gilbert rather liked that, which shows there's some little sense in the old man. I wonder if Phœbe is up. Ah! Phœbe, Phœbe. Dear me, I'm sorry she ain't the old man's daughter. He might have been my jolly old father-in-law—the fine old grandfather of a number of infant Miggleses!

> " 'It's of no use a moping,
> It's of no use a hoping,
>   For Phœbe the Maid of the Mill;
> Tim Miggles is settled,
> Tim Miggles is nettled,
>   For the place in her heart he don't fill.'

Well, I'll just go and tell Phœbe herself. She has a soul for poetry. She is a rum 'un."

With this determination Tim Miggles rapidly descended from his high situation with the intention of immediately seeking Phœbe, and imparting to her what he had seen, which, if he had succeeded in doing, he might have saved her from much alarm, although, in the result, it was better that the designs of Providence should take their course.

Tim arrived at the cottage, and popped in his head.

"What does 'e want?" said the miller, "popping thee fool's head in here?"

"Phœbe, Phœbe, the flower of the ——"

"Get thee gone," said the miller, enraged as he always was at Tim's metaphorical speeches.

Tim drew out his head, for he anticipated that, perhaps, the bellows, or some other hardy missile, might be discharged at it.

"It's all very fine," muttered Tim. "That old miller is the rummiest old chap as ever I knew. He's dreadful passionate. He's like the Baron of Flummerwhistle,—

> " 'Who swore and cursed for an hour or more,
>   'Cos he wouldn't walk on the ceiling instead of the floor.'

I won't tell anybody, that I won't, till George comes. I'll be jolly well a-hem'd if I do, that's all."

So saying, Tim Miggles retired, in great indignation, back to the top of the mill, where he remained, with his elbows resting upon the ledge of the narrow window, gazing most intently upon the roof of the carriage, upon the constables, and upon Mr. Scrimp and Mr. Pomander, who were still in deep conversation under the hedge, in fancied security.

Suddenly the village-clock struck, and Tim counted the strokes very deliberately.

"One, two, three, four, five, six, seven, eight—eight o'clock," he said. "Well, who cares? I sha'n't turn on the mill, I'll be d—d if I do."

CHAPTER LXIII.

Giles had passed a night of extreme mental suffering, and after his morning's interview, which he had had with Phœbe, he retired to the mill in bitter agony of spirit.

The conviction was hourly creeping over him, and gaining strength from every little circumstance that occurred, that the wild, mad scheme of eloping with Phœbe, contrary to her inclination, must fall and end in increased anguish and disappointment. Giles, as the reader is aware, was not a bad man. His consent and accession to crime was merely the result of a train of circumstances, which had wrought his mind to such a pitch of intense excitement as for a time to unseat his reason, and leave his mind save upon that one point, a complete chaos, as it were, in a boisterous sea without a rudder, and tossed to and fro at the mercy of every wind that blew.

All affection is selfish to a certain extent, and it is a common error for those who love to suppose that the extent and intensity of their own passion must, of mere necessity, ensure the happiness of the beloved object. Hence in most quarrels among rivals a great point is usually made with regard to who loves the lady with the greatest fervour, as if excessive passion was all that was required, when the truth is, a very moderate and small quantity or love will suffice to bring two parties together, but then it must be mutual. A very small stock of reciprocal affection will suffice to keep up a very steady and endearing union. Now Giles, in his own heart, felt that this desirable reciprocity of feeling did not exist between him and the fair object of his affections. He loved, madly, devotedly loved, but Phœbe's feelings were not of an answering description. His passion, like a mountain torrent, rolled headlong forwards, disregarding all obstacles, and spurning all obstructions. Its passage might produce desolation—people might shrink from the war and splash of its impetuous progress—but, except by its sound and its fury, it produces no effect upon the mind, and, with a passing remark, is allowed to plunge onwards to its destination.

The more violent and intense Giles's passion became the more Phœbe was alarmed, and his wild protestations of eternal undying love awakened no tender feelings in her breast. Giles began himself to feel these truths, and to believe that love was not created by love, but by some undefinable qualities in individuals, which arrested the imagination, and awakened the warmest feelings of the heart.

With his hands clasped round his brow, he paced the large loft of the mill after his interview with Phœbe, and his heart beat with wild and tumultuous feelings.

The moment was now rapidly approaching—the moment that he had longed for—the moment that he had at one time imagined would end his doubts and anxieties, by convincing Phœbe of the fervency and sincerity of his passion; but now, how he shrunk from the proceedings to which he had so rashly pledged himself. What worlds would he not have given to be now as he was before his fearful compact with the attorney! Once he thought of flight. He paused in his hurried walk, and calculated how many miles he might be from the mill before the hour of eight, and then, again, his resolution wavered, and he asked himself if it were possible that the specious reasonings of Mr. Scrimp could be true?

Thus, in a state of the greatest nervousness, and oppressed by the most fearful and heartrending doubts and anxieties, Giles passed some hours. At length he heard the village clock strike seven. Each sound, which proclaimed the progress of time, seemed to dart through his brain like a ball of fire.

"Seven!—seven!" he cried; "the—time be near. I—I know not what to think. My heart do beat like a bird—a wild bird against the bars of a cage. I do think I be nearly mad! yet no. This be the old mill—I know everything—I be to meet Phœbe—Phœbe—Phœbe—oh, Phœbe, what hast thou brought me to? I do hate myself as much as I do love thee; it is— it is for thee happiness that I do it. Seven o'clock—the time be drawing near—the meadow—the meadow."

He rushed from the mill to the meadow, nor paused until he had taken a station close to the hedge, where he could not be seen from the cottage.

In spite of his utmost exertions to calm the agitation of his frame, he trembled excessively: a cold feeling pervaded his heart, and his brain seemed incapable of further thought. With great difficulty, and only by continually repeating, in a low voice, the name of Phœbe, he kept his mind from wandering from the purpose which he had in hand. He fixed his eyes upon the little wicket-gate, through which he knew she must pass, and for half an hour he never changed his position.

Still Phœbe came not, and Giles's impatience became insupportable. He never for one moment took his eyes off the little wicket-gate, and now, as he began to feel doubtful of her coming, all his old, wild, ungovernable feelings revived, and, with clenched hands and set teeth, he uttered curses against George, who, he believed, must have returned from where he had been sent by the miller, and was, in all probability, detaining Phœbe in the cottage beyond the specified hour of her appointment, or, perchance, had induced her to break it altogether.

Now eight o'clock sounded from the church steeple, and Giles sprung to his feet, and his whole countenance became distorted by wild rage. He shook his clenched hand at the cottage, and uttered wild and incoherent threats against George, who, he firmly believed, could only have prevented Phœbe from meeting him according to his promise. Suddenly, however, he paused in his attitude of rage and imprecations. The wicket-gate opened, and Phœbe, fresh and blooming as a rose at the opening of the day, tripped into the meadow.

Giles's hands sunk powerless to his sides, his heightened colour subsided, and gave place to a deadly paleness, and an universal tremor shook his whole frame, deep sighs burst from his breast, and his whole appearance presented a picture of terror and mental desolation.

"She—she be coming," he muttered; "she be true, and I—I be false, for I be going to deceive her—yet, oh, Heavens! it is because I do love her. She do look beautiful, oh, so beautiful, that she do outshine the morning. Oh, Phœbe, why did thee come?—why did thee come?"

Giles pronounced these last words in a tone of such bitter and heart-rending anguish, that his worst enemy, if he had one, must have pitied him.

Looking around her to see if Giles was in the meadow, the unsuspecting and innocent Phœbe now rapidly approached to where he was lying, for he had, in the wild agony of his feelings, thrown himself upon the verdant sod, and seemed as if he dared not trust himself to look upon the pure fair being who he was about so wickedly to betray.

He heard the light footstep, and he kept muttering—

"She be coming—she be coming."

In a moment or two more Phœbe was by his side, and he suddenly sprung to his feet and confronted her.

The expression of Giles's face terrified Phœbe, and she shrunk back instinctively several paces, as if about to fly from the spot.

"Do," he cried, "get thee gone; there be yet time. Get thee back——back—back!"

"Oh, no, Giles," said Phœbe; "I—I do not wish to go till I have heard what you wish to say. Forgive me that, for a moment I felt alarmed, but you—you look ill, Giles, indeed you do."

"Thee will not go from me?—thee will not fly?"

"No, Giles," she replied. "I know that from you I have nothing to fear."

"Then God help thee!" he said, in a calmer voice.

"He helps us all, Giles," replied Phœbe.

"Yes, yes; the wicked He helps, even. I—I love thee, Phœbe. Thee know that I do love thee?"

"Oh Giles, do not talk of that again. Believe me, you pain my heart to hear you."

"Phœbe," Giles exclaimed, "it be in thee nature to love those who do love thee?"

"What affection I may give to one who has ever been kind to me, Giles," replied Phœbe, "I freely give to you. More I cannot say. You know the secret of my heart—or, rather, there is no secret in my heart—George is my brother, or my husband."

"Devils!" shrieked Giles, stamping wildly; "you tell me this, Phœbe?"

"Giles, Giles, you know it well."

"And — and —" continued Giles, — "you love him because he do love you?"

"He does love me," cried Phœbe. "We loved each other when we scarce could lisp the word. It is a dear affection, which has grown with our growth, and strengthened with our strength. Oh, yes—yes—George does love me."

"And thee will be happy with him because he does love thee?"

"Yes—yes. Love is dear happiness."

"Enough, enough," cried Giles; "that be enough."

"Wherefore, Giles," said Phœbe, "did you ask me to meet you at this hour? You see I have done so in pure confidence and esteem for you as a dear friend."

"Phœbe," he replied, "I—I have something to say to thee. I—I——"

Giles drew his breath with extreme difficulty, and for a few moments his agitation was so great that he could not give utterance to what he was about to say.

"Why this unusual agitation, Giles?" said Phœbe. "You are not well. Your cheek is of an ashy paleness. Speak to me. You alarm me, Giles. Shall I call for help? The good miller will hear me."

"No! no! no! no!" he gasped, laying his trembling hand upon her arm, and casting an uneasy glance towards the high road.

"Some fearful mystery hangs upon your tongue, Giles," said Phœbe. "Oh, speak! If it concerns any one dear to me, speak! Is it of George?"

The name of George acted as a spell upon Giles. His fear and violent agitation gave way to passion. His eyes flashed with fury.

"Yes, yes," he cried; "it concerns George. Come—come this way, and I will tell me. Further—further—come——"

"But why move from this spot?" said Phœbe.

"Because—because," replied Giles, "there be something to see as well as to hear."

"You terrify me," cried Phœbe, "but I will not shrink from a knowledge of anything that may concern him."

"Thee will trust theeself with me?"

"Freely," replied Phœbe; "but why do you fix your eyes in the direction of the road so very earnestly, Giles?"

"Because there be something that thee must see. Come—come, Phœbe, my—my Phœbe—come."

"Oh, Giles," she cried, "you—you cannot mean me harm?"

"Harm?—no. Love, thee said, be dear happiness. Come—come."

He grasped her arm, and led her hastily towards the hedge which separated the meadow from the road.

Notwithstanding her confidence in Giles, a feeling of alarm, from the peculiarity of his manner, had began to find a place in the innocent breast of Phœbe, and she suffered herself to be led rather reluctantly across the the meadow.

She strove to rally her spirits as she proceeded.

"What can I have to fear?" she thought; "I am close to home. A single cry would reach the ears of the good miller, and George, I dare say, has returned."

There was a gap in the hedge which looked into the high road, through which any one might force themselves with ease, and towards this Giles directed the steps of Phœbe.

"Whither are we going, Giles?" she said. "I cannot—will not leave the meadow."

"Come, Phœbe, come," he cried. "Love be dear happiness."

Now they neared the gap in the hedge, and Phœbe perceived the figure of a man, in a plain suit of livery, standing by it, on the road-side of the hedge.

She shrunk back instantly.

"Giles," she cried, as she tried to free her arm from his grasp, "I will go no further. There are strangers in the road."

"I cannot go back," he cried, "nor can thee. Mine—mine—ha! ha! —mine—Phœbe, thee be mine. Love be dear happiness."

As he spoke he released her arm, and suddenly clasping her round the waist, he raised her from the ground, and rushed towards the opening in the hedge.

Phœbe was taken so much by surprise that she had no power to resist, and she was actually in the road before she could utter a cry for help.

"The door! the door!" cried Giles. "Open the carriage-door some of thee!"

Phœbe screamed loudly, and cried,—

"Help! help!—Oh, Giles, help!—Save me! save me!"

The carriage-door was immediately opened, and Giles was about to place Phœbe within it, when he saw Mr. Perk already occupying it, and he hesitated for a moment.

Perk stretched out his arm and caught hold of Phœbe.

Phœbe uttered another scream, and then lay an insensible burthen in Giles's arms.

"In with her—in with her," cried Perk; "you are losing time, man."

As he spoke, he seized Phœbe by the arm, and strove to drag her into the carriage.

Giles had his right arm at liberty, and the only reply he made to Mr. Perk was, to dash his fist full in his face, and with such force, that Mr. Perk's head went through the glass of the opposite door.

Mr. Scrimp and Mr. Pomander were now both in the road, and the former cried to the constables, at the same time pointing to Giles,—

"That's your man! Be quick, my lads!"

One of the constables immediately seized Giles round the waist from behind, and called to his comrade:—

"Now, Jem, the ruffles—the ruffles."

Giles heard the speech of Mr. Scrimp, and in a moment the conviction flashed across his mind that he was betrayed. A curtain seemed drawn from before his eyes, and he comprehended in an instant the whole plot. On ordinary occasions Giles was a powerful young man; but now his blood boiled and hissed through his veins like liquid fire, and the party that was around him might as well have attempted to control a maniac in one of his wildest bursts of passion.

Mr. Perk was lying insensible in the carriage, and Giles let Phœbe gently drop from his arms, partly resting in the vehicle. He, then, with the rapidity of lightning, twisted himself round in the embrace of the constable, and seizing him by the waist, he, by an extraordinary effort of strength, lifted him from his feet, and threw him head foremost to at least six or eight yards distance. One stride then brought Giles to the hedge, from whence he plucked a stake, which was deeply embedded in the earth.

The remaining constable and the coachman, who had dismounted from his box to lend a helping hand, now made a rush towards him.

Giles was especially expert in all athletic exercises, and by a slight turn of his foot, he caught the leg of the coachman, who immediately fell heavily to the ground, while at the same moment Giles brought the hedge stake down upon the constable's head with such force that he completely doubled up under it.

Mr. Scrimp and Mr. Pomander had not time to run round the coach and interfere, if they had the inclination, but admitting that they were well disposed so to do at the commencement of the fray, that disposition was effectually put an end to when they witnessed the discomfiture of the constables, and they, with one accord, set off at great speed from the scene of action, leaving Giles completely master of the field, which boasted now but of one opponent who was unwounded, and that was the footman, who had,

No. 49

in extreme terror, forced himself into the middle of the hedge, and could get neither one way nor the other.

With a wild shout of rage and exultation, Giles now lifted Phœbe, as if she had been an infant, from the carriage, and flourishing above his head the hedge stake, he rushed into the meadow, and made, with great speed, towards the cottage with his insensible burthen.

Tim Miggles had been from his post near the top of the mill a transfixed spectator of the whole scene, and so short a time had it taken in acting, that he had not recovered from his surprise at its commencement, when it was over, and Giles was rushing like a madman across the meadow, with Phœbe in his arms.

When Tim saw that the contest, of the nature or cause of which he could form no idea, was over, he descended from his post with such rapidity that he lost his footing, and rolled down a long flight of stairs, to the great detriment of his clothes and person.

Tim Miggles, however, was in an unusual state of mind, and he immediately rose again, and made the best of his way to the cottage, at the door of which he arrived just a moment before Giles, who had three times the distance to traverse.

"Hilloa!" shouted Tim.   "Murder! murder! fire!"

The door of the cottage opened in an instant, and George, who had just arrived, sprung out, exclaiming,—

"What is it?   What's the matter, Tim?"

The first sight that met George's gaze was one calculated to excite the most dreadful emotions in his breast.   He saw Giles; his eyes blood-shot, and his whole appearances indicating the wildest disorder, standing, with the apparently lifeless form of Phœbe hanging upon his left arm, while in his right he held, in an attitude of defence, the formidable hedge stake with which he had done such execution.

George uttered a loud cry of horror, and made a rush towards Giles. The miller, however, who had hastened from the cottage immediately behind him, twined his arms round him, and although the old man was dragged forward some paces, still he succeeded in keeping George and Giles asunder.

"Keep off!" shouted Giles; "keep off, all of thee! I fought for her. She be mine, mine only.   I would die for her!"

"Monster!" screamed George, "you have killed her!"

"No, no," cried Tim Miggles, "I saw it all; he saved her."

"Dame, dame," cried the miller; "dame, I say, stir thyself, and take the dear child."

Phœbe now opened her eyes, and cried, faintly,—

"Help! help! George, help! Save me! save me!"

"Back, George, back; I command thee to keep back," cried the miller.

The dame now took Phœbe from the arms of Giles, who still stood in the same attitude, glaring wildly upon everybody.

"Phœbe, Phœbe," cried George, " say that you are unhurt.   One word— one word, or my heart will break."

"Dear George," said Phœbe, faintly.

"Thank God," said the miller, " my dear child is safe.   Can any one tell us the meaning of all this?"

"Master, master," cried Tim, "look! look at the mill!"

All eyes were turned towards the mill in an instant.

A dense smoke was seen to rise from it, and in a moment a bright flame appeared curling from one of the small windows.

The miller uttered a cry of despair, and sunk insensible in the arms of George.

CHAPTER LXIV.

WE must now return to Cury and Freegrove, who we left disputing about the propriety of wasting time in delaying their daparture for London until Freegrove had revenged himself in some manner upon the miller.

Cury followed Freegrove with a moody and discontented air, when he found that no argumentation would induce him to forego his revenge, and he merely said,—

"In what manner do you intend to proceed, Freegrove?"

"Why, I'll light a fusee, which I have in my pocket; it's a kind of thing that keeps burning for a long time, and attaches itself, by reason of having a deal of pitch and rosin in it, to any place at which it is thrown. I learnt the way to make such things of a man in London."

"But don't you see," said Cury, "the light is increasing every moment? You don't mean, surely, to risk walking direct to the mill and firing it?"

"Why, no," replied Freegrove, "not exactly. Any side of the mill where there is a window will answer my purpose. We will reconnoitre a little, Master Cury, from the thick plantation that skirts the meadow."

"Freegrove, Freegrove," cried Cury, "give up this dangerous exploit, and take at once the high road to London."

"Don't you wish you may get me," replied Freegrove. "I tell you that d—d fellow, George, as they call him; the half-sailor, half-miller, sleeps in the mill, and by everything devilish, he'll have a singing to get out if he rests heavy."

"Well, well," said Cury; "to the plantation, then, let us hasten. Fool," he added, in a suppressed voice, "your blood be upon your own head!"

As he muttered to himself, Cury felt in his pocket, and then, with a meaning smile, he followed his companion, who walked with rapidity towards the plantation, or little wood, which joined to the meadow, on the side opposite to that on which stood the mill on its little hillock.

A long streak of light was beginning to illumine the east as Cury and Freegrove came within sight of the mill; the birds were beginning to twitter on the hedges, and each moment the outline of the old mill became more distinct against the brightening sky.

They crossed several fields, the high grass in which was dripping with moisture from the quantity of dew which had fallen during the night, and gained the high road, at a point less than a quarter of a mile distant from the meadow.

"We can walk down the road, and have a good look at the mill from the hedge that leads to the meadow," said Freegrove, "although it's the least likely time of all for any one to be stirring."

"Hark!" said Cury, "I hear some one tramping across the fields. Creep close to the hedge."

They both crouched down under the hedge, and the rapid step of a man was heard to proceed along the field, which was within a few yards of them.

"Who can that be?" said Freegrove.

"Some rustic," replied Cury, "going over early to his work."

"A poacher, I'll be sworn," said Freegrove.

"Very likely," replied Cury.

It was George, whose steps the murderers heard; and had there been sufficient light to distinguish him, he might, possibly, have sealed by his blood the desperate acts of the two ruffians, whose hands were already reeking from the assassination of one whose bread they had eaten for many years, and who, whatever might have been his faults and crimes as a member of society, was a liberal and indulgent master to them.

"Come on," cried Freegrove; "I see the meadow from here."

"When was this affair of the Miller's Maid to come off?" asked Cury.

"At eight o'clock, or somewhere thereabouts, I believe," said Freegrove. "We shall be far enough off by that time, I hope. We play a better game than that, Cury."

"A higher game we certainly do play," replied Cury. "Our stakes are heavy."

"Well, and haven't we swept the tables?"

"Yes, we have, Freegrove; but we are not yet at home with our winnings."

"Why, you are a regular croaker, I'm d—d if you ain't," said Freegrove. "You seem to take quite to heart the burning of this old mill."

"You might burn down all the mills in the country," replied Cury, "without disturbing me, provided you did not take so bad an opportunity as the present, when every moment is more precious to us than a drop of blood."

"Come on—come on," cried Freegrove; "you are always snivelling about something or another. I tell you we shall be in London now to dinner."

"Hush!" said Cury; "don't speak so loud. Here's the meadow. Come, now, get through the hedge, and do your work at once."

Freegrove scrambled up the bank, at the top of which was the luxuriant foliage of the hedge, and looked into the meadow.

Cury on the instant drew a pistol from his pocket; but before he could make any use of it Freegrove turned his head, and the valet had barely time to hide his weapon from the observation of his companion.

"D——n!" said Freegrove; "these people surely don't go to bed at all. There's the girl now in the meadow talking to some one. Why, Cury, what's the matter with you?"

"The—the—the matter?" said Cury. "I—I—oh, nothing—nothing."

"Why, you look as pale as ashes."

"Do I?—I—oh, nothing. What should be the matter?"

"Nothing new, that I know of," replied Freegrove; "but when I turned round just now you had an uncommonly strange look."

"Ha! ha!" laughed Cury, faintly; "it is the morning light. You—you look so yourself. It's the pale grey morning light."

"May be it is," said Freegrove. "It's a d——d uncomfortable look though."

"So," said Cury, "there are people in the meadow?"

"Yes," replied Freegrove, "but I won't be baulked. We can get into the wood by going a little further down the road, and from that we can see right across the meadow to the mill."

"Yes," said Cury, "that will be the most prudent."

"Come on, then," replied Freegrove, "and don't on any account give us any more of those queer looks."

"It's the morning air, the morning air," said Cury, dropping a pace behind Freegrove, as he walked down the road towards the little wood.

The meadow was not very wide, and they soon reached the wood, into which they immediately plunged.

"Now, as soon as the meadow is clear," said Freegrove, "I can skulk across to the mill by the hedge, and if I can once throw in at any of the windows my fusee, there's nothing can save it. It's all old wood, and must go. Ha! ha! It will blaze like a torch."

"Oh, yes, yes," said Cury. "It's cold, very cold."

"Why, it's not so warm, Cury, as it might be," replied Freegrove; "but you are trembling, man, like the very deuce."

"It's—it's only the cold," said Cury. "The air among these trees is damp and chilling."

"Well, here's a bank," cried Freegrove, "and I'll just pop my head over it, and watch till the meadow is clear for me to run across. What the deuce does the wench mean by meeting her fellows at this time in the morning?"

Phœbe and Giles it was who were in the meadow, as will be recollected, so very early; and the fair girl little imagined that by her seeking an interview with Giles, she was saving the old mill from destruction, the loss of which would have been a severe blow to the heart of the kind old miller, whose whole soul was wrapped up in the ancient building, which had been in the family for so many years.

Freegrove now laid himself down upon a sloping bank, and resting his head upon his hand, he intently watched the meadow.

Cury stood a few paces from him, and kept his eyes steadily fixed upon his recumbent companion.

"This heedless fool," thought Cury, "will bring himself and me to destruction. That I—I should be forced to follow such a clod while he executes his vulgar revenge, when my very life hangs upon a thread, and yet I could not leave him; for were he taken, which, with his own blundering, would have been almost certain, to save his own neck he would, doubtless, have denounced me. Hell's fury! that I should have to watch over the safety of such a fool. There is, however, a way to rid me of the trouble, and calm my fears for ever."

He stole his hand gently into the breast of his coat, where he had suddenly concealed the pistol from Freegrove, and clutched it with a nervous grasp.

"It may be done," he thought, "in a moment; but if it should miss fire, or I should miss my aim? My hand trembles, yet I must try it. Closer—closer."

"D— them," said Freegrove, "they are there still. I think they are quarrelling about something, for the fellow is making strange antics."

"Yes, yes," said Cury; "a—a—yes."

"Yes, a—a—yes," said Freegrove, turning to look at Cury, "why, what do you mean? Hang me, if you haven't put on your queer look again. Why, you look like a corpse."

"So do you," replied Cury; "so do you. It's a green tint from the leaves."

"Is it?" rejoined Freegrove. "Well, it may be, but it's the most disagreeable tint ever I saw in my life."

"Are they gone?" said Cury.

"No, they are still there, d— them. Patience is a good thing. I see there's a little window in the mill just within reach, that will answer my purpose beautifully."

"Yes, oh, yes," said Cury; "I see it; the very thing; the very thing."

Freegrove continued to watch the meadow as before, and Cury again suffered his hand to creep slowly into his breast, and grasp the pistol.

Freegrove's attention was quite fixed on the meadow, and Cury slowly crept nearer and nearer to him, but so cautiously, that not a leaf rustled beneath his gliding tread.

"Now, now," he muttered; "I will do it now. My own life is unsafe while this man lives. A steady hand for one moment, and I may be rid of the only man I have to fear; nay, I might almost return to Haredale. The suspicion, the guilt of Sir Herbert's death would fall upon Freegrove. His body would be found, and—and it might be thought that remorse had induced him to lay violent hands upon himself. Yes, it's a good scheme, an excellent scheme. While Freegrove lives, I am in constant dread. He is a fool as well as a ruffian; he has not judgment enough to care for his own safety, much less mine. He must die! die! yes, yes, then all will be safe. Part of the plunder from the jewel-room will be found upon him, and that will fix the deed."

Still nearer and nearer to Freegrove did Cury creep, keeping his hand in the breast of his coat on the stock of the pistol, the fellow to which lay in the armoury at Haredale, by the lifeless body of Sir Herbert Foster.

Now he was within a couple of yards of Freegrove, when he suddenly paused, for the latter spoke, although turning his head from the meadow.

"They are separating at last," he said, "and high time, too, for the sun is already gleaming on the top of the mill, for the last time I expect."

"Which way do they go?" said Cury, making a strong effort to speak with composure.

"Why, the man is going to the mill," replied Freegrove, "and now I see who it is; it's the one they call Giles."

"And the girl?" said Cury.

"Why she," continued Freegrove, "is hastening to the cottage. The meadow will be clear in a few minutes."

"And so will the wood," muttered Cury.

Freegrove did not alter his position, but continued to peep through a small opening in the thicket, without dreaming of the danger that was behind him.

"Closer, closer," muttered Cury. "My hand trembles. I cannot trust myself to aim. I must touch him—touch him with the muzzle."

Nearer still to Freegrove he crept, till, by reaching out his arm, he could have touched him with his hand.

"Now," said Freegrove, "your troubles will be over, in a minute, and we can be off for London, for it won't take me any time scarcely to do for the mill."

"Yes, in a minute my troubles will be over," thought Cury; "and so will yours."

He slowly drew the pistol from his breast, and stooped over Freegrove till the barrel of the weapon nearly touched his head.

"The meadow's clear," cried Freegrove, suddenly turning and encountering the face of Cury within a few inches of his own.

For about half a minute the two associates in crime continued to glare at each other, without altering their relative positions. Freegrove then sprung to his feet, and cried,—

"Why, what the devil are you at?"

Cury opened his mouth several times as if inclined to speak, but he could not find words to say.

"D——n! Master Cury," continued Freegrove, "I suspect you."

"Suspect me?" said Cury, attempting to smile, but producing only an awful contortion in his countenance.

"Why, what the devil do you mean?" cried Freegrove; "you are enough to frighten a horse with such hideous faces."

"Oh, you—you jest," said Cury, "I am fatigued, that's all."

"Oh! that's it," replied Freegrove, "You had no occasion to lie down nearly on top of me, though. I tell you what it is, Master Cury, if I catch you within several yards of me again, I'll brain you. I don't like your looks, d—n me, if I do."

"Why," said Cury, trying to rally his spirits, "you don't mean to say you suspect me of any foul play?"

"Yes, I do, and yet I ain't quite sure. I am tolerably sure you meant some mischief; but if I was d—d sure, mind me, I'd plaster one of these trees with your brains."

"I might," said Cury, "with greater justice, I suspect you, for you threaten me, which I have not done by you."

"Well, well," replied Freegrove, "let it rest. I'm not afraid of you, Master Cury."

"I—I hope we are friends," said Cury, in a fawning tone. "Our mutual interests, you know ; our——"

"Hold your tongue," cried Freegrove. "You are an infernal coward, and I don't care whether you are a friend or an enemy. Recollect, you are further in the mess than I am."

"Your hand," said Cury, "and your knife, which even now lies by the —the body, struck the first blow."

"But your pistol did the job," cried Freegrove. "I was a cursed fool for forgetting the knife, but your pistol lies there, too."

"The pistol was not mine," said Cury, quietly ; "it belonged to Sir Herbert himself ; and if I recollect rightly, your name is engraved on the knife."

"D——n ! we must not quarrel, Cury," cried Freegrove. "Give us your hand. You, perhaps, didn't mean any harm, but those looks of yours were uncommonly queer."

"Upon my sacred honour," said Cury, "I——"

"Well, well, never mind—never mind. You wait here while I cut across the meadow, and do this little job that has delayed us longer than I thought."

"It's past six o'clock," said Cury. Be quick, Freegrove, be quick, or we are lost !"

"Lost, be d—d !" said Freegrove. "I'll go round by the road, and get into the meadow by the other end, close to the mill."

"Cury was now left alone, and he struck his forehead with his clenched fist, as he exclaimed :—

"Fool ! fool ! that I was to let him escape when my finger was on the trigger, and the least pressure would have done the deed. I used not to be weak. Die he shall—die he must—my life or his. I shall have no peace while that man lives. I must have been infatuated ; his life was in my hands ; and now his suspicions are awakened, there will be greater difficulty,—yet he must sleep sometimes. Iron as his frame is, it must have repose. Let him but close his eyes, and they shall never again open. I must have that man's blood. Beware, Freegrove, beware ! Your time is at hand. I may, then, perhaps, get up some specious tale of following him as the detected murderer of Sir Herbert, detected by me. Humph ! that requires consideration. The first thing to be accomplished is his death. This pistol, which he seems to have quite forgotten that I have about me, shall yet do the deed. Freegrove, we shall not reach London together. You are no companion for me. I associate with subtler spirits than such clods as you. You leave not this part of England alive, if there is any faith to be placed in a pistol bullet."

Cury now folded his arms across his breast, and leaned against a tree, while a demoniac smile lighted up his sallow features at the thought of the death of Freegrove, who he hated as much as he dreaded.

Freegrove returned in about ten minutes ; and Cury, as he heard him approaching, assumed a careless indifferent air and appearance, for his prime object was now to dissipate the dark suspicion which he felt confident was still lurking in Freegrove's mind, notwithstanding his apparent frank and open reconciliation.

"I have done it," said Freegrove, in a tone of exultation. "The window was open ; I threw in the fusee, the beauty of which is that it don't burst into a flame too soon, but goes on heating and smouldering all around it for a little time."

"Now then," said Cury, "let us begone."

"Why, d— it man," said Freegrove, "half an hour can't make much difference. You wouldn't surely go till we have seen some of the fun?"

"Fun?" cried Cury; "why, what on earth do you wait for now?"

"Oh, I must see some smoke, if not flame, from the mill before I can stir."

"Freegrove," cried Cury, "this is absolute insanity."

"Well, go yourself, then," replied Freegrove, sharply; "I don't want to keep you."

"And leave you here to be taken," replied Cury; "in which case ——"

"You think I'd peach, I suppose?" said Freegrove. "I don't know but what I should if I saw no other way. Self-preservation, you know, Cury. Ha! ha! ha!"

"Curses!" cried Cury.

"Come, tell the truth," said Freegrove. "You're afraid to stay, and afraid to go."

"As you please," replied Cury, folding his arms with an air of resignation. "You will, I firmly believe, ruin us both."

"Nonsense, man, nonsense!" said Freegrove. "The little affair at the hall will never be known for some hours yet. Nobody ever dreams of going to the armoury; and who, I should like to know, would think of disturbing Sir Herbert early in the morning? No, no; they'll all wait, I tell you, for you to go to Sir Herbert's bed-room and awaken him, and it's very likely to be quite the middle of the day before anything is at all found out about the business."

"It may be so," replied Cury; "but we should have been half way to London by this time, and once there, we should be comparatively safe."

"Hold your bother," cried Freegrove.

"How long shall we have to wait for some indication of fire at the mill?" said Cury.

"It can't be very long," replied Freegrove. "What's the time, now?"

"Past seven."

"D— it, it's getting late. Well, it's no great matter; you know it won't be any lighter than it is now, so a little time can't make much difference."

"We shall see," said Cury, with a groan.

"I should think so," replied Freegrove. "I tell you I wouldn't miss seeing that mill in a flame for ever so much, no, not for the finest dinner that was ever placed upon a table, Cury."

"You shall never see another dinner," thought Cury, "if I can help it. Only give me such another opportunity as that I so foolishly threw away, Master Freegrove, and I will put it out of your power to torture me any longer by your insane delays. To think that, by an unlucky train of circumstances, I, who have spent a life in finesse and fine-drawn stratagems, should be at the mercy of such a fool as this."

CHAPTER LXV.

For a few moments the party assembled in front of the miller's cottage were paralyzed by the sight of the flames bursting from the mill.

George was the first to recover his presence of mind. He carried the miller into the cottage; but before he could place him in his chair, the old man recovered, and starting to his feet, he cried:—

"George—Giles—Tim. My lads, all of thee save the mill—the dear old mill! Water—water! Stir theeselves. Quick—quick! Water—water!"

"Giles," cried George, "let us forget everything but the means of averting this calamity to our best friend and benefactor."

"Remember your promise, Giles," said Phœbe, laying her hand upon his arm. "You have saved me from worse than death. I will never think that you meant me harm. You promised, Giles, never to lift your hand against George. You will keep your word?"

"I will, Phœbe—I will," said Giles, in a voice of deep emotion. "I have been deceived—much deceived. God bless thee, Phœbe. I—I cannot speak to thee. Thee will hate me."

"Never! never!" cried Phœbe. "Oh! look at the dear old mill."

Giles said not another word, but throwing down the hedge stake, he bounded towards the mill with the speed of an antelope.

George and Tim were already there, and had partially succeeded in smothering the flames, but dense clouds of smoke rose from the old building, and the alarm rapidly spread to the village that the old mill was on fire.

The inhabitants, old and young, hastened to the spot, and soon every person was collected who could possibly be of any assistance in arresting the flames.

Giles was everywhere. He worked with the energy of three or four men combined in one person, and by his cheering shouts and encouraging cries he excited every one to increased exertions.

While all are thus occupied in endeavouring to save the ancient building, which for three or four generations had been a landmark to the surrounding country, we can turn our attention to the beaten and defeated party in the high road, which had been left by Giles in so utterly discomforted and routed a state.

The coachman recovered first from his fall, and sitting up in the middle of the road, he stared about him with an air of great consternation and alarm, the more particularly as the coach and horses had altogether vanished from the place.

He looked up and down the road in very great surprise, but he could see no indications whatever of their presence.

The fact was, that the horses had been frightened at the affray around them; and when Mr. Perk, partially recovering, and feeling an indistinct idea that he had suffered some material bodily damage, popped his cut face and damaged nose from the carriage, and screamed murder! the horses started forwards, and finding in a moment that they were uncontrolled by a driver, they quickened their pace to a gallop, and went tearing down the road, with the carriage bounding and swinging at their heels, at a pace which completed Mr. Perk's bewilderment and terror.

"Hilloa!" cried the coachman. "Hilloa! Is there anybody alive?"

"Ben, is that you?" cried the footman from the hedge.

"I think it is," replied Ben. "Where the devil are you?"

"Here, in the hedge. I can't get no ways at all."

"Where's everybody else?" cried the coachman.

"Here's somebody," said one of the constables, rising, and rubbing his head very hard. "That was the devil, I do think, that pitched me over. Hilloa, Jem, where are you?"

"I think we are all nicely in for it," said the coachman.

"I am," growled the footman. "For God's sake, some of you lend a hand, and get me out of the hedge. It's all tangled round my feet in such a way as never was, and my clothes is pretty well full of spiders."

"Where's the gentlemen?" said the constable.

"I'm blessed if I know," cried the coachman; "and there's the coach and horses gone too, the devil knows where."

Mr. Pomander and Mr. Scrimp, as we have already stated, started off with great speed from the scene of action, but the attorney, being rather short-winded, was soon obliged to give in, and he in vain tried to call to Mr. Pomander to stop, and not leave him, perhaps, in the power of ruthless enemies. Mr. Scrimp had not breath to utter a word; and, as a desperate resource, he took up a stone and threw it after Mr. Pomander with all his force, and by good fortune, rather than skill, hit the medical gentleman just in the middle of the back.

Mr. Pomander at once imagined that he was shot, and, with a roar of agony, he fell flat on the ground, which enabled Mr. Scrimp to gain upon him, and finally arrive close to him.

"There is n—no danger," gasped Scrimp. "They ain't f—f—following us."

"I'm shot," said Pomander, "an inward hemorrhage will be my death. Oh! oh! oh!"

"Shot! Nonsense," said Scrimp.

"Yes, shot," replied Pomander. "The ball struck the spinal column."

"It was a stone," said Scrimp. "I threw it."

"A stone?" cried Pomander, rubbing his back, and sitting upright. "Bless me, you don't say so? Upon my word it was very unfriendly of you."

"You wouldn't stop."

A confused hum of voices now came from the direction of the village; and Scrimp and Pomander, upon casting their eyes in that direction, saw a crowd of men, women, and children, all apparently rushing towards where they stood.

"What is the meaning of this?" said Mr. Pomander, turning pale and red by turns.

"Good gracious," cried Scrimp; "it must be after us. Run, Pomander, run."

"They are saying something, Scrimp," said Pomander. "Don't you hear? They keep on shouting something."

As the crowd from the village approached, their shouts came more clear and distinct to the ears of the confederates.

"It is fire they are calling," said Scrimp. "What can they mean?"

"Fire!—fire! The mill!—fire!" shouted the villagers.

"The mill?" cried Pomander, turning round and looking in the direction of the building. "It is the mill. The mill's on fire; and d— me if the great bin won't be burnt to ashes! Hurrah! hurrah!"

"They see us," said Scrimp; "we must go back, or we shall excite suspicion."

"It's our safest plan," answered Pomander.

"Besides," said Scrimp, "I don't think we were at all seen by the ruffian Giles, who knocked everybody about like so many nine pins."

"Most probably not," replied Pomander. "Let's call fire as loud as everybody, and go with the crowd."

"Fire! fire!" shouted the foremost of the crowd.

"Fire! fire!" cried Mr. Scrimp, with all his might.

"Fire! fire!" roared Pomander. "Come along, Scrimp, let's follow the current; you see popular opinion sets towards the mill, and be hanged to it. I hope there won't be one rafter left on another."

"Come on—come on," cried Scrimp. "Fire!—fire!"

The crowd had now fairly reached the spot on which Scrimp and Pomander stood, and they were carried on by the torrent without the power to extricate themselves, even had they wished to do so. They, however, thought that the best policy was decidedly to proceed with the villagers to the mill, and they did so accordingly, making themselves quite conspicuous by their loud shouts of "fire!—fire! The mill!—the mill!"

We must now, in order properly to connect together the various occurrences of our story, convey our readers once more to the Albion Hotel, Bungleum.

Bungleum was not further from London than the village of Haredale, and the direct road from Bungleum to London, passed within a mile and a half of the village.

Colonel Grainger rose with the first dawn of day, and resolved to lose no time in repairing to London, in order to make the most urgent inquiries in that great capital for the children, whose safety and happiness was now the only wish of his heart.

His mind had been very much disturbed with his interview with Mrs. Marrables, from which he could not but come to the conclusion that his darling Phœbe had endured the hardest usage, and been forced to fly from treatment which was beyond the endurance even of her gentle and patient nature. And what miseries and sufferings might have been her portion in London? The thought was agony to the colonel, and the whole night he had lain awake picturing to his tortured imagination all the evils which must surround his dear child in a large capital, without a friend in the world, and totally inexperienced.

Such thoughts as these were truly agonizing; and when Colonel Grainger rose in the morning, it was with a feverish pulse, and such indications of ill health, that he trembled to think that he might die before he could satisfy the one wish of his heart, to hold in his arms his dear child—his innocent Phœbe.

There was no one stirring in the "Albion" when he rose, and he walked out into the open air with the hope that the morning breeze would impart some degree of tension to his nerves, and vigour to his exhausted frame.

His impatience, however, would not permit him to remain long from the house, and he very shortly returned to the cold, uncomfortable coffee-room of the hotel, where still lay all the litter of the previous day.

Colonel Grainger paced the long, solitary apartment for some time, with the hope that some one of the inhabitants of the house would make his or her appearance. He looked at his watch—it was but half-past five o'clock.

At last, wearied with waiting, he rung the bell; but even that measure was unproductive of any results. Again, and again he rung; and at length a shuffling sound announced the approach of some one, and the door was opened by Sam the waiter, in a morning costume, consisting of a very dirty, blue-striped jacket, and greasy unmentionables.

"Yes, sir—yes, sir,—coming, sir,—coming," said Sam, popping his head into the room, and keeping the rest of his person on the outside.

"The chaise," said the colonel. "Let it be ready as soon as possible."

"Chaise, sir?—chaise and four, sir?"

"Yes—yes,—quick—quick! For London—I wish to start early."

"Yes, sir,—certainly, sir,—quick as possible, sir. Post-chaise and four to London. Sir,—coming directly, sir."

It appeared, however, that the chaise was not "coming directly," for Colonel Grainger heard six o'clock strike before he again saw Sam.

When the waiter did return, it was to say,—

"Bring your breakfast in a moment, sir. Eggs—ham—French rolls—coffee—tea—chocolate—cream, sir. Anything, sir. Everthing, sir."

"Bring what you like," said the colonel, "and do what you like, only tell me the moment the horses are put to the chaise, and tell your master to bring me my bill, for I may not return here ever again."

"Never again, sir?" said Sam,—"very sorry, sir—very, indeed. Certainly, sir; everything for breakfast. Coming—coming—everything for colonel's breakfast. Post-chaise and four horses. Bill immediately. Colonel never coming back again. Coming—coming."

The host of the Albion would not have the post-chaise announced till an ample breakfast had been laid on the table for the colonel, whether he chose to eat it or not, was quite another matter—it was down in the bill.

"Chaise, sir, at the door," said the landlord himself, entering with his bill. "Hope you have everything to your satisfaction, sir?"

"Oh, yes — yes,—certainly," said Colonel Grainger, hastily rising. "What is your bill?"

"Nine pounds three, sir."

The colonel laid down a ten pound note and left the room.

"I could cut my throat," said the landlord, stamping on the floor; "he would have paid half as much again. I have only charged him double price for everything. Oh, I could—I don't know what I couldn't do."

The chaise was at the door, and the horses chaping their bits, were impatient to be off.

"Waiter, sir," said Sam, "waiter, your honour."

The colonel dropped a sovereign into Sam's expectant hand. Post-boys always look out for these little incidents, as affording indications of the kind of liberality they are themselves to expect. The sovereign produced its full effect. Smack went the whips, and away went the chaise and the colonel in gallant style for London.

Seven o'clock had just struck as the chaise cleared at ten miles an hour the streets of Bungleum. The sun was beginning to break through the clouds, and the rapid motion of the vehicle imparted a freshness to the air, which Colonel Grainger found peculiarly grateful to his feelings.

"Before another sunset," he thought, "I may hold my dear child in my arms—my darling Phœbe. Oh, grant that I may find that you have endured nothing but poverty. Let me find you pure and innocent, and I shall ask of Heaven no other blessing."

The chaise had now got quite clear of the town, and was rolling rapidly between corn-fields, which extended many miles in all directions—some towards the sea.

Milestone after milestone was rapidly passed, and as eight o'clock was indicated by the colonel's watch, they were better than eleven miles from Bungleum.

Still onwards the foaming horses bore the chaise with undiminished vigour, and they shortly arrived at an inn where they were to change horses.

The fresh horses were put too in a few moments, and away they rattled again, soon leaving the little post-house far behind them.

Colonel Grainger had just dropped into an uneasy slumber, when he was awakened by a decrease in the speed at which he had been travelling, and he heard the sound of voices in excited tones.

He immediately put his head out of the window, and called to the post-boys to stop, which they had already nearly done, and were turned round in their saddles, all gazing in one direction.

The colonel cast his eyes around him and saw standing in the road about a dozen soldiers, who, by their dusty accoutrements and soiled muskets, appeared already to have travelled some distance.

"What is the matter?" said the colonel.

A sergeant who had the command of the party, with that quick tact which always enables a soldier to recognise an officer in any costume, immediately advanced to the side of the carriage, and with a military salute, said,—

"A fire, your honour."

Colonel Grainger's costume was that of an officer in undress, as he alighted from the carriage, the soldiers took but one glance at him, and immediately stood to their arms.

The colonel courteously returned their salute, and looking in the direction indicated by the sergeant, he saw at some miles distance, a dense smoke rising high in the clear morning air.

"Where is that fire?" he said.

"I think, sir, it's nigh Alton," said one of the post-boys.

"No—no," cried the other; "what are you thinking of, Alton lies there-away, to the left. It's as near by Haredale as possible—about three miles and a half off."

"It seems a large fire," said the colonel.

"It does, indeed," replied one of the postboys.

"I will not detain you," said the colonel, turning to the sergeant. "What are your orders?"

"To Chatham, sir," replied the sergeant.

Colonel Grainger touched his cap and walked back to the carriage-door.

"Slope arms," cried the sergeant. "March!"

The soldiers had hardly taken six steps along the road, when the sound of horses feet were heard coming at full gallop along the road. As yet nothing could be seen, for the road took a sudden turn near the spot at which the colonel's chaise had stopt. In a few moments, however, a horseman was seen approaching at a furious gallop, and as he came near, it was perceived by the colonel that he wore the dress of a groom, and was bare-headed.

As he approached the carriage, he reigned in his panting steed, and waved his arm, as if to bespeak the attention of the persons before him.

"Halt!" cried the sergeant to his men, and Colonel Grainger paused with one foot on the steps leading to the body of the carriage.

The man drew up within a few paces of the colonel. His appearance was wild and disordered, and he and his horse were covered with dust and foam.

The post-boys looked aghast, and even Colonel Grainger and the soldiers bent eagerly forward to hear what the rider of that panting steed had to say, as a reason for his haste and wild excitement.

"Murder!" cried the man, "murder! A dreadful murder!"

"A murder?" cried the colonel, in alarm, shrinking back. "Where?—when?"

"It was only found out," cried the man, "half an hour ago—my master's murdered."

"Who is your master? or rather, who was your master?" asked the colonel.

"Sir Herbert Foster, sir," replied the man. "Sir Herbert Foster, of Haredale Park. His body was found by the servants lying weltering in blood."

"And where are you going?"

"To Bungleum, for the magistrates, sir."

"Is any one suspected," said Colonel Grainger, "of being the murderer?"

"His valet, sir, and an old man named Freegrove, have absconded; and Freegrove's knife was found lying covered with blood, close to the body of my master."

"How far off is Haredale Park?"

"There is a cross road, sir," said the man, "that would take you there in half an hour; I have not left the house a quarter."

"I will go there," said the colonel. "This seems some horrible tragedy. Show us the road you speak of, my man, and I will drive to your master's house. If the deed has been so lately committed, its perpetrators cannot be far off."

"I can show your honour the road, or one of your honour's servants from the top of this mount," said the man, pointing to an eminence which was close at hand.

"Very well," said the colonel.

One of the postillions immediately dismounted and accompanied the groom, who spurred his horse up the hillock, which was sufficiently high to command a tolerable view of the surrounding country.

"I think I know the road," said the postillion, shading his face with his hands.

"There," said the groom, "you see the clump of trees by the turn of the road to the left there?"

"Yes, I do."

"Well, that's where the cross road begins. It goes straight through the fields to Haredale, and my master's house lies to the right, just as you come within sight of the mill. And egad, that puts me in mind of it. The old mill's a fire."

"What! the old mill at Haredale?" cried the postillion. "Old Gilbert Mark's mill?"

"Yes," said the groom, "the same. You may see it if it wasn't for the hedges right across the fields to the mill."

The man pointed with his finger as he spoke, and a flush of colour came over his cheek.

"Why, what's the matter?" cried the postillion, alarmed at his sudden alteration of manner.

"By Heaven!" cried the man. "I see them."

"See who?"

Down from the hillock the man spurred his horse, heedless alike of its safety and of his own. Then throwing himself off his seat as he came close to Colonel Grainger, he said in agitated accents,—

"I have seen them, sir; they are skulking under a hedge about half a mile off, in the direction of Haredale."

"Seen who?" said the colonel.

"The murderers, sir; the men I told you of."

CHAPTER LXVI.

COLONEL GRAINGER immediately sprung upon the hillock, followed by the man, and taking a small pocket-glass in his hand, he said,—

"In which direction?"

"Straight along, sir, by the row of chesnuts."

Colonel Grainger gave one long look, and then in a moment was in the road again.

"Sergeant," he cried.

The sergeant was by his side in a moment.

"Come here;" and the colonel led him to mount. "Do you see two men under a hedge some distance off, near six remarkable large trees, there by a corn field?"

"I do, sir," replied the sergeant. "They are skulking, your honour."

"Those men must be secured. I am Colonel Grainger, of his Majesty's Forty-ninth."

The sergeant touched his cap, and followed the colonel respectfully from the little hillock to where the soldiers were standing.

"Attention!" cried Colonel Grainger, when he stood opposite the men.

The men drew themselves smartly up.

"Have you ball cartridge?" he said to the sergeant.

"We have, colonel," replied the sergeant.

"Load," cried Colonel Grainger. "Trail arms. You will secure those men, sergeant. March! Leave a sentry at every road or foot-path."

Colonel Grainger then mounted the hillock, and, applying the glass to his eye, he watched, with keen interest, the result of the soldiers' proceedings.

Cury and Freegrove, after attempting to leave the neighbourhood of the mill by the road, were compelled, in order to avoid coming in contact with the advancing peasantry, who were hurrying to the scene of the conflagration, to cross a hedge, and fly through the open fields, a proceeding which was much more likely to draw marked attention upon then from distances, than as if they could have kept the road. They kept as close under the hedges as they possibly could, but the fields were so open, it being principally a corn country, that, as we have observed, they were seen, notwithstanding all their caution and excessive care.

Cury felt fully all the dangers of his situation, and even Freegrove began to shew signs of uneasiness.

"Hasten! hasten!" cried Cury. "If there be a discovery of what has occurred at Haredale while we are in the open fields, nothing can save us."

"Pho! pho!" replied Freegrove. "How should there be a discovery? It is not likely. We are safe for some hours yet."

"I hope so," said Cury. "But there is one thing I advise; and that is, that we bury in some spot, that we shall easily know again, all the jewellery that we have about us."

"There is something in that," said Freegrove, pausing. "If we do come across any d—d meddling people, these things in our pocket would do us up."

"They would," cried Cury, anxiously. "Let us not lose a moment."

"Here is a small oak tree," said Freegrove, "close to the hedge. Suppose we bury everything here?"

"Agreed," replied Cury. "Moments are precious. What we have in our pockets retard our progress, as well as expose us to danger."

"Have you a knife?" said Freegrove.

"No," replied Cury; "but here are plenty of pointed hedge-stakes. We can dig sufficiently deep with one of them."

Freegrove immediately commenced his work, while Cury, crouching down under the cover of the hedge, began emptying his pockets of costly trinkets and articles of value which he had brought from the jewel-room at Haredale.

Cury had had several opportunities of carrying into effect his intention of murdering his companion, but a new fear had come over him and stayed his hand. He felt that until they were quite clear of the open country, they were liable to be interrupted by some of the rustics, and he had great confidence in the strength and courage of Freegrove, and thought that in such an emergency it might be very desirable to have his strong arm and unflinching brute courage to depend upon, and as far as the destruction of Freegrove was concerned, the wily valet thought there was a time for all things, and he might as well have as much use out of his associate as possible before getting rid of him altogether.

It was while the worthy pair were thus engaged, that they were observed by the mounted groom, who had ridden from Haredale.

Freegrove was reasoning tolerably correctly when he said that it would, in all human probability, be late in the day before the murder of Sir Herbert Foster would be discovered, for, in fact, the armoury was rarely, if ever, visited by any of the household, and the events of the night were not likely to increase the desire of any domestics to do so, and run the risk of again seeing the apparition of Helen Wade.

It was, likewise, Cury's particular duty to attend upon Sir Herbert in the morning, and the ordinary servants of the house very rarely saw their master till late in the day, so it will be seen that, as we have said, there was every probability that the murder would remain unknown for several hours, at least, after the time that Cury and Freegrove left the neighbourhood of the mill; but it commonly happens that the most correct concatenations of probabilities are liable to be deranged by some accident which had never for a moment entered into the imagination of the sage calculator of circumstances and results.

So it was in the present instance. The armoury was never passed through, because it led to nowhere but the jewel-room, and the jewel-room led to nowhere at all; but past the door of the armoury, was a constant thoroughfare for the whole of the household, for various passages close to it branched off to different parts of the extensive establishment.

It happened that a female servant was walking quickly past the armoury door, when she felt that she was treading on something wet and slippery, and upon looking down she saw a narrow dark stain upon the floor, which seemed to come from the armoury-door. The girl sickened at the sight, for the idea that it was blood came over her in a moment, and she rushed, screaming, to the servants' hall. The cause of her alarm was soon told, and the domestics, in a body, repaired to the spot, and there, sure enough, creeping slowly from beneath the door of the armoury, and then spreading itself into a little sanguine pool, was a stream of blood.

In a few moments the door of the armoury was opened, and, to the horror of all, the ghastly body of their murdered master was discovered lying on the suit of armour which had fallen from the wall.

Thus was an early discovery of the fate of Sir Herbert Foster made, by a circumstance which neither of the murderers had ever in the most distant manner imagined could possibly happen, but which led to their destruction.

The murderers were now fairly in the toils. There was no escape for them. The sergeant's party was hidden by the intervening hedges from their sight, and, as it approached, a sentinel was left at every point which commanded a good view of the surrounding country, with orders to give the alarm should any one whatever attempt to pass the line of the high road.

Freegrove worked on with great diligence, and the attention of Cury was likewise quite taken by an examination of the various articles which he was dragging from every part of his apparel which would hold anything.

"That's deep enough," said Cury, "a foot deep is as good as a mile in this case."

Freegrove ceased from his work, and rising, wiped the perspiration from his brow. As he did so, he happened to cast his eyes in the direction of the furthest side of the field, and he instantly sprung back a pace or two, exclaiming,—

"D——n!"

Cury started at Freegrove's exclamation, and he looked instantly in the direction in which his eyes were fixed, and in an instant his face assumed the hue of death, and he trembled so violently that he could scarcely stand.

Half-a-dozen soldiers, with the sergeant at their head, were bursting through the hedge, and in another instant were actually in the same field with the guilty wretches, who saw that escape was impossible.

"Surrender yourselves," cried the sergeant.

"I'm d——d if I do," said Freegrove, making a rush to get through the hedge, close to which he was standing.

"Move a step, and we fire," cried the sergeant.

Cury fell to the ground with a deep groan.

The hedge was thick and high; and Freegrove, with all his strength and desperation, found it no easy matter to force his way through.

"Forward!" cried the sergeant, and he and his men dashed forward towards the prostrate Cury.

Freegrove just cleared the hedge by a desperate effort as the soldiers reached it, and he rushed across the next field.

"Make ready!—present!" cried the sergeant.

Freegrove heard the rattle of the fire-arms in the hands of the soldiers, but even that did not stop him. A new obstacle, however, presented itself to his progress, for the moment he arrived near to the enclosure of the next field, a voice cried, "Stop!" and he saw a soldier, with his musket at the charge, within a few paces of him.

No. 51

He looked around for a moment bewildered, and uttered the most fearful oaths.

The sergeant's party had by this time cleared the hedge, after leaving a guard over Cury, who made no resistance, but lay upon the ground apparently half dead with extreme terror.

"Forward!" again shouted the sergeant, and the men rushed across the field.

Freegrove now saw that he was virtually taken. He folded his arms, and biting his lips till the blood came, he stood like a statue, awaiting the arrival of his captors.

In a minute more he was surrounded by the soldiers.

"D——n!" he cried, "what do you mean by hunting me across the fields?"

"Our orders," said the sergeant, "are to arrest you and your companion. Fall in," he said to his men.

The soldiers placed themselves in double files, with Freegrove in their centre.

"March," cried the sergeant.

"Ha! ha!" said Freegrove, with a forced laugh. "These are times, indeed, when an honest man is to be marched along in this way. Perhaps you take me for a deserter?"

"Shoot your prisoner if he attempts to escape," said the sergeant, coolly.

"Ha! ha!" continued Freegrove. "I suppose a fellow must go when he's forced. Needs must when the devil drives. Ha! ha!"

The sergeant marched at the head of the little party, and, taking exactly the same route back that they had come by, they arrived to where Cury still lay upon the ground, with a soldier marching backwards and forwards on guard over him, as calmly as if he had been some inanimate object.

"Yes, yes—oh, yes," said Cury, rising and betraying by his whole bearing and manner the very extremity of fear. "Anything, gentlemen—anything you please. I am innocent. I—I don't know that man," pointing to Freegrove.

"You be d——d!" said Freegrove. "I tell you what it is, Mister Sergeant, we came to take a walk in the field, and found this property hid under the tree; there, you may see the hole."

"Yes, yes," cried Cury,—"oh, dear, yes, it's true, I'll take my solemn oath. You are in some mistake, sergeant; you will let us go?"

The sergeant now directed two of his men to take charge of the valuables which lay upon the ground, and upon the order to "March," the whole party, with their prisoners, set off at a quick step for the road, taking with them the sentinels as they came along.

Colonel Grainger had watched from his elevated position the whole of the proceedings with intense interest, and he was rejoiced to see the prisoners did not resist violently their capture. He descended to the road as the military party approached, and gave the word to "Halt."

"We found this property, colonel," said the sergeant, "in the possession of the prisoners."

"What do you want with us?" said Freegrove. "What have we done, I should like to know, that we are to be pulled about in this way?"

"Oh, yes, yes," cried Cury. "What have we done? We are honest men. I'll take a solemn oath we are."

"You are accused of murder," said Colonel Grainger, "and I shall detain you until I can deliver you to the proper authorities."

"Murder?" said Freegrove. "Stuff. We are servants of Sir Herbert Foster."

"Yes," said Cury; "murder, indeed. Our master—our kind master will protect us. We—we didn't kill him. He was always kind to us."

"Wretched man!" cried the colonel, "you have criminated yourself. I did not say your *master* was murdered; I merely said you were accused of murder, and your conscience directly tells you *whose* murder. Every one here present has heard what the prisoner said?"

Cury looked aghast from one to the other of the persons who surrounded him. All his cunning seemed to have deserted him, and he only muttered something about "mercy."

"We will not prolong this scene," said the colonel. "Let us proceed at once by the road which has been pointed out to the mansion of the murdered gentleman. Sergeant, look well to your prisoners. I will follow you in the carriage. Quick—march!"

The cavalcade immediately started. The soldiers proceeded at a rapid pace with their prisoners, and the colonel, with the chaise, kept close in their rear.

The feelings of Cury and Freegrove towards each other were now of the most deadly and exasperating character.

Cury considered that the whole of their present misfortunes had arisen from the delay occasioned by Freegrove's obstinacy in waiting so long merely for the gratification of his private revenge against the miller, and in his heart he bitterly cursed him as being the direct cause of his apprehension.

"We are lost—lost," he thought. "All is over. I might have been in London; but now, ruin—ruin—destruction—shame, and death. Curses on me for not taking his life in the wood; but yet, even yet, I will not die unrevenged!"

Cury's extreme nervousness and pusillanmity had caused him to make the two fatal mistakes which confirmed his guilt. His denial at first of any knowledge of Freegrove, and then his answer to Colonel Grainger respecting the murder, were sufficient of themselves to bring conviction to any mind, and Freegrove, justly enough, considered that Cury, by his weakness, had cut them off from all chance of clearing themselves from what before might have been but a mere suspicion of guilt.

Thus, as is universally the case, where persons are associated together for bad purposes, these two men came to regard each other with feelings of the most deadly hatred, and they thirsted for each other's blood more than they had ever thirsted for the glittering plunder which had brought them into unholy communion to do the unlawful deed which should make their names a disgrace, and their remembrance in after years a detestation.

CHAPTER LXVII.

MUCH grieved as was Colonel Grainger to postpone even for an hour his journey to London in search of his lost children, he still felt it to be his duty to carry out the adventure in which he had become so unexpectedly entangled, and to surrender the murderers, who had been captured through his interference, into the hands of justice, before prosecuting his own private affairs.

They had not proceeded very far when dense clouds of smoke completely obscured the horizon, and the little party came to a halt to gaze upon the fire, which was evidently in their immediate vicinity.

"That certainly seems to be a bad fire, your honour," said the sergeant, saluting Colonel Grainger as he spoke.

"There is, certainly, much smoke," answered the colonel. "Where, to the best of your knowledge, is the fire situated?" he said, turning to the postillion.

"I am quite sure, now, it's somewhere close by Haredale; if it bean't the old mill," answered the man.

Colonel Grainger hesitated a moment, and then said to the sergeant, in a tone of decision,—

"Keep a strict eye upon your prisoners, and make for the fire. We may render essential assistance there, without interfering with our duty as captors of these ruffians."

"Then, your honour, we had better push across the fields," said the sergeant.

"Do so," cried Colonel Grainger, "I will accompany you myself. You can remain here, postillion, with the carriage, and should I be detained above an hour, I will send to you, or you can come on by the high road."

"I will follow you, sir, by the road, if you please," said the man.

"Very well," said the colonel. "Now, my men, forward. To the fire, in as right a line of march as possible."

The soldiers set forward with animation, forcing with them their reluctant prisoners—Cury and Freegrove.

Cury seemed to have lapsed into a state of hopeless despair. He walked onwards, with his hands clasped before him, and betraying, by his countenance, the agonized state of his feelings. He continually muttered between his teeth,—

"Lost!—lost!—lost!"

Freegrove, on the other hand, seemed each moment to acquire additional ferocity, and he glared round him upon his guards with the most savage expression, as if meditating some dire and horrible vengeance against them all. But it was when his eye rested upon the trembling Cury, that he seemed wrought up to a pitch of the greatest fury, and his gaze was one of such concentrated hate and bloodthirstiness, that, had Cury noticed it, it must have added largely to his personal fears of the consequences of his deep criminality.

Rapidly they neared the old mill, from which many sparks were now rising into the morning air, accompanied by clouds of dense smoke.

"Forward," cried Colonel Grainger, in a cheering voice. "Forward, my lads."

The soldiers increased their speed, dragging their prisoners through hedges and over ditches.

Now the shouts of many voices came upon their ears, and the cries of "Fire! fire!" from the villagers, who were speeding towards the mill, came alarmingly upon the air.

"Forward!" again shouted Colonel Grainger, and trailing their muskets, the soldiers scampered across the fields with great rapidity.

Now they arrived at the field, skirted by the hedge, under the shadow of which Mr. Pomander and Mr. Scrimp had so lately ensconced themselves, to watch the progress of Phœbe's abduction, which, as we have seen, was so signally defeated by Giles.

Colonel Grainger seemed with the occasion to have regained all the elasticity of youth, for he was the first to force his way through the hedge, and bound into the road. He was followed immediately by the soldiers, who, with more speed than ceremony, dragged along with them Cury and Freegrove, who were both hurried along so quickly, that they had not time to think of resistance even if they had been inclined to offer it.

The road was crossed in a moment, and with a loud huzza the meadow was gained.

"Forward," again shouted Colonel Grainger.

"Another huzza from the men rent the air, and attracted the attention of the group at the cottage.

The wicket-gate was opened, and in a few moments more Colonel Grainger and his party were in the presence of the frantic miller and his family.

The villagers were now rapidly arriving, but all seemed much more ready in venting lamentations for the fate of the old mill, than in devising some means of stopping the conflagration.

"Halt!" cried Colonel Grainger, in a loud voice.

The soldiers immediately came to a stand.

"A file of men guard the prisoners carefully," he continued. "Shoot them if they attempt to escape. Now for the fire."

The good old miller stood aghast at this sudden apparition of a troop of military, who seemed to his bewildered faculties to have dropped from the clouds at his very feet.

Every one present, too, to a certain extent, shared in the look of astonishment which the miller cast upon Colonel Grainger.

George was the first to recover his faculties, and he was about to speak, when the colonel cried, in a loud clear voice,—

"Bring out all your buckets, and fill them with water instantly. Soldiers, take your stations at arms' length distance from each other, stretching towards the mill. You can then pass the buckets from one to another, and keep up a supply of water."

George comprehended in a moment, that if the mill was to be saved at all it should be by some such means as that which the colonel proposed, and he cried, in a cheering voice,—

"That will save the mill. Let the first man stand on the brink of the mill stream."

The miller seemed to rouse himself by a great effort, and he cried,—

"God bless you, sir. Save my old mill. Here, Tim, Tim,; the pails and buckets."

In a moment Tim Miggles, who had vanished into the cottage, returned, with a pail on each arm.

"Hurrah!" he cried; "that's the time o' day. Come on—come on."

> " 'The mill, the mill, the brave old mill,
> For once in a way shall have her fill
> Of water from the stream;
> The flour will all be turned to paste,
> And——' '

"Hold thee nonsense," cried the miller.

"Who is active and familiar with the inside of the mill?" cried Colonel Grainger.

"I," answered George.

"And I," cried Giles, advancing.

"Then stand both of you at the door, and we will supply you with water as fast as you can use it."

In a few moments more the arrangements were quite complete. The soldiers, assisted by some of the villagers, stood in a line, and handed the full buckets of water from one to another with great rapidity, and they were received by Giles and George at the mill, and emptied of their contents so judiciously, that in about ten minutes all the flames were evidently extinguished, and nothing remained of the fire but a little smoke, which still ascended from the heated rafters, and partially consumed corn with which the mill was stocked. To make all sure, however, they continued their exertions for some time longer, until they became convinced that every spark of the fire was extinguished.

With anxiety depicted upon every feature of his face did the old miller watch the progress of the exertions to save the building, which from the force of association, was so dear to his heart, that its loss would have affected him severely. Now, however, when he heard the voice of George ring clear and loud from the upper story of the mill, and the words, "Saved! saved!" smote his ears, the tears chased each other down the old man's cheek, and he uttered a fervent exclamation of gratitude to Heaven.

The soldiers had worked with energy and good will, and they now returned towards the cottage, headed by Colonel Grainger, with a glow of health upon his cheeks, which they had not exhibited for many a day.

CHAPTER LXVIII.

CURY and Freegrove had remained passive, but by no means uninterested spectators of the means adopted to quench the fire at the mill, and it was with deep execrations that Freegrove saw those means successful; and that the same persons who, under the guidance of Providence, had arrested him for the foul murder he had committed, were, likewise, the instruments of saving the honest miller from the consequences of the wild revenge of so bad a man.

The soldiers, who had been ordered to guard him and Cury, kept a wary eye upon their movements, for there was a restlessness about the eye of Freegrove which taught them to apprehend that he might commit some desperate act upon the impulse of a moment, which, while it would certainly ensure his own destruction, might yet prove dangerous to those against whom his ill-directed energies might be exerted.

With a deep oath he heard the exclamation of George from the mill that all was safe, and the fire extinguished; then sullenly crossing his arms upon his breast, he cast his eyes upon the ground, while dark and evil thoughts flitted across his hardened heart.

The throng of villagers crowded to the spot, full of curiosity to know the why and wherefore of the arrival of the soldiers, and to discover, if possible, who the "gentleman" could be who had exerted himself so manfully in quenching the flames.

The presence of Cury and Freegrove as prisoners in the hands of the military had, in the excitement of the moment, not been remarked; but now that the fire was extinguished, a general exclamation of surprise burst from all as these two well-known personages met their view, closely guarded by the soldiers.

The miller's first act was to spring forward and grasp the hand of Colonel Grainger in both his own, while he endeavoured to thank him for preserving to him the old mill, the dear companion of his life—his father's mill—nay, his grandfather's mill.

"God bless you, sir," he cried; "I don't know who you be, but you are a main friend to me and mine."

"I am doubly pleased," said Colonel Grainger, "that I have been instrumental in subduing this fire, since the building is endeared to you by old associations."

The colonel could not forbear a sigh as he spoke, for he thought of his own situation in life, uncertain, as he was, whether or not he was ever fated to renew any of those sweet old associations, which, amid war and tumult, and through the lapse of many years, had still always nestled round his heart.

The miller was about to speak again, when Giles rushed forward, and exclaimed,—

"Master, I—I have been wrong—mad, but don't let the villains escape." The miller looked inquiringly around him.

"There they are," continued Giles. "God Forgive me. They tempted me to steal her from you. Stop them! stop them!"

He pointed into the thickest of the throng; and the crowd, dividing and shrinking back, exposed Mr. Pomander and Mr. Scrimp, standing frightened and irresolute, by themselves.

"Villains!" cried the miller, rushing forward, but he was stayed by the arm by the colonel, who said,—

"What have they done, my friend? Do not be hasty. They shall be secured, if necessary."

"Done?" cried the miller. "They would have robbed me of my child—my dear child."

"And they shall not escape punishment, by Heaven," cried George, rushing forward.

"It's nonsense," cried Scrimp.

"It's all a black draught—I mean a black lie," cried Pomander.

"Then you need not run away," cried Colonel Grainger.

"Thank you for nothing," answered Scrimp, as he fairly turned and took to his heels, followed closely by the compounder of drugs.

"A hunt for a lawyer;" cried Tim Miggles, and in an instant he darted after them.

George and Giles both immediately joined in the pursuit, Colonel Grainger looked amazed, but he followed the direction of everybody else's eyes, and soon became as much absorbed and interested in the chase as any one.

Scrimp was rather outran by the son of Galen, whose legs being considerably longer, covered more ground than the lawyer's.

"They are hot and fast after us, Scrimp," he said, as he passed him.

"Who?" roared Scrimp;—"tell me who?"

"That madman, Giles, and the lover, George, they call him, as well as the fool, Miggles."

"Good God!" cried Scrimp, "we shall be murdered. "Pomander—euh! euh!—Oh, Lord, Pomander; for God's sake, don't leave me. Oh, Lord—oh, Lord!"

"The devil take the hindmost," muttered Pomander, as he shot a-head of his companion.

The chase now became really exciting and amusing, more especially to those who knew how well the pursued deserved any sort of punishment they might receive at the hands of the pursuers, who were evidently gaining fast upon them.

George sped onwards with the speed of a young antelope, nor was Giles many paces in his rear, while Tim Miggles seemed determined to be in at the death; and what he wanted in speed was compensated for whenever they arrived at a hedge, for then he passed easily through the gap, which it took George and Giles some few moments to make.

Pomander and Scrimp were evidently making hard for the village, and it appeared to the lookers on that George was purposely making a *detour*, relying upon his swiftness, with an intention of throwing himself between them and Haredale, and so forcing them either to surrender at discretion, or return back to the mill.

Now and then darting a hasty and terrified glance behind them, the fugitives pressed onwards. They clambered over fences, waded through ditches, burst, heedless of briars and nettles, recklessly through hedges, and with all the speed and franticity of despair, they urged themselves towards the village, hoping and thinking that there, at least, they should find shelter from what Lord Bacon would have called "wild justice."

"I—I,"—panted Mr. Scrimp, as he puffed and laboured on,—"I—I—don't—oh, dear—(puff)—mind being—Lord preserve us!—dealt with according to—(puff)—to—law; but to have these—(puff)—oh, Lord—mad-men coming after one in this—(puff, puff)—way, it's—it's—worse than—(puff)—being chased—oh, Lord—by a mad—(puff)—bull."

George now turned to Giles, saying,—

" Giles, slacken speed, but follow them right on, while I skirt round by Hodgson's farm, and meet them in front."

Giles nodded; and as George sprung over a hedge, in order to execute his project, he gradually slackened his speed, to the great delight of Mr. Scrimp, who was too terrified and confused to notice more than that he was increasing his distance from his pursuers.

"Pomander! Pomander!" he called, "you needn't go so fast; we've done them at last. I—I'm blown—quite blown; just go a little slower."

Mr. Pomander did relax his speed, but not in consequence of Mr. Scrimp's entreaties. The real cause was, that he had come to the brink of a wide ditch, so wide, that to jump it was out of the question, and so muddy and slimy, that it would have required some very powerful impulse, indeed, from behind to induce any one in his sober senses to wade through it.

"Where the devil does this ditch end?" cried Mr. Pomander, in a very frantic tone.

" That ditch!" said Mr. Scrimp, panting and surveying it with a rueful physiognomy,—" oh, Lord, I know it—it goes along here for half a mile, or more. There are stepping-stones—some—some-where, but——"

"D——!" said Mr. Pomander, " here's a dose."

"What shall we do?" cried the lawyer.

" We must try to jump it," said Pomander. " There's that mad fellow, Giles, coming on behind, with his eyes glaring like a hyena's."

"Good God!" cried Scrimp, " I can't jump it; it's quite ridiculous; I can't, indeed."

"Villains!" cried Giles, from the field behind them, which he had just entered.

" A chase for a lawyer," roared Tim Miggles.

Mr. Pomander looked behind him, and then at the ditch; for a moment he hesitated, and then gathering up his medical legs, he made a very terrific spring. Now Mr. Pomander had very long, wiry-looking legs, and it is just probable that he might have got clean over; but as it was, just as he was in the mid air, he saw George advancing from the other side of the ditch, and, with a cry of horror, Mr. Pomander fell into the very middle with a loud splash. Mr. Scrimp, with the fear of Giles, resolutely slipped down the clay bank, and waded into the ditch up to his middle; and had not the medical man come down just by his side with so awful a splash, he would have escaped better; as it was, however, the descent of Pomander covered him up entirely, and they both floundered about like gigantic eels, who liked the slimy mud, and gloried in it exceedingly.

CHAPTER LXIX.

SETTING aside the discomforts of the ditch, Pomander and Scrimp had certainly found an effectual means of keeping their enemies at bay, for George paused upon one side, and Giles paused upon the other, while Tim Miggles shook his head at the posture of affairs.

"Tim," said George, after a few moments' consideration, " n to the nearest farm-house, and borrow a long cart-whip."

A groan burst from the discomfitted lawyer as he heard this suggestion, and Mr. Pomander made a great splash all round him, in utter despair.

Tim Miggles ran off upon his errand, while George and Giles kept guard upon the fugitives.

"Young men—young men," said Scrimp, "you'll get yourselves into serious trouble. Assault and battery, you know, is no joke."

"You'll find it no joke," answered George.

"We will apologize," said Pomander.

"You shall," said George, "but it shall be to those you have tried to injure the most."

"What do you mean, my dear sir?" whined Scrimp.

"I mean this," answered George. "You shall both return to the miller's cottager, and on your knees you shall beg pardon of Phœbe and all there present."

"Oh, Lord," said Scrimp. "Pomander, I—I think we—we had better accept the—the proposal."

"The devil!" cried Pomander.

"Don't be in a hurry," said George, "My private account with you both I'll settle here. Do you confess that you had an intention of aiding in the abduction of the Miller's Maid?"

"Y—y—yes, we do," groaned Scrimp.

"Here you are," cried Tim Miggles, at this moment arriving, armed with a long cart-whip, with which he made smacks in the air as loud as the reporr of a pistol.

"Throw it over to me, Tim," cried George.

"We'll go!—we'll go!" shrieked Mr. Scrimp; "we'll go, quietly."

No. 52

"Yes, yes—oh, certainly," cried Pomander. "D— that whip, I say; we'll go anywhere."

Tim Miggles threw the whip over their heads to George.

"Now," said George, "you two unmanly scoundrels, you shall have a lash for everybody who would have been injured by your villany."

"Hurrah!" cried Tim; "I'll call the names."

"Do," said George, flourishing the whip.

"Mercy!" cried Scrimp.

"The devil!" roared Pomander.

"Phœbe," cried Tim Miggles.

Lash came the whip, with right good will, across the backs of the delinquents, a roar of rage and pain burst from them both, and they floundered about, kicking up the slimy mud fearfully.

"Giles," cried Tim.

Another salutation of the whip.

"The miller."

Lash again.

"Mercy!" shrieked Scrimp.

"Murder!" cried Pomander.

Then followed the "miller's dame," and "George," and himself, all sung out by Tim Miggles, with amazing glee.

"I think that's all," said George.

"No, there's one more," cried Tim. "Give it 'em well."

"Who is it?" said George.

"Snapallhecanup," said Tim.

Lash went the whip.

"The devil!" shrieked Pomander.

Lash went the whip again.

"Perhaps, gentlemen," said George, "you'd like to name somebody else?"

"Oh! oh! oh! oh!" shouted Scrimp, "that ever I was born. Oh, Lord! oh, Lord!"

"I'll trouble you now to get out of the ditch," said George, "and make the best of your way, both of you, to the mill, and, for fear you should catch cold, I'll follow you behind with the whip, you understand?"

"We—we can't get out—oh, Lord," cried Scrimp, who dreaded further punishment on dry ground.

"We'll see," said George. "Let them get out on your side, Giles."

With that George commenced a succession of long cuts with the whip, which so invigorated the lawyer and the doctor, that they scrambled out of the ditch in a few seconds.

George measured the distance across the ditch with his eye for a moment, and then by a tremendous leap cleared it, and alighted in safety on the other side, to the consternation of Scrimp and Pomander, who thought that, at least, they were out of his reach.

"To the mill! to the mill!" shouted George.

Pomander and Scrimp looked at the cart-whip for an instant, and then set off towards the mill at as quick a pace as they had run from it, followed closely by George, Giles, and the delighted Tim Miggles.

The whole attention of the parties assembled in front of the miller's cottage had been absorbed in watching the chase across the fields. They saw the capture of the pursued, and the punishment they received, and now every one was lost in wonder to see the whole party racing back again with with such headlong and desperate speed.

Whenever Mr. Scrimp or Pomander relaxed a little in speed, the sharp crack of the cart-whip behind them seemed to give them renewed strength, for they plunged forward again, with a roar of apprehension and fright.

Now the road was gained, then the meadow, and in a few moments more Pomander and Scrimp burst into the assembled throng in so awful a condition from black mud, that their most intimate friends would certainly have failed to recognize them.

"What is the meaning of all this?" said Colonel Grainger. "Tell me, some of you, what these men have done?"

"They are the mean and cowardly agents of a scoundrel," said George, "who would, by fraud or force, have taken from her home, and those who love her, an innocent girl, to force her to a life of shame and infamy."

"That be true," cried the miller. "Shame on them for the thought. May God forgive them."

"It is, indeed, true," cried Giles. "I am a witness against them, and God forgive me for listening to them for a moment."

"I saw 'em, too," said Tim Miggles. "I was a-top of the mill, and I saw 'em.

'Hang 'em, roast 'em, boil 'em, and fry 'em,
The devil will have 'em; he can't deny 'em.'"

"Their crime is a base one," said Colonel Grainger, "but graver matters call our attention at this moment."

"Let us send these rascals away, sir," said George. "Their presence is a contamination. I have only forced them here to ask for pardon of the innocence they would have injured so vilely and wickedly."

"Let them go, George," said Phœbe, advancing. "I forgive them freely; let them go."

"On their knees they shall solicit pardon," cried George. "I only regret that there is still another concerned in this wicked conspiracy who is not here. I allude to the scoundrel, Perk, who has made his escape, I suppose, for where mischief and iniquity was being enacted, there, for certain, would he be. Justice, however, will overtake him."

"I'll take the law of him," whispered Scrimp to Pomander. "He shall rot in prison for this."

"D— me," said Pomander, "if I think I shall ever recover to take any body to law. My stomach is full of mud."

"Lest you," said George, turning to Colonel Grainger, "should consider that these men have been treated with any undue severity, I will now read aloud a document which I have in my possession."

"A document?" murmured Scrimp.

"What now?" said Pomander.

"Hurrah!—Silence!" cried Tim Miggles.

CHAPTER LXX.

GEORGE took a piece of folded paper from his pocket; it was the confession which the reader will recollect Mr. Perk had been compelled to make and sign.

"This paper," said George, "is a confession, made and signed by a comrade of these men, but first let me tell you their names."

"I'll do that," interrupted Tim Miggles. "This here lanky one, with his nose a-bleeding, is Pomander, the doctor. This here littler one, all over blue mud, is Scrimp, the lawyer."

"That will do, Tim," said George.

He then unfolded the paper, and commenced reading.

"I, Stephen Perk, being a most contemptible and cowardly villain, did conspire with certain other vile scoundrels hereinafter mentioned, namely,

Sir Herbert Foster, baronet, Mr. Scrimp, attorney-at-law, Mr. Pomander, chemist, and Ralph Freegrove, steward to the aforesaid Sir Herbert Foster, baronet, to force away, by unlawful means, a certain young girl, known by the name ——"

"Stay a moment," said Colonel Grainger.

George paused.

"You mention Sir Herbert Foster?"

"Yes, that is the man, and a greater villain never ——"

"Hold!" cried the colonel. "Do you not know that ——"

"What?" said George.

"That he is *murdered?*"

"Murdered?" cried George, as the paper dropped from his hands "murdered?"

"Aye," said the Colonel, "most foully murdered, as I am given to understand, and these two men are in my custody on suspicion of committing the deed."

The soldiers moved aside, and all eyes were fixed in horror upon Cur and Freegrove.

"They are both his servants," said the miller.

An universal groan of execration burst from all asse ublel, and P clasped her hands in horror.

"Then, indeed," said George, "we will mention his name no more. He is in the hands of God."

Freegrove looked scowlingly around him, and strove to put on an air of defiance as he said,—

"I am innocent. Where's your proof?"

"I—I confess," said Cury, dropping on his knees, and covering his face with his hands. "Mercy!—mercy! I will tell all—all—all."

He dropped his chin upon his breast as he spoke, and kept muttering, "mercy—mercy."

Freegrove glared about him for a moment, then he struck Cury a violent blow at the back of the neck, before any one could prevent him.

"D——n coward!" he cried; and before any one had recovered from the surprise of the sudden act, he darted from the spot, and   j·ι γ·ιι wicket-gate.

A loud scream burst from Cury, and he dropped upon the ground.

"Take him alive or dead," cried Colonel Grainger.

The soldiers made a rush after him, but he had the start, and was unincumbered by anything to carry, while they had their muskets.

"By Heavens! the villain will escape," cried the colonel.

Freegrove was half way across the meadow before the soldiers had crowded through the wicket.

Colonel Grainger saw the pursuit was hopeless, and he cried, in a loud clear voice,—

"Halt!"

The soldiers paused.

"Make ready—present——"

Every musket was levelled. Still Freegrove kept on. The colonel waited till he saw him arrive at the hedge. In another moment he would have plunged through it, and most probably escaped.

"Fire!" cried Colonel Grainger.

A volley from the muskets immediately succeeded.

Freegrove sprung several feet into the air, and then, falling heavily to the earth, he rolled over upon his back under the hedge.

"They have hit him," said Colonel Grainger. "I regret it, but he would else have escaped."

The soldiers now ran across the meadow towards the fallen ruffian, and George, assisted by Giles, raised the prostrate Cury from the ground.

"He is dead!" cried George.

"Dead?" said every one, crowding around.

"Yes; Freegrove has killed him. See; there is a small knife thrust up to the very hilt in the back of his neck."

"I thought he had only struck him," said the colonel. "Good Heavens! how sudden has been the fate of these two men."

The soldiers now came back, bringing with them the body of Freegrove. Several shots had taken effect, and he was quite dead.

"Let them be laid side by side for the present," said Colonel Grainger. "This will be matter for judicial inquiry—an inquiry which, I fear, will delay me from proceeding upon an expedition which is near and dear to my heart."

George looked round, and missed Pomander and Scrimp. They had taken the opportunity of escaping in the bustle.

"They are gone," said George, "and, perhaps, it's better as it is. You, sir, however, had better see the remainder of the paper, which justifies me in my violence against them."

"Heed it not," said the colonel. "We must proceed to some magistrate's directly. This is altogether a most unexpected day's work."

"May it be the last of our troubles," said Giles, solemnly.

"Amen, young man," said the colonel, turning to him. "All here have the good wishes of Colonel Grainger."

"Colonel Grainger?" cried George.

"You did not say Grainger?" gasped the miller.

"Grainger is my name," repeated the colonel; "and I pray that none of you, who are now young and full of hope, may ever know the sorrow and anxiety that sits at my heart."

George advanced, and laid his hands upon the colonel's breast, as he said, in broken accents,—

"Your—your name is Grainger?"

"It is."

"You come from—from—from —"

' India," said the colonel.

"Phœbe! Phœbe!" cried George;—"Phœbe!"

"Phœbe?" said Colonel Grainger. "God of Heavens! what is this?" Phœbe advanced.

"Listen, Phœbe, oh, listen," said George. "Oh, God! oh, God! if this should be some delusion."

"George, George," cried Phœbe, "you are ill. Help! help! you are falling."

"I am better—better now," said George. "Repeat—repeat," he said, waving his hand to the colonel.

"My name," said the colonel, "is Grainger. I have newly come from India to seek my—my child."

"Your daughter?" gasped George.

"My daughter, Phœbe Grainger," said the colonel.

A wild shriek from Phœbe rent the air, and she fell insensible into the arms of *her father!*

"God of Heavens!" cried Colonel Grainger, "who is this?"

"Your child," said the miller, sobbing with emotion. "You hold in your arms Phœbe Grainger."

A paleness spread over the colonel's face. He moved his lips as if in prayer.

"If—if this should be some—some fond delusion," he said, "my heart is—is broken."

Phœbe now slowly opened her eyes, and her first word was "Father."

A cry of joy burst from the lips of Colonel Grainger.

"My child, my child!" he cried; "oh, speak to me. Tell me, your mother—"

"Died," said George, "and we were to the workhouse sent."

"At Bungleum?"

"Yes."

"Joy! joy!" cried the colonel. "She is my own—my long-lost—my child—my Phœbe! Just Heaven! what have I done to merit so much happiness?"

His tears fell fast upon his cheek as he strained her in his arms, and all were deeply affected by the scene.

With lips trembling with emotion, George stepped up to the happy father, and in a voice scarcely articulate, he said,—

"You—you had a son?"

"No," answered the colonel.

"A son, called George."

"My sister's child of that name was left an orphan, and was taken home by my wife."

"George!" cried Phœbe, springing from her father's breast.

"Phœbe!" he said, and in an instant she was folded to his heart.

"Are you George?" said the colonel.

"I am, I am," cried George. "Phœbe! dear Phœbe!"

"You are cousins," said the colonel.

"And lovers," cried the miller. "God has made them for each other. Through want and misery they have clung together; let them never more be separated."

Giles rushed forward, and taking George's hand, he placed Phœbe's in it.

"God bless you!" he cried, and then rushed from the spot.

"My children both," said the colonel, with deep emotion. "I live but to see you happy."

They both knelt at his feet, while tears of joy ran down the old miller's cheek.

"I'll give the bride away," blubbered Tim Miggles.

> "'While in despair my poor heart wriggles,
> It'll be a consolation she was guved away by Tim Miggles.'"

"This is a day of joy," said the colonel, "and may the remembrance of it gild our future lives."

"It will," said George; "and she who, as the Miller's Maid, won all our hearts—"

"Will prove a virtuous and a happy wife," said the old miller.

FINIS.